EYES OF A CHILD

Richard North Patterson

ALFRED A. KNOPF   NEW YORK   1995

FOR FRED HILL
AND SONNY MEHTA

THE NIGHTMARE

OCTOBER 16

ONE

RICARDO ARIAS'S face filled with fear and disbelief.

"If you're going to kill yourself," the intruder repeated softly, "you must leave a note."

Richie's eyes would not move from the gun. Pulled from damp and darkness, it had not been fired for years; the intruder wondered if it would fire now. But Richie Arias did not know this.

Sitting at his desk, Richie began groping for a pen.

His movements were sluggish, like those of a man struggling under water. Fixated on the gun, he seemed blind to the darkened living room: the worn couch and armchair, the cheap coffee table, the computer on the desk, the answering machine he used to screen creditors, the faded posters. A chrome standing lamp cast a pall on his skin.

His face was thin, with black eyes that shifted from softness to anger, as suited his needs, and yet never quite lost the alert, almost fevered expression of a bright graduate student running on too much coffee and too little sleep. Blood had begun to trickle from one nostril.

"I never write." His head twitched toward the computer. "Everyone knows I use that."

"Suicide is different." The intruder's voice was strained now. "The handwriting must be yours."

Richie's face looked drawn. Slowly, he picked up the pen, holding it gingerly.

" 'I am ending my life' "—the intruder spoke for him—" 'because I have faced what I am.' "

An instant's pause, the instinct to resist. Then Richie's pen began to inch across the paper. The effort was awkward and hesitant, that of a child learning to write, pausing in the middle of letters. Heavier on some than others, spidery at the end.

" 'What I am,' " the voice instructed him, " 'is selfish and pathetic.' "

Richie stopped writing. His eyes filled with resentment. *"Do it,"* the intruder ordered.

Wiping the blood from his nose, Richie stared at the paper. It was a moment before his hand moved, and when it did, there was a red smear on the back of his fingers. The word "pathetic" took too long to write.

" 'My only business is extortion. I have used my wife and child, out of greed and shamelessness, because I myself am nothing.' "

Richie flushed with anger. He stopped, staring at the words he had already written. His hand would not move.

The intruder hesitated, irresolute. Then saw, on the bookshelf next to Richie, a photograph.

Gun aimed at Richie, the intruder retrieved the picture and placed it carefully on the desk. A dark-haired girl, her solemn brown eyes gazing at Richie Arias.

It was far better than a note, the intruder realized: a last expression of cheap sentiment would seem so very like him. A shrine to his own suicide.

Turning from the picture, Richie's face showed that he understood the rest.

"You see," the intruder said softly, "I know who you are."

As if by instinct, Richie stood, backing from the chair. "Wait," he cried out. "No one commits suicide from across a room."

Their eyes met. The intruder did not speak.

"You can just *leave*." Richie's tone became a shrill wheedle. "I won't tell anyone. We just let it go, okay?"

All at once, staging a suicide did not matter. "Only *you*," the intruder said quietly, "would think that I could 'let it go.' Only *you*."

Richie's gaze darted to the gun. Slowly, the intruder started toward him.

Five feet, then four.

Richie's face was taut with fear and calculation. Backing toward the coffee table, he seemed to have forgotten it was there: his eyes flickered toward the bedroom hallway, searching for a way out. His throat worked. "Shoot me now, and it's murder."

The intruder stopped, raising the gun.

Richie's eyes changed. In that moment, he seemed to accept—despite his deepest instincts—that one person could truly love another.

"I'll give her up," he whispered.

In silent answer, the intruder's head moved from side to side.

Richie turned to run.

The gun jerked up at his first panicky step. As he stretched forward, straining for the hallway, Richie's leg slammed into the coffee table.

There was a sharp sudden scream of pain.

The next few seconds were like freeze-frames. Richie snapping at the waist, arms flailing. Sprawling forward in a face-first dive, head bobbing like a rag doll. Temple hitting the corner of the table. Another sound: a sickening crack. And then Ricardo Arias rolled sideways, flopping onto the carpet, and was still. He lay on his back, staring at the ceiling. The lamp bathed him in a circle of light.

Gun hand trembling, the intruder knelt beside him.

There was a red gash on his temple. Blood dribbled from his nose. The luminous wristwatch on his arm read 10:36.

Tentatively, almost gently, the intruder pushed open Richie's lips with the barrel of the gun.

It did not require much room. As the barrel slipped into his throat, Richie's mouth clamped down, the reflex of choking. The only sounds were Richie's shallow breathing, the whir of air-conditioning.

Eyes shut, the intruder took one breath and pulled the trigger.

A metallic snap. It was only an instant later that the intruder, forced to look at Richie's face, knew the ancient gun had not discharged.

Richie blinked, the first tremor of consciousness. Watching him taste the black metal, then discover it in some state of half awakening, the intruder prayed that the gun would fire.

Four more bullets.

Richie's eyes widened in terrible comprehension. His head rose, twisting feebly. His mouth opened around the barrel to form a single word.

"Please . . ."

* * *

The child shuddered.

It was dark. She was damp from the struggle to escape: her legs could not move, and her voice could not cry out. Knees drawn up tight against her stomach, she lay there, waiting.

The banging on her door grew louder.

As the door burst open, the little girl awakened with a soundless scream, torn from her nightmare.

She did not know where she was. But in her dream, she had imagined what would break down the door: a savage dog, with bright teeth and black curly hair, eyes searching the room for her.

A shadow moved toward her.

The girl shivered, stifling her scream, hugging herself so tightly that her fingers dug into her skin. And then her grandmother spoke softly, in Spanish, and Elena Arias stopped trembling.

"It was only your dream," her grandmother repeated, and swept Elena into her arms. "You're safe now."

Elena held her tight, tears of relief springing to her eyes, face buried in her grandmother's neck. She would know the smell of Grandma Rosa anywhere, sweet skin and perfume, the scent of cut flowers. As her grandmother gently lowered her head onto the pillow, Elena shut her eyes.

Elena felt Rosa's fingertips gently touch her forehead: in her mind, she saw her grandmother's jet-black hair, the slender face still almost as pretty as that of Elena's own mother, Teresa, whose room this once had been. The sounds of Dolores Street came to her then: Latin voices on the sidewalk; the squeal of cars at a stop sign. Outside, the streets were not safe, and Dolores Park, where Elena could not play, was filled with men who sold drugs at night. The window that her mother once could open wide was nailed to the frame. But here, with her grandmother, there was no black dog.

"Where is Mommy?" Elena asked.

Tonight, before bedtime, her grandmother had taken her mother's old world globe and traced a line with her finger from San Francisco, showing the route that her mother would fly tomorrow. But now Rosa repeated the words like a favorite story.

"Your mother is still here, at her house. Tomorrow she's flying to a place called Italy. But she'll be back in ten more days. And in the morning, when you get up, we'll find Italy on the map again."

Elena was silent for a moment. "But Daddy's not with her, is he? Mommy's going with Chris."

"Yes." Her grandmother's voice was quieter still. "Mommy's going with Chris."

Elena opened her eyes. In the faint glow of the night-light, her grandmother's gaze looked tired and sad.

Turning to the window, Elena listened for the sounds of the world outside. "Will I see Daddy tomorrow?" she asked in a tentative voice. "After Chris and Mommy leave?"

Her grandmother watched her, fingers still resting on her forehead. "No, Elena. Not tomorrow."

Tomorrow was as far ahead as Elena wished to think. She turned back to Rosa. "Please, Grandma, sleep with me. I'm afraid of being alone."

In the dim light, her grandmother started to shake her head and then stopped at the look in Elena's eyes.

"Remember what I told you, Grandma? About being scared?"

Her grandmother looked into her eyes. "Yes," she said gently. "I remember."

Neither spoke again. Her grandmother rose slowly from the bed and then, pulling her dress over her head, slid into the bed next to Elena, wearing only her slip.

Nestled in her grandmother's arms, Elena felt the rise and fall of Rosa's wakeful breathing as the caress of love and safety, until she fell asleep.

THE ESCAPE

OCTOBER 19–OCTOBER 24

ONE

THREE DAYS LATER, seven months after they had first made love, Teresa Peralta found herself in Venice with Christopher Paget, astonished to be in Italy, fearful that their time together was coming to an end.

Chris stood on the balcony of what had once been a thirteenth-century palazzo. He was dressed only in shorts, the late-afternoon sun on his skin. From the living room of their suite at the Danieli, Terri watched him as she held the phone to her ear.

Halfway around the world, Richie's telephone rang again.

Listening, Terri imagined its sound filling his small apartment. It was her third call in an hour.

Ten rings later, Terri slowly put down the telephone.

She was fresh from the shower, a slim, dark-haired young woman who barely came to Chris's shoulder, with olive skin and a sculpted face that he kept trying to persuade her was beautiful: a chiseled nose, too pronounced for her liking; high cheekbones; delicate chin; a quick smile that transformed her seriousness without ever quite changing her green-flecked brown eyes, watchful by habit. Pulling the towel around her, she studied Chris in silence.

Chris did not see her. He gazed out at the Grand Canal, standing in the posture Terri had come to know: hands in his pockets, head tilted slightly, taking something in.

She walked toward him, making no sound, until she could see what he watched so intently.

At another time, it would have enchanted her. A broad stone walk below, filled with people ambling among food and curio stands and the white-covered tables and umbrellas of outdoor restaurants, the edge of the walk lined with gaslights and gondolas and cigarette boats, their pilots chatting with each other as they waited for business. And, beyond them, the Grand Canal.

The azure sweep of water stretched in glistening wavelets through a city of stone and marble, gray and dusty rose, blue water, blue sky. Across the canal, perhaps a half mile, San Giorgio island appeared as an orange sphere, a white marble dome, a great hall with columns, Byzantium meeting the Renaissance in some gentle suspension of time. A faint sea smell came with a breeze that cooled Terri's skin. There were no cars; save for the motorboats, there was little Terri saw through the iron frame of the balcony that was not as it had been five hundred years before.

"It's timeless," Chris said without turning. "I don't know why, exactly, but I take comfort in that. As if we can survive Richie after all."

Terri was quiet for a moment. "How did you know I was here?"

"Because you're wearing almost nothing. It's a sixth sense I have."

As Terri smiled, Chris turned to face her.

He looked ten years younger than he was: his face was barely lined, his coppery hair had no hint of gray, and spartan self-discipline kept him trim and well-muscled. The ridged nose, a certain angularity, lent his features strength. But what struck Terri now was the startling blueness of his eyes, and the concern for her she saw there.

"His machine is off," she said.

Chris's eyes narrowed. "Perhaps they're out."

"No way. It's eight in the morning, California time. Richie picked Elena up from my mother's last night for her week at school." Her voice quickened. "We've been gone two days, and now I can't reach her. It's part of the mind games Richie plays with her—'Your mommy doesn't love you like I do.' Richie's far too smart to ever hold her incommunicado. But as long as he doesn't answer, Elena will never know I called."

Chris studied her face. "It's hard," he said at last. "But somehow, at least for a few days, we have to leave him behind." He smiled a little. "After all, we're two people in love, who've never been away together, alone in a beautiful place. We ought to be able to do *something* with that."

His tone, as so often, combined irony with seriousness. Terri knew by now that this was another way he protected them both: to say how deeply he felt made him too vulnerable, and Chris did not want others to feel responsible for him. But buying these few days of freedom had been the only thing that Chris could do for her.

He kissed her forehead. "Until we get to Portofino," he said in the same quiet voice, "I'd like to talk about this mess we're in—Richie and our children—as little as we can. It's quiet there, and we'll have time enough. Even to decide our future."

Silent, Terri took his hands in hers.

His right hand, she saw, was still swollen and discolored. Just as it had been two mornings ago, when he picked her up to drive them to the airport.

"Terri?" His voice was tentative, an inquiry.

Looking up at him, Terri met his searching gaze. And then slowly she backed away from him, letting her towel drop to the floor.

"Make love with me, Chris. Please."

His eyes changed.

Terri led him to the bed and, lying skin to skin, looked into his face. His hand, slowly tracing the bone of her back, made her shiver.

Her eyes closed. In the last instant before becoming lost in Chris entirely, Terri thought of the day eight months before when her life—and Elena's—had changed forever.

It began, quite unexpectedly, when Terri had taken her five-year-old daughter to the beach at the end of the Carelli hearing. As they walked along the sand, hands entwined, the late-afternoon sun glistened at the water's edge, and the sound of the waves was deep and lulling. She was only Chris's associate then, not his lover; her sole thoughts were of Elena.

They found a small cove carved into the cliffside, sheltered from the wind. As Terri gazed out toward the Golden Gate Bridge, Elena played at her feet: with a child's solemn concentration, she arranged toy people around pieces of plastic furniture. There seemed, Terri realized, to be a mother, a father, and a little girl. She wished that she could see into Elena's mind.

Elena began talking to her plastic people. "You sit *here*," she insisted, "and Daddy sits there."

"Who are you talking to?" Terri asked.

"You. You're sitting next to Daddy."

"And where do you sit?"

"Right there," Elena said triumphantly, and placed a little girl between its plastic parents.

A child, Terri thought sadly, ordering the world of adults. Terri had been certain that she had given Elena no sign of the marital problems she felt like a weight inside her—the fights over money and Richie's failure to get a job; the fantasy businesses he had used her money to finance; the ways he chose to isolate the three of them from others; the subtle manipulations, always denied, intended to erode her sense of self. But Elena must have some intuition; she had spent an hour at this game of family. Terri had seldom seen her so intent.

"Do you like playing that?" she asked.

"Yes." Elena stopped, gazing at her imagined family, and then looked up at Terri. "Why are you so mean to Daddy?"

Her daughter's voice was part inquiry and part accusation; there was an eerie certainty in it, as though Elena were speaking an indubitable truth.

Terri was momentarily speechless.

Keep it neutral, she told herself, as if you're merely seeking information.

"How am I mean to Daddy?" she asked.

Elena did not answer. But her voice held deep conviction. "Daddy cries, you know."

"Have you seen him?"

Elena shook her head. "No. He doesn't want to cry in front of me. He does it when he's alone, after you hurt his feelings."

Terri felt herself stiffen. Quite calmly, she asked, "Then how do you know?"

"Because he tells me." Elena's voice held a kind of pride. "When we're alone, and he tucks me in at night, we talk about our feelings."

Terri recognized the note in Elena's voice now: the false wisdom of a child, flattered by the contrived confidences of a manipulative adult. When she spoke again, it was without thinking. "Daddy shouldn't say those things to you."

"He *should*," Elena said almost angrily. "Daddy says I'm old enough to know things."

She had been foolish, Terri realized. This could not—should

not—be resolved between Elena and herself. But it would not do, she realized, to confront Richie with this conversation fresh in Elena's mind: the child might see the cause and effect.

"Can I play with you?" Terri asked.

Elena's mood changed. "Okay," she said, and smiled up at her mother.

For a half hour, Terri forced herself to remember that she had come to play with her daughter. They did that, talking about everything and nothing, until the breeze grew cold.

As they drove home, Terri only half listened to Elena. Her mind felt as cold as the breeze had been.

Richie was in the kitchen. At the sight of Elena, he flashed an incandescent smile, bending his dark-curled head to hers. "How's my sweetheart?"

His voice was almost crooning. Perhaps it was her mood, Terri thought, but something about it made her more edgy. "Can you put away your toys?" she asked Elena abruptly, and watched the little girl scamper down the hallway. She was unusually cooperative, Terri thought; she found herself wondering if, subconsciously, Elena had begun trying to keep her parents happy.

"How was *your* day?" Richie asked. "Court all right?"

"Fine." Terri's voice was cool. "And yours? Or did you spend it crying?"

Richie looked startled and then tried a puzzled half smile. As he looked at Terri, it died there.

"The funny thing," she said, "is that you never cry. Sometimes I'd feel better if you did. But the deepest feeling you can dredge up is self-pity, and that's only to manipulate me. Of course, Elena doesn't see that yet."

Failing sun came through the window. It was dusk: facing Richie, Terri felt darkness closing around them. "Quit being abusive," he finally said. "People express their emotions in different ways, you know."

"What have you been telling Elena?"

Richie's wiry body straightened; Terri saw the faintest glint of satisfaction in his bright black eyes. "I'm just being a parent," he said coolly. "I want Lainie to know the difference between real love and infatuation."

There was something frightening, Terri thought, in the way Richie appropriated a five-year-old to justify his needs. "Oh, and what *is* real love? I'm not sure I'd recognize it."

"Then let me explain it to you." Pausing, Richie spoke with exaggerated patience. "Real love is when people make a commitment to family and carry it out, even through the bad times. It's the opposite of this stage you're in with Christopher Paget, an infatuation with surface instead of substance. . . ."

"Then maybe I'm too shallow to deserve you." Terri stopped there; what she felt was too deep for sarcasm. "Don't you understand? I like working with Chris. Period. He has nothing to do with this and never has. And *I* never cared if you were the world's greatest promoter. That was *your* dream. I just wanted us to live a real life."

He shook his head. "Nothing makes you happy. It's like right now. You want me to parent Lainie, and then you complain when I do. I can never win."

Terri replied softly. "You always win, Richie. But this time I won't let you." Her throat felt dry. "I won't let the rest of Elena's life be about her father."

Richie placed his hands flat on the kitchen counter. "Lainie's *not* like you, and she'll never see me like you do. She's imaginative, like me. We communicate on levels you don't understand." His voice filled with authority. "You should rise above your jealousy and learn to see how good I am for our daughter."

Terri could not answer. All that she could do was let the truth sink in—his deep certitude, his irreparable self-involvement. He would always see Elena in terms of his own desires, and if one of his needs was to use her to control Terri, he would do that without hesitation, certain it was best for Elena. Perhaps, Terri realized, *that* was the most frightening perception of all. Richie was *not* merely calculating: some unfathomable part of him could make himself believe that Elena's happiness derived from his own.

"I'm leaving you," Terri said.

Richie stiffened. They watched each other in the semidark.

"You can't do that," Richie said at last. He made his voice calm. "Not without counseling. I'll set up an appointment. Six months down the road, we'll see where we are."

It took her a moment to accept what she had said, another to tell him what she believed most of all. "You have an uncounselable problem, Richie. And so do I."

Richie looked wounded. "What's so wrong that we can't fix it?"

His voice was suddenly plaintive; for an instant it made Terri want to comfort him. But it was too late. "You can't see other people as separate from you," she told him quietly. "Elena most of all. I can't change it, and I won't fight it."

"You can *help* me, Ter. That's what marriage is about."

His shoulders slumped. He looked so alone, Terri thought, and then she remembered Elena. "No," she answered. "Only *you* can help you. It's too late for us, and I have Elena to think of."

His voice rose. "If you were thinking of Elena, you'd give her an intact family."

Terri's chest felt tight. "It's all I ever wanted, Richie—a family. But there's a difference between 'intact' and 'healthy.' We're no good for Elena."

The room was dark now. Richie moved closer. "It's not up to you to say what's good. It's up to a judge, and he'll listen to me."

Terri realized that Richie was prepared for this moment, perhaps had been prepared for months. "And what will you tell 'him'?" she managed.

"That *I've* been the caretaking parent while you've worked long hours with a man who just may be your lover. That I want Elena." He paused; the smile that followed seemed a reward for his own cleverness. "That I can't provide care for her without sixty percent of your income."

"That's crazy."

His voice filled with triumph. "It's the *law*, Ter. I've checked it out. And even if you get custody, you think it's easy to find a man who wants to raise someone else's kid? You'll be all alone." His tone became insinuating. "You should know by now how much you need me, Terri."

Terri tried to keep her own voice steady. "I don't love you," she said. "I don't think you're a good father for Elena. I don't think our 'family' is good for Elena. So if I have to be alone, I will. And if I have to fight you for Elena, I'll do that too."

"You'll lose." His next words were softer yet. "But don't worry, Ter. Every other weekend, I'll let you see my daughter."

It was near the surface now: her fear of Richie, which connected them more deeply than love. Richie could not let Terri go and so would not let Elena go with her. Instead some stranger Terri did not know would decide whether she could raise Elena and, in deciding, would set the course of Elena's life. Richie would be smooth and plausible; how could Terri explain to a judge how things really were? Even the thought made her tired.

She forced herself to speak slowly and evenly. "I'm taking Elena and going to my mother's. We need to decide what to tell her."

Richie moved closer, biting off his words. "*We're* not telling her anything."

"We should. And we should do it together."

He was standing over her now. In the dark, she could barely see his face. "We're not telling her anything," he repeated. "And you're not going anywhere."

His voice trembled with an anger she had never heard in him before. When she tried to step past him, he moved with her, blocking her way. Terri felt her own voice quaver. "Please, don't make this worse."

"You don't understand, Ter. I'm not letting you do this."

Terri's heart was racing. She put her hand on his shoulder, trying to move past him.

"You bitch," he spat out.

She flinched as his hand jerked upward in the darkness. "*Don't...,*" she managed.

"Do you still want to leave, Ter?" Unless she shook her head, his upraised hand might strike. "Or are you ready to talk?"

As his hand rose higher, Terri flinched. Turning, she fumbled for the light switch, flicked it on.

Richie stood blinking at the light, his hand still raised, two feet from her. Terri was breathing hard. "Do it, Richie. Do it twice. That way the family court won't miss it."

Crimson spread across his face. But his hand did not move.

Terri looked into his eyes. "At least you weren't abusive, I used to tell myself. Not like my father with my mother." She stopped herself, catching her breath. "Now I know why. Before I ever met you, I was trained to give in."

Richie was silent, flushed, staring. Terri did not know where her words had come from. "But not anymore," she heard herself say.

"Whether you hit me or not, I'm leaving. And if you *do* hit me, I'll make sure it's the last time you'll ever hit anyone."

He stared at her, and then anger became another expression—embarrassment, exposure. His hand dropped to his side.

Don't let him see your fear, Terri told herself. She knew that this was not over; with Richie, things were never over until he won. Right now her only goal was to take Elena with her.

Terri made herself stand straighter. "I'll think of something to tell Elena," she said. And then she walked past him, going to get their daughter, not looking back.

TWO

TWO DAYS AFTER leaving Richie, sleepless and afraid for herself and for Elena, Terri found herself on Chris's doorstep.

He knew nothing about what she had done. For what she had said to Richie—that Chris had nothing to do with their marriage—was what Terri believed.

Chris and she were too different for it to be otherwise; even his home, a sprawling three-story Edwardian in the Pacific Heights section of San Francisco, reminded her of all the ways in which their lives were not the same. Chris had become famous sixteen years earlier, at age twenty-nine, for his part in exposing the Lasko scandal, the corruption of a President; Terri was barely twenty-nine now, and her career had hardly begun. Chris's forebears had founded a railroad; Chris himself had been raised with wealth and a sense of entitlement Terri could never imagine; his only marriage had been to a well-known ballerina, graceful and elegant. Terri was from a family of Hispanic immigrants, a scholarship student who had worked her way through college and law school and still never felt quite secure; the daughter of an auto mechanic who had drunk too much and abused her mother, Rosa—the one person, Terri had sometimes felt, to whom she truly mattered.

Standing at Chris's door, Terri wondered how it was that Christopher Paget, and not Rosa Peralta, had become the person she would turn to.

The first six months she had worked for Chris, she would not have guessed this. Something at the core of him had seemed unknown and unknowable: Terri did not even know then that, as Elena was to her, the center of Chris's life was his fifteen-year-old son, Carlo. And then the television journalist Mary Carelli, Carlo's mother and Chris's onetime lover, was charged with the murder of America's most celebrated writer.

Chris and Terri had defended her. The fact that Carelli was certainly a liar, and quite possibly a murderer, would have been hard on Chris even had it not been for the strain it caused between Chris and Carlo, who needed to believe things about his mother that Chris knew could not be true. But for Terri, the crucible of *People v. Carelli* made her see Chris as he was. As Chris came to trust her with the Carelli defense, and then with parts of his life no one else knew, Terri saw that the man he showed to others—ironic and aloof—concealed such feeling that she sensed it frightened him.

But this discovery, Terri realized, made her feel safe with him. She told Chris things so painful to her that she had never told them to anyone. He listened without judging, asking questions until the shape of her own feelings became clearer to her. In some deep way, intuitive and never spoken, Teresa Peralta knew that Christopher Paget was helping her become truer to herself. For that, and for being who Chris was, Ricardo Arias hated him.

This was not fair, Terri told herself; surely she was entitled to a friend. Especially now.

Standing straighter, she knocked on Chris's door.

When he opened it, Chris looked startled. It was so uncharacteristic that Terri felt disconcerted.

He smiled then, as if to cover his surprise. "The Carelli case is over now," he said lightly. "You can go home. Sleep, even."

Terri hesitated, suddenly abashed. "I'm a little at loose ends, I guess."

"Sometimes that happens after a trial." Chris paused and then looked at her more carefully. "I was just out on the deck. Care to join me?"

Please, Terri thought. But all she said was, "Maybe for a while."

Chris led her to his deck. The morning sun was bright. A few sailboats flecked the bay; in the foreground, homes of pink and white stucco glistened in the light. Terri went to the railing; she leaned on it with her palms, gazing out at the water. A light breeze rippled her hair.

Chris moved beside her. He stood there, watching with her. When he turned to her, his blue eyes were intent. "Are you all right?" he asked.

Terri could not seem to face him. "Yes and no," she finally answered.

Chris started to ask something, then stopped at what he saw.

"I've left Richie," Terri said softly.

Chris seemed unnaturally still. Terri wanted to ask what was wrong and then saw the realization in his face at the same moment that the sudden knowledge left her own face hot, her skin tingling. She had not come for his help, Terri realized, or his advice. She had come because she had fallen in love with him.

Chris murmured, "Ah, Terri . . ."

All at once, Terri felt alone. "Is this all right? My being here?"

As if to himself, Chris shook his head. Humiliated, Terri could not look away from him.

"I'm forty-five years old," Chris said at last, "with a teenage son. You're twenty-nine. You're newly separated. And you work for me." Pausing, he looked so unsettled that Terri found it painful. "Any counselor in America would tell you I'm a bad idea, and that you just need time to see that."

Chris was looking for a way out, Terri was certain, too kind to hurt her. "But how do *you* feel?" she said miserably.

Terri saw him search for words. He could not seem to find them. Then, quietly, he asked, "You'd have me live in Richie's shadow?"

Surprise ran through her, warm and sudden. She hesitated, afraid that she had misunderstood. And then Christopher Paget smiled at her.

"Please," Terri managed. "As soon as possible."

She felt herself grinning. He said something, then she gave an answer. What they said went past her. As Chris reached out for her, she could feel her own pulse.

Chris's mouth was warm.

Terri felt years of loneliness become wanting, something moving deep inside her. She closed her eyes, burying her face in his neck, caught between the undertow of Richie and Elena and the sudden fierce desire for Chris that pierced her exhaustion. She pressed herself against him.

Suddenly Chris pulled back, breathing hard. "I should know better." His voice was strained. "You're tired, strung out, running away from Richie. . . ."

The sentence trailed off. When Terri faced him, his eyes were filled with wanting her. "Don't patronize me, Chris."

He shook his head again, as if to clear it. Terri walked away from him, gazing out at the bay, trying to collect herself. "Then tell me why you're leaving him," he said gently from behind her. "I'd like to understand this, at least a little. As one friend to another."

The irony eased Terri's hurt. After a time, she began to talk, and then the dam of her emotions broke.

She told him everything.

Chris leaned on the railing next to her, listening intently, careful not to touch her. But as Terri described the night she had left Richie, his hand grazed her cheek.

"Has he ever hit you?" he asked.

Terri shook her head. "Until the day before yesterday, not even close. Maybe he didn't need to. Somehow, I was always afraid of him."

Chris studied her. "You're *still* afraid, aren't you?"

It was hard, Terri found, to speak her fears aloud. "It's like he has this instinct for other people's weaknesses," she answered finally, "but they're not *real* to him. So that nothing he does to them matters. Even me."

"Whatever else, Terri, I *am* your friend. I can represent you, or lend you money."

Terri turned to him, suddenly fearful for reasons that she could not put into words. "That's not why I came here. I don't want you involved with him."

"Why? Richie's not the same thing to you that he is to me. There's nothing he can do to me."

Terri shook her head. "I don't want to make him part of your life. It's bad enough that he's part of mine." Her voice became determined. "Whatever I feel for you has zero to do with Richie, and it *can't* have anything to do with Elena. I need to do this on my own."

Terri watched him study her, decide not to argue. A smile appeared at one corner of his mouth. "Then what *I* should have done is make love with you. Before you changed your mind."

Terri felt her tension ease. "Don't worry," she said magnanimously. "Sometime I may give you another chance. If you can manage to believe that I'll respect you in the morning."

His grin, boyish and surprising, was like a gift. She went to him again; this time, he held her, quiet, for what seemed like minutes.

"Tired?" he murmured.

"Exhausted." It was, Terri realized, more true than she had known.

Chris led her to a padded couch, faded by the sun. Terri lay with her legs across his lap. When she closed her eyes, his closeness became a warmth inside her.

"Whatever you *do* feel," he said, "I'm glad you came."

Terri smiled, eyes still closed. What she felt seemed too deep to explain: it was somewhat the same, she thought idly, as when her mother had held her at night when she was small, offering and perhaps seeking comfort from the rages of Terri's father. Her mind wandered as she felt the sun on her skin and the breeze from the water. And then, for the first time since leaving Richie, Teresa Peralta fell asleep.

THREE

LEAVING CHRIS'S HOUSE an hour later, Terri smiled to herself, an instant before she saw Richie parked across the street.

He leaned through the window on the driver's side, as if waiting to pick her up. His look was almost casual; his eyes had the strange blankness that she knew meant danger.

"Hi, Ter." His voice was friendly, curious. "How're things?"

Walking toward the car, Terri felt numb. "What are you doing here?"

"Waiting for him to finish with you." His voice was still chatty. "It was sheer luck. If I hadn't decided to drop by Rosa's to talk with you, I wouldn't have seen you leaving."

That was a lie, Terri saw. He had not shaved; she guessed that he had been parked near her mother's since the early hours, hoping she would go to Chris.

"I understand," he said amiably, "you're embarrassed," and he handed her a sheaf of papers.

A form petition for divorce. The caption on the cover page read *Ricardo Arias v. Teresa Peralta.*

With the odd detachment of a lawyer, Terri scanned the pleading for its essentials: the date of their marriage; Elena's name and birth date; a listing of Terri's sole asset—her pension plan—and Richie's request for half of it; the much longer list of debts incurred by Richie, for which Terri shared responsibility by law; dollar amounts for Terri's salary and Richie's projected expenses; his demand for alimony. And at the bottom, a signature showing that Ricardo Arias, attorney at law, would serve as his own lawyer.

"You look bad, Ter." His voice was silken. "What's the problem?"

Terri turned to him. "You're representing yourself?"

"I can't afford a better lawyer." Terri caught the gleam of satisfaction. "Unless I ask the court to make you pay for one. I *can* do that, you know. There's even a box for it in the form."

Terri stared at him. Her world seemed to have narrowed to the man in front of her, her husband, and the papers in her hand. Softly, she asked, "What about Elena?"

A faint smile appeared at one corner of his mouth: it told her, as it was meant to, that she was performing on cue.

"Read on," he said. "They really do have a box for everything."

Beside the line that read "Physical custody of children," Richie had checked the box next to "Petitioner." Himself.

"Of course, I can't support her without money," he added, and handed Terri another form.

A request for child support to be paid by respondent, Teresa Peralta, collected by means of a wage assignment: a portion of her salary from the law offices of Christopher Paget, to be paid directly to Ricardo Arias.

"Does your friend Chris sign the checks himself?" Richie asked. "I might want to frame the first one."

How many hours, Terri wondered, had he spent planning this. Choosing the sequence of papers to give her. Rehearsing what he would say as she read them. Perhaps typing his lines on the computer screen, smiling as he changed a word.

"This little performance of yours needs work," she told him. "Frankly, I've seen better."

"It's no act, Terri. You *forced* me to do this." His voice hardened. "I'm just responding to the crisis in my daughter's life. You're so swept up in your affairs that you've got no time for her *or* me."

Terri felt a pounding in her temple. "I've got the time, Richie. Right now."

"Then sit down and talk to me, Terri, like the person I used to know. We're *married*, remember?"

Slowly, Terri walked to the passenger's side and got in. The inside of his beat-up car seemed hot and close. She leaned against the door.

He rested his hand on her knee. "It's all right, Ter. It's really not fair—someone like him picking on someone like you."

She turned to him, carefully removing his hand. "What do you want, Richie?"

A red flush appeared on his face, the stain of anger and resentment. His mouth twisted in a smile. "A blow job, Ter, like the old days. If you've still got room." He raised an eyebrow in inquiry. "Or do you spit his out?"

Too stunned to snap back, Terri imagined what had passed between her and Chris through the prism of Richie's warped portrayal. Then she said, "You don't need Elena, Richie. You need help."

"Help?" She watched him decide deliberately to misunderstand her and then assume a wounded, puzzled look. "You did those things out of love for me, Terri. I'm sure even your new boyfriend would understand that."

"Leave Chris out of this," she said coldly. "He has nothing to do with us, and we have enough problems of our own."

The strange smile reappeared. "*You* leave him out of this. Because as long as you see him, he has everything to do with the welfare of *my* child and your ability to devote suitable attention to her in the limited time your job and relationship allow."

Certain phrases sounded stolen from a primer on family law. His mutability had always jarred Terri: if Richie needed to seem a compassionate parent, he would read six handbooks on what compassionate parents did, weaving what he had learned into his persona of the moment. But what scared her was how facile he was.

"Giving up your boyfriend," he went on calmly, "is what's best for our daughter and best for you. That should be obvious to anyone. Unless you're too far gone to see."

Our daughter, suddenly. A phrase meant both to seduce and to confine. Like "our family." The family Richie had always seen in his mind's eye, as he slowly worked to isolate Terri from her own family and friends, until there was no one left for her but him.

"What's obvious to me," Terri answered, "is that Elena is a five-year-old girl who needs her mother. Please don't use her as a pawn."

"I'm not *using* her, Terri. I'm *saving* her." Richie reached into the back seat and gave her another document. His tone became authoritative. "Read this. Any expert on child custody would tell you that this is what's best. In fact, I've already talked to several of them."

It surprised her. "How can you afford that?"

"I can't. I'm submitting the bills to the court as expenses to be borne by you." His voice took on an eerie placidity. "I'm sure you'll want to pay them without a court order. I can't imagine you'd want to tell the judge you oppose my getting the expert advice about our daughter you've been too busy to get yourself."

Our daughter again. She was tied to Richie, Terri thought bleakly, for as long as Elena was a child. That was what Elena's birth had always meant to him.

She stared down at the agreement he had given her. "What's in this?" she asked.

"Only what's in the best interests of the child." It was a catchphrase of the family courts: he sounded pleased to have mastered it so quickly. "Custody to me. Appropriate spousal support, and child support at forty percent of your annual income to keep me at home with Elena. And to make sure I *can* stay with her, you'll assume our community debts. So that I'm not forced to work outside the home."

"That's a real sacrifice. Considering how much you like working." Terri fought to control her anger. "Just out of curiosity, when do I get to see her? In between the two jobs I'll need to employ you as a day care center?"

"Every other weekend." Richie's voice was that of a man too reasonable to be baited. "And under certain conditions, a dinner with Elena one night a week."

Something in his calm was enervating. "What conditions?"

Richie nodded toward the agreement. "You'll live within three miles of Elena's and my home. So you can get her back at a reasonable time." He rested his hand on her knee again. "It's good for you too, Ter. If I have plans some night, I can drop Elena with you instead of getting a sitter. I'm happy to make those kinds of informal accommodations as long as it doesn't affect support."

He looked content, almost happy. All at once she saw the future through Richie's eyes: a guaranteed income that would force Terri to work too hard ever to seek custody of Elena; Terri kept near him by the need to see the daughter she could not raise, grateful for the last-minute calls from Richie whenever Elena was in his way.

"I may even give you more time than that," he added quietly. "But there's another condition. Now." He paused for emphasis. "Outside of work, you will never see Christopher Paget again. If that's too hard, find another job."

The car felt stifling. As Terri cracked open the door, Richie grasped her arm. "We're required to meet with Family Court Services." His tone became confident and conversational. "To see if we can work out custody without going to court. Our meeting's in ten days. Just sign this, Terri, and we won't even need to go through that."

Richie had begun to sound as if she had already agreed; five years of marriage had taught Ricardo Arias that he could always break her down. He took her hand, eyes suddenly soft. "It's him or me, Ter. Please get rid of him, okay?" His fingers squeezed hers. "Then maybe there's a chance for us."

Terri pulled her hand away, pushed open the door. "The only chance for us," she answered slowly, "was for me to never see you as you are. And, in a way, I wish I never had."

She got out of the car and, with deliberate softness, closed the door behind her.

FOUR

WHEN TERRI HAD RETURNED to her mother's from Chris's house, still clutching Richie's divorce papers, Elena was waiting.

"Did you go to make up with Daddy?" she asked.

"I *saw* your daddy." Terri placed the papers on the mantel in Rosa's living room; Elena could recognize her own name in print, and Terri did not wish her to see it.

"Is Daddy still sad?" When Terri did not answer, Elena followed her to the fireplace. "What did you talk about?"

"Just grown-up things." She knelt, hugging Elena. Her eyes were so much like Richie's, Terri thought, except that their fear and insecurity came from deep within her daughter's unschooled heart.

"But were you nice to him?" Elena asked. "Are you guys going to be married again?"

Instinct caused Terri to look past Elena to the hallway and see her mother watching them both, eyes as dark and somber as Elena's own. Terri focused on the child's face; it was hard enough to find the words for her alone.

"I know you're sad, sweetheart. And I know you want your daddy and me to stay together." There was a spark of hope in Elena's gaze. Gently, Terri added, "Your daddy and I both love *you*, Elena, and always will. But we don't love each other anymore. And I don't want you *ever* to see us fight."

She felt Elena stiffen, and then the little girl began to cry, body trembling with stifled sobs. Terri drew her close. "I'll help you," Elena managed. "I'll talk to Daddy."

Terri glanced up at her mother. In the gaze that passed between them, Terri saw Rosa remember, as vividly as she did, the night in this same living room when Terri had stepped between her father and her mother, begging him to stop. Terri faced her daughter again.

"That's not your job." Terri's voice was firm now. "Kids can't fix things for adults, and you shouldn't worry over us. It's your daddy's and my job to take care of *you*."

"But you *can't*." Elena leaned back, a child's anger at deception filling her voice. "If you and Daddy aren't still married, you can't live with us."

It startled Terri. "Who told you that?"

"Daddy." Elena drew herself up; Terri sensed her pride in being included in the world of adults. "I *am* going to help him take care of things. When I'm older, he says I can even cook dinner for him. When I'm seven or eight."

You bastard, Terri thought. She kept her voice steady. "Your daddy and I haven't decided *who* you're going to live with. But you'll see both of us. Because we both love you very much."

Terri watched the thin veneer of the grown-up Elena vanish in the tears of a frightened five-year-old. "Then why can't you love Daddy?" Elena's look became pleading. "Daddy's nice. If you didn't work with Chris, you could be friends again."

Terri stiffened. "Have you talked to Daddy about all this?"

Elena nodded. "We went to dinner, just the two of us. At La Cantina. It's my favorite."

Terri had never been to La Cantina. Distractedly, she wondered how it could have become Elena's favorite restaurant. Then it came to her: all those nights that Terri was preparing for the Carelli trial. The thought led her to another, deeper and sadder: how could a court, or even her own daughter, understand that Terri's career was not that of a woman who had chosen work over family but of a mother whose husband had given her no choice.

Facing Elena, Terri brushed the little girl's hair back from her forehead. "I know you're sad, sweetheart. But you don't need to be scared. I'll make sure that everything's okay."

Elena studied her intently, as if trying to believe. Rosa appeared, touching Elena's shoulder. "I have a coloring book for you, precious. At the desk in your mommy's old room upstairs. If you color a picture for me, I'll put it on the refrigerator."

Elena hesitated. And then, choosing the world of a child, she went with Rosa to find her crayons.

Terri sat on the couch, thoughts tired and diffuse, looking around the house where she had become who she was. A small, square living room with a low ceiling; the smaller dining room where Terri and her younger sisters used to sit, talking to their mother, watching their father from the corners of their eyes; the dark stairway to the bedrooms. It was the same, yet different. After her father's death, Terri and Rosa had repainted the inside. No one said why; they hardly spoke of her father again. But the eggshell white they chose was a color that Ramon Peralta had despised.

There were other changes as well. Gone were the things of Terri's father: the crucifix, a family photograph he had commissioned during a sober period—Ramon surrounded by Rosa and his dark-haired daughters, smiling tightly in a new suit he never wore again. It was as if he had tried to make the picture become reality by placing it on the wall. Terri had taken it down, silently handing it to her mother. Terri never saw the picture again.

Her father had been dead for fifteen years now. Yet she could never sit in this room without the guilty fear that she had done something to displease him. Even the silence reminded her of the school friends she could not have over, the things Terri and her sisters could never speak of outside this house. Like the cracking sound of his open palm as it struck their mother's face.

Footsteps sounded on the stairs.

Rosa crossed the living room and sat next to Terri, folding her hands. Somewhere between Terri's childhood and now, her mother had lost the habit of smiling; her face often seemed as somber as a Velázquez oil. But there were flashes of humor, and she was striking yet: the arresting brown-green eyes, the even mouth and well-defined features that Terri knew to be her own, although she could never think of herself as pretty like her mother. Today, as always, Rosa's jet-black hair was drawn back and her makeup applied carefully: it was part of Rosa's dignity that nothing was out of place. She watched her daughter with a look of sadness and expectation.

"I can't go back," Terri said.

"No?" Perhaps because English had not been her first language, Rosa spoke it carefully, with a correctness and perfect diction that Terri or Elena would never have. "Is it really so bad?"

"I think so." Terri tried to find words. "I think maybe he's *worse* than I know but that I've never had a way of really understanding."

Rosa's eyes were unnaturally still; Terri sensed that she understood Terri's reference to her father. Then her mother surprised her by asking simply, "Until now?"

There was no mistaking what Rosa meant, or who. Not for the first time, Terri reflected that her mother knew her all too well. "I don't know yet," she said at last. "Perhaps."

"And Richie?"

"He served papers this morning." Terri glanced upstairs. "He wants custody."

Rosa leaned back in the couch. "Where were you?"

Terri felt her gaze. "At Chris's," she answered. "Richie was waiting."

"That is like him." Rosa's eyes were grave; Terri sensed that she was not surprised, and then remembered that this was also like Ramon Peralta. "What did he say?"

In a flat voice, leaving nothing out, Terri told her.

Rosa listened with an averted gaze, as if to make this easier for her daughter. Only when Terri finished did she look up again.

"He means to make you pay for Chris," Rosa said with weary certainty. "The price will be Elena."

Terri shook her head. "It goes deeper than Chris. Or jealousy. Richie wants me alone, without anyone except for him. He always has."

"Then he did well." The remark was dispassionate, but Terri could feel her mother's hurt: over the years with Richie, concealing who he was from others and from herself, Terri had become more distant from her mother and sisters. "I would have wanted a better life for you, Terri. And for Elena."

There was an emphasis on the last three words. Terri chose not to answer.

"Ricardo frightens me," Rosa said slowly. "And I do not think that he should ever raise Elena. So I have to ask: should you leave him without trying? At least for a time."

"I don't think I *can* try anymore. There's something damaged about him, and we're terrible for Elena." Unbidden but powerful, the thought of Chris came over her. "I can't stand to have him touch me."

"But this is not just about Richie, is it?" Her mother leaned forward. "You're my daughter, and I love you more deeply than you will ever know. For many years, it was you, before anyone, who gave my life its meaning. But you're also Elena's mother now. And mothers are not free."

It was close to the surface, Terri thought, the unspoken thing that lay between them. "I know how important a family can be," Terri answered coolly. "That's why I left him."

Her mother did not flinch. "Then you know what you must do. Stay away from Christopher Paget, as Richie asks. Leave your job, if necessary."

Terri felt her stomach tighten. "I don't know if I can. Or even should. For Elena's sake as well as mine."

Rosa shook her head. "Elena has no interest in your love life. When you chose to have Elena, many years before you met this man, you chose to put her first. *Hers* is the new life, fresh and unspoiled, and it was given to you to protect. That's how it must be now, however hurtful."

Terri paused for a moment. For years, Rosa Peralta had been her only security, the person who, for Terri, defined what love was. It still pained Terri to quarrel with her: when she spoke again, her voice was strained. "I don't know *what* this will become. And *you* don't know Chris."

"I know enough. I watched the trial on television, after all. I heard you speak of him." She stopped. "And I hoped, in spite of what I saw in your face, that you would never fall in love with him."

"Well," Terri answered softly, "I have."

"And I understand. He is smart and successful. He's quite handsome. He may even love *you*." Rosa looked into Terri's face. "And only someone your age would think that is enough."

"What do you mean?"

"Chris will cost you Elena. Can you forget so quickly who Richie is? After she's gone, you will see Elena every time you look at Chris's face."

"I'm not choosing Chris over *Elena*." Her voice rose. "He's a wonderful father, Mama. You should see Carlo. . . ."

Her mother touched her arm. "And then you must ask: 'Does Chris *really* love me? Or is a man who wants a woman so much younger more in love with his youth than with her?'" Rosa took her hand now. "How old did you say he is, Teresa? Forty-five?"

"Yes."

"Three years younger than I am. He should call *me*." Her mother smiled, but Terri heard the bitter joke beneath: Rosa's interest in men had died with Ramon Peralta, as if he had branded her, heart and memory. When Rosa spoke again, her voice was quiet and sad. "Do not make this decision, Teresa. Not just for Elena's sake, but for your own."

Terri stood. "I *won't* let myself lose her, Chris or no Chris. But Chris may be my chance to be happy, Mom. If we choose to be together, it will be because I've found out what that means."

Rosa stared up at her. "And what is that," she said at last, "without Elena? That when Christopher Paget dies, far too soon yet not soon enough, you will remember once having loved him."

Terri was quiet for a time. Softly she asked, "And what do you remember?"

Rosa did not answer. Terri turned and walked from the room, ashamed at her question, not wanting to see her mother's face.

FIVE

THE NEXT MORNING, Terri returned to Chris's, with Elena.

Carlo was eating cereal at the kitchen counter, a baseball cap shoved backward over his black curly hair, lean body arranged in the pose of languid cool that only teenage boys can manage. Elena walked directly up to him.

He looked down at her with a slightly bemused smile, as if a cartoon character had just walked into his kitchen. Even now, in Terri's memory, the moment made her smile.

"Hi, squirt," Carlo said casually. "Remember me?"

Terri knew the answer. Three weeks before, when Elena had met Carlo for the first and only time, he had contrived to let her beat him at a game. Winning was something Elena did not forget.

"You're *Carlo*," Elena responded. "I beat you at Blockhead. I'm the champion of this house."

Carlo looked askance at her. "Only as long," he said with feigned annoyance, "as I let you be."

For the first time in days, Elena's eyes danced. "I can beat you," she teased. "I can beat you all the time."

Glancing quickly at Chris and Terri, Carlo rolled his eyes. "Who do you think I am, Munchkin. My *father?*"

Sensing the joke, Elena turned to Chris. "No," she decided. "He's too old."

"You've got *that* right." Carlo flashed the crooked smile that had so engaged Terri, and then turned to his father with a fond but discomfited gaze. "Although I guess you're never *too* old. If somebody's nice enough to give you a break."

The oblique remark, Terri recognized, was Carlo's way of telling her that he knew things had changed.

"Someone has to," Chris said equably. "I get so few at home."

"It's my developmental role, Dad. You've said so yourself." Turning back to Elena, Carlo saw her watching the adults with a puzzled look. "Tell you what," he said to the child. "Let me finish my cereal, and I'll play you another game of Blockhead. If you can get my dad to dig the game out, I'll even bring you a bowl of Happy Loops." He grinned down at her. "They've got lots of sugar in them—I eat 'em all the time."

Chris and Elena went to the library. Carlo resumed munching his cereal, while he gave Terri a veiled, expectant look.

"I guess your dad said something," Terri ventured.

Carlo nodded at his cereal. "A little."

This was touchy, Terri thought. In their own way, children—even teenagers—were the most moral people in the world; through the Carelli trial, she and Carlo had become warm friends, and she did not wish to disappoint him.

"I know this must be strange for you," Terri told him, "but I guess I have to say it. Your dad had nothing to do with my leaving Richie. He more or less found me on his doorstep yesterday. I'm not even sure it's fair to him. Or you."

Carlo gave a slight smile. "Don't worry about me. He was in such a great mood last night it was absolutely obnoxious. Think I should ask him to up my allowance?"

It was, Terri decided, a teenage effort to make this easier. "Maybe a car phone," Terri answered dryly. "To go in the Maserati Chris has ordered for your sixteenth birthday."

"I'm sure," Carlo said, and then angled his head toward the library. "Does Elena know?"

"Not really." Terri hesitated. "It's hard explaining divorce to a five-year-old who just wants things the same."

He nodded. "She won't get it for a while. She probably thinks her dad's a saint."

Once more, the remark surprised her. "More like a martyr," Terri answered. "It would be easier if he were."

Carlo gave a philosophical shrug. Terri could almost read his thoughts: Richie was not part of his life and never would be, which was fine with him. The world of adults—even the ones closest to him—could hold only so much interest.

"This won't be a regular thing," Terri told him. "Doing *Sesame Street*."

Carlo grinned. "Suits me," he said. "I've got a social life to work on. People who've passed puberty. But I'll make an exception for the 'children of divorce'—if they're yours." He turned to Terri. "You don't have any *more* of them, do you?"

Terri laughed. "Only Elena."

"Good deal." Carlo poured some Happy Loops and milk into a bowl. "I'd better go amuse the munchkin."

Chris was back shortly, glancing over his shoulder. "Talk about the Odd Couple. This is a side of Carlo I've seldom seen."

"He's a good kid, Chris. And he's had a good dad." Terri glanced toward the library. "Think we can go for a walk? I don't want Elena to hear this."

Chris nodded. Telling Elena they'd be back soon, they passed through the dining room and living area, the high ceilings and bright art, and stepped outside. Terri found herself looking for Richie's car.

They turned on Pacific Avenue, walking up Pierce Street to Alta Plaza, a gently rolling park that looked back down Pierce as it sloped for over a mile of city blocks to the blue water of San Francisco Bay. The bay was in front of them; to their left, on the rolling grass of the park, a group of kids played with a foam rubber football; the rhythmic volley of matches on four tennis courts sounded from behind them. They sat on a wooden bench, looking out at the bay.

"You must feel pretty isolated," Chris said at last.

A few simple words of understanding, Terri realized, could bring her close to tears. "I should never have come yesterday," she said simply. "Richie sees you as a threat."

"I'm sure that's how he *wants* you to feel." Chris's voice had a trace of suppressed anger. "It's not that I don't understand. My first instinct would be to protect Carlo—whatever it took. If you really think seeing me means losing Elena, then you can't see me. At least outside the office."

Terri felt her throat constrict. "I don't need you to be rational. I just need you to hold me, all right?"

His face softened, and then he brought her close. "Someone once told me," he murmured after a time, "that men have more answers than women have questions. I should remember that."

Terri rested against his chest. "I can't take the money you've offered," she said finally. "And you can't be my lawyer."

"Why not?"

"This morning, Richie handed me a subpoena for my bank records." She leaned back, looking into his face. "You *know* what that's about: if you're giving me money, he'll claim that I can afford to pay him even more support. Plus he'll use it to imply that you enticed your impressionable young associate to leave her happy home. Which won't help me at all when it comes to Elena."

"For God's sake, Terri. It's not like we've committed adultery—in fact, we haven't committed *anything*. And even if we had, it's not relevant to custody."

"He'll *make* it relevant, and he'll try to make any relationship we have seem bad for Elena. Trust me about this." Her voice rose. "We're lawyers, Chris—we know what lawsuits can be like. And this is going to be a bad one, with all the dirty tricks, twisted facts, and psychological warfare Richie can imagine. Except that it's about *my* child."

"There must be *some* way for you to buy him off."

"Not in exchange for Elena. He *needs* her too much." Terri felt bitterness overcome her. "It's all about *Richie*, of course. He'll do almost anything to win Elena over—play the martyr, lie about me, treat her as a little wife—because he's in love with the man he sees in his daughter's eyes. And because she's his one excuse for not working."

Chris gave a grimace of disgust. "Lots of people have jobs. What's *his* problem?"

"I don't think he *can* work for anyone. Before he stopped working entirely, he lost three law jobs. Or quit them; I could never quite tell. It was always someone else's fault—they were stupid or didn't understand him. But as long as I made money, and we could meet new people, every night was opening night—the great promoter-father and his loyal wife, coming soon to a cocktail party near you." Her voice filled with self-contempt. "Elena became part of it too. Whenever Richie made dinner, we'd both praise him, as if he'd done something wonderful."

"Why on earth did you stay with him?"

How to explain, Terri wondered, what she herself did not understand? "I've always told myself that he might have problems," she said at last, "but that he wasn't so bad. And *he* kept telling me that we were a *family* now and good for Elena. That was what I'd always wanted: a real family, where the parents loved each other and the kids felt safe." She turned to him. "He *knew* that, Chris. Sometimes I think there's a part of me that Richie knows better than I ever can. Like all my life, Richie was waiting for me, sure that one day I'd be there for him."

Chris's look was searching. Terri sensed him wanting to know more, then decide that this was not the time. "What will you do now?" he asked.

All at once, Terri felt the pressure of facing Richie alone. "The next couple of weeks are key," she said slowly. "First, we have to meet with the mediator. If that doesn't work, we're off to court to see who gets interim custody of Elena. For at least nine months, until there's a trial.

"Richie's going to make a good impression, at least to start with—he always does. Two weeks isn't enough time for anyone to figure out who he is. Unless I show them the real Richie, he's got a chance of taking Elena." Terri looked into Chris's face again. "Once I start doing that, he's going to retaliate any way he can. You're already on the list."

Chris gave a dismissive shrug. "I'm only concerned that you won't let me represent you. Unless you mean to handle this yourself."

Terri shook her head. "I don't know family law, and from what I hear, the judge in Alameda County hates parents in custody suits who represent themselves." Her voice softened. "I can't do it, Chris, and neither can you. I don't want you near this. For your sake *and* Elena's."

Chris stood, hands on his hips, looking away from her. "Maybe you can pacify him. Maybe I'm buying you a fight you don't need. Maybe if he's the first to find someone, he'll go on to other things."

Terri got up and went to him. "I want custody of Elena," she said. "And then I want to spend time with you. I have to be careful, that's all. Just until this hearing's over."

Chris became narrow-eyed with thought. His quiet made Terri anxious. "Is there anything you even want?" she asked. "Because for me, I have to put Elena first."

"What's bothering me is yesterday. All that restraint, and I'm paying for it anyhow." He smiled down at her. "Two weeks is a long time to live with the knowledge that I'm an idiot."

In her relief, Terri found herself laughing. "Two *hours*," she said, "is a long time with Elena, unless you're seeking custody. We should rescue Carlo."

When they returned, Carlo and Elena were still in the library. Elena had planted herself in his lap, and the floor was a mess. Carlo glanced at his watch with a look of mock annoyance, an important man with places to go and teenagers to see. "We've done a trip down memory lane," he reported. "My childhood from seven to thirteen—puzzle by puzzle and game by game." He looked at his father. "You saving this stuff for my kids or something? Or for the Smithsonian?"

Chris smiled. "Cooperstown," he rejoined. "Along with your baseball glove and first athletic supporter. From Little League."

"What's an athletic support?" Elena asked Carlo.

"Great, Dad." Turning to Elena, Carlo grinned at her. "My dad wouldn't know. And I won't tell you till you're six. Give you something to look forward to."

Elena put her arms on his shoulders, bumping her head against Carlo's. "Tell me *now*," she said. "Or I'll never marry you. Ever."

Watching their children, Chris and Terri shared the smile of parents.

SIX

THE MEDIATOR'S OFFICE was a bare rectangle in the Alameda County Administrative Building, in Oakland. Terri and Richie had sat against a blank wall, several feet from each other; Alec Keene—a fortyish mediator with a salt-and-pepper beard, horn-rimmed glasses, and a quizzical expression—had turned his chair from his desk to face them.

Terri had felt tense, concerned about Keene's first impression. In a gray suit and white blouse, she looked like what she was—a lawyer who had come from work. But with his corduroy slacks, checked shirt, and sweater with its sleeves pulled up, Richie resembled the benign head of a creative preschool for children whose parents valued ceramics and free play. He gazed at Keene with a pleasant, expectant expression. Keene would need to have been a mind reader to know, as Terri did, that Richie had studied the local family-law procedures so carefully that he could have given Keene's opening speech himself.

"So my central purpose here," Keene summarized, "is to see whether we can resolve custody of Elena without the ordeal of the courtroom."

He paused, gazing from Terri to Richie. "I'm sure we'd both like that," Richie said. His voice was hesitant, humbled by their joint responsibility. "I love Elena very much, and I know that Terri does too."

Richie wanted to establish a persona, Terri saw at once, to make it harder to attack him. "We have thirteen days," Keene told them, "before the hearing on support and interim custody. If the two of you can't come to some agreement, this office will make a recommendation to the court regarding interim custody until you *do* reach an agreement or permanent custody is awarded by the court."

The not-so-tacit message was that compromise was better. "How can you do that," Terri asked, "without any background beyond whatever we tell you?"

Keene nodded his acknowledgment. "That's why we'd much prefer that the parents, who really *do* know the child, try to work this out." He looked to Richie and back again. "But if they can't, someone has to resolve—and pretty quickly—the child's immediate situation."

Terri leaned forward. "But doesn't that put too great an emphasis on this one meeting? As I understand it, interim custody orders tend to become permanent."

Keene's eyes opened in an expression of candor. "Not always. But I admit that if the status quo seems to be working, the court may be reluctant to change it. Absent compelling reasons."

"What are those?" Richie interjected. "Can you give me an example?"

Keene touched his beard. "I'd say the real hot-button issues are child neglect, substance abuse, the mental instability of a parent, or evidence of physical or sexual abuse." His tone became cautionary. "Those kinds of allegations are becoming more and more common. In cases where parents start playing to win, it's sometimes hard to tell whether we're dealing with truth or tactics."

Richie shook his head, as if to signal his wonderment that people would exploit such problems. "That's not the situation here. Not between me and Ter." He turned to Terri for affirmation. "I mean, we may disagree, but I'm sure that neither one of us questions each other's sincerity."

Terri met his eyes, letting a quizzical smile play across her mouth. She could only hope that Keene would get the message: her husband was an actor, and she was too polite to say so. Richie turned back to the mediator, eyes narrowing in pretended hurt. How terrible, Terri thought, to play games for the future of a child.

Keene seemed to watch them both more closely. "Let me gather some data, just to get the mundane out of the way." He turned to Terri. "Where do you work, Terri?"

His manner was that of a man too well-mannered to show his boredom with routine. Terri knew better: her trial lawyer's instincts told her that he had already read this as a potential custody fight and was trying to determine who could best spend time with Elena. The next few answers could damage her beyond repair.

"As a trial lawyer." Her voice was cool and measured. "At the law offices of Christopher Paget."

She felt Richie stir. Keene glanced at him quickly, then leaned toward Terri, as if something had just struck him. "You defended the Carelli case, didn't you?"

Terri nodded. "I was co-counsel, yes."

"That must have been an incredible challenge." He stopped, as if at another thought. "In the past year, what have been your normal hours of work?"

"Nine to five-thirty." There was no point in trying to fool him. "Sometimes later."

"Weekends?" he asked sympathetically.

"Sometimes. Only when I was in trial, really."

"When you were later, or in trial, who watched Elena?"

"Her preschool, the Discovery School, has her until six. Sometimes, on the weekend, I'll take her to my office." She glanced at Richie. "As of twelve days ago, when we separated, I told the partner I work for that I really can't travel, that weekends are out, and that I have to leave promptly at five-thirty. So I'm ready to give Elena a predictable routine and to be with her pretty much anytime she's not in school."

Keene raised an eyebrow. "And your boss understands?"

Richie turned to watch her. "He's a single father," Terri answered simply.

Keene paused at that. "Okay," he answered, and turned to Richie. "I believe when you called me, Mr. Arias, you said that you work at home."

"I do." Richie's face became alight with pleasure. "On a new computer program, called Lawsearch. I really think it'll revolutionize legal research."

Looking for a weakness, Terri wondered if he would go too far, overplaying the great promoter until he seemed too preoccupied to parent Elena. As if reading her thoughts, Richie added, "It's been a good compromise."

His tone suggested that his meaning was evident to Terri. But as Richie had intended, Keene asked, "Between what and what?"

"Between work and parenting." He leaned back, spreading his hands. For Terri, his gestures had the same quicksilver quality as his expressions, as if nothing about him was quite real. But the look he turned on Keene radiated conviction. "Terri and I have always hated this yuppie-parent syndrome—you know, the overachieving two-career couple who come home burned out around the kids' bedtime, grab a drink, and ask the nanny how her day went." He gave Terri a confiding smile, as if warmed by the memory of their joint concern. "We tried having both of us work in offices for a while and decided it just wasn't right. So we agreed to put the emphasis on Terri's career and have me at home for Elena. It just makes sense that way—of the two of us, I'm the entrepreneurial one. It turns out I was also the lucky one. Watching Elena grow has been more rewarding than I ever dreamed." He paused, seemingly touched by the thought, and softly said to Terri: "No matter what, Ter, I'm really proud of what we've done."

It was a test, Terri realized: in the conspiracy that had been their marriage, it was Terri's role to cover for him, and he counted on that still. "I'm proud too," she said to Richie. "Of some things. The only problem is that none of the things *you* just described ever happened."

Richie's face was turned from Keene; only Terri could see his reflexive look of anger and surprise. But she kept on speaking to Richie. "So let's talk about what *did* happen," she said. "When I got pregnant with Elena, before we were married, I told you that I wasn't sure we should be married at all. You answered that you wanted a family, that our child would be the center of it. So I asked if I could just stay home with her. At least for a while."

Richie's eyes shone with resentment; Terri felt the guilt of her betrayal, the habit of five years. She forced herself to look straight at Richie. " 'Of course,' you answered. 'I want you home for our baby too. That's part of why we should get married.' "

"So we did." Terri's voice went flat. "And as soon as Elena was born, you quit your new job without telling me and decided to get an M.B.A. To help secure Elena's future, you said."

"That's not how it happened—"

"That's *exactly* how it happened." Terri leaned toward him. "So I had to return to law school when Elena was six weeks old and then scrambled to find the first job I could, at the P.D.'s office, while you took out a loan and went to grad school. I'm still paying off the loan.

"In the first year after you got out of grad school, you quit or got fired from two more firms. When your credit card charges got too high for me to carry, I left a job I'd gotten to like and took one with Chris's office." Her voice grew quiet. "When I came home that night and told you what I'd be making, you said you were proud of me because now you could 'work at home.' I started crying—I was so damned tired. You got angry and stormed out. But I couldn't even go after you to argue, or to plead. I had Elena to put to bed. As I do every night." She turned to Keene. "Elena has one stable parent—me. I want custody of our daughter."

Keene looked at them both, mouth half open. His quizzical smile seemed to have frozen in place.

With a look of deep sorrow, Richie shook his head. "Why are you saying this, Terri? We made those decisions together. Remember all those long dinners. *My God* . . ." He seemed to choke on the words, looking to Keene for help. "They say divorce does this to people, but I just can't *believe* that it's done it to us." He bowed his head, raising his hand to ask for time. "Sorry."

It would not do, Terri saw, for her to interrupt. Richie sat straighter in his chair, as if fighting to recover his dignity, then spoke to Keene. "The simple fact is that for the last year and a half, I've been home with Elena. In the structure of our family, I'm the one she turns to. We can talk about anything Elena wants to talk about." He stopped for a moment. "She's the center of my life, all right?"

"How many times," Terri asked, "have I left work to pick up Elena because you were too busy? And when you do talk to her, its about *your* problems. Elena's a *child*, not a little adult." Terri caught herself; Richie's edge was that Keene could not know where reality lay, so that the truth might sound too harsh. "Parenting is more than hanging around the house. And in this case, it's not collecting child support, either. I need you to help support her."

"What is this, Ter? An attack on my entire life? Character smears?" Richie's voice rose with hurt and anger. "Under the circumstances, I think I've been damned restrained."

"All right," Keene interjected. "I think I've got the flavor of your disagreements. Have you discussed solutions?"

"I've tried," Richie put in quickly, and then made his tone more soothing. "Look, I *know* Terri. She's a good mom. Elena loves her and she should see her. I just think that I should raise her, that's all."

He turned to Terri, voice softer still. "I think *you* think so too, Ter. At some other time, when your thing with Chris has calmed down a little, I'm sure we can work this out in Elena's best interests. Just give me a three-month trial period, that's all."

Keene removed his glasses, placed one stem beside his mouth. "I missed something," he said to Richie. "This 'thing with Chris' . . ."

"It's hard for me to face—traumatic, actually." Richie took a deep breath, gazing at the floor. "Terri's having an affair with her boss. Christopher Paget. Since it started, it seems I can't do anything right. He's good-looking and rich—everything Terri wishes *I* was. I simply can't compete."

Keene watched him. "That's a little out of my realm," he said gently.

Richie glanced up quickly. "Look, I know I need to separate my feelings about *that* from my positive feelings about Terri as a mom." His voice grew stronger. "The only thing is, I can't help but think it's affecting *her* judgment about Elena. The last thing that little girl needs is to be suddenly forced to rely on a distracted mother with a demanding job and a new boyfriend who isn't the dad that Elena's grown up loving."

"*That,*" Terri answered, "is not true. Chris and I are friends, and I *may* be seeing him. But I wasn't during our marriage—"

"We *are* married," Richie broke in. "Two weeks ago, we were living together. We've never even seen a marriage counselor. So don't tell me that Christopher Paget has nothing to do with the hell we're putting Elena through."

"All that Chris has to do with Elena," Terri shot back, "is that he's given me shorter hours so that *I* can raise her. Which is far more help than you've *ever* given me."

Richie flushed. In the silence, Keene looked glumly at them both. "Our time is up," he said finally. "Unfortunately, absent some change, I'm going to have to make a recommendation to the court that someone won't like. Maybe both of you."

That was it. A quick handshake, a neutral word of encouragement, and she and Richie were in the hall.

Terri felt suddenly empty; Elena's future, she thought in wonderment, might just have been decided.

Richie clutched her arm. "You said a lot of crap in there, Terri.

Nothing but lies. But it won't get you a thing. Because you've got no idea of how to *reach* people." His voice grew quiet with contempt. "Which is why you're going to lose her. Big time."

She turned to face him. "You said I was attacking your whole life. There's just one thing I forgot to mention." She moved close, staring up into his face. "You're a shitty lover, Richie. I mean really, really bad."

He reddened and then managed a faint, superior smile. "And there's something *I* forgot to mention—something I picked up from a lawyer I've been consulting." He almost whispered now. "Alec Keene's wife just left him. For a lawyer. See you in court, Ter."

SEVEN

FOR SECURITY REASONS—chiefly the potential for disappointed fathers to run amok with guns—the family court was housed in the Municipal Court building, a bleak and dingy building whose cramped entryway housed a guard and a metal detector. As an urban criminal lawyer, Terri was inured to such surroundings; passing through the metal detector with her lawyer—a pert, red-haired divorce specialist named Janet Flaherty, whom Terri had found through Chris—Terri the mother had felt a rising dread.

A cheery voice spoke out behind her. " 'Abandon all hope,' " it quoted, " 'ye who enter here.' "

Turning, Terri saw Richie's too bright smile. Part of him, she realized with amazement, enjoyed the attention he was about to receive. "Have you been lurking outside, reading *Bartlett's Quotations?*"

"Such a cynic." Still grinning, he extended his hand to Janet Flaherty. "Janet? I'm Richie Arias. We've spoken on the phone. Can we talk for a moment"—his head twitched toward Terri—"without your client?"

Terri felt her face tighten: unerringly, Richie knew how hard it was for Terri to speak for Elena through someone else. Flaherty regarded him with a blank expression. "Can we talk for a moment," she asked, "without *your* client?"

Richie laughed with great good humor. "I think only caterpillars can do that." The smile flashed again. "Or worms."

Flaherty's face did not change. "Exactly."

They took the elevator to the third floor, stood in the green tile hall outside the courtroom. Ignoring Terri, Richie fixed Flaherty with a gaze of profound seriousness. "I just wanted to avoid any undue emotion. What I was hoping, Janet, is that you might help mediate between Terri and me. We don't seem to be talking too well."

Richie with his party manners, Terri thought grimly. But Flaherty stayed level and unimpressed. "One reasonable step," she said "would be for you to look for work. As we've requested the court to direct."

Richie shook his head in disappointment. "At this critical time in our daughter's life, the last thing she needs is two absent parents. I *do* work. At home."

Flaherty suppressed a grimace. "We've plowed this ground before. So what's the proposition now?"

"A package deal. Nonmodifiable spousal support of a thousand a month for the next three years. Child support: fifteen hundred a month—"

"That's half my take-home," Terri put in. "Setting aside that *I* want custody."

"Let me finish. Please." He turned to Terri with limpid eyes. "I've worked this out, Ter, in a way that's fair to both of us. For one year, I get weeks and you get weekends. At the end of that year, we sit down and see how it's working. If we can't agree, then we can come back to court for a permanent order." His voice softened. "Look, this is the kind of mature solution the court will really respect. Besides, I'm taking a haircut on spousal—I'm sure the judge would give me more."

Terri watched him. "I'll up your spousal," she said. "But I want preponderant custody of Elena. Weekdays and every other weekend."

"You know that's a nonstarter, Ter." He spoke slowly and seriously, as if rehearsing for the judge. "This isn't a matter of money. I'm willing to sacrifice my career if it means Elena's happiness. And it does."

Frowning, Flaherty looked at her watch. "We're due inside," she put in. "Terri and I should talk."

They walked down the hallway, Terri glancing over her shoulder. Richie was walking in aimless circles.

"He's nervous about spousal," Terri murmured.

Flaherty nodded. "By making spousal support nonmodifiable, he avoids having to report to the court about looking for work and maybe getting cut if he's been sitting on his ass. He's not bad at this, really." Flaherty gazed down the hallway. "Thinks he's good with women too."

Terri felt concern overcome her. "Did you follow the rest of his scam?"

Flaherty's quick nod mingled impatience with understanding. "Richie knows that child support is his meal ticket—unlike spousal, he can live off that till Elena turns eighteen. Come the end of the year, he won't agree to any changes, even if she's obviously troubled. What he'll do instead is tell the court that it shouldn't disturb the status quo." She paused, glancing at Terri. "In family law, a year is long enough that the court will probably buy that.

"Once he has permanent custody, he can ratchet up child support every time you get a raise. As I understand his history, that means threats and tacit blackmail for the next thirteen years. And every time you try to force him to work, he'll start citing Elena's best interests.

"And last," Flaherty finished, in astringent tones, "he's got every weekend free. In short, the deadbeat's version of a perfect life. Have I missed anything?"

Terri found the mordant summary depressing in its accuracy. "There's no way," she said emphatically, "that I can let him raise Elena."

"Then we've got no choice but to go in there and fight him." Flaherty touched her shoulder. "But I should warn you again about how quirky Judge Scatena can be. Twenty years as a family court judge has taught him to hate pretty much everyone—lawyers included. Who he hates most depends more on how his synapses and dendrites connect that day than it does on the merits of a particular case." Flaherty glanced down the hallway. "We could luck out. Richie's not exactly a real guy, at least by Scatena's standards." She looked at her watch again. "Two minutes. Better go in."

As they moved toward Richie, he was whistling to himself.

"I can't agree," Terri said. "Not about Elena."

Irritation crossed Richie's face. Then he shook his head in solemn wonderment. "It's such a mistake, and really so sad. You give me no choice but to stand on my rights."

He turned on his heel and walked into the courtroom. Watching him, Flaherty looked pensive. "I have to ask you, Terri, do you have my retainer?"

Terri could follow her thoughts. Dealing with Richie would not be easy; the fees could mount quickly, and Flaherty, a solo practitioner, was too pragmatic to take chances with her cash flow. But once Terri wrote the check, she was out of money: the five thousand dollars Terri had borrowed from Rosa were a last resort.

"Do you want the check now?" Terri asked.

Flaherty shook her head. "I trust you."

They went inside.

The judge's chair was empty. The wall behind the bench was covered with gold paper; the American and California state flags stood to each side. The chief oddity was a black wrought-iron eagle, staring at the courtroom from atop the judge's bench. In front of the bench were two wooden tables, each with a brass nameplate, marked "Petitioner" and "Respondent"; a low wood partition with a swinging door separated the litigants of the moment from those waiting their turn—an assortment of men and women with lawyers, looking anxious and uncomfortable. Terri had never found a courtroom so dreary.

Gazing around her, she spotted Alec Keene in the front row. Richie had taken a seat next to him and was chatting amiably.

"What's Richie *doing?*" Terri murmured to Flaherty.

"Don't worry—Alec's already met with the judge to make his recommendation." She paused at the look in Terri's eyes. "He won't tell me how he came out on Elena, but Alec's a pro. And as far as I know, what Richie told you about his wife is bullshit."

Terri nodded. Trying not to look at Richie, she glanced toward the other side. The judge's deputy sat at the edge of the courtroom, a moonfaced man who looked too bored to move. But when a door at the rear of the bench swung open and Judge Scatena abruptly entered, the man rose slowly and intoned, "*All rise.* The Family Court for the County of Alameda, the Honorable Frank Scatena presiding, is now in session."

The spectators rose a few at a time—the newcomers confused and looking about them for cues. Scatena was an erect white-haired man in his sixties with a seamed face, a hooked nose, and, it appeared, painfully arthritic hands; surveying the room with jaded bureaucratic displeasure, he kept twisting his fingers and wincing. "All right," he said in a throaty, incurious voice, "what have we got first?"

The deputy glanced at his docket. "Case No. 94-716," he announced. "Ricardo Arias versus Teresa Peralta. Petitioner's motion for alimony, child support, and interim custody; respondent's cross-motion for interim custody and that the court require petitioner to seek employment."

Richie rose and walked through the swinging door. Terri glanced at him with a sense of wonderment; the last time they had stood before a judge was the day that they had been married. The memory of how she was then, scared and hopeful and pregnant with Elena, came to Terri with piercing sadness.

"I'll hear petitioner," Scatena said to Richie. "The first issue is spousal support and whether you'll get work."

Richie went to the podium, head held high, looking Scatena in the face. "Good morning, Your Honor. Ricardo Arias, appearing in pro per—"

"I know that," Scatena cut in. "And there's nothing much worse than a male lawyer representing himself in a custody suit. Why haven't you got your own lawyer?"

Richie paused for a moment, then smiled. "I agree," he said with an air of candor. "No matter how I try, I'm too emotional to always be objective. Plus I have no experience at this." He shrugged helplessly. "If I had any money, I wouldn't be standing here."

Terri inclined her head to Flaherty, whispering, "The *last* thing he wants is a lawyer to control him."

But Flaherty was watching Scatena. The judge leaned forward. "You can ask me to order your wife to pay for a lawyer. *She's* retained one, so there's some money there."

Richie nodded in agreement. "She makes a very high salary, that's true. But it's my position that any resources should be preserved for Elena's benefit to the maximum extent." His voice became humble. "I can only promise that in any appearance before this court, I will behave as professionally as I can."

"He's doing it right," Flaherty whispered. "Don't make this judge mad."

Scatena assessed Richie. "Why don't you just get a job, Mr. Arias? You seem able-bodied enough to me."

"Well, to start, it's a critical time in our daughter's life—"

"Yes, and it's too bad. But there are millions of divorces a year. And in most families these days, both parents work. I may not like it, but there it is." Scatena resumed twisting his fingers. "This situation isn't unique."

Richie looked down. "I guess to a parent, Your Honor, each child is unique. That's what makes families so important. But you're right, of course." He paused, brow furrowed. "The thing is, Terri and I agreed that I would raise Elena. As a result, my law career has fallen way behind now—I can't earn half of what Terri makes. Half of *that* would go to child care. And there would be no one home for Elena after school or during the summer."

Scatena sat forward. Richie met his eyes, speaking with the unassuming candor of a man sitting in a coffee shop. "Then there are the equities to consider. I'm here only because I agreed to sacrifice my career to Terri's, in Elena's best interest." Richie's gaze broke again, and his voice grew soft and shamed. "Terri has resources: a high-paying job and a wealthy boyfriend who happens to be her boss. Because I thought we would always be married, I have none. It's not fair—to Elena or me—to push me out of the house."

Terri felt herself gripping the table. The sudden reference to Chris was deft: a passing mention, meant to suggest that Terri had left him for her employer.

"That depends, doesn't it," Scatena told Richie in a neutral tone, "on who gets custody."

Richie looked up again, voice gathering strength. "When I say fair to Elena, Your Honor, I mean to include economics. I *intend* to help support my daughter—it's part and parcel of my concept of parenting. It may well be that in the long run, *I'm* the primary support of Elena." He spread his hands. "I certainly haven't been sitting around. I've taken my role in the family—the at-home parent—and used it to start my own business. The computer program I'm putting together is on the cutting edge of research technology for lawyers." He stopped, smiling at his own enthusiasm. "If it works, who knows?"

It was, Terri saw, another nice touch: Richie might look optimistic, even silly, but he was no longer a deadbeat. "So how much do you want?" Scatena asked.

"Spousal only?"

"Yes."

Richie cocked his head. "My petition says fifteen hundred a month. But that's based on my wife's current salary, of course." His voice turned soft. "I believe that she has reason to expect a raise."

Terri grasped Flaherty's sleeve. "He's making it sound like I'm fucking my boss for money. That Chris broke up our marriage."

Flaherty shook her head. "We can't start denying that to Scatena," she whispered. "It's a sideshow—all we would do is move Chris front and center. And it's irrelevant to the issues here, even if it *were* true."

That was right, the lawyer in Terri knew. But Richie had planted the thought quickly enough to get away with it, certain that it would damage Terri no matter what she did.

"All right," Scatena said. "Let's hear from Mrs. Arias."

Walking to his table, back to Scatena, Richie allowed a self-satisfied smile to play across his mouth. Then, as if remembering Keene, he erased the smile in an instant.

Flaherty went to the podium. "Janet Flaherty, Your Honor, for respondent Teresa Peralta."

"Yes," Scatena amended dryly. "Ms. Peralta."

Terri did not like the sound of that. But Flaherty looked unruffled.

"Mr. Arias's position—on *everything*—stems from the assertion that Teresa Peralta implored him to stay home. If that were correct, then his argument might carry some weight.

"The truth, Your Honor, is that Ms. Peralta implored him to work and he refused." She paused. "The *truth* is that Mr. Arias has been on a self-declared sabbatical from his responsibilities—both to Teresa and to his daughter, Elena.

"Who supports Mr. Arias? Teresa does.

"Who supports Elena? Again, Teresa.

"Who *watches* Elena?" Here Flaherty paused. "*Not* Mr. Arias. A day care center. Paid for by Teresa Peralta—"

"What about summers, Counselor?"

Terri flashed on the bitter argument she had with Richie when money was tight last summer and Elena had stayed home: leaving work early, Terri had found Elena camped in front of the television, hungry because Richie had forgotten lunch.

"Last summer, Mr. Arias," Flaherty answered. "But that was an economic necessity—he had again declined to work. And Elena's summer was *not* satisfactory."

Scatena grimaced. "But she did leave her with Mr. Arias, correct?

I don't suppose she'd have done that if the child's life had been in danger."

Flaherty stared at him. "We don't think that's the standard, Your Honor—"

"According to Mr. Arias," Scatena interrupted in a hectoring tone, "he was also working."

"According to Mr. Arias," Flaherty replied. "But his so-called enterprise has yet to generate a dime. Where is his business plan, I wonder, or a cash flow projection? Where are the buyers for his supposed breakthrough?"

"I have no clue, Counselor. Maybe Mr. Arias doesn't, either. He says this is a start-up." Scatena leaned forward. "Come the final hearing, Counselor, you can lawyer this case to death. Call in experts, give his plans the complete Harvard B-School analysis—I don't care. But our business here is determining what he gets in the meantime."

For the first time, Flaherty looked disconcerted. "What Mr. Arias should 'get,' in our view, is a directive to find work."

"She makes over twice the national family average, Counselor."

The argument, Terri saw, was sliding downhill. "In *San Francisco*," Flaherty rejoined. "The most expensive city in America. Look at our income and expense statement." Flaherty jabbed the finger of one hand, ticking off the last. "Rent, fifteen hundred a month, for no great apartment. Child care, over five hundred. Car payments, two hundred. Food and household, four fifty. Charge cards, six hundred—"

"Which is obscene, with the picture you're painting."

"Those charges were Mr. Arias's." Flaherty lowered her voice. "The point, Your Honor, is that my client's take-home can't go any farther than it's going. The reason she's in this position is that Mr. Arias won't work."

Scatena gave a theatrical shrug. "Mr. Arias says otherwise. So what am I supposed to believe?"

"The numbers," Flaherty responded. "They're not in dispute. Ms. Peralta's paycheck can't stretch anymore."

Scatena folded his hands, a man who had heard enough. "Well, it's going to have to, Ms. Flaherty. The man has no job. I'm going to award him interim support, and I'll decide how much after we ad-

"No, parenting is a number of things—love, understanding, stability, and financial support—which flow from a single source. A sense of responsibility."

She paused, turning to look at Terri until Scatena's eyes followed. Terri tried to read his face.

"Teresa Peralta," Flaherty said slowly, "is the *responsible* parent. The one who calls Elena's teachers. Who takes her to the doctor. Who puts her to bed at night, drives her to day care in the morning. And, yes, who supports her.

"Mr. Arias talked about security. Ms. Peralta *is* this child's security. She is the one who does everything." Flaherty paused again. "Including take care of a man who has not, for whatever reason, provided for himself or his family.

"To give Mr. Arias custody would be to get things backward. Teresa Peralta needs help, *not* another dependent. Not still more burdens." Flaherty paused again. "The reward for being the responsible parent should be the responsibility of parenting. That is what Elena needs, and that is what she has in Ms. Peralta."

Scatena held up a hand. "You pose me the same problem, Counsel. How do *I* know?" His voice became biting. "Frankly, if Mr. Arias had hired you first, I'm sure you could make him sound as much like Walt Disney as Ms. Peralta sounds like Snow White."

From the corner of her eye, Terri saw Richie repress a smile. She rose from her chair without thinking.

Flaherty's voice sounded parched. "All that I'm doing, Your Honor, is addressing the facts—"

"As *you* see them," Scatena snapped. "They're not so apparent to me. Anything else?"

"Yes, Your Honor." The words were out before Terri heard the desperation in her voice, and then she forced herself to sound calm. "It is simply not possible for this court, or any court, to make an informed decision in so short a time, with so little information. I ask the court to defer any ruling until there's been some chance for Mr. Keene to see Elena—"

"*Sit down.*"

Terri froze, and then slowly sat. She was, by reflex, still a lawyer.

Scatena glowered from the bench. "Ms. Flaherty speaks for you. Which, as an attorney, you know very well. I'll find you in contempt if you *ever* speak out again." He leaned back, wincing as he wrung dress custody." He glanced at Richie, then added in a sarcastic tone, "If Mr. Arias were an unemployed wife, there'd be no question about spousal support, and we wouldn't have spent twenty minutes debating it."

Richie nodded to himself, as if deeply impressed by the judge's sense of fairness. Watching Flaherty return to her seat, Terri could not repress her fear. "He's buying Richie's act," Terri whispered.

"It's okay," Flaherty murmured back. "Custody is a separate deal. A lot depends on Alec Keene."

"Next," Scatena snapped, "is custody. Mr. Arias?"

Richie walked slowly to the podium. "It's exactly as the court said," he began. "I'm at home, and Terri isn't. At least in the near term, that should decide custody. But I want to take just a moment—because I know the court has people waiting—to talk about *why* I'm home."

He paused to collect his thoughts. "For better or for worse, the last twenty years have been a time of social change. Women have been entering the workplace in greater numbers, for greater rewards. There are more two-worker families. And of course, there's more divorce."

The message was subtle but unmistakable. Terri leaned close to Flaherty. "He's guessing Scatena doesn't like the women's movement. . . ."

"In this environment," Richie went on, "there's been more experimentation with the family unit. In *our* experiment, I was the one to be with Elena. That's her security now."

He drew himself up. "I love my daughter," he finished softly. "I don't think we should experiment with her, anymore."

He gazed up at Scatena as if in search of understanding and then abruptly sat, his last obeisance to a busy man.

"Make *him* the issue," Terri whispered to Flaherty. "Don't let him get away with this."

Flaherty rose with a look of introspection, prepared to give the argument that Terri had helped her craft. "As we know," Flaherty began, "being a parent is very complex. It isn't any one thing. And it certainly isn't as simple as who's home between nine and five—a time during which, for most of the day, Elena Arias will be in school.

his hands. "You know, Ms. Peralta, professional couples are the bane of this court, and lawyers are the worst. The child might as well be a football." He paused. "I advise you to remember *that* if you can't work things out with Mr. Arias."

The courtroom was still. Scatena wheeled on Flaherty. "You can sit down too, Ms. Flaherty. Seeing how your client doesn't seem to need you."

Flaherty walked back, mouth a grim line. Scatena did not wait for her to sit. "Here's my order," he snapped. "Interim custody to petitioner, Mr. Arias. Interim spousal support to Mr. Arias: one thousand two hundred fifty dollars until the final hearing. Interim child support to Mr. Arias: a thousand dollars." The judge looked back at Terri, his face glowering with the residue of ill temper. "Visitation to Ms. Peralta: alternate weekends, Friday evening to Sunday evening. Work out the details with your husband—this court doesn't have time for that." He turned to his deputy. "Next case."

Terri sat there.

Flaherty touched her shoulder. "Come on," she said gently. "Let's go."

Scatena cracked his gavel. Terri started, rising from her chair like an automaton. She did not see the courtroom as she left it. She felt numb.

Outside, Terri found herself leaning against a wall. Flaherty was next to her, she realized. "I'm sorry," Flaherty said in a chastened voice. "He's like that."

"It's okay. You did everything you could."

Flaherty squeezed her hand. "Are you all right?"

"Fine. I'll call you later."

The lawyer hesitated. "Go ahead," Terri told her. "You've got other cases. Please."

Flaherty nodded. Terri listened to the tap of her heels as she left. Less than a month, and Elena was gone.

Terri felt a hand on her shoulder. She turned, ready to face Richie.

It was Alec Keene. "Things like that should never happen," he said.

"Shouldn't they?"

"No, they shouldn't." He began fidgeting. "And I shouldn't tell you this, either. But that wasn't what I recommended. Half the time, the man doesn't listen to us."

Terri stared at him. " 'The man,' " she said tersely, "doesn't know anything about my daughter."

"He doesn't need to." Keene's tone mingled weariness and disgust. "He's had a lifetime of experience—just ask him. He can tell more about the parties from their decorum in his courtroom, he told me once, than by reading our reports."

It made Terri feel sick. "Then Richie won that one. He's a con man. I'm just a fool."

Keene watched her a moment. "Try this for three, four months," he said. "Then come see me."

He left.

Terri took a deep breath. Put one foot in front of the other, she told herself. Get out of here and think about it later.

She left the way she had come, down the elevator and out the glass door, alone.

Terri hurried to her car.

She made it to the passenger side, cracking open the door. Then she bent forward over the pavement and vomited.

EIGHT

THE LOOK in Elena's eyes, frightened and inconsolable, made Terri fight back tears.

They stood in Rosa's living room. "I don't *want* to just live with Daddy," Elena said. "I want to live with *both* of you."

Terri hugged Elena before the child could look at her. When Terri glanced up at her mother, standing beside them, Rosa's face was stone. Rosa turned and left the room.

"It's just for a while," Terri said to Elena. "Only for a while." Said it almost like a mantra, to herself.

"But *why?*" The little girl pulled away. "Why don't you want to be with me?"

Elena's defensiveness of Richie had vanished: she was a child who needed her mother. But all that Terri could do for her was not to cry. "I *do* want to be with you," she said, and then spoke the lines she had rehearsed. "But Daddy's at home right now, and I have to work. So we decided he should take care of you. Just for now."

"But who's going to take care of Daddy?"

In her bitterness, Terri wished she could take the child to Scatena, demand that he answer her himself. But the custody trial would not be for at least nine months, and after yesterday Terri could not imagine winning. "I'll still help him," Terri said quietly. "Daddy will be fine, and some weekends you'll come live with me. Next weekend, if you want, we can go to the zoo."

It did not seem to reassure Elena, and Terri wished she had not said it: the image that came to her was of driving Elena and Richie to Tilden Park and thinking that—whatever their own problems— she did not envy the weekend parents she saw there, could not imagine accepting a few hours of pushing a swing in exchange for the constant presence that, without any schedule or sense of moment, would make Elena who she was.

There was a knock at the door.

"It's your daddy." Terri mustered a smile. "It's time now."

"How's my princess," Richie exclaimed, and swooped to pick up Elena. Then he turned and asked Terri in a businesslike voice, "Got her stuff?"

Silent, Terri handed him the suitcase.

"I'll need my check," he told her. "The whole amount."

Terri stared at him. "It's not the first yet."

"Well, I need it, and that's just how it is." He kissed Elena on the cheek. "I promised Lainie we'd go to the movies, and there's not enough food."

Terri saw Elena's eyes, fearful and confused. In silence, she hoped that there was a special place in hell for men who made their daughters worry about them.

She went to her purse and wrote him a check.

"Okay, Lainie," Richie said in a cheerful voice. "We're off."

He walked briskly away, Elena looking over his shoulder.

Terri made herself watch them go. It was not until the car disappeared that Terri climbed the stairs to her old bedroom and closed the door behind her.

The next night, after Carlo was in bed, Terri came to Chris.

For a time, they stood in his darkened living room, Chris holding her in silence. And then Terri took his hand and they walked upstairs to his bedroom.

They stood facing each other, a few feet apart, as they undressed. The sheets felt cool on Terri's skin. Only their fingers touched.

Until he reached for her.

He seemed to know her. There was no fear, no haste or overeagerness: in the last moment before she became part of him, Terri thought with a shade of ruefulness that Christopher Paget had made love far too often, to far too many women, for him to feel these things as she did.

And then nothing else mattered.

Terri felt his mouth and hands moving across her face and nipples and body, stopping where they would as she became caught up in their discovery, his partner, doing as he did until she told him, in every way but speech, the one thing that was left for him to do.

She felt him with an intensity that shook her.

Conscious thought stopped: all Terri knew was that he could not be close enough, deep enough, unless she pushed still harder. Time vanished. And then her body tightened, thrusting against the length of him as the first shudder ran through her. She barely recognized the woman's voice, crying out with passion and release, as hers.

"Stay inside me, Chris," she whispered. "Lose yourself." And then Terri realized that he had.

Silent, he held her.

Terri let her mind go free, feeling the breeze through Chris's windows, listening to the rustle of trees outside, the city sounds drifting from below. A foghorn sounded. All at once she felt disoriented: her child was gone, the life she had lived was over, she was lying in the darkened bedroom of a strange house. It seemed that Teresa the mother had vanished, and the woman she had left behind did not know who or where she was.

"I know you feel lost," Chris murmured.

It was as if he had read her thoughts. "I do," she said simply.

Chris brought her closer. Near dawn, she fell asleep in his arms.

In the days and weeks that followed, Chris tried his best to give her a life she could cling to without Elena.

They found Terri a place she could afford, a bright five-room apartment in a sunny part of the city, Noe Valley. Terri enjoyed the outdoors; on a weekend without Elena, they drove across the Golden Gate Bridge to Marin County in Chris's convertible, with the top down and the stereo blasting—he liked the Gin Blossoms, REM, and the Spin Doctors, Terri found to her surprise—to hike to the beach. They both enjoyed modern art, so the next day they went to galleries along Hayes Street. As a child, Terri had imagined herself as a dancer; Chris got them tickets to the ballet. Most of all, he gave her his time, without demands or even plans beyond the moment.

As for Carlo, he was far too secure to resent Terri's presence. And he was good to Elena. At moments, Terri felt so close to Chris that it scared her, but then, as always, Elena pulled her back. Terri devoted her weekends with Elena to the child alone; they would visit Chris and Carlo only for a few hours, and only when Carlo would be there. Chris and Terri did not touch in her presence. But as gentle and nonassertive as Chris was, Elena would say little to him; angry that the loss of Elena had not destroyed Terri's relationship to Chris,

Richie had made it clear to their daughter that Chris was his enemy, a source of hurt. Carlo was different: to his seeming embarrassment, the little girl worshiped him.

"*Carlo*," she would shriek, and run through the house to find him. The boy reacted with amusement and chagrin; his charm, he remarked to Terri, was sure to end at kindergarten.

"I'm not so sure." Terri smiled. "As far as Elena's concerned, you've got it all—no wrinkles, money to buy ice cream, and plenty of time to play."

"Rrright . . ."

But Carlo was indulgent with her. He carried Elena on his shoulders; let her win at Blockhead; introduced her to the friends who kept dropping by to shoot pool. Once, Carlo and his red-haired girlfriend, Katie, had read Elena stories; Elena had cast a proprietary eye at Katie and positioned herself in Carlo's lap.

"I'm going to marry Carlo," Elena announced to Katie. "When I'm twelve."

Carlo checked his watch. "In exactly five hundred seven thousand, one hundred thirteen hours and eighteen minutes," he told Katie, "your time is up."

That was enough for Elena. And the next weekend, on an afternoon when Carlo seemed particularly tolerant, he walked her to the park near Chris's house. Terri watched them go, a tall, handsome boy in a baseball cap with a raven-haired child who came to his waist but insisted on holding his hand. Unlike Terri, and perhaps Chris, Carlo seemed to make her forget how angry she was.

Closing the door, Terri decided that this was a blessing. For Elena—when she wasn't listless—was so angry that she seemed out of Terri's reach.

At first, this anger seemed sporadic, the fruits of a bitter separation. There were times when the child seemed wholly engaged in her favorite activities: pounding on the electric keyboard; painting with watercolors at Terri's apartment; climbing playground structures so fearlessly that only the joy in her face stopped Terri from coaxing the child down to safety. Terri had quick reflexes and unusually fast hands: Elena, who shared these gifts, delighted in playing jacks with her mother, snatching the metal pieces before the rubber ball bounced twice. But at other times, the normally spirited little girl would become recalcitrant, ignoring her mother or throwing toys;

telling Terri that she hated her apartment; demanding to call her father so that he would not be lonely. Whether spoken or silent, the message was the same—the divorce was Terri's fault.

"You hug and kiss Chris now," Elena said flatly.

They were tie-dyeing T-shirts at the kitchen sink; Terri had thought it a happy day. She searched her memory of the time since the separation for some slip in Elena's presence, found none. "How do you know that?"

"Daddy told me." The child's voice was accusatory. "He's all alone."

For a moment, Terri found herself so angry that she wanted to scream, What about *me*—the one who loves you and pays his bills and works until I can't see straight. "Chris is my friend, Elena. He's nice to me." She paused and then asked, "Don't you think I deserve *someone* to be nice to me?"

Elena frowned. "*I'm* nice to Daddy," she said, and put down her T-shirt. "I'm bored with this."

That night, when Elena had gone, Terri called Richie. "What are you telling her about Chris?" she asked.

"Why is everything always 'about Chris'?" His voice was mock innocent. "What makes you think I even care?"

"Whether or not you care, we need to get this straight."

"We already did," he said. "In court. Anyway, can't talk now—we're playing Blockhead." His voice grew silken. "You know, the game that Carlo likes so much."

He hung up.

Terri waited until ten and drove to Richie's.

Elena answered the door. Surprised, Terri bent to hug her. "It's past your bedtime, sweetheart."

The little girl pushed her away. "It's *not*. Daddy said there was no bedtime tonight."

Walking past Elena, Terri saw Richie in the living room, an empty bottle of wine in front of him, candles on the coffee table. Instinctively, Terri looked for a second adult, then perceived from Richie's flush that he had drunk the bottle alone. For an instant he looked cornered, and then his eyes took on a strange glitter. "We've stayed up playing games," he said. "Just like you, Terri. Coming here."

The words had a sibilant hiss; their overprecision reminded Terri of Ramon Peralta.

Without answering, she picked up Elena and tucked her in bed, read her stories until it seemed that the little girl was asleep. But as Terri left, Elena whispered, "Can you stay, Mommy? I like it when you're here."

When Terri at last went to find Richie, the living room lights were off. That and the smell of wine gave Terri the trapped, eerie feeling of her childhood: a man sitting alone in the darkness, ready to explode.

"Miss me, Ter?" Richie's voice from the darkness was slurred and insinuating. "We're all alone now, and Christopher Paget's nowhere in sight. Just the way it should be."

She forced herself to face him. "If you ever do this around Elena," she said softly, "I'll kill you myself."

Terri turned and walked out. She did not know whether she had only imagined Richie laughing as the door shut.

NINE

"HE DOESN'T DRINK," she told Chris the next day. "At least not much."

They sat in his office. "Maybe he's beginning to unravel," Chris answered. "I'd start keeping a journal. Everything Richie does."

"Assuming anyone will believe me." She paused. "Elena's not right, Chris. I may go back to Alec Keene."

Chris nodded. "I think you should."

As Terri stood to leave, he raised a hand to stop her. "Have another minute?" he asked. "There's something I need to talk to you about."

His tone was somehow different. Slowly, Terri sat again, watching his face.

Chris folded his hands. "I've been asked to consider running for the Senate, Terri. In the Democratic primary, two years from now."

It startled her. "As in *United States* Senate?"

Chris nodded. "Amazing, isn't it. 'The Decline of the West.' "

"That's not what I meant, Chris. I'm just surprised, that's all."

"So was I." Chris was trying to make this sound like a mere curiosity. "When Wally Mathews called, I thought he wanted money again. Instead he wanted *me*, for whatever reason."

She was quiet for a time. "You might be good, Chris."

"So Wally claims," he said dryly. "According to him, I'm famous twice over—for the Lasko case and for the Carelli hearing. He also pointed out that winning the primary would cost at least seven million dollars and that I happen to have it. Wonderful system, isn't it." His voice became a shade less casual. "Part of it is that some people want a senatorial candidate who hasn't been handpicked by James Colt, Junior. Our inevitable next governor."

Once more, Terri felt surprise and a little unease. James Colt was a prominent Democrat of about Chris's age: besides his vast wealth and ambition, one reason for his power was public veneration for his father, a charismatic senator from southern California who had died before he could run for President. Most local politicians, including the ambitious district attorney, McKinley Brooks, were already allied with Colt; it would not be easy for Chris to build support.

"What reason," Terri asked, "does Wally give for wanting someone independent of Colt?"

Chris shrugged. "The same reason a lot of party people give, under their breath. That beneath his public charm, James Colt is as mean as a snake and utterly devoid of principle. Wally thinks that I could be a counterweight."

Why, Terri thought, did she feel a sense of loss and apprehension? She and Chris had never discussed the future and, until the court awarded final custody of Elena, could not consider living together even if they wanted to. "And you're thinking about it," she ventured.

"To my surprise. After Lasko ended, I wanted nothing more to do with politics. But when Wally called, I realized that there are things I'd like to say, and this may be a last chance to say them in any way that matters." Chris turned to the window. "At my age, you start to ask yourself what it's all meant. My answer has always been Carlo. But outside of that, I really don't know. And in two years, Carlo leaves for college."

"How does *he* feel about this?"

"Carlo claims to be all for it, although I worry about being gone too much. Another part is us." He turned back to her. "James Colt will not be thrilled, and politics can be pretty savage. Even when it's not, it tends to eat up lives."

Something told Terri that she did not wish Chris to do this. But she did not know what Chris might want for them, or where his self-interest ended and hers began; until the final custody hearing, there was no point in imagining their future. "It might be nice for you to have a hobby," she said with a smile. "It's just that I worry about Richie, all right? He's jealous of you, Chris."

"*Richie?* What can *he* do to me?" Chris seemed to watch her for a moment, and then changed the subject. "Whatever Richie does when he has Elena," he told her, "don't save him, and don't cover for him. Without your help, he may start screwing up Elena's life in a way that other people notice." His voice turned cool and clear. "No matter how painful, let him. Because Elena will end up with you."

This, Terri knew, was the best advice Chris could give. But the mother in Terri found it hard to follow.

Perhaps Richie knew that she could not help but salvage him if Elena was at risk. When Richie suddenly "gave up" the old apartment because he had stopped paying rent, he had let her know that he was looking in neighborhoods Terri knew to be unsafe; after a week of this, Terri found them another apartment in the city, so that Elena would be closer, and when the landlord balked at Richie's credit, Terri cosigned the lease. She hated herself for it, just as—in the twisted logic of a custody battle—she despised herself for finding Elena the best possible school for kindergarten, once it was clear that Richie would not bother. Richie knew nothing about the school, and did not seem to care. But when Terri dragged him to observe the classroom Elena would enter in the fall, Richie cornered the teacher, Leslie Warner, a willowy dark-haired woman with wide-set eyes and a credulous demeanor. In his proud and confiding manner, Richie described to Warner how he "participated in Elena's fantasies," so as to "help her imagination come alive"; smiling and nodding, Warner did not take her eyes off Richie. Terri could not stand to watch.

But neither, it seemed, could she truly help Elena.

It was not any one thing, but a series of disturbing changes. Elena, though still defensive of her father, no longer asked whether he and Terri might reconcile. Instead she would sit alone for long listless periods, barely speaking. She would not sleep by herself, began demanding the night-light she had proudly discarded a year before. She complained of stomachaches. She smiled less, painted less, went to the playground at Terri's suggestion rather than asking to go. When Terri called the school, the teacher said that Elena was polite to her but had made no real friends. Yet Richie claimed to see nothing.

They were standing in her kitchen after Richie had dropped off Elena. "She's always fine with me," he told her. "That leaves you and your boyfriend. If you were a little more sensitive, Ter, you'd see that your premature relationship is a form of abuse and give him up."

Terri controlled her temper. "She's been listless at school too. And she used to make friends so easily."

Richie grimaced. "I'll keep an eye out, okay? But Leslie keeps me posted, and I think *you're* the problem. In fact, I think that all you're proving is how right Scatena had it. I don't know why you imagine you can change his mind—especially when you're still screwing Paget."

Through her anger, Terri heard the reference to "Leslie"—dropped, perhaps, to make Terri wonder. It would be just like him, Terri thought; a chance to ingratiate himself with an attractive young woman by playing the anxious father. "This isn't a contest, Richie—"

"You're damn right it isn't." His voice turned low and angry. "I'm broke all the time now—no money for Lawsearch, no nothing. It's a good thing some women like me enough to take me out." His eyes glinted with resentment. "Except for my sex life, you really fucked me over."

Terri simply stared at him. "It's so sad," she said then. "In some ways, you understand me so well. But you don't understand yourself at all. So you'll always end up blaming me for everything that happens to you. All the way to the bottom, taking Elena with you."

His face changed; it was as if the softness of her voice had drained the anger from him. He sat down at the kitchen table, chin propped in his hands. "It just isn't going well, Ter." His voice fell. "It hasn't, ever since you left me."

His body seemed to slump. For an instant, from some buried instinct of their marriage, Terri wanted to comfort him. "I'm sorry," she said. "I want things to be good for you. Really."

He looked up. "For Elena's sake," he said flatly.

"For Elena's. For your sake. And for mine." She paused. "If your life is a shambles, nobody wins. I don't want a lifetime of worrying about you or what you'll do to keep afloat."

He gazed up at her and then looked away. "Sometimes, without you, I just feel so lost." His voice fell. "Sometimes I feel like things will never be right again."

Even Richie could not tell, Terri thought with sadness, where his vulnerability became artifice. It was that knowledge that kept her from touching Richie's shoulder. And then, at the instant when she stopped herself, Terri sensed all the unknown ways—planted deep in her subconscious—that she still was Richie's wife.

He looked up at her, eyes brimming. "We can still make it, Ter. I know we can. Then you can be with Elena."

Terri could find no words.

Standing, Richie took her hands in his. "We'll go to a counselor." He stopped, feeling the lifelessness of Terri's hands, and then flashed an edgy smile. "Look, I *know* things have gotten a little out of hand with this custody deal, okay? But that was just a lawsuit, Ter— you do what you have to do. Nothing's happened we can't put behind us."

She stared at him. "I'm real, Richie. I have feelings of my own. Not just whatever you want me to feel."

He seemed to blink; there was a blankness in his eyes as he searched for the right emotion. Something in the moment frightened Terri more than violence would have. "I know, baby," he said softly. "I know this has been scary stuff. But it's over now. For all of us."

Terri felt a knot in her stomach. She stood there, mute and rigid, until his arms enfolded her.

"No," she murmured. "*No.*"

He stood back from her, eyes widening in puzzlement.

"I can never be with you, Richie. Ever again." She gripped his shoulders, as if to make him see. "It's all wrong. It's like we call out the worst in each other."

He stared at her. "But what about Elena, Terri? What about what *she* wants?"

Terri walked away from him, leaned against the wall. "She wants what *any* child wants—two parents who love each other. But she can't have that, ever." She turned to him. "The next best thing is two parents who love *her* more than themselves."

Smiling slightly, he put his hands on his hips, his eyes narrowed. "I get it, Ter—another attack on me. That way people won't figure out that it's Christopher Paget who stands between Elena and the family you won't give her—"

"Please, Richie, just let me have her for a while. I'll see you're taken care of. Please. I'm frightened for her."

"Elena *needs* me." Richie gave her a look of bitter knowledge. "You think you can take everything away from me, don't you. But you can never kill my daughter's love."

He turned and walked from the kitchen.

Terri stood there awhile. Then she heard him in the bedroom, talking to Elena.

"It makes me sad too," he was saying quietly. "I'll come back for you just as soon as I can."

As he drove away, Elena watched him from the window. She did not want dinner.

That night, Terri found Elena sitting rigid in her bed, tears streaming down her face.

Terri got in bed with her. "Was it a nightmare?" she asked gently. But Elena would not speak.

In the morning, Elena's eyes were puffy with sleeplessness. When Terri asked about the dream, the child shook her head.

Back off, Terri told herself, try to leave her alone. Do something. Take a shower. Think of Chris. Anything at all.

It worked for a while. And then, applying eyeliner, Terri found Elena next to her.

To her relief, the sight brought Terri close to laughter: dressed only in cotton underwear, Elena stretched to see herself in the mirror, her child's belly sticking out a little, solemnly applying imagined mascara with a toothbrush in an absurd pantomime of her mother.

"What are you doing?" Terri asked.

"I'm going to my office," Elena answered matter-of-factly. "I'm *very* busy. I have to be in court, you know."

The answer left Terri both amused and ambivalent: Terri's memories of her own mother were of someone who was always there.

"For court," Terri told Elena, "you'll need a briefcase," and she went to the closet for an extra one.

Taking it, Elena's smile was impish. "Now I'm *you*," she said, knowing this was funny, and then started across the living room, a half-naked child with a briefcase that dragged on the carpet.

Terri smiled after her. "Do you want to be me?"

Elena turned to her, eyes still and serious. The laughter was gone.

"Yes," she said. "So *I* can take care of Daddy by myself."

Terri shook her head. "I already told you, sweetheart. You don't need to take care of grown-ups. Including your dad."

"I *do*." The child seemed angry now. "You don't want to take care of him anymore. So *I'm* going to."

Speechless, Terri watched the little girl strain to stand straighter, holding the briefcase stiffly. The smudges beneath her eyes were like bruises.

TEN

ALEC KEENE's venetian blinds cut the afternoon sunlight into ribbons on his gray tile floor. "Terri's been pretty specific," he said to Richie. "Listlessness, insecurity, lack of sleep. And, lately, repeated nightmares."

Richie looked at him with folded arms. "I haven't seen it, Alec." His voice was polite but cool. "I hate to say so, but these things seem to happen when Elena's with Terri. If they happen at all."

His voice was a shade less deferential than previously, Terri noticed; it was as if Judge Scatena had placed him in control. Quietly, Keene asked, "Are you saying that Terri made all this up?"

At once, Richie's tone became apologetic. "Okay, maybe that last wasn't fair. What Terri says surprises me, that's all."

Keene appraised him. "Do you have any suggestions?"

Richie gazed at the ceiling; the expression was that of a man reluctant to express his thoughts. "I do," he said slowly. "Terri's a good mother, I know. But since her involvement with Christopher Paget, she has a hard time thinking about Elena." He turned to Terri. "And you *are* involved with him, Terri."

"Yes." Terri kept her voice steady. "*Now* I am. But that has nothing to do with Elena."

"*Oh, Terri,*" Richie said with a knowing smile. "*Any* expert can tell you that a new relationship can be upsetting to *any* child, let alone one that occurs so soon after a breakup." His voice softened. "Or, in this case, before."

"You'd better find something else, Richie. That one's getting old. . . ."

"Look, Ter, I'll learn to live with the fact that you've changed lovers quicker than *I* can change a tire, all right? But it's not so easy for Elena." He turned to Keene, voice softening. "I apologize, Alec. It still stings a little. But I'm trying to be objective. All that I'm asking is that Terri agree not to expose Elena to Christopher Paget."

Terri kept her eyes on Richie. "It's not that frequent. Besides, Elena adores Carlo. It would be wrong to tell her that she can never see him."

"On some level, Terri, she'll be relieved. And parents make hard decisions all the time." Richie's tone became pleading. "I'd make *this* decision, if I could. Please, put Elena first."

Terri turned to Keene. "Anytime I talk about Elena, Richie brings up Chris. It's meant to get you off track."

Keene looked glum. "Would it be so difficult, what Richie asks?"

"Not difficult," Terri answered. "Pointless. Chris and Carlo aren't giving Elena nightmares—"

"No?" Richie cut in. "Then you are."

Terri ignored him. "Our daughter needs professional help," she said to Keene. "Now."

"With whose money? Christopher Paget's?" Richie's voice rose in amazement. "I propose a simple solution, and rather than even try it, you want to put Elena in the hands of yet another stranger."

Keene looked from one to the other. "We're getting nowhere," he said. "There's a final custody hearing in just a few more months, and the two of you can't even agree on how your daughter is acting." He leaned forward. "What I'm going to recommend, as soon as possible, is a family evaluation."

Richie looked puzzled. "What's that?"

"It's an assessment of both of the parents and the child, conducted by a child psychiatrist or psychologist paid for by the two of you. The evaluator will interview you, Terri, and Elena at length, as well as others who may be in contact with the child. The interviews will also involve intensive psychological testing for the adults and age-appropriate tests for Elena." Keene turned to Terri. "In addition to allowing the evaluator to make a recommendation on final custody, it may well help you assess the nature of Elena's difficulties."

Richie stared at the floor, his expression troubled. "What *I* worry about," he said, "is the trauma to Elena. The separation has been hard on her."

"I *thought*," Terri said coolly, "that she was just fine with you. So how do you know it's been hard?"

"Because she *talks* to me." His tone became one of forced patience. "Frankly, about how upset she is with *you*, although I do my best to tell her how confused you are." His eyes flickered, and he turned back to Keene. "If this evaluation is done, will it include Chris Paget?"

"It might. If Terri intended to live with Mr. Paget, it probably would."

"Good." Richie shot Terri a quick glance. "I want him tested."

Terri simply looked at him. Keene, too, said nothing; the silence in the room seemed to focus on Richie. He leaned back in his chair, expelling a deep breath. In a different, more subdued voice, he said, "Gotten a little tense here, hasn't it." He flashed a self-deprecating smile. "Look, if there's any way to work this out, I want to. Just let me calm down for a moment and think."

It was, Terri knew, Richie at his most deceptive. He sat in his chair, eyes hooded, and then nodded to himself.

"Here's what I propose." He looked up at Keene. "I don't see these problems Terri's reporting, and I sure don't see that there's a problem with the current custody arrangement. In fact, I've *told* you what I think the only problem is—Terri's relationship. But I don't want to get sidetracked here. Whatever else, I know Elena misses her mom." Richie turned to Terri. "Tell you what, Ter. I'll give you Lainie every weekend, and we'll see how that works. If she's okay, maybe we could make it permanent." His voice grew pointed. "And if there has to be an evaluation, at least we'll know how Elena does with much *more* time with you."

Terri shook her head. "I want an evaluation now—"

"And in three months, if you still want one, we'll *have* one. With all of us *and* Christopher Paget." Richie spread his hands. "I'm offering you more time, without even requiring you to keep Elena away from Paget. Although I think you should."

"You're stalling, Richie."

"Stalling? I'm *giving* you something. A lot more than I need to."

Feeling Keene's gaze, Terri saw that Richie had boxed her in: if she contested custody after turning down more time, and Scatena ever learned of it, she would have no chance at all. Meanwhile, Richie's preponderant custody would be that much more the status quo, and his checks from Terri would continue. He would even have the free weekends he had always wanted.

But *she* would have more time with Elena.

Terri exhaled. "All right," she said slowly. "We'll try it. Just for a few weeks."

Keene gave a hopeful smile, then shook hands with both of them. Richie walked with Terri through Keene's door and the crowded waiting room, chatting pleasantly until they reached the hallway and the two of them were alone.

He took her elbow, speaking quietly, a man giving firm but friendly advice. "I told you to stay away from Paget. But you wouldn't listen. So now *this* is the best you'll ever get from me. And it's far, far better than you'd get from my 'friend' Scatena, as you've called him." His voice grew softer still. "You'll never beat me, Terri. So don't fuck with me again. Ever."

Turning on his heel, Richie left.

As Terri watched him go, she tried to be grateful for her weekends with Elena, resolving to spend all her time *this* weekend with Elena alone.

And except for Chris's debut in politics, she would have.

His speech was scheduled for Saturday. Terri had not expected to have Elena then: Rosa was in Los Angeles, visiting Terri's twin sisters both on scholarship at UCLA. So Chris, who wanted Terri to come, offered to pay Carlo to watch Elena.

Carlo was saving money for a car; Elena, of course, was delighted. When Terri dropped her at Chris's that morning, she ran through the door after Carlo, armed with a dollhouse and a basket full of Fisher-Price people.

Terri watched her climb the stairs. "Poor Carlo," she said to Chris. "I bet he can hardly wait."

"At twenty bucks an hour?" Chris smiled. "As much as he wants a car, Carlo would play with hand grenades."

Terri looked at him wryly. "*You're* unbelievable, and Carlo must not know what cars cost. Even used. There's a lot of Fisher-Price people between him and anything that runs."

Chris grinned. "Oh, *he* knows that. What he figures is that if he shows a little character, I'll end up helping him buy the car."

"Is he right?"

"Of course."

They walked into the bright morning sun, laughing.

But it was not, they found out on the way, a good morning for politics.

It should have been. The venue was well chosen, the annual convention of the California Society of Newspaper Editors. Without committing himself to run, Chris had assembled a small group of consultants and met with the editorial boards of some of the state's major newspapers. He had done this without the ritual obeisance to James Colt, Jr. Colt had quietly made it known that to support Chris was an act of disloyalty, and Terri herself wondered if Chris had been unwise. But the reaction otherwise had been at least polite: Chris had resources and name recognition of his own, and he was too interesting and attractive to write off. The speech he was prepared to give—a call for reform of the justice system—played to his strengths and experience. And then an unbalanced father, angered by a custody fight, took an AK-47, walked into a recreation center in Oakland, and slaughtered his two children and five others.

Chris and Terri heard the news while they were driving to Moscone Center. "Oh my God," Terri murmured automatically. In the passenger seat, Chris merely listened.

"The right to keep and bear arms," he finally murmured. "Our most sacred freedom. No cost can be too great."

His voice, Terri thought, was almost conversational. "The other day," he went on, "Wally Mathews and I were discussing what to focus on. I mentioned gun control. Wally shook his head. Make that a focal point, he said, and you're asking for trouble—the gun lobby would start gunning for *you*, and a lot of others will think you're against law and order." Chris's voice grew softer. "He's no doubt right."

Something in his tone silenced Terri. They listened to the radio until they reached the center.

Terri sat in the first row. The news had not yet filtered through the audience, a group of perhaps five hundred, mostly white and middle-aged. When Chris was introduced, she did not know what he would do.

For what seemed minutes, he gazed out from the stage. "This morning," he began, "while I was polishing my speech, a man walked into an Oakland play center with an assault rifle and butchered seven children. Two of them were his own; five more just happened to be there. All seven are dead."

A groan went up. Even Terri felt Chris's flat words in the pit of her stomach.

"My speech," Chris went on, "was quite well written. It was a balanced review of the shortfalls of our criminal justice system. Had I given it, it might well have served the purpose of showing how qualified I am to be a United States senator. And like most speeches on crime—even by liberals—it mentions gun control only in passing." His voice held the barest trace of irony. "*That*, I am certain, was an affirmation of my growing political maturity."

There was silence now. "I don't own a gun," Chris said quietly. "Outside the army, I've never fired one. Perhaps that makes it easier for me to notice that the chief use of handguns in America is domestic violence and robbing the corner store."

He paused; for the first time, his words had an undertone of passion. "Since when, I have to wonder, is an AK-47 a tool for sportsmen? Empty one into a deer, and there wouldn't be enough left to hang up on the wall. The truth is that other countries use assault weapons to fight wars; we use them to butcher people in our streets and stores and homes." His voice grew quiet again. "We used one of them this morning. To murder children."

Terri heard murmurs from the crowd. Chris's voice rose above them. "And I do mean 'we.' Most of us have a piece of it. The gun lobby which pours money into politicians' coffers. The politicians who take it and then vamp for the rest of us, conducting empty debates about meaningless legislation that preserves this country as the world's shooting gallery. And all of us who fail to call them to account. Like me—a cocktail party advocate of gun control, who has done nothing meaningful in his entire life to stop this kind of tragedy, other than not to shoot anyone himself."

Part of Terri wanted to look at the crowd. But she could not take her eyes off Chris. "I suppose this speech is impolitic," he continued. "I really don't care. Because what passes for our politics is a joke. We have politicians whose slogan seems to be 'Love them till they're born.' We have an economy that is more and more based on unproductive people—lawyers included—exchanging money with other unproductive people. We mouth nonsense about an information society that ignores the most basic maxim of the computer age: garbage in, garbage out. Because our public education system is a shambles. And we have a seemingly permanent underclass of poor people and minorities that we've all but written off, except as targets for politicians who want to hide the truth—that it's things like Social Security and Medicare that are bankrupting us; that we could starve every welfare recipient in America without making a dent in the budget; and that the real cost of our welfare system is that it changes nothing for the better.

"In short, our politics isn't serious anymore. It's not about serious things. If anyone requires proof of that, consider that seven children died today because our political system is too cowardly and indifferent to protect them."

He lowered his voice again. "This is an easy speech to give," he said. "Anyone can be angry about dead children. But going forward, I'm going to try something more difficult: to talk about serious things, and to propose serious answers. Otherwise there's no point to this."

Chris stood straighter. "I hope that people listen. But if they don't, at least I won't feel any worse than I do this morning.

"Thank you."

He sat abruptly. Only after a moment did Terri realize that people were standing, feel the waves of applause washing over Chris, one upon the other.

An hour later, a pensive Terri drove them home. "You were good," she said at last. "Much better than good. People were saying you could win it—despite James Colt."

Chris gazed out the window. "I'm just sorry for those parents." He turned to her. "Know what I feel like doing? Something with our kids."

But when they got home, Chris's house was silent. They turned to each other, listening for sounds; it was the instinct of parents, Terri thought, to worry for their children when other children have died. "I guess they've gone to the park," Chris said. "Carlo must have tired of plastic people."

Terri smiled. From upstairs, they heard a faint noise that might be a child talking.

The sounds came from Chris's bedroom. Together they went upstairs, and then Terri heard water splashing in Chris's bathroom.

They walked through the bedroom and found Elena in Chris's oversize bathtub. Carlo was sitting against the bathroom wall, watching Elena and listening to a Giants game on his transistor radio. Elena was surrounded by the bobbing plastic heads of miniature people. "I'm taking a bath," she explained to Terri. "With Carlo and my friends."

"I can see that."

With a comic expression, Carlo pulled the baseball cap down on his head. "She wanted to get in the tub, she said. Wouldn't even go for ice cream." He looked at Terri. "Do you leave her in there alone? I can't remember much from being five."

"I keep pretty close." She turned to Elena. "Do you like Chris's tub?"

"Yes. It's *big*."

As if to show her mother, the little girl spread her arms and legs, arching her back to stretch the full length of the tub. It threw Terri off for a moment; something in her daughter's pose was not that of a little girl. "I'm staying here, Mommy. With Carlo."

As too often lately, Elena's voice held a trace of challenge, the false maturity of a child who wished to believe herself adult. Terri turned to Carlo with a smile. "I'll take over from here," she told him. "I think you've done enough."

Carlo stood, looking relieved. "I'm going to see Katie," he said to Chris. "If that's okay."

"Sure."

Chris and Carlo went downstairs, talking about Chris's speech, leaving Elena staring after them. For the rest of the afternoon, the little girl was sullen.

Terri passed this off as her devotion to Carlo. And then, on a Friday shortly after Elena entered school, Leslie Warner called Terri at work. "I don't mean to disturb you," Warner said. "But something happened at school today, with Elena."

"Yes?"

There was a pause. "Elena's quite embarrassed. So please, when you talk to her, try to be low-key about it."

"Fine." Terri bit back her impatience. "But I don't know what to be 'low-key' about."

"Oh, of course. It was a playground incident. At the back of the school are several Dumpsters. Sometimes the kids will hide behind them." Warner paused. "Today I found Elena there with a little boy, Matthew. She had pulled her panties down, to show him her genital area."

Terri sat back in her chair. "What did she say?"

"Nothing." Warner paused again. "According to Matthew, Elena asked him to look at her."

"What do you think I should do?"

"Nothing, really. There's a lot of acting out at this age." Warner's tone took on a touch of condescension. "Plus there's a divorce going on, I know, and these things overstimulate children. New relationships, whatever . . ."

The phrase trailed off; Terri knew at once that Warner had already spoken to Richie.

Terri made her own voice level. "Have you called Elena's father yet?"

Warner seemed to hesitate. "Yes, actually. I know that Richie's the primary caretaker. But he told me Elena would be with you tonight."

Terri gave herself a moment. "She will be," Terri said politely. "Thank you for calling."

When Terri hung up, she went looking for Chris. But he was in court. Terri worked absentmindedly, thinking about Elena, until she found the words she wanted.

But it did not matter. Before dinner, when she asked Elena what had happened, the little girl turned her face to the wall, arms clasped, as if holding herself together.

"I love you, sweetheart," Terri said softly. "You can talk to me whenever you want to."

Elena shook her head, mute; Terri could see only her black hair, moving from side to side. When Terri bent to touch her shoulder, Elena twisted away.

That night, Terri could not sleep. Around midnight, when she went to check Elena, the little girl was crying. Her nightmare had come again.

ELEVEN

"You want an evaluation *now*?" Richie had demanded. "Two weeks after we agree to a new arrangement?" His voice rose in irritation. "That was a compromise, Terri, meant to resolve this for all time. It's like you never get enough."

Terri kept looking at Alec Keene. "Elena's still not right," she said quietly. "And now there's this thing at school."

Keene propped his chin on tented fingers, gazing at them both. "I'm inclined to agree with Terri," he said at length. "It may be time for a psychologist to take a look at this." He glanced at Richie. "What can it hurt?"

"Elena," Richie retorted. "She's been through enough." He paused, easing the indignation from his voice. "Look, I don't want to be irresponsible about this. But I can't agree to a process that's not objective."

For the first time, Keene spoke to Richie with the exaggerated calm of someone straining for patience. "It's not a matter of the parents agreeing. If there's no settlement, a family evaluation report is mandatory." His voice became gentler. "But we need to work toward a methodology that satisfies both parents. Let me ask what you mean by objective."

"It's simple." Richie leaned forward. "I'll object to any evaluation, as strongly as I know how, that doesn't include intensive scrutiny of Christopher Paget and his son."

Keene looked puzzled. "Perhaps—depending on Terri's plans—some time with Mr. Paget might be helpful. But at this point, his son seems pretty peripheral."

"Peripheral?" Richie gave Keene an opaque stare and then turned on Terri. "Let's take your extra weekend time, Ter—the time *I* gave you with Elena. How much of it does Elena spend with *you* and how much with Chris and Carlo Paget?"

Terri felt nettled. "Almost none—"

"Define 'almost,' " Richie cut in. "An hour? Two hours? More?"

"How much, I'm not sure. Not enough to call for your Gestapo act."

"Yes," Keene interjected. "This is supposed to be a dialogue, not cross-examination."

Richie held up his hand to Keene, still gazing fixedly at Terri. "Then let me make it simpler. Tell me, Terri, how much time Elena spent alone with Carlo Paget on the *first* weekend after our agreement."

"I don't know." Terri was edgy now. "Chris was giving a speech, and I didn't have a sitter. It wasn't long."

"And where were they? Elena and Carlo."

Terri hesitated. "At Chris's house."

"At Chris's house," Richie repeated, his tone gentle with suppressed anger. "Who else was there?"

"No one."

Richie nodded. "That's right, Terri. No one. And what did they do?" His voice was even softer now. "Draw pictures? Play with dolls? Or maybe they played dress-up."

For Keene's sake, Terri held her temper. "I wasn't there. That's why I asked Carlo to stay with her."

"You're not being very helpful. To me *or* to Alec." Terri glanced at Keene; he was silent now, caught up in Richie's oddly menacing puzzle. Richie leaned forward. "But you *do* know, Terri, what they were doing when you and your boyfriend came home."

Terri felt her pulse quicken. "Elena was taking a bath."

Richie's voice was silken now. "Alone?"

"No." Terri paused again. "Carlo was watching her."

Richie leaned back now, eyebrows raised. "And where is the bathroom?"

"Upstairs, off Chris's bedroom." Terri's voice was flat. "Spit it out, Richie. I've had enough of your little cat-and-mouse game."

Richie's eyes darted from Keene to Terri, but his tone was still soft. "Just one more question, Terri. Do you usually turn your daughter's intimate care over to adolescent boys? Or does Christopher Paget's son rate this special little privilege?"

"All right," Keene interrupted. "What's your point, Richie?"

Richie turned to him with an oddly pleasant expression, as if they had just been introduced. "It's this, Alec. The last time we were together, Terri began ticking off symptoms: listlessness and absent-mindedness; lack of close peer relations; stomachaches and regression; sleeplessness, needing a night-light, bad dreams. Things our daughter had left behind at the age of four. When Terri and I were together, and she was living in our house."

He smiled faintly, as if remembering a happier time. Then his head snapped up. "What Terri said puzzled me—I hadn't seen these behaviors when Elena was with me. But like any responsible parent, I wanted to keep an open mind. So I went to the library and took out some books. And as I read, I began to worry."

His eyes narrowed. "I didn't want to believe it, of course. No parent does. So I wrote it off to the divorce. And then there was this incident at school—sexual acting out, they called it. And everything Terri had told us suddenly fell into place." He turned to Terri, eyes suddenly hard. "It's a symptom of sexual abuse, Terri. Of *our* daughter, by your lover's pervert son."

It startled Terri. "That's crazy. . . ."

"*Is it?*" Richie demanded. "Then how did I know about that bath?" His voice lowered. "Because Elena, our daughter, told me."

"Carlo was just *watching* her," Terri began. Suddenly she flashed on Elena in the bathtub, back arched; was the look somehow provocative, or had Terri imagined it? Her stomach felt hollow. "What did Elena tell you?"

"It was more what she didn't tell me." Richie stopped, eyes open and candid. "She was withdrawn, spacey, obviously upset. Just as you described. When I asked her what was wrong, she turned her face to the wall and folded her arms." His voice grew troubled. "Have you ever tried to get her to answer you, Terri, and she just shakes her head and turns into a ball? Because that's how she was." He turned to Keene. "All she said, Alec, was, 'I took a bath with Carlo.' "

Through her disbelief, Terri felt a visceral fear. "Why didn't you tell *me?*" she demanded.

Richie opened his palms. "These kinds of charges are *very* serious. I wanted to think it over—I was in kind of a tough position here, and I didn't want it to look like I was playing games." His voice took on an edge. "After all, Terri, *I* was the one who asked you to keep her away from Carlo."

"Then what changed your mind?"

"This thing at school." He turned to Keene. "When Terri called you about it, Alec, I was glad. Because I was coming to the conclusion, however reluctant I might be, that I had to put this on the table. For Elena's sake."

Keene faced Terri. "At any other time," he asked, "have you left Elena alone with Carlo?"

"Hardly at all." She hesitated. "Maybe once or twice. One time he took her to the park."

Keene touched his eyes. "I don't know what's happened here," he finally said. "These behaviors don't necessarily mean child abuse. But once the charge is made, people don't back off. And it affects everyone, for a long time." He looked at Richie. "Including Elena and this boy."

"I know," Richie answered gravely. "Believe me, I know. The only good thing is that this doesn't involve Terri. At least in the sense that she's the abuser." He turned to Terri, voice suddenly crisp. "That means you can fix it, Terri. By keeping her away from Carlo Paget."

"It's not that simple," Keene put in. "Terri has a relationship with the father." He turned to Terri. "Is it possible you may live together?"

Terri hesitated. "I don't really know," she said, and then made her voice firm again. "As a parent, I can't dismiss what Richie says. But I don't believe that Carlo would abuse Elena. What I *do* believe is that Richie's been saving this as a bargaining chip—"

"My God, Terri." Richie's voice rose suddenly. "Are you still clinging to Paget after all this? What does it take?"

"I want Elena tested—"

"That's a cop-out." He stood. "Look damn it, I want some guarantees from you."

Terri stood to face him. "You've got one. Elena won't go near Carlo, all right? For *both* their sakes. But there *will* be an evaluation. Elena *will* get help. We *will* get to what's happening with her."

"You're damned straight we will. By having a professional turn Paget and his son upside down and inside out. If that's what you want, then we're going to do it right."

Keene stepped between them. "All right, both of you. *Enough.*"

Terri sat down; after a moment, so did Richie. She gazed at him across the room. It was strange, Terri thought; suddenly she did not feel anger. What she felt was sadness; what she saw was Carlo, holding Elena's hand as they walked to the park, the little girl smiling up at him.

Even Richie seemed subdued. "I'm sorry it's come to this," he murmured.

Keene shrugged. "So am I. But it has. I'll be in touch, with names of three prospective evaluators. Try to agree on one, all right? Otherwise Judge Scatena will have to choose one for you."

Keene had little else to say. As they left his office for the final time, he wished them good luck.

The halls were empty. Richie nodded toward a quiet corner. "Let's talk settlement," he said.

"Settlement? I can't even stand to look at you."

"I did it for our daughter." He shook his head portentously. "This has gotten ugly, Terri. Unless we agree, it will only get uglier. For everyone."

Terri forced herself to stay there. "You mean you'll *make* it ugly," she said. "So what do you want now?"

"My original deal. The one you turned down so Scatena could give you even less time with Elena." He ticked off the points. "Twenty-five hundred a month to me. Elena to me during the weeks. Weekends to you." His voice became commanding. "If, and only if, Elena never sees Paget or Carlo again. No handshake deal on that one, Terri. I want it in writing."

Terri stared at him. "It's always the same sick little game with you, isn't it? Drop the bomb, add a few soft words about settlement, and then try to make sure I'm as isolated as possible. But now you've found the perfect wedge between Chris and me—our children."

"Can you really be that infatuated with him?" He gave her a derisive smile. "Then consider *his* best interests. Your boyfriend wants to go to the Senate, I read. I doubt that raising a child molester is the kind of family values Danny Quayle had in mind. Or, for that matter, whoever Paget may run against."

Terri felt her fists clench. "I think you'd better spell it out for me, Richie. Every slimy nuance."

"Oh, I have your attention now. Good." His smile vanished abruptly. "What I'm saying is that Elena's and your boyfriend's interests are finally the same. That may free you up to think about Elena. For once."

"You'd use Carlo." Her voice was flat. "Against Chris."

Richie slowly shook his head. "You've got it backward, Terri. I'd do *anything* to make you protect our daughter." His voice lowered. "Anything at all."

Terri turned from him, walking away.

"*Oh,*" he said behind her. "There *is* one more thing."

Terri faced him again. "Which is," she asked coldly.

"I need some money. In settlement of my community property interests." His voice was placid now. "I want you to sign a loan application for ten thousand dollars. To make up for the ground I've lost, staying with Elena and all."

Terri looked at him in disbelief. "There *is* no community money. Just furniture."

Richie shrugged. "So call it a legal fiction, Ter. And it doesn't need to be a bank loan." His eyes widened, as if at a sudden new thought. "Maybe you could talk to your boyfriend...."

TWELVE

WHEN TERRI HAD CALLED about Richie's charges, from a phone booth outside the Administrative Building, the softness in Chris's voice scared her more than anger would have.

"Do you know what comes to me, Terri? Something Carlo told me just before he came to live with me, when he was seven.

"What he said was: 'I hate myself. I want to kill myself.' " His tone was still quiet. "He wasn't joking," Chris continued. "Though he looked at me with a funny smile when he said it. He was testing me. To see if anyone gave a damn about whether he lived or died.

"For eight years, the major purpose of my life has been to tell Carlo, less by words than by being there, that no one in the world was more important to me. The funny thing is, it worked. But while I was trying to change Carlo's life, someone else's life changed too. Mine." His voice grew softer yet. "I love that boy more than Ricardo Arias will *ever* comprehend."

Terri wished that she could see his face. Wearily, she answered, "I wish this had never happened, Chris."

"It never did." For the first time, Paget's tone was hard. "You were there, Terri. Carlo was giving her a bath because *we* asked him to watch her."

"I don't think it happened, either. But Elena told Richie *something*." Her own words became firmer. "I like Carlo a lot, and I also know who Richie is. But Elena's a mess, Chris. I can't pretend that Richie never raised this."

There was another silence. "I'll talk to Carlo," he said in a flat voice, and got off.

Terri made one more telephone call, then drove to Elena's school. When Terri appeared, the little girl ran into her mother's arms.

Terri held her close. A moment later, she realized that Leslie Warner was standing there and that she seemed to watch Terri with an air of vigilance and disapproval.

"Come on, sweetheart," Terri murmured. "We're going to see Dr. Nash—it's time for your checkup." She left without acknowledging the teacher.

Elena's pediatrician was a brisk, no-nonsense woman in her mid thirties. As Elena lay on the examining table with her eyes shut, stoic and silent, Terri hoped that her explanation had soothed her. Elena, she thought sadly, had just turned six.

Afterward, Dr. Nash took Terri aside. "I can pretty much rule out intercourse," she said bluntly. "Beyond that it's always hard to tell. Unless the child says something."

Terri looked around the examining room: Elena was engrossed with coloring books. "You can't tell me *anything?*"

The doctor frowned. "Nothing physical," she finally answered. "She was awfully quiet for such a talkative girl. Perhaps she sensed something. But she went through the pelvic all right, and the first time can be scary."

In the examining room, a baby started crying. "Look," Terri said, "I need to find out what happened."

Nash paused, then clasped Terri's hand in hers. "I've got people waiting," she said. "I wish I could tell you more, but I can't. If something else comes up, please call me." She hurried off.

At least, Terri realized, it was Friday; she could take Elena home with her.

They sat together on the living room rug with Elena's plastic people. But Elena—whose rich imagination once had invested these figures with distinctive personalities—now seemed to play by rote. When Terri put away the toys, Elena did not protest.

Terri pulled her daughter close to her. "Do you remember," she began gently, "when we talked about good touching and bad touching?"

Elena glanced at her, eyes veiled and cautious. She gave an almost imperceptible nod.

"Tell me about bad touching, okay?"

Elena would not meet her eyes. In a small voice, she said. "It's when someone wants to touch my 'gina. That's all."

"Can you think of anything else?"

Elena stood abruptly and walked to the corner of the room. Terri went to her, kneeling. "Are you all right?"

A brief nod. The girl's eyes opened wide, as if to see whether Terri would accept this. "Do you remember," Terri asked, "the day you took a bath at Chris's house? When Carlo was with you?"

Elena's eyes froze.

Terri forced herself to stay calm. "Did Carlo ever touch you, Elena? In a good way, or a bad way?"

Elena turned sideways. Her profile was a line of tension—pursed lips, folded arms, stiff body. Terri slid in front of her. "Did you say something to Daddy about Carlo? Or a bath?"

The child's eyes flickered. Terri knew what it meant: six-year-old children, when planning to lie, do not disguise it well.

"*No,*" Elena said, and turned away.

Frustrated, Terri clutched her shoulder. "You can *talk* to me, Elena. Just like with Daddy."

"I *can't.*" Elena whirled abruptly, eyes angry and accusing. "You want to take me *away* from him."

Terri was startled. "From who?"

"From Daddy. I can *never* talk to you."

Elena turned and ran to her bedroom.

Terri found her on the bed, crying. When she would not come out for dinner, Terri brought a bowl of ice cream to her room, worried and miserable.

A half hour later, Elena straggled to the living room with a blanket and a book. "Read a story, Mommy. Please?"

Terri took Elena in her arms and read the story. When she had finished, Elena kissed her on the cheek.

"I love you, Mommy." The little girl laid her head on Terri's shoulder. "I wish you would live with us again."

Whoever first conceived of a broken heart, Terri thought to herself, must have loved a child.

An hour later, Chris called. "Carlo wants to talk with you," he said. "We both do."

Terri touched her eyes. "I'll try to get my mother."

It was nine when she got to Chris's. Carlo was in the library. For once, he did not wear the baseball cap.

She sat across from him, with Chris standing to the side. Carlo was pale; the effort to look stoic made him seem younger than his age. But his eyes did not waver.

"I never touched her. Not that way. Not even close."

His voice had a slight hoarseness. Terri fought to withhold her sympathy. "Richie claims she was upset."

"She wanted to take a bath, she told me." His words were shot with pain. "Jesus, Terri, she's a *little kid*."

Terri glanced up at Chris. Impassive, he seemed to be appraising Carlo. "Did you help her undress?" Terri asked. "Anything like that?"

"No way. She had her clothes off before I even started the water. All I did was make sure she wouldn't drown."

"How did taking a bath come up?"

"Kids *do* things, that's all." He shook his head in wonder. "What *else* does she say?"

"Nothing. Just folded her arms and denied talking to Richie. Which is a lie."

Carlo exhaled. "She's a nice kid," he said finally. "But I wish I'd never met her."

Terri felt a sliver of sadness; whatever the truth, the good between Carlo and Elena had vanished. And, perhaps, between Carlo and Terri herself.

"I've got something else to say." Carlo's voice was tight now. "Maybe *he* believes this shit. Maybe he doesn't. Either way, he thinks he's going to put me through a lot of crap—social workers, shrinks, whatever." His voice turned raw. "Let him. I didn't do this stuff."

Terri leaned forward. "There'll be an investigation, Carlo. The evaluator will want to interview you. Give you all sorts of tests . . ."

"So let's get it over with. So I can go back to some sort of normal life." He stopped, seeming to imagine the questions he would face, and his voice grew strained again. "I have a *girlfriend*. I'm not some pervert."

Terri watched his face. Abruptly, Carlo turned to his father. "Is that it, Dad?"

Chris's gaze had filled with sadness and affection. "Yes," he said. "That's it."

Carlo left the room without looking at Terri. Chris watched him climb the stairs, until he disappeared.

"*This,*" he murmured to Terri, "is one of the worst nights of my life."

What would be left of them, Terri wondered, however this might end? "How is he?" she asked.

"Exactly as you saw him—scared, angry, confused." Chris's voice was level. "I know Carlo better than I know anyone. If he'd done what he's accused of doing, Carlo would lie about it. Most people would. But Carlo's not lying."

"Are you saying that Richie put her up to this?"

Chris turned to her. "Think about it, Terri. I know you're worried for Elena, and so am I. But the first time you sat down with Keene, Richie asked him to spell out the hot-button custody issues— including child molestation. The hardest thing to prove or dis- prove." Chris's tone filled with contempt. "When Elena came home that weekend and told him about the fun bath 'with Carlo,' Richie must have salivated. All he had to do was tack on the disturbed be- havior you'd already described to him and take it to Keene."

"The behavior is *real*. And Elena won't talk."

Chris shrugged. "That's why you need an evaluation."

Terri held his gaze. "Even one that involves Carlo?"

"*Especially* then. He didn't do this, Terri. How would he feel if he ran away from it?"

Terri walked to the window. "Richie also mentioned your Senate race," she said after a time. "What would people think, he asked me, if they knew that Carlo was a child molester? He's *desperate*, Chris, looking for money—"

"Richie," Chris cut in, "doesn't know what desperate is."

Turning, Terri gave him a questioning look. She saw Chris's anger as a change in his eyes, nothing more.

"I'm going to wait," he told her softly, "until you've got Elena. And then I'm going to destroy him."

Terri tried to imagine what Chris meant. She went to him, grasp- ing both his arms. "What about *us*?" she asked. "*All* of us. Whoever he is, he's Elena's father."

Chris's face turned cold. "That's not a father. That's a sperm do- nor. Elena would be better off without him."

When Terri returned home, she was exhausted.

Rosa waited in the living room. With a calm that seemed accusa- tory, she said, "Elena had the nightmare again."

The child lay sprawled in her bed. The position in which she had at last found sleep looked like someone running.

Terri thanked her mother and then showed her out as quickly as she could.

Closing the door, she leaned against it. Then she walked to the kitchen, picked up a vase of flowers, and flung it against the wall.

It shattered: shards of glass on the floor refracted dull light from the ceiling. Terri stared at the jagged pieces and then walked away.

In the morning, Terri cleaned up the glass. She was paying bills when Richie called.

"We have a deal, Ter?"

Terri had not slept; she was far too tired to temporize. "No deal," she said. "No money, no custody agreement. Nothing except an evaluation."

For a long time, Richie was silent. "I can't tell you," he said quietly, "just how sorry you both will be."

She waited for more. He said nothing; still Terri listened, connected to him by his silence. When she heard the click at last, she imagined him placing down the telephone with exaggerated softness.

Die, Terri told him. Please, just die.

THIRTEEN

ALTHOUGH TERRI could not have known this, their fatal turning point began with a call from a reporter.

It came at a moment of frustration. Terri had just put down her office phone after talking to the evaluator Alec Keene had recommended, a warm-sounding child psychologist named Denise Harris, only to learn that Harris could not start with Elena for at least eight weeks. The phone rang and Terri, distracted, picked it up again.

"Ms. Peralta? Jack Slocum. Have a moment?"

Slocum worked for the morning paper, Terri recalled; his voice had the nervous aggression of the daily reporter. "Concerning what?" she asked.

"The article in this week's *Inquisitor*. I wonder if you have any comment."

Terri could not fathom why she should care about a supermarket tabloid filled with celebrity gossip and citings of spaceships. "I missed that one," she said. "Did Elvis die?"

"They didn't call you?" Slocum's voice was incredulous. "On page seven, your husband claims that Christopher Paget broke up your marriage."

It was as if, Terri thought, she were dreaming.

"Ms. Peralta?"

"Let me ask *you* something," she said at last. "The *Inquisitor* pays for slime like this, right?"

"Uh-huh. Mr. Arias got ten thousand dollars."

Terri sat back in her chair. "This isn't news," she said. "It's compost."

"Come on, Ms. Peralta. Christopher Paget may well run for the Senate. You don't think we're obliged to explore questions of character?"

"Whose character?" Terri snapped, and hung up.

She found Chris at his desk. He did not look up. Slocum had called him, she realized: the *Inquisitor* was spread out in front of him.

At the center of page seven was a news photo of Chris and Terri emerging from the Carelli hearing, and next to that, a color picture of Richie holding Elena. Elena looked bewildered; Richie's expression was pained but resolute, the abandoned and embattled father. The photo caption read: "Ricardo Arias raises six-year-old Elena by himself. 'She's all I have now,' Richie says. 'We're barely making it.' "

"What's so pathetic," Chris said quietly, "is that all he has to offer is lies and self-pity, and all it's worth to him is ten thousand dollars. It's like something from *Queen for a Day.*"

Terri felt a rush of shame. She forced herself to keep on reading.

The writing was florid but effective: the story of a stay-at-home father, abandoned by his wife for her rich and powerful boss. "We had so much in common," the article quoted Richie. "We were both Hispanic and poor, working together for a better life. Our first years were so happy with Elena, and I thought our marriage was strong. Then Terri became caught up in another world. *His* world. One day she just demanded a divorce and then ran away to be with him." Terri did not know what made her angrier: the grotesque portrait that Richie had sold to them, or the way the *Inquisitor* referred to the "alleged" affair to prevent Christopher Paget from suing.

"It seems," Chris said in a flat voice, "that there's a price for everything we do."

Terri shook her head. "Has anyone else run this drivel?"

"Not yet. But there's not a chance in hell that James Colt won't find out about it. And even without his encouragement, journalists love this sort of thing—in some newspaper, somewhere, some reporter with the ethics of a slug is already looking for a libel-proof way to print this. Something like: 'Political insiders are privately concerned that the *Inquisitor* has placed a cloud over Paget's embryonic campaign.' Sound about right?"

It was as if he were discussing a client. Terri kept herself from apologizing for Richie: it was pointless and would sound too pitiful. "*I* could sue him," she said. "I'm not a public figure. It's easier for me to bring a lawsuit."

"Not as long as he's got Elena. It can't seem like you're seeking custody to spite him." When he looked up at last, his expression held sympathy. "If it weren't for my flirtation with politics, Richie would rate no interest at all."

Terri looked away. "I can't believe he's done this."

She knew that it was the wrong thing to say even before she saw the look in Chris's eyes. But all he said, very quietly, was "Really?"

She made herself gaze back at him. "What are you going to do?"

"Play by the rules, of course." Suppressed anger crept into his voice. "Within the rules, I've already done what I can. Our friend Slocum's publisher agrees with me that this isn't news—at least for now. If all this turns out to be is an *Inquisitor* story, it'll probably go away."

"But you don't think it will."

He stood and walked to the window. "That may depend," he finally answered, "on what else Ricardo feeds them. Or what the media, or perhaps someone like Colt, dig up on their own."

Terri hesitated. "Carlo, you mean?"

"Yes." He turned to her, eyes hard now. "It's time for me to have a talk with Richie."

Terri felt her nerves tingle. "You *can't*, Chris. Not yet. It will only make things worse."

"Carlo's my son, damn it." Suddenly Chris's anger burst into the open. "This little weasel thinks he's *immune*, Terri. We sit here like two corporate lawyers, discussing our legal remedies, while he distorts our lives and victimizes *my* son. How he must laugh."

Terri forced herself to be calm. "Richie and I are contesting custody. Whatever he's done to Carlo, or you, you're not in court with him. I don't want Richie telling Scatena that you tried to prevent him from learning the 'truth' about Carlo and Elena. And that's exactly what he'll do."

Chris stared at her, and then his voice turned cool. "He has a certain genius, doesn't he. He's put us on opposite sides: anything I do to protect Carlo may hurt Elena. And as long as he can keep on claiming that Carlo abused her, no one can touch him. Especially me."

It seemed so long ago, Terri thought sadly, that Chris had dismissed Richie as a nuisance and a failure. Perhaps what was most painful was that Richie had become *real* to Chris: in his complete lack of scruples, the absence of anything to lose, Richie was beyond the weapons a normal man would use. "I'm so sorry about him," Terri said finally. "But if he keeps on doing stuff like this, he's going to reveal who he really is. I'll try to tell him that."

Chris's shrug was dismissive. "Do whatever you like. I'm sure he'll listen."

There was no point in saying more to him, Terri realized—not now. She went back to her office and picked up the phone.

"Richie Arias," he answered in a cheery voice.

"I've read the article," Terri said calmly.

"Terri?" His tone was still upbeat. "What did you think?"

"That it captured you perfectly." Her own voice remained level. "In a way, I'm glad you did it. You're usually better at concealing what you are."

"Oh. And what is that?"

It was strange, Terri realized. Richie was trying to sound derisive, but part of him was insecure without her. "I won't bother to tell you," she answered. "It's much better if you're still in the dark about how normal people think." She kept her voice flat. "You're tone-deaf, Richie. You can read the notes, but you can't hear the music."

"What the hell does that mean?"

"I'll give you one example." Terri paused, speaking slowly and succinctly. "If you drag Carlo Paget into the newspapers, you'll be publicly exploiting a teenage boy *and* your own six-year-old daughter. And no competent psychologist can miss the meaning of *that*."

"Look, I'm out of money." His voice rose. "You think I wanted to embarrass myself? You and your boyfriend made me."

"No, we didn't. As I told you once, you're a self-made man. It's not much to show for the only work you've ever done."

There was a tense silence. "And now you've found the perfect lover, haven't you. The one man who could help you out of this terrible marriage." Richie's voice grew quiet. "Tell me, Terri, what makes you think that he'll choose you over the Senate? You know, when things get *really* hard for him?"

"What do you mean by *that*?" Terri snapped. Said it without thinking, as Richie had known she would.

He laughed softly and hung up.

FOURTEEN

ROSA HAD SAT DOWN on the couch; it was as if the weight of what she felt required this. "You're going to Italy," she repeated to Terri. "With Chris, because he has asked you to go. Eight months after leaving Richie."

Her tone was flat. Rosa did not say the rest: that Chris's son stood accused of molesting Terri's daughter. That Terri was in the midst of a custody fight. That Richie would try to punish her.

"The evaluation doesn't start for almost a month." Terri kept her own voice calm. "Chris and I *need* this time, Mom. Somewhere away from the office and Richie's constant presence, where we can think through whether there's any way to make this work."

Rosa closed her eyes; it was moments before they opened and she spoke again. "For months," she began quietly, "I've said nothing to you. The courts have taken away your daughter. The man who you claim loves you is a millstone. The child *I* love is a shell. And still I've said nothing."

Terri folded her arms. "What is it you'd like to say?"

"That your decisions have been wrong, Teresa. Every one of them. Beginning with Christopher Paget." Her eyes were hard now. "And that Elena has paid the price."

"Chris isn't responsible. *I* am."

"Oh? And then why are we talking about Chris yet again, and not Elena? This is a precious child, Terri. It hurts me even to look at her now." Her voice softened. "I understand that you and Chris are not adulterers, at least in the sense that Richie means it. But the existence of this man has colored every decision, and tainted every issue, surrounding Elena's welfare." She paused, stressing each word. "Including your decision to leave Ricardo Arias."

Terri shook her head. "I left because of Elena."

"Did you?" Her mother's smile was filled with bitter irony. "And now Richie *has* Elena."

"I'm trying to change that, Mama."

Her mother shook her head. "I don't believe you can, Teresa. Not *this* way." She leaned forward. "Richie is a given. Chris is not, and he is much too costly. Please, ask him to step aside."

"Just like that." Terri's voice rose. "Tell me, Mom, do you know what it's like to *want* someone—I mean really want them? Or even just to laugh with someone?"

Rosa folded her hands. "No," she said slowly. "Nor do I know what it is to lose a child. Your laughter has come at a price."

Once more, Terri felt the guilt of all that had happened. "That's why we're going to Italy—to talk all these things through and to see if there's any future for us that is good for our children. Like the adults we happen to be." Terri heard the edge in her voice. "You'd be surprised how well that works—talking."

Her mother's face remained impassive. "Are you so certain, Teresa, that Carlo didn't molest your daughter?"

In the silence that followed, Terri held her gaze. "I can't swear to it," she said finally. "But I don't believe he's capable of that. The evaluator will try to find out."

"The *evaluator*." Rosa's voice was tinged with scorn. "Is that like the *judge*? Someone to help you?"

Terri felt her throat tighten. "It's different. This person is *trained* to deal with children."

"And so, naturally, you now will place your hopes in her." Rosa's face was still a mask; only her eyes showed the anguish behind it. "To abuse a child is a terrible thing. Whatever else you blame me for, it is something that I *never* would have let happen to you. Or to *any* child of mine."

For an instant, in what Rosa did not say, Terri felt the presence of her father. "What makes you think," Terri answered, "that you and I are different?"

As at other times, Terri's tacit reference to her father drew from Rosa a veiled look of scrutiny. But as always, her mother did not mention Ramon Peralta.

"I imagine," Rosa said in a tired voice, "that you've already told Ricardo."

"Yes." Richie had hardly reacted: he had simply taken the dates down, asking questions to be sure he had them right. "If there's an emergency, Richie has to know where I am. I would never leave, Mama, if Elena were with *me* for more than weekends. But she isn't. If you take Elena on the weekends I'll be gone, it'll be good for both of you."

Rosa fell silent, defeated. It was only then that Terri saw the sheen of tears that her mother would not permit to fall.

Terri kissed her, the offering of peace, and left.

It was dark, a little past ten. The inside stairs to her apartment were quiet, empty. Climbing them, Terri promised herself a good night's sleep.

The door was ajar.

Terri gazed at it, stepping back for a moment. Then, slowly, she pushed it open and peered into her living room.

She saw nothing. The lights were out; Terri sensed that the room was as she had left it.

She stepped forward, head turning to each side. Still nothing. And then, softly, someone shut the door behind her.

Terri turned, a scream caught in her throat. In front of her door stood the shadow of a man.

"*Don't.*" Her voice trembled. "*Please.*"

The shadow moved toward her. In the pale glow from the street, she saw one arm reach out.

A light switched on. Ricardo Arias stood by her floor lamp, grinning at her.

"What's wrong, Ter? You used to like a little excitement."

Her heart was pounding. "What are *you* doing here?"

"You seem jumpy tonight." He raised his eyebrows. "Waiting for your boyfriend? That *would* be fun."

She fought to control her voice. "How did you get in?"

"Remember when I borrowed the car to drive Elena, when mine was in the shop?" He grinned again, flipping Terri a set of keys. "You shouldn't keep your extras in the glove compartment, Terri. Someone might steal them."

Terri looked down. Her keys lay on the floor: to her apartment, to her mother's home. To Chris's house.

"You scum," she said softly.

"That's really not fair. Actually, I came here to effect personal service of an important set of legal pleadings. Regarding Elena. You remember her, don't you? Our daughter?"

Beside her on the carpet, Terri saw, was a flat sealed envelope. "Pick it up," Richie told her.

There was something in his voice, an edge of anxiety beneath the air of confidence. "Do it yourself," she snapped. "I'm sick of picking up after you."

Richie stared at her. Then he bent to retrieve the envelope, and placed it in her hand. "I'm not leaving," he said. "Not until you've read this."

What, Terri wondered, was so important to him? She turned away, sat in a chair. "If it means that much," she said, and pulled back the clasp on the envelope.

Inside were a set of pleadings, marked "Filed under seal." The caption read: "Petitioner's Motion for Preliminary Injunction." The relief requested was simple: that respondent Teresa Peralta cease all contact between her daughter, Elena, and her lover, Christopher Paget. And his son, Carlo.

Terri gazed down at the papers. The petitioner, Ricardo Arias, wanted the court to issue an injunction: restraining respondent from exposing their daughter "to the unstable and immoral sexual patterns that pervade the Paget household."

She could not help but read the rest.

Richie's first ground was a reprise of the *Inquisitor* article: Christopher Paget had destroyed Richie's marriage and left Elena without a family. But the words "Carlo Paget" stopped her.

Terri looked up at Richie in disbelief. "So you're bringing Carlo into this," she said quietly. "You just can't help yourself, right?"

"I'm *protecting* Elena." Richie folded his arms. "I thought it was time that Judge Scatena knew the facts."

"You'd drag them *both* into a courtroom." Her voice filled with anger. "Elena too."

"Only if you make me." He assumed a stiff, self-righteous posture. "You'll notice that I've been *very* responsible—everything filed under seal. So none of this becomes public unless you force me to a hearing." He smiled briefly. "Not even the press has to know."

Will they print this? she would ask Chris. It may depend, Chris would answer, on what else they come up with.

"I see the light dawning, Terri." Richie draped an arm around her. "Just think what a *truly* vindictive person would do with this—someone in politics, for example. Something far more painful than interrupting a vacation."

Terri stared at him. "The hearing date. You scheduled it for when we'd be in Italy."

"In Portofino, according to your itinerary. You know, *I've* never been there." He paused, giving her shoulder a friendly squeeze. "In light of our daughter's crisis, I had to move quickly. But you could always ask Judge Scatena to postpone the hearing. Something about being on the Italian Riviera with your boss."

Deliberately, Terri took his arm off her shoulder. "Tell me what you want. Tell me, and then get the fuck out of here."

Richie's eyes glinted. "Call off the evaluation, and I'll call off the hearing. I want permanent custody, the support I've asked for, *and* fifty thousand dollars." His voice flattened. "It's more money than I asked for last time. But I bet you can figure out somewhere to get it. *Now*."

She stared at him. "And if I don't?"

"We go to a hearing." He nodded toward the papers in her hand. "And those become public documents. Open to *anyone*." He paused, speaking more softly. "Politics is such a dirty business, Terri."

Terri's telephone rang.

"That should be your boyfriend," Richie said cheerfully. "He must have read his courtesy copy."

Turning, Terri answered the telephone.

"So Colt found Richie," Chris said. "I suppose it was only a matter of time."

He did not sound himself. "You found the papers," Terri said.

"Carlo did. I need to see you."

She glanced over at Richie. "Oh, *I'm* leaving," he told her. "I know you lovers need time to talk."

"All right," Terri said to Chris. As she hung up, Richie kissed her on the forehead and vanished.

Terri locked the door behind him and sat down again.

She could not seem to hold a thought. There were too many: making love with Chris; the look on Rosa's face; Richie's smile of pleasure; Carlo.

Elena, stretching out in Chris's bathtub.

There was a knock on the door. Terri went to open it. Standing in the doorway, Chris tilted his head sideways, searching her face. He looked tired.

"Are you coming in?" she asked.

He stepped inside. She closed the door, turning to him with her hand still on the knob. He looked, Terri thought, completely miserable. But his eyes did not leave her face.

"Most couples have bad moments," he said at last. "But they don't have them in public, with their children at risk. Unless one of them runs for office. I couldn't be sorrier, Terri. For both of them. And for you."

Watching him, Terri could see the price he might pay for Richie: the Senate race, the painful talk with Carlo. But right now, what seemed to matter most to him was how she felt.

"Unless I give him Elena *and* money," she said wearily, "she'll go through a hearing. You and Carlo will be spread all across the papers. The Senate will be history."

"And if you *do* give Richie Elena, *we'd* be history." Chris gazed at her. "One way or the other, he means this to end us. Just as, I suspect, Colt means it to end *me*."

"Do you think that's what made Richie do this?"

Chris nodded. "In part. One of his people read the *Inquisitor*, I'm quite sure, and got in touch with Richie. Just in case he needed more encouragement."

Terri found it hard to look at him. "That gives us only one way out, doesn't it?"

Chris had made his face impassive. "You agree not to see me. Now or ever. And just to be safe, I get out of the race."

Nodding, Terri turned away from him. "That way there's no hearing; everything stays under seal; he can't put Carlo and Elena through all this. Then I press forward with the evaluation, try to get custody."

Chris sat on the couch, staring at the ceiling. "Don't do it for my sake," he said finally. "Or Carlo's. If you do that for anyone, it should be Elena."

Terri began picking up Richie's papers, like a lawyer straightening her desk. "The hearing's not for three more weeks. We've got that long to decide."

"Three weeks to be together." For the first time, Chris seemed almost angry, though his voice was very gentle. "Just time enough to go to Italy."

Terri turned to him in surprise. "We could cut four days off the trip," Chris said, "and still be back to prepare for court. Richie or no Richie, we owe that much to whatever we have."

Terri sat next to him, hand resting on his arm. "We can't, Chris—not now. I won't be able to stop thinking about Elena. It would be a nightmare...."

"Perhaps it would be." He stared at the floor and then went on. "Maybe we couldn't be ourselves. But we'd be far away from Richie. Maybe, somehow, we can think our way out of all this." He paused for emphasis. "Whatever I've faced in life, I've never let anyone just run me over. I won't start now, for Ricardo Arias. And neither should you."

Terri found that she could not answer. As if feeling her hesitancy, Chris gently touched her face. "Come with me, Terri. If after Italy, we're not together, we'll have all the time we need to live with that."

FIFTEEN

"IT'S ALL RIGHT," Rosa said. "I'll make sure Elena's safe."

They were standing in the doorway of Rosa's home, on the night before Terri left for Italy. It was seven o'clock; Elena was in her nightgown already. When Terri let the little girl go, and looked into her mother's silent gaze, she felt unutterably sad. "I know you will," she said to Rosa, and pulled Elena close again.

Arriving home, she felt suddenly sure—in spite of Chris—that she should not go away with him. She snatched at clothes, unable to get started.

The telephone rang.

It was Chris, she knew, calling to take her to dinner. After that, she would stay with him; right now, Terri felt, only that would get her to Italy.

"Hi," he said. "Ready yet?"

"Getting there. What's for dinner?"

"Actually, I think I'm coming down with something. Is it okay if I just pick you up in the morning?"

"Sure," Terri said automatically, and then felt the loneliness overcome her. "Are you all right?"

"A little queasy. I've got the twenty-four-hour whatever, I think. I don't want to give it to you, or take it with us on vacation. We're taking enough as it is—"

"That's fine," Terri cut in. But when she hung up, she found that she had far too much time to think, and too much need to talk.

An hour later, she had not started packing.

Terri sat on the edge of the bed, lost in the past. Remembering the night she had packed for her honeymoon, filled with hope and uncertainty. Knowing, already, that Elena would be born. Looking across the bedroom into the face of her new husband, Ricardo Arias.

She picked up the telephone, to call him.

In the stillness of night, Terri knelt before the confessional.

The priest was silent. Behind the screen, his profile was a shadow. The church was dark and cold.

Terri was afraid. But she could find no peace, and there was no one else to tell.

Trembling, Terri confessed what she had done.

The church was hushed. The priest had turned toward her.

As he rose from the confessional, Terri could feel his anger. The only sounds were his footsteps on the stone.

The priest appeared from behind the screen, a shadow. Terri could not bear to see his face.

She turned to run. Behind her, he called out.

"Teresa . . ."

Terri awoke, the terrible image lingering on her brain.

Her eyes adjusted to the dark. Voices drifted through the window from the walk below. A church bell, deep and sonorous, echoed across the water. The lulling rhythms of an ancient city, where Terri lay next to her lover, unable to forget Ricardo Arias.

Venice, Terri realized. She was with Chris.

He reached out to touch her. "Are you all right?"

With Chris, she told herself again, for the last two days. Together with him in Italy, and yet lost in the past.

Silent, Terri tried to retrieve the last pieces of reality. They had made love, slow and sweet and passionate, and then, in fitful sleep, the dream had reached out for her. She could not have slept more than two hours; the evening sky framed in the wrought-iron balcony had a faint sheen, the death of sunlight moments before; the voices below their window were quickening with anticipation, people rushing toward the night.

"You cried out," Chris said.

Terri still felt shaken. "What did I say?"

"You were afraid of something. Richie, I thought for a minute. But I couldn't make it out."

Terri touched her eyes. "It wasn't Richie."

"What was it, then?"

Terri lay back on the pillow. In the darkness, the crystal chandelier above their bed looked like shards of black obsidian, falling toward them. "It's an old nightmare," she said. "One I haven't had for years." Terri found that she could not look at him; she spoke to the ceiling, voice drained of emotion. "I'm in the chapel at Mission Dolores. It's as it was when I was a child, except that the confessional is in a dark alcove, one where I've never been before.

"I'm alone, confessing my sins. I can't see the priest's face, of course; he's a shadow on the other side of the screen. But I recognize the profile; it's Father Anaya, the parish priest.

"There's a last sin, one I've never confessed to anyone. I lean my face to the screen, as close to Father Anaya as I can get, and whisper it."

Terri did not wish to remember. Her words were slow, reluctant. "The shadow moves. I hear footsteps; something about my sin is drawing Father Anaya toward me."

Terri closed her eyes. "I want to run. But I just stand there, waiting, as the shadow appears beside the confessional. A priest in monk's robes and a cowl.

"At first, I can't see his face. But I know that he's filled with hate. His arm rises to point at me, and then he steps into the light."

Eyes opening, Terri turned to Chris. "It isn't Father Anaya, Chris. It's my father."

Chris looked at her intently. After a time, he asked, "And that's how it ends?"

"Yes. It's always the same." Suddenly Terri felt angry. "Except that I thought I was rid of it, years ago. It's so arrested—like wetting the bed or something."

Chris fell quiet. Terri lay back, feeling the breeze through the window, watching the shadows in the room. Her forehead was damp. A tendril of hair stuck to her cheek.

Chris brushed it away. "A lot of people have recurring dreams," Chris said at last. "I just wonder why you'd have this one now. With all that's going on."

"Do you remember your dreams?"

"Not really." Chris seemed to reflect. "The only one I can recall is where I'm in elementary school, on a bus, except that the driver is Daniel Patrick Moynihan. If you can figure *that* one out, get back to me."

Terri stared at him. "You're making that up. You have to be."

"I'm not. Haven't you heard? WASPs don't have *dreams*, Terri. They have cartoons."

Even now, making her smile was a gift Chris had. "That's because WASPs don't believe in sin," she retorted. "Unless they're fundamentalists."

Smiling slightly, Chris touched her face. "This particular sin of yours," he asked. "What have you done that's so terrible?"

"I've never known. I'm always afraid that my father's going to say it aloud. But the dream just ends."

"Do you have any idea what it means?"

Terri felt a sudden impatience. "It's obvious enough. Somehow, I feel guilty about my father, perhaps for how I felt when he died. I don't waste a lot of time on it."

Once more, Chris seemed to watch her closely. "The nightmare started after he died?"

Terri turned from him. "It's nothing, all right? Except that I seem to have passed my talent for recurring nightmares on to Elena, like some family curse."

Chris reached for an ice bucket beside the bed, poured a glass of Pinot Grigio, and handed it to Terri. "I thought she wouldn't tell you what she sees."

"She won't." Terri sipped the wine, tart on her tongue. "But she always calls it 'the dream.' I'm left with this little girl in my arms, damp and trembling, not knowing how to make it stop." She faced the window. "Sometimes, Chris, I wonder what I've done to her."

He reached out, cradling her face. "Why don't you try to call her again."

Terri kissed his palm and went to the other room.

Dialing Richie's number, she watched Chris flick on a bedside lamp, refill the ice bucket. The lamp caught the slim line of his body. Richie's telephone rang.

Terri began counting. At twelve rings, she hung up.

Gently replacing the phone, Terri was still. Enough, she told herself. Be with Chris while you can.

"Nothing?" he asked her.

"Nothing."

Chris pulled his hand from the ice bucket. Perhaps the purple discoloration had faded a little, Terri thought, but Chris still winced when he used it. "You should have had that x-rayed," she said. "For all you know, it's broken."

He shrugged. "I doubt it. And I'd have had to spend the night before we left in an emergency room, endlessly waiting for some rookie doctor to tell me I shouldn't go at all. Getting *you* to go was hard enough."

Terri looked at his hand again. "I've never been the victim of a falling trunk. I can't imagine how you did it."

"Your reflexes are faster. I only wish you'd helped me pack."

Terri gave him a wry look. "It's *your* trunk. And it was *you* who canceled dinner at the last minute and left me alone all night."

Chris turned to the window. "I'll make it up to you," he said at length. "It's a fine night to take the vaporetto, and I know just the place for black squid pasta."

"*That,*" Terri answered, "was the real subject of my nightmare. The other stuff I just made up."

They caught the vaporetto near the Danieli and took the long, slow ride to the Rialto Bridge.

The floating bus hammered along the dark canal with the deep throb of a motor straining to capacity. Chris and Terri walked through the glassed-in compartment filled with tourists and Venetians, and stood in the open air of the fantail, breeze in their faces. The night was purple; the lights of the vaporetto swept the black water of the canal. They seemed far away from everything.

For a half hour, they cruised past the three-story facades of the grand houses that rose from each side of the water. Some glowed with light, which illuminated a room—tall ceilings and crystal chandeliers, books and oil paintings—others were deserted and almost spectral. Feeling Chris sway with the water as he held her, Terri recalled the moment of sheer happiness, surprising and intense, as she stepped from Chris's house that first morning, before she had begun the long, dark slide toward wishing Richie dead.

Briefly, Terri shivered.

Chris slid his leather jacket around her. Together they gazed across the water at the Rialto Bridge.

It was a light, almost floating structure from which five covered arches rose on each side, silvery in the night, to meet above the black water of the canal. The piers were lined with gondolas and vaporettos and private boats; the walk near the bridge was bathed in the light of outdoor restaurants where groups and couples sat eating or drinking cappuccino; on the left bank a stream of tourists and Venetians strolled through the stalls of street merchants. Voices and laughter carried across the water.

All at once, Terri had the almost weightless sensation of having stepped in an instant from one life to another—the Teresa Peralta who shared this time and place with Christopher Paget could not be the one who had spent six dreary years as Richie's wife. With a fierce suddenness, Terri felt the desire to immerse herself in Italy and Chris. When the vaporetto docked, she hurried them off.

They left the pier, crossed the bridge, and wandered between the dark medieval buildings of narrow stone streets until they found the restaurant Chris was looking for. But Madonna was not the intimate *ristorante* Terri was learning to expect of Venice. The wooden door opened into two large and brightly lit rooms, with white walls and vivid modern prints. Both rooms were jammed with diners; waiters in starched white jackets bustled between their tables and the kitchen, calling quickly to each other above the warm cacophony of voices mingling. It was like her favorite restaurant in the Mission District, where Terri had grown up—families and laughter and argument, kids spilling drinks and no one much caring.

Terri smiled at the thought, and then Chris, glancing over her shoulder, held two fingers in the air. Suddenly a short, mustached waiter was whisking them to a corner table. Terri looked around them. Even past nine o'clock there were dark-haired Italian children at some tables, other kids still among the groups waiting. Terri could not help thinking of Elena: it was hard to imagine Chris and Terri ever bringing her on such a trip.

"Cocktails, signorina?"

The hell with it, Terri thought. "Tanqueray martini, please. Straight up, not much vermouth."

Chris grinned; he had introduced her to martinis only a few months before, when Terri had been in an escapist mood. "The same," he told the waiter.

As he left, a little girl in the corner caught Terri's eye. She was perhaps four and knelt in her mother's lap, touching her gold earrings with the air of great discovery. Even as a baby, Elena had done these things with Terri; from a few weeks old, when Elena was still breast-feeding, the little girl would spend long minutes gazing into Terri's face as if discovering the person into whose care she had been given. When Richie's fecklessness had forced her to return to law school, Elena was not yet two months old.

Please, Terri told herself, forget him. At least for tonight.

The martinis arrived. Terri touched her glass to Chris's. "To us," she said. "And to staying up late."

The first sip had the crisp, almost medicinal taste of a good mar-tini. A second sip and the gin hit her, a first bracing shock, then warmth. The third sip seemed to flow down her tongue.

As Terri watched, the little girl touched her mother's face, as if to learn its features. "I can't believe you never wanted kids of your own," Terri said to Chris. "Not the way you feel about Carlo."

Chris considered her for a moment; since they had come to Italy, this was Terri's first mention of his son. "Until Carlo came to live with me," he answered, "I never thought I had much talent for it. Besides, by getting him at age seven, I not only skipped the terrible twos, fours, and sixes, I never changed his diapers." His smile did not quite touch his eyes. "I think it lends our relationship a certain dignity. Never once will Carlo have to listen while I tell his college girlfriend about the night he spit up on my tuxedo."

Terri laughed and decided to order another martini.

When it arrived, the dark-haired girl was resting against her moth-er's shoulder. The second martini, Terri discovered, was even easier than the first. She did not know why she had never had two before.

"I love you," she said to Chris. "I love you a lot."

Chris smiled again, more easily. "I love you too, Terri."

When the waiter took their dinner orders, Terri asked for red wine. Chris did not question this; there was some consultation with the waiter, and soon a bottle of Chianti appeared. The first sip was tart, almost peppery.

"This is good," Terri assured him. "*Really* good."

The little girl was leaving, she saw. Her mother had passed her to her father, who carried her through the crowded restaurant, sliding around the people who still waited. Her head bobbed on his shoul-der, but her eyes did not open; at times like this, the world of a small child was smells and closeness, the people who cared for her. The thought felt warm and then, as Terri remembered holding Elena, turned to sadness in an instant.

Chris had followed her gaze. "Cute kid."

It was nice that Chris had noticed, Terri thought. She treated herself to more Chianti.

About the time she finished her second glass, time and space changed.

She saw hardly anything but Chris. Dinner came; the waiter filled their glasses; Chris grinned when she liked squid pasta. Time moved like slides in a projector, one image suddenly replaced by another—the wine bottle in the waiter's hand, the check arriving. Everything but Chris seemed part of a silent movie; she could barely remember what the two of them were running from. Italy felt fine.

The night air was a shock to her—cool, hitting her face like water. Chris's gaze at her seemed far too serious.

"Let's go dancing," she said. "We've never done that."

Suddenly Chris was laughing again. "I can't dance worth a damn."

"You just move your body." Terri could not see what was funny; suddenly it seemed quite important that they dance together. "Come on, Chris. I'll show you."

Chris did not argue. There were winding streets, her hand in his, and then the dark cave of a nightclub; American music blasting from a sound system that drowned out voices; brandy; mouths opening but making no sound; bodies streaked by purple and red strobe lights. Terri went with the music, body moving, head thrown back, hair flying. Her forehead was damp, her body loose and sensual; she barely saw Chris in front of her, saw no one else at all. The songs did not matter; only the pulse of the music, the beat of her own heart. Terri was free.

No music, suddenly. Harsh lights went on, dissolving the streaks of red and purple. The club was a stale-smelling cubicle filled with tables and half-empty drinks.

Chris took her hand. "They're closing up."

The night was cold now. "Let's go somewhere," Terri said. "Please, I don't want to stop yet."

"It won't help," Terri thought she heard him say. She ran away, toward the night.

They were in an empty piazza—shadowy buildings, bare stones, the dark shape of a fountain. Terri's heels clattered on the stones,

gray in moonlight. She kicked off her shoes and hurried toward the
fountain. The water was cool on her feet; the hem of her dress clung
to her legs. Chris stood watching her, hands in his pockets.

"It's nearly three," he said. "We're out of places, Zelda. This is the
last fountain in Venice."

It made Terri laugh. She looked down at Chris, slim and beautiful
as a statue, and wondered if she could ever look that way to him.

"It doesn't matter," she said, and got down from the fountain.
"There's something I want to do with you."

She took his hand, stepped into her heels again. Each move felt
sure and perfect.

"Come on," she said. "Let's hurry back."

They ran through the streets, twisting and turning, until the last
one opened on the Grand Canal.

When they were inside the hotel room, time stopped.

Terri turned off all the lights. It was so quiet that she could hear
herself breathe.

The dark was softened by moonlight, the faint glow of the gaslights on the walk below. Terri could see nothing but his face.

"Stay there," she whispered.

He stood by the bed, perhaps ten feet away. Taking off her earrings, Terri placed them on the dresser behind her. His reflection in
the mirror was a shadow above her shoulder, so still that it was as if
he were captured by her image. Terri turned to him again.

There was no sound. "I've been wanting to do this," she said
softly.

Slowly, she began to move for him.

The pulse of the music in her head was slow and sinuous. Her
dress as it fell was caught for a moment by the sway of her hips.

She slid her bra down over shoulders, imagining that he had never
seen her like this.

It fell to the floor. Her rhythm was slower yet; Terri wanted him
to feel her across the room.

"*Jesus.*"

His voice was husky now. Yet as clear as her own.

"I want to take us away, Chris. From everything."

When she was naked, Terri asked him to watch her.

Seconds passed. In the silver light, moving as he watched, Terri
felt beautiful at last.

When his shadow came toward her, Terri did not stop. Face-to-face with him, she saw how dark his eyes seemed.

"Right here," she said.

They slipped to the floor together. Everything he did was right. Even his silence as he filled her.

The rest was wanting, mutual and desperate, nothing held back. For a long time after, neither spoke.

"Sleepy?" Chris asked.

"No," Terri answered quietly. "Not sleepy."

Slowly, his mouth moved across her stomach, and then nothing else mattered. In the deep quiet of release that followed, Terri at last forgot Elena.

SIXTEEN

WHEN TERRI AWOKE, the morning sun shone with a savage brightness, and the room looked like a bad dream: clothes strewn on the floor; her bra draped over the mirror; the sheets half torn from the bed. The back of her skull throbbed.

Chris handed her a glass of water and three aspirins. She took them without comment, then squinted up at him.

"How come *you're* so chipper?"

"A cold shower." He grinned. "Otherwise I'm walking the thin line between civilization and barbarism. Much as we did last night."

Terri sat up in bed. She was naked; it took her a moment to realize that the rawness on her shoulder blades was rug burn. A flush spread across her face.

"How much," she asked, "do you remember?"

Chris sat beside her. "Every bit of it. Care for a detailed description?"

She shook her head. "I've never done *that* before."

"I'm flattered." He kissed her forehead. "I just wish we'd gotten back a little earlier. Anytime before three-thirty."

Terri managed a smile. "If I'm going to start taking my clothes off like that, I should probably pace myself." She looked at him askance. "How many times did we make love?"

"Three. But only twice on the rug." Chris pulled a damp wash-cloth out of the ice bucket, wrung it out, and gave it to her. "Put this over your eyes for a while. It helped *me* this morning, and I needed it."

It was a good idea; everything in the room had sharp edges. Darkness was better, and the cloth soothed the pounding that ran from her neck through her eyes. "Speaking of last night," she heard Chris ask, "you didn't happen to use a diaphragm, did you?"

"Are you serious? Did *you* use a condom?"

"I was afraid of that," Chris said. "The amateur hour."

He slid the cloth from her eyes and kissed her. Terri took his hand, held it to her cheek. "Can you pass me the phone?" she asked.

A shadow crossed his face. And then he turned, reaching, and handed her the telephone.

"Thanks," she said, and dialed Richie's number.

No one answered.

Holding the telephone, Terri imagined that Elena must feel as if she had lost her mother. As if it were now, Terri remembered the morning when Rosa had gone to the doctor, her face bruised, and Terri had hidden from her father in the bedroom. Looking out the window for her mother, Terri had been frightened that Rosa might tell the truth about what had happened, that they would never let her come home. When at last she did, pausing on the sidewalk until she saw Terri's face in the window, Terri the child felt relieved for herself, a guilty sorrow for Rosa. Remembering now, Terri understood the power of Elena's wish that *she* return to Richie; Terri had no scars that Elena could see.

Watching Chris, Terri dialed again.

No answer, still. All at once, Terri felt the venoms of her hangover—guilt and nausea and self-contempt. "God," she said bitterly, "I wish he were dead."

The words echoed inside her. But all that Chris said was, "I should call Carlo."

Terri handed him the telephone. Dialing, he turned from her.

The moment that Carlo answered, Chris's voice lightened. After a time, Terri left the room.

When he was finished, she picked up the telephone again. Her head still pounded.

"Nothing?" Chris asked.

"No. And Elena should have been in bed for hours."

Putting down the phone, Terri drifted to the balcony. The morning was bright; the sidewalks stirred. "If I can't reach Richie by tonight," she said, "I'm calling the school."

Chris said nothing.

After a time, they put on sunglasses and went to an outdoor café on the Piazza San Marco, that immense stone rectangle, the size of two football fields, lined on three sides by two- and three-story buildings with terraces and ornate columns. Chris and Terri chose a table; ordered croissants and two double espressos; and surveyed the rest of the piazza. It was, Terri realized, quite wonderful.

"I'm sorry," she said finally. "Not just about being so worried. About everything." She looked him in the face. "I wonder, sometimes, if you can ever forgive me for what he's done to you. Even if we could find a way to go on."

Chris pushed his chair back from the table, stretching his legs in front of him. He stared at the espresso he cupped in both hands. "I think that's more a matter of whether you'll forgive *yourself* for staying with him. Enough to stay with *me*."

"You still think I need a shrink, in other words."

"Is *that* a sin too? Like the one in this dream you've started having again? Or whatever feelings you've never faced about your mother and your father?"

Terri turned away. "I don't like thinking of *him*," she finally said. "When I do, it scares me. Anyway, a lot of it I hardly remember now." Suddenly she felt angry. "It's done, all right? My father's dead."

Chris gazed at her over the edge of his cup. "How *did* he die, Terri? You never really say."

As if by reflex, Terri shut her eyes.

The image was like the shock of a flashbulb, leaving a painful shadow on the retina. Her father's head at her feet in the first morning sun, a ribbon of dried blood running from his temple. She felt her mind flinch, close down; then there was nothing.

Terri did not answer. Softly, Chris asked, "What is it, Terri? That you blame *yourself* somehow?"

Terri opened her eyes, dispelling the terrible image. But she did not look at Chris. "The house felt safer afterward," she said at last. "Maybe I blamed myself for liking that." Her voice grew tired. "Sometimes, Chris, I think that's why I was so determined to become a lawyer. Because there were *rules*: no one got hit, and everyone had their turn to speak. The law protected even children, I thought."

Turning to the piazza, Chris fell silent. As Terri had known he would.

SEVENTEEN

TERRI STOOD in a phone booth near the Doges' Palace.

No one answered Richie's telephone. As before, the machine, with its despised cheery message, did not switch on.

Chris paced outside, squinting in the noonday sun. As she dialed again, he turned away.

Terri pushed open the glass door. The breeze felt cool.

Chris shoved his hands in his pockets. For a moment, Terri thought, everything about him looked tight. "It's three a.m. in San Francisco," she told him. "Richie's *there*, Chris—he's just not answering."

"At three a.m., *I* might not answer, either. For all we know, he's turned off the ring mechanism as well as the machine." Chris's voice had a slight edge. "Who knows—by tonight, he may be weary of tormenting you. There's only so much fun a man can stand."

By tonight, Terri thought, she would call the school. She had almost forgotten who she was with.

"Care for lunch?" Chris asked.

"Not yet." She took his arm. "Do you mind if we just walk for a while?"

Quiet, they strolled along the Grand Canal. The spacious walk was busy but not crowded; the wind was fresh, the sea smell light but pleasant. The people were a mixed bag of Venetians and tourists with cameras, stopping at the curio stands and sidewalk restaurants. Many of the tourists were Italian, reminding Terri that few Americans could travel in the way that Chris was sharing with her. It made her feel grateful and uneasy all at once: thinking of Elena, Terri wondered if she could stay in Italy.

Chris had stopped, gazing at a street artist drawing pen-and-ink portraits of whatever passersby would let him. The man had parlayed a red scarf and a handlebar mustache into a remarkable resemblance to Salvador Dalí: his work, Terri thought wryly, was a bit more mundane. But his execution, complete with brush flourishes and dramatic pauses to gaze narrowly at his subject, a middle-aged German woman with bleached-blond hair, was delivered with the almost comic solemnity of a master. Terri could see that this scene had softened Chris's mood: he had a warmer sense of people—even their foibles and vanity—than Terri had at first known.

"He's wonderful," Chris murmured. Terri knew that he did not mean the drawing; Chris found something admirable in the brio and sense of self that impelled this man to get up every morning, wax his mustache, and venture forth with his artist's kit to become the Dalí of his chosen piece of sidewalk.

With a certain ceremony, he presented his drawing to the German woman. She did not seem pleased. Some haggling over the price ensued; when it was over, the woman went off without a word of thanks. The artist looked glum: left without a subject, he sagged, and his search for fresh customers bore a trace of humiliation.

"Care to perform a service?" Chris asked Terri.

Terri did not feel a fitting subject for art. "*Me?*"

"A keepsake," Chris said lightly. "I've wanted your picture since the first day I saw you."

The artist had discovered them standing behind him and was eyeing Terri with an air of hope. "The thought never occurred to you," she told Chris. "And I hate my nose. If I volunteer to do this, *I* pick the closet it hangs in."

"It's going in my bedroom," Chris answered, and went over to the artist.

Terri sat for him patiently, purse at her feet, while the artist complimented her and smiled at Chris, a man who could appreciate another's good fortune. Terri began to enjoy herself, to take pleasure in *Chris's* enjoyment.

After a time, another man stopped to watch—a young Italian, by the look of him, curly-haired and slight. He stood behind Chris; his eyes moved from Terri to the painting, as if critically comparing portrait to subject. "A fine likeness," Chris told the artist. "Even better than I'd hoped."

Squinting at his palette, the artist smiled at this compliment. "A pleasure, sir. Your wife is beautiful."

Chris caught Terri's eye: given their circumstances, the mistake was so ironic that she could not suppress her mischief. "He needs to hear that," she told the artist. "I go for days without the smallest sign of affection."

Chris turned to keep from smiling. There was a sudden blur of motion; Terri flinched, startled, and then saw the young Italian snatch the strap of her purse and begin running.

"*Chris . . .*"

But Chris had seen him. "Wait here," he snapped, and started after the thief.

The purse snatcher was ten yards ahead. But he had not counted on a tourist with Chris's passion for fitness.

Instinctively, Terri ran after them.

The man burst through a clump of tourists, scattering them with open mouths and startled faces. Glancing over his shoulder, he saw Chris behind him; the thief's legs churned faster, carrying him away down the broad sidewalk. Chris followed in a path cleared by the man's own flight. There was something lethal in his pursuit, a release of anger so intense that Terri could see it in his lengthening strides. Their figures grew smaller.

Terri's heart pounded. "*Chris,*" she called out. "*It's all right.*"

Chris could not hear her. She saw the man glance over his shoulder again, a pantomime of fear. When the thief suddenly swerved through the umbrellas of an outdoor restaurant, knocking dishes to the cement, Chris hardly broke stride.

Terri ran faster.

Bursting past the last umbrella, the thief disappeared between two buildings, down a side street. His only hope, Terri thought, was to lose Chris in the maze of Venice. Part of her hoped he would.

Chris vanished down the side street.

Terri ran along the walk and through the restaurant. An old woman had fallen to the cement, food scattered in her lap. There were shouts and cries; broken plates crunched beneath Terri's feet.

Entering the side street, she spotted a man running twenty yards ahead—Chris disappearing down an alley to the right. Terri was panting now; as she started running again, her side ached and her head pounded, and the feeling in the pit of her stomach was like morning sickness.

Turning the corner, she entered a Venice that startled her. The alley was a slit of light, a shadowy passage between stone buildings and an inky canal, still and faintly rancid. There was mold on the walls; laundry hung like rags from the windows above her head. It was a world so cramped and dank that Terri felt entrapped.

In the iron doorway of a house with boarded windows, Terri saw two profiles.

Chris had his hand on the thief's neck, shoving his head against the door. Their faces were inches apart.

Terri ran toward them. *"No,"* she called out.

Chris did not turn. His forehead glistened with sweat; he seemed scarcely to breathe at all. The man stared back at him, angry and frightened. Terri's purse still dangled from his hand.

Chris gazed into the thief's face as if he were not human. "From his breath," Chris said, "he's a smoker. Otherwise I never would have caught him."

He could have been discussing a dead animal. Terri felt their tension: the rich American, filled with a repressed anger that only Terri could understand; the purse snatcher who must despise him. The thief's curly hair reminded her of Richie.

He spat in Chris's face.

Chris's expression did not change. Just a slight turn of the head, as if interested that the man had understood him.

"Let him go," Terri pleaded softly. "Please."

Chris's hands seemed to tighten. "Check your purse," he told her. "Make sure you've got everything."

As she took her purse from the thief's fingers, Chris twisted the collar of his T-shirt. She could see the man's Adam's apple work, his spittle on Chris's face. Chris's hand still looked swollen.

Terri did not look into the purse. "It's all here," she said quickly.

Chris jerked the thief by his neck. Then, as if they were partners in a dance, he turned the man, dragged him a few feet, and bent him backward over the canal—knees flexed, feet on the sidewalk, back and head above the water. The man began struggling, face contorted.

"If I let you go," Chris inquired softly, "do you think you can keep your balance?"

Terri froze at something in his voice. Even the thief stopped struggling. Then he gave a belated shrug, pretending that he did not understand.

"That's too bad," Chris said, "because I guess we'll never know," and gently pushed him into the canal.

There was a splash. For the first time, Chris turned to Terri. She was staring past him into the water, at the thief. The man's hair was soaked; his arms paddled randomly.

"Can he swim?" Chris inquired.

"Yes."

"Perfect justice, at last." Drained of his anger, Chris sounded weary. "Better this than calling the police. Or, for that matter, American Express."

Terri took a last look at the thief, who was clambering awkwardly into a motorboat at the foot of the wall, and then she dabbed Chris's face with a tissue. Looking at her, his eyes were troubled, as if he had returned to himself.

"Let's go," she told him. "We never paid the artist."

They made their way back through the side street. Stopping at the restaurant, Chris apologized and left some lire for the damage. Then they returned to the Grand Canal. Except to thank him, Terri found little to say.

When they saw the artist, Terri held her purse aloft. The artist smiled his delight. But as he presented Terri with her drawing, the face she saw was not hers but Chris's, filled with an anger he had never let her see.

EIGHTEEN

THAT EVENING, Chris and Terri walked back to the Danieli from dinner at Harry's Bar. Other lovers, more carefree, drifted arm in arm beneath the gaslights. Part of Terri wished to join them. But she would have no peace until she spoke to Elena.

When they reached the hotel, she hurried through the ornate lobby and up the staircase, ahead of Chris. Opening the door, she switched on the lights and began jabbing at the buttons of the telephone.

Once more, Richie did not answer.

She put down the phone. From the doorway, Chris watched her. Then he stepped inside, closing the door behind him. In the dim light, Terri looked up at him, silent.

Chris began pacing the room: since the incident of the thief, Terri had understood that his nerve ends were wired to hers.

"I'm sorry," she said finally. "Maybe I was crazy to come here."

Turning, Chris looked stung. "Maybe," he answered tersely, "you should have left your husband at home."

"I'm not going to respond to that. Not now." Terri looked at him straight on. "I'm sorrier about what he's done than you can *ever* know. And maybe he's achieving exactly what he wants—us sitting here quarreling over him, as if he were pulling the strings from seven thousand miles away." She paused for emphasis. "But right now all that matters, Chris, is that I can't find my daughter."

"So here we are," Chris snapped back. "In Venice, waiting by the telephone for the sound of Richie's voice."

His eyes, clear and cold, seemed to stare into the depth of his loathing for Richie. It came to Terri with bittersweetness that, in light of all they had been through, she and Chris fought very little. "Sometimes," she said more softly, "I worry he'll just take her."

Chris looked at her in surprise. "Kidnapping? Two weeks before the hearing? I wish he *were* that dumb."

Terri fell quiet. "I'm calling the school in an hour," she said at last. "Either Elena's there or she's not."

Chris turned to look out at the night. But his gaze seemed absent, meant only to lend him distance from his own hurt. It gave Terri a sense, once more, of the immensity of his self-control, and of the isolation that was its price.

"Maybe it would be easier," she said softly, "if you just let yourself blow up."

Chris gave a small shake of the head, more to himself than to Terri. "I watched my parents get angry," he said after a while. "They threw vases at each other in boozy rages, said things so wounding that they could never be forgiven. The words, I came to realize, were worse than the crockery—it was the things they *said* that gutted their marriage." He turned to her again. "It's one of the ways that you and I are alike. You believe that anger is a sin." His voice grew quiet. "We're the same species, you and I. But I'm not sure you know that yet. Or how important it can be."

Terri thought of his damaged hand, the purplish hue of his injury, and then of the thief. "But have you ever let yourself get angry, Chris? I mean *so* angry that you stopped wanting to control it?"

Chris did not answer; it was as if he had not heard her. "I can't make you stay here," he said at last. "But before you call the school, you should at least find out if Rosa's seen Elena. One thing you can't appear, to people like Scatena or Alec Keene, is spiteful or alarmist."

Glancing at her watch, Terri did not answer. She felt Chris's hand on her shoulder.

Reaching for the telephone, she placed a call to Rosa.

Six rings, then seven. Chris's hand seemed to tighten. "No answer?" he asked.

"No. And my mother doesn't have a machine."

Chris was silent for a moment. "Try her again," he said. "Perhaps you dialed wrong."

I know my own mother's number, Terri almost snapped. Instead she calmed herself and dialed again. She listened to the telephone ring, her own phone pressed to her ear.

"Hello?"

The connection was bad; the woman's voice was so thin that Terri could hardly make it out.

"Mom?"

"Terri?"

"Thank God you're home."

A second's pause, then the echo of delayed transmission. "I was in the basement," Rosa's hollow voice answered. "Looking for something. How are you?"

"*I'm* looking for Elena. I'm worried sick about her."

Another delay, seemingly infinite. "Elena?"

"Yes. I want to know if you've talked to her."

A longer pause. "She's *here*, Terri."

"With *you?*"

"Yes." This time the pause was punctuated by static. "She's at school."

Terri's eyes shut. "Elena's with my mother," she murmured to Chris, and then, as if in delayed reaction, leaned back against him.

Her mother said nothing more; it seemed a long time before Terri asked the next question. When she did, it was in a different tone, tentative and tight.

"Where's Richie?"

There was more static, and then Rosa answered, "He never came."

Terri sat up. "Have you tried to reach him?"

She felt Chris stand, walk away. "No." Rosa's long-distance voice sounded faintly surprised. "Should I?"

"I don't know. Is Elena upset?"

"Only at first. Actually, she seems quite happy."

Terri could imagine that, at least for a time. "Just a minute, Mama." Covering the telephone, she turned to Chris. He was standing near the window again; Terri could not see his face. "Richie never showed," she said. "What do you think I should do?"

Chris shrugged. "Nothing."

Terri gave him a questioning look. "Devoted fathers aren't supposed to blow off custody," he said. "Why remind him."

Terri frowned. "I was thinking about Elena."

"So am I. Let him rot awhile."

After a moment, Terri spoke to Rosa. "Leave him be. He'll show up whenever he decides to."

"All right." Rosa's voice sounded clearer now.

Still gazing at Chris, Terri was silent again. "You should have called me, Mama. This has been pretty tough."

"I'm sorry, Teresa. I had meant to. Later on this morning."

Perhaps she imagined it, but Terri heard a faint rebuke beneath Rosa's measured apology—if Terri had not gone to Italy, she would not have lost touch with Elena. There was no point in prolonging the conversation: she was quite certain that Rosa would never ask about her trip.

"Tell Elena I'll call her," Terri said. "And if you hear anything about Richie, please call *me*."

"I will." Her mother's tone was gentler. "But don't worry, sweetheart. Everything is fine."

When Terri got off, she saw that Chris had drifted to the balcony. He gazed out at the canal: the sinuous dance of streetlights on black water, the groups and couples passing below, a lone cigarette boat vanishing in the night as it moved toward San Giorgio island.

"I wonder where he is," Terri said.

Chris did not turn. "I could care less."

Terri walked behind him. "He's never taken off like this, that's all. I mean, Richie's not reliable, but he doesn't just disappear."

Chris's shoulders moved, a half shrug. "How long has he been missing?"

"I don't know, really. Since Sunday, when he didn't pick Elena up, it's been two days."

"*Two days.*" Chris turned to her. "We know Elena's safe, all right? If it's all the same to you, I'd prefer not to waste any more time obsessing over what might have happened to *Richie*. Frankly, I don't want to get my hopes up."

Terri put her hands on her hips. "For *us*, I feel the way you do. But not for Elena. Like it or not, Richie's part of her security."

"Jesus fucking Christ." From the shadows, Chris's voice had a quiet intensity. "I refuse to sentimentalize this weasel as a father, and I refuse to listen to you do it."

"He *is* her father, and she loves him. I can't pretend she doesn't, just to please you." Terri paused, then resumed, her tone more level: "We're talking about a feeling that just *is*."

"And would be less harmful," Chris shot back, "if Richie *never* showed. Because if a parent isn't around, kids simply invest them with imaginary qualities, like God or a movie star. Which is what

Elena would do with Richie." His voice became sardonic. "Assuming that you could stand to let her."

Terri watched him. "Are we arguing about Richie? Or are you trying to tell me something else?"

Chris leaned against the balcony, backlit by moonlight. A cool breeze from the canal swept past him and touched Terri's face. Softly, he said, "You really don't know, do you."

Something in his tone, low and quiet, unsettled her. The wind chilled Terri's skin; she could not see his face. "Know what?"

He turned away. "A half dozen times, just in the last few days, I've told myself that I should let you go. Sometimes I even want to. But I never can." The raw feeling in his voice startled her. But when he spoke again, it was gently. "Sometimes I *do* blame you for Richie."

Terri stopped herself from going to him. "I understand, Chris. It's just that I can't live with it."

"You shouldn't have to. Perhaps, with someone else, you wouldn't."

"But that isn't something wrong with *us*, Chris. It's something wrong with *him*. The question is whether there's any way for us to deal with what he's done."

Chris shook his head slowly. "Not if I take Richie out on you. You're right about that too."

He sounded tired. Then he stepped from the shadows, leaning his forehead against hers.

"I'm screwing this up," he murmured. "Always watching you, never knowing what to do or say." He paused again. "I *was* wrong to bring you here. I'm sorry for that, and for talking you into it."

Gently, Terri kissed his face. "*I* was wrong," she said at last. "For the next few days, we should try to live our life."

NINETEEN

THE NEXT AFTERNOON, after a leisurely drive through the Tuscan countryside, Chris and Terri entered the most charming place Terri had ever seen.

Like many towns in Tuscany, Montalcino had been built atop a steep hill, the first defense of the Middle Ages. The cobblestone streets were too narrow to drive: they parked near a gray-stone fortress with three square turrets and a large stone courtyard. Once inside, Terri entered another time and place: she could imagine lookouts gazing from the turrets and the courtyard filled with soldiers and horses. The garden in back, with low stone walls and fruit trees planted in straight lines, commanded a sweeping view of hills and valleys. To Terri, the site felt safe, inviolate.

The town itself was quaint yet lively. Church bells sounded; children kicked a soccer ball in a town square surrounded by benches and people talking; a bent old couple walked arm in arm in the oddly formal posture of aged Italians, bent but observant, their slow steps seemingly imprinted on the bone and brain, a matter not merely of age but of a life spent in a place that existed outside change or even hurry. Watching them, Terri felt more peaceful, attuned to Chris again.

"Can you imagine *us* like that?" Terri asked.

"Sure. Only I'm in a wagon."

Smiling, Terri took his arm. They stopped briefly to buy mineral water, and then meandered through the town. As they walked, she realized that at the end of the street Montalcino seemed to drop into space. They went there and found themselves gazing down at the tree-covered grounds of a centuries-old church, which ended abruptly at a precipice and a startling panorama of hills and fields and val-

"I have no clue."

"When I saw you cross-examine a witness."

Terri looked at him. "God, Chris, I think you're serious."

He smiled again. "I am, sort of. As I often tell Carlo, sexual attraction can be complicated."

The reference to Carlo was a reflex, Terri saw. His smile vanished; for a painful moment, Terri thought about Richie.

"Penny for your thoughts," Chris said softly.

"I was thinking about my dream," Terri answered after a time; only then did she realize that this memory had followed her image of Richie. She rested her head on Chris's shoulder. "It makes me feel like Mrs. Rochester," she said finally. "In *Jane Eyre*. Except that I'm not crazy."

Chris seemed to consider this. "Of course," he ventured, "you'd be the last to know."

Terri moved closer to him. "You really are a help."

"When the dream is over, what kind of feeling are you left with?"

It was hard to answer. "It's like guilt," Terri said finally. "Only worse, because I don't know *why*. Like I've done something too terrible to remember."

Chris turned his face to hers. "Until we came here, Terri, when did you last have it?"

That she remembered so precisely bothered her. "Six years ago," she said at last. "The night before I married Richie."

Chris fell into silence. Terri stood, walking toward the church.

The outside was simple: white stone, a triangular roof, the bell tower beside it. As she looked up, the bell sounded—one deep chime, then another—drawing her inside.

Terri hesitated at the entrance, feeling like a trespasser. Then she pushed open the heavy wooden door.

The church was hushed and empty. The inside was exquisite: walls of blue and pink marble, a ceiling with bright seraphim painted on its three domes; rich frescoes; intricate marble statuary, lovingly preserved. But it was intimate, human scale, a place not for processions but for prayer.

The benches were close to the altar. Terri sat, remembering for a moment the chapel of Mission Dolores on the morning of her father's funeral mass. In the quiet of the half-lit church, she seemed to lose herself between then and now.

leys receding into the distance until they seemed less to end than to vanish.

Chris and Terri sat on a bench beneath a white flowering tree beside the church, drinking their water from cool green bottles. Before them were fields of tiny wild flowers and, farther off, rows of staked grapes on the hills that sloped down and then up to country homes. The failing sunlight deepened the green of the hills and softened the burnt-orange walls of the villas. The breeze smelled faintly of flowers; the grass was cool beneath their bare feet.

Chris seemed to contemplate the bell tower of the church. "I love making love with you," he said.

His head had not turned; the observation was delivered casually, like a comment on the architecture. "What brought that to mind?" Terri asked. "The bell tower?"

"Oh, I don't know. I think about it all the time—in court, at baseball games, whatever. So I suppose it could have been anything." He smiled slightly. "Last night, even."

Terri slid down in her chair, the sun on her face, remembering the feel of their lovemaking. "It's not so bad," she conceded. "You're pretty well-adjusted about sex. I could probably do worse." She smiled. "In fact, I *used* to do worse."

"Oh." He turned to her with polite interest. "When was that?"

"All the time."

Chris's grin, white and sudden, made him look impossibly young; only the faint lines at the corners of his eyes suggested someone much older than thirty.

"You," she said, "are deeply appealing to me."

What was it, Terri wondered, that still reached her after all they had been through? Part of it was that she felt a liking for Chris so deep that she wanted him as close as he could get; part, more mystical to Terri, was the way he turned his head; the way he moved through a room, tensile and alert; the way his eyes changed when he reached for her. After they made love, she would lie next to him, looking into his face, not needing or wanting to speak. As she had last night.

It was as if, Terri thought now, she could stop their time from running out.

Chris put down his mineral water. "Know when *I* first decided you were truly sexy?"

When at last she rose, Terri knelt before the altar and crossed herself. Only then did she understand why she had come.

Bowing her head, Terri asked forgiveness for her sins. It was some time before she stepped into the sunlight.

Chris was gazing out at the hills and valleys, drinking from his bottle of mineral water. His swollen hand, she noticed, had almost healed.

He looked up at her, curious. The church, Terri realized, had left her with a feeling of lightness. "Somehow it felt familiar," she told him. "Maybe, in another life, I was married here. To someone other than Richie, of course."

Chris smiled at that. Sitting next to him, Terri left the dream behind her. "Did *you* ever go to a shrink?" she asked.

He smiled a little, as if tracing her thoughts. "Uh-huh. For a couple of years, after I became a parent, I decided to give my own parents some thought."

Terri turned to him, curious; Chris seldom spoke of his family. "What were they like?" she asked.

"If you mean 'who were they?' I have no idea." Chris still scanned the countryside. "They drank and fought and had no purpose. Their only life was in the society pages."

Terri realized that she had seldom imagined Chris as a child. "How was *your* life?"

"It was what I knew." His voice was dismissive. "When you're four or so and you begin to realize that your parents' love is conditional, if it exists at all, you don't get a condominium and a new set of parents. What you decide instead, without even knowing it, is that if your parents don't seem to like you much, they must be onto something. Fortunately for me, they were also strong believers in boarding school." He paused, then added, sardonically, "Naturally, as an adult, I put all that behind me."

Terri smiled at his not-so-subtle point. "All right, Chris, I'll go enlist some mental health professional. If only because I'd rather fuck you than have you for my analyst."

Laughing, Chris took her hand.

Soon, Terri thought, they would be in Portofino. The end of their trip and, perhaps, of more.

"I wish that we could just stay here," she said. "Hide out in Montalcino."

He smiled, knowing what she meant. "And what would we *do*, day after day?"

"Avoid reality, of course. Or any decisions at all." She took his hand. "We could enter some sort of time warp between the thirteenth century and now, where we never get any older, and Richie's deadline never comes."

"Too late," Chris said softly. "In the real world, where we live, it's nearly here."

TWENTY

PORTOFINO, on the Italian Riviera, was surrounded by steep hills that tumbled to sparkling green water. The hills were covered with palms and tall, slender evergreens, leafy boughs, and bright flowers with multicolored blossoms. Tucked amid the riot of vegetation were the iron gates of private villas and the sprawling Mediterranean hotel where Chris and Terri stayed, the Splendido.

Chris and Terri sat at the glass table on their balcony. The view was sweeping: the orange and pink storefronts of the fishing village; the sun-blinded harbor, azure spiked with the white masts of sailboats; and across the bay, tree-shrouded hills with, rising above the green, an ancient stone fortress. On the grounds below them, the pool and patio were surrounded by palms and a garden filled with flowers imported from every continent. The only sounds were birdsongs from the surrounding hills.

So beautiful, Terri thought, and so very painful. When she drifted to the bedroom to make her call, Chris stayed on the balcony.

Elena was painting pictures with her grandmother. "*Mommy,*" she exclaimed. "Where are *you?*"

Terri found that she was smiling, as if Elena's voice had changed something inside her. "In a place called Portofino, sweetheart." Terri did her best to describe it, and then said, "I wish you could see all of this."

"I can *draw* it for you," Elena answered. "There are palm trees outside Grandma's house too. On Dolores Street."

Terri laughed a little, imagining Elena's rendition of an Italian fishing village. "I've missed you *so* much, Elena."

"I miss you too, Mommy. How many more days is it?"

Thinking of Chris, Terri felt sad again. "Only three," she said softly. "Then I'll be home."

Elena was quiet for a moment. In a different voice, quiet and afraid, she asked, "Do you know where Daddy is?"

Terri hesitated. "He hasn't called you yet?"

In the silence, Terri imagined Elena shaking her head, forgetting that her mother could not see her. "Do you think he had an accident, Mommy?"

The plaintive question left a chill on Terri's skin. "An accident? No, sweetheart. Your daddy's just gone somewhere."

"But *where?*" There was a long pause. "Mommy, I think Daddy's dead."

Terri felt a chill. "No, Elena," she said calmly. "Daddy's not dead."

"He *is*, though. I know it."

Terri stopped herself from turning to Chris. "Why do you think that?" she asked.

"Because he's lonely." Elena's voice was frightened now. "Daddy wouldn't leave me alone."

Terri felt herself inhale. Chris was standing in the doorway to the balcony, watching her now. "I think he just took a trip," she said firmly. "He told me he might."

"Promise?"

"Promise. So don't worry too much, all right? Besides, you've got a picture to draw for me."

"Okay, Mommy. I will." There was a voice in the background, and then Elena added, "Grandma wants to talk to you now."

Terri heard instructions to find crayons, and then Rosa said in a muted voice, "Do you want me to call the police, Teresa?"

Terri glanced over at Chris. He had opened the refrigerator, she saw, and was making them drinks. "No," she answered quietly. "At least not until Elena makes you."

"As you wish. But she's sure that something is wrong now. I don't know how much longer I can wait."

Terri took the gin and tonic Chris had made her. "I'll call back to-morrow," she said at last, and rang off.

"How is she?" Chris asked.

Terri turned, watching his face. "She thinks Richie's dead."

Chris's eyes narrowed. "Your mother?"

"Elena."

Chris sat on the end of the bed. "Does she say why?"

"Only that he never came for her. It's like she knows that Richie depends on her so much that if he's not with her, he must be dead."

Chris seemed to reflect. "Elena's world is pretty small," he said at last. "In the eyes of a child, everything that happens is about herself."

Terri walked to the balcony, looked down into the blue harbor. "A long time ago," she said finally, "my mother lost her belief in happy endings. Perhaps Elena has too."

She could feel Chris behind her. "And you?" he asked.

After dinner, they followed the stone pathways that wound through the hillsides above Portofino, the moonlit boats in its harbor like silver ghosts, and found a bench beneath an arbor. They sat in the balmy Italian night, gazing down through the boughs of trees at the lights of the Ligurian coast.

They were too high to hear sounds from the water. Fireflies flickered in front of them; the tulips at their feet wavered in a faint wind.

Terri leaned against him. "Tomorrow," she murmured, "we can talk. But not tonight."

They walked back to the room. Slowly, as if to remember each moment, they made love.

Terri did not fall asleep for hours. When she did, too exhausted for worry, the nightmare broke her restless sleep.

Until the final moment, it was the same. But this time the priest was not her father; it was Richie.

Terri woke up with a start, heart racing.

Chris, she saw, was sleeping at last. When he stirred, reaching out for her, Terri did not awaken him.

TWENTY-ONE

TERRI DID NOT TELL HIM of her nightmare.

"If we're trying to decide our future," she said in the morning, "let's at least get out. I don't want to sit around in our hotel room like two depressives in a Bergman film."

They took a stone path winding down through the hills to the harbor below. The water glistened with early sun; in close-up, the storefronts and the flats above them were frescoed with painted-on moldings or shutters. They bought cheese and fruit and mineral water, hired a motor launch and a gap-toothed fisherman to pilot it, and cruised from the harbor along the steep irregular line of the coast until they reached a small fishing village nestled in an inlet carved by the water from sheer cliffside. There, beside a few bars and cafés, a tiny church, a rocky beach with fishermen's nets strewn near the water, the pilot left them.

They sat facing each other on the sand, the food spread between them. This morning, Terri realized, Chris had hardly touched her.

She spread her hands in a gesture of helplessness. "Where do we start, Chris? Elena, Carlo, the Senate, the hearing? How could we live with all the wreckage? And why would *you* even want to?"

Chris picked up a seashell, tossed it in his hand. "That's why you're a lawyer," he said finally. "You know all the right questions."

"And none of the answers."

"Then maybe I should start. As hard as this kind of thing is for me." Chris looked up from the shell, into her face. "I love you, Terri. More than I've loved any woman. And more, I know, than I will again."

For a moment, she was too moved to answer. But this was a time for truths to be spoken. "I don't believe I'm worth it, Chris. And even if you believe it now, you won't later on. Not after your career in politics is finished and Richie has dragged Carlo through the mud."

"That's not for you to say, Terri. Unless saving me from myself is your excuse for backing out."

Terri shook her head, stung. "I'm not a fool. You can have pretty much anyone you want—including women who don't have crazy dreams—without turning your life inside out. I don't know what you want for us, exactly. But how do you expect *me* to live, waiting for the first moment that I see you regret ever staying with me?" Terri paused to slow the rush of feelings. "Maybe in a week, when Richie puts Carlo on the stand. Or perhaps in a year, if we last that long, when your chance for the Senate is gone and you're disappointed with what your life has come to—"

"As if women are interchangeable," Chris cut in sharply, "as long as I'm a senator. Just find someone who's prettier, or more sophisticated, or perhaps has a master's degree in art history and the freedom to travel when Carlo gets older, so that when we visit the Louvre *she* will know even more than I do. Jesus Christ." His voice filled with passion. "Your mother's right about one thing—I *am* forty-six. Old enough to place a value on what I feel about you.

"Where do you suggest I go to find *you* again, after I've thrown us away because, six years ago, you married Ricardo Arias. Someone who, when I talk to her, feels right. Someone who's so real to me that everything she says makes sense. Someone with the character to make her own life in the face of hardships most people never knew. Someone I trust to love the people I care about. Even Carlo, in the end." His face softened. "Someone who, when I touch her, or even look at her, makes the world different. Or just someone with whom to have a child of our own."

Suddenly Terri felt tears in her eyes. "I never knew you wanted that."

Chris gazed at the shell in his hand. "I know," he answered quietly. "Perhaps I should have said these things sooner, or not at all. But as long as you were fighting for Elena, what difference would my feelings have made? What difference *should* they have made?"

Terri reached for his hand. "At least I'd have known what you were waiting for."

Chris gazed at her hand, resting on his. But he did not take it. "I didn't tell you that to change things, Terri, or to make you feel for me. That's no basis for a life, or even another week together."

"Then why *are* you saying all this?"

Chris seemed to hesitate, and then his hand closed around hers. "Because I want to live with you, as soon as we straighten out this mess. And—if it's as good for our children as I believe we still can make it—to never stop."

Terri could not trust herself to speak. Chris continued, looking away: "I know that it's different for you. You're barely thirty. Maybe for you there's some other thirty-year-old to share what you hoped for with Richie—as many children as you want, buying a house together, having friends the same age, growing older at the same time." He paused, as if uncertain of her feelings. "I used to think that once you got custody of Elena, you could see more clearly the life I wanted for us. But you have to be able to do that now. To decide whether you would want the same things *I* want if somehow Richie weren't a problem." Chris dropped her hand, scooped up the shell again. "Because if you're not sure you want to be with me, then what Richie does, or where he is, matters not at all to us."

Terri touched her eyes. "Really, you are such an idiot."

The quizzical smile he gave her was the reflex of surprise: his eyes searched out her meaning. "So Carlo tells me," he responded after a time. "I guess that makes it unanimous."

"It does, Chris. And I'd love to have a child with you."

To Terri's wonder, it seemed to startle him. She gripped both his hands. "What do you think is making me so sad? God, Chris, if you just eliminate Richie, being with you is more perfect a life than I ever could have imagined." That thought stopped her, like the discovery of something painful, and then the vehemence left her voice. "But that's not how it is. If I'd known what I was bringing through your door that morning, I never would have come."

Chris looked at her. "You mean that, don't you?"

"Of course I do. Look what we get for staying together. Public charges that Carlo is a child abuser. Elena being asked to testify against him, maybe in a courtroom filled with reporters. And— whatever the truth of Richie's claim—plenty of time after that to blame each other if *either* of our children is damaged or I lose Elena for good." She paused. "I listen to you, Chris, and it's like you've forgotten that Richie exists."

Chris stood, turning away. At the water's edge, two fishermen gathered nets into a boat; except for that, the beach was empty. Although the steep hills surrounding the inlet sheltered them from the wind, it seemed colder now; watching the deep, slow waves die in the rocky sand, Terri saw Chris fold his arms for warmth. "You'll have plenty of time to blame yourself," he said finally, "if you let Richie define your choices. Or Elena's."

Against her will, Terri allowed herself to imagine that Chris could help make Elena more whole than Terri herself could ever become. She caught herself, shaking her head. "Elena would take too much patience, Chris. It's not just Carlo—so much of Elena is tied up in protecting Richie. I'm not sure you know how troubled she is."

"So was Carlo when he came to live with me." He put his hands in his pockets, gazing down at her. "I have another chance now, with *your* daughter. That would mean something to me."

Terri fought the impulse to go to him; the thing she must say instead—*needed* to say—was far too hard. "If Carlo *did* molest Elena, that would be impossible. *We* would be impossible."

"I know." Chris's gaze was steady. "But that's another reason to face down Richie."

"In public? What a burden that would place on Carlo."

"So would cowardice."

Looking up at him, she shook her head. "I don't think that's a decision you can make for him."

Chris sat across from her again. "It's a decision *Carlo* made. Before we came to Italy."

Terri imagined them together, father and son. Saw Carlo decide to do this because he wished his father to be happy. "You'd let Carlo do that?" she asked. "For us?"

"For us, and for himself." Chris paused. "Elena never said that Carlo molested her—she simply refused to talk about it. Somehow, Richie floated across the idea to her that absolving Carlo was a betrayal of *him*. But for her to say what isn't true would be a betrayal of Carlo. So Elena resolved it the only way a child could: by going mute. It's sad, really." Chris's voice grew firmer. "For *both* their sakes, Elena and Carlo have to be relieved of this. If we don't stand up to Richie, that will never happen."

Terri touched her temples. "Richie thinks Scatena is his friend. If I force him to court, he'll go. And take all of us with him. Along with your hopes for the Senate."

"Will he, I wonder? Because this time, I'll be your lawyer."

Terri looked at him in astonishment. "You're joking . . ."

"Hardly. Scatena runs the family court like a satrap because he thinks no one's really watching. The day *I* walk into his courtroom, and put Ricardo Arias on the stand, *everyone* will be watching. And by the time I'm finished, unless Richie backs off, there won't be enough left of him for even Scatena to scrape up. Nor," Chris finished softly, "will Scatena want to."

Terri's mind felt sluggish. "First," she parried, "he'll give Richie his turn with Carlo and Elena."

"I doubt that seriously. Before we left, I drafted a motion asking Scatena to defer any testimony by Carlo and Elena until *after* this psychologist has reported on her evaluation of Elena and the rest of us. Under the circumstances, not even an idiot like Scatena will want to be the judge who—in front of God and everyone—subjected a teenager and a six-year-old to questioning that anyone but Richie would know is better handled in private and by a professional."

Terri studied him. "You've thought it all through, haven't you? Well before we came."

"Whatever made you think," Chris answered, "that I'd just wring my hands and let Richie do whatever he wanted." He smiled a little. "I love you dearly, Teresa Peralta. But a saint I'm not. Or, for that matter, a victim." Chris's smile vanished. "The evaluation's *your* job, Terri. You have to make this psychologist see Richie for who he is."

Terri shook her head. "You're forgetting how good he can be. Even if there's no sign at all that Carlo abused Elena, Harris may believe that Richie's the better parent: each step of the way, he's come out ahead. I'm going to have to take her through every neglect of Elena's interests, every lie, every manipulation, every attempt to extort money. Right down to the night I found him in my apartment." Terri paused for emphasis. "Richie's been very careful to ensure that there are no witnesses to *any* of that. Harris may not believe me."

"Maybe not. But consider the *Inquisitor* article and Richie's threat to put Elena through a hearing. He did all that to keep Harris from *ever* looking at Elena." Chris's eyes narrowed. "He doesn't want this evaluation, and not just because Carlo's innocent. On some level, Richie knows there's something wrong with *him*. He's afraid he'll flunk the Rorschach test, Terri. He's right to be. Because the man you married is mentally ill."

Even now, Terri found that the label startled her.

Chris took her face in his hands. "Your mother's wrong," he said. "Not about Richie—I think she gets him well enough. It's just that Rosa can see Richie far more clearly than she can imagine anything better." His gaze was intense. "Don't let her life become yours, Terri. It's enough that your mother lived it."

Terri met his eyes. "But if I'm to be with you," she said after a time, "I need to be able to love you with a whole heart. Even if I lose Elena."

For once, Chris had no answer.

Terri turned from the look on his face. "Please. I just need to think awhile."

They ate together, quiet. But an hour later, when they had cruised back to Portofino, Terri asked to be alone.

She walked in the garden, thinking of Elena and Carlo and Rosa, Judge Scatena and Alec Keene, and how they would react should she decide to be with Chris. Then of the man she had married and the man whom she now loved and the way that, by also loving a child, Terri had set one upon the other.

A little after four, she found Chris on the patio.

As she approached, he tried to keep his face impassive, concealing his apprehension. But Terri knew him now; it no longer quite worked. It was the knowledge, she thought to her surprise, that a wife might have of a husband she knew too well, and loved too deeply, ever to share with him.

She sat across from him at a small round table. "Hi," he said casually. As if the moment were nothing special.

Terri touched his hand. "You're precious to me, Chris. I'm still learning, I'm afraid, how much a part of me you've become."

Chris started to reach for her, then stopped himself: he did not know where she was going. She gathered her thoughts, began again.

"I don't know, really, what this trip was supposed to tell us. If it was that we can escape our problems because we love each other so much, it didn't work. It's been too hard for both of us." She looked down. "What it taught me is something different. That as bad as things are, and as much as we thrash around, you and I keep trying.

And that in the end, life is better than before." She took his hands now, gazing directly at him. "I believe in you, Chris. We have to solve this terrible thing with Carlo and Elena. But if we can, I'll live with you, and have our child. Because that baby, and our life, will be something no one can ever take from us. Not even Richie."

Chris's eyes shut; it was only then that Terri saw, beyond anything he could say or do, how deeply Christopher Paget loved her. And then he raised his head, and gave her a smile that seemed to stop her heart: this was the man Terri would spend her life with, she was suddenly certain, and what that meant to him was what it meant to her. "We have so much," he said. "And there's so much more we can do."

Terri grinned. "You mean like sleeping through the night?"

Chris laughed at that; it seemed to Terri that he might laugh at anything. And then his smile vanished.

The elderly concierge was approaching their table, grave and tentative, sensing his interruption. "I apologize," he said. "But I have a message for Ms. Peralta." Turning to Terri, he added, "We've been looking for you since this morning."

It startled her. Terri thanked him and read the slip of paper.

"What is it?" Chris asked.

She looked up at him. "My mother." Her voice felt thin. "The message says it's urgent."

All at once, Chris seemed edgy. "Maybe Richie's popped up," he said at last. "You asked her to call."

But Terri was hurrying to find a telephone before she knew she had not answered him. "It's all right," she remembered Rosa saying. "I'll make sure Elena's safe."

Slowly, Terri put down the phone.

It was a while before she stood. The miniworld of the hotel lobby went on around her, unnoticed; walking past the lush Italian gardens, to Chris, she saw nothing but his face.

He watched her with a look of unease. Terri thought this strange, and then remembered hurrying from their table, fearful, in the moments before everything would change for them.

Terri found that she could not sit.

"What is it?" Chris asked.

She brushed the hair back from her face. "Richie's dead."

His eyes did not change. Perhaps widened slightly, that was all. Terri watched him, taut. "*Say* something, Chris. *Please.*"

He stood wordlessly, walking slowly to the iron railing at the edge of the patio. He seemed to watch the bay.

Terri clutched his arm. "What *is* it?" she asked.

"Would you care for me to put it into words? All right. I'm glad he's dead, and I hope that it was slow and painful." He turned at last, eyebrows raised in an expression of mild curiosity. "How *did* he die, by the way?"

Terri kept her voice steady. "He shot himself. Apparently. My mother called the police last night, and they found him." Pausing, Terri realized that she had not let go of his arm. "That's not like him, Chris."

He gazed down at the bay. "Is killing oneself 'like' anyone? I'm just surprised he had the discernment to do it." He expelled a deep breath, the first hint of suppressed emotion. Then he turned again, his face newly gentle. "You're in shock, Terri. But Richie can't hurt you anymore, or Carlo. Most important, you have Elena now."

Terri tried to focus on that. "I need to be with her," she said. "Oh, Chris, it will be so hard to tell her."

In silent answer, Chris's arms came tight around her.

They stayed like that for a time, quiet and close, heedless of anything else. And then Chris murmured, "At least no one can blame us for *this*. Not even Elena."

Terri leaned back, looking into his face again. "Only because it's suicide," she answered slowly. "From what the police told my mother, Richie may have died the night before we left."

In his eyes, Terri saw the flicker of some new emotion. But she could not identify what it was, perhaps only imagined it. "We'd better pack," Chris said at last. "We can catch a plane in Milan."

THE INQUIRY

OCTOBER 27–NOVEMBER 30

ONE

CHRISTOPHER PAGET was not surprised when, three nights after Ricardo Arias was found, two homicide inspectors came to his home. The technique was familiar: they appeared unannounced, armed with a tape machine to record whatever Paget might say. In itself, this was not too worrisome—it was competent police work to check into an apparent suicide. But one of the inspectors was Charles Monk: the odds against coincidence were high, and Monk would not have forgotten the Carelli trial, where it had been Paget's role to ask the questions. Within an instant of opening the door, Paget found that he was thinking like a lawyer, alert beneath the surface.

"Come on in," he told Monk easily. "We're through with dinner."

Monk said nothing. Ushering in Monk and his partner, a graying and taciturn Irishman named Dennis Lynch, Paget sensed Monk taking in the surroundings with the silent impassivity that suspects found unnerving: it was Monk's gift that he could reduce the normal range of human response to a stare and a voice that never changed. Monk's appearance was striking—a six-foot-four-inch black man with the grooved planes-and-angles face of an African mask and the gold-rimmed glasses of a scholar—and off the job he had a certain laconic charm. But Paget thought of him as a monotone with eyes and a brain that forgot nothing; an hour with Monk and his machine had ensnared Mary Carelli—a frighteningly clever woman—in a trial for first-degree murder.

"Why don't we sit in the library," Paget said, and led them into a high-ceilinged room with a fireplace and two sofas.

Terri sat on one of them, drinking coffee. "You remember Terri Peralta," Paget said to Monk.

Monk neither spoke nor shook hands, but his brief wary look

gave Paget a moment's satisfaction: Terri was also a potential witness, and Monk would not want his witnesses to hear what each other said.

"You can talk to us both," Paget said pleasantly. "I'm sure that Terri is on your list."

Monk paused. Paget could follow his calculations: neither Paget nor Terri was under arrest, and to insist that someone leave was beyond his power. "We were trying to find you," Monk said to Terri.

She looked at him over her coffee cup. "I was out all day," she said. "Trying to distract my daughter any way I could. It's been hard."

Monk nodded. He did not ask how Elena was. But the child Terri had described to Paget had moved from tears to numbness, burrowing deep within herself. It was as if, Terri told him, Elena blamed herself for Richie's death. Paget hoped that Monk would let the child be.

"Where is she now?" Monk asked.

"With my mother." Terri glanced at Paget but did not explain her presence here. To Paget, the fatigue etched in her face said enough; she looked like a woman who should be with a friend. Monk set the tape machine in front of her.

"Can you answer a few questions?" he asked.

Terri nodded. Monk glanced at Paget: he wanted him to leave, Paget knew, as surely as Paget intended to stay. Smiling at Monk, he took a chair to the side of them.

Belatedly, Dennis Lynch introduced himself to Terri. A pose of diffidence came easily to Lynch, Paget sensed, which cast him as the good cop in any partnership with Monk. Lynch eased his slender frame onto the couch next to Monk, facing Terri with a half smile of sympathy, ignoring the tape machine on the coffee table between them. Paget found their presence invasive; he had dealt with the police for years, but never in his home.

Monk pushed a button. The tape seemed to have a mesmeric effect, Paget noticed; all four of them watched it spin. Then Monk began speaking.

"This is an initial investigation into the death of Ricardo Paul Arias." Monk's voice was methodical; each word stood alone. "It is October twenty-seventh at seven-thirty-five p.m. I am Inspector

Charles Monk; with me is Inspector Dennis Lynch. The witness is Teresa Peralta, and we are at the home of Christopher Paget, who is also present." Monk turned to Paget with a bland expression. "Are you representing Ms. Peralta?"

It was a game, Paget knew. "No," he said evenly. "I was just here with Ms. Peralta when you happened to show up. This is, as you point out, where I live."

Monk looked at him, then turned to Terri as if Paget were not there. He skipped the Miranda warnings; Terri was not in custody, and he could ask whatever he wanted. Within moments, Monk had Terri's age, her work and home addresses and telephone numbers, and enough background information for him to find her at will, subpoena her bank records, and interview her neighbors for the last five years. Then he turned to the subject of Richie.

"Were you related to Ricardo Arias?"

The question seemed to surprise her. "I was his wife," she answered simply. "For over six years."

"Do you have children?"

"A daughter. Elena Rosa."

"And she is how old?"

"Six." Terri's voice was flat. "Also."

Monk watched her. "At the time of Mr. Arias's death, were you still living with him?"

"No." Quite deliberately, it seemed, Terri did not look at Paget. "We were separated."

"For how long?"

Terri still gazed at Monk. "Since the end of the Carelli trial. However long that's been."

Paget suppressed a smile; he was certain that Monk remembered the date precisely. Calmly, Monk asked, "And where did Elena live? Before your husband died, that is."

"Richie had preponderant custody." Terri's voice had the first tinge of wariness. "You've already interviewed my mother. So you know all this."

Monk did not respond. "Was there some question about custody?" he asked.

"*I* had some questions." Terri flicked her bangs. "I didn't think that Richie should raise her."

Monk leaned back, hands folded in his lap. The room seemed quieter now. "Why not?"

Terri breathed audibly, as if thinking about Richie made her weary. "He had emotional problems," she said at last. "I don't think he was stable."

"Did you ever go to a counselor? Seek help of some kind?"

Terri hesitated. "No."

Monk glanced at Paget. "Why not?"

Terri seemed to draw inward; her gaze became self-questioning. "For years," she said at last, "I told myself that Richie was just unusual. At the end, when I saw him more clearly, I thought that nothing would help."

Monk caught Lynch's eye. In a sympathetic voice, Lynch asked, "What did you think was wrong with him, Terri?"

"People weren't *real* to him." As if hearing Paget's silent warning, she caught herself, and the vehemence left her voice. "However he needed someone to be or feel, that's what he imagined they were."

Lynch nodded his encouragement. "Did he go to a psychiatrist, anyone like that?"

"No." Terri gazed down. "Richie thought he was fine."

Lynch paused, blue eyes narrowing slightly, as if sorting something out. "*Was* he going to a psychiatrist?" Paget asked.

Monk turned to Lynch; Lynch saw this, faced Paget, and shrugged. No one answered.

"Did *you* ever consult a mental health professional?" Monk asked Terri.

Terri glanced at Paget. "Only to talk about Elena."

"Concerning what?"

Terri hesitated; Paget watched the thought of Carlo cross her face, and then she answered simply, "Emotional problems."

"Of what kind?"

Terri folded her hands. "Since the separation," she said slowly, "Elena has seemed troubled. I thought it was getting worse."

Monk leaned forward. "Did Mr. Arias agree?"

For an instant, Terri looked cornered: as if thinking along with her, Paget imagined the police interviewing Alec Keene and combing through the files of Terri's divorce case. He was glad that Carlo was at a friend's tonight.

"I don't know whether he agreed or not," Terri said coolly. "There wasn't much about Elena we did agree on."

It was a calculated answer, Paget thought: by conceding the depth of their disagreement, Terri avoided the particulars and thus kept the focus off Paget and Carlo. Yet Monk, he suddenly realized, must have impounded Richie's papers. He watched the same thought come to Terri; she composed herself, waiting for the next question.

But Monk dropped the subject abruptly. "Did your husband own a gun?" he asked.

Terri looked down. She shook her head.

"Is that a 'no'?" Monk said. "The tape doesn't pick up shakes of the head."

Terri raised her eyes. "It was a 'no.' "

"Did he have any interest in guns?" Here Monk paused. "Because the gun we found with him was quite unusual."

"How so?" Paget asked.

Monk kept looking at Terri. "It was a thirty-two-caliber Smith and Wesson safety model. Five cylinders." His voice grew more deliberate. "The last one was made in 1909, Ms. Peralta. It's practically a collector's item."

Terri looked puzzled. "Richie wasn't a collector," she said. "I don't know what he knew about guns. If anything."

Monk regarded her. "Do *you* own a gun?"

"No." Her voice was emphatic. "And if I'd known Richie had one, I'd have asked him to get rid of it."

"Because you thought he was unstable?"

"Because guns *kill* people. Including children."

Monk sat back. Softly, he asked, "Do you think Richie killed himself?"

Terri rested her head on the back of the couch, staring up at the ceiling. Her face looked drawn. "I can't imagine *anyone* killing himself," she said at last. "But people do. So I don't know how to answer that."

"What about Richie?"

Terri still watched the ceiling. "I'm not sure I understood him. Now I'm less sure than ever. But there was something wrong with him." She paused. "Toward the end, he seemed angry and more desperate. His mood swings were wider."

"Do you know why?"

Terri lowered her eyes to him. "He had lost me," she said simply. "And he had very little money."

"Was he employed?"

"No." Terri's voice was cool again. "Richie didn't like working for people. He liked it better when I worked for him."

"Did he ever ask you for money?"

Terri hesitated: Paget saw her flash on the fifty thousand dollars Richie had wanted her to extort from him, to protect Carlo and Paget himself.

"I *gave* him money," Terri answered. "Nearly twenty-three hundred a month. Much of that was child support."

Monk adjusted his glasses. "Are you sorry he's dead?"

His tone was one of mild inquiry. But Lynch had started to fidget; the gestures had the suppressed nervousness of a thwarted smoker. Terri gave them a look that combined tolerance with exhaustion.

"Not for me," she said. "But for Elena, yes."

"How is she?"

Terri gave a shrug of helplessness, as if Elena's reaction defied easy description. "You'd have to know her," she said tiredly. "During the separation, Elena imagined she was responsible for him. So if Richie's dead now, in Elena's mind it must be her fault. As if she could have stopped this."

The words lingered in the room. The lights from the lamp looked pallid now; the large window behind Terri was a black rectangle. It felt too quiet.

Monk leaned forward. "Elena was expecting to see him, wasn't she?"

"Yes. On Sunday evening."

"And when did you first know that he hadn't come for her?"

"When I called my mother from Venice." Terri glanced at Paget. "It was Tuesday, I think. At night."

"Did you consider having the police check on him?"

Terri was silent for a moment. "Elena was safe at my mother's." She glanced at Paget. "That was all I cared about, really."

"Did you discuss that with your mother—the fact that he was missing?"

"Yes. A few days later. I told her not to call."

Monk let the answer hang there for a while. His eyes did not leave her face now. "Had he ever done that before? Not show up?"

Terri gave him a level gaze. "I was in a custody fight," she said at length. "If Richie didn't show, I wasn't going to force him to. I never thought he'd killed himself."

Monk raised his head a little. "When," he asked slowly, "was the last time you spoke with him?"

Terri glanced quickly at Paget. "The night before I left for Italy. By telephone."

Paget was surprised; Terri had not told him this. He wanted to stop the interview. But he could not, and now Terri would not look at him.

"That reminds me," he said to Monk. "Did you check his answering machine? When Terri tried to call from Italy, it wasn't on."

Monk turned, annoyed at the interruption. "Someone turned it off," he said tersely. "Seems like he erased the tape."

He faced Terri again. "What time did you call him? The night before you left, that is."

Terri was regarding Paget; she seemed to catch herself and then gave a small shrug. "I don't know. Maybe nine or so. It wasn't for long."

Paget felt himself tense. "What did you talk about?" Monk asked.

Terri stared at the tape recorder. "I'd been packing. Somehow, it made me think of my honeymoon, how much hope I'd had and how sad things were now." She looked up. "So I called to ask if I could see him."

Paget felt a surge of anger: this man had threatened to destroy Carlo and smear them all. Even now, that Terri had called him felt like a betrayal.

"Why did you want to see him?" Monk asked.

Terri looked at Paget again. "To beg him," she said softly. "To ask him for Elena. To see if there was something I could give him in return."

"Such as?"

"Money." She shook her head, as if at her own foolishness. "I knew it was hopeless, even then. People like Richie never stay bought."

Why, Paget asked her silently, didn't you tell me?

"What did he say?" Monk asked.

Terri turned from Paget. "That he had an 'appointment' that night."

Paget watched her, edgy. "Did he say who with?" Monk asked.

Terri's expression was one of distaste. "No. But I thought it must be a woman—'appointment' had a sniggering sound." Terri shrugged again. "Maybe there was no one. That would be like him: trying to impress me, or to string me out till I got desperate."

Monk folded his hands. "Did he sound like someone about to kill himself?"

"No." Once more, Terri seemed to stop herself. "But I'm not sure, really. Bravado was something he was good at—Richie needed people to think he was on top."

Monk was still for a time. "What," he asked then, "did you do after you hung up?"

"Packed. Then I went to bed."

"Alone?"

Terri nodded. "Alone."

"Did anyone see you that evening?"

Terri glanced at Paget. "Only my mother and Elena, when I dropped her off. That was around seven."

"Did you talk to anyone else?"

Now Terri focused on Monk. "Just Chris."

Monk inclined his head. "Do you mean Christopher Paget?"

"Yes."

"And when was that?"

"I don't know." Terri hesitated. "Before I called Richie."

"And did Mr. Paget call you or did you call him?"

"He called me."

"Concerning what?"

Terri paused again. "Our arrangements. We decided he'd pick me up the next morning."

"And that was all?"

Terri glanced at Paget's hand. He raised it slightly; the bruise and swelling had vanished. "That's all I remember," she said.

Monk touched his chin. "Your flight," he said. "When did it leave?"

"Very early. Eight o'clock, I think."

"You didn't go to Mr. Paget's the night before?"

"No."

"Or to see Mr. Arias?"

Terri stared at him. "No," she answered finally.

Monk stood, stretching himself, taking in the art on the walls with a slow sweep of the head. Paget found the gesture oddly territorial, as if Monk had appropriated his library. "Did you ever visit Mr. Arias's apartment?"

Terri nodded. "I found it for him."

"Were you there often?"

"Not often. Sometimes. When I dropped off Elena."

"When was the last time you were there?"

Terri seemed to think. "The Sunday before I left. Again, taking Elena back."

"Did you go inside?"

Terri's eyes narrowed. "I really can't remember. But I think so."

Monk shoved his hands into his pockets. "Mr. Arias had a computer, didn't he?"

"Yes." Her tone was flat again. "I'm still paying for it."

"What did he use it for?"

"Everything—addresses, recipes, checkbook, business plans. You name it."

"Letters?"

Terri looked askance at him. "Letters too, I think. Sure."

Monk began pacing, two or three steps, then back again. He stopped abruptly. "When did you last have intercourse with Mr. Arias?"

Terri stared at him. Paget stood at once. "Why is *that* important?" he demanded.

Monk was unruffled. He continued to look at Terri. "Because you were living with him, Ms. Peralta, and then you weren't. I'd like some sense of your relationship."

Terri glanced at Paget. She looked pale now. "The night before the Carelli trial started," she answered.

"And what," Monk prodded in the same monotone, "is your relationship with Mr. Paget?"

"Just that." Her voice was terse. "We have one."

"A romantic relationship?"

"Yes."

Monk turned to Paget and back again. "And when did *that* part—

the romantic part—begin? Before, during, or after the Carelli trial? Or all of the above?"

Paget stepped forward. "That's enough—"

"*After,*" Terri interjected. "And *after* I left Richie. Is that what you wanted?"

Monk gazed at Paget and then turned to her. "Yes," he said with surprising courtesy. "And only because it's my job. The man's dead, after all, and we have to ask questions to find out why." His voice grew softer. "For all I know, he killed himself over you and Mr. Paget."

Paget watched Terri lean back on the couch, tired and drained of anger. But the last thing Monk did before moving on to Paget was to take out an ink pad and, with surprising gentleness, help Terri put her prints on a white card with boxes for each finger. She sat there, silent, gazing at the black tips of her fingers; to Paget, the moment was more humiliating than any questions Monk had asked.

Monk turned to him. "Mind answering a few questions?"

Paget glanced up from the card. "If you don't mind *my* asking a few," he said coolly.

The only change in Monk's expression was a deliberate widening of the eyes, to convey the message that Paget must be joking. But his silence suggested that he might grant a moment's sufferance to his involuntary host.

"Exactly how," Paget demanded, "did Arias die?"

Monk shrugged. "Gunshot wound."

"I meant where?"

Monk seemed to watch him. "The bullet lodged in the brain stem."

Paget's eyes narrowed. "What was the point of entry?"

Monk turned briefly to Lynch, who grimaced slightly: the expression suggested that Paget would find out anyway. In the same flat voice, Monk said to Paget, "It looked like he ate his gun."

Paget saw Terri wince: the laconic phrase was police argot for a not uncommon suicide—a cop who shot himself through the mouth with his own weapon. The image that lingered was not pretty.

Paget folded his arms. "You find gunshot residue on the roof of his mouth?"

Monk nodded. "There was powder on his tongue and palate, a little on the back of his throat." His tone was indifferent. "The gun got in his mouth, sure enough."

Terri stood and walked to the window. "Did he leave some sort of note?" Paget asked.

Monk paused a moment. "There was a note," he said tersely, and inclined his head toward the tape machine. "Mind sitting over there, so we can get this done with."

Terri turned to watch them. Her face was still pale; it made the green in her eyes seem brighter. When Paget sat, she walked to the edge of the sofa and rested her hand near his shoulder. To Paget, the gesture felt instinctive, the reflex of a lover. His partner, Teresa Peralta.

Chris's gaze at Monk was that of a lawyer, Terri thought, not a witness anxious to ingratiate himself.

"So," Monk said to him, "the night before you left for Italy, you didn't see Ms. Peralta. Is that right?"

Chris took his time answering. "That's right. I spoke to her by phone."

"About what time was that?"

Chris seemed to think. "I don't really know. Perhaps eight-thirty or so." He leaned forward. "There *was* one thing Terri's forgotten. We had plans to go to dinner that night, and then to my house. The first part of our conversation was me calling to cancel."

Terri felt a moment's surprise; it was not Chris's nature to volunteer information. Then she saw that he had made it clear that Terri could not have planned to call Richie or to visit anyone but Chris himself. That Chris thought it important to protect her told Terri something more.

Monk fixed Chris with the same impassive gaze. "Why did you cancel?"

"I felt sick." Chris shrugged. "It was some twenty-four-hour thing. By morning, I was fine."

"Did you see anyone that night?"

Chris rested an arm on his knee, propped his chin in one hand. "Carlo," he said after a time. "My son."

"Was Carlo home with you?"

Chris shook his head. "He had a date. He came home around midnight. I waited up for him."

"Even though you were sick?"

"Carlo's a new driver." Chris cocked his head. "Do you have a teenager, Inspector?"

Monk hesitated. "One daughter."

"How old?"

Another pause. "Sixteen."

"Ever wait up for her?"

Monk sat back and looked at Chris: the effect was of someone smiling without ever having changed expression. Terri had a sudden sure image of Monk lurking by the front door, checking his watch until his daughter came home. It seemed to drain a little tension from the room; for the first time, Monk himself seemed tired.

"How," he asked Chris, "did *you* feel about Mr. Arias?"

Chris leaned back. "Based on my observations," he said after a time, "he was a completely undesirable human being. Terri had more patience than I ever could have managed."

"What do you base that on?"

"Richie's undesirability, or Terri's patience? I base them both on the divorce proceedings. Richie's devotion to using Elena as a meal ticket was matched only by Terri's determination to keep that from Elena." He glanced up at Terri. "Truth to tell, that much forbearance amazes me."

It was, Terri saw, a clever response: in one answer, Chris had placed her in the most favorable light while avoiding his deepest reasons for despising Richie. Or, for that matter, Carlo's.

Lynch leaned toward Paget. "Can you think of any reason why Mr. Arias would kill himself?"

Chris shrugged. "I'm no mind reader, and I didn't know the man. But his life was in a downhill spiral: divorce, financial problems, apparent difficulty finding or holding a job, perhaps some dawning appreciation that the world didn't see him as he wished to be seen. Those are on anyone's top ten reasons for suicide." He looked back to Monk. "What did his note say?"

Monk ignored that. "So you stayed home that night, correct?"

Chris nodded, silent, and then cocked his head. "Satisfy my curiosity for a moment. We've spent a fair amount of time talking about a single night, and yet you found Richie a week later. All that time at room temperature couldn't have helped him much." Chris leaned back on the sofa, gazing at Monk with an expression of pleasant inquiry. "The last body I saw anything close to that old was a little Japanese woman who, by the time the police found her, looked something like a two-hundred-pound male Eskimo in green makeup, with claws for hands. You can imagine the rest—the poor lady had become part of the food chain. The medical examiner couldn't have given you time of death if she'd had a Ouija board."

Terri half shut her eyes.

Monk removed his glasses and began to wipe the lenses. "Mr. Arias," he said slowly, "liked air-conditioning."

"At thirty degrees Fahrenheit?" Chris raised his eyebrows. "When did Richie stop opening his mail? Not until Saturday, at least. *That's* what you must be going on."

Monk did not answer. But the look on his face, or rather its absence, told Terri that Chris was right. Chris did not have to make his larger point: that Richie might have died the next morning, while Terri sat with Chris on an airplane to Milan. "Anyhow," Chris said carelessly, "it's kind of an academic issue, however interesting. The man *did* leave a note."

Monk seemed to appraise him for a moment, and then spoke into his tape recorder. "We are terminating the interview," he said, "at approximately nine-oh-two." He switched off the machine and looked up at Terri. "We may have more questions."

"That's fine. But please come to my office, not my home. I don't want Elena upset."

"Of course," Lynch said quickly. Monk did not say another word as Chris ushered them out. It occurred to Terri that he had not asked Chris for prints.

When Chris returned, he crossed the room to take her in his arms. "Sorry," he murmured.

Terri leaned back to look at him. She said, quietly, "They don't think he killed himself, do they?"

Chris tilted his head. "You were divorcing him, Terri. Plus we're together. Monk's going to ask the questions." He frowned. "After all, if he doesn't, the press may get ahold of this and pillory him. Even without that, Sir Charles isn't going to cut *us* any slack. Not after the Carelli case. This is his chance to remind us that we're just citizens."

Terri shook her head. "You think it's more than that, Chris. You were pretty careful to cover for me."

He shrugged. "It seemed like the thing to do. Besides, I was also pretty careful to cover for *me*. As were you."

Chris was, as usual, impassive. "Do you think there's any chance he'll miss the *Inquisitor?*" Terri asked. "Or those court papers about you and Carlo?"

"Oh, he's already seen the *Inquisitor*. As for missing the stuff on Carlo, almost none. I just wasn't going to trip over myself to help him on *that*." He shrugged once more. "At least the media have been quiet—no one in the press seems to have picked up on Richie's death, although I suspect James Colt knows he's dead. But one way or the other, Monk will come around again. Chances are he was holding back."

Terri studied him. "It bothers me, Chris. My mother says that they were particularly interested in where we were on the night before we left for Italy and when she had last seen me."

"Monk didn't try to talk to Elena, did he?"

"Elena? My mother didn't let them near her." Terri was quiet. "I should get home to her now. She's been having that dream again."

Chris watched her face. "And your dream?" he asked softly.

"It still comes. If that matters."

"It does to me." Chris kissed her hair. "I wish there was something I could do. For both of you."

"The only thing you can do, for either of us, is to love me. Because Elena's going to need all the patience I can give her." Terri looked up at him. "I'm starting her with Dr. Harris. But what she can find out, and how long that will take, I just don't know."

"It's all right, Terri. Suddenly we have nothing but time."

Terri was quiet: she knew that Chris, like her, wished to start a life that must wait for Elena to be better and, with Harris's help, to clear Carlo. "It seems that we're always waiting, Chris."

"I'd rather wait for you than live with anyone else." He smiled a little. "Care to go dancing sometime?"

It made her smile back, and then she looked into his face. "I won't be in tomorrow," she said. "If that's okay."

Chris gazed down at her ink-smudged hands. "Of course," he answered. "Spend the time with Elena."

They walked together to his door. Stepping onto the porch, Terri remembered that Richie was not spying on her and would never spy again. The night was cool and silent.

She turned back to Chris. He stood inside the doorway, watching her with the barest trace of a smile. "For what it's worth," he said quietly, "I didn't kill your husband. I could never work out the details."

Terri found herself speechless. And then Chris leaned forward, hand cradling her neck, and gently kissed her. "So don't worry about me, all right?"

TWO

DENISE HARRIS had been a surprise to Terri. On the telephone, Harris was crisp, quick to ask questions. But in the flesh, the forty-ish black psychologist was a person of much softer edges: quieter and slower to speak, with a welcoming manner and luminous brown eyes which suggested that nothing was more important than whatever Terri had to tell her.

They sat in Harris's office, in the second story of a brightly painted Victorian in Haight-Ashbury. The first floor served as her home, a mishmash of African art, art deco, and Victoriana, which Harris referred to as "cross-cultural confusion" but to Terri implied a preference for favorite things over stylistic symmetry, an impression reinforced by several pictures of Harris's twelve-year-old daughter at various ages. That Harris did not conceal her own life put Terri more at ease, and her office had the same suggestion of warmth, with its bright colors, upholstered chairs, shelves of toys for children, and sunlight streaming through a large bay window. No hard edges anywhere.

"How was it with Elena?" Terri asked at once. "She wouldn't say."

"About what I expected," Harris answered easily. "For fifty minutes, we sat on the rug here, not playing with toys, while Elena didn't talk to me."

Harris sounded undismayed, but Terri was overcome by worry. "She wouldn't say *anything?*"

"Not a word." Harris leaned forward. "It may take a while, Terri. For whatever reason, I think Elena's quite afraid. Of *what*, I can't know yet."

"Isn't there anything you can do with her *now?* Anything at all?"

Harris shook her head. "This isn't a test," she answered gently, "and Elena didn't flunk it. Six-year-olds generally don't articulate their inner traumas for at least two or three sessions."

Terri could not help but smile; as was the clear intent of Harris's mild joke, she felt like the overeager parent who wanted her child to read by the end of kindergarten. But what was at stake was a child who no longer cried over her father but sat by herself for hours, refusing to say much of anything. A child whose last reference to Richie, two days after Terri's return, was, "Daddy died because I left him all alone."

"How was she at Richie's funeral?" Harris asked now.

"The same." As tearless as Terri and Rosa, filing past the closed casket in Mission Dolores beneath the piercing stare of Richie's mother, Sonia, which softened only for Elena, and only until she saw the child's dissociation. Richie had been Sonia's prize: the worth of others—even Richie's older brothers—was measured by their devotion to her youngest son. In her obsession with Richie, Sonia saw Elena's withdrawal as insulting. But the little girl's delicate profile, twinned with Rosa's, gave Terri a sudden jolt of memory: the morning sixteen years before when they had celebrated the funeral mass for Terri's father in this same church. Then, as now, the face of Terri's mother had the ravaged silent dignity of a woman whose feelings were too complex and powerful for weeping or shows of grief. Then, unlike her sisters, Terri had fought back tears, refusing to cry so that her mother would not stand alone. Stood tearless by Rosa, as Elena did now.

Tearless even as they left Richie's graveside in a bleak drizzle, the three of them holding hands, and Sonia had said to Terri, "Ricardo did not kill himself—he did not commit this sin," in a voice so accusatory that Terri had taken her to the side of the funeral cortege and softly said, "I'm sorry that he's dead, Sonia. But if you ever do anything to upset Elena, you will never see her again."

"Terri?" Harris asked.

Startled from memory, Terri found herself gazing at the psychologist. Everything about Harris seemed round: her face and mouth and body; her eyes, which conveyed without a word a remarkable range of messages—concern, amusement, caution, sympathy, compassion, even surprise. But Terri sensed that nothing truly surprised

Harris, and that she had the persona of an extremely skilled actress whose job it was to draw people out without conveying how carefully she studied them.

"I was just wondering," Terri said at last. "Are these conversations privileged? Yours and mine."

Harris seemed to reflect a moment, chin resting on two fingers. Her hands, Terri noticed, were surprisingly slender and graceful. "Elena is my client," Harris answered, "but she's also a child, and you're her parent. I can't effectively treat her—or even understand her—without your help. And I can't be sure I have your help unless *you're* sure it's confidential." She leaned back. "With two exceptions that, as a lawyer, I'm sure you understand."

Terri nodded. "If you discover abuse, you have to report it. And there's no privilege regarding a crime yet to be committed or potential violence to someone else."

Harris did not ask why Terri had raised the question: they had made a compact, her uncurious look suggested, and Terri's reasons for it were not her concern. "So," Harris said casually, "where were we?"

Terri paused a moment. "At Richie's funeral," she answered. "His mother said, within earshot of Elena, that she didn't believe Richie killed himself."

Harris raised an eyebrow. "Do you think Elena understood?"

Terri paused again. The question could be taken two ways: did Elena understand that Richie's death was not an accident or that Sonia believed that Richie had been murdered. Harris's bland expression gave Terri no clue.

"I don't know," she answered. "All the way home, and ever since, Elena said nothing about his death at all. But when we got into the car, she curled up in a ball, hugging herself." Terri flicked back her hair. "What's so terrible," she finished slowly, "is that Richie's death, which is devastating to Elena, is in certain ways good for everyone else. *I* have Elena, and Richie can't hurt Carlo. Chris can even run for the Senate, if he wants to risk it. I'm scared that Elena may sense all that."

Harris appraised her. "For sure you can't be acting glad he's dead. But you can't pretend you're grief-stricken, either—kids have radar for hypocrisy. The best thing you can do is live your life day to day, give Elena a stable home." Harris spoke gently. "This is a child who's undergone a great deal in the last half year or so: her parents' separation, possibly some form of sexual abuse, and now her father's death. Some of what she must feel is impossible for a child to verbalize, and *all* of it is complicated by something pretty powerful—the combination of Richie's apparent desire to make her feel responsible for him, and a six-year-old's inherent belief that everything happens because of her. Although, I have to say, I find Elena's comments about Richie's death interesting for other reasons."

"What reasons?"

"In the sense that Elena may have had some heightened sense of danger to her father." Harris gave a deprecating smile. "I don't mean that in the parapsychological sense. She may well have felt it from *him*."

"But how will you get her to talk?"

"Slowly." Harris bent forward in a posture of entreaty. "You'll need to be as patient as you can. Originally, you came to me about an accusation of child abuse, and to understand why Elena had become so withdrawn. Some of the behavior you've described— listlessness, regression, acting out, even the nightmares—*could* be consistent with abuse. But even if that happened—and please understand how I mean this—sexual abuse is no longer the worst thing in Elena's life." Harris paused, and then added softly, "Her father has died from a bullet in the head. That dwarfs anything she's ever experienced."

Terri felt despair. "But what will you *do?*"

Harris shrugged. "I may spend weeks just getting her to play games with me. Perhaps, by playing with doll figures, I can get some sense of how Elena sees herself in the world, what's bothering her. With all that's happened to her, it could be easier to express herself through surrogates. Which, necessarily, requires me to interpret quite a bit." She gazed at Terri. "That may be something you can help with."

"How?"

"I want to understand Elena's life. You can tell me about *her*, of course. But I'd also like you to tell me something about *you*. Not just your marriage to Richie but how you think you got there."

The question made Terri edgy. "That's kind of complicated. I'm not sure I even understand it."

Harris smiled a little. "I'm not trying to be your therapist—I can't be. But I do need some comprehension of the family Elena got born into." She folded her hands. "Before you married Richie, what did you know about him? His family, for example."

"Not much." Terri reflected. "Richie never said much about his childhood, except that he'd always excelled at everything. And that his mother used to call him her little prince." A thought struck her, a connection. "Sonia's version of Richie was the same as his—that he was wonderful and that anything bad that happened to him was someone else's fault."

"What about his father?"

Terri shook her head. "His parents were in New York, and I only met Ricardo senior once or twice before he died. He was pretty grim: Richie said he used to cuff him and his brothers around when they got out of line."

Harris touched her hair, a tight coiled Afro faintly flecked with gray. The gesture, seemingly distracted, struck Terri as an effort to distract *her*. "Would you say Richie was more comfortable with women? Or men?"

Terri hesitated a moment. "He thought he could manipulate women better, I think—perhaps that they would like him more. That may be why he agreed that you would be the family evaluator. The other two psychologists Alec Keene recommended were men."

Harris's eyes narrowed a bit, as if considering whether to say something. "Alec set it up that way," she finally said. "Because he thought that Richie would pick a woman. And because, Alec told me, he wanted me to see him."

Terri was startled. "Did Alec say why?"

Harris shook her head. "He left me to puzzle that out. I don't think, really, that it was anything specific." Her voice had a shade of irony. "Maybe, as you've said, it was just that Richie was so clever."

Terri sat back: for a moment, unbidden yet powerful, she could feel Richie in the room with them. Harris leaned her head on her elbow, the casual attitude of a woman at leisure. "Tell me, Terri, what do you remember about being Elena's age?"

The seeming change of subject took Terri by surprise. "About being six?"

"Yes."

Terri hesitated. "Nothing, really."

"At all?"

"Nothing specific." She felt like a specimen under a microscope. "Isn't everyone like that?"

"No, actually." Harris seemed to appraise Terri over her smile. "*Some* people are like that. Tell me, what *are* your first memories? At any age."

Terri glanced at her watch; there were ten minutes left in the session. "Frankly, Denise, I don't see what this has to do with Elena."

Harris seemed unruffled. "Understanding you may have a great deal to do with our understanding of Elena. Yours *and* mine. So humor me." Her voice became quiet. "Try to lean back, close your eyes, and pretend that Elena's happiness depends on your coming up with something. Pretend, just for a time, that you're her."

Terri gave Harris a sardonic half smile, to signal that this was foolish. But when she shrugged and closed her eyes, blackness descended.

"Anything at all," she heard Harris say.

Blackness descending, like a blanket pulled over her head.

Her mother is crying. Terri cannot help her; the crying comes with the night. She grips the blanket, pulling it tighter. Perhaps if she can stop the sound, her mother will stop hurting. The cries grow fainter.

Terri opened her eyes. "Nothing," she said. "I can't remember anything."

THREE

CARLO PUT DOWN the sports page. "So what exactly did the cops want?" he asked.

They were sitting on the deck; the weather was unseasonably warm, and white sails dotted the bay. Carlo had been leafing through the *Chronicle*, Paget the Sunday *Times*. Their companionable silence felt familiar, the routine of two old friends; it reminded Paget that since Carlo had gotten his used convertible, they spent less time together. It was the way of things, he supposed: the son eagerly embracing the wider world, the father proud but a little rueful and—in Paget's case—careful to keep quiet about it. Carlo, he thought, was entitled to become an adult without his father serving as his personal Greek chorus.

He turned to Carlo. "They're trying to figure out why our late friend Ricardo killed himself. And, in the process, to ensure that his resignation was voluntary."

Carlo shook his head in mock dismay. "You have a great way of putting things, Dad. Law do that to you?"

Paget smiled. "Nope. My warm human qualities are all my own. Although the subject of Richie's passing stretches them a bit."

"I can tell." Carlo pushed the baseball cap back on his head. "Do they think he *didn't* kill himself?"

Paget shrugged. "They're considering it. They have to, really. It's part of their job description."

Carlo's face was serious now; gazing at his son's profile—clean jawline, thin face, dark lashes over narrowed blue eyes—Paget was struck again by how much the boy looked like his mother. Except that the sense of calculation and self-control, so strong in Mary

Carelli, was absent from Carlo. "Do they know the stuff about Elena?"

"By now, they pretty much have to."

Carlo was quiet for a while. "You know, Dad," he finally returned, "I wouldn't make jokes about Richie. Not where anyone can hear you."

Paget was oddly touched; for the first time he could remember, he was aware of Carlo looking out for him. "Don't worry, I only share my bad taste with you. And, on her lucky days, Terri. Although this is a subject on which I exercise some restraint."

Carlo looked curious. "How's *she* dealing with all this?"

"Terri's all right. The problem, really, is Elena. Now that Richie's dead, Elena seems to feel she killed him. Metaphorically speaking."

The mention of Elena, Paget saw, still unsettled Carlo: his gaze at the water had a preoccupied quality. "Why would she think that?" he asked.

"Who knows? It's magical thinking, Carlo—placing herself at the center of the world. Kids do it all the time." Paget decided to shift the focus. "How else did you know I'd buy you that car?"

Carlo grinned. "Just rational thinking, Dad—predicting the behavior of indulgent adults. Kids do it all the time."

Paget laughed. "At least you could have acted surprised."

"Would you settle for grateful?" Carlo gave his father an awkward pat on the shoulder. "Surprises aren't nearly as good as knowing you can count on someone."

Paget covered Carlo's hand with his own. "You always can, son. Just buy your own gas, okay?"

Carlo smiled again, and then he cocked his head. "Was that the doorbell?"

Paget listened. The second rasp of the bell was clearly audible. "It's one of *your* friends," he told Carlo. "Mine have better manners than to drop in on Sunday morning."

Carlo disentangled himself from his chair with the agonizing slowness of an arthritic octogenarian. Amusedly watching his son— the three-sport athlete—make standing look like an act of will, Paget reflected that there is nothing in the world more put upon than a teenage boy who does not wish to move. "The next step," he advised Carlo, "is learning how to walk."

Carlo gave him an exaggerated grimace. "Funny, Dad," he said, and began moving toward the door with the alacrity of a man on a treadmill.

He returned with Charles Monk. Trailing behind them was Dennis Lynch, carrying a tape recorder.

Paget looked up. "Morning," he greeted Monk amiably. "If we'd known you were coming, I'd have invited you."

Monk's eyes widened slightly; in his range of expressions, Paget thought, this might mean amusement. Monk turned to Carlo and back again. "We have more questions," he told Paget. "I'd like to talk to you both. Alone."

All at once, Paget's thoughts felt sharp and focused. "No, thanks," he said coolly. "Just because we *didn't* invite you doesn't mean that you're not our guests. You care to talk to my son, you do it with me here—right now, *once*. Afterward, *we* can chat alone."

Monk stared at him in silence. The message was that he understood that Paget meant to force them to take Carlo first, in his presence, so that the police could not ambush either of them. Only Carlo, standing uncomfortably to the side, seemed left out of the edgy dynamic.

"We'll do it right here." Paget gestured at two canvas folding chairs. "Have a seat."

Monk gazed at the chairs for a moment. They were rather like hammocks. Sinking into them, the two homicide inspectors looked immobilized and a little foolish. Monk, suddenly all arms and knees, did not seem amused.

Carlo watched Monk balance the tape recorder in his lap and then turned to Paget, as if for help or guidance. Paget kept his face and voice calm. "It's all right," he said easily, and placed a hand on Carlo's shoulder. When Paget nodded to Monk, smiling a little, Carlo's face seemed to ease. He turned to Monk, waiting.

"You'll have to speak up," Monk said to Carlo, and began his litany: that the interviewee was Carlo Carelli Paget; that his father was present; and that it was ten-forty-five on a Sunday that, to Paget, had been bright and pleasant just minutes earlier. Carlo stared at the tape machine.

"Ready?" Monk asked him.

Looking up, Carlo gave a brief nod. He seemed composed, but

nothing about him was languid anymore. By contrast, Monk's gaze seemed almost dreamy.

"Did you sexually molest Elena Arias?" he asked.

The question struck Paget like a slap in the face. Carlo straightened in his chair.

"No," he said.

The answer had a simple dignity—no protest, no elaboration. What Paget himself would do. But it did not stop the rush of anger. Monk had gained his petty revenge: walked into *his* home, humiliated *his* son, and made Paget watch it. And then, suddenly realizing that Monk was watching *him*, Paget understood his deeper reasons.

"Nicely done," he told Monk in conversational tones. "Is that all, or do you mean to ask Carlo about the Lindbergh baby?"

Paget saw his son's faint smile. Shrugging, Monk turned back to Carlo. "Have you ever met Ricardo Arias?"

A quick shake of the head. "No."

"Or spoken to him?"

"No."

"Or been to his apartment?"

Carlo watched the tape. "I don't even know where it is."

Monk seemed to study him. "Are you aware of the materials Mr. Arias filed in the family court?"

Carlo tried to look stoic. "Stuff about me and Elena." His voice became deliberate. "It's bullshit."

Monk glanced at Paget, then back to Carlo. "Did you and your father discuss that?"

"Uh-huh." Carlo propped his chin on his hands. "He said that Terri's husband was using this stuff to try to break her."

"Did you and he discuss what to do about it?"

Carlo seemed to choose his words. "Only that we might have to go to court. To prove it was a lie."

"Did you discuss the possibility of publicity?"

"Yes." Carlo looked down now. "Dad said the papers might be there."

"What was his attitude?"

A quick glance at Paget. "He was pretty upset about it. So was I."

"Were you willing to testify?"

Carlo nodded. "If I had to. I told Dad that."

"And what did he say?"

Carlo seemed to breathe in. "My dad said he was sorry. And that he was proud of me."

Monk studied Carlo with new concentration. "Do you remember the night before your father went to Italy?"

Carlo shifted in his chair. His answer came in an undertone. "Uh-huh."

"Where were you?"

Lynch, Paget realized, seemed just a little more tense.

"With friends," Carlo answered slowly.

What was *this*? Paget wondered: surely they did not suspect Carlo. But Monk's face showed nothing.

"Between when and when?" he asked.

Carlo shrugged. "I'm not sure, exactly. But my dad makes me get in by twelve-thirty. So maybe from around seven."

Paget was momentarily amused; even talking to Monk, Carlo was annoyed enough by his curfew to complain about it. But Monk's next question cut him short.

"When you left," he asked Carlo, "was your father here?"

"Yes."

Carlo's repeated nods, Paget noticed, seemed like a nervous tic. It was hard to watch a son as if you were assessing a witness, unable to coach him.

"What about twelve-thirty, when you returned?" Monk asked. "Was your father also here?"

Another quick nod.

"You'll have to speak up."

"Yes." Carlo's voice was a shade too loud now. "He was here then too."

Lynch's gaze had turned to Paget. "And where," Monk asked Carlo, "were you in the meanwhile?"

A moment's hesitation. "With friends. Like I said."

Monk's voice seemed a little colder. "Give me their names."

"There were a bunch of us." Carlo looked reluctant to go on. "My girlfriend, Katie," he said finally. "Katie Blessing. Danny Spellman, Darnell Sheets, Jenny Havilland, Joey Arroyo. Maybe Rachel Rubenstein—I'm not sure about her."

"Were you with them the whole time?"

A longer pause. "Mostly," Carlo answered.

Monk watched Paget's face. "Was there a period," he asked Carlo, "when you weren't with them?"

The nod again, quick and nervous. It was the time, Paget knew, when an inexperienced witness would start to demonstrate his sincerity, giving voluble answers to the question and a half-dozen others that Monk had never asked. So that Carlo's terse "Yes," coming after a pause, disturbed him.

"When was that?" Monk prodded.

"Maybe eight-thirty." Carlo had begun to fidget; when Monk did not fill the silence, Carlo added, "It wasn't very long."

Monk let the answer sit there awhile. "And what were the circumstances?"

"We were all at Darnell's house, and we decided to go to a movie. Maybe later, Katie and I were going to a pizza place." He shot his father a quick glance. "I'd forgotten my wallet."

Paget felt himself becoming very still.

"What did you do?" Monk asked.

Carlo folded his arms, looking down. "Tried to borrow money."

Carlo, Paget saw, was trying to stretch this out, hoping that the reckoning would never come. His heart went out to him: the questions *would* come, and for the first time, Paget knew where they would end.

"What happened?"

"Nothing." Carlo's voice was lower now. "There wasn't enough to cover us."

"What did you do?"

Answering, Carlo would not look at Paget. "We decided that I'd meet the rest of them at the theater—you know, the Empire in West Portal."

Monk, Paget knew, would have to drag this out of him. Monk watched Carlo intently now. But for the last five questions, Lynch's eyes had not moved from Paget's face.

"And between Darnell's house and the Empire," Monk asked softly, "how long were you gone?"

Carlo's brow furrowed; it was the expression of someone stalling for time. "Forty-five minutes, maybe."

"Were you alone?"

Carlo seemed quite miserable. The nod, when it came, was brief; the "Yes" almost inaudible.

Monk leaned forward. More softly yet, he asked, "And where did you go, Carlo?"

Carlo turned to his father. Paget knew that Carlo could not help this. But Paget's face could tell him nothing.

Carlo faced Monk again. Suddenly composed, he said simply, "I came home."

"And what did you do here?"

Carlo leaned back. "I went to my room and got my wallet. Then I left."

"Where did you park?"

Carlo looked puzzled; only Paget, it was clear, understood the question. "In the driveway," Carlo answered.

A slight pause. "Was there any other car here?"

Comprehension appeared as a stain on Carlo's cheeks. "My dad parks in the garage," he said. "I didn't go there."

Tensely watching, Paget thought that Carlo's body was in retreat, Monk's in pursuit. "While you were home," Monk asked quietly, "did you see anyone?"

Carlo stared back at Monk. He did not look at Paget now; this seemed as deliberate as turning to his father, just a moment before, had seemed involuntary. In his son's silence, Paget implored Carlo not to lie.

"No," Carlo answered. "I was just looking for my wallet. I ran upstairs to my room, got the wallet, and ran back down the stairs again. It took less than two minutes."

"To get to the stairs," Monk asked, "you pass the library and living room, right?"

The nod again, slower now. "Right."

"Did you see anyone?"

Carlo shrugged. "I wasn't looking."

Monk's face was stony; only the rhythm of the questions changed, a little faster now. "But someone in those rooms could see *you*, right?"

The nod again, barely perceptible. "Yes."

"Where is your dad's room?"

Carlo seemed to blink; Paget willed himself not to move. "Next to mine," Carlo answered.

"And no one called out to you?"

Slowly, Carlo shook his head.

"You have to give me an audible answer, son."

He's not *your* son, Paget thought. "All I can tell you," Carlo said, "is that I didn't *hear* anyone call me."

"Did you hear noises in your father's bedroom?"

Carlo leaned back, folding his arms. To Paget, he looked suddenly pale. "I can't remember," he said.

That, Paget was certain, was true; most people quickly forget nonessentials, and the memories of police witnesses are often the well-intentioned imaginings of those to whom the normal absence of recall suddenly feels like a sign of guilt. But Carlo could not know this: he had begun to watch the spinning tape as if it were an enemy.

"Tell me," Monk asked him softly, "was there any sign that your father was even here?"

Paget's stomach felt tight. Carlo's mouth opened; Paget saw him straining to think. "All that I remember," he said in a low voice, "is thinking maybe I heard footsteps in the attic, above my room."

"So you're not sure."

"No." Carlo's voice was cool now. "But that would make sense. The attic's where Dad and I keep extra suitcases."

"Did you hear *Carlo?*" Monk asked abruptly.

It was a moment before Paget realized that Monk had turned to him. "No," he answered.

Monk glanced at the tape. In a voice that seemed almost indifferent to the answer, he asked Paget, "Where were you, anyhow?"

To Paget, Carlo's eyes seemed almost pleading. "I'm not sure," Paget said evenly. "But Carlo's right: we keep our bags in the attic. So I spent some time there."

"How much time?"

"Five minutes, perhaps. It wasn't an eventful trip." Paget looked at Lynch and then back to Monk. "If we're through with Carlo, and on to me, I believe that Carlo had some plans."

Carlo shot him a quick glance. "If that's all right," he said to Monk.

Monk paused. Then, drawn by the trade that Paget offered—Carlo's freedom for a shot at Paget—he nodded.

Rising, Carlo gave his father a look that mingled concern with apology. No, Paget told him with a look, it's I who should be sorry. Even before Monk stopped Carlo from standing, asked him to stay for a moment, and took a set a fingerprints.

Rising, Carlo gazed at his ink-smudged fingers. Much, his father thought, as Terri had.

"Have a nice time," Paget told him easily. "And wash your hands."

Carlo managed a smile. "Thanks, Dad."

Taking his cue, Carlo had made his voice sound close to normal. Paget wondered where Carlo, who had no plans, would choose to go. Then the boy left, and Paget turned to Monk.

"All right," he said. "Let's get this done."

FOUR

"DID YOU EVER MEET Ricardo Arias?" Monk asked quietly, and Paget felt everything change.

He was in a field of evidence not yet discovered: questions yet to be asked, facts not yet sifted, connections yet to be made. But the questions *would* be asked—of Terri, of Carlo, of people Paget had never met and perhaps did not know existed—and the connections drawn, like lines between dots in a child's puzzle, until a picture emerged. Paget could not yet see the picture, and perhaps never would: it was Monk who would ask the questions, and draw the lines. Paget's role was to stare at the tape as at some coiling snake, and guess.

"No," he answered.

"Did you ever *see* him?"

"Yes."

"Where?"

A moment's pause. "In the *Inquisitor*. With a touching caption beneath him. Something like 'For ten thousand dollars, you can feed this boy.'"

Monk sat back, staring at him. Even Lynch's face hardened; no one was screwing around anymore.

"Where were you that night?" Monk asked.

"Here."

"Did you ever visit his apartment?"

Paget's temples began to feel constricted, as if in a vise. "No," he answered.

Monk handed the tape machine to Lynch; the gesture was like that of a man loosening his tie, settling in for a while. "Do you believe your son sexually abused Elena Arias?" he asked.

"Absolutely not."

"Do you know why Mr. Arias made that charge?"

"Yes." Paget's voice was firm now. "He was a worthless deadbeat who wanted to live off child support. The best way was to trash his wife and anyone who might help her."

Monk leaned back. His eyes were an unusual brown, Paget thought, almost a shade of muddy yellow. "Mr. Arias," he said, "filed papers in his child custody proceeding charging your son with child abuse and you with adultery. Are you aware of that?"

Paget squinted; the noontime sun had begun to hurt his eyes. "Of course."

Monk pushed the gold-rimmed glasses up the bridge of his nose. "Let's start with Teresa Peralta. Did you take her from her husband?"

For the first time, Paget understood what his clients must feel as they saw their lives sliced and diced and rearranged to suit the police, their pettiest and most private acts exhumed for use in court. "Take?" he said. "Terri's not for taking—or keeping. And our relationship—other than as friends—didn't start until she left Richie."

"You're running for the Senate, aren't you?"

There was a faint undertone in Monk's voice, perhaps the bone-deep distrust of a cop for a defense lawyer, his opponent in a world too morally complex to allow for a common view of justice. "I may," Paget answered more easily. "But the race is almost two years away."

Monk gazed at him, silent: Paget sensed that the message Monk intended to convey was that he should not run. But whether that reflected a weariness of lawyers and politicians, or something deeper and more specific, Paget could not tell. Then, quite slowly and deliberately, Monk asked, "Why did Ricardo Arias file these papers under seal?"

That Paget was expecting this did not numb the jolt he felt. "I can only speculate," he answered. "Clearly, he intended to put pressure on Terri to give him permanent custody. Through me, if necessary."

Monk leaned forward. "Was Mr. Arias blackmailing you?"

It was as if Richie were not dead; his plans and schemes lived on in the minds of the police, entwining those he had plotted against. "No," Paget answered.

Monk seemed to stare right through him. "Tell me," he asked in a tone of mild curiosity, "did Ricardo Arias ever ask you for money?"

A second jolt: the insidious beauty of the question was the question buried beneath it—whether Paget and Ricardo Arias had ever spoken.

"No."

Monk sat back, waiting for Paget to say that he had never talked to Richie. Watching the recorder in Lynch's lap, Paget saw that the tape appeared to be close to ending. "Care for some iced coffee?" Paget asked.

"No. Thank you." Monk's voice was very polite now. "Did you and Mr. Arias ever speak by telephone?"

The recorder clicked.

Monk fumbled in his pocket for another tape. It gave Paget a brief moment to ponder whether Ricardo Arias might have recorded phone calls. And then he realized, quite certainly, that Richie could not have done so.

Monk inserted the new tape, identified Paget as the witness, and handed the machine back to Lynch. "Did you and Mr. Arias ever speak by telephone?" he repeated.

"No," Paget said.

"So," Monk said, "the night before you left for Italy, you didn't speak to Ricardo Arias by phone."

"No."

"Or see him?"

"No."

"Or visit his apartment?"

"No."

Monk's rapid-fire cadence made Paget feel cornered. "Did Richie ever call *your* home?" Monk asked.

Paget hesitated. "I wouldn't know. Theoretically, it's possible."

"Who, besides you, answers the telephone."

"Carlo, obviously. Sometimes Cecilia, the housekeeper. And, when it's working, the answering machine."

"What are Cecilia's hours?"

"Two-thirty to six-thirty, five days a week. She runs the laundry, cleans the house. Sometimes fixes dinner for us."

"Have an address for her?" Lynch asked.

Paget turned to him. "You can talk to her here. When I'm present, after I've spoken to her, at our convenience. I'm not going to have you scaring her to death."

Monk glanced at Lynch. "We'll get back to you," Lynch said.

Monk folded his hands. "Do you own a gun?"

"No."

"Have you ever had one in your possession?"

"Only in the army."

"Ever fire one?"

"Again, not since the army. I don't like them."

Monk leaned back. "How about Ms. Peralta?"

It took Paget by surprise. "Terri told you already. She hates guns too. I can't imagine her owning one and have no reason to think that she did."

"What about Ms. Peralta's family?"

Paget tried to decipher the question. But Monk's face, as usual, was opaque. "Gun ownership, you mean? Terri's father has been dead for years. In San Francisco, that leaves her mother. And I somehow doubt she's supplying Terri with weapons. If that's your question."

Monk shrugged. "Have you ever met her?"

"No."

"Do you know what her relationship to Richie was like?"

"No. . . . Of course, she *knew* him. So I'd have to guess she didn't like him."

From Lynch, a shadow of dark laughter. Monk's expression did not change. "What about Ms. Peralta?" Monk asked. "How would you classify her relationship to Mr. Arias?"

"Strained. Although, for Elena, Terri tried her best."

Monk's gaze was attenuated and unimpressed. "Do you think that Ms. Peralta intended Mr. Arias any harm?"

Paget shook his head. "All the time we were in Italy, Inspector, Terri worried that he hadn't shown up. Again, for Elena's sake and in spite of everything." Paget decided to give them a piece of his personal life, to divert them from Terri. "While we were there, we had long and agonized discussions about whether our relationship was possible in light of Richie's malice. You don't put yourself through that for a dead man."

Monk's gaze hardened into a stare. "Unless one of you is an actor."

It jarred Paget, as Monk intended, putting a different spin on Italy: the charade of a murderer building an alibi by toying with the emotions of a lover, hoping that the decay of Richie's body would obscure the date of his death.

"How did *you* feel about Arias?" Monk asked abruptly. "You weren't exactly forthcoming with us about your reasons for disliking him. Your son, for example."

"I didn't like him then, and I still don't." Paget folded his arms. "You weren't asking me about Carlo but about a death. About which, as it happens, I know nothing."

Monk appraised him. "So you don't have any information on how he might have died?"

"None. Except from you."

"On whether someone might have killed him?"

"No."

"Not even a theory?"

Paget stared back at him for a while. "Theories are your job. Not mine." He tilted his head. "Although suicide's not a bad one. If I were you, I might take Richie's note as a sign of his sincerity."

Monk simply watched. "A man will do a lot of things," he said, "if someone holds a gun to his head."

Paget smiled a little. "Including swallow it?"

But Monk, it was clear, knew he had said enough. And he had what he had come for: answers, impossible for Paget to run from, recorded on tape. Noting the hour and minutes, he clicked off the machine. "We appreciate your time," he said.

Even this small courtesy haunted Paget a little. "Sure," he answered.

The response felt insufficiently outraged. But Paget had entered a territory without a map: he no longer knew what to say, or even how to act. Only a couple of hours had passed, and now nothing in his life felt natural.

Shepherding Monk and Lynch to the door, Paget said little. From the window of his library, he watched them leave.

Damn Ricardo Arias to hell.

For the next hour or so, his thoughts cold and clear, Paget entered the mind of Charles Monk. When he rose from his chair, his skin felt clammy, like the aftershock of a nightmare.

He went to the kitchen, took out an oversize green garbage bag.

Then, glancing at the front door, Paget climbed the stairs to his room.

His walk-in closet was filled with suits. For years, Paget's response to depression, or even boredom, had been to buy an Italian suit: about twenty-five suits were jammed so tight that it was hard to find the one he was looking for. A gray suit, with a speckled stain on the cuff of one sleeve.

He pulled it out, examining the cuff. The dry cleaner, he decided, could do nothing with it. Even if that still made sense.

Paget took the suit off its hanger and stuffed it into the garbage bag. It was only when he was outside, standing over the garbage can, that he realized the police might search his trash.

Paget went to the library, gazing into the fireplace. But Carlo, he realized, might come home.

He hurried upstairs to his room.

Randomly, he pulled out three more suits. Then he put the gray suit back on its hanger, threw it on his bed with the others, and began looking for the shoes.

This was easier. Paget was indifferent to shoes; the three pairs of dress shoes wedged between the running shoes and Dock-Siders were all that he owned.

Which ones were they?

The simple black ones, he remembered. They were almost new; he had worn the pair before that until Terri had pronounced them older than she was. Putting them in the garbage bag, he felt a twinge of sadness. And then, more deeply, felt furtive and alone.

He had no choice, Paget thought; he could not keep the suit and shoes.

He walked outside, into the bright sunlight, and drove to the Goodwill bin at the supermarket. It was gone: a sign said that the only drops now available were at the Goodwill stores.

He sat there in the parking lot, apprehensive now, considering his choices. The image of Charles Monk, coming to his home at random, kept breaking through his thoughts.

Nervous and irresolute, he drove to the Goodwill outlet in the Mission District. Not far, he reflected, from where Terri had lived as a child.

The outlet was a dark room with a long counter, where a pleasant Hispanic woman with vivid makeup and round beautiful eyes was taking donations of clothes and scribbling out receipts for tax deductions. There were two men in the line ahead of him: Paget looked at the floor, still debating with himself. And then the woman looked up, smiling brightly, and met his eyes.

It was a moment before he showed her what he had brought. "Suits," she said. "Nice ones too."

"Thank you." Paget hesitated and then placed the bag on the counter. "I also have some shoes."

She pulled them out of the bag. "They look new."

Paget nodded. "They don't fit quite right. It's sort of like walking on roller skates."

She laughed at that, looking into his face, flirting a little. "You should be more careful with your money."

Would she recognize him, Paget wondered, or remember him? "So my girlfriend tells me," he said.

The woman laughed again. But now she turned to the receipt pad in front of her. "Oh, don't bother," Paget said.

She glanced up. "No? I'll be happy to give you one. Help with taxes. I mean, this has got to be over a thousand dollars, even used."

Too much conversation. "Okay," Paget said. "Thanks."

The woman scrawled out a receipt. "The name?" she asked.

"Paget."

He watched the woman write "Padgett." He did not correct her; as he took the receipt, Paget saw the woman slide her copy into a drawer.

"Thanks," he said, and quickly left. Glancing over his shoulder, he saw her smiling after him and waved. A few feet down the street, looking back again, he crumpled the receipt and tossed it in a trash container.

Paget drove home, fervently hoping to become a shadow in the mind of a busy woman. That was likely, he tried to tell himself, unless she saw his face again. With that thought came another, as insidious as superstition: he had made a mistake that he could not correct.

When Paget entered the house, it was not Monk he found in the library, but Carlo.

It was a surprise. Carlo did not spend much time there anymore; Paget sensed that his son had been waiting for him.

"Where've you been?" Carlo asked.

His voice had a touch of anxiety. "Running errands," Paget answered, and stopped to look at Carlo. In another voice, far less careless, he said, "I'm sorry about today."

Carlo looked away. "I was worried I'd say the wrong thing."

Paget smiled. "As I've always said, just tell people the truth. It's less confusing."

Carlo gave him a sideways glance. "I wish I'd seen you that night."

Or even *heard* you, Paget sensed him thinking. "Don't worry," he said. "They're just acting like police. They treat any unexplained death as suspicious, and anyone who was connected with the dead guy is going to get a visit." Paget paused. "I'm sorry they dredged up that stuff about Elena. But I was proud of how you handled it. The whole thing, really."

Carlo watched him closely. "You sound pretty calm."

Paget had thought his unconcern plausible enough. But he knew his son very well. Well enough to know that this was not a statement but a question; more than well enough to hear the worry that crept into Carlo's voice. But then not every teenager was as perceptive as Carlo.

"In two weeks, Carlo, they'll have disappeared. Meanwhile, don't talk to them about this. Or, for that matter, to anyone."

Watching his son's face, Paget felt the sadness return: it was as if the fears of his clients, the consciousness of being hunted, had silently entered his home. Then Carlo gave a fatalistic shrug that did not conceal how strange he must feel.

All at once, Paget wanted to be with him, to be as normal as possible. "What are you up to tonight?" Paget asked.

Carlo considered this. "Nothing, really. Katie's parents are putting her through family night—happy faces around the table, that kind of thing."

Paget smiled. "Some families are like that. Especially ones with mothers."

Carlo smiled back a little. "You're like that too. Anyhow, what are *you* doing?"

"Zip. Terri's tied up with Elena."

Carlo scrutinized him. "Ever miss all those women without kids?"

"Nope. Just the ones without husbands."

Carlo laughed now. "Oh, well."

Paget leaned back in his chair. "So why don't we go to a movie?"

Carlo raised an eyebrow. "What are you offering?"

"I don't know. What are you suggesting?"

Carlo pondered that for a moment. "Arnold Schwarzenegger."

Paget tilted his head. "Clint Eastwood?"

Carlo grinned. "Sold," he answered. "Arnold was just my opening move."

FIVE

PAGET KISSED Terri's neck, the line of her chin. She laid her head against his shoulder, baring her throat; Paget could smell her skin and hair, hear her murmur of contentment.

They were in the library two nights after the police had come, stretched out on the Persian rug, with Paget's shoulder against the couch, Terri's back to his chest as she rested in his arms. The room was dark and quiet; the only light was from the fireplace, flickering tongues of orange and blue, wood crackling as it burned. The fire glistened in the crystal snifters on the coffee table, burnishing the cognac Terri and Paget had forgotten to finish. He felt content.

It had been a leisurely evening, their first in days. They had eaten cheese and smoked salmon, talked about their day. They knew that they would make love; there was no rush. Time, drifting through their talk, their touching, felt sensual and easy. Tonight, Paget thought, they were a lot like any couple.

"This Dr. Harris," Paget asked. "What is she like?"

Terri shifted her weight slightly, settling against his chest. "Fine, I guess. With shrinks, I don't have a big frame of reference. The problem is that we've spent more time on *my* childhood than Elena's."

"To what end?"

"I don't know, exactly." Terri reached for her snifter of cognac. "What do *you* remember about your childhood, Chris? Say at around Elena's age. Anything at all?"

Paget reflected. "I haven't thought about it for a while. But a fair amount, I think. Both good and bad."

"What's your first childhood memory?"

"The clearest? I think it's a tie between getting spanked for lying and a big toy car I got for Christmas, with pedals so that I could ride it like a tricycle. I thought it was a Rolls."

Terri smiled. "Of course you did. How old were you?"

"A little younger than Elena. Perhaps four or five." Paget took a sip of Terri's cognac, warm and velvety. "What's yours?"

Terri was quiet. "My mother being beaten," she said at last.

Paget's eyes narrowed. "What brings all this up?"

"The other day, Denise Harris asked for my memories at around Elena's age. There was just a blur. And then I suddenly remembered pulling the blanket over my head so I couldn't hear my mother crying." Terri sipped some cognac. "It was like if I couldn't hear her, then my father had stopped hurting her. But I was protecting myself, of course."

"Where were they that you could hear them?"

"In the bedroom. It was next to mine. I think, somehow, he wanted me to hear."

Paget watched the fire. "You must hate him. Still."

He felt her shrug, a small movement of her shoulder blades. "I don't feel anything. I don't think about him, really. It's fine now."

It would do no good to question this, Paget knew. "What did Harris make of that? If anything."

Terri fell quiet. "I didn't tell her," she said at last.

"Why not?"

"I couldn't." Terri turned to him. "It's hard to explain, Chris. It was like I was afraid to."

"Afraid of what?"

"I don't know, really—it's more instinctive. It's like I'm still sitting at the table, watching him, hoping to get through dinner without some kind of an explosion." She shook her head, as if to herself. "At school, I was always the quiet one. A pleaser. Like if I didn't make trouble and got good grades, no one would get angry. *He* wouldn't get angry."

"Where was your mom in all this?"

"She loved me." For the first time, Terri sounded defensive. "She couldn't change him, that's all."

"That's no way to live, Terri."

The small shrug again. "Lots of people do. And I came out all right, in the end."

Paget was quiet again. How much, he wondered, did she truly remember? "Are you going back to Harris?"

Terri sipped more cognac, placed the snifter in his hand. "When I left, I didn't want to. I hate talking about that stuff. Except, some-times, to you." She paused. "But I'm going to. I have to trust Denise—God knows *I* haven't helped Elena. I can't let her go on like this."

Paget watched the fireplace, the spit and dance of flame, sinuous and hypnotic. "One of these days, Terri, you might try out that dream on Harris. Just for the hell of it."

Terri delayed in answering. "Maybe I will, all right? I just don't want to talk about this anymore. Not tonight, at least."

The best response, Paget thought, was silence: there was an edge to her voice, as if she regretted telling him about the dream. But when, moments later, he kissed her, the feel of her mouth was grate-ful, ready.

They went upstairs to Paget's bedroom.

Terri undressed. Her body, a profile in the moonlight, was slim and silver. His first touch brought it to life.

Paget held her close. So many women, he thought, and yet the first time Terri and he were skin to skin it was like coming home. Except that this was a place where he had never been before and never knew to find. He could feel her heartbeat.

"I love you," Terri said.

The sheets were cool and crisp. There were no more words.

Later, she lay with her hair strewn across the pillow, one arm out-flung, a woman surprised by sleep. Her breathing was deep and even.

For a time, he watched her as she slept. Sometimes he would do this: it was as if he could discern the child Terri in her woman's face and yet still see the strength that had brought her through so much, and that he honored more than she could ever know. Perhaps, some-day, they would have a child of their own; Paget knew that he would love that child with the depth of his love for Terri. And, in loving them both, have what he had never had before.

Turning, Paget gazed at the luminous numbers of the clock radio, read 11:15. He could let her sleep awhile longer. But he could not sleep himself, even if he had been able.

He rose from the bed, watching Terri's face for signs of waking, and slipped on a pair of shorts.

In the hallway, no light came from beneath Carlo's door. Paget walked through the silent house, down the stairs from the deck off the kitchen, and entered the garage.

It was musty, the smell of cement and dirt, dampness and wood. The nose of the car pointed to where he had hidden it: behind a cinder block, loosened from the others holding back the dirt at the end of the garage.

Kneeling, Paget pried loose the block.

It was still there, although smudged with dirt. Paget reached above him, pulled the chain that hung from a bare bulb. The bulb flickered; the leather-bound journal opened in his hand.

The script, small and distinctly feminine, moved across the page in tight, relentless coils. Beneath the yellow bulb, Paget read the last entry. Pensive, although he had read it several times before.

It was hard to believe that no copy existed. But with every day that passed, this seemed more likely.

Tomorrow, after Carlo had left for school, he must find a safer place for it.

Paget hid the journal where it had been and slipped back through the house.

In the bedroom, Terri's head tossed on the pillow. A soft cry came from her throat. When Paget bent over her, her jaw was working, her eyes shut tight.

Gently, Paget kissed her, then raised his head to look into her face.

Terri's eyes flew open. She stared at him in fright.

"It's me," he said softly. "Chris. Your white knight."

Her eyes focused. Her body gave a shudder. In a tone soft with self-disgust, she murmured, "Jesus."

"The dream again?"

"Yes. Please, don't say another word."

He sat by her, silent. Her breathing was still rapid. In a cold, clear voice, she said, "This is really fucked, Chris."

Paget took her hand. "You all right?"

"Now I am." She turned to look for a clock, as if for a frame of reference. "What time is it?"

"Around midnight."

It seemed to startle her. "God, I've got to go. My mother's waiting up."

Paget gave a short laugh. "This is the part that *I* don't like. Where you turn into a pumpkin."

"No help for it." Terri still sounded distant; seemingly aware of that, she touched his face. "All the rest of it was good, Chris. Every part."

After a moment, Terri stood, flicking on a bedside lamp. Watching her dress, Paget realized that there was a part of him, even now, that found their intimacy a kind of gift. That loved their nakedness together; her touch as she lay with him. That lightened at her voice on the telephone.

"Something's occurred to me." He said it softly, reluctantly. "About our phones."

Terri stopped, finger resting on the last button of her blouse. "Monk?" She paused to look at him. "They can't wiretap us, Chris. They'll never get authorization for it—not in this state."

Nodding, Paget felt the pressure of his own fear. "I know. But I'm in politics now, and there are such things as illegal taps, by people other than Monk." He spoke more quietly. "I just think we should be careful. Not talk too much about Richie, or Elena, or even your sessions with Harris. Anything at all personal."

Terri watched him. "I just never thought about anyone doing that to *us*, that's all. We don't say anything, really."

Paget smiled. "When I talk about your body, it says something to *me*. I don't want an audience."

Terri finished the button. "Don't you think that's a little paranoid?"

"Maybe. But spying is not unknown in politics. And McKinley Brooks has all sorts of political friends. Particularly James Colt, who continues to let it be known that my own ambitions don't jibe with his."

Terri stepped into her shoes. "Screw them, Chris. We don't get to talk much as it is. I've gotten to *like* calling you after Elena goes to bed. It's like being a teenager, phoning your boyfriend in bed."

"Your mom let you do that?"

Terri smiled. "As long as I did my homework, she pretended not to know. But she did, of course."

Paget stood. "Humor me, okay? Just for a couple of weeks."

In the dim light, he felt her watching him more closely. "All right," she said slowly. "I'll just breathe into the phone a lot."

* * *

Terri sat alone, watching the rise and fall of Elena's breathing.

It was past two o'clock. Perhaps an hour before, she had heard her daughter crying. Rushing to the bedroom, she had found Elena rigid and frightened; it had taken the child a moment to recognize her mother, hold out her arms for comfort. But in the moment that she did, there were no barriers between them. Elena was simply a child again, seeking comfort from her mother, the only parent she had.

Her face was wet. "I'm *scared*, Mommy—so scared. Please, Mommy, *hold* me."

Terri squeezed her as tightly as she could. "What is it, sweetheart? In the dream, what happens to you?"

Elena did not answer. She buried her face in her mother's neck. "Stay with me, Mommy. I'm afraid to be alone."

Elena, Terri knew, would not tell her. But if she did, what difference might it make? "Of course I'll stay," Terri said. "I'm your mommy, and I will *never* leave you."

She had said this automatically. And then suddenly remembered that it was what her mother had said to her at night, over and over, when Ramon Peralta was alive. Knew that when she herself had said this to Elena, it was in her mother's voice.

Now Teresa Peralta, Elena's mother, watched her daughter's sleeping face.

I'll remember, Terri silently promised her. I'll remember everything I can. And in time, perhaps I'll understand.

SIX

WHEN TERRI ARRIVED at the office the next morning, Charles Monk was sitting at her desk, her telephone propped under his chin.

Monk listened intently, taking notes. He looked up, stared directly into her face, and then resumed writing as if she were not there. Over his shoulder was Terri's picture of Elena.

The room was quiet. Monk's concentration seemed so total that Terri found herself closing the door with extra care, so as not to break his thoughts. Then she noticed Dennis Lynch sitting calmly by her window with the tape machine and studying the progress of the Sixth Fleet as it moved across the bay.

Turning, Lynch gave her a small wave. For a moment, Terri felt like a visitor; only the cops looked at home.

Continuing to ignore her, Monk spoke a few terse words into the telephone, like a lawyer whose time was too valuable to waste. From a couple of phrases, Terri guessed that he was talking to a bank.

Only when Monk put down the telephone did he look at her again. "Would you like your chair back?"

"Yes. Thanks."

Rising, Monk stopped to study Elena's picture. "When was this taken?" he asked.

"Last year. For school."

Monk turned to her. "Was your husband particularly attached to it?"

Terri paused. "He had the same picture in his apartment. If that's what you mean."

Monk did not answer. He walked around the desk and sat down. Lynch pulled his chair up next to Monk's.

"We have more questions," Monk said.

Terri managed a smile. "I was sort of hoping you were going to play a Beatles tape backward. The one where it says 'Paul is dead.' "

" 'Abbey Road,' " Monk answered. "Never liked it."

Lynch switched on the machine.

Monk gave his preface again, then asked abruptly, "Did you ever threaten to kill Ricardo Arias?"

It startled her. "Of course not. Does anyone say I did?"

Monk ignored that. "Did you ever quarrel over Elena?"

"Yes." Terri felt the sudden anger of someone whose space had been invaded. "That was what the custody suit was about."

"But you never threatened to kill him? Not even when you were fighting over Elena?"

This time, there was a faint tingle in Terri's skin. Much more slowly, she said, "I can't remember saying that. And I certainly can't remember meaning it."

Monk sat back. "Did Christopher Paget ever threaten Mr. Arias?"

"Not in my presence."

"Or say that he wished Mr. Arias was dead?"

A slight pause. "No."

"Do you have any reason to believe that Mr. Paget is capable of violence?"

Terri folded her hands. "Chris," she said slowly, "is the most self-controlled man I've ever known. He doesn't do anything without thinking."

"That's not what I'm asking." Monk's voice had a relentless patience, the march of one word after another. "My question was whether Mr. Paget is capable of violence. Not premeditation."

Terri felt herself flush. It was time to preempt these questions. "Chris is not a murderer," she said coldly. "Either in anger or without it."

Monk did not blink. "Are you?"

Terri folded her hands. "Not even in my dreams."

Monk studied her for a moment. Quite softly, he asked, "Do you know where Christopher Paget was that night?"

"Yes." Her voice was cool now. "At home."

"And *how*, exactly, do you know that?"

Terri met his eyes. "Because he told me."

Monk leaned forward. "But you don't *know* he stayed home, do you?"

Terri folded her arms. "Not as a matter of literal fact."

"And how did his health seem the next morning?"

Fine, Terri thought. And then, although Monk did not know to ask about it, she thought of his swollen hand. "All right," she answered. "He seemed a little tired, like he hadn't slept well. That's what flu will do to you."

Monk leaned back. "Whose idea was the trip to Italy?"

It was time to collect her thoughts. "I need a cup of coffee," she said. "Would either of you like one?"

"No, thank you," answered Lynch. Monk, still watching her, simply shook his head.

Terri went to the coffee station. Before opening her office door again, she drew a deep breath. Her palms felt damp.

Reentering her office, Terri walked to the window and gazed out at the bay, ignoring the two policemen.

They were more than twenty stories up; immediately beneath them, on a tennis court, two tiny figures in white chased an invisible ball. But the gray steel ships of the Sixth Fleet seemed to shear the bay like knives; distance, and silence, lent them a lethal quality. Terri counted a cruiser, a battleship, and two destroyers; it was odd that, having forgotten so much, she could remember so precisely the day that Ramon Peralta had taught her this.

She had been eight then. The Sixth Fleet had sailed into the bay for Fleet Week; her father, who had served four years in the navy before Terri was born, had decided to leave Rosa and Terri's sisters at home. For the only day she could remember, Terri had her father to herself.

He was sober; the day was bright and clear. Terri had on a crisp white dress. She could remember watching the ships on the water from a hill above the bay, Ramon's rough hand holding hers, listening to him name each ship for her and explain what they did. Being part of this navy, she realized, had been his proudest moment; in the afternoon, when they toured the grim cocoon of a destroyer and Ramon had shown her the kind of cabin he had slept in, Terri did not say how cramped it seemed. What was important was the sinewy feel of the iron ship, the sound of her father's voice. "Teresa," he had said simply, "ours was the greatest navy in the history of the world." She looked up at him, saw his black mustache and white smile, saw beneath it his need for her approval. In that moment, Terri realized why her mother had fallen in love with him.

The glow of that day had lasted for weeks. Until the next time her father had beaten Rosa Peralta.

She turned from the window. "Did you ever watch those ships come in?" she asked Monk. "Take your kids?"

Silently, he shook his head.

"You really should," Terri said, and sat across from him again.

"Whose idea," Monk repeated, "was the trip to Italy?"

Terri sipped her coffee. The cup was a centrifuge of warmth in her hand; her voice was firm and calm now. "Both of ours. We needed to get away."

Monk waited a moment. "Who scheduled the trip?"

It was Terri's turn to hesitate. "Chris did."

"Including the plane to Milan?"

"Yes."

Monk leaned forward. "Remind me of the first day you tried to call Ricardo Arias and couldn't find him."

"Monday morning. Sunday night, San Francisco time."

"Did you mention that to Mr. Paget?"

"Yes. Of course."

"And what did he say?"

"To call him again. Which I did. Monday night, and again on Tuesday morning, and throughout the day."

"And when he didn't answer, you still didn't know that Elena was with your mother, correct?"

Not unless I killed Richie, Terri thought. "That's right," she answered. "I didn't know where she was."

"Did you think about calling the school?"

All at once, Terri saw how clever Monk was. His face looked calm, almost bored—like Chris, she realized, when he wished to hide his thoughts. "I thought about it," she answered. "Then I decided to call my mother first."

"Why not call the school? They would know for sure if Elena was there."

"I didn't want to seem panicky." Pausing, Terri tried to make herself believe she had thought this on her own. "I thought my mom might have talked to Elena."

The last phrase sounded halting: the answer did not help her, but any other did not help Chris.

Monk studied her. "Did you discuss *that* with Mr. Paget? Whether to call the school or call your mother?"

Don't you know? Terri thought silently. Chris and I talk about everything: he's the first man, ever, who has truly been a part of me. Putting down the coffee, she looked directly at Monk. "I don't remember."

Monk's voice was soft now. "And after you called your mother, and found Elena there, you decided not to look for Mr. Arias."

"Yes."

"Did you discuss *that* with Mr. Paget?"

Let him rot, Chris had said.

Terri hesitated. "I believe so."

"And what was the substance of that conversation?"

Suddenly Terri could see the scenario Monk was building in his mind. A trip to Italy, planned as cover. A night alone, hours before they left. And all the days after that, knowing he was dead, letting his body decompose in that apartment. Until no one could tell if he had died before they left.

"It was *my* decision," she told Monk, "not to call Richie. We were in a custody dispute, and I was willing under those circumstances to let him be neglectful. Because in my mind he was very much alive."

In the quiet, Terri watched the tape, silently winding her answer around a plastic spindle. "Thank you," Monk said politely. "We hope this wasn't an inconvenience."

Something in Terri would have preferred him to accuse her. It was so unnatural: a civil conversation with a tape recorder playing, a word of thanks at the end, with Monk noting the hour and minute. As if people did this all the time.

They packed up their tape machine and left.

Terri waited until she was certain they had caught the elevator, then she went to Chris's office.

He was putting down the telephone. "That was the phone company," he told her. "The cops have a search warrant for my phone records. Bank records too."

"I know." Terri sat across from him. "I just had a visitor. Chris, I think they're serious about this."

SEVEN

"MY MOTHER took care of me," Terri told Harris. "The best way she could. And how could *my* childhood affect Elena's?"

"There could be lots of ways," Harris answered. "Tell me, why do you think your mother didn't leave?"

Terri found herself staring at a print on Harris's wall, two fawns in a lush African landscape with surreal birds and multiple suns, their displacement all the more striking because of the innocence with which they grazed. Chris admired the same artist, Jesse Allen; contemplating the fawns seemed to make it easier for her to talk.

"Money," Terri answered automatically. "I mean, that's what kept a lot of marriages together then, wasn't it? The women couldn't make it."

"Doesn't your mother work now?"

"Uh-huh. As a bookkeeper." Terri reflected. "Somehow, I remember her working for a while. Then it stopped. I don't know why."

Harris was watching her, Terri discovered, with a thoughtful half smile. "Did something else occur to you?"

Terri hesitated. "I don't know. Just that I was thinking that it was hard for *me* to cope, too, because of money. Not because *I* didn't work, but because Richie wouldn't."

"Do you think that Richie set it up that way?"

"I don't know." Terri resumed looking at the African landscape. "When I agreed to marry Richie, I told myself that he wasn't like my father at all. That he wasn't abusive. That he never lost his temper. That he wouldn't mind having a wife who'd accomplished something. I couldn't see any parallel between Richie and my father."

"And that was important to you."

"Yes." Terri's voice was firm now. "I didn't want Elena to be afraid. Of her father, or of anything."

Harris touched her chin. "Were *you* afraid, Terri?"

Terri had folded her arms, she realized.

"Terri?"

In her mind, Ramon Peralta's face was contorted with drunken fury. Her mother's mouth was swollen; her eyes shone with tears. Still she refused to cry.

He raised his hand to strike—

"Did he beat you, Terri?"

Terri closed her eyes and slowly shook her head.

"What are you remembering?" Harris asked softly.

It is night.

Terri is fourteen now; she can no longer hide beneath the covers or inside the closet, as she has taught her younger sisters to do. Her mother's cries have drawn her from the bedroom.

Terri creeps down the stairs. Unsure of what will happen, afraid of what she will see. Knowing only that, this time, she must stop him.

The first thing she sees is her mother's face.

In the dim light of a single lamp, it is beautiful and ravaged, drained of hope. Her mouth has begun to swell.

Ramon Peralta steps into the light.

His hand is raised. Rosa backs to the wall. Her eyes glisten with tears. By now Terri knows that the tears will never fall; it is Rosa's pride that she endures this without crying. But she cannot stifle the sounds when he hits her, cries from deep within her soul.

"Whore," Ramon says softly.

Helpless, Rosa shakes her head. Her shoulders graze the wall behind her.

"I saw you look at him," Ramon prods. His accusation is sibilant, precise; Terri can imagine his whiskey breath in her mother's face. Ramon comes closer.

Watching, Terri freezes.

She stands there, trembling, ashamed of her own cowardice. No one sees her; there is still time to turn away.

Her father's hand flashes through the light.

Terri flinches. Hears the crack of his palm on Rosa's cheekbone; the short cry she seems to bite off; the heavy sound of his breathing.

In the pit of her stomach, Terri understands; her mother's cries draw him on for more. Rosa's lip is bleeding now.

"*No,*" Terri cries out.

Tears have sprung to her eyes; she is not sure she has spoken aloud. And then, slowly, Ramon Peralta turns.

Seeing her, his face fills with astonishment and rage. But Terri cannot look away.

"You *like* this," she tells her father. "You think it makes you strong. But we hate you—"

"*Teresa, don't!*"

Her mother steps from the wall. "This is *our* business—"

"*We* live here too." Without thinking, Terri steps between them. "Don't *ever* hit her," she tells her father. "Ever again. Or we'll hate you for the rest of your life."

Ramon's face darkens. "You little bitch. You're just like *her.*"

Terri points at her chest. "I'm *me. I'm* saying this."

His hand flies back to hit her.

"*No.*" Her mother has clutched Terri's shoulders, pulling her away from him. Her father reaches out and jerks Terri by the arm.

Blinding pain shoots through Terri's shoulder. She feels him twist her arm behind her back, push her face down on the sofa. Terri wills herself to make no sound at all.

"What," her father asks softly, "would you like me to do now?"

Terri cannot be certain whether he asks this of Rosa or of Terri herself. Can sense only that her mother has draped both arms around her father's neck.

"Let her go, Ramon." Rosa's voice is gentle now. "You were right. I shouldn't have looked at him that way."

Terri twists her head to see. But she can only see her mother carefully watching Ramon as she whispers, "I'll make it up to you. Please, let her go."

In her anguish, Terri senses her father turning to Rosa, sees the look on her mother's face. The look of a woman who has met the man she was fated for. Lips parted, eyes resolute, accepting her destiny.

With a sharp jerk, Ramon Peralta releases his daughter's arm.

"Go," Rosa tells her. "Go to bed, Teresa."

Standing, Terri turns to her mother. Her legs are unsteady, but

Rosa does not reach for her. She leans against her husband now, one arm around his waist. Two parents confronting their child.

"Go," Rosa repeats softly. "Please."

Terri turns, walking toward the stairs. Knowing that, in some strange way, her father has accepted Rosa as a substitute for Terri. Her arm aches, and her face burns with shame. She does not know for whom.

At the top of the darkened stairway, Terri stops. She cannot, somehow, return to her room.

She stands there. It is as if, from a distance, she is standing guard over Rosa.

From the living room below, a soft cry.

Terri cannot help herself. The second cry, a deeper moan, draws her back toward the living room.

At the foot of the stairs, Terri stops.

Two profiles in the yellow light, her mother and her father.

Her father wears only a shirt. Her mother is bent over the couch, facefirst, as Terri was. Her dress is raised around her waist; her panties lie ripped on the floor. As Ramon Peralta drives himself into her from behind, again and again, she cries out for him with each thrust.

Terri cannot look away. Her mother's face, turned to the light, is an unfeeling mask. Only her lips move, to make the cries.

And then Rosa sees her.

Her eyes open wider, looking into her daughter's face with a depth of pain and anguish that Terri has never seen before. She stops making the sounds. Silently pleading with her daughter, her lips form the word "Go."

In Rosa's silence, Ramon Peralta thrusts harder.

"Go," her mother's lips repeat, and then, still looking at Terri, she makes the soft cry of pleasure her husband wants.

Terri turns and slowly climbs the stairs, footsteps soft so that her father will not hear. Her eyes fill with tears.

Harris listened, impassive.

"Did you ever talk about this?" she asked quietly. "I mean, with your mother."

Terri touched her eyes. "No."

"Not at all?"

Terri gazed at her a moment. "A few nights later," she said simply, "my father died. My mother and I never spoke of him again."

EIGHT

TERRI DIVED for the yellow ball, flailing with her racket, and fell skidding chest-first on the green surface. It took a moment for Paget to notice; he was distracted by the flight of the shot she had hit, a laser forehand that flashed through the noonday sunlight and nicked the baseline, impossible to return. When he turned, he saw Terri sprawled on the court, laughing.

"If you weren't left-handed," Paget said with an air of petulance, "you never would have gotten there."

Lying in a patch of light and shadow, Terri tried to look aggrieved. "I could have abrasions," she said. "Maybe even contusions."

A light wind stirred the pines surrounding the court and the grassy park of which it was part. Paget walked to the net and stood with his hands on his hips, gazing down at her. "I'm finding it easy to withhold my sympathy. In fact, I think I've been hustled."

"I would never lie to you," Terri protested. "At least about tennis. I've hardly ever played."

That was true, Paget guessed. Which only made his problem worse; Teresa Peralta was a natural athlete, with the reflexes of a cobra and no interest at all in losing. Paget's future in tennis did not look bright.

"Get up," he demanded.

Terri gave him a look, rolled on her back to inspect her knees for scrapes, and got back up to play. "Do you always lose this gracefully?" she asked.

"Hard to say. I haven't had much practice."

When she settled in near the baseline, alert and ready, Terri's intent expression had the trace of a smile. Paget served to her backhand, the weak point of the novice.

Terri's wrist flicked. The ball dropped over the net, landing two feet on Paget's side with a little bit of backspin. Paget got there quickly, strained to reach the ball and loop it back. His ball landed in front of Terri with absolutely nothing on it.

It bounced to the level of her eyes; Terri raised her racket, seeming to study it with a certain interest, and then casually batted it toward the spot Paget had vacated to return the shot before. For all the chance he had to get there, Paget might as well have been in Venice.

"Tie," Terri announced innocently. "What do they call that in tennis?"

Paget stared at her. " 'Deuce,' " he answered. "They call it 'deuce.' "

Terri nodded. "Deuce," she repeated. "Thanks."

The last recourse of the bully, Paget decided, was a killer serve. It was the hardest thing for a beginner to master and the hardest to return. Preparing to serve, Paget called on the memories of youth, trying to reconstruct the perfect form.

He tossed the ball above his head, stretched to his toes, and brought the racket down in a savage arc that ended with a snap of the wrist. There was a deep ping; a yellow blur slammed past Terri's feet and skipped to the fence. She stared at it a moment and then turned back to Paget.

"Lessons," he said.

Preparing for his next serve, Terri's smile was grim.

Something had locked in; when Paget tossed the ball again, stretching to hit it, the serve sped toward Terri's backhand.

Quickly, smoothly, she turned to the side and swung. A low, clean shot, clearing the net by two inches, zipping past Paget before he could even think to be surprised. Landing on the far side of the baseline, a foot too long.

Terri stared at the ball in disgust.

"Aren't you going to congratulate the winner?" Paget asked. "Jump the net or something, like the graceful loser that you are?"

Terri turned to him with an inscrutable expression. Then she slowly placed the racket on the court, bent forward, and performed a handstand.

To Paget's astonishment, Terri began to walk on her hands. She did that all the way to the net, turned around, and backflipped over to land in front of Paget.

"Congratulations," she said.

Paget stared at her, suspended between laughter and amazement. "What was *that*?" he asked.

"I used to be a gymnast, till I was about fourteen. My mother was my biggest fan; I guess she figured it helped me get out of the house." Terri grinned. "Elena still loves to watch me do it. So if we ever do have a kid of our own, she can tell all the other kids that her mom can walk on her hands. They'll think I'm terrific."

Paget laughed. "*I* think you're terrific. In any position."

"That's for later." Terri took his arm. "In the meantime, don't worry about yourself too much. You're really not bad at tennis."

They picked up Terri's racket, collected the balls and racket covers, and traded them for the picnic lunch in Paget's convertible. They had resolved to set their worries aside and spend a day together; the fact that it was easier to do that by skipping work, when Elena was at school, only enhanced his pleasure. "It's not that easy," he told her, "to be forty-six years old. Let alone to have an erratic backhand and a girlfriend who leaves palm prints on the tennis court."

Terri's mouth flickered. "A *committed* girlfriend," she amended, "who thinks you're sexy. At any age."

They spent two more hours, picnic spread on the grass, talking about everything and nothing, watching mothers or nannies play with kids too small for school. It was easy to be with him, Terri thought, the sun on their faces, to feel the deep friendship she always felt when they had time together. Perhaps, in months or even weeks, she would know what had happened to Elena and to Richie, and then the pieces would fall into place.

Suddenly she remembered to glance at her watch. "I've got to go," she said. "Another mom is picking up Elena, but I can't be late. The way things are, she'd think something happened to me."

Chris smiled. "*Nothing* happened to you. But it was a nice day, anyhow. At least for me."

The drive home went easily. Chris had a new Bonnie Raitt disc; they cruised in warm sunlight all the way to Noe Valley. Terri felt so relaxed that when she kissed Chris goodbye, she nearly promised to call him. Not even remembering the police could dampen her mood.

She was humming a Bonnie Raitt tune as she climbed the stairs to her apartment. But when she arrived, her door was ajar. A two-inch crack.

Terri felt fear on the back of her neck; it was a moment before she realized that she had thought of Richie, on the night she had found him inside. Another moment until she realized who must be on the other side of the door.

But when she pushed it open, it was not Monk who looked up from her desk, but Dennis Lynch. He gave her an apologetic smile. "Sorry," he said pleasantly. "We thought we should do this when your daughter wasn't here."

Terri stifled her anger. "I guess you have a warrant."

"Oh, yeah. Showed it to the manager already." Lynch pulled the warrant out of his coat pocket and gave it to Terri, waving her to a couch. "Make yourself at home. We'll only be ten, fifteen minutes."

Terri sat. From Elena's bedroom came the sounds of drawers opening and closing. "Find anything interesting?" she asked Lynch. "Like a drawer full of spare bullets? Or are you dusting Fisher-Price people for fingerprints?"

"Just the usual routine," Lynch said. He was watching a crime lab cop in a white jacket, perched on his hands and knees in a far corner of the living room, picking at Terri's rug with tweezers.

"If you're looking for fibers from Richie's rug," she said, "they're probably all over. I've been in his apartment, and he's been in mine. In fact, this particular search is a serious waste of taxpayer money."

Except, Terri thought, if you want to frighten someone. And then it occurred to her: perhaps they were trying to frighten Chris, to see what he would do. Lynch, she saw, was watching her; he was not Monk's partner for nothing, Terri thought—his deferential mask was an act.

Another crime lab cop came from the hallway with Terri's gray suit. "We'll want to keep that for a while," Lynch told her calmly. "We'll give you a receipt, of course."

It was that, strangely, which made her angry. "I don't have that many suits, Inspector. And I don't have *any* with gunshot residue, blood spatters, or traces of cerebral cortex on the hemline. I'd like you to leave that here."

The crime lab guy turned to Lynch. When Lynch gave him a querying look, the man pointed to a round spot on the lapel.

"Ketchup," Terri said disgustedly. "From McDonald's. Elena spilled it when she was sitting in my lap."

Lynch shrugged. "Got to check it out, that's all."

Terri stared at him. "I'm sure you've been to McDonald's. Why don't you just lick it?"

Lynch shook his head, as if disappointed by how hostile Terri seemed. Ignoring him, she began to read the warrant. It told her, as it was designed to, nothing at all. Nor did Lynch say anything much before he left, taking with him two crime lab cops, three evidence bags of rug fibers, a woman's gray suit, and the tape from her answering machine. It was the last which reminded Terri that she could not call Chris to warn him.

NINE

WHEN PAGET ARRIVED HOME, still dressed in tennis clothes and sunglasses, there were two squad cars in the driveway, and Carlo was waiting for him on the front porch. His face was pale; the door was open behind him, and Paget heard voices coming from inside. Carlo held some papers.

"Monk?" Paget asked under his breath. When Carlo nodded, Paget took the warrant from his hand. It allowed a broad search; as always, it did not explain the basis on which the police asserted that there was "probable cause" to comb Paget's home for evidence in the death of Ricardo Arias.

"I tried to keep them out," Carlo murmured. "One of the cops grabbed my arm and told me to stay in one place and be quiet."

His tone was shaken and embarrassed. Paget paused to touch his shoulder.

"There was nothing you could do," he said reassuringly, and stalked into his house in search of Monk.

A red-haired cop was standing in Paget's library, peering into his fireplace. Carlo's childhood games had been pulled out of their cabinet and turned upside down: Monopoly money and playing cards were strewn across the Persian rug. To Paget, it was a violation of the life he had shared with his son; his rage was so deep that he found it difficult to think.

"Where's Monk?" he demanded.

The cop turned to him, surprised. "You're not supposed to be in here."

"I *live* here," Paget snapped. "I asked where Monk was."

The cop's youthful face turned cold. "You'll have to sit on the porch, sir. Unless you want me to cuff you."

Paget tilted his head. "Are you aware that I'm a lawyer?"

The cop shrugged his contempt: the police, Paget knew, often considered criminal lawyers to be as dirty as their clients, cynical profiteers in a conspiracy to break the law. To tear apart the house of a wealthy defense lawyer was more than a duty; it was a deeply satisfying act of class warfare. When Paget did not move, the cop took the handcuffs off his belt and started toward him.

"Because," Paget said coolly, "your warrant is fucked up. So before you do something truly stupid, go find someone who's capable of understanding why."

Paget's voice was tight; maintaining calm seemed to cost him a great deal. But the cop had stopped halfway across the room, the first flicker of hesitation in his eyes. "I'll give you a clue," Paget continued. "When you find Charles Monk, take him aside and whisper the words 'Special Master' in his ear. He'll be quite impressed with your insight."

The cop flushed at Paget's tone of contempt; the stain on his face emphasized freckles, making him look like a teenager out of his depth. Like Carlo, just moments before.

"You wait right here," the cop ordered, and went upstairs. The petty satisfaction Paget felt vanished abruptly: Monk was prowling through his bedroom, he knew, with special attention to his clothes and shoes.

Suddenly Paget heard the voice of his housekeeper.

Walking to the living room, he saw the dark-haired Cecilia, a Nicaraguan woman with haunted eyes and a husband who had been murdered by guerrillas. She sat beneath the Matisse print of a dancer, warily answering the questions of a plainclothes detective with a tape machine. The sense of his own impotence hit Paget with a rush: the cops could ask what they wanted of whomever they wanted, take whatever they wanted, and Paget could do nothing but apologize to Cecilia.

As he walked across the living room, the detective turned to him. "I'm sorry," Paget said to Cecilia. "But this will be over soon."

She looked up at him with a look of fear and shame; in the depths of her soul, she knew that authority had no limits. The detective, a brown-haired man with a brush cut and sad eyes, said to Paget, "You'll have to go outside."

"Oh, I'm waiting here," Paget said. "For the Special Master."

Eyeing Paget with a look of wary thought, the man pulled some glasses out of his pocket, as if about to read the fine print on a contract. Paget looked past him to Cecilia. "Tell them whatever they want," he said softly. "Nothing you say can hurt me."

Paget felt a gentle hand on his shoulder. Turning, he discovered Monk, with the young cop next to him.

"I told him not to move," the cop told Monk.

Please, the cop's tone said, bust this asshole. Paget smiled at him. "There are more games in the library. Carlo used to like the one called Masterpiece." He shrugged. "Of course, you'd have to know something about art."

Monk stepped between them; something in his yellow-brown eyes suggested that he had understood Paget's anger. "Are there any legal files in the library?" he asked Paget.

"No."

He addressed the young cop. "Finish the library, then. And check with me before you do anything else."

Monk's voice, calm and professional, suggested that Paget's sarcasm was beneath the young cop's notice. The cop's face relaxed a little, and then he left the room.

Monk folded his arms. "You shouldn't do that," he remarked to Paget.

It was odd; Monk's invasion of Paget's home seemed to bind them in a kind of intimacy, within which Monk could advise Paget on how to accept this new reality. Paget shrugged again. "What difference would it make, Charles? You going to go easier on me?"

"Nope." Monk peered at him. "You keep files here?"

Paget nodded. "So let's review where we are. To inspect legal files, you need a Special Master to screen them for privileged materials. You haven't got one, or the warrant would have said so."

"True," Monk said calmly. "But if the lawyer in question is a target of the inquiry, you don't need one."

Paget stared at him. "Am I a target? If you could justify that, you'd have enough to arrest me for murder. Which you damn well don't, or I'd be downtown right now." He paused. "The D.A. screwed up."

Monk appraised him. "Even if you were right," he said slowly, "just tell me where your files are, and we won't look at them. 'Cause I don't give a damn about files."

But Paget was determined to eke out this small victory. "It won't work—they're mixed in with other stuff. Besides, I bring work home at night, and sometimes I forget where I put my papers. So wherever you go, *I* go. Or you don't go anywhere."

Monk was silent. Paget could follow his calculations: Paget might be playing games with him, but by going through the wrong papers, Monk could risk suppression of the evidence he did obtain. Paget guessed that he was wondering if, in his unsettled state of mind, Paget might betray some piece of evidence that concerned him or make an unguarded remark.

"Where have you been so far?" Paget asked.

"Just your bedroom."

"Then let me speak to Carlo, and we can go back upstairs. But the deal is that we take it a room at a time, with me present. Anyone who isn't with us waits outside the house."

Monk gazed past him at Cecilia and at the plainclothesman. "You about through?" he asked the man.

"Uh-huh."

"Then you can pack up your stuff and leave. I'll do the rest."

Paget turned and went to the porch. It was perhaps five o'clock; Carlo was on the steps, sitting in the shadow of the incongruous palm tree that, when he was seven, he had loved so much that he begged Paget to buy the house.

Paget sat down next to him. "Sorry," he said softly.

When Carlo turned to him, Paget was startled to see that his eyes were moist. "This scares me, Dad."

Paget touched his shoulder. "It's hard to realize that they can do this to you. But what they're looking for is evidence of some crime. There's nothing to find here."

Carlo clasped his hands. He looked like a young boy holding on tight; for his son's sake, it was all Paget could do not to hug him.

"Didn't you and Katie have plans?" Paget asked. "I remember something about a movie."

Carlo gave a listless shrug. Suddenly, desperately, Paget did not wish for him to be here when the cops tore apart their home. He took some money from his wallet. "Here," he told Carlo. "Take Katie to dinner. Don't let Monk ruin *her* night too."

Carlo shook his head. "I just want to stick around."

"There's nothing you can do. I've got to deal with the cops, and they won't even let you back inside." He squeezed his son's shoulder. "After dinner, go see a movie. By the time it's over, we'll have our house back."

Carlo turned to him, hesitant. "Please, son," Paget said quietly.

Carlo scanned his face more closely; in that moment, Paget saw him understand how much this pained his father. He stood, still looking at Paget, unsure of what to say. "Call me," Paget told him, "if you're going to be past ten or so."

It made Carlo smile a little. "Ten-thirty," he said, and walked down the steps to his car.

Turning, Paget encountered Cecilia in the doorway. With mingled embarrassment and fear for him, she looked into Paget's face. "They ask me to leave," she explained. "But I can come back later, Chris. To help clean up."

To hear his name pronounced "crease," as Cecilia spoke it, sometimes made Paget smile inside. It did not make him smile now: in Cecilia's mind, the America where Paget lived had been a safer place than the Nicaragua where her husband had died, and no amount of explaining would change her first instinctive reaction to what the police would leave behind.

Paget shook his head. "Go home, CiCi. Read to the children. Tomorrow, if I need it, you can help me."

He squeezed her hand and went inside.

They were already in his bedroom. Monk had permitted the young cop to stay; when Paget entered, he had taken a pair of Terri's panties from the nightstand on her side of the bed and was holding them to the light. He waited until Paget saw him and then, as Monk started in on Paget's closet, turned the drawer of the nightstand upside down and spilled Terri's perfume bottles and diaphragm onto Paget's bed.

An hour after sunset, Paget sat in the dining room amid the ruins of his home, drinking Courvoisier from a snifter Monk had left out on the table. At his feet were broken pieces of his grandmother Kenyon's china serving platter, a gift at her wedding eighty years before: the young cop had knocked it off the china cabinet and, when Paget turned at the sound, blandly apologized for his clumsiness.

It was the last room they had reached. By then the house was a wreck: Paget's and Carlo's drawers overturned; clothes strewn on the carpet; books tossed about like refuse, and silverware scattered on the kitchen floor. Paget had expected this: from his own clients' experience, he knew that the police never picked up what they did not take.

They had taken very little, mostly from Paget's bedroom. Three gray suits, to check for bloodstains or traces of Ricardo Arias's hair or bone or brain matter. Several pairs of shoes, to inspect for fibers from Richie's rug. A checkbook register that might reflect the purchase of a Smith & Wesson older than his grandmother's broken china. All that Paget had expected; only when Monk demanded the keys to Paget's Jaguar convertible, explaining that the crime lab people would return it in a week or so, did Paget notice that the last item on the warrant called for the impoundment of his car.

The crime lab, the warrant stated, would need to check the car under ultraviolet light. Paget watched the young cop drive it away; it seemed to Paget that he had stopped at the head of the driveway, despite the absence of any traffic, and gazed at Paget in the rearview mirror.

When the police had left at last, Paget went to close his empty garage. The block that had formerly hidden the leather-bound journal was tossed to one side; carefully, Paget replaced it.

They had found nothing, he knew, in the library.

Now he sat alone in the dining room.

A few moments before, Terri had called for the second time: she had said just enough to tell him that she, too, had been searched. But she could not come to him, nor he to her. Rosa was unable to watch Elena that evening, and Paget had a house to make less ravaged before his son returned.

Looking around him at the mess, he took the last warm swallow of brandy.

His run for the Senate was in serious trouble. Tomorrow he would think about that; it seemed a small thing now.

Why, he wondered, had Monk chosen suits that were gray?

He went to the kitchen, threaded his way through the pots and pans on the floor, and picked up the telephone.

Outside, through his windows, the city dropped toward the bay, a smooth oval of blackness, and the lights of Marin County twinkled in the hills beyond. The telephone he had dialed rasped in his ear.

"Hello?" the woman answered.

"Caroline? This is Chris Paget."

"*Christopher.*" The woman's well-bred voice, nasal and faintly New England, conveyed a certain ironic pleasure. "What a pleasant surprise."

"Not for me, I'm afraid. It seems I'm in need of a lawyer."

"For *you?*"

"Uh-huh."

Briefly, Paget heard the silence of her surprise. "Well," Caroline Masters replied, "at least you can afford me."

quired a certain bearing: she carried herself so perfectly that the first
impression she gave was of some electric combination of aristocrat
and stage actress. She was an extraordinarily handsome woman, a
year or two younger than Paget—aquiline features; glossy black
hair; deep-set brown eyes beneath a high forehead and widow's
peak—and Paget was certain that she knew how striking she was.
But the public Caroline Masters seemed designed in part to divert
attention from the private one, about whom people knew almost
nothing. Even her office was decorated like a résumé—her law
school diploma; her judicial appointment; a seascape of Martha's
Vineyard—which added nothing to the known facts of her life. But
for Paget, one fact was enough: Caroline Masters was a superb
lawyer.

"Well," she said after a time, "there's no doubt you have motive
enough for three murders. It also appears that, depending on when
the lamentable Mr. Arias died, you were either in Italy, on an airplane or—on the night before you left—without an alibi worth
mentioning."

"All true."

Caroline tented her hands. "What do the police know," she asked
carefully, "about where you were that night?"

"What I told them is that I was home all night."

Caroline's eyes narrowed. "And the police have that on tape?"

Paget turned to the window: the day was sunless, and the tops of
buildings vanished in morning fog. "That's right."

"And now they've taken three gray suits." Letting the statement
linger, Caroline seemed to watch him more closely. "I don't need to
tell you what that may mean, Christopher."

Paget felt an eerie helplessness, as if at the discovery of an unknown enemy. "A potential eyewitness."

Caroline nodded. "At least one. Perhaps someone who believes
that he or she saw a man in a gray suit, somewhere near Richie's
apartment, on the night before you left for Italy."

Paget fell silent. He was already certain that Caroline would not
ask if he had murdered Ricardo Arias. For a defense lawyer, this restraint was common sense—the answer, if it was yes, would prevent
her from preparing the best defense. What Caroline would want to
know was far more practical: what had Paget told the police, and

TEN

"IF I WERE YOU," Caroline Masters said the next morning, "I might have considered torturing Richie first. But I gather you killed him straightaway."

Paget nodded. "More time-efficient. Getting the gun in his mouth was hard enough."

Caroline smiled over her cup of black coffee. "It's good to see you again, Christopher. I'm just sorry it's because the police made themselves so at home."

But Caroline was merely surprised. Paget was disoriented. Part of it was the lingering disbelief that he needed a lawyer; the other was seeing Caroline Masters again. Caroline had been the judge in the Carelli hearing, the star of a televised morality play watched by millions of viewers. Offers had poured in, Paget knew—law, politics, even the media: in the end, Caroline had accepted a partnership in San Francisco's largest firm, Kenyon and Walker, because it best served her ambitions.

It made sense for both sides. Caroline not only was a draw for clients but had been an exceptionally skilled defense lawyer; with her combination of criminal-law toughness and Eastern pedigree, Caroline could make the most arrogant board chairman feel well represented. For Caroline, it meant four hundred thousand dollars a year; a panoramic view of the city; and a new base of supporters for her ultimate ambition—a high federal judgeship. All of this confirmed Paget's sense that life had a certain ironic symmetry: his great-grandfather Kenyon had founded the firm in the 1870s, to service his own father's railroad, and Paget had never set foot in its offices.

Caroline herself seemed quite at home. She had greeted him with the brisk assurance of someone who graced the firm by being there. At five feet eight, Caroline had long since learned that height re-what else might they think they knew. Only the system, Paget knew, presumes a defendant's innocence; his lawyer cannot. That this reality now applied to him felt alien and depressing.

"A word of advice," Caroline said. "No more chats with Monk. As it is, we're going to have to live with what you've said already."

In retrospect, Caroline was right, and she was only saying what Paget would have said in her place. But to receive the advice felt different than to give it. "Do you know why I talked to them?" he asked.

Caroline raised an eyebrow; she did not look convinced that she wished to hear this. Paget leaned forward. "Because I didn't kill him."

Caroline picked up her coffee cup, still watching him; she sipped briefly and put it down again, as if the contents had grown cold. "No?"

"No. In fact, I assumed that the little scumbag shot himself."

"And what do you think now?"

"That the cops think someone killed him. But it wasn't me. If it had been, I'd have come to you before I said a word to Monk."

Caroline shrugged. "Which, in Monk's eyes, would have drawn suspicion like a magnet. You'll get no credit from *him* for talking." She toyed with her reading glasses. "Unless, of course, he thinks you answered his questions truthfully."

It was as subtle as Kabuki theater, Paget knew: Caroline had already guessed that he would not respond to this. When he did not, she said, "So let's continue with the possible reasons for our friend's skepticism. If you don't mind."

Her tone was so arid that Paget almost smiled. "No," he said. "I don't mind."

"For example, Christopher, what do you think they meant to accomplish by turning your house upside down?"

"Scare me into doing something funny, I suppose. Perhaps trying to destroy evidence."

"Possibly. But what evidence could they hope to find?"

Paget shrugged. "The obvious. Bullets. A receipt for the purchase of a gun. Some small memento of the late Ricardo—blood or hair or tissue. Perhaps some fibers from his rug. Which may be why they wanted the car."

Caroline nodded. "Fibers might help them. But only if you'd never been to Richie's at any *other* time. What did you tell them about *that?*"

"That I never had. At *any* time."

Caroline paused for a moment. "So what do you think they'll find?"

"Nothing," Paget said softly. "Except maybe fibers from Richie's rug."

Caroline's eyes narrowed. "That," she said, "would not be helpful."

"You forget Terri. She went to Richie's regularly, to pick up or drop off Elena. And, of course, she's often at my place. So it depends on where the fibers were found—on my shoes, for example, or just on the rug."

Caroline's mouth formed a smile. "It seems that your relationship with Terri has complicated a number of things, Christopher. Including the evidence." She leaned back in her chair. "Are you sure it's not *Terri* that Monk's after? They searched her apartment, after all."

Paget shook his head. "Maybe, in the middle of the night, Monk imagines that we plotted Richie's death together. But I'm pretty sure it's me they want."

How, he saw Caroline wonder, can you be certain? But of course she did not ask. "Still, this makes me sad for her," she said finally. "When she worked for me, at the P.D.'s office, Teresa was among the best of my young lawyers. But I thought her clearly the best *person*—fair, nonjudgmental, and compassionate. Some people become as hard as their life. It never seemed that Terri was."

Paget tilted his head. "Did you ever meet Richie?"

Caroline looked surprised, and then guarded. "You never did?" she asked.

Paget met her eyes. "Monk asked me that, of course. I told him no."

Looking down, Caroline touched an earring; the gesture seemed designed to cover an awkward conversational transition. "I met Richie once or twice," she said. "At Christmas parties, that kind of thing."

"What did you make of him?"

Caroline was thoughtful. "That he was very engaging," she said at last, "to whoever was put in front of him. And that whoever it was didn't matter to Richie at all."

"A performer?"

The phrase seemed to connect with her. "My least favorite people, Christopher, are cocktail party joke-tellers. Because what matters to them is not who's laughing but only the sound of laughter. Richie was something like that." She looked more closely at Paget. "Why do you ask?"

Her repeated use of "Christopher"—formal, familiar, and ironic all at once—made Paget smile momentarily. "Because if there's ever a trial, Richie's state of mind may be an issue. Including the likelihood of suicide."

Caroline considered him. "We're a little ahead of ourselves," she said at last. "At least about a trial. Unless there's something the police know, or think they know, that you haven't told me."

The elliptical formula drew a second smile from Paget, smaller and briefer. "Only," he said with irony, "if the police know, or think they know, something that I don't know they know."

A fleeting smile from Caroline. "What about Teresa?" she asked. "Is she looking for counsel?"

"Not yet."

"Whoever, Christopher, it can't be me. You understand why."

Paget nodded. "In theory, one of us may have killed him. Which would create a small conflict between clients."

Caroline nodded. "Thank you for being so professional about it. Also, *both* of you may be witnesses. Which means not only that the three of us can't meet but that you can't talk to Terri about anything we say."

"I understand."

"You look a bit unhappy with that."

Paget hesitated. "The rules for targets," he said finally, "are the opposite of the rules for lovers."

Paget watched Caroline consider this thought and then saw it lead to another. "Isn't there something curious about all of this?"

"You mean how nasty they've been?"

Caroline nodded. "It's not like Charles Monk and, normally, it's not like the district attorney. Even if McKinley Brooks is still pissed off about the Carelli case."

"If it's the Carelli case Mac's mad about," Paget responded, "I should get any other lawyer except you. But I don't think it's the Carelli case, at least not directly. Try the magic words 'James Colt'?"

Caroline's lips parted; the expression was somewhere between the dawn of comprehension and the beginning of a startled laugh. *"Junior,"* she said. "Of course. McKinley Brooks's new best friend, ever since Mac conceived ambitions to be something more than district attorney."

Paget nodded. "Junior not only wants to be governor; he wants to control the party in this state should *his* ambitions become even loftier. He does *not*, he's made quite plain, wish for me to be a senator, and I'm equally sure Brooks knows that. I think I've just been warned."

Caroline folded her hands. "Knowing that could be useful to us. If it's true."

"Now? Or at trial? When we suggest that they're on a witchhunt?"

Caroline did not smile. "You don't want a trial. But what I *will* do, soon, is go see Brooks and whatever assistant D.A. is monitoring Monk's adventures. To see whether I can talk them out of this, or at least hear what's on their minds."

Paget sat back. "As we talk, Caroline, a question occurs to me. Is this case very good for you?"

Her eyes narrowed a bit; the expression this left was the cousin of a smile but much keener. "Are we referring to the rumors that I harbor certain ambitions?"

"I'm referring to the fact that if he becomes governor, James junior is the one who passes out state judgeships."

Only the ghost of a smile now. "True. But state court bores me. And it's United States senators, as you well know, who recommend on federal judgeships."

Paget laughed aloud. "I'm yours, Caroline. For whatever *that's* worth after all this is over."

Caroline shrugged. "Well," she said, "that's *my* job, isn't it."

Turning, Paget gazed out the window, pensive again. It was a typical San Francisco morning: the fog was thinning, and shafts of sunlight had begun to bring color to the high-rises, a sheen to the glass. Coming here was the best thing he could have done: much more than sympathy, he found a certain astringent comfort in Caroline's sheer intelligence and lack of sentiment. "Anyhow," he told her, "I'm glad you're doing this. For my sake, at least."

Caroline gave him an ironic look. "For your sake," she said dryly, "so am I."

Paget stood. "I guess that's it, then," he said, and shook Caroline's gracefully extended hand. "Please let me know if you have any other thoughts."

"I shall. In the meantime, Christopher, try not to worry about this more than is necessary to help me. And do give Terri my best."

Paget headed for the door. "Actually," Caroline said, "there *is* one other thing."

Paget turned to her. "What's that?"

"When they give you back the Jaguar, put it in the garage. And mothball the Armani suits, or whatever they are. From now until you're off the hook, I'd like you to imagine yourself on camera and the television audience as jurors."

When Paget raised his eyebrows, Caroline smiled. "You're a very attractive man, Christopher. I've always thought so. But for a prospective defendant, you're just a bit too elegant."

ELEVEN

TERRI SAT on her living room couch, wearing a flannel nightgown and her first pair of reading glasses. Legal files were scattered around her, and the television news was on "mute." The apartment itself was bare—worn couch and borrowed chairs, a cheap wooden breakfast table for Terri and Elena—and the one floor lamp she had gotten from Richie highlighted the room's bleakness. It was just past eleven.

"We're a long way from Italy," she said to Paget.

"Not as long as I'd like."

She gave him a look that mixed worry and inquiry. It was the first time they'd been able to talk since the police had searched their homes. Wary of the telephone, and tied up in trials, they'd been reduced to meeting at Terri's once Elena had fallen asleep. "What do you think is wrong?" she said.

Paget hesitated. "Politics is my guess. I think James Colt wants to stop me from running for the Senate."

Terri frowned. "Do you have any proof of that?"

Paget felt a moment's discomfort. His mind and Terri's usually followed the same paths; tonight Terri's professional skepticism seemed to open a distance between them. As foolish as it was, what Paget most wanted was an accepting lover.

"No proof," he said finally. "Just logic."

Terri shook her head. "Politics only takes you so far. They think Richie was murdered and that one of us has lied. Maybe, because of politics, someone hopes it's you."

Paget considered her. "I don't think they even need *that* much. James Colt is clever enough to know that the stench of a criminal inquiry would scare most politicians and prejudice most voters. Particularly when the subjects are murder, adultery, and child abuse." Pausing, Paget realized how trapped he felt. "Never, in his wildest dreams, would Richie have believed that his obsession with us would outlive him."

Terri appraised him. Softly, she said, "Not unless he killed himself."

Her watchful expression, the few quiet words, hit Paget like a shock. "What does *that* mean?"

Terri placed her hand gently on his wrist. "That there's something you're not telling me, Chris. Perhaps more than one something."

He withdrew his hand, as if from a flame. "Would you care to give me an example?"

Terri stared at his hand, then into his face again. "What I'd like, really, is for you to tell me."

Suddenly Paget felt cornered. "All right," he snapped. "I murdered the little bastard. So that you could afford new furniture."

There was a first flash of resentment in Terri's eyes. "Do you think I *like* this? Wondering if there's something I don't know?" Her voice slowed. "My entire relationship with Richie—maybe my whole life—was based on questions I never asked and thoughts I told myself to stuff. You and I can't be like that. . . ."

"This isn't relationship counseling, damn it. It's a possible homicide, in which you and I are potential witnesses. And as long as we're not married, there's nothing I could say to you that Monk or McKinley Brooks or some hotshot assistant D.A. couldn't grill you about for hours." Paget forced himself to speak more softly. "One of us might have to testify about anything we say to each other, perhaps against the person who says it. That's why I so seldom ask you where you found the gun."

Terri gave him a startled look. "You don't think that *I* killed him."

"No, as it happens. But if we're ever forced to testify, even asking you the question could do great damage. Unless, of course, I simply lie about this conversation." He paused. "Or, perhaps, forget we ever had it."

Terri's gaze broke. "Jesus," she murmured. "How can we *be* like this?"

Paget raised the hand that had been damaged. He kept it there, in front of Terri, until she looked up. "Isn't that what you've been doing? Forgetting things? Especially for Monk."

Terri could only stare at him.

"Forgetting isn't much fun," Paget went on. "Is it, Terri? Especially when your forgetfulness is just another form of lying."

Terri's face composed itself, and then she looked at him directly. "And not talking," she answered, "makes me feel dead inside."

Paget turned away. "I know. About that and several other things, I'm very, very sorry."

She searched his face for meaning. "You don't have to be sorry. Just tell me the truth, please. No one else will ever know it."

Paget looked back into her eyes. "Only this, Terri." He emphasized each word. "*I did not kill Ricardo Arias.*"

Terri stared at him. "And you have no idea who did."

"None. Unless it was Richie. Just as you said."

Terri glanced down the hallway to the bedroom, as if Elena might hear them. Paget saw a tremor run through her, half shudder and half sigh. Beside them, the television flickered silently: talking heads and news tapes—a fire, a double murder, an interview at a homeless shelter. Terri turned to him again. "But you think there's going to be a trial, don't you?"

To answer truthfully, Paget found, made him feel as if he were calling down a curse. "I don't know," he said finally. "But I no longer assume there won't be. That's why I hired Caroline. And it's why, as much as I might want to, you and I can never talk about this."

Terri sat back, as if absorbing this new reality, and then something at the edge of Paget's vision became part of his consciousness.

Turning to the television, he saw the face of James Colt, his lips moving without words. Terri had followed Paget's gaze; reaching for the remote, she switched on the sound.

"I'm running for governor," Colt was saying to a microphone, "on the basis of trust." His voice was light but pleasant; his suntan and his white-gold hair brought a touch of southern California to the blue-gray eyes and cleft chin, a replica of his father's. "Private character is the key to public leadership. I believe that any person seeking high office in the state of California should live a private life that voters can respect and their children can admire. And no one who fails to meet that test has any place in *public* life."

"Maybe I'm paranoid," Paget murmured, "but did you just hear a message?"

Terri looked at him as if about to ask a question, and then she seemed to think better of it. When they turned back to the television, Colt was gone.

TWELVE

"So Elena had the nightmare again," Rosa said to Terri.

They sat on a bench in Dolores Park, where Terri and her sisters once had played. It was a sunny morning, and the rolling sweep of grass, sheltered by thick and leafy palm trees, did not look like the drug exchange and gang refuge it became after dark. There were swings and slides some distance away; Elena, active for once but plainly tired, had climbed a playground structure to the top and was gazing out at the park, alone. She showed no interest in the children playing beneath her.

Terri watched her daughter. "After Chris left," she answered. "For a moment, when I came to her room, she thought I was Richie."

"How do you know that?"

"She called out 'Daddy.'" Terri shook her head. "Maybe she'd heard Chris's voice."

When Rosa turned to watch Elena again, it was with a heightened attentiveness. After a time, she asked, "Did Elena say anything else?"

"Not really. She seemed to realize where she was, and then she put her arms around me."

Pensive, Rosa fell quiet, and Terri let the subject drop. She could not mention her conversation with Chris; whatever problems they had must stay between them, and Terri preferred that her mother believe the police to be satisfied and Richie's suicide a settled matter. As far as Terri knew, this was so: since Richie's death, her mother's concern had been its effect on Elena, not its status with the police.

Now, as usual, Rosa seemed to watch her granddaughter. Even sitting on a park bench, she was impeccable—a turtleneck sweater and wool slacks, earrings and makeup, a gold bracelet on her slender wrist. Looking at her, Terri sometimes imagined a second Rosa, an elegant woman who lived in the hills above Acapulco and flew to Europe when she wished to get away. A woman, Terri thought sadly, who would never allow a man to beat her.

"And you?" Rosa asked finally. "Are you still having *your* dream?"

It was the closest Rosa came to speaking of Terri's father. All Terri had told her was that she was having her dream again—"the one from junior high school." Terri did not have to tell Rosa whom the dream concerned. She had done that the first night it had come: Rosa, her husband barely two weeks dead, had held Terri close without speaking a word.

"Every few nights now," Terri said. "I've been wondering if I should talk it over with Dr. Harris."

Rosa grazed her hair with her fingers. "Do you think that's wise, Teresa. To stir things up inside you?"

It was, Terri knew, the credo by which her mother had learned to live. All at once, it struck Terri that there was too much silence in her life. Softly, she asked, "Why did you never leave him, Mama?"

In profile, her mother's eyes widened. But what cut to Terri's heart was the way her body became rigid; it was how she had held herself when Ramon Peralta slapped her. Only when the silence continued did Terri realize that Rosa meant to act as if she had not heard the question.

"Mama?"

Rosa flinched, almost imperceptibly. Terri put a hand on her thin shoulder. "I love you, Mama. Talk to me, please."

Slowly, Rosa turned to her. The look on her face was frightening; each line seemed etched with pain, and her eyes had a depth of passion that was almost fierce. "*You* ask why I stayed with him?"

The simple words carried the anguish of a life lived for others and, beyond this, of Elena's problems now. Their impact on Terri was like a blow.

"I know," she said quietly. "You stayed for us."

"For *you*, Teresa." Her mother stared into her eyes. "I do not say this easily, and never to your sisters. But when I lay next to him at night, it was *your* face I saw."

Terri felt this with the certainty of the girl who had watched her mother in the living room, her face bruised, silently urging her child up the darkened stairs as Ramon Peralta took her from behind. It was as if Ramon had bonded them for life; yet Terri, the woman, felt Rosa use the guilty underside of this unspoken bond to silence her. "I believe you," she answered. "But what I need from you now is to help me understand my life. *Our* life."

Her mother's eyes hardened. "For what?" she demanded. "So that we can wallow in something that's best forgotten?"

Terri gripped Rosa's shoulder. "The 'something' is my *father*. And he's *never* been forgotten. I dream about him. Even our conversations, the ways we find not to speak of him, are like a memorial to what he did to us. Like how we used to whisper when he passed out on the couch, afraid that he'd wake up and hit you again."

Rosa turned pale: suddenly Terri felt her mother's humiliation at being confronted with what their life had been. "Mama," she said softly, "I don't judge you. I *never* will. You loved me, and you got me to where I am, a mother with a child we *both* love more than anything. But there's a part of you, a part of my life, that is lost to me. Sometimes I think, because of that, I've failed Elena without knowing why." She looked into her mother's face. "Can you understand that?"

Rosa lowered her gaze and then slowly shook her head; Terri could not tell whether this was Rosa's answer or a plea to be left alone. But after a moment, Rosa asked in an ashen voice, "What is it you wish to know?"

"Why, whether for us or for me, you stayed with him. And what happened to you because of that."

In silence, her mother peered up at Elena. The little girl was sitting atop the play structure, doing nothing of note; Rosa watched her still. "Elena's so passive," she murmured.

"I know."

Rosa exhaled slowly. "All right, Teresa. We will do this once. And never again." She gazed off into the distance. "The answer is this: I stayed with him because a girl I barely remember now, but who in my mind seems much like you, thought that all Ramon Peralta needed to escape his fears was her. And because by the time she knew better, her first daughter had been born."

Terri felt unspeakably sad. "What was he afraid of?"

"Himself." Rosa's voice was filled with irony. "His father used to beat him. Ramon was afraid of ending up like that."

"*My God*, Mama." Suddenly, Terri had the eerie sense of watching her mother head toward a fate that only Terri could see. "Before you were married, did you know that?"

"You must understand the Ramon I met." Rosa leaned back, smoothing her slacks; she did not face Terri. "He was just out of the navy, handsome and eager for life. I thought it nice just to watch him. But then I saw how uncertain his smiles were, how much he wanted me to like him—that was when my heart went out to him. This man, who could be so much, needed me to help him." Her mouth set in a grim line. "I was right, Teresa. For as long as he lived, Ramon needed me."

Terri felt a kind of strange relief. Turning to her mother, she said, "So you *didn't* know how he would be."

Rosa tilted her head, as if asking the question of herself. "I'm not sure," she said slowly. "There was this one night, after a dance at the Latin Palace. Ramon had been drinking, and I had danced with someone else. When we got in the car, Ramon slapped me out of nowhere. There were tears in his eyes before I even knew that he had seen the blood on my lip." Again her voice took on an ironic edge. "He laid his head in my lap and began sobbing, begging my forgiveness. The next day, he sent roses."

"But weren't you afraid of him?"

"Because of that?" Rosa gave a small shrug. "To be truthful, Ramon wasn't so different from a lot of other men I had known, starting with my father. Except that Ramon *wanted* to be different." Rosa's voice grew soft. "I had never seen a man cry, you see. It convinced me that he wasn't like my father, brutal and unfeeling. Ramon, I told myself, had so much more love inside him."

Terri tried to recall Rosa's father, her own grandfather. The memory was dim—a stern-looking man who spoke no English but once had bounced her in his lap. There was the faintest sense, perhaps a trick of the mind, that her mother had watched them closely. "After that one time," Rosa continued, "it was as if Ramon had scared *himself* even more than he'd scared me. He never drank when he was with me. And until we were married, he never hit me again." She turned to Terri. "Do you know who reminded me of Ramon before our wedding? Richie. So watchful to see the impression he made on me, with all his plans and dreams and love for you. As if he had something to hide."

Terri felt herself flush. But Rosa, she saw, was not sparring with her; for this moment her mother spoke more honestly than she ever had before. Only the look in her eyes, remote yet touched with shame, betrayed how hard this was.

"And after?" Terri asked.

Rosa reached for the thermos at her feet; on these mornings when they brought Elena to the park, Rosa made thick black coffee from Costa Rica. But until now, this morning's coffee had gone untouched. Rosa filled a plastic cup and handed it to Terri, poured another for herself. "The night we were married," Rosa said at last, "we slept together for the first time. It wasn't much, and it was over quickly. But I was happy we had done this. And then, as I waited in the dark for him to hold me, Ramon said that I was not a virgin. When I began to cry, he slapped me, and took me without asking. It was much more painful than before." Rosa's voice became hushed with memory. "For two weeks after, out of anger and embarrassment, Ramon never touched me.

"It no longer mattered." Rosa's eyes became softer. "For the next eight months I wondered whether you were conceived the first time, filled with my hope, or the second time, the product of his hate. But when you were born, Teresa, and I looked into your face, I knew."

Terri met her mother's gaze. "Couldn't you still have left him, Mama? Even then?"

"To where? A jobless woman with a child? And there was no question, back then, that I *would* have this child." For a moment, silent, Rosa turned to watch Elena. "When I told Ramon I was pregnant," she resumed, "tears leapt to his eyes. He called our families, made a crib for you with his own hands. We were having our firstborn, he said, and would build our family around you.

"After that, he treated me well for a time, and I tried to be happy again. Only later did I understand what a baby truly meant to him." Rosa's eyes were hard now. "He was afraid of more than being his father. He had never loved his father or felt love in return—only fear. Once he *became* his father, he was afraid that no one could love him of their own free will or stay with him *except* from fear. In his mind, you took away my will and gave me something to fear for." Her voice softened. "The child I loved much more than him."

Terri took her mother's hand. "It was as if," Rosa told her quietly, "Ramon knew I could not leave now. A month after you were born, the drinking started again."

Rosa paused, and Terri saw her eyes shut. "Drink changed him, Teresa—brought out all the demons of his nature. One night he saw me nursing you and imagined you were not his. He waited for me to put you in the crib he had made. Then he slapped my breasts until milk came again and I cried out for him to stop. And then, when *you* began crying, he wept and begged my forgiveness. Just as he had before."

Terri's stomach felt tight. But her mother's words kept coming, flat and steady, like raindrops on a stone: Terri had wished to hear this, and now she would. "The next morning," Rosa continued, "I went to see Father Anaya. You remember him, don't you?"

Her mother's eyes had opened again: the question, almost conversational, had a certain lethal quality.

"Yes," Terri said slowly. "I was afraid of him, in his black robe and white collar. But he seemed kind enough."

"Oh, he was *very* kind to me. He took my hand and told me that what Ramon had done was a terrible sin. We were in his chapel, where it was cool and quiet, and for a moment I felt better." Removing her hand from Terri's, Rosa swallowed some coffee, wincing as if at its taste. "And then he explained to me that the kingdom of heaven was God's but that in our home, the man must rule. If I obeyed Ramon in all things, took extra care not to anger him, then our home could be peaceful and happy.

" 'I've done nothing to anger him,' I answered. 'He's just *angry*.'

" 'Then you must be sure never to provoke him,' he told me. 'You have a daughter now, a marriage and family, which are sacrosanct in the eyes of God. If you must do a little more than your part, then console yourself that it is for a reason, to strengthen your family and surround your daughter with love. In time, when you have more children, you will know that this is right.'

"In that moment, I realized that I had ceased to matter. Assuming that I ever had."

Rosa gazed past her: Terri sensed her remembering, as if it were fresh, the truth of her own insignificance. "As I spoke to Father Anaya," Rosa told her, "you slept in the corner of the chapel. I picked you up and looked into your face. You were very small then, Teresa, a funny little face with a few tufts of black hair. But then you opened your eyes and looked back at me, and I saw your eyes were mine. And I swore to you then that the one thing I'd do was take care of you, always. So that you did not end up like me."

Terri shook her head. "You were nineteen years old, Mama."

"I was *married*, Teresa, and a mother. I knew my family would never take me back, even if I had wanted that. There was nothing but to go on with the life I'd made. As Ramon's wife and your mother.

"When I came back, I looked around our home, as if to imagine my future. No one else was there. I remember staring for minutes at the crucifix Ramon had glued to the living room wall. Then I took you upstairs and, in the quiet, nursed you until you fell asleep again.

"When Ramon came home that night, I went to him as a wife.

"He took me twice. There was no tenderness at all. It was as if he had heard Father Anaya speak to me.

"As I lay in there in the dark, it came to me that I would have more children. I was Catholic, and Ramon's wife—there was nothing to prevent this except abstinence, and Ramon would have me as he wished. That was when I saw my life as Father Anaya saw it: I would bear children at the whim of my husband's desire for me, and each one would bind me that much longer to Ramon.

"I turned my back to him and cried. But softly, so he would not hear me. In the morning, as first light came through our window, I promised myself that I would never cry again.

"It just went on like that. There were weeks Ramon would not drink at all: he would go to the garage where he worked, come home at five-thirty, eat without complaint the dinner I had cooked for him. And then something would go wrong—a cross word from his boss, an expense we did not plan on—and he would not be home on time. There would be no call from him; I did not need one. I knew where he was." Rosa sipped coffee, eyes reflective; the gesture had the eerie normality of a woman musing about a contented past. "And then he would come home and beat me for what the world had done to him, until my cries excited him. By the time I was twenty-six, I had five daughters, and the pleasure of knowing that Ramon would *never* have a son."

There was a bitter satisfaction in Rosa's voice. She turned to Terri now. "You were to have been his son, Teresa. He wanted one so desperately that, in the depths of his drinking, he beat me for not giving him one. When Maria was born, and then Eva, the beatings grew worse. For me to then have twin girls was the final insult: after Ynez and Elizabeth were born, he would look at me with hatred in his eyes. But only *I* knew that he would have to beat me forever." Her mouth formed a smile that seemed like a curse. "On Mission Street, in a room above a furniture store, was a woman who read palms. But her real business, people whispered, was abortion. I went to her when Ramon was visiting Guatemala and told her that I wished to have no more children. Only when she realized that I was not pregnant did she understand what I wished for. But she had made enough mistakes aborting babies to do what I asked. . . . "

"Oh, Mama."

Rosa's smile faded; the grasp of her worn hand grew tighter. "I bled for days. But I was very sure that I would *never* give Ramon Peralta a son he could make like him." She sat back, staring into her daughter's face. "Now you know, Teresa, why I never wept when he hit me. It was the price I paid for defeating him."

There was nothing, Terri realized, that she could say. Through her horror, a kind of calm overtook her: she was old enough to face the buried secrets that had bound her family and, in the end, to feel compassion for her mother. "Do my sisters know this?" she asked.

"No. And they never will."

As if by some instinct, mother and daughter turned to watch Elena, Rosa's hand still clasped in Terri's. Elena seemed to gaze at a homeless man pushing a shopping cart across the grass. It struck Terri that, alone in her perch above the park, Elena did not wish to rejoin the world. "At least," Rosa said at length, "you and your sisters had a place to come and go, clothes to wear and food to eat, some sort of structure to your lives. Sometimes, Teresa, I cling to that. As I clung to you."

Terri understood this: of her few memories, the best were of her mother. Rosa showing Terri the things she knew, like cooking and sewing. Helping with Terri's homework. Crawling into Terri's bed at night and holding her close until she fell asleep. With the simplicity of a child, Terri had thought her mother perfect; when Rosa's face was unmarked, it was Terri's deepest wish to look like her mother. This wish had been granted, and perhaps more; to the depths of her soul, Terri suspected, she had become her mother's daughter.

"But how did you *live?*" she asked.

Rosa turned to her in surprise. "You truly wish to hear more?"

Terri looked at her steadily. "Yes, Mama. All of it."

Rosa's eyes narrowed in disbelief. But she did not argue; Terri watched her steel herself. "It grew worse," she said simply. "Much worse. Although I tried to hide that from you."

"You couldn't, Mama. It was like all of us lived in a prison. Except that *we* got out for school."

"A prison—yes. Do you remember that, after the twins were finally in school, I worked for a time?"

"Not really."

Rosa shrugged. "It didn't last for long. We needed the money, and even then I was good enough with figures to be a bookkeeper for a truck rental company. But Ramon was insulted by it. I had never asked him, you see. The night before I was to start, he struck me so hard that my eye was swollen. I went anyway."

Her voice took on a hopeless quality. "Within two weeks, Ramon believed that I was sleeping with my boss. He began calling me at work, dropping in without notice. The beatings, when they came, seemed intended to disfigure me. When still I did not leave, Ramon entered the office one day, knocked all the papers off my desk, and accused me of 'fucking' Joe Menendez—the man I worked for. There were no walls around my desk, only a partition. Everyone heard him." Rosa gazed at the grass in front of her. "The next day, Joe—a nice man with two children—explained that having me there had become too disruptive. He could barely look at me: he had seen Ramon and knew what was happening. But he had an office to run."

Terri touched her eyes. "Wasn't there anyone to help you?"

"The police, you mean?" Rosa gave a mirthless smile and then leaned back against the park bench; it would have seemed the posture of reminiscence, except for her eyes. "A few nights after I was fired, after you were in bed, Ramon tore apart the house. Do you know what he was looking for, Teresa? My birth control pills. The ones that I must be using to deny him a son.

"When he couldn't find them, he began to hit me—on the face and arms and stomach. The bedroom was dark; I could barely see his face. All that came to me was the pain, the whiskey smell of his breath, the hatred in his voice as he said he would not stop until I told him where the pills were. And then he wrenched my arm behind my back until I thought that it would break.

"My face was pressed against the mattress; I could hardly get the words out. 'All right,' I managed to cry, 'I'll tell you the truth. Just let me go.'

"He did that. I waited until my head cleared, and then I reached for the lamp and turned it on.

"Ramon was on his knees, naked to the waist, staring down at me as I lay on the bed. I looked him in the face and, as clearly as I could, said, 'You're not man enough to have a son, Ramon. You're just a man who beats up women.' "

Rosa seemed to shiver at the memory of her pain and hatred. "And then," she said quietly, "the man who was your father beat me until I lost consciousness."

Terri closed her eyes. "When I awoke," Rosa went on, "my vision was blurred. But it was morning; I knew that I should get you to school. And then I heard him downstairs, explaining to you that I was too sick to get up, that he would walk you to Mission Dolores for school. A few minutes later, I saw him crossing the street with you and Maria and Eva, hands linked together and looking both ways for cars. A nun at the crosswalk, waiting for children, smiled at him. The dutiful and loving father." Rosa's voice turned cold. "It was very important, you see, that no one know what happened in the privacy of our home. So important that Ramon threatened to kill me if I ever told.

"Watching him cross the street with you, I decided to call the police. Before he killed me for *not* telling.

"That night, two uniformed police came to our home and asked for Ramon. They took him outside on the steps; I went upstairs, listened through the window. I could barely hear them, but it was enough. They'd had a complaint, they said; they wouldn't make trouble for him this time, but he should know better than to beat me. And then one cop patted him on the shoulder, and they left.

"I could hear his footsteps on the stairs. I was so frightened that I found myself counting each step. But then the sound of his steps turned from our bedroom. For a moment, I was relieved, and then I realized that he'd gone to *your* bedroom. To make sure that you and your sisters were asleep."

Terri swallowed; she had a fleeting memory of her father leaning over her bed to kiss her good night. "What happened?" she asked.

Her mother looked away, toward Elena. "Ramon hit me, of course, and then he turned me over on my stomach. He'd thought of a new way to have me, he said. One that involved no threat of pregnancy." Rosa's voice softened. "I never called the police again."

Terri flinched; all at once, she was at the foot of the stairs again, watching her father take her mother from behind. Only now she understood what she had seen.

"Oh, Mama . . ."

"You wanted to know, Teresa." Rosa's voice was clear again. "After that night, I never knew how much money we had. Ramon hid his checkbook, gave me just enough for food. No one, not even your friends from school, was to be allowed in the house unless he had consented. And I was to tell you, as I did, that no one was to discuss our family with others.

"Ramon was very clever. He knew that if I asked this of you, you were certain to obey. Because *I* was the one you loved, and he was the one you feared. His father, come again."

"People *knew*," Terri said. "I could feel it."

Above her ironic smile, Rosa's eyes were curious. "But did you tell them?"

"No. Never."

"Then they could *pretend*, Teresa. That's all that people want. Because, just as Father Anaya told me, the family is sacrosanct."

Terri shook her head. "I can't accept that people are like that."

"Deep down, we *want* them to be like that. We want to help them not to know." Rosa turned to her. "Just as you did with *your* family, year after year. Helping Richie hide who he was, and others not to see him. You were so determined to marry him, to build the family you thought you'd never had. Only gradually did I see it." Her mother's tone grew softer, and a little sad. "I hadn't given Ramon Peralta a son like him, Teresa. I'd given Ricardo Arias a wife like *me*."

"But I *left*, Mom."

"Yes. You did." Now Rosa's tone became sardonic. "It's an independent woman who can make such choices for her children. But then everything is so different now, isn't it. And Elena has reaped the benefits."

The edge in the words was only the surface, Terri knew, of a grief and anger that Rosa found hard to express. It was that knowledge, and the story Rosa had told, that caused Terri to soften her answer. "And we were better off," she said quietly, "because you stayed."

"Yes. And because I would *threaten* to leave." She turned to her daughter. "You remember, I'm sure, that there were periods of peace in our home, when Ramon did not drink. When he would play with you, even take you places he wanted to go. Perhaps you wondered why, and hoped it would last."

Slowly, Terri nodded; the thought of Fleet Week came to her again, or watching the stars with her father. "I *knew* why," Rosa said. "Just as I knew that it would never last." She smiled a little. "You see, there was one other thing that scared Ramon—being without me. Because deep down inside, just like Ricardo, he was weak. So every few months, when things got too bad, I would tell him I was going away.

"The tears would come, and the begging. 'Please,' he would say, 'I'll change.' " Rosa's voice became ironic again. "If you think about these periods of peace, Teresa, they always began with roses. A gift from your repentant father, sent with a card promising to love me all his life."

All at once, Terri remembered. A dinner: Ramon, smiling at Rosa, had placed roses on the table. At that moment, Terri had thought him wonderful.

"Jesus," she murmured.

Rosa looked at her, as if trying to fathom her feelings. "But he never harmed you, did he?"

"No, Mama. Not with his hands."

"There are men who do worse. Ramon was jealous of me because he was so frightened. And he was right about one thing: when I married him, I was not a virgin.

"One drunken night, when I was fourteen, and more terrified than I can ever tell you, your grandfather found me alone. We never spoke of it again." Her voice was quiet and bitter. "So you see, Teresa, Ramon Peralta was nothing special. My own father taught me that."

THIRTEEN

FROM HER FIRST few moments in the office of McKinley Brooks, Caroline Masters knew that there was something wrong.

It started with Brooks himself. His smile was a little tight; his eyes did not smile at all; and his manner—the easy bonhomie of the city's most successful black politician—for once could not obscure the constant workings of his mind. But what concerned her more was that the assistant D.A. with him was Victor Salinas.

To look at them, Brooks and Salinas were opposites. Brooks was rounding amiably into his mid forties; a decade younger, Salinas had the leanness and intensity of a man who played his daily squash games not for exercise but to win, and his carefully trimmed mustache and handpainted tie lent him a touch of the dandy that Brooks was careful to avoid. But Salinas burned with an ambition as deep as Brooks's own and far less well concealed; there were few in the D.A.'s office who did not know that Salinas was waiting restlessly for a chance at Brooks's job. That Brooks would give this case to Salinas told Caroline that it was something special: either Brooks the lawyer had decided that his need for Salinas's relentlessness outweighed the risk of giving him exposure, or Brooks the politician had decided that the situation called for an assistant as political as he—in which instance, Caroline reflected, Brooks had indeed begun to imagine some higher and better office. To Caroline, either prospect suggested that Christopher Paget was in trouble.

Brooks passed her a cup of the coffee he brewed fresh in his office. "This really *is* a treat, Caroline. I thought you'd gone to a better place, as my granddaddy the Baptist preacher used to say."

This was delivered with a touch more satire than usual: Brooks referred to his Southern roots only as a humorous affectation, and his down-home pronunciation of "Car-o-line" somehow suggested that

Lady Bountiful had come to visit the plantation. But what it told Caroline was that Brooks was a little on edge, and that her handling of the Carelli case still rankled him.

"I'm sure your grandfather was referring to the dead, McKinley. I've just been resting."

From the side, Salinas flashed her a quick smile; like many of his gestures, this seemed his idea of what was appropriate rather than something felt. As a trial lawyer Salinas was not a natural, but he made up for this with a ferocious preparation. Caroline found it easy to imagine him in a gym, pumping doggedly on a bicycle with a grimace on his face and a faraway look in his eyes, planning his day in minute detail.

"Whatever," Brooks was saying to Caroline, "you certainly *look* wonderful. After a while, folks here at the Hall of Justice begin to look like a Hogarth painting—grotesque and a little stooped. Maybe it's the fluorescent lights."

He *does* want out, Caroline thought. Certainly it was ambition, not amenities, that kept Brooks in this job. The Hall of Justice was a rabbit warren of worn green tile and crabbed quarters, and even Brooks occupied a charmless rectangle with a view of a highway overpass. But Caroline doubted that Brooks could easily imagine himself in her place, with no audience to applaud him.

Caroline smiled. "You wouldn't like my new life, Mac—having to perform your wonders in private. That's what makes *your* life so exciting: the high-wire act, with all those avid voters and ambitious rivals waiting to see if you fall off. Or, for that matter, seek higher office."

As he listened, Salinas's eyes seemed to narrow; it struck Caroline that if Brooks fell off the wire on *this* case, Salinas might go with him. "Indeed," Brooks responded, folding his hands across his stomach. "But I'm sure I can count on you to steer me right, Caroline. I always have."

The comment, amiable on the surface, changed the atmosphere abruptly; the reference to the Carelli case was so unsubtle that Caroline wondered if Brooks was trying to distract her. "I don't have any advice," she said amiably. "Just a question. Is there some sort of pent-up demand for Christopher Paget's scalp that I've managed to miss? Or has it become the new style to badger defense attorneys, harass their girlfriends, fingerprint their children, and trash their homes like some mob of French peasants in search of Marie Antoinette?" Caroline smiled. "Oh, and make off with their sports cars—a particularly nice touch, I thought."

Brooks shot Salinas a quick glance. "We don't tell the police how to carry out their job."

Caroline smiled again. "Bullshit."

Brooks leaned back in his chair. "Are you suggesting, Caroline, that we should intervene to make sure that Chris Paget is treated *better* than the average citizen?"

Caroline rolled her eyes. "Oh, McKinley, come *off* it. Name me a multimillionaire from an old family who isn't treated at least a little better than a drug dealer, let alone a famous lawyer and senatorial prospect from the very same political party *you* happen to grace. You can't possibly be *that* livid about the Carelli case."

Brooks shrugged. "Any favors I owe Chris Paget have long ago been discharged. Put it that way."

The failure to deny a grudge was so unlike Brooks that Caroline was sure of her ground. Softly, she said, "It's not the Carelli case, Mac. Please don't insult me."

Salinas, she realized, was giving her the fixed look of someone hoping to learn something. Brooks shifted in his chair and then glanced sideways at the other man.

"Chris has a problem," Brooks said finally. "As you say, he *is* prominent. A possible race for Senator makes him more so. Which makes any case involving him a potential embarrassment to me."

Caroline appraised him. "I wouldn't concern yourself," she said coolly, "with charges of favoritism."

Brooks seemed to sit straighter, as if she had turned the screw another notch. "I can't let people think I'm affected by who he is," he said blandly. "Or what he might become."

"Really? I would have thought by now that you'd have had a conversation or two about the very seat that Chris may run for. Perhaps someone seeking your support for some candidate other than Chris." She paused. "James Colt, for example."

Salinas gazed out the window as if this did not involve him; what Caroline felt was his intense interest in learning—or guessing—what Brooks had kept to himself.

"I can hardly take a position," Brooks answered, "in a race where one of the prospective candidates is involved in a case under active investigation. It's not an inspiration to play politics, Caroline. It's an inhibition."

Caroline smiled. "I never suggested that you were playing politics. Merely that someone with lesser ethics might have an interest in Chris's downfall. So do be sensitive to that particular nuance, Mac. Lest some cynic think that your public-spirited hounding of Christopher Paget is politics in disguise."

Brooks spread his hands in a show of wonder. "Seems like anything Monk does, or doesn't do, must have some hidden meaning for this office. And all because the dead body in question comes with a widow whose boyfriend happens to enter politics."

The last observation, seemingly random, struck Caroline as carefully planted. "Are you suggesting," she asked, "that Chris might be better off if he *left* politics?"

Brooks's eyes widened. "Who am I to say? The only thing I know is that *I'd* be better off. But that's no reason for Chris to *want* to, is it. So I'll just have to keep myself on the straight and narrow." He fixed Caroline with his most candid smile. "A tightrope, just like you said."

Caroline made her own smile puzzled. "Then why walk it at all? After all, Christopher Paget is the least likely killer this side of James Colt."

Brooks looked startled; for a moment, Caroline thought she had gone too far. "Explain that," he said with an air of puzzlement. "About Chris, I mean."

It was time, Caroline knew, to shift the focus. "Just this: Christopher Paget has wealth, political promise, a considerable public reputation, and a son he treasures above any of that. He'd never throw it all away on a piece of scrofula like Ricardo Arias."

"Scrofula?" Salinas put in. "Here's a broke young guy in a custody dispute, with a little girl he's worried sick about, up against his lawyer wife, a boyfriend who's got more money than God, and a kid who may be a child molester. And yet, somehow, Arias manages to fight for what he thinks is right. Talk about an underdog—if there's anyone to feel sorry for here, it's a guy like that who ends up dead."

Caroline was momentarily startled. Salinas, she realized, identified with Ricardo Arias. But what bothered her was something more—he was already thinking about his opening statement and had begun auditioning its politics for McKinley Brooks. And that Salinas's version of Richie was a fun-house mirror of the real man was a depressing reminder of how completely a courtroom can distort reality.

"Nicely done," she said to Salinas in her dryest voice. "And very populist. If only the late Ricardo were fully worthy of your talents." Turning back to Brooks, she added, "If you have something better, enlighten me, and then we'll talk."

"Your *client* has already talked," Salinas put in. "To the police, on tape. Does he have anything to add?" A brief but pointed smile. "Or change?"

Brooks tapped his chin, looking from Caroline to Salinas. "Victor's right," he said finally. "What do you have to offer us that's new?"

The word "offer," elliptical in itself, might suggest some sort of deal. But Caroline could not know. "Right now," she said in a matter-of-fact voice, "your complaint against Chris is that he had reason to dislike Ricardo Arias. Frankly, *I* didn't like Ricardo Arias, and I only met him at cocktail parties. And if Richie *wasn't* trying to blackmail Chris but was the saintly single father you describe, then it's all the more likely that he killed himself in despair over Elena and the plight of children everywhere. Who, I might add, he supported in about the same proportion as he did his own daughter." Turning to Salinas, she smiled again. "No matter how you play him, Victor, Ricardo's sort of a tar baby. I suggest that you consider him more carefully before you imagine the jury weeping."

Salinas's eyes flashed his combativeness. But Brooks's body began to rumble with a suppressed chuckle, all the more theatrical for its silence. "Lord, Caroline," he said finally, "you *are* entertaining. And you *do* make me think. So let us think alone for a while."

Caroline stopped smiling. "Mac," she said in her most clipped tone, "you haven't told me a damned thing. Except that—for whatever reason—you'd rather vamp than talk. Which is the strangest part of all."

Brooks's face went cold. "What I've told you," he answered quietly, "is that we have an investigation, and that it's ongoing. Until *you* tell me something better than that Chris is too pleased with life to shoot someone—no matter how good his motive—that's all I have to say. Although, as always, it's a real treat to see you."

Caroline gave him a small smile. "As always," she said, and turned to Salinas. "You too, Victor."

Standing, Salinas flashed a smile so wide and quick and lacking in warmth that it lent his spectral eyes an eerie deadness. And then he excused himself, and she and Brooks were alone.

Caroline nodded toward the door. "He's an impressive lawyer, Mac. Remember Richard Nixon when he used to smile?"

For a brief moment, silent but intimate, Brooks permitted himself a smile of his own. "Very well," he said finally. "And he became President."

"Only for a while."

Brooks was watching her now. "Speaking of politics, Caroline, not in front of Victor. He might not know when we're just chewing the fat."

"Of course," Caroline said. For the next fifteen minutes, riding a cab to her office, she pondered the meaning of that.

At four-thirty, her telephone rang. "Find out anything?" Chris asked.

"Two things. First, you told Monk something that they don't believe. Maybe about where you were that night."

There was a pause. In a level voice, Paget asked, "What do they think they have? A witness?"

"They won't tell me that." Caroline exhaled. "But the second thing, Christopher, is that you're right. Whatever Mac's doing, James Colt's fingerprints are all over it."

FOURTEEN

"WHAT DO YOU REMEMBER," Harris asked, "about your father's death?"

It was the question Terri had been dreading. "I try *not* to remember it," she answered.

"Why?"

Terri gave her an incredulous look. "Because it was traumatic, Denise. Maybe some people remember more about being young than I do. But how many of them dwell on finding a parent dead?"

Harris raised her head, as if considering Terri's question. "Not all of them repress it," she said at length. "Which perhaps is one reason for your dream—a sort of jailbreak for your subconscious."

Terri felt defensive again; what she had done was so natural that she resented having to explain it. "What do you think I should have done? Taken pictures for the family album?"

"I'm not saying you should have done *anything*." Harris smiled a little. "I'm just asking for whatever you recall after all these years of forgetfulness, all right?"

"But what does this have to do with Elena? Or, for that matter, my relations to Richie and how they might have affected her?"

"I don't know, Terri. But something, perhaps—particularly in terms of how Elena saw *you* react to *her* father. And just like Elena, this nightmare you've had is troubling to you. Perhaps it's better to think about your father's death a little less symbolically."

Terri hesitated. She could think of it, she found, only by shutting her eyes. But when she did this, all that she saw was black; all that she felt was that she should not do this.

"Take your time," Harris said calmly. "I don't mind just sitting here."

Terri shut her eyes again.

The first wisp of memory, breaking through the darkness, was not an image. It was a sound: the closing of a screen door.

A shiver ran through Terri's body. "What is it?" Harris asked.

Terri shook her head. "We had a screen door," she said slowly. "On the back porch. When you closed it, the catch on the door made a kind of soft click. I can hear the sound."

"Where are you?"

The darkness seemed to change slightly: it was no longer the gray light and shadow of eyes held shut but something dark and close. Terri's chest felt tight.

"I don't know," she said softly. "I just don't know."

An image. Rosa behind her, perhaps catching the door as it slipped from her hand. The cat, hungry, rubbed and purred against her leg.

"What's the first thing that comes to you?" Harris asked. "Anything at all."

Terri leaned back in the chair. With her eyes shut, the image was like the particles of night broken by the first light of sunrise. The chair felt as soft as the warm mattress that Terri sank into as a child. As a girl.

Terri cannot sleep.

She has the sensation of broken slumber. The rectangle of her bedroom window, once black with night, frames the first gray sheen of morning, the palm tree outside becoming a dark form, more distinct as minutes pass.

Something is wrong.

She does not know why. There is no sound from her parents' bedroom: this silence is what, when first waking, she always wishes for. Yet the quiet now has a deeper quality, as if something—or someone—is missing. There are goose bumps on Terri's skin.

To calm herself, she takes a kind of mental inventory, recalling the faces of her family the night before. After dinner, her mother had cooked soup, and then Terri had washed dishes. By Rosa's fiat, that job now fell to Maria and Eva—Terri had more homework. But last night her sisters had played Monopoly at the dining room table, laughing and quarreling a little; Rosa had let them do this because their father was not home. Washing dishes, Terri had not asked where he was. There was no need; she could read the tension in

Rosa's body, the distracted way that she wiped the dishes Terri gave her to dry.

Afterward, Terri had gone to her room and finished her algebra. Some part of her listened for her father, the sound of a door opening and closing. She had fallen asleep still listening.

Now, this morning, something is wrong.

Watching the first light through her window, Terri can recall the hours before only as a feverish jumble, the half-light between waking and sleeping. Her eyes feel scratchy with sleeplessness, and her sheets are damp; the restless images of twisting and turning are indistinct, perhaps borrowed from some other night, or from her imaginings, the clammy feeling of the sheets on her skin. As she stumbles from bed, uncertain of her purpose, the hardwood floor is cold beneath her feet. She has left the window cracked open, and the chill of fall hits her face and body.

Terri pauses at the door of her bedroom, feeling the silent house.

It is not quite six. Terri does not know what draws her down the stairs. As she takes them, walking softly, something tightens inside her. And then, perhaps only in her mind, she hears the screen door shut.

She stops there.

It could not have been. There are no footsteps in the house, no sound of the door behind the screen opening or closing. Yet for what seems like minutes, her only instinct is to climb the stairs and plunge into a sleep so profound that she will never awaken to learn what made the noise.

Instead she sits down in the stairwell. Deprived of light, it feels like a prison in which she can neither move nor see. Her heartbeat is light and quick.

The only sound is Terri's breathing.

She tries talking to herself: fourteen is far too old for a child's fears. Standing, she continues. Yet when she reaches the end of the darkened stairs, she half expects to find her parents as they were just days ago, her mother bent over the couch, silently urging Terri up the stairs with her eyes as her mouth makes the cries that Ramon Peralta needs.

Silence. And then, as light breaks into the living room, comes the first sound that Terri senses is real. Something faint but distinct, defined more by direction than by anything it tells her. But the direction frightens her so much that she stops moving.

It is coming from the screen door, or through it: she is certain now. What she cannot comprehend is the bitter taste in her mouth, the pulse in her throat.

Instinctively, she looks around her, as if Rosa will be there for her. There is no one. As she edges through the dining room, toward the kitchen, where the door is, she hears a sound that she knows by heart.

It is La Pasionaria, the cat. At the entreaties of Terri's sisters, Rosa had consented to the adoption of a calico female when Ramon was not there to protest. Rosa had picked the name. Her sisters thought it romantic, and Ramon had taken no notice; only Terri knew that her mother, the most conservative of women, had named the cat after a Communist heroine of the Spanish Civil War and sometimes smiled when she called it.

The sound, more insistent now, is that of a cat clawing the screen door.

Still, Terri delays going to the door.

Entering the kitchen, she fishes beneath the sink for a bowl and cat food: they have learned to feed the cat outside so that Ramon Peralta cannot curse or kick it. Pouring the dry cat food, Terri glances up: the inner door is glass, and Terri sees the outline of La Pasionaria standing on her hind legs, with her front claws digging into the screen. Spotting Terri, the cat cries out to her.

Terri goes to the door.

She opens the glass one first. Stepping through it, she speaks softly to La Pasionaria, just before unlocking the screen to find Ramon Peralta staring up at her.

The cat's dish, falling from her hand, scatters food across his chest.

Ramon does not move. A ribbon of dried blood runs from his temple past his mouth, caught in the rictus of a man gasping for air, and then onto the stone in a carmine pool that looks sticky to the touch. But her father's eyes seem as dry as the blood on his face. One hand, stretching backward, must have clawed at the screen like the cat. There is the smell of urine.

Terri does not make a sound.

It is as if some part of her has expected this. Another part, filled with horror, stares into his face; the shock of how he looks becomes a ragged shiver. Calmly, La Pasionaria eats the cat food off his shirt; then, as if in distaste, she walks across his body and into the house.

Terri begins to shake; the handle of the screen door rattles in her fingers. She does not need to touch her father to know that he is dead.

"Teresa!"

Terri starts, heart thumping wildly as she turns toward the sound.

Already dressed, Rosa stares past her at Ramon and then into Terri's face. It is what her mother sees there that seems to make her move.

Silent, Rosa sweeps Terri into her arms. In the back of Terri's mind she hears the whisper of the screen door closing; as tightly as her mother holds her, as softly as she speaks, still she senses Rosa looking over her shoulder into the face of her dead husband.

"Oh, sweetheart," Rosa says, with trembling voice. "Oh, sweetheart, that this should happen to you." It is that which Terri remembers now: she cannot know, and will never ask, to whom it was that Rosa spoke.

She does not know how long they stayed there, holding each other as her father lay on the porch. She only knows that Rosa's next words, steadier and directed to Terri, are: "Do not look, Teresa. Do not look at him again."

Terri never did.

After a moment, her mother leans back from her, hands clasping Terri's elbows. "You must listen to me now," she says. "I must call the police. But I do not wish your sisters to see him, or to know until I am ready to tell them. Do you understand?"

Terri is not certain. Mute, she can only nod.

"Good." Her mother's grip tightens. "I am going upstairs to wake them now. Then I will serve them in the dining room—anything they want from the kitchen, you and I will get. After that, you will go with them to school as early as you can. Tell Sister Irene that there's a problem at home and that I will call to explain. But do not tell her what the problem is."

Looking into her mother's face, Terri nods again, less in understanding than at the intensity of Rosa's eyes and voice. Her mother would take care of this, as terrible as she thought it: from now on, Rosa would take care of everything.

"What should *I* do?" Terri asks.

Her mother thinks. "Stay at school," she says quietly. "Just until I come for you. It won't be long."

Terri cannot imagine sitting in class, away from her mother, alone with the knowledge of her father's death. "But I want to stay with you," she says.

Rosa shakes her head. "I don't want the police to bother you, Teresa. You help me most by helping your sisters. It will be bad enough for them that your father, filled with drink, has died from a fall on his own back porch."

Terri cannot answer.

"Come," Rosa says softly. "Help me with your sisters. From now on, if we are to survive, I will need you."

Terri takes her mother's hand, turning from the body of her father. Her shock seems deeper now. Only a part of her knows that, hand in hand, they have begun climbing the stairs to awaken her sisters for school.

Harris expelled a breath. "You seem to remember quite a bit," she said after a time.

Terri slumped in her chair; she had the faint, somewhat remote feeling of someone who has gone too long without food. "More than I thought," she finally answered. "But nothing about that night, and the days after are just a blur. Except for my father's funeral, and then taking his picture off the wall."

"And it was after that when you first had the dream."

"Yes."

Harris was quiet again. Oddly, Terri found herself smiling, not in amusement but in irony.

"What is it?" Harris asked.

"The cat. La Pasionaria. She was never the same."

Harris cocked her head. "How so?"

"She avoided everyone but me." Terri shook her head. "She began to sleep with me at night, to follow me around the house. When I went to college, she stopped eating."

"What happened to her?"

"I had to smuggle her into my dorm at Berkeley." Terri smiled, again without humor. "Actually, you could say that she changed my life. . . ."

Even in the dorm, where she is walking contraband, La Pasionaria tries to follow her everywhere. It's as if Ramon Peralta's death unbalanced the cat more than it did his wife or his oldest daughter.

One night, while Terri studies late at the library, her blond roommate, Sue, talking to a boy she likes, becomes careless. By the time Terri comes back, Sue is hysterical: La Pasionaria has escaped to go looking for her owner.

Terri and Sue comb the corridors, the common areas, the basement. It is Terri who, entering the dim dungeon of the laundry room, can hear the cat's faint cries above the spinning washers and the tumble of clothes in the dryers. But the only living thing she can see is the curly-haired boy sitting cross-legged on the floor in front of his laundry, reading a computer magazine.

"Do you hear something?" Terri asks.

He looks up at her; in her anxiety, Terri does not really take him in.

After a moment, he nods. "A cat," he says.

"*My* cat," Terri answers. "But I can't see her."

He tilts his head, smiling a little. "She's here somewhere."

Terri, peering behind the washer and dryer shoved against the basement wall, can see nothing. The cries grow louder.

"Here," the boy says. Leaning against the wall, he begins pushing a dryer toward Terri. The boy is slim but strong: the dryer begins to move. And then the boy reaches suddenly behind the dryer and pulls forth a trembling, mewing calico bundle.

The cat struggles to escape his grasp. "This must be yours," the boy says, and hands the cat to Terri.

La Pasionaria calms in her arms. It is only then that she looks at the boy. He has bright black eyes and a thin face; from the cast of his features, he is Hispanic like Terri. But her first thought is a strange one: the boy looks nothing like Ramon Peralta.

"Thanks," she tells him. "I really love this cat."

"I like cats too," he says. "They're independent, and they take care of themselves. Like we have to."

Terri is not sure what this means. But he seems nice enough, and he has just rescued her cat. And she feels, if forced to admit it, a little lonely: most people she meets here seem to have more money and more time.

"I'm Terri Peralta," she says.

He looks into her eyes. "Ricardo Arias," he says, and smiles at her. "My friends call me Richie."

FIFTEEN

PAGET'S TELEPHONE RANG.

He had been enjoying a peaceful breakfast with Carlo, their first in days. They had talked about easy things—pro football, Carlo's new basketball coach, and Katie's parents' refusal to let her drive—and Paget felt his son accepting, warily and with deep reservations, the idea that their life might still be normal. They did not speak of Monk or of the fact that, when Carlo came home five nights before, the kitchen they now sat in was still a shambles. But their knowledge that this was deliberate did not devalue this time together—if anything, it was enhanced. So that when the phone rang yet again, Paget was tempted not to answer.

It was Carlo who changed his mind. "Better get that," he said; when Paget looked at him, he saw the concern in his son's eyes again, as if even the telephone ringing carried the threat of something unpleasant and unexpected. Paget doubted this—the police would not call, nor was Terri or Caroline likely to report bad news by phone. But the only way to reassure Carlo was to answer.

"It's Katie," Paget predicted, "wanting a ride to school. Her parents have decided to save on gas until you graduate."

When Paget answered the phone, Carlo was smiling.

"Mr. Paget? Jack Slocum."

The thin voice was intrusive, almost insinuating. Paget knew the voice at once: the reporter who had found—or been led to—the *Inquisitor* article on Ricardo Arias. "I'm over in Alameda County, at the family court," Slocum went on. "There are some files in *Arias versus Peralta* that the clerk won't let me have. Apparently, they're sealed."

Slocum's tone—bewildered and a little righteous—was as transparent as his pretense that Paget would wish to help him. Paget said nothing.

"Mr. Paget?"

Carlo was watching now, his spoon poised over his cereal. "Yes?" Paget responded.

"I was hoping you could help me. See, from what I understand now, Mr. Arias is the one who wanted them sealed. And he's dead."

Paget fought to control his anger. "That makes him a little hard to reach, doesn't it. Have you tried the 510 area code?"

Carlo put down his spoon and folded his hands; he had heard the edge in his father's voice. Slocum himself sounded nettled. "I hear you might have copies."

At that moment, looking at Carlo, Paget despised the press with the fierceness of a man who loved his son. "Oh," Paget said quietly. "And where did you hear that?"

Slocum ignored the question. "Actually, I hear the files involve you, Mr. Paget. And some members of your family."

Turning from Carlo, Paget made his answer soft. "Does that excite you, Mr. Slocum? Is it *that* slow a day in Bosnia?"

A pause, and then Slocum let his aggression show. "Look, are you going to give me copies or not?"

"No. But I'll try explaining health care to you. Have a minute?"

"This is *news*, Mr. Paget. Your character is news. As is your family." Pausing, Slocum tried to make his voice sound careless. "Maybe the police have a copy. I hear they're looking into Arias's death."

"I doubt the police will open their files. Anyhow, you'd have to do some work, and why pretend? Why not just go to the person who fed you this tidbit and get a copy from him?" Paget's tone was quieter yet. "You know, from the man who was feeding your predecessor, the late Mr. Arias."

There was silence. "I see," Paget continued. "Your source prefers anonymity. So you'd like to get copies from somewhere that can't be traced to him. Just in case there's a lawsuit and his name came out."

Another pause. "Are you *blackmailing* me, Mr. Paget?"

Paget gave a short laugh. "No. Just talking about something you *do* understand."

There was more silence. "Our paper," Slocum retorted angrily, "can go to court and get those papers unsealed. Most courts believe that the public interest outweighs personal privacy. Especially for people who think we should elect them to something."

"I'll remember that," Paget said, "if I ever find you crawling through my sock drawer. Anything else?"

Now Slocum tried sounding aggrieved. "Look, I'm giving you a chance here, out of fairness, to come down on the side of being open about your life. If you don't cooperate, I'll have to write that you refused me. And *this* time no one will keep me from printing that."

"Fine. But when you do, be sure to mention that you're *not* on the list of people I discuss my life with." Paget's voice went cold. "Perhaps you think you're damaging me politically. Perhaps you're right. But I suggest to you, very seriously, that you leave my *son* alone."

Paget hung up.

Carlo had walked to the window and was staring out at the bay. Without turning, he asked, "That was a reporter, wasn't it?"

Paget rested both hands on his son's shoulders. "They're trying to dig up Richie's molester stuff. And dirt about Terri and me, real or imagined."

Carlo faced him, worry filling his eyes. "Can they?"

"Probably. The only way to stop them is to give up on the Senate. As quickly and as gracefully as possible."

There was hesitancy on Carlo's face. Paget could read his thoughts: Carlo already imagined the shame of being labeled as a child molester—his name in the newspapers, the snickers of peers and even friends, the questions of reporters for whom, indifferent to Carlo, Richie's accusation was a fact in itself. "I don't want you to give up, Dad. It's not right."

But this was said without conviction. It was Carlo's own life that was most real to him: whether his father became a senator was not something he would carry with him, day to day. And Paget understood this.

"What wouldn't be right," he told Carlo, "is to sacrifice you to my ambitions." To ease the moment, Paget tried self-mockery. "I mean, what kind of father would do that?"

"About any politician I ever heard of." Carlo gave his father an awkward hug. "So maybe you're not one, Dad."

"Maybe I'm not." Paget spoke softly now. "I'll have to take care of this reporter right away. The best way I know how."

But Carlo's thoughts had moved past Slocum. "What about the police, Dad? What about Richie?"

Paget looked into his face. "All that I can tell you, Carlo, is what I've said before. Because I didn't kill him, they can't prove that I did. It really is that simple."

The boy was silent, still watching his father for cues. Paget smiled a little. "I've got to deal with this now, okay? It may take me a few hours to make life perfect again. And you've got school."

Carlo hugged him once more. This time it was very tight. He hurried to his car without saying more.

There was, Paget thought, one call to make. If only to satisfy his doubts.

From Los Angeles information he got the telephone number of James Colt's office. When a secretary answered, Paget identified himself and asked for Colt.

For over five minutes, Paget was on hold. More tense with each moment.

"Mr. Paget," a crisp voice said. "This is Jack Hamm. I'm Mr. Colt's chief of staff. Can I ask the nature of your call?"

"It's personal," Paget said mildly. "You might tell him that it concerns my family."

There was silence. In a cool tone, Hamm answered, "Please wait a moment."

Taut now, Paget waited for several moments.

"Mr. Paget?"

It was Hamm again. "Yes," Paget said calmly. "I'm still here. Waiting."

"I'm sorry." A long pause. "At the moment, Mr. Colt does not consider it appropriate to speak to you."

"Might I ask why?"

Paget felt the man choose his words with care. But the answer, when it came, had a rehearsed quality. "These personal matters are not something Mr. Colt should be involved in." The voice slowed for emphasis. "Particularly when you may be seeking public office, as he will be. Like it or not, Mr. Paget, candidates pay a price."

Paget decided to push harder. "Their families shouldn't—"

"And Mr. Colt understands that." Hamm's tone became tinged with regret. "If you were an ordinary private citizen. . . . "

Hamm let his voice trail off. His message was delivered, this said; it was pointless to be indelicate.

"I understand," Paget answered, and hung up.

* * *

"I don't think this problem with Slocum came from Brooks," Caroline said to Paget. "At least it didn't start there."

Paget watched her. "Colt?" he asked.

Caroline nodded. "Colt's the one with the most to gain. Even if Slocum doesn't get the files, the pissy little article he's planning to run does you real damage, politicswise. And it gives Brooks no way out: if Richie's death *and* these files hit the media together, Brooks would have to pursue you even if you were his brother."

Only then, satisfied, did Paget tell Caroline about his call to Colt.

Her eyes widened, and then she thought for a time. "It's not unreasonable," she said at length, "to believe that Mr. Hamm was making a suggestion. He seems to have hinted pretty clearly that Colt knows the nature of your personal problems. Which, if they come from him, he certainly does."

Paget felt a wave of depression. "Through most of my life, Caroline, I've had the illusion that I could control things, if only I tried hard enough. But I can't get my arms around this. I don't even know where all the pieces are, or who holds them. I'm not even sure how best to protect Carlo."

There was something puzzled in Caroline's look, a touch of fallibility, as if for once she did not know what to say. Paget tried smiling. "I really didn't mean to distress you," he said. "And I don't expect you to make me feel any better."

She shook her head. "It's not that. I was just thinking what a flimsy foundation any of us have—our work, a handful of friends, children if we're lucky—and how something we don't anticipate can bring it down so quickly." She caught herself and smiled. "But no one has died here—no one we care about, that is. And you've the great good fortune of having me for your lawyer. So let's think this through."

She leaned back in her chair. "The first piece," she said slowly, "is politics, where 'who shot Richie' doesn't matter. What's at stake *there* is Carlo's privacy, and the immediate way to ensure that is shutting off the press.

"What someone—Colt, I'm quite certain—wants you to do is drop the Senate. The carrot is that once you do that, it guts the media interest in Richie's charges—"

"Which is why I *should* do that," Paget cut in. "As much as part of me hates to, I hate what would happen to Carlo more. Colt wins, and I learn to live with that. That's all."

"Not so fast, Chris." Caroline held up her hand. "Here it gets kind of murky, but have you stopped to consider what you lose by dropping out? Not on piece one, but piece two—the police investigation, where 'who shot Richie' matters quite a lot."

Paget stared at her. "A deal," he finally said. "Never stated, but understood: I drop out of the race, and perhaps Brooks lets Richie stay a suicide. Have I caught the essence?"

Caroline appraised him. "More or less."

"Pretty cynical, Caroline. It attributes the lowest possible motives to Brooks as well as Colt, and further assumes that no one but Richie's mother—and certainly not Mac—gives a damn about *why* he died."

Caroline gave him a cursory smile. "Does that seem so far-fetched? Really, Christopher, you *are* an idealist."

But Paget did not smile back. "It also assumes that Brooks has no case against me."

Caroline's own smile vanished. "Not *no* case," she said finally. "Just not a case so strong that, in the exercise of his discretion, Mac can't decide to drop it."

The question, couched as a statement, carried within it a buried inquiry. Paget turned to the window: the morning sunlight, glinting on the windows of high-rises, left them opaque. Quietly, he said, "I'm getting out, Caroline. Not because I'm afraid of what Brooks has. But because the one thing I *do* control is whether or not I run. And this is the only thing I can do to prevent the notion that Carlo molested Elena from becoming a media plaything. As early as tomorrow."

"If you're indicted," Caroline said slowly, "Richie's charges against Carlo will become your principal motive for premeditated murder. And the notion that you tried to keep it quiet will hurt you all the more."

Turning, Paget looked at her steadily. "But it won't hurt me tomorrow, will it?" He shrugged. "Besides, once I drop out, Colt may lose his interest in Richie's death. Which could mean that Brooks will too."

Caroline raised an eyebrow. "It must be extraordinary," she said finally, "to love a child."

"There are *two* people I love, Caroline. First, and always, there's Carlo. And now there's Terri. I don't want either hurt."

"And how would Terri be hurt?"

"Through Elena, of course. Terri's trying to work out her daughter's problems with an analyst, not the press or the police."

Caroline folded her hands. "All right," she said at length. "How's this: I call the publisher of our morning paper and inform him that any public interest in his boy Slocum's story has gone aglimmer with your candidacy. Which is a good thing, I'll add, because Slocum's devotion to purity in politics has been satisfied without the risk of a lawsuit." She smiled briefly. "Child's play, if you consider what we do a fit activity for children."

"Sometimes, Caroline, not even for adults. Not even for adults like us."

Her smile faded. "I'm sorry, Christopher. I really am."

After that, Caroline said little. Walking to the elevator, she touched his arm. "Take the day off if you can. Take Terri with you."

Paget meant to. But when he arrived at the office, shortly before noon, Terri was gone.

SIXTEEN

WHEN THE FIRST telephone call came to her office, and even more intensely when her phone rang again, Terri hoped that the caller would be Chris.

But the first call was from Denise Harris. She was brisk and to the point. "The police were here this morning," Harris said. "A man named Dennis Lynch."

Terri stood, telephone clasped to her ear. "What did they want?"

"Any notes or records I had regarding Elena's therapy, or any conversation with you." Harris paused a moment. "They also wanted to interview me. When I asked them why, they told me it was about Richie's death—that you, or even Elena, may know something about it."

Harris sounded quite calm, a good professional imparting information to a mother. But Terri found herself pacing. "What did you say to them?" she asked.

"Only that I couldn't help them. Not without your consent." Harris paused. "I guess they haven't asked you."

"No."

Harris was silent for a time, then quietly said, "I don't need to hear any more about this, Terri. Not unless it has something to do with Elena."

"It doesn't. But just for the record, we're seeing you for Elena's benefit, and whatever the police are thinking about Richie is a separate thing." Terri paused for emphasis. "I don't want them bothering Elena. Ever."

"Then they won't." Harris's voice was neutral; for the first time, Terri sensed her discomfort. "Call me if anything happens with Elena, all right?"

For an instant, feeling frightened and alone, Terri considered telling Harris about Jack Slocum, the threat of an article that might include Elena. But perhaps that was more than the therapist wished to know; either the article would appear or it would not, and meanwhile there was nothing she could do. "I will," Terri answered. "And thanks for calling, Denise. I appreciate your concern."

"Anytime," Harris said easily. Terri sensed that she was grateful to get off.

A rush of half-formed thoughts flooded Terri's mind. The eerie sense that her words to Harris—that she did not wish the police to bother her daughter—echoed Rosa's on the morning when Terri had found her father dead. A deep resentment of Chris for being elsewhere when she needed him. The desire to rush to Elena's school and take her child home. A wave of guilt she could not define. A thought of piercing clarity: Denise Harris might well believe that Chris and Terri, or perhaps Terri alone, were responsible for Richie's death. And another: that other people she knew might come to think that Elena's father was murdered and that Terri wished to marry his murderer.

It made her remember what she felt in her father's home: That any happiness was transient. That she had done something wrong. That her only security was escape.

The night before, the nightmare had come again.

Get a grip, Peralta. Feeling sorry for yourself is a waste of time, and so is expecting someone else to take care of you. That much she had learned from Rosa.

Terri began pacing. Her desk was strewn with work she could not do.

The telephone rang.

A woman's voice, taut and upset, speaking too quickly. "Mrs. Arias, this is Barbara Coffey, Elena's day care supervisor. You remember?"

Terri checked her watch: Elena would not be in day care for a good three hours. "Is something wrong?"

"Yes. I came in early, to bring some posters while the room was empty for lunch." Her voice rose. "Elena was there, with two men— one white and one black. They were asking questions . . ."

Terri stood. "You mean the school just let . . ."

"Yes." The woman paused. "Her teacher's *with* them, Mrs. Arias."

* * *

Terri found them in the schoolroom. Four desks were arranged in a circle. Monk and Lynch sat on top of theirs; Leslie Warner sat next to Elena, holding her limp hand as Monk asked questions. Behind them, a bulletin board had spelling words and cutouts of Halloween pumpkins. Monk's tape machine sat on Elena's desk.

"*Mommy,*" Elena said, and got up, looking uncertainly from her mother to the teacher who gripped her hand.

Terri gazed down at Leslie Warner. "Let her go," she said softly. "Right now."

Warner opened her mouth to speak, then shut it again. Elena's hand slipped free.

Terri picked her up. "Hi, sweetheart," she said. Elena's arms came tight around her neck.

"I'm sorry, Mommy," the little girl said.

Through her anger, Terri's nerves tingled; she did not ask what Elena meant. "I've come to see you," Terri told her. "Just wait outside for a minute, okay?"

The little girl nodded against her shoulder. Terri carried her to the doorway; Barbara Coffey waited, looking fearfully over Terri's shoulder at Warner and the police. "I'll take Elena to the playground," she said.

"Thank you," Terri said. "You're the only one who thought of her."

Coffey took Elena's hand; as they left, the little girl looked back at Terri. It was all Terri could do to wait until Elena disappeared.

She turned, walking back into the room. She stopped two feet in front of Monk.

"You scum," she said. "Both of you."

Monk's returning gaze was not angry; Terri had the sudden intuition that this had not been his idea and that he would make no excuses. He turned to Warner. "Thank you," he said politely. He turned back to Terri, nodded slightly, and left. Lynch trailed after him without looking at anyone.

Facing Warner, Terri simply gazed at her. The teacher's gray eyes were at once defensive and defiant; she backed away one step.

"How could you allow this?" Terri asked.

Warner raised her head. "I have an obligation. To Elena, *not* you."

In that moment, Terri understood. "*You* called them."

Warner folded her arms.

"Why?" Terri asked softly.

"You threatened to kill Richie." Warner's voice rose. "Elena *told* me, months ago."

Terri felt her body stiffen. Slowly, it came to her: the night she had found Richie drunk with Elena. She had tucked the child in bed and then, thinking her asleep, had told Richie that she would kill him if he again became drunk around their daughter. And then, suddenly, Terri remembered Monk asking if she had ever threatened to murder Richie.

Gazing at Warner, Terri shook her head. "Do you have any idea," she said slowly, "of the harm you may have done? Do you understand my child at all? Or any child?"

Warner seemed to draw resolve from the weariness in Terri's face. "You shouldn't raise her," she retorted angrily. "Not with what Elena knows. She's *lost* without her father."

Terri looked into Warner's eyes. She made herself wait until she was certain of what she wished to do. And then, quite slowly and deliberately, she took one step forward and slapped Warner across the face.

There was a sharp crack; a jolt ran through Terri's arm. Warner reeled backward, eyes shocked and filling with tears, mouth open in fear.

"You fool," Terri said softly, and went to find Elena.

Elena pointed at the sea lion, leaping to catch a silvery fish tossed by a curly-haired woman in a blue zookeeper's outfit. "Look, Mommy," she said. "He's having dinner."

It was all that Elena had said in minutes, and one of a handful of words in the hour since Terri had picked her up at school. On first seeing her mother, the little girl had worn a fearful, guilty look. Being questioned about a parent would turn a child's world inside out, Terri knew, and that Elena did not mention the police showed how fearful and ashamed she was. To take Elena home for a "talk" would only make things worse; when Terri asked Elena if she wanted to go to the zoo, the little girl nodded, and her anxiety seemed to ease.

But the zoo itself had seemed to overwhelm her, and none of her formerly favorite things—the petting zoo, the orangutans, or the merry-go-round—drew any response. Finally, Terri suggested a ride through the zoo in a motorized train; Elena could sit in her lap and take things in as she chose.

Now, moving past the seal pool, Elena settled back against her mother. The day was gray and a little chilly. The train was not crowded, and Terri and Elena—sitting alone near the end—could talk as they chose. The rolling, parklike setting seemed far away from police or questions, and the bump and rattle of the train had a certain lulling quality.

The next animals they saw were polar bears. Mammoth and white, two shaggy white bears lumbered across a rocky terrain with a moat to keep them from escaping. For no discernible reason, one of the bears reared on its hind legs and emitted a growl toward Terri and Elena. A year ago, Elena might have shivered with a child's delight at being frightened; the child she had become buried her face in Terri's shoulder until her mother assured her that they had moved past the creature.

Elena looked tentatively into her mother's face. "Were you scared?" Terri asked.

Elena nodded. Slowly, she said, "The policemen scared me too."

Behind her, grizzly bears went by unnoticed, and then a rhinoceros. "How did they scare you?" Terri asked.

Elena looked away. "Miss Warner said not to be. But they asked all about Daddy."

Terri tried to sound casual, as if she were curious only because Elena had mentioned it. "What about Daddy?"

The little girl gazed at Terri's lap. "When you guys were fighting."

Terri studied her. "Even grown-ups argue sometimes, Elena. Do you remember anything about us fighting?"

A short nod. "You said you would kill Daddy."

The words, fearful yet certain, made Terri's skin feel cold. Even at six, part of a child's mind was literal: Richie's death lent meaning to things that Elena could not comprehend. And then, struggling to explain, Terri thought of Ramon Peralta.

"Your father was drunk," she said softly. "Do you know what 'drunk' means?"

Elena hesitated. "You act crazy?"

Terri nodded. "Very crazy, sometimes. And I love you too much returned as fresh as when he was alive. "Your daddy was a selfish man," Terri said without thinking. "He didn't love me or you or anyone. All that he wanted was *you* to feel sorry for him, and *me* to take care of him."

Elena's eyes filled with tears. "That's not true," she exclaimed. "Chris was Daddy's enemy. I told them all about it."

"Who?"

"The policemen." Pausing, Elena's voice took on a new determination. "I wouldn't leave Daddy, and so Chris killed him with a gun. He's going to jail, Mommy. Forever."

When there was a knock on his office door, Paget turned, hoping for Terri. And then Lynch and Monk came through the door with a bearded medical technician.

They've come to arrest me, Paget thought at once. Steeling himself, he asked, "What do you want?"

Monk watched Paget's hand, frozen halfway to the telephone: Paget knew that Monk had followed his thoughts perfectly. Then Lynch shook his head. "All we want is prints," he said evenly. "And blood."

In his self-disgust, Paget almost laughed.

Monk and Lynch sat at Paget's desk like two corporate lawyers ready to negotiate a deal. Lynch put fingerprint cards and an ink pad on Paget's blotter, while Monk handed him some papers. A search warrant, much like the one for Paget's home and car. Except this warrant authorized the holder to take fingerprints and sample blood from Paget's body.

Paget looked at the ink pad, then at Lynch. "You could have done this a while ago," he said, "instead of stringing things out."

Lynch, pushing forward a card, shrugged his apology. Paget held out his right hand. Silent, the technician took it; he placed one finger at a time on the ink pad and then on the card, rolling it from side to side. Paget turned to Monk. "In fact," he continued, "you *would* have, Charles. If it had been up to you instead of Brooks."

Monk looked him in the face. But he said nothing: to acknowledge the question would be to admit that he could not answer.

The telephone rang. It might be Terri, Paget thought. As it rang, to have let your daddy be like that around you. I was just trying to tell him that."

For the first time, Elena looked up at her. The zoo train cruised by a jaguar and two Indian elephants, ignored by the dark-haired child whose eyes now searched her mother's. "Did you want to kill Daddy?"

Though Terri was prepared for this, the question shocked her. "Of course not," she said finally. "Why do you ask that?"

Once more, Elena turned away: Terri found that something in the child's profile, so much like Richie's, unsettled her. "Because of me," Elena said.

Terri pulled her daughter close to her, kissing her forehead. "I love you more than anything, sweetheart. But killing people is wrong."

As if in answer, Elena's arms tightened around Terri. "I didn't tell them, Mommy. Only Miss Warner, a long time ago."

"Tell them what?"

"What you said to Daddy." Elena's voice was soft and fearful. "I won't get you in trouble. I promise, okay?"

Terri felt her stomach wrench. "You don't need to promise, Elena. You don't need to be afraid for me."

Elena shook her head. "They'll take you away from me. If a mommy or daddy gets in trouble, that's what they do. Then I could never see you again."

Terri pulled herself back, holding Elena to see her face. "Who told you that?" she asked.

Instead of answering, Elena insisted, "I didn't tell them. I wouldn't talk about you."

Terri remembered asking Elena about Carlo, the child's face turning to the wall, the silent refusal to speak or even look at her. "Daddy told you that, didn't he?" Terri said softly. "About taking parents away."

Elena nodded, her voice hovering between pride and confusion. "He told me about *all* his feelings. All the things that scared him."

"Like what?"

Elena looked down again. "Chris took you away from Daddy," she answered. "He was helping you take *me* away too. I had to stay with Daddy, or he'd be all alone."

The simple words, repeated like a catechism, frightened Terri for Elena more than anything the child had said. Her hatred of Richie the technician turned the tips of Paget's fingers into prints on a white card.

The telephone stopped ringing.

Paget's mouth was dry. The technician pulled out a thin silver needle and a glassine bag. Silent, Paget undid a shirt cuff and rolled up the sleeve of his left arm.

The technician punctured the inside of his arm. With a fixed expression, Paget watched the bottom of the bag turn a deep red, and then the cop put a Band-Aid where the needle had been.

"Thank you," he said.

Leaving, Monk did not look at Paget. Lynch and the technician trailed after.

Checking voice mail for messages, Paget left inky smudges on the numbered buttons of his telephone. The inside of his arm stung.

The call had been from Terri. There was a problem with Elena; Terri could not explain by telephone. Her voice, coming from an outdoor pay phone, sounded strained and preoccupied. When Paget called her apartment, no one answered.

Paget went home and made himself a drink, waiting for Carlo to return from basketball.

SEVENTEEN

"IN A SINGLE DAY," Harris said the next afternoon, "Elena finds herself being torn between her teacher, the police, her dead dad, mom, mom's boyfriend, and maybe even the boyfriend's son. If I had known all that was happening, I'd have gone to the school myself."

Terri slumped in her chair. "I'm taking her out of there as soon as I can."

"I don't see that you have much choice. Even without having slapped that foolish woman." Harris paused. "You look exhausted."

Terri shrugged helplessly. "I couldn't sleep, and then Elena had her dream again. This morning she looked worse than I do."

Harris seemed to reflect. "Elena needs protection from whatever this is about Richie." She paused for emphasis. "No matter what comes next."

Terri gave her a direct look. "I don't know where Elena's thing about Chris is coming from, Denise. Unless it was Richie telling her that Chris was his enemy."

Harris's eyes met Terri's. "Is there any possibility," she said softly, "that Elena got this suspicion of Chris from *you?*"

Terri felt herself flush. "No."

Harris fell silent. Finally, she asked, "Who are the people Elena feels most loyal to?"

"Loyal?" Terri repeated. "My mother, me—Richie when he was alive, and maybe still. Anyone else is pretty well down the list."

"Including Chris?"

"Definitely including Chris. Well below Carlo, I think."

"Because it's funny," Harris went on. "Working with Elena, I tend to agree with you that—for whatever reason—she blames *herself* for

Richie's death. It's nothing she says. But whenever I mention Richie, she gets a shamed, almost furtive look, as if she feels guilty. If that's right, she *could* experience blaming Chris as a kind of relief."

"Relief?"

"From holding herself responsible. For Elena, blaming Chris has got to be easier than placing the onus on someone much closer." Harris watched her. "Especially if the alternative is you."

Suddenly, Terri's weariness verged on sickness. "Why can't she accept that Richie's death was an accident?"

Harris seemed to form a bow with her lips: the effect was the most openly pensive look Terri had yet seen from her. "I don't know," she answered. "I just don't know."

Terri touched her eyes and then slowly shook her head. "All I ever wanted was some sort of normal life. For a moment, in Portofino, I almost believed I'd have one."

Watching her, Harris was quiet. And then Terri remembered Chris in Portofino, smiling at her, in the moment before Rosa had called. "What is it?" Harris asked.

Terri turned away. "Poor Chris," she murmured.

Naked, Terri lay against Chris's chest.

"Do you think this will end it?" she asked. "Quitting the race?"

Chris gazed at the bedroom ceiling. The look in his eyes was distant. "I turn this over in my mind now," he said finally. "Again and again, night after night. What do they have? I ask myself. What do they *think* they have? All I ever get from it is another night without sleep."

Terri had never seen Christopher Paget so lost. She had gone from Harris's office to find him, driven by the instinct that he needed her. Now, lying in his bed in the light of late afternoon, the duality of the moment left her without words: the man she loved, and wished to comfort, was suspected of killing the father of her child.

"What are you afraid of?" she asked. "Tell me, Chris. Please."

Chris did not seem to hear her. But she could see the truth in his eyes: whatever Chris might believe about James Colt, he knew that this was not merely politics. "Sleeplessness does funny things," he said finally. "I have these visions of being put away somewhere, without you, without seeing Carlo through to manhood. It's mental melodrama, like a road company *Les Misérables*."

Terri lay there, silently stroking his hair, trying to remember his expression and tone of voice when he told her he did not kill Richie.

"So what do we do now?" she asked softly.

Chris turned to her at last. "Right now?"

"Yes. I can't see past this moment, Chris. You're going to have to help me."

He touched her face. "Feeling lonely?"

"Not lonely, Chris. Alone."

Slowly, Chris nodded. "I understand. If, after this is over, I never again feel distant from you, I'll have what I most want in life."

It was the first time today that he really seemed to be *with* her. She slid across his chest, her face over his.

Chris gazed up at her. "This may be a stupid question," he said. "But how *are* you, anyhow?"

"Lousy, thanks. My daughter's seriously depressed, my boyfriend can't talk to me, and the police think that one of us killed my late husband."

"That's all?"

"Not quite." Terri's voice changed, and she looked into his face. "I have the nightmare almost every night now. It's like my subconscious won't leave me alone."

Chris's eyes met hers. For a strange moment, Terri imagined that he was about to tell her something—she did not know what, or why. And then Chris kissed her, and the moment passed.

"I love you," he said.

Terri slid her hand down his body, lightly resting her fingers on his stomach. "You're lonely," she said softly. "And I'm lonely."

He smiled into her eyes. A moment later, Terri could feel him responding to her touch.

Paget felt himself come alive. All that he could think about was Terri.

His mouth moved across her stomach, her breasts, the warm hollow of her neck. The scent and feel of her skin and hair filled his senses as he touched her. The sounds she made were like a pulse inside him.

In his life, only Teresa Peralta had done this to him.

Right now she was all that mattered. As he entered her, Terri's eyes met his. For that moment, time stopped for him.

Terri blinked. Something changed, like the breaking of a current. Her body beneath him was still.

"Listen," she whispered.

He heard it now. A knocking on the door. Slow and insistent, almost like the tolling of a bell.

They looked at each other. The knocking, unvarying and inexorable, seemed louder now. They did not need to speak their thoughts aloud.

Terri shook her head.

"I have to," Paget said. Sliding from inside her, he stopped for a moment, looking into her face again.

The knocking kept on.

Gently, Paget kissed Terri's mouth and got up from the bed. She watched him as he dressed—a sweater and jeans and moccasins—taking his time.

By now they knew that the knocking would not stop.

And then, quite suddenly, it did.

Silence. There was a cracking sound, like wood snapping. Terri pulled the sheet above her breasts.

Footsteps now. In the doorway, Paget glanced back at Terri. "Lock the door," he said. "And call Caroline."

Slowly, Paget walked down the winding stairs, hand grazing the rail.

The front door was broken open. Monk and Lynch were in the alcove, waiting with the young policeman who had searched Paget's home.

"Three of you?" Paget asked, and then the young cop took the handcuffs off his belt.

Monk raised a hand, motioning the cop to wait. His gaze at Paget was steady and without pleasure. "You have been indicted by the grand jury," he said with grave formality. "We have a warrant for your arrest in the murder of Ricardo Arias."

Monk began reading his rights.

Paget felt a moment's lightness, like an oxygen shortage. As if by reflex, he nodded when Monk was finished, and then Monk took his arm. When Paget heard the bedroom door open, he did not look back. Monk guided him past the splintered entryway.

The street was cool and quiet. A neighbor, walking her basset, turned to watch them.

There was an unmarked car in the driveway. Monk and Lynch steered him to the car and pushed Paget into the back seat. Then the young cop got in next to him, snapping the cuffs on his wrists. He sat next to Paget with a narrow look of authority and pleasure.

Lynch and Monk got in front, and then Monk turned over the engine. As they pulled from the driveway, Paget saw Carlo's car.

Carlo braked abruptly. Monk turned into the street, and Paget looked through the side window into the stricken face of his son.

"I'm all right," Paget tried to mouth. The car kept moving; Paget saw Carlo calling out to him, and then his son's face vanished like a mirage.

The next several minutes were a blur. A collage of half-noticed images, ending in the bowels of an underground garage. The car drove into a steel cage and stopped.

They were at the Hall of Justice, and all that Paget could think about was the look on his son's face.

The cage shut behind them.

The young cop jerked Paget out of the car, and then Monk opened the front of the cage to take them into a smaller mantrap surrounding an elevator. As the elevator enclosed them, Paget leaned his back against the wall.

With a shudder, the elevator creaked slowly upward. Then it opened at the sixth floor, into another cage, and Paget's mind reentered the moment.

A thick-bodied sheriff's deputy in tinted glasses was waiting on the other side of the cage. He unlocked the bars, then steered Paget and his escorts down a hallway and through a steel door into a cacophony of sounds: a room filled with deputies herding the dregs of the urban underclass newly busted for felonies, some of them yipping or moaning from the rise or fall of drugs taken in their last moments of freedom. At the far side of the room, more deputies at three tellerlike stations booked whoever stood in front of them, shouting to be heard above the din, entering crimes as coded numbers on a computer screen. In one corner, a black transvestite sat with his legs spread, crying to no one and urinating on himself; Paget smelled urine everywhere, as if it had seeped into the concrete. The young cop unlocked Paget's cuffs.

"In here," the deputy snapped, and pushed Paget into an empty concrete room with a steel toilet. "Strip," the man ordered in an indifferent voice: Paget was merely another body in a nameless parade that had no past or future, no faces or lives or souls.

As the man watched, Paget took off his clothes.

"Bend over," the man said.

Paget knew what this was about: some of the human traffic had drugs or handguns secreted in their rectums. Bending, Paget tried to think ahead.

When Paget had dressed again, the man pushed him into a bare concrete holding tank to the side of the room and ordered him to wait.

The twenty or so inmates of the holding tank, blacks and Latinos and a few Asians, seemed to study him with the lassitude that comes from the shock of arrest. Paget knew that it was on the other side of the booking process, in the cells where they would put him, that assaults and rapes waited in the middle of the night. He did not look at anyone.

Paget had to keep his thoughts focused, and clear. Once he got out, he could think about Carlo again, and Terri.

Monk opened the door and walked over to Paget. "I'm going to walk you through this," he said. "Express check-in."

Another series of images: Monk shoving through the crowd to the booking window. A mustached Latin deputy booking Paget for the murder of Ricardo Arias—name and address, fingerprints and photo. More fingerprints in a concrete room that smelled like a latrine; another photograph in a wooden seat that looked like an electric chair. Through a bulletproof window, Paget could see his comrades in the holding tank, still waiting to be booked; from the other side of the glass, a muscled young black man stared back at him, resentful and unblinking, as if to tell Paget that he would remember his special treatment.

"I'm checking with my lawyer," Paget told Monk.

Monk shrugged. Paget went to a telephone on the concrete wall and tried to call Caroline. No answer; only Caroline's voice on tape, elegant and a little dry, soliciting a message.

"This is Chris," Paget said to the tape. "I'm at the county jail. I need a security cell."

When he turned, Monk was holding out an orange jumpsuit. Paget stared at him. "I want my own cell," he said.

Monk shoved the jumpsuit in Paget's hands. "Put this on," he said.

"Look—" Paget began, and then the telephone rang.

"It's for you," a deputy said to Monk. Monk took it, listened for a moment, and said a few terse words. Hanging up, he turned to Paget and repeated, "Put that on."

Paget did. A deputy put his clothes in a bag and took them away to a storeroom.

"All right," Monk said. "Let's go."

A few steps later, Paget found himself standing in front of the barred door to the county jail, flanked by Monk and the deputy who had watched him strip. Through the bars was a two-hundred-foot-long corridor with cells on either side and sheriff's deputies spaced in front of them. The sound of inmates shouting at each other echoed off the walls. The light was a sickly yellow.

Someone pushed a buzzer, and the door opened. Monk steered Paget through the door. He heard it shut behind them: a whisper, then the soft metallic click.

Paget felt frightened and alert at once: he was like a piece of meat on a conveyor belt, moving into the belly of the criminal justice system without any way to stop. On both sides of him were cells full of milling, stinking prisoners—blacks on his left, Hispanics and Asians on his right, separated so that they would not attack each other. A few steps further were the cells for the insane, with a psychiatric tech stationed in front, the inmates babbling or staring at him as if in catatonia. A pool of urine glistened on the floor.

"Where am I going?" Paget asked.

Monk stopped moving. "Shopping," he said. "Your assignment is to pick out five guys who look like you. If you can find that many."

Paget turned to him in surprise. "A lineup?"

Monk nodded. "Pick your prospects. Of course, they have to be volunteers."

Think, Paget ordered himself.

Slowly, Paget and Monk made their way down the corridor, staring through the bars of the next communal cell. The inmates, hostile or bored or curious, gazed back at him or shouted like captives in a zoo. A pockmarked Latino with a beard and marine tattoos came to the bars and put his face as close to Paget's as he could manage. "Oh, *sweet meat,*" he said in a caressing voice, "I can hardly wait for *you.*" The man's torso began to undulate.

Paget looked past him. About twenty prisoners stood around or lay on bunk beds; none of them were Caucasians. "Great material," he murmured to Monk. "Think whoever your witness is will be able to figure out I'm white?"

Monk grunted; to Paget, the sound was halfway between agreement and disgust. "Let's go," Monk said.

They went to the next cell.

Inside, a twentyish olive-skinned Latin with reddish hair leaned against a bed. He shrugged when Paget pointed at him; he was bored, the shrug said—why not. The sheriff's deputy unlocked the cell, beckoning, and the man stepped into the corridor.

Cell by cell, Paget added prospects. A thin-bearded man with brown hair. A saturnine Latin of about Paget's height and age. A much shorter man with brown hair but blue eyes. They trailed sullenly after Paget and the cops, silently shuffling to wherever they might go. No one spoke; none of them were as fair as Paget.

At the last cell, Paget stopped, gazing at a Caucasian prisoner.

The man was younger than he, perhaps thirty-five, and his hair was redder than Paget's copper-blond. But their height was similar, their skin tone the same, and the man's eyes were as blue as Paget's. The two men watched each other, the bars between them.

Silent, Paget beckoned. The man was still, gazing at Paget, and then walked over.

"What's happening?" he asked.

A faint Southern accent. "I need you in a lineup," Paget said.

The man shrugged. "Why should I?"

Paget angled his head toward the line of prospects. "Man," he said slowly, "*you* are my only ticket out of here."

The man surveyed the prisoners with narrowed eyes, a faint sardonic recognition that no one looked like Paget. "All right," he said, and stuck his hand through the bars. "My name's Ray."

"Chris," Paget answered, and shook his hand, clammy and cold to the touch. It was all that they seemed to have to say to each other.

Monk and the deputy let Ray out of the cell.

Paget and the five prisoners filed back down the corridor, Monk to one side, the deputy behind them. The jail door swung open; two other deputies waited to escort them down one corridor, then another, and into a barred mantrap that faced a metal door.

"There had better be a lawyer," Paget said to Monk, "on the other side of the door."

The metal door opened, and Paget and the others stepped through.

They were standing on the stage of an auditorium. The stage itself was lit from above, but the theater seats were shrouded in darkness: gazing out, Paget could see shadows moving, hear people whisper whom he could not see.

"Christopher," a voice called from the shadows. "I'm over here."

Silent, Paget nodded. The fact that Caroline had spoken to him meant that, for whatever reason, the witness was not yet there.

"All right," Monk said. "Spread out."

The six men formed a line. Monk gave them each a numbered card: Ray was three, Paget five. The men stared into space.

A flash cube went off. Paget blinked: it was the photo of the line-up, to be used in court. And then more flash cubes flickered in the darkness, as pictures were taken of each participant, one by one.

There was silence, then a reshuffling of the unseen bodies who watched them. It was as if the atmosphere had a new density; Paget sensed that the witness had been brought in.

From the darkness, a cop's bored voice began reading: "The person charged with the crime may not be here. You don't have to pick anyone. Don't pick anyone to please us. You don't have to pick anyone unless you're sure. . . ."

Somewhere in the darkness, the witness watched them.

"Number one," the cop's voice called out.

The short dark-haired man stepped forward from the line.

More silence, then whispers. "That's fine," the cop called out. "Number two."

The same: silence, whispers, a dismissal.

"Number three."

Ray stepped forward. He squared his shoulders, gazing out at the audience.

"Turn right," the cop's voice said.

Ray did so; Paget felt himself grip the card he held.

"Turn left."

Ray turned again. Paget started counting the seconds that passed. He was at twenty-one when the cop called out, "Step back. Next is number four."

Number four passed quickly. Swallowing, Paget hardly listened.

"Number five," the voice called out.

Paget stepped forward.

He gazed out at the darkness. In the silence, he felt the unknown witness. The absence of sound was oppressive.

"Turn right," the cop called out.

Paget did that. It was thirty seconds, with muffled voices talking in the dark, before the cop called out, "Turn left."

Paget's palms were sweating. He had stopped counting; he only knew that it seemed too long before the cop told him to step back.

Number six went quickly.

The six men stood there, facing their unseen audience.

"Could I see number three again?" a new voice asked.

A woman's voice, low and a little hoarse. Paget could not recognize it.

Ray stepped forward. He turned to the right again, then left, and then faced forward for what seemed quite long.

"Step back," the cop called out.

There was silence. And then, more softly, the woman said, "I want to see number five."

Paget stepped forward, facing the darkness again. No one asked him to turn.

"That's him." The woman's voice was shaking now. "I'm sure of it."

THE JURY

FEBRUARY 1—FEBRUARY 2
THE FOLLOWING YEAR

ONE

CHRISTOPHER PAGET watched the jury pool—eighty or so strangers with no connection to his past—wondering which twelve of them would now decide his future.

Judge Jared Lerner's spacious courtroom was a curious amalgam of sterility, majesty, and urban dinge. The walls were a cheap blond-wood paneling; the fluorescent squares overhead cast a pitiless light; and the worn theater seats behind the low wooden divider, packed with potential jurors, gave it the institutional look of an over-crowded classroom in an underfunded school. But the presence of a black-robed judge lent gravity, and the room had the taut hermetic feel unique to a high-profile murder case about to begin. Reporters lined the walls; the lawyers fidgeted or stared into space; Lerner himself—a sharp-featured man with a dark beard like the prow of a ship—looked edgy and alert.

Paget, sitting next to Caroline, could not enjoy an unconsidered moment: minute to minute, he was aware of each potential juror watching him. He sat very still, hands folded in front of him, trying to look serious yet composed, as ordinary as Caroline's artifice could make him.

The Italianate ties were gone, along with the double-breasted suits and the breast-pocket handkerchief. It was unsettling to realize how much of one's sense of self was superficial: the protective blandness he had assumed at Caroline's instance added to the diminishing effect of being brought before a court on a charge of murder—dependent on Caroline and a random group of strangers whose quirks he could not know and whose response to Paget's every look or gesture must be his constant concern. Part of him could still not believe that Ricardo Arias had brought him to this.

Of course, it was some comfort, he thought with irony, to have the best defense that money could buy: Caroline Masters and, seated discreetly behind them, the detective Johnny Moore. But neither Carlo nor Terri was here: as potential witnesses, they had been barred from court by Judge Lerner, on the motion of Victor Salinas.

Salinas had swiveled on his chair, hands in pockets, eyeing the jury pool with ostentatious casualness. The ease, Paget knew, was feigned: Salinas was gauging the ethnic composition of the panel, honing his strategy for selecting the jury that, on the basis of prejudice or predilection, was most likely to convict Paget of first-degree murder. They were about to begin the chess game where cases are won or lost—the strange mixture of intuition, sociology, pop psychology, and racism through which Caroline and Salinas would winnow eighty people down to twelve.

On the surface, Judge Lerner's rules were simple enough: the bailiff would call out twelve names at a time, and the candidates would shuffle forward to the jury box to be queried by Judge Lerner for competence or bias. If some disqualification was obvious, Lerner might dismiss a juror on his own accord, or Salinas or Caroline could ask him to do so for cause. But the real art lay in the lawyers' use of peremptory challenges: the precious occasions, twenty in number, on which each side could demand dismissal of a juror it did not want—either immediately or at any time before a jury was impaneled. Peremptories must be husbanded: Paget had seen defense lawyers, their peremptories exhausted, forced to accept a nightmare juror who then led his fellows to a verdict of guilty. And it was not hard to see trouble ahead for Caroline: the first prospects sitting in the jury box did not fit the profile she had hoped for, and there was an ominously high percentage of young Hispanic males.

"All right," Lerner said. He had a thin, reedy voice, but these first words brought down a curtain of silence. He turned to the first twelve panelists. "As you know," he continued, "this is the case of *People versus Christopher Paget*. The defendant, Christopher Paget, stands accused of murdering Ricardo Arias. My role, and that of counsel, is not to embarrass or discomfit you but simply to determine whether you can judge the facts fairly and impartially."

Caroline touched Paget's arm, as if to reassure him. But Paget knew that Caroline Masters must do more than pick jurors who claimed to be unbiased: somewhere in the panel, she must find twelve people who would acquit a man who would not testify in his own defense.

"First," Paget had said to Caroline, "Salinas has to prove beyond a reasonable doubt that Richie didn't kill *himself*. If he can't do that, I go free."

They had sat in the quiet elegance of Masa's restaurant, cool and dark and modern, the night after Paget's arrest. Paget had spent the preceding night on a cot in a solitary cell, listening to the low voices coming from the dark cages around him, the odd cry of protest or insanity, the footsteps of guards as they paced the corridor. After an angry session between Caroline and McKinley Brooks, they had agreed to the amount of bail. But arranging a half-million dollars had taken until early afternoon; after that, Paget had needed to wash away the smell of jail and the feel of prison clothes, then to reassure Carlo and Terri as best he could. Both conversations had been painful: it became clear that the best thing Paget could do for them, and for himself, was to start building a defense as quickly as he could. It was Caroline's grace note to take him to Masa's, a slice of Paget's normal life as far removed from prison as she could manage.

She sipped her Manhattan. "Suicide's a possible defense," she answered. "But based on the crime scene and the condition of the body, the medical examiner seems convinced that Richie was murdered. We not only have to shake her but have to give the jury some reason to believe that Richie wanted to kill himself." She frowned. "Other than good taste, that is."

The mordant comment was meant not as a joke, Paget knew, but as a spur: she did not yet know enough about Ricardo Arias to build an alternative to murder. "The script for suicide isn't hard to see," Paget answered. "He'd lost his wife, he had no job, and he was involved in a custody fight."

Caroline looked unimpressed. "Maybe. But it's not enough. I want a detective, Chris—I'd prefer your friend Johnny Moore, if that's all right. Among other things, I want to know every slimy little thing Ricardo ever did—I don't care if it was in grade school. I'll bet money that he didn't start with you and Terri."

"Maybe not. But the fact that Richie was a maggot isn't relevant to murder. At least in and of itself."

Caroline touched one finger to her lips; the brightness of her eyes, a half smile, lent the thoughtful gesture a faintly sensual quality. "I want the jury to despise him. All I need is an excuse, and then I'm going to trash him."

"All you need," Paget answered, "is a judge who'll let you get away with it. I can only think of one or two."

Caroline looked away; her eyes narrowed a little, but the smile remained. "Leave that to me."

The comment, quiet and ambiguous, lingered there a moment. "Maybe," Paget finally remarked, "you can say you're proving a lifetime of emotional instability. Or that, starting in kindergarten, eleven other people had good reason to kill him. Perhaps his sixth grade teacher."

Without responding, Caroline looked around her. Their table was in a quiet corner; three waiters, attentive but deferential, glided among the well-dressed diners—couples and business people on expense accounts—there to enjoy an elegant three-hour presentation of dishes. Quietly, Caroline said, "As of now, you know the only other decent suspect as well as I do. Better, in fact."

Paget felt himself stiffen. "Is that a serious observation?"

Caroline looked at him steadily. "She's not my client, Chris. I have to put this on the table. In some respects, Terri's a far more likely murderer than you."

Paget put down his drink. "There's no way."

Caroline watched his face. "As a matter of strategy? Or as a matter of fact?"

"Both."

Caroline gave the half smile again. "So I suppose I needn't mention Carlo. Who also has no alibi."

In his surprise, Paget almost laughed. "No," he answered. "I'm sentimental that way."

Caroline angled her head. "Then we have a lot of work to do, don't we. Just for the record, I assume you want to waive your right to trial in sixty days."

Paget sipped his martini, cold and bracing and medicinal. "No," he answered. "I don't."

Caroline's gaze became a stare, and she sat straighter; everything about her was intended to convey her restraint in not calling him a fool. "The prosecution is way ahead of us. We—*I*—need more time to assemble a defense."

Paget stared into the bottom of his drink. "But then," he said softly, "we'd be giving Salinas and Monk more time, wouldn't we?"

Caroline leaned back in her chair. The distance between them was more than physical; she studied him with a new air of reserve. "That assumes, Christopher, that there's something else for them to find."

The question, tacit yet pointed, left Paget with a feeling of vulnerability: except for Caroline, he was alone in this. "I don't want to live with this hanging over me, Caroline. Every day will be tainted, borrowed."

She shook her head almost angrily. "Then imagine the days you'll spend in *prison* if we don't give them our best. For God's sake, at least you're *free* now. Once the trial's over, the *best* thing that will have happened to you is that you're where you are right this minute—not in prison." She touched his arm for emphasis. "There's another practical thought to consider. This witness they've found is *not* a young woman. Given enough time, memories fade and witnesses even die. Without her, I think we win."

Paget met her eyes. "Before yesterday, Caroline, I'd have given the same advice. But I've had twenty-four hours of living with a charge of murder, and already everything has changed—my relationship to Carlo and Terri, the way I think about time. I doubt I'll even taste this dinner."

"Then think about Carlo—just that." Caroline leaned forward. "Suppose you're found guilty. If we stretch this out and then take an appeal, you'll have seen Carlo well into college before you go to prison. He's what now—a junior? Each month could be precious."

The combination of pragmatism and sentiment jarred Paget as much as having his own lawyer imagine the consequences of a guilty verdict. It was odd that Caroline, who had no children of her own, had put her finger so acutely on his fears. "I can't tell you," Paget said quietly, "how much—for Carlo's sake as well as mine—I don't want to go to jail."

Caroline's face went blank. "Then you might try thinking of Carlo, Chris. Rather than just using him as an excuse."

Paget gave her a level glance. "You play rough sometimes. Don't you, Caroline?"

The comment seemed to startle her, and then her face softened a little. "Only when I should."

He exhaled; the effect was somewhere between the release of tension and a plea for understanding. "I've tried to weigh everything, more carefully than you know. Including the effect of a delay on my chances of acquittal."

Caroline gave him a long, quiet look, as if to decipher his last comment. "Have you also considered," she asked for the first time, "whether you're going to testify?"

The seeming change of subject, Paget saw, was not a change at all. He tried to sound dispassionate, as if he were discussing theory with a colleague. "The conventional wisdom is that I don't. The jury might not like me, or Salinas might make me look bad."

Caroline propped her chin on folded hands, studying him keenly. "That's always possible. But you're an appealing man, and you have a fine record. Most important, you're a good father—one who would never risk leaving Carlo in the lurch, correct? And you just may be the only witness we have." Caroline narrowed her eyes, as if considering whether to say something more, and then continued in a quiet voice. "Juries can forgive someone they like, Chris, for lying to the police. Deep down, most jurors can imagine circumstances where *they* would lie to Charles Monk. They just won't forgive you for lying to *them*."

Behind Caroline's impassive gaze Paget sensed some obscure embarrassment. It took him a moment to understand: contrary to all her training, and against her better judgment, Caroline wished him to be innocent. "As of now," he answered calmly, "assume that I won't testify. I can always change my mind."

Caroline's eyes were very still for a moment, and then she shrugged, glancing down at the menu. "Have you had the salmon mousse here?" she asked. "It's quite wonderful."

Sitting next to Caroline, Paget watched Jared Lerner, the defense bar's favorite judge, question the first potential juror.

According to Johnny Moore's inquiries, the middle-aged redhead, Alice Mahan, was an Irish Catholic mother of four, a telephone operator for twenty years, the wife of a parochial school teacher, and the sister of a security guard. Paget, Caroline, and Johnny Moore had rated Alice four on a scale of one through five, placing her toward the bottom of the list, on the theory that Alice might be rules-oriented and inclined to trust authority. Which could be nonsense, Paget knew. But they had to start somewhere, and if Alice got past Lerner, Caroline must decide whether to use a peremptory challenge to strike her from the jury.

Which was one reason drawing Jared Lerner was such good fortune. Within moments, Lerner had asked Alice whether she believed that a defendant was innocent until proven guilty; whether she knew that guilt must be established beyond a reasonable doubt; and whether she understood that the prosecution bears the burden of proof. All of which principles Lerner was drilling into the potential jurors before the trial even started.

To each question, Alice Mahan had answered yes.

Lerner leaned forward from the bench, beard pointing toward Alice, bald head glistening under the fluorescent lights. "Some people," Lerner said, "feel that if a defendant doesn't testify, he or she may have something to hide. What do you think about that?"

It was perfect for the defense, an open-ended question that gave Alice permission to state her true beliefs. Glancing at Caroline, Paget silently thanked her for Jared Lerner.

"How did you do *that*?" he had murmured earlier that morning, as they were sent to Lerner's courtroom: with ten other judges available, the odds against Lerner seemed too high for coincidence.

Caroline smiled. "I didn't do anything, really."

"Define 'really.' "

She shrugged. "I saw him the other night, at a reunion for ex-public defenders. When he asked me what I was doing for fun, I told him a little about our case—which he'd read about, of course—and said that the trial would be fascinating." Another fleeting smile. "Judges are human, after all, as you no doubt calculated about *me* prior to the Carelli hearing. So I suppose that Jared Lerner might have *asked* for this assignment."

Now, as Alice Mahan formed her answer, Paget watched Victor Salinas scowling.

"If a defendant doesn't testify?" Alice asked in a puzzled tone. "I really don't know about that."

Lerner gave her a pleasant smile. "I'm sure you've never had to give it any thought. Why don't you just take a moment and do that now. For example, try to imagine Mr. Paget not testifying, and tell me how you feel."

Alice cocked her head, squinting. "I don't think I'd be satisfied, really. I mean, a man on trial for murder shouldn't want to leave us with any questions."

It was the very mind-set Caroline and Paget feared. Their focus on the judge was as taut as Salinas's.

Contemplating Alice Mahan, Lerner stroked his beard. "Do you think," he asked slowly, "you could judge the case fairly if he decides *not* to testify?"

Alice hesitated and then gave a small nod. "I'm not sure," she said finally. "But I'd certainly *try*, Your Honor."

Tensing, Paget saw Salinas turn to Lerner with a hopeful expression. "Strike her," Caroline said under her breath. "Please."

Lerner gave Alice a nod of approval. "I'm sure you'd try, Mrs. Mahan. And I appreciate the help you've given me. But in fairness, I think I should excuse you."

Salinas turned away. "Bingo," Caroline murmured.

"One of the nasty little racist secrets of picking San Francisco juries," Johnny Moore had said to Caroline, "is for defense lawyers to strike as many Asians as possible. Is there anything about Chris's case that makes you disagree?"

They were meeting in Caroline's office—the detective, Paget, and Caroline herself—to strategize on the selection of a jury. But where Paget and Caroline Masters looked as if they belonged there, Moore—with his white beard and the ruddy face of a reformed drinker, his wool sport coat and corduroy slacks and tennis shirt open at the throat—seemed more like a pro bono client who had been sent to Caroline by Legal Aid.

"Asians?" Caroline answered. "It depends. If we're talking immigrants or the unassimilated, I suppose I agree: they tend to defer to authority and to forget the presumption of innocence. But give me a second- or third-generation Asian, especially a professional with an advanced education, and things start to look quite different. At least there I don't worry so much about class bias." She leaned back in her chair, hands behind her head, reading glasses halfway down her nose. "All right," she said dryly to both Moore and Paget, "who's next? Now that we've covered Asians."

"Latins," Paget said. "For two reasons. One living, one dead."

Caroline nodded. "Salinas and Richie. Too much chance of identification."

"No argument there," Moore put in. "I wouldn't take a Latin male. Period."

Caroline shrugged. "There are no absolutes," she said, "in jury selection. But let's move on. The prosecution case is a law enforcement package: Salinas is going to give them the M.E.'s take on Richie's body, then Monk's investigation, and ask the jury to trust that it was murder. Part of *my* story is going to be that the D.A. played dirty and that this is a prosecution and police vendetta. So we have to be wary of blue collar folks who dislike the rich and identify with cops."

Moore glanced sideways at Paget. "Or," he said slowly, "people who are uncomfortable with incomplete stories."

Caroline smiled with one side of her mouth. "Yes," she said with irony. "Chris and I have discussed that."

There was an awkward quiet. Caroline did not look at Paget; her gaze settled somewhere above his head, as if fixed on a thought. "I'd add lawyer-haters," Paget said to fill the silence.

"Of course." Caroline folded her arms. "So who *do* we want?"

Paget thought for a moment. "As a gross generalization, the old civil rights coalition—Jews and blacks. Jews because of a humanist bent that goes with a certain sympathy for the accused, blacks because the black community knows that cops are not always free from bias."

Caroline looked dubious. "Monk complicates that, don't you think? They'll listen to him and respect him. What I need, frankly, is *anyone* who doesn't trust authority."

Moore frowned. "That's why education is so important here, as long as it's combined with imagination. Chris's case depends on finding a jury that is capable of abstract thinking—imagining alternative scenarios you may never be able to prove. If we were lucky, we'd get a jury of white Yale-educated poets who vote the liberal line and come from East Coast cities."

Caroline shook her head. "Even if we could find them, Salinas would mow them down." The smile she gave Moore was somewhat grim. "Maybe you can find us an artichoke or two."

Moore looked puzzled. An artichoke, Paget knew, was defense lawyer's argot for any juror who looked weird enough to hang a jury for no discernible reason, and picking one was the greatest art of all: Paget had once hung a jury in a case he should have lost by sneaking in a juror who—once the case was over—asked him with a bug-eyed stare if the world would survive the twentieth century. "An artichoke," he explained to Moore, "is a juror who knows I'm innocent because his dead mom tells him so."

Moore smiled at this but said nothing.

"Artichokes come in all forms," Caroline put in helpfully. "You might want to comb the jury pool for women with an obsessive attraction to blond, silent males."

The comment, delivered in a tone of mock innocence, carried a pointed barb: it reminded Paget uncomfortably that his lawyer was headed for a trial earlier than she wanted, for reasons Paget refused to explain, and in which he would say nothing. "Some of our premises may be debatable," Paget said evenly. "But a few aren't. We can't have people poisoned by pretrial publicity. And, whoever else is on the jury, we can't risk anyone with an emotional connection to suicide or custody fights." He paused, adding softly, "Or, for that matter, child molestation."

Caroline's face changed; she gave him a brief look of sympathy, and then her voice turned crisp. "This is all very well," she said at last. "But everything we've said, Salinas knows too. He'll bump our theoretical dream jurors as fast as they pop up. And in the end, we'll wind up in a lottery, compromising and picking jurors on feel." She paused for emphasis. "At some point—perhaps more than once— Victor and I will *both* gamble on the same juror. And one of us will be wrong."

Paget felt unsettled. "What's your point, Caroline?"

She looked at him directly. "That when it comes right down to it, I'd trust my instincts over Victor Salinas's. Or even yours." She paused, then finished quietly: "If we're down to the last juror, Chris, and there's any question about what to do, *I* want to make the call. Because *I'm* the only one of us who'll be telling that juror that *you* are not a murderer."

Victor Salinas, Paget had begun to perceive with apprehension, could project a certain charm.

He was questioning the twenty-third of the first twenty-four initial panelists, a process that had yielded three jurors: a white male public school teacher; a black bank officer; and a middle-aged Filipina stenographer. These were compromises. None fit the jury profile for Christopher Paget or, with the possible exception of the Filipina, whom Caroline thought persuadable, for the prosecution; it was Caroline's assessment that they were the best the defense could do and that Salinas was likely to keep them as well. As for the remaining twenty, Jared Lerner had struck three who looked bad for the defense, Victor Salinas had used seven of his peremptories in a pattern that would have seemed random had his targets not all been well educated, and Caroline had already expended ten—five Latin males, punctuated by two Asian immigrants, a Japanese doctor who had lost a bitter custody fight, the nephew of a New York cop, and a retired black army sergeant, who, in Caroline's murmured aside, seemed more military than militant.

The problem was the jury pool. Except for the Filipina stenographer, Caroline had stuck to the script. But she was using up peremptories too quickly, both she and Paget agreed, and she was unhappy for yet another reason. "We're striking too many minorities," she whispered to Paget. "The jury panel may begin to think *we're* prejudiced."

Paget had nodded. But the ten panelists Caroline had stricken had seemed ripe for Victor Salinas. Now, helpless, they watched Salinas question the juror Paget most wanted: an attractive sixty-year-old Jewish woman named Marian Celler, whose husband was a cardiologist; whose daughters were a professor of Romance languages and a graduate student in anthropology; and who had helped administer several significant charities. When Johnny Moore leaned forward to say that they take her, both Caroline and Paget had agreed.

Standing near the jury box, Salinas smiled at Celler. "Your family has distinguished itself," he said pleasantly, "by not having sent a single member to law school. Is this an accident, or is it another re-flection of good parenting?"

The prospective jurors laughed at the mild joke, seemingly a throwaway. But Paget knew the joke had been planned for days. Sa-linas intended to disassociate himself from his own profession: he was not one of *those* lawyers, his manner suggested, but someone who protected his fellow citizens from the worst of lawyers' tricks.

Celler gave Salinas a perfunctory smile. "It's an accident," she said. "Neither of our daughters wanted to be a doctor, either. And *I* married one."

Salinas jammed his hands in his pockets. "Have you had any expe-rience with members of the legal profession?"

"Yes, Mr. Salinas. My husband and I have had the same lawyer for twenty-five years."

"And have you been satisfied?"

Celler gave a vigorous nod. "Oh, very. Harold helped my hus-band set up his professional corporation, and he has our estate in good order. He's not only our adviser but our friend."

"She's dead," Paget whispered to Caroline.

As if to confirm this, Salinas said, "That's all *I* have, Mrs. Celler," and sat down.

Caroline rose. "Good afternoon, Mrs. Celler."

Celler smiled. "Good afternoon."

Caroline walked toward the jury box. "I'm sure you're aware, as Mr. Salinas's questions suggested, that Mr. Paget is himself a lawyer."

"Oh, yes."

Caroline glanced briefly at Salinas, then back at Celler. "Based on your experience, Mrs. Celler, what is your opinion of the integrity of the legal profession?"

Celler leaned forward. "Oh, it's quite high. Our lawyer, for one, is a man of great integrity. And I'm aware from my charitable work of how much lawyers give back to the community, both in money and in services."

This time, facing Salinas with raised eyebrows, Caroline gave him a one-sided smile that lingered until the jury panel saw it. Only then did she turn back to Celler. "It's been nice to know you," Caroline said dryly. "However briefly."

There was coughing from the press contingent, the sound of suppressed laughter. As Caroline sat down, Salinas gave her a look of anger: with one subversive comment, Caroline had made it clear to the panelists that Salinas was trying to cash in on antilawyer bias. Now he had the choice of confirming it or letting on a juror that he plainly did not want.

A certain amusement flickered in Judge Lerner's eyes. "Mr. Salinas?" he asked.

Victor could wait, Paget knew, deciding later whether to strike Marian Celler. But it was his practice to decide right away, relying on his initial instincts. He composed himself, standing straighter for the jury, pride and indecision crossing his face. A little too loudly, he said, "The people pass Mrs. Celler."

"Oh, Victor," Caroline murmured under her breath, "that really wasn't very smart."

Just after five-thirty, they adjourned.

Marian Celler had been Caroline's finest moment. She had used fourteen peremptories, with only six left; had Jared Lerner not stricken two propolice jurors for cause, matters would have been even worse. Among the eight jurors passed, Caroline had been forced to accept the first two Asians, a Chinese medical technician whose parents came from Hong Kong and a twenty-year-old Vietnamese immigrant. Most of her peremptories had been used on Latins: Caroline did not like the message this might send, and tomorrow's panel was even heavier on Asians, Latins, and the less well educated than today's had been. When Paget had suggested that they spend the evening reviewing their approach to the jury pool, Caroline had readily agreed.

They drove from the underground garage in Caroline's black Mercedes-Benz. Paget was surprised to see that the sky was dark; the onset of the trial had broken his connection to the outside world. Tonight, he knew, they would sit in an interior conference room, sandwiches and jury questionnaires spread out on the table; he would briefly call Carlo, then Terri, and then spend the next several hours trying to enter the minds of strangers who lived only on paper.

Caroline turned down Mission Street, the towers of the financial district looming to the left, dark forms with squares of light. "Mind if I open the sunroof?" Paget asked. "I'm feeling stale, like we've spent all day on an airplane."

Caroline smiled. "Whatever helps."

Paget pushed the button and leaned back, trying to pick a star or two out of the city sky, which was dulled by the reflection of artificial light. Lately, he had tried to experience life as a series of moments, small and still and as perfect as he could make them. With the breeze on his face, Paget, finding what he thought was a star, remembered the night sky the last time he and Terri had gone sailing.

It was perhaps five weeks before. Paget could not stand being inside, and there was no place they could go where heads would not turn. When he had proposed to sail at night, Terri had not questioned him.

The sail had been quiet and cool. Terri sat in the stern of Paget's boat, wearing an oversize leather jacket Paget had bought in Venice. After a time, the wind almost died, and they drifted in the middle of San Francisco Bay. The water was black; the lights of the city climbed the hills; the beams of cars crept like soldier ants across the Golden Gate Bridge. Above them, the sky seemed to break away from the lights of the city, becoming deeper and darker as it moved north toward Marin County, filling with stars. Paget gazed at the sky and then at Terri; her hair was black and glossy in the moonlight, and her face seemed more beautiful than Paget could remember. All he wanted was to look at her.

Her eyes were still and serious. After a time, she asked, "Why won't you testify?"

"I was hoping to get away from all that, Terri," he answered. "At least for tonight."

He felt her gaze. "Do you and Carlo go through this too?"

"All the time. There's nothing I can say to him that Salinas couldn't ask about."

Terri shook her head. "But not to testify . . ." She let the sentence drop there; she did not need to finish it.

Paget did not answer. In the silence, Terri shook her head again; this time, the gesture had an absent quality, a sense of numb amazement. "Warner Books called me this morning. They want to do a book and then package it as a miniseries."

Paget gave a short laugh. "Who plays you?"

Terri did not smile. "Rosie Perez is hot, the guy told me. I guess all Latinas must look alike."

Paget gazed up at the sky. "In *this* version," he asked finally, "am I innocent or guilty?"

Terri folded her arms. "We never got that far."

Her voice was cool with remembered anger. Paget turned to her; in that moment, her profile reminded him of the cover of a glossy magazine, perhaps two weeks ago, with Terri taking Elena from school beneath the caption: "Did Christopher Paget Kill for Her?" Inside, there was an account of Paget's life and Richie's charges; beside the part that discussed the claim of child molestation was a picture of Carlo and yet another of Elena. Near the end of the article was a quote from Sonia Arias, saying that Terri's role in her late son's "murder" had not been probed to Sonia's satisfaction.

"How *is* Elena?" Paget finally asked.

"About the same, as far as I or Denise Harris can tell. Although I like her new school better." Terri's voice grew tired. "She started to make her first real friend, and then the girl told her that her mommy's boyfriend killed her father."

The weight of things felt so oppressive that to express regret, Paget realized, would sound banal. "And Rosa?" he asked finally.

"Is being very quiet. As she should." Terri's voice softened. "I keep thinking about Carlo. When we first knew how we felt, it seemed like it could be so good for both our kids."

"It *would* have been, except for Richie." Paget leaned back, gazing at the outline of the Golden Gate Bridge, dark towers rising from the glow of car lights moving. "As for Carlo, his friends are standing by him. But he seems tougher somehow, less trusting. Which I suppose makes sense if the person you've depended on may disappear."

Terri looked away; Paget felt her exhale. "You're really afraid they'll find you guilty, aren't you?"

Paget made himself look into her face. In the dim light, he thought—or perhaps imagined—that there were tears in her eyes. "I know this has been terrible," he said. "Not only for Elena but for *you.*" He took both her hands in his. "Six years ago you married Richie, thinking in the back of your mind that there was something wrong but telling yourself to believe in him, if only for the sake of the child you would have. Now it's happening to you all over again, isn't it?"

Terri seemed startled. The tears, Paget saw, were real. "I'm afraid of losing you, Chris."

Slowly, Paget shook his head. "No," he said softly. "You're afraid I'm *not* me."

TWO

THE SECOND MORNING of jury selection, Christopher Paget went to court with the wired alertness that came from rigorous exercise and too little sleep. Since his arrest, his workout regime had gone from strenuous to harsh; he drank only wine; he went to bed at ten o'clock. The result was a rush of energy; he felt keen, alive, more fit than he had in years. But there was nothing he could do about broken sleep: the times that he awoke suddenly, wondering what else he could have done, and could not rest his mind any more than he could change the past.

Now Paget studied the faces in the jury box, searching each stranger for some spark of shared humanity or, perhaps, charity. At Caroline's request, Judge Lerner had just stricken for cause a forty-ish graduate student whose demographic profile was good but who, Caroline's questions uncovered, was amid bitter divorce proceedings in which she had accused her estranged husband of child abuse, and who ultimately was forced to concede that she might not be fair. The current panelist, a Korean engineer named James Rhee, had seemed to please Salinas; as Caroline Masters rose to question him, he watched her with wary politeness. Moore had rated Rhee a prosecution juror: his notes included "inclined to defer to authority" and "engineer—may not like loose ends."

Caroline herself was down to four peremptory challenges, and it appeared that four jurors still remained to be picked. "Prior to these proceedings," she asked, "were you aware of who Mr. Paget was?"

Rhee gave a cautious nod. "Sure. There were so many articles about this case—I especially remember the one in *Newsweek* with Mr. Paget on the cover. And there was a program on *20/20*."

Caroline raised an eyebrow. From tabloids to *The New York Times*, the publicity had been massive and unrelenting. It was time, she had told Paget this morning, to remind the jurors that he had done things much more favorable than to be charged with killing Ricardo Arias. "Was that the *first* time you'd ever heard of Mr. Paget?"

Rhee removed his wire-rimmed glasses, wiping them carefully. "Oh, no. I remember Mr. Paget from when he was planning to run for the Senate."

His tone was decidedly neutral. "Did you have an impression of Mr. Paget *then?*" Caroline asked.

For the first time, Rhee smiled. "Yes. That he was not of my political party."

With that, Paget was ready to strike him. But Caroline was not sitting down. Wryly, she said, "I take it you're not a Democrat."

Watching Salinas, Paget saw him frown. Seventy-five percent of San Franciscans, and at least that much of the jury pool, were Democrats with a decidedly liberal bias; Paget recognized this as Caroline's first chance to make that connection between Paget and the jury panel. Ruefully, Rhee shook his head. "No," he said. "In San Francisco, it gets kind of lonely. Even my kids think Michael Dukakis got elected President."

There was a wave of laughter from the jury pool and, in particular, the press. Even Judge Lerner smiled a bit. "Don't worry, Mr. Rhee," he said. "In this courtroom, Republicans are cherished, and preserved. Rather like the spotted owl."

More laughter, this time with an undertone of warmth; that people seemed so eager for relief reminded Paget that the jury selection had become a grim contest. Belatedly, he reminded himself to smile for the panel's sake.

But Caroline's smile at Rhee seemed genuine. "Despite being an endangered species," she said, "do you feel you can judge this case fairly?"

A brisk nod. "Sure. That's my job here."

Caroline appraised him for a moment and then nodded. "Every jury can use an owl," she said. "Spotted or no. Thank you, Mr. Rhee."

Paget felt a hand on his shoulder. Moore was leaning forward; as Paget turned, he whispered, "Don't let her take this guy."

But Caroline was walking toward the defense table with a satisfied expression. "Mr. Salinas?" Lerner was asking.

Salinas stood. "The people pass Mr. Rhee."

As Caroline sat down, Johnny Moore scooted his chair forward. "Ding him," he whispered. "He's bad news."

Caroline turned to him, eyes narrowing. "The man has a sense of humor, and the jury likes him. I'm damned near out of peremptories, and I think I can work with him."

"Ms. Masters?" Lerner was asking.

Caroline looked at Paget. Almost imperceptibly, he shook his head.

Quickly, she turned toward Judge Lerner. "Might we have a moment to confer?"

"Of course. As long as that's what it is—a moment."

Caroline leaned forward, looking at Paget. Their faces were inches apart, Moore's to the side. Ignoring Moore, Caroline asked, "What is it?"

Tense, Paget felt the courtroom watching. "Too risky," he answered. "I agree with Johnny—he's not a natural for us. And if he goes on, *he's* the foreman. Count on it."

"Maybe," Caroline said tersely. "But Rhee won't like the Richie we're going to give them. He's much more likely to admire *you.*"

"Not *Chris,*" Moore interjected. "The one he'll admire is Victor Salinas. The hardworking representative of law and order."

Caroline's eyes remained on Paget. "I want him, Chris. What'll it be?"

Paget took a deep breath. "Strike him."

Caroline watched him for a moment; rising, she gave Moore a look of something close to anger. But when she turned to Lerner, her face was calm. "With deep regret," she said, "we've decided to excuse Mr. Rhee."

During the morning recess, Caroline was quiet, studying jury questionnaires at the defense table. Paget was still troubled by the decision he had made; in the hallway, he could not resist seeking reassurance from Johnny Moore.

Moore looked around them for reporters. "I think we were right, of course. But if *you* were trying the case, and Caroline was the client, you'd have taken him."

"Why do you think that?"

"Because, like Caroline, you bet your instincts. And because she may think that I've found enough to give Salinas a rude surprise, assuming he's fool enough to try marketing little Richie Pondscum as the poster boy for the American Dream."

It was, Paget thought, exactly what they had asked Moore to do, the day they first met at Caroline's office.

There had been just the three of them in an oversize conference room lined with Oriental murals. The oak-paneled table was large enough for a directors meeting and so shiny that Paget could make out his reflection. "Ample quarters," Moore observed to Caroline. "I can almost hear the meter running. How many lawyers have to work to keep this up?"

"Nearly five hundred."

Moore shook his head. "And to think," he said in his soft Irish lilt, "that this country can't even make a decent refrigerator."

The comment was very like the Johnny that Paget had always known, a curious combination of cynic and sentimentalist who for years had lived the risky and duplicitous life of an undercover agent for the FBI and yet still believed—or so Paget suspected—that he wanted the family and children he had never stopped to have. Moore had a particular fondness for Terri, Paget knew, but seemed to have a certain aversion to Caroline Masters—perhaps because Caroline, so steely in her desire for privacy, betrayed no flaws with which Johnny could sympathize. Sitting across from him, Caroline gave Moore an enigmatic smile, somewhere between courtesy and amusement.

"The reason," she said, "that there are so many of us is that Americans hate every lawyer but their own, and every lawsuit except the one they want to bring. Just as they respect every law but the one they want to *break*. When a people's social conscience dies, the law thrives; all these lawyer jokes are simply cover for their own complicity."

Johnny gave a soft chuckle; the comment, offhand yet telling, seemed to remind him that Caroline was very smart. "If my *refrigerator* dies," he said, "I'll come to you."

"Oh," she said dryly, "*we'll* be representing the manufacturer, of course. But let's move on."

Johnny nodded briskly. "Ricardo Arias. An inferior product if there ever was one." He glanced at Paget. "Chris says you'd like my thoughts on where to start."

"Indeed."

"With Charles Monk." Johnny stretched back in his swivel chair. "Specifically, with the crime scene report. Monk is a good detective. But people—including jurors—have a total misconception of what homicide cops do. They think someone like Monk shows up with an empty mind and then, like a vacuum cleaner, gathers the facts in a thorough and objective inquiry to come up with the perpetrator. It's a lovely notion. And, of course, it's absolutely preposterous."

Paget found himself smiling; it was good to remember why he had such faith in Johnny. "Police are human beings," Moore went on. "They arrive at a crime scene, like Richie's apartment, take it all in, and then start to come up with a 'hypothesis'—which simply means a guess too lacking in support to be dignified as a theory.

"It's no different than trying one of these damned jigsaw puzzles they make too difficult for children. You have to start with an idea of how the puzzle will look when all the pieces fit, and then work toward that. There really is no other way to attack a puzzle— whether it's a kid's game or a homicide." Pausing for a moment, Moore smiled. "Monk's problem—*every* cop's problem—is when you start *trying* to make the pieces fit. Sooner or later, Monk tried to do that. It's human nature."

Caroline folded her hands. "We need everything Monk missed, Johnny, and every lead he didn't follow. One point I'd like to sell to the jury is that this is a political vendetta, whether because Brooks lost the Carelli case or because Chris had the nerve to enter politics without being anointed by James Colt, Junior."

Moore shrugged. "You can probably make it *look* like that, whether it's true or not. There'll be *something* Monk didn't do— there always is. Fortunately for Chris, jurors become disenchanted when they discover the cops aren't perfect."

Listening, Paget realized how much more cynical defense strategies sounded now that he was the client. "I'm sure there *was* politics," he put in. "All the while, I got the opposite of preferential treatment, right down to breaking the crockery. I could feel Colt's hands on the levers, whether I could see him or not."

Moore turned to Caroline. "This may be off the subject, Counselor, but don't *you* worry a wee bit about offending Mr. Colt. He'll likely be our next governor, after all."

Caroline gave him a look that was less serene than simply without expression. "Why would I worry?" she asked.

Moore let it go; Caroline, Paget saw, meant to leave him with no choice. Paget wondered if she understood Moore's intentions: Paget was his friend, and Moore wanted to ensure that Caroline would not place ambition above her client. "Next," Moore said without skipping a beat, "we have this eyewitness. You'll want eyesight, drug or alcohol use, any prescriptions, whether she's reported crimes before, what the neighbors say. And, for that matter, whether she has visions of Warren G. Harding on odd Wednesdays."

Caroline nodded. "Everything," she said in a flat voice. "I also want you to go over each of her dealings with the police. We can't let this woman survive."

Over his smile, Moore appraised Caroline Masters with cool gray-blue eyes. "Good citizenship surely has its price, doesn't it? Which gets us back to Richie. I assume you mean to sully the poor man's posthumous reputation."

Caroline met his gaze, answering sardonically, "However did you guess?"

"There seems to be a pattern here. Frankly, if you didn't try to make Richie's death seem like a public service, I'd suggest a saliva test for both of you." He turned to Paget. "Didn't Monk say something that made you wonder if Richie was seeing a psychiatrist?"

"Uh-huh."

"If that's true, and if the shrink is prepared to say that Richie wasn't suicidal, Salinas may want to call him. Either way, I'll find out." He faced Caroline again. "I'll run Ricardo's life through the grinder—neighbors, schools, family, girlfriends, finances, jobs, business associates, doctor visits, traffic tickets, legal problems. I assume you'd like him to look dirty and, better yet, to have had a deep-seated desire to simplify his life through suicide."

Caroline nodded. "If possible. I'd also like the names of anyone but Chris with a reason to dislike him."

Something in Moore's face changed, as if Caroline had reminded him that his friend Christopher Paget had enough reason to kill Ricardo Arias so that even Moore could not be sure. "Yes," he said softly. "Other suspects would be nice."

There was silence. When Moore turned to Paget, his eyes were wary but nonjudgmental. "Do *you* have any ideas, Chris? Other than Terri, that is."

His voice, as Caroline's once had, held a buried plea for help. Not just with the case, Paget knew, but with his doubts.

Paget was quiet for a time. "If it were me, Johnny, I'd work very hard on suicide."

Luisa Marin was a slender young Hispanic woman with red-brown hair, pale skin, and a fragile, almost haunted look. Caroline had noticed her among the jury panel about an hour before; there was something about her expression, inward and yet tense, that set her apart. Caroline had guessed at emotional problems, some deep-seated fear that disassociated her from the world at large. But when Caroline had begun to question her, Luisa seemed focused if wary; in the same way that had seemed to satisfy Salinas, she answered Caroline in a few brief words. She was troubled, Caroline sensed, but not one of the deracinated shells Caroline saw talking to themselves on the streets: Caroline guessed that there was something beneath the sparse facts—jobless, Catholic, lightly educated—that had placed her near the bottom of Chris's list.

"I see that you're at home," Caroline said. "Have you been looking for work?"

Luisa did not really answer. "I was an inventory clerk," she said quietly. "Before."

Her eyes moved from Caroline's face; the effect was of someone looking at another part of her life. "Before what?" Caroline asked.

Luisa looked back at Caroline with a directness that was somehow disconcerting; it reminded Caroline of the "thousand-yard stare" she had sometimes seen on veterans of Vietnam. "After my father died," she said simply, "my mother had a stroke. I take care of her now."

Somewhere within that answer, Caroline knew, hid a problem she could feel on the back of her neck. Her next question was instinctive. "How did your father die?"

Luisa folded her hands, drawing her shoulders in. The impression was of a woman being violated. "He was a policeman," Luisa answered.

For an instant, Caroline imagined some urban tragedy. It was only as she repeated her last question that, with something like horror, she sensed the answer.

"How did he die, Ms. Marin?"

Luisa's face became immobile, almost waxen. In a soft, firm voice, she answered, "He was cleaning his gun."

Caroline realized that she was standing very still. "Was there," she asked gently, "a question of suicide?"

Focused on Marin, Caroline felt the silence as a vacuum. With sudden vehemence, Luisa shook her head. "He would never kill himself," she said fiercely. "He was a good Catholic and a good man."

"But people do," Caroline answered softly, "all the time. Even Catholics, and especially policemen."

There was a sheen of tears on Luisa's face now. Caroline half expected Lerner to break in. But he did not; surely he must understand that suicide was critical to Chris's defense, and that Caroline had too few peremptories not to push every juror to the limit. "Is there a question?" Salinas broke in. "Or are you done, Counselor?"

Caroline ignored him. Marin's lifeless expression had become the stricken look of a woman recoiling from her own doubts. "Do you believe," Caroline asked, "that suicide is a sin?"

A moment's silence. In a parched voice, Marin answered, "That is what the Church teaches."

"It also teaches, does it not, that sins are forgiven."

Marin sat straighter. "He would not do that to my mother. It nearly killed her."

Caroline nodded. "But you're not sure," she said finally. "Are you?"

Marin only stared at her. "Ms. Masters," she heard Jared Lerner say, "how far do you intend to pursue this?"

When Caroline turned, Lerner was studying Luisa Marin with an air of unhappiness. "I need some latitude," Caroline said. "With your indulgence, Your Honor, this is important."

Lerner gave her a long contemplative look and then nodded. Once more, Caroline faced Marin. "There are parts of a policeman's life," she said softly, "that even those closest to him cannot know. Do you understand that?"

Marin's tears had vanished. Silent, she nodded.

Gently, Caroline asked, "What does your mother believe?"

Marin seemed to flinch. "When she found him," she answered, "she went into shock. That night, the stroke came. The last words I ever heard her speak were the day before my father died."

Caroline paused a moment. In a tone of sympathy, she asked, "I take it there was no note."

"No."

Caroline paused, letting her reference to a note sink in among the jurors. "But still," she asked, "you can't be sure, can you?

Marin's eyes flickered. "Only in my heart."

"Because you knew him as your father." Caroline paused. "If not as a policeman."

Marin bobbed her head. It was not clear what she was answering.

Caroline walked to the railing of the jury box, looking at Marin, in the second row. The effect was intimate, as if she were speaking to the woman alone.

"Of course," Caroline said, "you didn't know Ricardo Arias at all."

"Speak up, Counselor," Salinas interjected from behind her. "I'm having trouble hearing."

It was, Caroline knew, an effort to break whatever connection she might be developing with Luisa Marin. Looking straight at Marin, Caroline murmured, more softly yet, "Quit playing games, Victor."

Salinas stood. With a certain dignity, he said, "I'm not the one who's playing games, Counselor."

Caroline turned to him. "Then I'll keep speaking in a softer voice, Mr. Salinas. So that you can hear me."

There was muffled laughter from the press, and Salinas looked stung. But when Caroline turned, Luisa Marin's face had relaxed a little.

"Do you believe," Caroline asked her, "that the police are free from prejudice?"

Marin seemed to hesitate; it seemed as if the question was beyond her experience, and then she looked away. "My father didn't," she said reluctantly. "Sometimes it bothered him. 'They pass good laws,' he used to say, 'and then we enforce them against people we don't like.'"

To a criminal lawyer, the comment had an unnerving accuracy. "Did your father ever worry that the innocent are punished?"

"Yes." Marin's voice was firmer now. "As I said, he was a good man."

Caroline nodded. "And are you willing to accept the possibility that, in *this* case, the police have been unfair to Mr. Paget?"

"Yes."

Pausing, Caroline looked into Marin's face. "Even if that means, Luisa, that the prosecution has overlooked the reasonable possibility that Ricardo Arias killed himself."

It was more statement than question; as if, by answering, Luisa Marin would make a compact with Caroline Masters. Marin seemed to steel herself. "Yes," she said in a determined voice. "I can."

Caroline nodded. "Thank you, Luisa. I believe that." She turned to Judge Lerner. "I have nothing more, Your Honor. I appreciate your indulgence."

Lerner gave her a courtly nod and glanced at Salinas. "Mr. Salinas?" he asked.

Just before Caroline turned, walking toward the defense table, she saw Salinas's frown of uncertainty. She had almost reached the table when she heard Salinas say, "The prosecution passes Ms. Marin."

Chris, she saw, was regarding her with a contemplative expression. "Well?" she murmured.

The corner of Chris's mouth twitched. Caroline studied him for a moment; his eyes, she saw, held a warmth she had not seen for days. And then, almost imperceptibly, he shrugged.

All at once, Caroline felt the full weight of defending him. So that it was a moment before she could turn and say, "The defense accepts Ms. Marin."

But then Caroline had felt this weight since the morning, three weeks before, when Teresa Peralta appeared at her office.

This was not like Terri, Caroline thought; ever since she had worked for Caroline, at the public defender's office, Terri had been careful to observe the protocol of a professional. Even her suits, well tailored but cautious, had fit the role: it was as if the young Hispanic woman, without models of her own, was adhering to the script until she could find her way.

Caroline had never doubted that she would. Beneath the careful exterior, Terri had combined compassion with an almost unnerving directness; life had taught her to strip things to the bone yet given her the intuition to look into someone's heart. Except—and here Caroline thought of Richie—when that someone was very close to her, and a man. It was something Caroline understood.

Without preface, Terri sat at Caroline's desk. "I'm sorry to come like this," she said. "But if I'd called first, you might have told Chris. And that's what I don't want."

Over the last two years, Caroline had not seen Terri much: she seemed older now and, though still polite, much less deferential. Caroline wondered which part of that, and for what reason, came from being with Christopher Paget.

"Chris *is* my client, you know. I can't promise you confidentiality."

Terri gave a dismissive smile. "Of course not. But at least this way, once you've heard me out, you can decide for yourself without having told Chris that I was coming."

Terri was so cool in manner that it seemed she hardly knew Caroline at all. Quietly, Caroline asked, "Are you all right, Teresa?"

The question seemed to startle Terri; Caroline realized that she had come here with business on her mind and was trying to hang on to that. But Terri's face—strong and delicate and beautiful— suddenly conveyed such worry that Caroline remembered how young she still was. "No," Terri said tersely. "Nothing's all right. But the reason I'm here is that unless something changes, Chris is going down."

Somehow the words hit Caroline hard. "How can you know that?"

"Because I knew Richie." Terri was almost too still: now she could not look at Caroline. "Once I leave here, Caroline, we never had this conversation. You don't have to worry about what I'll say"—here Terri paused—"anywhere else or to *anyone* else. But there's no way that Richie killed himself. I don't believe it, and I don't think you believe it, either."

Caroline felt the blessed nervelessness kick in, twenty years of being a lawyer, fighting the unruliness of her own emotions. Calmly, she answered, "Let's stick to what *you* don't believe. And why."

Terri faced her again. "Part of it's the way that note is written."

"Why? It's only a fragment—a few words."

"It's enough." Terri leaned forward. "Richie would never admit to being 'selfish and pathetic' to anyone, even if it would be read when he was dead. His whole life was spent trying to hide the truth—not 'facing' it, like the note says. There's this tone of moral disapproval that just isn't Richie. He didn't hold himself to normal standards."

A strain in Terri's voice, an uneasy combination of stress and remembered anger, lent her words conviction. Caroline asked, "What about the picture on the desk?"

Terri's eyelids fell. "That seems more right," she said finally. "Except that it's the kind of thing Richie would do to touch someone's heart, for money. Not to make someone feel sad when it wouldn't do him any good."

To Caroline, this had the uneasy ring of truth. "Is there anything else," she asked softly, "about Richie? Or about Chris?"

Terri seemed to pause; for a moment, Caroline thought that she might blurt something out. Instead Terri chose her words with care. "Ever since my mother called me in Portofino," she said finally, "I've been sure that Richie would be the last person on earth to hurt himself. Other people, yes. But to kill yourself you have to despise yourself, I think, or to feel such shame that you can't stand it. The man I married wasn't capable of either emotion."

Caroline leaned back in her chair. "Why are you telling me this, Terri?"

Terri's gaze was steady now. "Because I don't want Chris to spend his life in prison. He's already suffered for Richie, far too much."

Caroline gave her a curious smile. "And you somehow think that this stuff *helps* him?"

"No. I'm making a point."

"Which is . . . ?"

"That if you're trying to get Chris off on suicide, he's in serious trouble." Terri's voice fell. "Is there any chance that Chris will change his mind about testifying?"

Terri's real question was unspoken; she hoped that Caroline would give her hope that Chris was innocent. But they were both professionals: Terri could not ask, and Caroline would never answer. "I don't know," Caroline said.

Terri shook her head impatiently. "And you don't have anything else, do you? Except to say that the D.A.'s case isn't enough and that they're screwing Chris out of spite." Abruptly, Terri stood. "If I were still working for you, Caroline, you'd tell me to take the best deal I could."

Still sitting, Caroline gazed up at Terri. "Remember Richie's note?" she asked with some asperity. "Pretty hard to plead this down to a spontaneous crime of passion. Given that Victor's theory is that *Chris* dictated the touching final words that *you* don't believe were Richie's own. It smacks a little too much of premeditation, don't you think?"

Terri stared at her momentarily and then sat down again, deflated. Suddenly Caroline felt ashamed. "I'm sorry," she said softly. "As it happens, Chris refuses to bargain for a lesser. But you didn't come here to tell me things that *you* already know that I know."

Terri shook her head. "You need another suspect."

"I know that too. Any ideas?"

"One." Terri drew a breath. "Me."

Caroline nodded. "Somehow I was expecting that. Just for fun, Teresa, tell me what your reasoning is."

Terri folded her arms. "The same reasoning the police followed until they landed on Chris. Like him, I've got no alibi. And my reason for killing Richie is even better—he took my daughter, ruined my reputation, destroyed my finances, and then threatened to drag Elena, Chris, Carlo, *and* me to court." Terri paused; it was somehow touching, Caroline thought, to hear her try to convict herself in the dispassionate summary of a trial lawyer. "My fingerprints were in his apartment. His rug fibers were on my shoes. And once I was in Italy, I told my mother not to call the police. At one point, my own daughter heard me threaten to kill Richie." A quick, bitter smile. "I've even got a predilection for violence—look at the way I slapped Elena's teacher. Except for the eyewitness, it's a carbon copy of the case against Chris. And I've seen firsthand what you can do with eyewitnesses."

Caroline appraised her. "You've thought it through, it seems."

Terri cocked her head. Quietly, she asked, "Haven't *you?*"

Caroline laughed softly. "Of course. It's clear, Teresa, that I taught you well."

"Yes. Thank you."

"A question, then. Have you considered what might happen to *you* if I did too good a job?"

Terri nodded. "Nothing. Except for more damage to what's left of my reputation."

"How do you figure that?"

"Is this a quiz?" Terri's eyes flashed impatience. "Because even if Chris is acquitted, the fact that they indicted him means that the police thought *he* murdered Richie. Which translates to an acquittal for *anyone* else, on the grounds of reasonable doubt. The D.A. would never even try me."

The curious pride Caroline felt in Terri's clear-eyed toughness was followed by a much deeper regret: the Terri she felt she knew could not live with a man she thought a murderer, even if Chris was acquitted. Caroline wondered if she was watching the end of a relationship, Teresa Peralta discharging her debts to Christopher Paget as best she could.

"I've considered it all," Caroline said finally. "I even ran it past another lawyer, whose judgment I deeply respect. He pointed out two problems. First, trying to make you a suspect brings it too close to home. You and Chris are lovers, and *both* of you might wind up looking guilty.

"Second, as my friend suggests, trying to prove your girlfriend guilty of murder is not the act of a gentleman. The jury might just hate Chris for it. I'm forced to agree." Caroline made her tone more gentle. "All in all, Teresa, I'm going to have to win this case without skewering you. Trust me to do that, please. For Chris and for you."

Terri looked at her directly. "Chris is the client, Caroline. At least you should ask him yourself."

Caroline sat back, considering whether to say more. And then, out of kindness, she did. "I've already asked him, Teresa. The lawyer friend I mentioned was Christopher Paget." She smiled briefly. "Chris likes sounding practical. But, as usual, I doubt he gave me *all* his reasons."

Terri seemed startled. For a moment, it appeared as if she would lose her composure, and then she simply turned away. "Please, don't tell Chris I came here."

Caroline nodded. "I won't. For his sake." Her tone was quiet. "I'm sure that Chris would appreciate the sentiment, Terri. But I'm also sure that he'd grasp the implications of your visit. Every one of them."

* * *

By afternoon, both sides appeared to have agreed on three more jurors—a white physical therapist, a Japanese accountant, and a recently naturalized Irishman who was a dispatcher for a moving company. Neither Paget nor Caroline was sanguine about any of them. But two of her last peremptories had been used on an elderly Chinese woman with a language problem, who might lack the verbal skills or cultural inclination to hang a pro-prosecution jury, and on a white bookkeeper who believed that the root of the city's social problems lay in a disrespect for the police. As time wore on, Paget felt the jury slipping away from them.

Now, with the next two panelists blue-collar Asians, Paget watched Caroline question Joseph Duarte, an upwardly mobile Hispanic businessman in his early thirties, with the cocksure manner of a leader and an absolute lack of deference—to Caroline, in particular, which might be either a dislike for high-profile women or some unspoken social resentment.

Even before the questioning, Paget had mentally stricken Duarte; Salinas's questions had been so perfunctory that Paget sensed him trying to conceal how much he wanted the man. For himself, Paget was beginning to regret his decision on James Rhee: if Caroline let Duarte go, *he* might well become the foreman. But if Caroline used a peremptory on Duarte, one of the two Asians following might become the twelfth juror.

"Mr. Duarte," Caroline said pleasantly, "you are aware, are you not, that Mr. Paget is quite wealthy."

A brisk nod. "Sure."

"What experiences, if any, have you had with people who you would consider more than usually affluent?"

A skeptical smile. "Do you mean 'rich'?"

To Paget's surprise, Caroline grinned. " 'Rich' will do just fine."

Duarte's smile became broader, as if he had won a point. "I used to caddy at the Olympic Club, to make money toward college." His voice became flatter. "There were plenty of rich people there."

Caroline tilted her head. "You mean there were plenty of rich *men* there, all of them white." She paused, adding dryly, "And, of course, their wives."

It was a shrewd probe: the Olympic Club had a long and distinguished history of restricting minorities and barring women altogether. Duarte's smile flashed again. "I remember that," he said in a tone that suggested he had made it a point to remember. Watching, Paget sensed that it was ethnic and class resentment, and not a dislike for women, that underlay Duarte's manner.

It seemed that Caroline guessed so as well. "How," she asked, "would you characterize your experiences with the rich folks at the Olympic Club?"

Duarte touched his mustache and gave her a guarded look, as if deciding how much of himself to reveal. "Some treated me all right," he said finally. "Others treated me like dirt. One way or the other, it was hard to forget that you were only welcome as a caddy."

Caroline gave a nod of understanding. "Do you think," she asked quietly, "that this unpleasant experience with wealthy people would affect your ability to judge this case?"

Duarte sat straighter, as if she had insulted him. "No," he said tersely. "*I* can take people as individuals."

The unspoken comparison to the wealthy golfers of Duarte's youth could not be missed. "I appreciate that," Caroline said respectfully. "And it may help you to know that Mr. Paget can too. Which is why he abandoned his family's membership at the Olympic Club and refuses to let his law firm entertain at clubs that discriminate against *anyone.*"

Instantly, Salinas was on his feet. "Your Honor, could you instruct Ms. Masters to skip the unsupported testimonials about her client. This isn't the trial, and *she* can't testify for him."

It was a clever thrust; while reining in Caroline, Salinas was tacitly leading the jury to expect Paget to take the stand. Caroline shot back, "What are you afraid of, Victor? That the jury won't hang Chris for being wealthy?"

It was a distraction, Paget knew, and seriously out of line. Judge Lerner leaned forward. "Enough, Ms. Masters. I won't tolerate personal attacks among the lawyers. And Mr. Salinas's point is valid: your role is to question Mr. Duarte on his qualifications, *not* to gild Mr. Paget's defense."

Caroline dropped her eyes for a moment; humility did not come easily to her, Paget knew, and her prior life as master of her own courtroom made it harder yet. But when she looked up at Lerner, her mien was respectful and her voice soft. "I'm sorry, Your Honor, if my desire for fairness to Mr. Paget caused me to cross the line." Then she turned to Salinas and said with apparent contrition, "My apologies, Victor."

It was gracefully done, Paget thought: Caroline had acknowledged her error, which was wholly intentional, while reminding the jury that her client was entitled to justice. As if nothing had happened, Caroline faced Duarte again. "You made a reference to saving for college. You went to San Francisco State, did you not, and graduated with honors?"

"Yes."

Caroline's expression became admiring; the look was something that Salinas, as a man, could not pull off. "And you also worked?"

Duarte nodded. With a note of mingled pride and resentment, he said, "Summers and nights. Except for scholarships, I paid for the whole deal myself."

"Does any of that lead you to resent others who, as Mr. Paget did, had it so much easier?"

Duarte shrugged. "Resent? Let's put it this way. I'd hire *me* before I'd hire them—it's all about what I call 'walking-around sense,' knowing how to cope. But I don't want my kids to work like I did, and I'm not going to resent them when they don't."

Caroline smiled. "Then they're fortunate, because lots of parents do. But what about a stranger, like Mr. Paget?"

Duarte gave her a sardonic look. "Well," he said, "I *did* notice he had a Latina girlfriend."

All at once, Paget was on edge: it was impossible to tell whether this was a satiric gibe at Caroline for doubting the objectivity of a nonwhite; an expression of dislike for the rich man who became involved with Richie's wife; or a grudging concession that, in at least one area of his life, Paget was himself not biased. Caroline put her hands on her hips, smiling at Duarte as if he had her complete interest. "Are you determined to be hard on me, Mr. Duarte?"

He spread his hands. "It's like this," he said, in the tone of someone whose patience was being tested. "I didn't like being judged on ethnicity, all right? So even if other people do it, *I* don't. I came here to listen to the facts and make a judgment. Just like I do in my business."

To Paget, the response sounded grudging. Though Duarte might try to be fair, he would make no connection with Paget as a person—he had not ever mentioned Paget's name. But Caroline was giving him a look which managed to suggest that Duarte had impressed her deeply. Paget surprised himself with the thought that his lawyer was a very attractive woman and, for all her air of certainty, a subtle one. Without a word, she was having an effect on Duarte: his face eased, and his gaze at Caroline became equable again.

"Thank you," Caroline told him quietly. "I appreciate your time, and your patience."

Her voice carried an undertone of respect; it suggested that she had met someone interesting and that he had won her over with his fairness. It was not until she turned away from Duarte, eyes narrowed in doubt, that Paget saw the extent of her artifice.

"Mr. Salinas?" Lerner asked.

Salinas stood. Firmly, he answered, "The people pass Mr. Duarte."

When Caroline reached the defense table, Moore leaned forward. "Take him," he whispered, "and you're looking at the jury foreman."

Caroline nodded. "Beginning to miss Mr. Rhee?" she whispered to Paget.

"You bet. This guy says he'll judge me fairly. But class and race are like a little worm inside him."

"I know that."

"Ms. Masters?" Judge Lerner said from the bench.

She glanced over her shoulder. "Please, Your Honor, a moment."

Her tone was unintentionally curt, and she did not wait for an answer. As if sensing the strain of this decision, Lerner folded his hands and waited.

"There's another thing," Paget murmured to Caroline. "At least to a point, this guy could be Ricardo Arias—the disadvantaged Latin, struggling to make it. On some level, he may feel like it's *his* wife I 'stole.' Which is one way to decipher that little crack of his."

Caroline looked at him intently. "But he *isn't* like Richie, and we can turn it around if he believes that Richie was a bum. And the race thing works both ways, Chris—we've bumped every Latin male on the panel."

"So why keep this one?"

"Because we've got two Asians next, and based on Johnny's data, both of them look bad to me. This guy believes he's made a commitment to me, and—whatever else goes on inside him—he'll try to honor it as a point of pride."

"Ms. Masters?" Lerner asked again.

Ignoring him, she gazed at Paget. "Last juror, Chris, remember? It's judgment time, and I want to make the call."

He had seconds to decide. Paget felt himself draw breath. Softly, he answered, "This is no time for pride, Caroline. Yours or mine."

Caroline studied him until she understood what he was telling her. Then she nodded, her expression grave and troubled. But when she turned, facing Joseph Duarte, the look she gave him was one of triumph and complicity. "The defense," she said, "passes Mr. Duarte."

Duarte gave her a short nod, as if his honor had been satisfied. Watching, Paget saw Victor Salinas smile to himself.

"Then we have a jury," Judge Lerner said. "Thank you, Counsel *and*, of course, the ladies and gentlemen of the panel. The trial will commence tomorrow at nine, with opening statements. The clerk will now swear the jury."

Lerner's clerk stepped forward facing the jury and instructed them to raise their right hands. "Do you solemnly swear," he intoned, "that you will well and truly try this case, based on the law and facts, and render a true verdict, so help you God?"

In ragged chorus, the jurors affirmed the oath. Lerner's gavel cracked. "All rise," the stubby bailiff called out, and Jared Lerner left the bench.

There was noise again, jurors stirring, reporters talking among themselves or leaving to file stories. Victor Salinas made his way across the courtroom with a look of undisguised pleasure. Ignoring Paget, he said to Caroline, "The district attorney would like to see you. I think it's time, don't you?"

Still sitting, Paget looked up at him. "Sure," he said before Caroline could speak. "I haven't seen Mac in months."

Salinas turned to him with a neutral expression. "I don't think he was asking you."

"And *I* didn't ask to be here. If Brooks wants to talk, he can damned well talk to both of us."

In a mute appeal, Salinas looked at Caroline. Paget was sure that she did not want him there. But Caroline simply smiled and said, "Where I go, Chris goes."

"I hear the jury's for shit," McKinley Brooks said in matter-of-fact tones. "Unless you're Victor."

Caroline gave a generous smile, which took in both Brooks and Salinas. "Victor's very excitable. He also has a sporadic hearing problem."

Salinas moved his mouth in a perfunctory smile of his own. "Don't kid a kidder," Brooks responded. "We basically got the folks we wanted, and your risk of losing just shot up. Even," he added pointedly, "if you got the *judge* you wanted, however you pulled *that* off." He leaned back. "Jared Lerner lets in everything, and damn the rules of evidence. You think you can win by attacking Arias, and maybe this office. But Victor's more than ready for a fist-fight, if that's what you want. This is our last chance to work things out before the free-for-all begins."

It was past six o'clock; the windows were dark, and the room was the sickly yellow of artificial light. Although Caroline and Paget sat across Brooks's desk, with Salinas next to Brooks, they spoke as if Paget were not there. He sensed that this was more than aversion to talking in front of a defendant; Brooks and Paget had once been nominal friends, and the handling of the inquiry seemed to have made Brooks uncomfortable. "What do you have in mind?" Caroline asked him.

Brooks leaned back, folding his hands across his stomach. "We might consider," he said carefully, "dropping this to murder two."

Caroline raised an eyebrow. "How do you intend to do that? Say that Richie composed his own suicide note and then Chris decided to help him in a spontaneous fit of rage?"

It was eerie, Paget thought, to listen to himself being bargained over. But he was glad that Caroline seemed unimpressed; it was what he would have done. "Come *on*," Brooks was saying. "Have you ever seen a judge turn down a deal that the lawyers rec-ommended, no matter how bogus? *Our* problem is politics—persuading the public we haven't sold poor dead Richie down the river."

"Oh, you can fix *that* part," Caroline rejoined. "So, bottom line . . ."

"Fifteen to life, plus three for using a gun, which means Chris is eligible for parole after twelve. We'll tell the court we think that he acted under great emotional stress, due to all the problems with Richie, and remind Lerner of what we have to prove for first-degree murder: 'calm and careful reflection,' the 'considered decision to kill,' evidence of planning in advance—all that stuff."

"Which," Salinas interjected, "is more than *you* can argue, isn't it, Caroline?"

Caroline turned to him. "You'll have to explain that."

"I think you're going with suicide." Salinas gave her a derisive smile. "Once you do that, your choices narrow. You can't just tell the jury, 'We think Arias killed himself, but if Chris *did* kill him, it was because he was all excited.' I mean, it just doesn't work, does it? Especially"—he shot his first quick glance at Paget—"because your client has this little problem about testifying. If he *doesn't* testify, there's no one to say that it wasn't murder one. And if he *does*, he has to say either that he didn't do it or that he did, but only in a blind rage." He gave Caroline another smile. "Without a deal, your client's choice is not guilty—probably by trying to sell this bullshit about suicide—or being convicted of murder one and going away for twenty-five to life. Because no parole board will let him out any earlier."

It was, Paget thought miserably, a telling description of the box he was in. "There is another choice," he said. "Maybe *Mac* could testify."

These, his first words, brought a reluctant gaze from Brooks. In a tone that suggested he was humoring Paget, Brooks responded, "What about?"

"All the conversations you had with people about this case." Paget paused, adding mildly, "Beyond the ones with people in law enforcement, that is."

Brooks examined his hands as if they were of real interest. "Why don't you tell me what that means."

"Manslaughter," Caroline said in her most astringent voice. "Three years max. Assuming that Chris condescends to take it."

Salinas looked from Caroline to Brooks; Paget could see him

wondering what the district attorney had not told him. "I'm not prepared to give you manslaughter," Brooks said slowly. "The papers would kill me for it."

Caroline shook her head. "Oh, McKinley," she said. "It really is a thankless business, isn't it? Carrying water for the mighty."

Brooks's face grew hard. "There's nothing there," he said tersely. "And I'd hate to see you play with matches. You could get burned."

"*Someone* might." Caroline's eyes glinted. "As for me, I'm going home tonight, turn out the lights, and lie there in the dark wondering what I *ever* did to make you think I'd sell my soul for a politician I wouldn't wipe my floor with."

Brooks seemed to sit back in his chair, and then he gave her a wintry smile. "You always were the cat who walks alone, Caroline."

She looked him in the face. "I still am."

They stared at each other for a moment, and then Brooks's gaze broke, moving from Caroline to Paget and back again. "You're going to lose," he said to Caroline. "Murder two is the best I can offer."

She turned to Paget. "Is this even worth discussing?"

"No," Paget answered softly, then turned to Brooks. "And no. Because you fucked with me, Mac. You trashed my home, scared my kid, and hassled Terri and her six-year-old daughter. All so *you* could curry a little favor with Colt by running me out of politics." He paused. "And because, eyewitness or no, *I didn't do it.*"

Salinas was quick to ask, "Does that mean that you're going to testify?"

For another moment, Paget kept looking at Brooks. "I don't know," he said to Salinas. "It depends on whether you catch my interest."

Salinas sat back, studying him.

"Is that all, McKinley?" Caroline asked.

Brooks slowly nodded. "Yes," he said. "I guess that's all."

Caroline and Paget stood. "See you tomorrow," Salinas said brusquely, and opened the door.

Without another word, Caroline and Paget walked to the elevator.

Alone with him in the elevator, Caroline expelled a deep breath. Somehow, Paget thought, she looked smaller.

"You're doing a great job," Paget said.

Caroline gave him a half smile. She said nothing.

They reached the underground garage. Caroline walked beside him to her car, still silent. She unlocked the door, and then stood there as if seized by a thought, turning back to Paget. "Buy me a drink, Chris, and tell me we did the right thing."

For a moment, he thought, Caroline Masters looked tired and a little lonely. Paget shook his head. "I have to get back to Carlo. You understand."

"Of course."

Paget looked at her. Impulsively, gently, he kissed her on the forehead, and then looked into her questioning eyes. "We did the right thing, Caroline. No matter what happens."

"Want to shoot some hoops?" Paget asked.

Carlo pushed his chair back from the dining room table, stretching his legs and studying his father with veiled eyes. In the almost ten years they had lived together, Paget had recently calculated, they had eaten perhaps three thousand dinners in this same room—usually just the two of them, sitting under the eighteenth-century crystal chandelier at a walnut table that seated twelve—discussing the events of the day, or sports or politics or Carlo's school friends or whatever came to mind. Paget had reviewed Carlo's second-grade math homework there; admired the watercolor that won the school art contest when Carlo was ten; helped him write his first term paper and fill out his applications to high school. Since his arrest, every moment with Carlo seemed to resonate with earlier moments; sitting here, it seemed to Paget that he had watched Carlo grow up at this table.

Paget was not a nostalgic man; he had enjoyed Carlo more at every age and looked forward to Carlo as an adult, the son who would also be his friend. This sudden tendency to remember Carlo as a younger boy, with tenderness and regret for the passage of years, was a trick of the mind, Paget knew, another symptom of the palpable desire to stop time that had begun with his arrest. On the eve of a trial that could end their life together, Paget felt such regret and self-blame that only clinging to the past provided relief.

Now, with an almost desperate longing, Paget wished to shoot baskets. To remind himself of the weekend he had put up the hoop; the first day he had taught Carlo to shoot; the time that, watching

Carlo fill with pride, he had raised the basket to its full ten feet. But Carlo could not know this: he was living in the present, Paget saw, where his father had been indicted for murder and might spend the rest of his life—and much of Carlo's—in prison. It was the thought that Paget awoke to in the middle of the night; he did not wish to dwell on it. All he wanted was to play Horse.

"One game," Paget said.

Carlo frowned at him. "Would you mind just talking, Dad?"

His son's tone was so flat that it brought Paget up short; he had been expecting Carlo to fill *his* needs for escape, when what Carlo needed was the father he had always had. Suddenly Paget felt ashamed; he reserved his deepest contempt for parents who ignored their children's needs or, worse, expected their children to take care of *them*.

"Sure." At dinner, Paget realized now, he had been silent. "Sorry. I was just looking for distraction, I guess."

Carlo seemed to take a second look at him, and then his face grew softer. "We can talk while we shoot," he said. "The ball's in my closet."

Carlo went upstairs; Paget took the stairs down through the basement to the driveway and flicked on the lights he had installed to illuminate the hoop at night. He stood there, gazing up at the hoop; Carlo, who had once been so tentative, should be all-league next year. Paget wondered if he would be free to watch him.

He heard the screen door open behind him, close with a swish, and then the rubbery thump of his son bouncing the basketball. Paget smiled to himself; the sound had so many associations with Carlo that he could replay the memories for hours.

A basketball flew over Paget's head, arcing through the light and shadow, and hit the backboard of the hoop above the garage, barely grazing the rim.

"Shit," Carlo said.

Paget laughed. Carlo had all the tools except for a good outside jump shot: speed, dexterity, and reflexes Paget had never possessed at any age. But the one thing Paget had maintained from prep school was a soft jumper he could still hit about half the time. It was why his only means of challenging Carlo was to play Horse, alternating shots until a player sank one and the other had to make the shot or receive a letter. The first one to spell out "horse" lost; in recent years, Paget could still win a game by camping outside and, with cheerful sadism, shooting jump shot after jump shot. "My object is to improve your game," he would explain straightfaced to Carlo, who would mumble in disgust and wait until Paget missed, so that he could return to the repertoire of drives and hook shots his father could not match.

Paget picked up the ball, dribbled to a point about twenty feet away, and fired. With a smooth arc, the ball rose in the dark and then suddenly seemed to fall, flashing through the net without touching metal. "True greatness," Paget said admiringly. "Vintage Christopher Paget."

"And the fans go wild," Carlo said with naked sarcasm. He retrieved the ball and went to the spot of Paget's shot. He eyed the net carefully, bounced the ball twice, and then fired it in a flat trajectory that hit the rim, bouncing the ball toward Paget. Carlo seemed to study the net and then jumped as if he had the ball, flicking his wrists in a pantomime shot. "There," he murmured.

" 'H,' " his father answered.

Paget backed away from the net, took roughly the same shot, and missed.

Carlo gathered up the ball. "So," he said, "how's your jury?"

"All right." Saying this, Paget wished that it were so. "A lot depends on how they respond to the lawyers. A friend of mine once said, 'A trial is where you choose twelve people to decide which lawyer they like best.' It's a little cynical, but there's something in it."

Carlo walked to where his father had stood and gazed at the basket, gauging his shot. "Yeah," he said. "How do you feel about that? I mean, Caroline's smart and all. But she doesn't seem that warm and fuzzy."

Without waiting for an answer, Carlo replicated Paget's jump. This time it landed inside the rim, swirled once, and came out again.

"Trying to beat me at my own game?" Paget asked.

Carlo shrugged. "We'll see."

Paget retrieved the ball. "About Caroline, I picked what I'm comfortable with, and I'm happier with cool and smart than some folksy gunslinger who thinks he's Mr. Populist." He paused for a moment; Carlo's tenuous early life had made him a careful observer, and with his usual good instincts, he had hit upon Paget's only real doubt about Caroline. "Jurors don't like arrogance," Paget continued. "But they *do* admire style and intelligence, and a lot of people seem to have a secret longing for aristocracy—which is why admiring the Kennedys became a national exercise in self-improvement. Wit and style seem part of Caroline Masters' birthright, and she can adapt her touch to the audience. She'll do fine with these people."

Paget hoped that was right. He bounced the ball once and arched another jump shot, which fell through the hoop. "The pressure's on," he said to Carlo.

Carlo got the ball. "Is Caroline going to talk to me again? Before I testify?"

"Sure." Paget turned to him. Inside, he ached for Carlo; not only would Salinas try to make him testify against his father, but he would drag him through Richie's charges that he molested Elena. Paget wished that he could help his son prepare, and blamed himself that Carlo had to face this at all. But it would not help to say this now.

"You couldn't be in better hands," Paget added calmly. "Caroline will prepare you not only for everything *she'll* ask you but for everything Victor Salinas will ask you. That way, you'll be as comfortable as possible."

Carlo turned to him. "I really *am* feeling the pressure," he said quietly. "But not from your stupid jump shot. I just want you around to shoot it, okay?"

Paget smiled. "Okay."

Carlo shook his head. Even more softly, he said, "I wish I could talk to you about what to say."

Paget gazed at him across the half-lit driveway. "I know, son. But we can't."

Carlo was staring at him now. "Dad," he said slowly, "I really don't want to screw up."

"Then just tell the truth. That way you *can't* screw up."

But Carlo only looked at him. Oh God, Paget thought, you're not really sure, are you? "Look," Paget went on, "we really *can't* talk about this, okay? But I've never told a serious lie that I haven't paid some price for, and there are some I've had to live with for a long time." He paused, finishing softly: "Don't try to do that for me, Carlo. I'll know you're doing it, and it will hurt me. And if Salinas catches you at it, that could hurt me quite badly."

Carlo rested the ball on his hip, looking back at Paget as if to fathom his meaning. "All this evidence they say they have ..."

"Will be explained. Just be patient, for two more weeks." Paget tried to smile. "Meanwhile, shoot the ball, okay?"

Inside, through the screen door, came the distant ringing of a telephone. With an anxious expression, Carlo turned. "It's probably Terri," Paget said, "calling to wish me luck. I'll call her in a while."

Carlo gave his father a questioning look. "It's fine," Paget said. "We've got a game to play."

Carlo hesitated, then he turned to the basket, breathing in once, and sank the jump shot.

"Grace under pressure," Paget remarked. As Carlo flipped him the ball, he heard the phone still ringing.

Something in the conversation, Paget realized, made him remember the times when Carlo was much younger and Paget had cheated to help him win, missing easy shots or miscounting the letters of "horse." It was one thing that Paget did not miss; all at once, he wished that he could talk to his son, his friend.

The phone stopped ringing. For a brief instant, Paget thought of Terri; the sudden silence felt like losing her.

Distractedly, he shot the ball.

From the side, Carlo seemed to study his form. But this time, Paget's shot bounced off the rim.

"I'm taking your jump shot," Carlo announced. "I've decided it's time to learn."

With perfect form, suddenly quite like Paget's, he swished the ball through the net.

"Nice shot," Paget said.

Carlo retrieved the ball. But instead of tossing it, he walked over to his father and handed him the ball, looking into his face.

"I think I'll feel a lot better," Carlo said, "when you've finally gotten to testify."

Silent, Paget took the ball. He backed up two feet, to where Carlo had stood, and carefully faced the basket. But his shot, falling, grazed the outside of the hoop.

" 'H,' " Paget said.

THE TRIAL

FEBRUARY 3–FEBRUARY 16

ONE

A MURDER TRIAL is like a cocoon, Paget thought: the world outside seems barely to exist.

He sat at the defense table with Caroline Masters, waiting for Salinas to begin his opening statement. He could imagine the routines of daily life only by attaching them to Carlo, who had no choice but to go to school, or to Terri, whom Paget had asked to mind his cases. But his sole concrete image was that of the satellite trucks of news services, set up outside the Hall of Justice to feed live reports from the trial.

At Paget's insistence, the trial itself would not be televised. But there was no help for the reporters who jammed the courtroom; or the fading novelist who had decided to write a true-crime book; or the producer who hoped to make a miniseries—all waiting for that dramatic moment that would reveal Paget's character and which, translated into words or images, would put their own distinctive signatures on the death of Ricardo Arias.

For what mattered was not truth but entertainment, and here the plot was far too good. "The Christopher Paget trial captures the essence of the nineties," a television news report had begun; Paget had switched it off before he could find out what the essence of the nineties was.

Caroline, he knew, had worries of her own. She was facing by far the biggest case of her career, and the pressure was compounded by her ambitions. As if she had heard his thoughts, Caroline turned to him with a slight smile. In fresh makeup and gold earrings and a well-tailored black suit, she seemed nothing like the tired woman he had seen the night before. "Forgive me," she murmured, "but some perverse part of me enjoys this."

"Then it's all worthwhile," Paget said dryly. But, for that moment, he felt better; during the next two weeks, no matter how many reporters and voyeurs packed the courtroom, the only people who would matter as much as Caroline were Judge Lerner and the jury.

Paget turned to scan the jury, among them Marian Celler, attentive and carefully dressed, with reading glasses on a silver chain around her neck; Luisa Marin, hands clasped and eyes half shut; Joseph Duarte, holding a notepad with a look of skeptical alertness, preparing to master this experience as he had mastered so many others. Paget wondered if he would ever become as real to them as they already were to him.

Finally, there was Jared Lerner. The judge alone would decide what these jurors would hear and how much latitude Caroline would have in creating a Richie different from the embattled underdog Salinas would put before the jury. From the bench, Lerner looked from Caroline to Salinas; beneath the judge's calm, Paget sensed the pleasure of a man who was about to conduct the biggest trial of his career and felt himself well qualified.

Lerner took a long last survey of the courtroom and then nodded to Victor Salinas. "Mr. Salinas," he said, and the trial began.

Approaching the jury, Salinas paused to underscore the moment. The jurors looked rapt. There was utter silence.

"*This,*" Salinas began, "is a case about secrets, and about lies. More than that, it is about arrogance."

He stopped, looking directly at Paget. "The arrogance of a man who decided that *another man* was too inconvenient to live, and too insignificant for anyone to question how he died."

Gazing back so that the jury could see him silently challenge Salinas, Paget wondered if the prosecutor's stare of distaste was theater or an effort to stoke his own intensity. Abruptly, Salinas faced the jury, speaking to Joseph Duarte.

"Ricardo Arias," he said softly, "was a man like you or me. He had a daughter he loved, a life built on family, a future he believed in—the dream of starting his own business. And most of all, he had his wife, Teresa."

His voice became flat with muted outrage. "That was the *first* time that Christopher Paget, Teresa's boss, found Ricardo Arias inconvenient. Because he wanted Teresa for himself.

"And so, ladies and gentlemen, Christopher Paget took her from her husband, and her home."

"Victor's going for it," Caroline whispered to Paget. "This is almost too good to believe."

"But Ricardo Arias," Salinas said with sudden steel, "*still* had his daughter. Elena, the child he adored.

"He fought to keep her, and he won. Ricardo was satisfied with that. But Teresa Peralta would not let go. In spite of his limited funds—because *he* had cared for Elena while Teresa 'worked' for Christopher Paget—Richie Arias suddenly found himself in a custody fight he never wanted."

Listening, Paget thought again of the way in which a life, packaged for the courtroom, could become the opposite of what it was. "And *then*," Salinas continued, "strange things began happening. Despite all Richie's efforts, Elena became moody and depressed. There was a call from a teacher, reporting sexual play involving Elena." Now Salinas turned to Marian Celler. "Reluctantly, and to his horror, Ricardo Arias concluded that his daughter—the person he loved most—had been sexually molested.

"*Molested.*" Salinas's voice fell to a half whisper. "By Carlo Paget. Christopher Paget's teenage son."

An involuntary flicker of distaste crossed Celler's face. Salinas nodded as if satisfied and resumed a normal tone.

"Like any loving father, Ricardo Arias went into action. He demanded that Teresa keep Elena away from Carlo Paget. And when, in the face of *all* that had happened, Teresa *still* insisted on trying to get custody, Ricardo Arias went to court.

"He accused Christopher Paget of adultery and began to strip the veneer of respectability which hid who this man really is.

"Most important, Ricardo Arias placed the evidence of child abuse before the court and demanded that the court keep Elena Arias away from the kind of household that bred these kinds of horrors."

Paget winced inwardly. An undertone of confidence had entered Salinas's voice as he burnished Richie's image for the jury. "In bringing his fears to the court's attention," Salinas went on, "Ricardo

Arias did the responsible thing. He filed the papers under seal, to shelter Elena's tragedy from public view. *Only* if Teresa refused to keep Elena from the Paget home would a hearing ensue, in thirty days, and Richie's concerns become public."

Salinas paused again. "It was an act of compassion," he said softly. "And it was a fatal mistake. For Christopher Paget was running for the Senate."

Turning to Luisa Marin, Salinas slowly shook his head. "Ricardo Arias's act of love for his daughter was a death warrant. If his charges became public, Carlo Paget could be exposed as a molester and his father as an adulterer. Not only would Mr. Paget's lover lose her child, but his ambitions for high public office might well be destroyed."

Caroline had been right, Paget thought; his withdrawal from the race had spared Carlo nothing and was now hurting Paget himself. Abruptly, Salinas spun on him. "*What*, Mr. Paget must have wondered, would life be like without Ricardo Arias?

"His son would be off the hook.

"His affair would remain buried.

"His girlfriend would have her daughter—at whatever cost to Elena.

"And most of all, Christopher Paget could become *your* senator."

Still facing Paget, Salinas let the irony hang there and then turned back to the jury. "The only problem," he told them quietly, "was that Mr. Arias would have to disappear within thirty days.

"Christopher Paget had planned a vacation to Italy with Teresa. And despite this critical hearing involving *both* their children, Mr. Paget wanted to go." Salinas's body was suddenly as still as an actor's. "Why? Because the night before they left for Italy was a perfect time for murder. For unless Mr. Arias was quickly found, Christopher Paget could suggest that Ricardo Arias died in San Francisco while Paget made love in Venice to Ricardo Arias's wife."

Flushed with anger, Paget spotted Joseph Duarte gazing at Salinas, hand frozen above the pad.

"*And*," Salinas added with indignation, "if people thought that Ricardo Arias had killed *himself*, no one would question Christopher Paget at all.

"How do we know he thought these things?" Still facing the jury,

Salinas pointed an accusing finger toward Paget and softly answered, "Because Christopher Paget *lied* to the police.

"When the police found Ricardo Arias, it looked like a possible suicide: he was shot in the mouth, a gun was found near his hand, and on his desk was the beginning of a note saying that he had decided to take his life." Salinas paused, lowering his voice. "But there were bruises on his legs, damage to his nose, a gash on his head—and there was nothing, not blood or even gunpowder, on the hand that supposedly fired the gun. And as the medical examiner will show you, the condition of the body and the circumstances of his death all pointed to one thing: murder.

"Murder," Salinas repeated. "Committed between roughly nine o'clock on October sixteen, the night *before* Christopher Paget left San Francisco, and noon the following day.

"And so, on Mr. Paget's return from Italy, the police decided to question him.

"And what did Mr. Paget say?

"That he had never met Ricardo Arias, or even spoken to him.

"That he had never been to Mr. Arias's apartment.

"And that, although not even his son or girlfriend can support this, he was at home on the last night of Ricardo Arias's life."

Caroline watched intently as Salinas surveyed the jury. "We will show that each and every one of these statements was a lie. Not only had Christopher Paget spoken to Ricardo Arias—he had been to his apartment." Pausing, Salinas lowered his voice. "Most important, ladies and gentlemen, we will show that Christopher Paget went to Richie's apartment the night before he left for Italy, and that Ricardo Arias was never seen alive again."

The jury was grim-faced now; Joseph Duarte had resumed writing. Covertly, Marian Celler glanced at Paget.

Salinas's voice rose abruptly. "By the end of the trial, you will know that Ricardo Arias was murdered.

"That Christopher Paget was there.

"That Christopher Paget lied about that.

"And that Christopher Paget profited from his death."

Turning, Salinas gazed at Paget, until the jurors followed his eyes. "You will know," he finished quietly, "that Christopher Paget made Ricardo Arias write his own suicide note. And then, quite coldly, killed him."

* * *

Facing the jury, Caroline Masters looked calm, almost serene. She took a moment to meet each juror's eyes; the look said that she had heard the prosecution and was not impressed.

"Let me tell you," she said in matter-of-fact tones, "what, when this trial is over, you will *not* know.

"You will not know whether Ricardo Arias killed himself.

"Or whether he died while Mr. Paget was somewhere over the mid-Atlantic.

"Or whether, even *assuming* that Mr. Arias was murdered, and assuming further Mr. Paget was in San Francisco, Mr. Paget had any part in—or any knowledge of—that crime."

Caroline paused, sweeping the jury. "And *that*, members of the jury, means that you must find Christopher Paget innocent of murder."

The jury seemed alert; by inverting Salinas's opening, Caroline had persuaded them to listen. But Duarte's eyes were narrow with doubt.

"What Mr. Salinas just told you," she continued evenly, "is a list of what Mr. Salinas needs you to believe.

"Mr. Salinas needs you to believe that Christopher Paget met Ricardo Arias.

"That he went to Mr. Arias's apartment.

"That he was there in some proximity to his death—perhaps hours, perhaps days.

"In fact, Mr. Salinas offered so many lists that it was easy to miss what was missing: proof that Christopher Paget killed Mr. Arias."

It was good, Paget thought; Caroline had put a subtly satiric spin on Salinas's style, without ever raising her voice. Listening, the jury seemed more open now.

"But Mr. Salinas's wish lists are not evidence," Caroline went on. "In truth, he cannot even prove beyond a reasonable doubt that Christopher Paget and Ricardo Arias were *ever* within two miles of each other at *any* moment of Mr. Arias's less-than-flawless life. *Let alone*," she said with irony, "that, beyond a reasonable doubt, Mr. Paget killed Mr. Arias." Pausing, she gazed at Joseph Duarte. "Because the truth, and please note this well, is that Mr. Salinas cannot prove that anyone killed Mr. Arias *but* Mr. Arias.

"And so," she said softly to Duarte, "Mr. Salinas asks you to share his prejudice."

Once more, Duarte put down his pencil.

"He does this," Caroline told him, "by offering you a cartoon.

"In this cartoon, Ricardo Arias is a simple and loving man, courageously fighting for his daughter's welfare. While Mr. Paget is the spoiled and arrogant son of wealth who stole Ricardo's wife.

"In short, Mr. Salinas wants you to convict Mr. Paget because you like Mr. Arias better.

"Aside from the total lack of evidence, there are two problems with this. And the first of them is the *real* Ricardo Arias."

Caroline, Paget saw, would not take her eyes off Duarte. "As to Mr. Arias, let me offer you a list of my own.

"This was a man of minimal honesty.

"A man unable to hold a job.

"A man who lived off his wife.

"A man who used his daughter for money.

"A man whose selfishness and callousness drove Teresa Peralta out of the house and *then*, because she was the only responsible parent Elena had, forced Teresa to support them by posing as the loving custodial father."

Duarte's face was attentive now. "Ricardo Arias," Caroline said with scorn, "who, for ten thousand dollars, used his daughter as the centerpiece of a self-pitying article in a scandal sheet." Her voice, quieter yet, seemed even more contemptuous. "Ricardo Arias, who charged an innocent teenage boy with child abuse so that he would not lose the monthly support check Teresa provided for their daughter."

Pausing, Caroline scanned the jury box. "Ricardo Arias," she repeated. "A man who, at the end of his life, was running out of excuses. A man who, after years of hiding behind his wife, faced a rigorous examination of his own life and motives by a psychologist appointed by the family court.

"A man about to be exposed for what he was—a con artist whose only means of support was the daughter he claimed to love."

It was nicely done, Paget thought. But in itself, an alternative vision of Ricardo Arias was not enough; it might well serve as a motive for murder.

Caroline, it seemed, had thought of this. "No one deserves to die," she said softly to Luisa Marin. "But I believe that we can understand why a man like this, faced with the truth of his life, might well consider ending it."

Marin looked pensively at Caroline and then at her lap. Caroline turned to Marian Celler. "What is far more difficult to fathom is why Christopher Paget would choose to *kill* him. And that is Mr. Salinas's *second* problem—Christopher Paget.

"Unlike Ricardo Arias, Christopher Paget already possessed those things he valued most: a warm relationship with his son, Carlo; a healthy and loving involvement with Teresa Peralta, *after* she had freed herself from the misery of her marriage; a distinguished career; and a chance to serve his larger community as a candidate for public office. Yet Mr. Salinas asks you to believe that *this* man—a man with an unbroken history of emotional balance, personal responsibility, and a deep distaste for violence—was driven to murder Ricardo Arias.

"In reality, Christopher Paget has faced far greater challenges than those Ricardo Arias posed to him. Sixteen years ago, *this* man earned his country's gratitude by exposing corruption in the highest levels of our government—at the risk of his own career and against the awesome resources of a corrupt President." Caroline paused, shaking her head in wonderment. "For a lawyer with the courage and talent of Christopher Paget, dealing with someone like *Ricardo Arias*—however painful his lies about Carlo—is something that Chris's entire life prepared him for. And yet Mr. Salinas asks you to believe that a man like Ricardo Arias drove *this* man to murder."

At the corner of his eye, Paget sensed Marian Celler appraising him. Caroline approached the jury box, speaking quietly. "You come to judge Chris Paget's life armed with the common sense and experience gained from your *own* life. Members of the jury, it is *all* that you will *ever* need. For *all* that Chris Paget asks is that you not set common sense aside.

"Ricardo Arias *was* who he was: an unstable man, capable of self-destruction. And Christopher Paget *is* who he is: a peaceful man, who loves his son far too much to kill Ricardo Arias."

One by one, Caroline met each juror's eyes, renewing their compact. "This prosecution," she finished simply, "makes no sense. In the end, if nothing else, you will know at least that much."

As Caroline sat, Paget realized that her words had touched him. But there were two things Caroline had not done and could not do: directly challenge Salinas's circumstantial evidence, or promise that Christopher Paget would explain it.

In the jury box, Joseph Duarte wrote feverishly.

"You look preoccupied," Denise Harris said.

Terri nodded. "I am."

It was a little past one; shortly before Terri had come here, Chris had called her from a pay phone at the courthouse. The phone booth had been surrounded by reporters, and Chris could say little: all that she could make out, less from his words than from his tone, was that Salinas's opening statement had shaken him. It seemed to her that her life now consisted of waiting for other women to do her job—for Caroline Masters to salvage Chris and for Harris to penetrate Elena's shell.

"Is it the trial?" Harris asked.

Terri nodded. "And Elena. In a way, they're inseparable, aren't they? They both have to do with Richie's death."

"It may all come back to Richie, in a way." Pausing, Harris looked into her face. "On the evidence of your dreams, you somehow feel responsible for your father's death—even though it was an accident—and, perhaps, for Richie's death. Now, Elena's nightmare *seems* to be different: it began while Richie was alive, although we don't know what she dreams about. But what appears quite clear is that *Elena* feels responsible for her father's death. Or at least *did*."

Terri stared at her. "What you seem to be suggesting," she said finally, "is that Elena believed that I wished her father dead and blamed herself."

Harris shrugged. "Does that seem so far-fetched? Given that, in their egocentricity, children tend to believe that *everything* relates to them."

Chris had said much the same thing, Terri remembered, in Portofino. She got up from her chair, walked to one of Harris's upstairs windows, and pushed it open from the bottom. Standing there, she gazed out into the sunlit street, feeling the cool air on her face. Three miles away, Chris was on trial for murder.

Still at the window, Terri said, "Elena seems to be past that now. Ever since she found out Chris was charged, she believes that *he* killed her father. Insists on it, really."

Harris was quiet for a time. "Whatever else, Terri, we know that *Elena* didn't do it."

Terri leaned on the window frame. "No one killed my father," she said finally. "And for all we know, no one killed Richie. The rest of this, from my supposed sense of guilt to Elena's, is Freudian guesswork."

"Which, to a child, can be something very real."

Terri turned. "And how is she doing with *you*, Denise? In the presumably real world."

Harris smiled a little, and then her face grew serious. "I play with the doll figures," she answered, "while Elena watches. But I finally persuaded her to start drawing."

"What does she draw?"

Harris rose from her chair and went to a drawer beneath a shelf of children's games. She took out a sheet of drawing paper, handing it to Terri.

Terri gazed at Elena's drawing. As best she could tell, it was the stick figure of a little girl on the jagged edge of a mountain. The drawing seemed incomplete; one of the girl's feet was on the tip of the mountain, while the other did not rest on anything.

"Has she drawn *other* pictures?" Terri asked.

Harris stood beside her, looking at the picture. "Uh-huh," she answered. "Several. But they're all pretty much like that."

"Like what?"

"A little girl in a position of danger, with no one else in the picture. My guess is that she's a surrogate for Elena herself."

Terri turned to her. "How do you mean 'position of danger'?"

Harris pointed to the leg that rested on nothing. "Here, for example, the little girl is falling off the mountain."

Terri gave her a skeptical look. "I'm no psychologist, Denise, but I've been to a bunch of parents' nights. Based on your interpretation, I've seen lots of drawings of kids in danger—in grade school, they give them prizes."

"If you're saying that kids don't draw precisely, I agree." Harris still studied the picture. "But this was *Elena's* interpretation, not mine."

Terri felt a faint alarm. "What did she say?"

Harris frowned. "That the little girl had been bad and was falling off the mountain."

"Did *you* say anything?"

"Yes. I suggested that she might want to draw someone else in the picture, to rescue her. As you can see, she wouldn't."

"Do you know why?"

"Only what Elena told me." Still Harris did not look at her. "What she said, Terri, was that there was no one who could save her."

TWO

CHIEF MEDICAL EXAMINER Elizabeth Shelton was a slender blonde in her late thirties, with a clear-eyed gaze, an air of composed attentiveness, and a well-tailored style that reflected taste and moderation. In his life as a lawyer, Paget had admired Liz Shelton: she was fair and professional, she spoke the truth as she saw it, and juries trusted her instinctively. There was no point in trying to break Shelton down, Caroline said, and the best thing one could try was to score some points and create a little doubt. Paget agreed; he had not looked forward to this moment.

Putting Shelton on the stand, Salinas appeared quite confident. He quickly established Shelton's extensive credentials in both forensic medicine and criminology, and took her through a summary of her physical findings and the tests and procedures she had performed. Then Salinas began to lay the groundwork for murder. "When Mr. Arias's body was found," he asked, "did you go to his apartment?"

Shelton nodded. "Yes, with a team from the crime lab."

Paget imagined several white-coated men and Shelton photographing Ricardo Arias's body, wearing masks to stifle the stench of decomposition. "Could you describe the condition of the body?" Salinas was asking.

"Of course." Shelton turned to the jury, her tone dispassionate. "Mr. Arias was lying on the floor with a revolver near his hand. I found what appeared to be a bullet entry wound through his mouth. He was obviously dead, and had been for some time."

Paget saw Luisa Marin look away. Salinas picked up a manila envelope and pulled out several photographs, which he passed to Shelton almost gingerly. "Dr. Shelton, I hand you what have been premarked as People's Exhibits 1 through 4. Can you tell me what these are?"

Shelton took out a pair of tortoiseshell reading glasses and inspected the photographs one at a time: the gesture seemed less for the sake of eyesight than for maintaining a certain professional distance. "Yes," she answered. "These are crime scene photographs of the head and hands of Ricardo Arias."

The jury seemed suddenly still. "Your Honor," Caroline interjected, "does Mr. Salinas intend to show these photographs to the jury?"

Salinas turned to her. "That's why I had them marked," he said with muted exasperation.

Caroline kept looking at Lerner. "To what end, I wonder, except to horrify our jurors? I think we can all agree that Mr. Arias is deceased. The question is not whether he's dead but whether it was a homicide. As to which these photographs prove nothing."

That was right, Paget knew: Salinas's aim was to make the jury *feel* Richie's death. "The prosecution is entitled," Salinas retorted crisply, "to show the manner of death and condition of the body." Glancing at Caroline, he added in an accusatory tone, "And the defense is *not* entitled to sanitize this man's death until it becomes a parlor game, like Clue or Let's Give a Murder."

Salinas, Paget realized, meant to try this case on moral outrage. Lerner looked unhappily from Salinas to Caroline and told her, "I'll allow these."

With a satisfied smile that the jury could not see, Salinas collected the photographs and tendered them to Caroline. She spread them on the table, and Christopher Paget looked into the face of Ricardo Arias.

Richie's eyes were frozen in shock and terror: he did not look like a man who had resolved to shoot himself and then pulled the trigger. His face was waxen and puffy, and his curly hair seemed to rise from his head. There was dried blood coming from his mouth, and flecks of blood on his face and chin. His nose appeared swollen.

Paget made himself study each picture. It was hard to believe that this staring corpse had once been a threat to Carlo.

In the final picture, Richie's hand was shriveled like a mummy's.

All at once, Paget had seen enough. He pushed them back to Caroline. "Easy to grasp why Salinas wants these in."

Nodding, she collected the photographs and gave them to Salinas. He handed them to the jury, his expression grave.

One by one, they inspected the photographs. Paget watched them: Marian Celler, sitting back from the pictures, mouth compressed; Joseph Duarte, studying each photo impassively and taking notes. Only Luisa Marin refused to look. "What bothers me is his eyes," Paget murmured.

Caroline glanced over at him. "The terror?" she asked. "Or the surprise?"

Salinas was walking back toward Shelton. "In the course of examining Mr. Arias," he asked, "did you form an opinion as to how recently he had died?"

Shelton nodded. "From the body, it was clear that Mr. Arias had been dead for some time."

"What made that apparent?"

"Several factors. The air-conditioning was set at sixty-five and the apartment was quite cold, which retards bloating or decomposition. But as the pictures show, Mr. Arias's hands were mummified and his skin had a somewhat greenish tinge, both indicating the passage of several days."

"Were you able to establish a time of death?"

Shelton shook her head. "No. However, we were able to establish from extrinsic evidence a probable *range* of time within which Mr. Arias died."

"And what was that evidence?"

"His mail, to start. It appeared that Mr. Arias had opened his mail for Friday, October sixteen—several bills were on his desk, bearing the postmark of October fourteen or fifteen. But there was a stack of unopened mail behind the mail slot of his apartment; the local mail bore postmarks from October sixteen until the day before we found him. Based on which we believe that Mr. Arias died sometime between the delivery of his mail on Friday, October sixteen, and the next day's delivery."

Paget turned to Caroline. But she was already on her feet. "Your Honor, I move that the last sentence of Dr. Shelton's answer be stricken as speculation. Given the performance of our postal service, it is utterly plausible that Mr. Arias picked up this mail on Saturday the seventeenth." Pausing, Caroline added with irony, "Or, for that matter, on the following Monday or Tuesday."

Salinas gave a quick, edgy smile. "The post office is a convenient whipping boy, Your Honor. But Dr. Shelton is stating one basis for her belief, not testifying to a fact. And we will be offering other evidence to establish the time frame of Mr. Arias's death."

Lerner nodded. "Based on that representation, Mr. Salinas, I will deny the motion. At least for now."

Sitting, Caroline looked unsurprised but pensive; the prosecution needed to show that it was likely Richie had died while Paget was still in the country, and this was Salinas's first small victory.

"What," Salinas asked Shelton, "were the *other* indicators of the range within which Mr. Arias died?"

Shelton folded her hands. "In the kitchen, we found a full pot of coffee. We determined that Mr. Arias had preset his automatic coffeemaker for seven-thirty a.m., suggesting that he died before the coffee was actually made."

It was a potentially damaging point, possibly narrowing the range of Richie's death to the hours between midevening and seven-thirty the next morning. "Objection," Caroline called out again. "Two of them, actually. First, it's quite possible that, in a state of despair, Mr. Arias lost all interest in his coffee. Second, we don't even know what *day* the coffee was brewed—unless Mr. Coffee has developed technologies beyond my imaginings."

For the first time that day, Paget smiled. Salinas approached the bench, shaking his head. "*Your Honor,*" he said with annoyance, "Dr. Shelton is giving us the basis on which she determined a probable range of death. Ms. Masters' recourse is to cross-examine, *not* to object to every question."

"Then ask one that isn't objectionable," Caroline shot back.

Jared Lerner broke in. "Overruled," he said to Caroline. "Dr. Shelton is stating the basis for her opinion. I'll give you plenty of latitude to challenge that basis on cross."

Frowning, Caroline turned to sit down. Before she had done so, Salinas asked quickly, "In your career, Dr. Shelton, have you ever known *anyone* to preset their coffeemaker and then turn around and shoot themselves?"

Caroline spun on Salinas. "So now there are rules for suicide?" she snapped. "Or are you offering Dr. Shelton as a mind reader? For that matter, how do you even know that it was *Mr. Arias* who set the coffeemaker—"

Lerner held up his hand. "If that's an objection, Ms. Masters, I'm sustaining it." He turned to Salinas, leaning forward with a stare of

annoyance. "And I'll admonish *you*, Counselor, not to try to prejudice the jury by asking questions you know very well to be
improper."

It was a necessary rebuke, Paget thought: Salinas seemed to take
each success as an invitation to go farther. "I apologize, Your
Honor," Salinas said quite calmly. Turning to Shelton, he asked,
"Were there *other* factors on which you based a range of death?"

Shelton gave a small smile, as if bemused that there was any question. "Of course. We found the morning newspaper for October sixteen on the kitchen table, open to the business page. But the
newspaper for the *seventeenth* was still outside the door."

It was neatly done: with one added detail, the medical examiner
made her guesstimate seem convincing and Caroline merely quarrel-
some. As she appraised Shelton, Paget saw Caroline's eyes narrow in
something like a smile. "In addition," Shelton went on, "there were
facts I learned from the police. According to Inspector Monk, several people spoke to Mr. Arias on the afternoon and early evening of
October sixteen, but the police found no one who claims to have
seen or spoken to him after about nine o'clock that evening. All of
which further suggested that Mr. Arias was shot sometime between
roughly nine o'clock on October sixteen and the early morning of
October seventeen, when he failed to pick up his newspaper." Once
more, she smiled briefly. "Or, quite possibly, to drink the coffee that
was waiting for him."

The seemingly casual remark, Paget thought, was artful: he
doubted that anyone on the jury did not now assume that Ricardo
Arias had died before Paget left for Italy.

Quietly, Salinas asked, "And were your physical findings, Dr.
Shelton, consistent with a self-inflicted gunshot wound?"

With this question, Paget knew, Salinas had reached a critical
point: before proving Paget a murderer, he must establish that a
murder had occurred. In the jury box, Joseph Duarte flipped a
page of his notepad and waited to hear Shelton's reasons. For the
first time, Shelton turned to Paget, giving him a look that seemed
to mix puzzlement and disappointment. "They were not," she
answered. "I concluded that Mr. Arias had died at the hands of
another."

Although she had not spoken his name, Paget felt accused. The jury was stiff, attentive. "What facts," Salinas asked, "led you to conclude that Mr. Arias was not a suicide?"

Shelton gazed up at the ceiling, as if to reconstruct her thought process. "When I first arrived at the scene, I assumed this might well be suicide. The cause of death—a gunshot through the mouth—was consistent with that, and there were no signs of forced entry at the apartment itself. And Mr. Arias apparently had left a note." Pausing, Shelton looked pensive, a woman reliving her own doubts. "But within moments, I found things that made suicide seem unlikely. By the time I left, it seemed apparent that this was a homicide dressed up to look like suicide." She glanced at Paget. "Not very well dressed, at that."

As she watched, Caroline took out a pen and began scribbling on a legal pad. "On what basis," Salinas asked, "did you determine *that?*"

"The *first* thing I noticed was Mr. Arias's hands." Shelton turned to the jury. "As I mentioned, the bullet which killed Mr. Arias did *not* exit his head. That causes something called blowback—blood splatter and tissue which, because of the pressure of the bullet, sprays *forward* through the path left by the gunshot. Which is why the pictures of Mr. Arias show specks of blood and tissue on his face.

"Similarly, the firearms examiner advised me that the gun which killed Mr. Arias was old, a Smith and Wesson safety revolver manufactured in the early nineteen hundreds, and firing Winchester silvertip bullets made roughly *thirty* years ago. A gun like that leaves a considerable amount of gunshot residue—what we call GSR—a sootlike deposit of unburnt gunpowder and the chemicals found within. There *was* a significant amount of GSR on Mr. Arias's tongue, the roof of his mouth, *and* his face. In fact, we even found blood spatter and traces of powder on a coffee table *three feet* from Mr. Arias's body." Shelton paused, surveying the jury. "My point is this: if Mr. Arias had placed the gun in his mouth and pulled the trigger, I would expect to find *at least* as much blood spatter and GSR on his *hands* and *arms* as on his face. But there was almost none."

The jury had a rapt look, Paget saw. Marian Celler, whose empathy Paget hoped for, seemed very troubled. "If that had been the *only* thing," Shelton said, "I would have had extreme difficulty in accepting that Mr. Arias shot himself. But there was additional evidence inconsistent with suicide.

"Perhaps most troubling was the *other* violence done to Mr. Arias. First, Mr. Arias's skull showed an abrasion—a gash on the back of his head—which was not caused by the gunshot wound. And in fact, we determined from traces of skin and hair that Mr. Arias's head had struck the corner of his coffee table.

"Then there were contusions and swelling to Mr. Arias's nose. Again, the fatal bullet did not cause this. And the fact that his nose had been bleeding was consistent with a blow struck *prior* to his death."

In an involuntary reflex, Paget thought of the suit he had taken to Goodwill, and then of Terri, glancing at his hand as she had concealed his injury from Monk. He was glad that she was not here.

"Our autopsy," Shelton continued, "revealed another anomaly: a bruise on the front of Mr. Arias's right leg. Although we could not determine the cause, its position reflected the approximate height of the coffee table."

Salinas folded his arms; his posture and expression were that of a master teacher listening to his most brilliant student. "Have you completed your answer, Dr. Shelton, regarding your basis for opining that Mr. Arias was murdered?"

"No, actually." Shelton turned to Caroline, nodding slightly. "Ms. Masters is quite correct: there *is* no protocol for suicide. But in my experience, people tend to shoot themselves in three positions: standing up; sitting in a chair; or lying in bed. Here, based on the pattern of blowback on the arms and the angle of the bullet, Mr. Arias would have had to shoot himself while lying on the floor *and* with his head slightly raised. I've never seen *anyone* who did that.

"Which brings me to the angle of the gun. Like the position of the body, it's unusual—even bizarre. If Mr. Arias had been holding the revolver in his mouth, you would expect it to be pointing *up* toward his brain. Instead the trajectory was slightly downward, toward his throat. Which would have required Mr. Arias to lie on his back, head slightly raised, and then take the gun, hold it above him—apparently over his nose—crook his elbow and arm to angle the gun downward, and *then* pull the trigger. Perhaps with his thumb."

Shelton's testimony was becoming deadly, Paget knew. But there was nothing Caroline could do but listen and wait.

Salinas walked to his table, producing a small black revolver with an exhibit tag. "Your Honor, this revolver has been premarked as People's Exhibit 5. With the permission of the court, I will ask Dr. Shelton to identify it."

"May we see it?" Caroline asked.

Without a word, Salinas placed the revolver on the table. Looking down, Paget saw a small and worn handgun, with a checkered handgrip monogrammed "S&W" and a safety catch inside the grip. He did not pick it up.

"Odd," he murmured to Caroline, "that it's so old."

"Counselor?" Salinas interjected.

When Caroline nodded, Salinas took the gun and handed it to Shelton. "Is this the murder weapon, Dr. Shelton?"

Holding the revolver by the barrel, Shelton examined it. "It certainly appears to be," she answered.

With sudden fluidity, Salinas took the gun from her hand and lay on the floor, head slightly raised. "In your opinion, was *this* Mr. Arias's approximate position at the moment of death?"

Caroline rose. "Is Mr. Salinas about to levitate, Your Honor? Otherwise I really don't know what this proves."

But the jury seemed riveted to Salinas. He peered up from the floor at a somewhat bemused Jared Lerner. "I'm simply helping Dr. Shelton demonstrate her point regarding the contortions required for Mr. Arias's presumptive suicide. Quickly, I hope, before I get a crick in my neck."

There was muffled laughter. "All right," Lerner said with an air of amusement. "Go ahead."

But what was coming, Paget suddenly saw, would not be funny. Slowly, Salinas placed the gun to his mouth, asking disingenuously, "Is this the right angle?"

Shelton gazed down at him with a fleeting look of distaste. "No," she said tersely. "Raise the gun above your nose and point it down."

Salinas followed her instructions; the result—elbows bent, wrist twisted, thumb on the trigger—looked grotesque. "Like *this?*" he asked in a tone of disbelief.

"Approximately. Yes."

Salinas maintained the awkward position. "But this *isn't* what you believe happened. Could you help me illustrate what you think *did* happen?"

Gingerly, Shelton walked over to Salinas and knelt. The jury watched as one.

Gazing into Shelton's face, Salinas opened his mouth. With her right hand, Shelton slid the gun into his mouth.

Salinas's eyes widened. "Like *this*," Shelton said quietly, and pulled the trigger.

There was a soft click. In the jury box, Luisa Marin turned away. Salinas's eyes stayed frozen: in that moment, Paget knew, the murder of Ricardo Arias had become real.

Slowly, Shelton removed the gun. But Salinas's eyes did not change. "Which reminds me," he asked quietly, "did you find anything peculiar about Mr. Arias's eyes?"

She looked down at him. "I did," she said with equal quiet. "Virtually all the people I've seen who shot themselves died with their eyes shut."

Luisa Marin was staring at Shelton; in that moment, Paget was certain that she had seen her father's body, and that his eyes were closed.

"Pardon me, Counsel," Jared Lerner broke in. "Are you through lying on the floor?"

Salinas seemed faintly annoyed. "Yes," he answered. "Thank you, Your Honor."

Turning, Elizabeth Shelton walked back to the stand. "She just *loves* Victor," Caroline whispered dryly.

Shelton faced Salinas again, her face studiedly neutral. Hands on hips, Salinas asked, "Based on the medical evidence, Dr. Shelton, do you have a belief as to the sequence of events which led to Mr. Arias's death?"

Shelton glanced at Paget; for a brief moment, their eyes met, and then she turned to the jury. "I do," she said firmly. "The medical evidence is consistent with my belief that Mr. Arias sustained a blow to the face and that he spun and fell over the coffee table, resulting in an injury to his head. Together, the blows to the face and head rendered Mr. Arias unconscious." Pausing, Shelton spoke more quietly. "The evidence further suggests that as he lay there on the floor, someone inserted the gun in his mouth and pulled the trigger twice.

But, as ballistics discovered, the bullets had been kept in a damp place, and the first shot did not discharge. Finally, the medical evidence suggests that before the gun was fired again, Mr. Arias awoke. So that, in the last instant of his life, he was aware of the gun in his mouth."

The sentence lingered there. Shelton reached for the glass of water on the railing of the witness box, took a sip, and continued. "I cannot *know* what happened. But my thesis accounts for the medical evidence—the injuries to Mr. Arias's nose, head, and leg; the tissue on the table; the blood spatter and GSR on the same table as well as on his face; their anomalous absence on his hands; the peculiar angle of the bullet; the strange position of his head; and"—here Shelton's voice fell—"the look of terrible fright, captured by the moment of death."

She folded her hands. "I may be off about a detail or two. But the medical evidence is *not* consistent with suicide. Of *that* I'm quite confident." She paused again. "To put it more baldly, Mr. Salinas, this man was murdered."

Beneath the table, Caroline's fingertips grazed Paget's knee, a fleeting gesture of reassurance. "Victor went a little too far," she murmured, and then she was on her feet, walking toward Shelton.

Shelton gave Caroline a look of polite interest. "Was Mr. Arias's alarm set?" she asked abruptly.

Shelton looked surprised. "No. I believe not."

"Perhaps," Caroline said dryly, "he didn't plan on getting up."

"Objection," Salinas called out. "Calls for speculation."

"Precisely, Victor," Caroline asserted, still gazing at Shelton. "And it's at least as reasonable as your questions about the coffeemaker."

The corner of Shelton's mouth flickered. "Sustained," Lerner said. "Perhaps you may wish to ask the question another way."

"I do, actually. Dr. Shelton, would you consider Mr. Arias's failure to set his alarm to be as consistent with suicide as his supposed action in setting the coffeemaker is consistent, in your thesis, with murder?"

Shelton gave a disinterested shrug. "I suppose so. Neither proves much, and my opinion isn't based on coffee grounds."

"That's just as well. Let's stick to the evidence, then. For all you know, waking or sleeping, Mr. Arias was alive when the newspaper was delivered, correct?"

"It's possible, yes."

"And, indeed, it's possible he slept well into the morning? Until ten or eleven."

Shelton's eyes, alert and a little amused, told Paget that she had followed Caroline perfectly. "In theory, yes."

"So that even accepting your hypothesis, if Mr. Paget was driving to the airport before seven and on an airplane by eight, it's quite possible that Mr. Arias died thereafter."

Shelton nodded. "It's all possible, Ms. Masters."

Caroline raised her head; her profile, handsome and aristocratic, seemed to draw the jury. "Then you have no opinion on whether *Christopher Paget* shot Ricardo Arias. Or even *could* have."

"None whatsoever."

These were easy questions to ask, Paget knew; other witnesses would try to show his guilt. But it allowed Caroline to establish a rhythm, making a point or two with the jury. "Speaking of the revolver," she continued, "it's a rather weak caliber, is it not?"

"Yes."

"Which would cause a lesser amount of blowback?"

"Yes." Pausing, Shelton decided to anticipate Caroline's next question. "But not in a pattern which reached the coffee table but excluded Mr. Arias's hands and arms."

Caroline smiled. "It didn't really *exclude* them, did it? As I recall, the autopsy report showed traces of blood and GSR on Mr. Arias's right hand."

"A *small* trace," Shelton corrected. "But there was far more on the gun itself. From which I concluded that someone else held it, receiving blowback on his or her hand or sleeve, and then placed it in Mr. Arias's right hand, leaving only the small trace of blowback and GSR."

Caroline walked forward, as if to demonstrate her persistence. "Mr. Arias was right-handed, was he not?"

"I believe so."

"Then isn't it possible that he shot himself using *only* his right hand, explaining the absence of GSR and blowback on his left hand and arm?"

Shelton frowned now. "*That* much is possible, Ms. Masters. But *not* the paucity of residue on *either* hand. Particularly when compared to the revolver itself."

Restless, Marian Celler gazed at the clock. Move on, Paget urged Caroline. But she did not do so. "There was also blood, was there not, on Mr. Arias's hand near his wrist. Quite a bit, in fact, and *also* Mr. Arias's blood."

"Yes," Shelton said. "But that was a *smear* of blood, completely inconsistent with the speckling caused by blowback."

"Oh? And what *did* cause it?"

Shelton folded her hands. "In my opinion," she said evenly, "the smear was caused when Mr. Arias wiped blood from beneath his nose."

Caroline raised her eyebrows. "How did you determine *that?*"

"It just makes sense. And, as the pictures show, there was also a smear of blood beneath Mr. Arias's nose."

Suddenly Paget saw Shelton's mistake and knew what Caroline would do next. But instead she simply asked, "But you're quite certain the blood on his hand was not blowback?"

"Quite."

"And you never considered that it *was* blowback but that Mr. Arias's hand, falling after he shot himself, smeared the blood as it crossed his face or body or even the rug?"

Shelton appraised her. "I found no blood, anywhere, which caused me to entertain that possibility."

"But is it *possible?*"

"I wasn't there, Ms. Masters. But I found no reason to believe it happened like that."

Shelton was looking annoyed; Caroline's persistence in raising the question of blowback, Paget saw, seemed to have disguised what she meant to do. But then, abruptly, Caroline shifted subjects. "Mr. Arias *did* leave a suicide note, correct?"

"There was a note, yes."

"Do you believe he didn't write it?"

Shelton shrugged. "As far as I know, the fact that he *wrote* it isn't in dispute. But I would have to question the circumstances."

Paget saw Luisa Marin clasp her hands together, her expression strained and tight. "In other words," Caroline said, "your opinion simply ignores the letter."

Shelton leaned back. "In reaching my opinion, I took its *existence* into account. But I concluded, based on the medical evidence, that this was not a suicide."

"All right. Then let's return to the medical evidence." Smiling, Caroline turned to Salinas. "Do you think you can play Mr. Arias again, Victor? You were so good the last time."

Salinas half stood, looking surprised and a bit nettled. "Why can't you stage your own demonstration?"

"Humor me, Victor. Besides, your suit's already dirty."

There was laughter in the courtroom, a small smile from Marian Celler. "She has you," Judge Lerner said to Salinas. "Your public demands an encore."

There was a second wave of chuckles. Salinas opened his palms and smiled. "For you, Your Honor. But after this, I'm giving up acting."

"Oh," Caroline said with a smile, "I doubt *that*. But I appreciate your help, Victor. You wouldn't mind coming over here and lying on the floor, would you? And do bring your gun."

Paget suppressed a grin: so this was how she would do it. Walking over to Caroline, Salinas did not look happy.

She smiled again. "At my feet, Victor. Please."

Salinas executed a mock bow. "Always," he responded with irony, and lay on the floor near Caroline.

"My, you look natural," she said, and turned to Liz Shelton. "And you, Dr. Shelton, would you mind stepping down?"

Shelton gave Caroline a quick, appraising glance and then walked over to Salinas. "You may take the gun," Caroline said. "And then if you would, could you replicate the murder scenario you staged for us earlier?"

Caroline had captured the jury now. They watched with strict attention as Shelton knelt by Salinas. "As I recall," Caroline said, "Victor's head was slightly raised, and he looked quite uncomfortable. Please do that again, Victor, while Dr. Shelton puts the gun in your mouth."

Salinas raised his head with a look of distaste. Slowly, Shelton slid the gun between his lips. Caroline peered down at Salinas with a critical expression. "Eyes a little wider, please, Victor. You were much better the first time."

Someone coughed in the courtroom, suppressing laughter. "All right," Caroline said to Shelton. "Now, as I recall your thesis, some unknown person struck Mr. Arias, who then took a pratfall over his coffee table, struck his head, rolled onto the carpet, passed out, and came to just in time to see his killer and gaze up with horror. Although *not* long enough to grab for the gun. Is that about it?"

Shelton kept looking at Salinas. "Approximately."

Caroline looked puzzled. "Didn't you leave something out?"

"And what would that be?"

"The part where Victor wipes his nose."

The startled laugh, Paget realized, was Jared Lerner's. But now Caroline was not smiling. "Can you answer my question, Dr. Shelton? Just when did Mr. Arias find time to wipe his nose?"

As Shelton gazed up, Salinas pushed the gun from his mouth. "Down, Victor," Caroline said, and looked back at Shelton.

Shelton shook her head. "I don't know."

Caroline stared down at her. "I mean, it's a little implausible, isn't it? If *I* were Mr. Arias, I might have gone for the gun before cleaning myself up."

Shelton set down the gun. "You're assuming that's when he wiped his nose. It could have been some other time."

"Oh? So now your 'thesis' is that he wiped his nose shortly *after* he was hit but *before* pirouetting over the coffee table?"

Salinas sat up. "Are we through here?" he snapped.

She looked down at him. "Completely," she said, and turned to Shelton. "You may return to the stand, Dr. Shelton."

Shelton did so. "Do you have my last question in mind?" Caroline asked.

"Completely," Shelton responded, with a certain wry dignity. "And as I testified before, it's possible that I'm wrong about a detail or two. For example, the intruder may have struck Mr. Arias at some earlier point. Temporizing with his potential killer, Mr. Arias may have wiped his nose. And then, believing his situation hopeless, may have turned to run, striking the coffee table." Shelton paused, her voice gathering force. "Whatever else, it is *not* my thesis that Mr. Arias beat himself, bruised his leg, banged his head on the table, and shot himself in a weird position, covering his right hand in some inexplicable way, all in order to conceal his passionate desire to kill himself."

It was a devastating counter. But Caroline merely smiled. "Assuming that your earlier string of 'may's adds up to something, let me try yet *another* theory. In a state of extreme distress, Mr. Arias begins to write a suicide note but can't bring himself to finish. He starts pacing in an agitated state, holding the gun, oblivious to his surroundings. Blindly, he trips over the coffee table, hitting *both* his head *and* his nose, and lands on the floor with the gun." Caroline paused, speaking more slowly. "Stunned, he wipes his nose—the kind of reflexive thing an agitated man, addled and alone, has time for. And then his thoughts clarify, and he knows what he wants to do. And does it." Gazing at Shelton, Caroline spoke quite softly now: "Just as he said in the note."

"It's completely inconsistent," Shelton answered promptly. "Because it fails to account for the lack of blowback and GSR."

"But it *does* account for his injuries, doesn't it, Dr. Shelton? *And* for the smear of blood." Here Caroline paused for a deadly moment. "Unless, of course, that *was* blowback."

Shelton gave her a level look. "There was no GSR on his wrist at all. In my opinion, the only way Mr. Arias could have fired that gun was if he were wearing a glove."

"But then," Caroline retorted, "he wouldn't have that mysterious blood on his hand. Which you can't really explain, can you?"

"Not as an isolated fact, no. But in the totality of the facts, I don't believe it matters."

Caroline, Paget knew, was running out of points to score. He saw her pause, hoping to end on a high note. "But it *did* matter to your initial thesis, didn't it? In which Mr. Arias is struck and plummets over the table."

Shelton hesitated, and then nodded. "It did," she conceded. "And in retrospect, I was a little ambitious in trying to tie everything together. But the essence of my opinion is this: the medical evidence—the lack of blowback, the absence of GSR, the injuries to Mr. Arias's head and body, the position of the gun—is *all* inconsistent with suicide. Period." Shelton paused again. "And there was one other thing," she finished quietly. "The look on Mr. Arias's face."

Caroline's expression did not change; perhaps only Paget knew how much she regretted her last question. "Wouldn't *you* be frightened," she asked, "if you were about to shoot yourself? Even if you wanted to?"

Shelton thought for a moment. "The circumstances are hard for me to imagine. But yes, I suppose I might."

Slowly, Caroline nodded. "I suppose I might too," she said softly. "Thank you, Dr. Shelton. I have no further questions.

All at once, it was over.

As Shelton stepped from the stand, staring straight ahead now, Paget looked at the jury. He knew what the television news would highlight: courtroom drawings of Caroline, standing over Victor Salinas. But in the faces of his jurors, Paget could see that Ricardo Arias had moved much closer to being a victim of murder.

THREE

THE NEXT MORNING, Salinas set out to prove that Ricardo Arias had meant to live forever.

He began with Leslie Warner. Taking the stand, Elena's former teacher arranged her long floral skirt and fingered her bracelets, smiling at the jury.

"What a cretin," Paget murmured to Caroline. "I still can't believe she fed Elena to Charles Monk."

Caroline nodded. "If I were Terri, I'd have whacked her too. But *you're* about to pay for it."

Warner folded her hands, looking at Salinas with an air of polite expectation. After a few introductory questions, Salinas asked abruptly, "You were going to meet Mr. Arias, were you not? The day after anyone last saw him."

Warner looked somber. "Yes. To discuss Elena."

"Were you surprised that he didn't appear?"

"Very much."

Slowly, Salinas asked, "In your acquaintance with Mr. Arias, that didn't seem normal?"

"Not at all." Warner glanced at the jury, as if to ensure that they were listening. "At our first meeting, before she even entered our school, he spoke to me about Elena for some time, how much he enjoyed her imaginative qualities and wanted to encourage them. That night, and in subsequent meetings or conversations once Elena was in my classroom, Richie—Mr. Arias—seemed a very warm, very concerned father."

Salinas nodded. "How often did you speak to him?"

"Quite often." Looking down, Warner twisted her bracelet. "Actually, after a particular incident involving Elena very early in September, he would drop by or call at least once a week. Or I would call him. I mean, I knew that Mr. Arias was the custodial parent and quite concerned."

Caroline's eyes narrowed. "I'll bet she could hardly wait for those all-important parent-teacher conferences."

Paget smiled a little; Caroline's instincts were good, and he sensed she was onto something.

"This early incident you mentioned," Salinas was asking. "Can you describe it?"

Here it comes, Paget thought. "Yes," Warner said in a flat voice. "I observed Elena behind a Dumpster, pulling down her panties and asking a boy to look at her genital area. When I pulled her aside and asked about it, she was too upset to talk. So I decided to call Mr. Arias."

Salinas looked disturbed. "Did the incident you observed raise particular concerns?"

Warner's own expression turned grave, as if mirroring Salinas. "Sexual acting out is fairly common; as a teacher, I see it a lot. Sometimes it's simply experimentation; at other times it may suggest deeper problems. In this case, Elena's distress when I spoke to her was *so* extreme that I decided to notify Mr. Arias." Her voice turned flat again. "And, of course, Elena's mother. Although the court gave *Richie* custody."

Paget leaned his head close to Caroline's. "He's using this supposed meeting as a wedge. To get in stuff about Carlo and how wonderful Richie was. It's flat objectionable."

"Except in Jared Lerner's courtroom," Caroline murmured. "But I'm about to give it a try."

"When you say 'deeper problems,' " Salinas asked, "what do you have in mind?"

Abruptly, Paget felt himself tense. Warner's eyes seemed to compress. "Under certain circumstances, it can be a symptom of child abuse."

Quickly, Caroline was on her feet. "I move to strike that answer, Your Honor. Ms. Warner has not been qualified as an expert on *anything*. Including child abuse *or* Ricardo Arias."

But Salinas was prepared with a rationale that played to Judge Lerner's liberality. "It is perfectly valid," Salinas said to Lerner, "for us to call on Ms. Warner's experiences as a teacher. With the court's permission, I'd like to establish that experience as a context for her conversations with Mr. Arias."

Lerner frowned. "I'll let it go," he said to Caroline. "The jury can hear it for whatever it's worth."

Caroline sat again. Angry, Paget braced himself for what would come.

Salinas turned to Warner again. "Prior to your call to Mr. Arias, did you have any incidence of child molestation among your students?"

"Yes. On four different instances over a six-year period, children in my class were determined by Child Protective Services to have been sexually abused."

"And did that experience influence your decision to contact Elena's parents?"

"Yes. In those four situations, the children—three girls and a boy—displayed some of the same behavior I saw in Elena almost from the first day: listlessness and inattention, detachment from other children, and sexually suggestive or aggressive play. These experiences definitely raised my consciousness in thinking about Elena."

"In turn, did you mention possible sexual abuse to Mr. Arias?"

"Yes."

Paget saw Caroline frown. By pinning his questions to Warner's conversation with Richie, Salinas legitimized Richie's concerns: the specter of child abuse had first been raised not by him but by a caring and enlightened teacher. It struck him that the "fistfight" before Lerner—which Brooks had forecast—did not necessarily favor the defense.

"And what," Salinas asked slowly, "was Mr. Arias's response?"

"He was quite disturbed." She paused, as if upset by the memory, and spoke more quietly. "I remember him saying something like 'God, Leslie, I hope not—this poor kid has gone through enough.'"

In the jury box, Joseph Duarte looked pensive, as if imagining Richie's anxiety. Caroline shook her head. "Jesus," she murmured. "Why don't we just have a séance." Paget knew what she meant: through Leslie Warner, Salinas was bringing Ricardo Arias to life.

"Do you remember what else Richie said?" he asked her.

Warner nodded firmly. "He wanted to meet with me, right away.

At the meeting, he peppered me with questions about Elena's behavior, taking notes of everything I said." Pausing, Warner shook her head. "Before, he seemed a cheerful man, upbeat and enthusiastic. But now he looked so upset for Elena that I thought for a minute he might cry. This worry about her just seemed to kill him."

As if hearing her last phrase, Warner put a hand to her mouth. Salinas waited a respectful moment. "Oh, *please*," Caroline murmured in disgust. But the jury, Paget noticed, was somber.

"What else do you recall about this conversation?" Salinas asked.

Warner folded her hands. "For all his obvious emotion, I thought Mr. Arias *very* responsible. He said, and I agreed, that with suspicions this vague he didn't want to upset Elena by confronting her. Instead he asked me for a reading list of books on sexual abuse and requested that I call him if *anything* happened with Elena." She paused. "Oh, and he asked if I was going to call Ms. Peralta. When I said yes, he told me that was good, that his wife needed to be involved."

Inwardly, Paget winced; the Richie the jury must now imagine was different from the one Terri had known. Salinas stepped forward. "When was that meeting, Ms. Warner?"

"Again, very early in the school year." Her voice fell. "Perhaps six weeks or so before Mr. Arias died."

"And after that, did Mr. Arias keep in touch?"

"As I said, at least once a week. Several times he dropped by after school."

"And what did you talk about?"

For a moment, Paget thought, Warner looked curiously defensive. "Elena. He wanted to know if there was anything new and how she was doing in school."

"And what was his demeanor during those visits?"

"Very concerned, but appreciative." Warner smiled faintly. "He was a very cheerful man, really. One time, because I'd told him I'd been to the opera and loved *La Bohème*, he brought me a book about Puccini."

Moving still closer to Warner, Salinas paused for emphasis. "Did there come a time, Ms. Warner, when Mr. Arias reported to you *his* concern that Elena *had* been molested?"

For the first time, Warner glanced at Paget. "Yes," she said in a tone of suppressed anger. "About three weeks later, he called me sounding very upset, and asked if I could see him. When he came to the school he looked as troubled as he sounded." She moderated her tone. "What he shared with me, in confidence, was his fear that Elena had been sexually molested by Mr. Paget's son."

From the side, Paget saw several jurors glance at him surreptitiously. But he could not control his look of outrage: after Salinas had raised this charge in opening statements, Paget had spent the night with Carlo, encouraging him to keep his pride in the face of the reporters clustered outside their home, the plummy news voices who made Carlo part of their lead sentence. It was hard to watch Salinas smear his son to get at Paget himself.

"And what," Salinas asked, "did Mr. Arias tell you?"

Warner's gray eyes were shadowed with disapproval. "That his wife let Elena spend time with Mr. Paget's son—Carlo, I believe his name is. It had bothered him, Richie said, once I voiced my concerns. But he hadn't wanted to say something irresponsible which might damage a teenage boy." She folded her hands. "*Then* Elena told Richie that Carlo had given her a bath. And when he questioned her, Richie said, she went into a shell—I could tell it frightened him." She shook her head. "It scared me too. Because that was how Elena had been the day that I questioned her. And in my experience, it's a symptom of abuse."

Paget saw Caroline begin to rise, and then reconsider. She was right, he knew: objecting would only aggravate the damage.

"Did Mr. Arias tell you what he intended to do?"

"Yes." Warner's voice became firm. "He intended to tell his wife to keep Elena away from Carlo and Mr. Paget. And if she refused, he was going to court."

"And when did he tell you this?"

Warner stared at Paget now. "Less than two weeks before his death."

"And when he told you, what was his demeanor?"

Warner gave a short nod, as if approving of the Richie she remembered. "Determined. Confident, I might even say, that he was doing the right thing and that he'd win."

Caroline rose. "I'd like to make a belated objection, Your Honor. Ms. Warner's not a mentalist, or a psychiatrist for that matter, and what we seem to be hearing are *her* mental impressions of Mr. Arias's mental state. Based on what, I have to wonder."

Eyeing Caroline, Salinas turned to Lerner. "Your Honor, the defense proposes that Mr. Arias killed himself. We're forced to show that he did not. And if Ms. Masters can find *anyone* to say that Mr. Arias was spotted on a park bench, looking brooding and morose, I *guarantee* we'll hear from them."

Salinas had anticipated each problem, Paget saw, and prepared a rationale that Lerner might accept. Against his will, Paget had begun to fear Salinas's thoroughness. As if to confirm this, Lerner nodded. "Overruled."

"Thank you," Salinas said, and turned to Warner. "Did you *ever* see any signs of despair in Mr. Arias?"

"Never. As I said, except for worrying about Elena, he was a very optimistic man. I don't want to be hokey, but Richie seemed high on life—in love with his daughter, excited about his new business, looking forward to putting the divorce behind him and getting on with his future."

Salinas assumed an almost mournful look. "And when, Ms. Warner, did you *last* see Mr. Arias?"

Warner looked down. "The day before his wife left for Italy with Mr. Paget."

"Can you describe that conversation?"

"By then Richie had filed his motion in court. He expressed disappointment that, with all that was at stake for Elena, Ms. Peralta had chosen to leave the country with her boyfriend." She paused. "We talked for a while, and then he asked if I could meet him the next morning, Saturday, at The Coffee Bean in Noe Valley. To talk more about Elena."

"And what did you say?"

"That I would." Warner shrugged, still looking down. "I live close to there, and so did he."

"During this conversation, did he sound normal?"

"Absolutely normal. If anything, more concerned than ever about his daughter."

Salinas nodded. "When were you supposed to meet him?"

Warner paused a moment. "I said around eleven would be good."

"And did you go there?"

"Yes." Warner's voice became almost wispy. "But Richie never came."

Salinas angled his head. "And what did you do?"

"I waited for a hour and then left."

"Did you try to call him?"

Warner gave a slight shake of the head. "I was too embarrassed. I thought Richie had forgotten." She gazed up at Salinas with an almost haunted look. "You'll never know, Mr. Salinas, how much I wish I'd called."

Watching Warner, Marian Celler leaned forward. In despair, Paget felt the jury slipping away. Quietly, Salinas said, "I have no further questions."

Careful, Caroline admonished herself as she approached Leslie Warner. Right now the jury likes her, and you're already on the edge; too supercilious, and you'll lose them altogether.

"Good morning," Caroline said pleasantly.

Warner regarded her with wounded gray eyes, as if interrupted from sorrow and remorse: it confirmed for Caroline that something in this woman enjoyed the role she was playing. "You seem quite troubled by Mr. Arias's death," Caroline observed.

Warner nodded. "I am."

Caroline gave her a puzzled look. "Is there a particular reason?"

Warner paused a moment. "It's tragic when someone dies so young," she replied. "Especially someone who seemed so full of life and so concerned for his daughter. Maybe that's the biggest tragedy of all—that Elena won't have a father."

Or that you won't have a date, Caroline thought. "Did you feel particularly close to Elena?"

Another pause. "I was concerned for her," Warner responded. "But she wasn't with me long. After Richie died, her mother took her out of school."

The last words were flat with disapproval. There were several ways to take this, Caroline thought; then, all at once, the path seemed to open up in front of her. "Did you have a social interest in Mr. Arias?" she asked.

Warner sat back a little. "I don't know what you mean," she said stiffly.

Caroline tilted her head. "For example, have you met for coffee with the father of any other student?"

Warner's mouth compressed. "No."

"Or any mother?"

"Not that I can remember."

"Including Teresa Peralta?"

"No." Warner's voice was flat again. "Elena was a particular concern of mine. When her father asked to see me, I didn't have a problem with that."

Caroline's look turned curious. "Just how well did you know Mr. Arias?"

Warner rearranged her flowing skirt. "Fairly well, I think. When you talk to someone almost twice a week for several weeks, you get a sense of who they are. Especially someone as open as Richie."

"Oh? Do you know how Mr. Arias made a living?"

Warner gave her a cool look. "He had his own business," she said emphatically. "Called Lawsearch. He was very excited about it."

"Did he happen to mention that he was living on a combination of spousal and child support, paid by Ms. Peralta?"

Warner folded her hands. "No."

"So I also gather you don't know whether he could have survived if he'd lost custody of Elena."

"No."

"Or even whether he had financial problems."

"No."

"Or *emotional* problems?"

"No."

"Or whether he was seeing a psychiatrist or counselor?"

"No." Warner's voice was cold now. "We didn't have the kind of relationship where he would tell me those things. Our conversations were mainly about Elena."

Caroline put her hands on her hips. "What kind of parent was Ricardo Arias?"

Warner looked annoyed. "He was concerned, as I said."

"And how do you know that?"

"Because we *talked* about her. Quite a lot."

"Did you ever actually observe them together?"

Warner looked bewildered. "I wasn't in a position to see their interactions."

"In other words, you knew Mr. Arias was concerned because he *said* he was concerned, is that right?"

"Parental contact with the teacher indicates concern to me."

Caroline made herself look pensive. "Would you say another sign of concern would have been to have Elena evaluated by a psychologist? One who specializes in children."

Warner gave her a tight smile. "Yes. I believe I mentioned that to Mr. Arias."

"Did *he* happen to mention that Ms. Peralta had *asked* for such an evaluation?"

Warner looked surprised. "I don't believe so."

"Did he tell you that once the abuse charges were made, Ms. Peralta had again asked that they be investigated by a professional?"

In the witness box, Warner seemed to edge away from Caroline. "We didn't discuss that," she said tersely.

"So you didn't discuss *why* he felt it necessary to bring his charges against Carlo in court?"

A vigorous nod. "To protect Elena."

"I see. And you believed that it was *your* responsibility to protect Elena as well. Is that correct?"

"Inasmuch as I could. As her teacher."

"As her teacher, when you called *Ms. Peralta* about the playground incident you mentioned, did you mention the concern that Elena might have suffered sexual abuse?"

Warner's shoulders seemed to curl in. She had begun staring at Caroline with open dislike; yet Caroline had never raised her voice. "No," Warner said. "She didn't seem receptive."

"Do you make it a practice to decide to raise child abuse only if a parent seems 'receptive'?"

Warner flushed. "Of course not. But I'd already told the custodial parent, Mr. Arias."

"Tell me, then, why Ms. Peralta didn't seem 'receptive'?"

Warner folded her arms. "When I suggested that Elena might be overstimulated by her new relationship, Ms. Peralta sounded annoyed. So I decided to leave it there."

Sometimes it helped, Caroline thought, to truly dislike a witness. "And how did you know about Ms. Peralta's 'new relationship'?" she asked.

"Because Richie told me." Warner looked angry now. "Apparently, Ms. Peralta had been involved even *before* the marriage broke up."

Still Caroline did not raise her voice. "According to whom?"

"Mr. Arias."

"And of course you took his word for that too. Because you knew him so well."

Warner stared at her. "I accepted what he told me. I had no reason not to."

"And on *that* basis, you made a moral judgment about Ms. Peralta as a mother."

"Elena's problems came from *somewhere*," Warner snapped.

You officious fool, Caroline thought. "Indeed they did, Ms. Warner. Don't you think that if you'd told Ms. Peralta of your concerns, she might have helped identify *where?*"

"I didn't consider that."

"And yet you had a series of meetings and conversations with one parent within the space of a few weeks, all supposedly premised on the specter of abuse that you never even *mentioned* to the other."

Warner gave her a hostile look. "Many of these contacts were initiated by Mr. Arias."

For the first time, Caroline moved closer. "And did either he *or* you raise the possibility of including Elena's mother?"

Warner shook her head. "No. On my part, I was confident he'd report to Ms. Peralta."

"Really? In truth, weren't these exclusive meetings a convenient way of ingratiating yourself with a father you found attractive and who was hostile to his estranged wife?"

"No," Warner responded angrily. "I was meeting with the custodial parent."

Caroline nodded. "The custodial parent," she repeated quietly. "Who, for all *you* know, was the one who had molested Elena."

"*Objection,*" Salinas called out. "That is outrageous, Your Honor. There is no basis for that kind of diversionary slander."

Caroline spun on him. "From the moment you entered this courtroom, Victor, you have been just delighted to slander a teenage boy so that you can convict his father. But I suppose it's not slander if it's also a career move."

"I *resent* that—" Salinas began, and then Judge Lerner's gavel crashed.

"Enough personalities—*both* of you." He addressed Caroline. "I agree that your question's germane—*if* rephrased. Press on."

Caroline turned back to Warner. "Did you ever consider,"

she asked softly, "that Mr. Arias might have molested his own daughter?"

Warner gave her a hostile look. "No," she said firmly.

"Or that telling Ms. Peralta might help Elena?"

Warner grimaced; with each question, Caroline thought, she looked a little less attractive. Stiffly, she answered, "I did what I thought was right."

Caroline gave her a long, silent look. "Is it fair to say," she asked finally, "that your entire assessment of *Mr. Arias* was based on your meetings with *Mr. Arias?*"

Another pause. "I think I'm a decent judge of character. In my business you see a lot."

Only if you're looking, Caroline thought. "You didn't know anything about his life—correct?—except what he told you?"

"I suppose not."

"So you didn't know how he acted when he wasn't with you?"

"No."

"Nor do you have any background in psychology or psychiatry."

"I don't."

Caroline paused, skipping a beat. "Or suicide."

Warner looked startled. "No."

"Has anyone you knew very well ever killed himself?"

A short shake of the head. "No."

"And yet you're convinced that Mr. Arias *didn't* kill himself."

Warner's mouth set in a stubborn line. "Yes."

Caroline half turned, taking in the jury for the first time. They were surveying Warner with a newly skeptical air; Joseph Duarte tapped his pencil to his lips, watching Warner intently over a semi-smile. It was that which persuaded Caroline to go for broke. Facing Warner, she said, "You don't like Teresa Peralta, do you?"

Warner blinked. Slowly, she answered, "No."

"Is there a specific reason?"

"Yes." Warner's eyes hardened, as if she saw an opportunity to regain the ground she had lost and could hardly believe that Caroline would give it to her. "Teresa Peralta slapped me."

"What was the occasion?"

"I was at school, in my room." A slight hesitation. "I'd suggested to the police that they should question Elena."

Caroline gave her an incredulous look. "Elena? As in Ms. Peralta's six-year-old daughter?"

"Yes." Warner's voice rose. "A few days before Richie died, Elena was moping around the classroom after the other kids went out to play. When I asked her what was wrong, she said that she heard her parents having an argument and that Ms. Peralta had threatened to *kill* Richie."

"Do you know the context?"

"No." Warner's voice dropped. "When I told Richie, he just laughed. He said his wife had a bad temper."

"Did you ever discuss this supposed threat with Ms. Peralta?"

"No."

"Did you see fit to inform Ms. Peralta that you were setting two homicide inspectors loose on her kindergartner?"

"No."

"For that matter, did you consult the principal?"

"No."

"Or a psychologist?"

"No."

"Did you consult *anyone* on how the violent death of a parent might have affected Elena?"

"No."

"Or how being questioned about it by the police might affect her?"

"No."

"And of course, because you never talked to Ms. Peralta about anything, you were unaware that she had engaged a psychologist to help Elena."

Warner sat rigid in the witness chair. "I did what I thought was right."

"You always do, don't you? Isn't it true that before she hit you, Ms. Peralta asked if you had any idea of the harm you were doing?"

Warner's eyes seemed to widen. "She *may* have said something like that."

"And didn't you respond by saying that she shouldn't raise her own daughter and that Elena was lost without Richie?"

A slow nod. "I think I did."

"And then she slapped you."

"Yes."

Caroline appraised her. "How long after *that*," she asked quietly, "was it that you called the police and offered to testify that Mr. Arias wasn't suicidal?"

Warner's shrug was like a twitch of the neck. "Sometime thereafter. I'm not sure when."

"Try the next day, Ms. Warner."

Warner held her head higher. "If you say so."

"Oh, I do." Caroline gave a sardonic smile. "One more thing. Before Ms. Peralta slapped you, did she also call you a fool?"

A brisk nod of indignation. "Yes. She did."

Caroline gave her a look of bemusement. "And after that, you *still* thought she was an unfit mother?"

The insult was so subtle that it took Warner a moment to flush, Salinas to object. There was a snicker from the press.

"That question," Salinas said angrily, "is sheer harassment, deliberately calculated to insult this witness."

Caroline turned to Salinas. "Please forgive me, Victor," she said in rueful tones. "I was just doing what I thought was right."

When Caroline abruptly turned her back on Warner, returning to the defense table, Joseph Duarte gave her a short nod.

There were moments during a trial, Caroline thought, when it felt like you could live forever.

FOUR

TERESA PERALTA sat in Denise Harris's waiting room, reading notes from Chris's murder trial while Harris saw Elena.

She had arranged for the notes through Caroline Masters, who assigned an associate to follow each day's proceedings. After Salinas barred her from the courtroom, Terri had resolved that she would know where the prosecutor was going right to the moment when Salinas put her on the stand. Salinas's opening statement indicated his intention to make Richie's charge of sexual abuse a centerpiece of the prosecution; it was doubly ironic that Terri, forbidden to attend the trial, was waiting here while on the other side of the door a stranger tried to learn from her own daughter where the truth might lie.

But even Chris felt like a stranger now. It was not only that he would not talk about the evidence against him; the demands of maintaining his composure, of trying to think like a lawyer while the father in him worried for Carlo, drained so much energy that he seemed to have withdrawn to another place. It was becoming harder to remember how she once depended on him; or the sudden surprising brightness when he smiled at her; or the belief that she knew enough to share a life with him. The unnerving sense that Chris was a series of compartments, with some that he opened for no one, had taken its place.

But there were few things, now, of which Terri felt certain. She could not believe that she had been a good mother—she had the evidence of Elena to tell her otherwise. She was no longer sure that she knew her *own* mother; there seemed to dwell within Rosa an ingrained solitude, a deep sense that she had always been alone. Terri did not know whether her own daughter had been molested; there was too much doubt to be sure of Carlo, and she did not know what secrets Chris was hiding.

Perhaps Caroline knew, or at least had guessed. Caroline was so smart that Terri had sometimes found her scary, and she was more like Chris than any woman Terri knew: Caroline acted according to her own personal code, which she did not explain to others, even if the price was to appear unfeeling. There was an honor to this, and a certain arrogance as well. But perhaps Caroline sensed things about Chris that Terri could not see.

That was part of it, Terri realized. She had been Chris's professional partner and now—when it mattered most—the role had fallen to Caroline Masters, who seemed so well suited to it. But there was something more. Defending Chris might be so inimical to Caroline's ambitions that Terri could think of only one reason that Caroline would take it on: that on grounds Terri did not know, Caroline sensed that Chris was innocent.

Pensive, Terri flipped the page.

Caroline had done well with Liz Shelton, but not well enough; Shelton knew that there was no way Richie had killed himself, and Terri was quite certain that Caroline could find no one who believed Richie suicidal. But what Terri believed, and what she might say, were different.

Caroline could do many things, Terri reflected, perhaps even believe in Chris. But only Terri could make the *jury* believe in a man they might never hear.

She resumed studying the notes, making her own notations to mark the key points of Salinas's case.

At certain angles, Harris reflected, Elena Arias was the image of her mother.

The child had long eyelashes, quick but delicate hands, a grave beauty. But the resemblance went far deeper: Harris was sometimes haunted by the almost ruthless determinism through which the trauma of the parent seemed to catch up with the child, generation after generation.

Buried in Terri's childhood or adolescence, Harris suspected, was something so deeply wrong that Terri herself had yet to face it. Harris's best guess was sexual abuse. But the deeper tragedy was apparent to Terri herself: in trying to escape Ramon Peralta, Terri had fled

to her own marriage carrying Rosa's troubles with her, and now—
for whatever reason—Elena was troubled as well.

An endless chain, Harris thought. Ramon Peralta's father had
beaten him; Rosa's father had raped her. They were a couple made
for each other, just as they had made Terri the perfect wife for
Ricardo Arias.

Of course, Terri had tried to end this and to take Elena with her.
So there was always the hope of change. Except that, Harris reflected wearily, she could not be entirely certain Terri herself had not
killed Richie: in an abusive relationship, beneath the victim's stoi-
cism, anger lives a life of its own.

Troubled, Harris turned back to Elena.

The child sat on the rug with crayons and drawing paper. Elena was
almost through with her drawing; working alone seemed to make her
feel peaceful, and beneath her air of listlessness, she had surprising
powers of concentration. But when Elena handed Harris the picture,
watching for her reaction, it was another drawing of a lone girl, this
time in what looked like a desert beneath a red-orange sun.

Examining the picture, Harris tried to sound brightly curious.
"What's she doing, Elena?"

Elena's shoulders gave a miniature shrug. "She's lost," the child
answered in matter-of-fact tones.

"Why?"

"Because she was bad. So they left her there."

"Who's they?"

But Elena's face had closed, the opaque expression of a child who
had suddenly tired of a subject. "No one."

Harris did not question this. Instead she went to a shelf, got out
a box full of plastic figures, and sat down with Elena. Silently, Harris
began to create a world without people: a plastic fence across a river,
which led to a wood full of trees, with a couple of hills and a log
cabin in the middle. Elena watched with interest; neither spoke.

At length, Harris said to Elena, "Your turn."

Elena studied the plastic landscape. "You're already finished," she
objected.

Harris shook her head. "There're no people in it," she said, and
pointed to the box of plastic figures. "You get to decide who lives
here and what kind of things they do."

Elena studied the landscape, eyes averted from Harris. She was an intuitive little girl, Harris sensed; on some level, Elena understood that to play with Harris was to reveal herself. Suddenly Elena turned to her.

"Why does Mommy bring me here?"

Harris smiled. "Because she loves you and knows things may be hard for you right now. She thought you might want a friend to spend time with."

"I don't need a friend."

"*I* do." Harris paused a moment, adding another tree to the woods. "Why don't *you* need a friend?"

Elena shrugged. "They're boring. All they want to do is play."

What was so disturbing, Harris thought, was that Elena had learned to scorn her own childhood. One explanation could be the trauma of her father's death. But there was a more troubling possibility: Elena's detachment from other children was common among children who had been sexually abused.

"Sometimes *I* like to play," Harris said, and started to build another fence.

It might go on like this, Harris thought, for weeks, or even months. Then, without saying a word, Elena placed a plastic figure in the middle of the woods.

She had chosen the black-haired girl, Harris noticed, from a box full of blonds and brunettes, mothers and fathers, sisters and brothers and dogs. "Does she live in the cabin?" Harris asked.

Elena shook her head. "No. In the woods, where it's dark."

"Who lives with her?"

"Nobody."

Harris busied herself with another fence. "Does she *want* anyone to live with her?" she asked.

Elena fell quiet, studying the woods. Silently, she placed the figure of the little girl next to a tree.

"What's she doing?" Harris asked.

"Nothing." Elena looked away. "The robbers have tied her to a tree."

"Where are they?"

Elena folded her arms. "She can't see them," she answered in a thin, flat voice. "It's too dark in the woods."

"Can someone help her?"

Slowly, Elena shook her head. "It's a nightmare, and she's all alone. The robbers have a black dog."

At the word "nightmare," Harris felt the smallest change in herself, a pricking of nerve ends. Time seemed to slow down. Carefully, she asked, "What does the black dog do?"

"Watch the little girl." Elena's voice was small now. "She can hear him in the dark."

For a moment, the child seemed transfixed by her imaginings. "What's going to happen to her?" Harris probed.

Again, Elena shook her head. Harris waited for an answer that never came.

"Can't she call 911, Elena?"

"There's no telephone."

The child's certainty was frightening, Harris thought; her vision of isolation was too vivid and complete. For a moment, quiet, she considered Elena. Then she reached into the box and brought out a plastic alligator.

The creature was fearsome-looking, with pointed teeth and black eyes painted on its dark-green face. Without comment, Harris placed the alligator beside the little girl, facing the darkness Elena had described.

Pointing to the alligator, Elena asked, "What's *that?*"

Harris smiled. "The little girl's secret friend. She looks scary, but she's very nice. She's come to protect the little girl."

Elena looked suddenly fearful, as if something dangerous would happen. She kept herself very still.

Look for a neutral question, Harris thought. "What's the little girl's name?"

Elena's eyes did not move. Reluctantly, she answered, "Teresa."

It made an odd kind of sense, Harris thought. Elena could not admit that she was the little girl, and her mother was the person with whom she most identified. Harris made her voice soothing. "Then Teresa will be safe now."

With sudden vehemence, Elena shook her head. "The alligator can't hear her. The dog will eat her up."

"Oh, *this* alligator has very good hearing. And she can see in the dark."

As she stared at the alligator, Elena's voice rose. "If the alligator stays, there will be a fight."

Gently, Harris touched her shoulder. "It's all right," she said softly. "The alligator's not afraid of the dog. Or the robbers."

Almost frenziedly, Elena grabbed the alligator and thrust it at Harris; startled, Harris saw the terror in the child's eyes. *"No,"* she cried out. "Someone will get killed."

All at once, Harris put her arms around the slender trembling body. "It's all right," she kept repeating. "No one will be hurt now."

Pressing against her, Elena Arias shook her head. She made no sound at all; it was a moment before Harris knew that she was crying.

FIVE

FROM THE MOMENT he first saw her, there was something about Sonia Arias that Paget found disturbing.

It was more than the bright, almost birdlike look of malice she gave him as she took the stand. For Paget, there were too many hints of some inner dislocation: the overplucked eyebrows; the brightly hennaed hair, at odds with both her age and her skin color, sallow as parchment; the stalklike legs and desiccated face of an anorexic; the way her head snapped with the looks she darted around the courtroom, an uneasy meld of paranoia and the narcissism of a fashion model, striking poses for a camera. She did not seem a part of her surroundings: when Paget struggled for an association, the closest he came was Gloria Swanson's frightening faded movie queen in Billy Wilder's *Sunset Boulevard*. For those looking to explore the darker pools of Richie's inner life, Paget sensed, Sonia Arias was a good place to start.

"Ever see *Sunset Boulevard*?" he whispered to Caroline.

Caroline's eyes narrowed in a half smile she could not show the jury, and then she made a quiet shivering sound. It captured his feelings perfectly.

"*This*," Caroline murmured, "should be entertaining."

From his opening question, Salinas treated Sonia Arias carefully: although his supposed evidentiary purpose was to establish that Richie had been scheduled to call her on the Saturday after he last was seen, his real intent was to present the jury with a grieving mother. But there was something imperious about the way she held her head high, peering around the courtroom as if to demand that people watch and listen. When Salinas asked his first key question, she looked straight at Paget, pausing to answer until every eye was on her.

"Ricardo," she said in a voice suddenly sharp with vengeance, "would never take his own life. He was *taken* from us. That's why he didn't call me."

Paget met her eyes with a calm expression. Her head snapped away, as if to snub him, and she stared fixedly at Salinas.

Gently, Salinas asked, "Why do you say that?"

She gave him a prideful look. "Ricardo was strongly Catholic— from his childhood, *I* saw to that. He knew that suicide was a sin."

By instinct, Paget glanced at Luisa Marin; her eyelids had dropped, as if she was drawn back into her own life. He wondered if she could ever accept his defense, so at odds with what she had made herself believe.

"Are you going to let this go?" he asked Caroline.

Still watching Sonia Arias, she touched his arm. "Wait," she said. "Victor's giving us an opening. Just let him run with her for a while."

"Aside from Richie's religious convictions," Salinas went on, "are there other aspects of his character which tell you he didn't shoot himself?"

"He never even *touched* a gun." Looking beyond Salinas at the jury, Sonia Arias seemed barely connected to the man who questioned her. "From childhood, he was a beautiful boy, with black curly hair a woman would die for. And always happy, an optimist, ready to make the best of things. There was a kind of magic about him: to meet Ricardo Arias was to fall in love with him." Sonia paused, her words becoming slow and authoritative. "People couldn't do enough for Richie. And if he ever needed *anything*, he knew that I would give it to him. He would turn to *me* before he would ever consider suicide."

Finishing, Sonia Arias peered around the courtroom, as if jealous of attention. "She's just as Terri described her," Caroline said softly. "I doubt she knows where Richie ends and she begins."

Salinas, Paget saw, was regarding Sonia Arias with a certain wariness. "How would you describe Richie's relationship to your granddaughter, Elena?"

"Devoted," Sonia answered with suppressed bitterness. "Totally in love, as I was with him. That little girl doesn't know how lucky she was to have a parent who held nothing back."

So even Elena was unworthy. Paget could not easily calculate the effect of this woman's "love" on Richie, but the thought that Elena had inherited both Sonia and her handiwork filled him with empathy and unease. "And did you and Richie discuss the effect of his divorce on Elena?" Salinas asked.

"It wasn't *his* divorce," Sonia answered grimly. "I want to make that clear to everyone who's listening. For the first time, millions of people are hearing about Ricardo Arias, and I won't rest until they know who and what he was." Suddenly Sonia turned and pointed at Paget. "*She* left my son, to take up with *this* man. She was always too ambitious to give Richie the support he needed, and then she left him with their daughter." Her voice filled with an odd satisfaction. "I *told* him about her, from the beginning. But Richie was too good a person."

All at once, Paget felt the anger run through him. Through gritted teeth, he said to Caroline, "I've had about enough of this."

"Easy," she answered quietly, and was on her feet. "Your Honor, rather than move to strike, I wonder if I could make an observation. Mrs. Arias is understandably upset. But her opinions regarding her late son's marriage may not be fair or even accurate—let alone relevant. I wonder if Mr. Salinas could help us hew more closely to objective fact."

Slowly, Lerner nodded, regarding Sonia Arias with a look of polite unease. "In responding to Mr. Salinas's questions, Mrs. Arias, try to answer them directly. With respect, I believe that's how you can be most helpful."

Turning, Sonia gave him a coquettish smile; it was so unlike her demeanor seconds before that it was eerie. "Of course," she said pertly. "I'd want Ricardo to be proud of me."

Lerner blinked. "Yes," he said. "Thank you."

Salinas cleared his throat. "I take it," he said, "that Richie's principal concern was for Elena."

Sonia folded her hands. "Always." Abruptly, Sonia's firm voice had returned. "I begged him to come to New York, take a rest from all the strain he was under. But he just couldn't bring himself to leave her."

Salinas paused a moment. "Did there come a time," he asked softly, "when Richie told you he believed that Elena had been molested by Mr. Paget's son?"

As the jury watched, suddenly intent, Sonia Arias folded her arms. "Yes. Of course, I can remember when Richie was a baby, admiring how beautiful he was—*always* was, until the day he died. But I can't imagine *what* a parent would have to do to turn his own son into a pervert."

Rising quickly, Caroline touched Paget's arm. Her voice was stripped of charity now. "Your Honor, I move to strike everything after 'yes.' And I ask this witness, if possible, to distinguish between fact and anger. Whoever may be its subject at the moment."

"Motion granted," Lerner said promptly. "Members of the jury, I am directing you to ignore Mrs. Arias's comments regarding Mr. Paget and his son as speculative and unwarranted." He turned to Sonia Arias. "I understand," he said more gently, "that you wish to help the prosecution. Please understand that you are not."

Sonia Arias sat straighter in the witness chair, turning from Judge Lerner. She did not answer.

Looking unhappy, Salinas asked, "What did Richie tell you about the alleged abuse by Carlo Paget?"

"He was disgusted and sick at heart. What was worse, Elena's mother had left him with no money for a lawyer, or to get a psychologist to help her own daughter." Sonia gave the jury another look of pride. "So *I* sent Ricardo a thousand dollars to hire one or the other. He was *so* appreciative and relieved."

Next to him, Paget saw Caroline look puzzled and then make a note. "To your knowledge," Salinas asked, "did he intend to fight for permanent custody of Elena?"

Sonia gave an emphatic nod. "To the bitter end, and I was going to help him. He didn't want that woman, *or* her boyfriend or his son, to make a mess of Elena's life." She paused for emphasis. "Nothing—and I mean *nothing*—was going to keep Ricardo Arias from having his daughter."

Once more, Paget thought, it was difficult to separate mother from son. He leaned closer to Caroline. "Remember when Lee Harvey Oswald's mother decided to write a book about him? She was going to call it 'A Mother's Place in History.' "

Caroline gave a soft laugh, all the while studying Sonia Arias with an air of intense reflection. But Salinas was utterly still now, drawing the jury to him.

"When," he asked quietly, "did you last speak to Ricardo?"

For a moment, Sonia Arias looked down. "That Friday. The last day anyone saw my son alive."

"And what did you talk about?"

"That Elena's mother was going to Italy with her boyfriend, despite all the worries about Elena and his son. Richie said it was the final proof that he needed to fight for Elena, any way he could."

Abruptly, the atmosphere in the room had changed. The jury leaned forward to listen. Marian Celler, who had been wiping her reading glasses, stared at Sonia with the glasses still in her hand. "Did you respond to that?" Salinas asked.

"Yes." Sonia still looked down. "I told him I'd come to help—that day if he wanted me. But he said he could take care of Elena, and said what would really help was if I could send him the money I would have spent on airfare. I told him I'd think about it and we could talk the next time he called." There was a wounded undertone in her voice, as if she was reluctant to believe that her nearness to Richie could be of less value than money. "He had powerful friends now, he told me. Other people who could help."

The last two sentences, Paget saw at once, were unrehearsed. For a split second, Salinas looked unsettled. "Colt's people," Caroline whispered.

Quickly Salinas asked, "Did you talk to Ricardo often?"

The question seemed to revive Sonia's pride. Looking directly at the jury, she said, "Every Saturday and Wednesday, since college. Ricardo always called *me*, and he never forgot. Not once in twelve years."

Salinas gave her a melancholy look. "But he didn't call on Saturday, did he? Or ever again."

Sonia looked down again. "No."

"Did you try to call him?"

"I wanted *him* to call *me*." Her mouth twisted. "I thought he might be upset about the money."

"Did you *ever* call?"

Sonia folded her arms. "I was very angry with him," she said, and suddenly the tears welled in her eyes. "You see, I'd forgotten who Richie was."

* * *

What Caroline needed to do, she knew, would not be easy.

Rising, she regarded Sonia Arias with a look of puzzlement. "When you said that Teresa Peralta didn't support your son Ricardo, what precisely did you mean?"

Sonia gave her a knowing smile. "I meant emotionally. She never appreciated how special he was—how imaginative, how attractive, how *different* he was than most men. I mean, how many fathers have that kind of commitment to their daughter?"

Caroline's gaze was a polite blank. "So when you said that Ms. Peralta never supported Richie, you weren't referring to financial support?"

Sonia's face seemed to tighten. "No."

"And in fact, she supported him through six years of marriage, did she not?"

"Only after he quit the law. And just so he could start his business."

"How many law jobs did Richie 'quit'?"

"Three." Sonia looked angry. "But one was to go to business school. Richie wanted to become more entrepreneurial, he told me."

"And Teresa also *sent* him to graduate school, correct? For an M.B.A."

A curt nod. "She did that."

"And then gave him money to start his business."

Sonia stared at her. "She may have. But so did *I*."

"Do you know what happened to the money? Terri's *or* yours?"

"No." A slight pause. "Richie had some bad luck."

Caroline kept her face and voice bland, civility without warmth. "Before Teresa married him," she asked, "who supported Richie?"

Sonia Arias hesitated. This part of the trial, Caroline thought, could be entitled "Who Was the Real Ricardo Arias?" At the corner of her eye, Victor Salinas showed signs of restiveness. "We supported him," Sonia said finally. "And let me set the record straight again. I helped them get through the law school years, when Teresa had the baby. By getting a job."

Caroline angled her head. "Did *Richie* ever work?"

"Objection," Salinas called out. "Mr. Arias's employment record is totally irrelevant."

"Really," Caroline shot back. "It was you who introduced the question of whether Mrs. Arias believed her son to be suicidal. That places his personal circumstances squarely on the table."

Lerner nodded. "Agreed, Counselor. At least within limits. Move on."

Caroline turned to Sonia Arias. Frowning, the witness said, "I can't remember what jobs Richie maybe had."

As if thinking of another question, Caroline paused. "What about when he lived at home?" she asked casually. "During high school. Did he ever work then?"

For what seemed too long, Sonia did not answer.

For Caroline, the scene had a certain horrible fascination: Sonia stared at her, trying to see into her mind before deciding on an answer. "That was a long time ago," she said at last.

"Let me help you," Caroline said pleasantly. "When he was seventeen, didn't Richie have a summer job clerking at a sporting goods store near your neighborhood in the Bronx? Called Bernhard's?"

Sonia's face turned to stone. Salinas half rose to his feet. "Yes," Sonia said coldly. "I remember that now."

"And didn't Mr. Bernhard call your husband and demand reimbursement? Because he'd caught Richie skimming from the cash register?"

"Your Honor," Salinas called out. "The prosecution requests a bench conference."

"Of course," Lerner said, and motioned Caroline to the bench.

She and Salinas stood face-to-face, with Lerner peering down at them. "What is this?" Salinas demanded in a taut undertone. "I called this witness to make two simple points. One, that Ricardo Arias showed *no* sign of any suicidal impulse. Two, that his failure to call on Saturday, as anticipated, suggests time of death. Whether he stole the milk money in fifth grade is petty character assassination, completely irrelevant to any issue in this case."

It was here, Caroline knew, that she needed Jared Lerner to rule as she had hoped for since the moment when she planted the trial in his mind. She spoke to him directly. "As Mr. Salinas will concede, he is attempting to show that Ricardo Arias was an emotionally stable man with no thought of suicide and, for that matter, no enemies in the world beyond my client and Richie's former wife. That's enough to justify these questions. But what Victor has *also* been trying to do, right from his opening statement, is to paint Ricardo Arias as the compendium of virtue." She turned on Salinas. "You've asked for this, Victor. *My* Ricardo Arias is a cheat, a liar, unable to hold an honest job, and, quite possibly, a textbook sociopath humbly disguised as a second-rate con man. Not only does that suggest emotional instability, but people like *my* Richie make other people mad—lots of them." She faced Lerner again. "This is a murder trial, Your Honor, not a memorial service for Richie's family and friends, assuming that he had any beyond the unfortunate Ms. Warner. Chris Paget is entitled to have me show *anything* suggestive of mental problems on behalf of Mr. Arias. And, I will represent to you right now, we believe there's plenty."

"That's an excuse." Salinas looked up at Lerner with new intensity. "Petty theft, if that's what we have, doesn't translate to suicide. Suicide's the loophole through which Ms. Masters intends to squeeze every piece of innuendo she can find, until the jury forgets this trial isn't about Ricardo Arias but about the man who killed him."

"*There's* a new thought," Lerner interjected. "But it's a little late, Victor. Next time you nominate someone for altar boy, you may want to screen him first." He looked down at Caroline. "I'm going to give you considerable latitude, Caroline. See that you don't abuse it."

"Thank you, Your Honor." And thank you, Johnny Moore, she added silently.

Salinas merely shrugged. On the way back to the prosecution table, he shot Caroline a sideways look, as if to remind her that the trial would be long and hard.

Turning to face Sonia Arias, Caroline saw a brittle woman, tensely guarding her image of her own son. Caroline felt a moment's pity, and then it was gone. Quietly, she said, "Do you remember the question?"

Sonia Arias sat straighter. "This man Bernhard never caught Richie stealing anything. We paid him five hundred dollars because he threatened to call the police."

"Wasn't there another reason you didn't want trouble? A problem at Bronx Science, about three months earlier?"

It was curious, Caroline thought; Sonia Arias seemed smaller now. "There was a misunderstanding," she said.

"There was a *suspension*, wasn't there? Because Ricardo was accused of stealing a math test from his teacher's desk?"

"So another student said. But *he* was the one who stole the test and then blamed it on Richie out of spite." Sonia Arias turned to the jury. "Ricardo was innocent. But he was a beautiful, talented boy, and people were always jealous of him. Going to the senior prom, in his tuxedo, he looked so handsome. Any girl would want to be with him—"

"Did there come a time in college," Caroline cut in quietly, "when Richie moved out of the dorm?"

"Yes." Sonia gave her a wary, wounded look and then frowned. "It was when he decided to live with Teresa. Of all the girls he could have had."

Caroline moved a few steps closer. "Did Richie tell you that the dorm committee had *asked* him to move out? Because he'd been accused of stealing from people's rooms?"

"*No.*" Sonia gripped both arms of the witness chair. "*She* must have said that. Richie never told me anything like that."

At the corner of his eye, Paget saw Salinas rising to object and then stop himself. Paget could read his thoughts: Caroline must have witnesses for her charges against Richie, and to object might make them part of the trial.

"No?" Caroline went on. "You mentioned that after law school Richie worked for three firms, correct?"

"Yes."

"Did he ever tell you that he'd been fired from two of them?"

"*No.*"

"And that one of the firms fired him for misrepresenting his grades?"

"No." Sonia's arms were rigid now, and her eyes darted from place to place. "And it's not true, either."

"How do you know that?"

Sonia mustered a superior smile. "Because I know my son."

I doubt anyone did, Caroline thought—except, perhaps, his wife. But she was satisfied for the moment: she was morally certain that Joseph Duarte, climbing his own ladder, had not stolen from employers or cheated on tests. "Did you know," Caroline asked Sonia, "that your son was seeing a therapist?"

Salinas, Paget saw to his surprise, made no movement to object.

"Of course." Sonia smiled, as if she had bested Caroline. "Richie told me all about it. He was very concerned about Elena and needed advice. So I helped him pay for it."

"How much did it cost?"

"It was expensive—one hundred dollars an hour. But Richie was worth it."

Caroline gave her a curious look. "Did you send the money to the therapist," she asked, "or directly to Richie?"

"To Richie, of course. I didn't want to embarrass him."

That, Caroline thought, would be impossible. "Tell me, Mrs. Arias, why wasn't *Richie* paying for a therapist?"

"*She* didn't send him enough money. So as usual, *I* stepped in to help."

"By 'she,' I assume you're referring to Ms. Peralta, and the spousal and child support she was sending Richie."

"Of course." Sonia shot a defensive glance at the jury. "Richie told me she was making over eighty thousand a year, while he struggled to support his daughter and start a business. You'd think the courts would be fairer."

"Indeed. Did Richie happen to mention that *Ms. Peralta* had wanted custody and that he not only fought for custody but refused to get an outside job. And that he demanded—and received—the *maximum* support the law required Ms. Peralta to pay?"

Sonia waved a hand. "Whatever, it wasn't enough to live on."

"Is that what he was doing? Living on Teresa's salary?"

"Of course."

"At the time you agreed to send him money for therapy, did he tell you that he had received ten thousand dollars from the *Inquisitor* for an article claiming that the defendant, Mr. Paget, had stolen his wife?"

Sonia looked surprised, and then she gave Caroline a smile that was close to haughty. "It was an important human interest story, and Ricardo looked and sounded wonderful. Of course they wanted to write about him."

"Perhaps you didn't understand the question, Mrs. Arias. Did Ricardo tell you that the *Inquisitor* paid him ten thousand dollars?"

The smile became a grimace of contempt. "I don't remember those kinds of details."

"Oh? Would you have paid for Ricardo's therapy if you knew he had ten thousand dollars? Or sent him the extra money he asked for, as you mentioned earlier?"

Sonia folded her arms. "Maybe I would have. I was Richie's mother, all right? *You* obviously don't know anything about what that's like."

For a long time, Caroline simply stood and looked at her, feeling the jury watch. "No," she said softly. "And I wouldn't wish your experience on anyone."

The comment, quiet and ambiguous, hung there as Sonia stared from the witness box. "But you've reminded me to ask *you* something," Caroline went on. "How well, I wonder, did you really know your son?"

Sonia raised her chin. "Very well, thank you."

"And yet you don't know if he stole from his employer, or cheated in high school, or was kicked out of his dorm for theft, or was fired by two law firms, or, for that matter, was flush with cash from the *Inquisitor* while you sent him money for counseling."

Sonia looked past her now, at nothing. "I can't know things that aren't true, just because you say them to me."

"But what if they *are* true? Would you *still* say that you knew your son?"

"I knew who he was at heart."

Caroline shook her head. "In fact, isn't your testimony that Ricardo wouldn't kill himself based on your belief that the Ricardo you *saw* was the man he *was?*"

Sonia looked white and haggard; she clasped both shoulders as if holding herself together. "I *knew* my son."

Caroline stood beside her now. "Isn't all you really knew about Ricardo Arias, from age eighteen to age thirty, whatever your son chose to tell you?"

All at once, Sonia Arias stood in the witness box. "Ricardo Arias had a passion for living," she said in a shrill voice. "And I was there for him. This young man would never do a selfish thing like kill himself."

Caroline watched the jury, looking at Sonia Arias with a kind of dread and pity. Marian Celler was pale; Luisa Marin's eyes had filled with tears.

"No further questions," Caroline said softly, and went back to her chair.

Approaching Sonia, Salinas seemed to walk with deliberate lightness, as if fearing to make noise. "Mrs. Arias, do you remember when I showed you the handwritten note? An alleged suicide note, supposedly written by your son."

Sonia seemed startled, as if interrupted from memory. "Yes. I remember."

"Do you also remember what you told me?"

"That I couldn't recognize the handwriting."

Salinas nodded. "And why was that?"

"Because it had been so long since I'd seen it." Suddenly Sonia smiled with a mother's fondness. "When Ricardo was seventeen, we saved to buy him a computer. We didn't have much money, but Richie made it all worthwhile. He was a wonder at it, and he loved typing so much that he even did shopping lists on the computer. Later, when he went away, every letter was typed—he was so good at graphics that he used it to make Christmas cards. They were like art." As if restored, Sonia faced the jury again. "Ricardo was a perfectionist. After that computer, he never handwrote anything. Like suicide, it was against his nature."

SIX

ON THE THIRD MORNING of the trial, Victor Salinas called Richie's therapist as a prosecution witness.

Diana Gates was a composed brunette in her early forties, with short straight black hair and a pleasant snub-nosed face whose soft angles and wide-set brown eyes conveyed a certain professional reserve. But the jury could not know how hard Gates had fought against testifying.

From the outset, the therapist had refused to speak to either Monk or, once he discovered her existence, Johnny Moore. Her position was clear: under California law, conversations between therapist and patient are confidential. In Gates's mind, the privilege survived Ricardo Arias. At eight o'clock this morning, urged by Salinas, Jared Lerner had ruled otherwise. No one knew what Gates would say.

What this told Christopher Paget was that Salinas was sufficiently confident Ricardo Arias was not suicidal that he was willing to chance a terrible surprise: Salinas clearly intended to explore Richie's state of mind. For Paget, an endorsement of Richie's character by a professional, combined with a disparagement of Caroline's suicide theory, could be devastating.

Even the jury seemed to feel the tension. Most looked alert and a bit fidgety: notebook in hand, Joseph Duarte wrote something, scratched a line through it, and started over. Gates sat with her hands folded as Salinas established her advanced degrees and extensive experience in family therapy; she answered the questions and no more. Her expression never changed.

"How long," Salinas asked, "did you treat Ricardo Arias."

"Twice a week," Gates answered, "for approximately four months. In other words, until his death."

"So you saw him how many times, roughly?"

"Between thirty and forty sessions, an hour apiece."

Sitting beside Paget, Caroline made a note of this. "When Mr. Arias first came to you," Salinas asked, "did he explain why he wanted therapy?"

Gates paused. "In general, Mr. Arias's concerns related to his daughter, Elena. At first, he wondered if *I* might perform the family evaluation if it came to that. But I was able to persuade him that I might be more helpful in an individual capacity."

There was something, Paget sensed, buried in the bland response. Salinas seemed to hear it as well: the prosecutor hesitated and then skipped to the heart of things. "In the course of seeing Mr. Arias, Dr. Gates, did you form an opinion as to whether he was prone to suicide?"

Caroline looked up from her notes. Although she could well have objected, she did not. The courtroom was completely still.

"It wasn't my mission," Gates responded, "to determine whether or not Mr. Arias was suicidal. I made no effort to."

A moment's frustration crossed Salinas's face. "But sometime in these thirty to forty hours, didn't you form an impression of Mr. Arias's personality?"

"An impression? Yes." Gates lowered her eyelids in thought and then looked directly at Salinas. "I'd prefer to put it this way. Nothing I saw gave me reason to consider that Mr. Arias might take his own life."

Paget saw Joseph Duarte write the comment in his notebook and then appear to underline it. Salinas moved forward with new confidence. "Did you see any characteristics in Mr. Arias which *contradict* the idea that he killed himself?"

Gates seemed to reflect. "The thrust of our conversations, Mr. Salinas, was forward-looking. Mr. Arias was determined to maintain custody of his daughter and brimming with ideas for doing that. And he wanted to know all about the evaluation process." Gates paused abruptly, and then finished, "The idea of suicide never crossed my mind."

Caroline's face, Paget noticed, had the carefully schooled blankness of a lawyer whose client was taking a beating. "Did you have a sense," Salinas was asking, "as to whether Mr. Arias was depressed by the breakup of his marriage?"

Gates considered this. " 'Depressed' is not the word I'd use. He was deeply offended that Ms. Peralta had chosen to leave him. He also expressed concern that his daughter had been molested."

"How did Richie react to this concern?"

Gates sat back. "By trying to educate himself. Mr. Arias asked me detailed questions about the signs of possible molestation, how likely a child would be to verbalize her feelings, how this might be analyzed and treated. He also asked me to recommend reading on the subject and, when I did, read *everything* and discussed it with me at some length."

"I take it, then, that Mr. Arias took the charges regarding Elena very seriously."

Gates appeared to study Salinas. "Mr. Arias seemed very much to want my help."

"Indeed," Salinas pressed on, "Mr. Arias seemed to take the *process* seriously, correct?"

Gates gave Salinas the same inscrutable look. "Mr. Arias always scheduled in advance, was always on time, and was always focused the entire hour. I would say that Mr. Arias was very engaged in what he was trying to accomplish."

"Again, Dr. Gates, would you consider these behaviors consistent with suicide?"

"I would not."

Paget leaned toward Caroline. "She talks about Richie as if he were a specimen. Think it's just her?"

"I don't know," Caroline murmured. "But there's *something* going on here. Just what did they *do* for those thirty to forty hours?"

"In your fifteen years of practice," Salinas was asking, "have you treated people with suicidal tendencies?"

For the first time, Gates dropped her gaze. "Two people I saw," she said quietly, "took their own lives. A teenage girl, and a wife and mother. Those were two of the hardest experiences of my life, to the extent that my feelings matter in such circumstances." She looked up. "Beyond that, Mr. Salinas, I've treated a number of people who I felt were potentially self-destructive. It's something I'm very aware of, all the more because I've lost patients."

Salinas nodded his understanding. "And are there characteristics you associate with potential suicide?"

Gates seemed to exhale; the troubled look in her eyes seemed to humanize her. "There's no one-size-fits-all prescription. But in general, I associate a higher risk with such things as extreme depression, self-loathing, radical mood swings, perhaps some feeling that the world is beyond the person's control. . . ." She paused again. "Those factors were present, to a greater or lesser degree, in the two patients who took their lives."

"Did you observe any of those characteristics in Mr. Arias?"

Gates shook her head. "None. In many ways, Mr. Arias's self-esteem was extremely high—if anything, he seemed unusually resilient and resourceful."

Salinas paused a moment, letting the jury absorb Gates's answer. "When did you last *see* Mr. Arias?"

"I believe it was on a Thursday, which I understand was one day before the last day *anyone* saw him. Our appointments were generally for Monday and Thursday, and before leaving he confirmed that he'd see me on Monday. So that I was quite surprised when he didn't show up."

"On that last Thursday, how did he seem?"

"The same, really—Mr. Arias's demeanor never changed much. He seemed generally upbeat, but very determined to maintain custody of Elena, and quite satisfied with his recent court filings, which were aimed at barring Elena from contact with Mr. Paget or his son." Gates leaned back. "He *did* seem quite angry with Ms. Peralta for sticking with her plans to go to Italy. He didn't feel she was reacting properly to the papers he had filed."

"Did he seem in a state of despair or depression?"

"Not in my observation."

Salinas turned to a brisk young woman who had joined him at the prosecution table. Within seconds, she and Judge Lerner's deputy had materialized an easel, on which she placed a photographic blowup of a handwritten note. *I am ending my life,* the note read, *because I have faced what I am.*

What I am is selfish and pathetic.

The handwriting itself, irregular and childlike, had a certain haunting quality. Staring at the note, Gates seemed for the first time to be deeply troubled.

"As the defense has stipulated," Salinas told her, "this is a note found near Mr. Arias's body, next to a photograph of Elena. I take it that you don't recognize the handwriting?"

"No. I've never seen Mr. Arias's writing, except on checks. I never studied it."

"But do those words, Dr. Gates, correspond with Mr. Arias's self-image as you perceived it?"

Reading with her, the jury was two rows of attentive faces: Luisa Marin seemed to scan the note over and over. "I don't believe this is how he saw himself," Gates answered quietly. "Or how he would wish others to see him." There was something fearful in her eyes now, as if she had come face-to-face with the reality that her patient had been murdered. "I simply can't believe," she said at last, "that the man I saw on Thursday would turn around and write this."

As she slowly rose, Caroline felt tense. She had never before questioned a prosecution witness without studying his or her statement to the police, carefully designing her cross-examination. But this witness had no statement: Gates, a smart professional with no ax to grind, had just done Chris Paget grievous harm, and Caroline had no path to follow. She had only the sense, instinctive and half formed, that something lay beneath the surface of Gates's answers.

"In meeting with Mr. Arias," Caroline began, "did you explore his family background?"

Gates met her gaze directly. "To some extent."

"For example, did Mr. Arias tell you that his father beat him in childhood and adolescence?"

Gates hesitated. "He said that, yes."

"In what context?"

"He was quite resentful. He mentioned several times that he had never touched Elena in anger. It was clear his memories of childhood were colored by that experience."

"But isn't it plain that child abuse is handed from generation to generation and that abusive fathers are quite likely to have been abused as sons?"

Gates nodded. "Yes."

Caroline tilted her head. "Is that *also* true of sexual abuse?"

This time Gates paused for a split second, locking eyes with Caroline. "Yes."

"I gather, Dr. Gates, that a considerable amount of your time with Mr. Arias was concerned with the question of whether his daughter, Elena, had been sexually abused."

"It was."

Caroline moved closer, feeling her own nerves. "In the course of these discussions with Mr. Arias," she asked softly, "did you consider whether Mr. Arias might be indirectly seeking help for some problem of his own?"

Gates folded her hands again. "That was *not*," she said finally, "the manner in which Mr. Arias approached the question. He seemed interested in studying Elena for clues and determining how likely it was that she would become able to talk about whatever had happened. If *anything* had."

Caroline put both hands on her hips. "But did you consider the *possibility?*"

Gates frowned. "Whatever I learned, I learned through Mr. Arias. In that context, I heard nothing which suggests the possibility you mention. In fact, his sexual interests seemed exclusively adult."

"Even though Mr. Arias had been abused as a child?"

"*Physically*, not sexually. They're quite different. And I had no reason at all to suspect that Mr. Arias would beat his own daughter. Which is much more clearly indicated by his history than is sexual abuse."

Caroline studied her. "Speaking of history, did you also discuss Mr. Arias's relationship with his mother?"

"To some extent."

"And what did you learn?"

"According to Mr. Arias, his mother adored him. He mentioned that several times, with something of an air of pride."

"What else did he say about Sonia Arias?"

"Very little, although he seemed to feel he could count on her." She paused, as if considering whether to say something more. "In general, Mr. Arias seemed more comfortable with women than men—he believed that women accepted him more readily. It's not unusual in this kind of family, where the father is angry or remote and the mother somewhat doting."

"Did you make any other assessment about Mr. Arias's relationship with his mother?"

Gates's eyes flickered, and then she looked down momentarily. "I suppose I should tell you, Ms. Masters, that Mrs. Arias once called me."

Caroline felt surprise. "What did she say?"

"Her primary concern was to find out how Richie talked about her and how *I* saw their relationship."

"How did you respond?"

"I asked if Richie knew she was calling. When she said no, I explained as gently as I could that I communicate with my patients in confidence." Pausing, Gates added pointedly, "It tends to promote trust in our profession."

Caroline smiled. "What was Mrs. Arias's response?"

"She wanted to know if Richie had told me that *she* was paying for his appointments."

"Had he?"

"No, actually. It wasn't a great deal of money." Gates paused. "I got off as quickly as I could. I didn't want to be in the middle of something."

"The middle of *what*, exactly?"

Gates leaned back. "My impression, to use the current cliché, was that Sonia Arias was somewhat lacking in boundaries. She didn't see Ricardo as a separate person: he was part of her own ego, her need for love and approval—which, perhaps, Mr. Arias had learned to play on."

"And how might that have affected him?"

Gates gave Caroline a measured look. "Without specific reference to Mr. Arias, the effect *can* be an inflated self-concept and the sense that people will and *should* gratify the child's wishes which persists into adulthood."

"Your Honor," Salinas interjected. "Is there some point to all of this? Or is Ms. Masters simply putting on a seminar in early childhood development?"

Without turning, Caroline addressed Lerner. "Whether suicide or murder, the psychology and character of Ricardo Arias are very much at issue here. If the court will indulge me, I'll try to stick to the pertinent."

Judge Lerner nodded. "Please do so."

Facing Gates, Caroline asked, "You mentioned that your charges to Mr. Arias did not involve a great deal of money. I understood your fee to be one hundred dollars per hour."

"Usually, it is. But after a couple of sessions, Mr. Arias told me that his finances did not permit that kind of charge." Gates paused a moment. "I thought about it and decided that I should continue seeing him. As I do for certain patients, I reduced his fee to twenty dollars an hour."

"He didn't tell you that his mother was sending him two hundred dollars per week to cover your fees?"

For what seemed a long while, Gates simply studied Caroline; at the corner of her mouth, Caroline thought she detected the faintest shadow of a smile. "No," Gates answered. "He didn't."

"Does that come as a surprise to you?"

Caroline saw no smile now. "No," Gates answered tersely.

The obvious next question, Caroline knew, was "Why not?" Instinctively, Caroline decided to avoid it.

"You perform family evaluations, do you not? Of the kind sought by Ms. Peralta?"

"Yes."

"Was your experience a reason that Mr. Arias sought you out?"

Gates nodded. "That's what he told me. He said I could help advise him about the evaluation process."

"Did Mr. Arias say what kind of advice he wanted?"

Gates gave Caroline a steady gaze. " 'How to make it come out right,' I believe was how he put it."

Once more, Salinas was on his feet. "Objection. Again, Mr. Arias's specific goals in custody proceedings are irrelevant to the question of suicide."

This time, Caroline spun on him. "Are they? According to you, they gave him every reason to live." She turned to Lerner. "The defense believes this relevant to Mr. Arias's state of mind at the time of his death, Your Honor. I'd like to develop that."

"See if you can, then." Lerner turned to Salinas. "Counselor, you opened this particular can of worms. Please show Ms. Masters a little patience."

Caroline faced Gates again. "Mr. Arias first saw you in July, correct?"

"Early July. Yes."

"In other words, *before* anyone raised the possibility that Elena had been sexually abused."

"As far as I know, yes. I don't believe that Mr. Arias mentioned it until after Elena returned to school."

"Did Mr. Arias explain what he meant by making things come out right?"

Gates folded her hands. "What he asked for, Ms. Masters, was a list of positive attributes he should present as a father. As well as what kind of negative factors might cause Ms. Peralta to lose permanent custody."

"Did you describe them to Mr. Arias?"

"Yes. The main ones, in any event."

"And what are they?"

Gates, Caroline realized, seemed never to blink. "Substance abuse. Child neglect. Violence. And, of course, sexual abuse."

Salinas started to rise, then stopped himself. "Did Mr. Arias say anything in response?" Caroline asked.

"I don't recall." A pause. "What I do recall is that he wrote down the factors I listed on a piece of paper."

The irony, Caroline thought, lay in the words themselves: Gates's tone seemed never to change. "Did you also discuss the evaluation process?" Caroline asked.

"In detail. Particularly after Ms. Peralta began requesting an evaluation in her mediation sessions. Mr. Arias was quite concerned to understand all the ins and outs. Including psychological testing."

"Could you describe the nature of the testing?"

Gates gave a short nod. "The principal test is the Princeton Personality Indicator, or PPI. The test subjects answer over five hundred true-false questions designed to reveal specific personality factors in great detail. They're also set up to detect when a person is trying to beat the test—that is, to appear to be someone he or she is not. The PPI is particularly helpful in diagnosing personality disorders."

"Did Mr. Arias ask for advice with respect to the PPI?"

"Yes." Gates's tone was still level. "He wanted to know how to give the right answers."

"What did you tell him?"

"That there was no way to help him."

Caroline cocked her head. "Do you know why he was so concerned?"

Gates, Caroline realized, was sitting quite still. "What Mr. Arias said was that he wanted an edge. But he also mentioned that his wife had told him he wasn't normal. It seemed to upset him."

"Do you know why?"

"No." Gates paused, as if considering something. "I do know that he was quite angry with her."

Caroline moved closer, turning so she could glance at the jury. "How did Mr. Arias evince this anger?"

Gates tented her fingers. "What I particularly remember was a statement he made early on. That he wanted Ms. Peralta to suffer."

In the jury box, Luisa Marin looked troubled. Caroline raised her eyebrows. "Mr. Arias seems to have been quite comfortable telling you things."

"He was," Gates said in a dry voice. "After he was assured that our talks were confidential, he seemed to enjoy sharing the workings of his own mind. Including how he intended to 'break Terri down,' as he put it."

There was something here, Caroline thought, that she did not quite understand. With professional dispassion, Gates was slowly painting a picture of Ricardo Arias, but how she saw her own role as his therapist was unclear. "Did he discuss *Ms. Peralta's* personality at any length?"

"Certain aspects of it. He seemed chiefly interested in those characteristics that he believed he could exploit. For example, Ms. Peralta's father was an abusive alcoholic, and Mr. Arias asked how a child of such a family might react to the pressure of a custody suit. His own observation was that Ms. Peralta was afraid of conflict when it got too close to home, and that he had doubted she could stick out a custody fight."

"Had she surprised him?"

"To a point." For the first time, Gates glanced at Paget. "He tended to blame that on Mr. Paget—he thought that Mr. Paget had propped up Ms. Peralta, while Carlo, Mr. Paget's son, was trying to displace him with Elena."

A certain calm came over Caroline now, the sense that she was about to enter another dimension, make all the connections at last.

"Do you recall *when*," Caroline asked, "Mr. Arias first mentioned the possibility of sexual abuse?"

"I believe there was a playground incident, something about Elena exposing herself—Elena's teacher had called him. That was when Mr. Arias started asking me about symptoms and began reading on the subject."

"Did he consider it an opportunity to put pressure on Ms. Peralta?"

"Clearly. And, perhaps, to get back at Mr. Paget and Carlo for their sins against him, real or perceived. One aspect of Mr. Arias's personality was to believe that if you'd 'done' something to him, he was free to retaliate by doing something to you, whatever it might be." Here Gates paused. "*But*—and I want to emphasize this—Mr. Arias didn't invent this concern: *that* originated with Elena's teacher. Nor could he summon Elena's symptoms out of nowhere. So I am *not* saying that nothing happened to this little girl."

"But do you have any insight on why Mr. Arias later made specific charges about Carlo Paget?"

Gates looked pensive. "Mr. Arias told me he'd been thinking about any new people Elena had been spending time with. The only people he could come up with were Mr. Paget and his son, and sometimes the boy and Elena were alone. Then, according to Mr. Arias, Elena said something disturbing about Carlo Paget giving her a bath, and it all came together."

"Do you have any opinion about the validity of Richie's charges?"

"None. But I didn't sense that this bath was Mr. Arias's invention, either. Even if, as you suggest, some part of Mr. Arias may have *wanted* Carlo to be a child abuser."

"Did you give Mr. Arias any advice?"

"Yes. To be very careful of Elena. I thought she might need help, and I didn't want her lost in all of this." She paused. "I also suggested that the family court mediator, Alec Keene, would help find the best evaluator for Elena."

For the first time, Caroline had a glimmer of understanding: Gates would offer no excuse or explanation, but she saw her role differently than Ricardo Arias had perceived it. "Did Mr. Arias agree?"

"He agreed that Elena should see *someone*. But he was still worried about how he would come out in this evaluation Ms. Peralta proposed. Particularly the psychological testing."

"How did you respond to that?"

Gates folded her hands. "What I told him," she said quietly, "was that I'd test him myself. If he wanted to find out."

Oh my God, Caroline thought. With equal quiet, she asked, "And did he take you up on that?"

"No." Gates paused. "Even after I assured him that *no one* but me would ever know the results."

Joseph Duarte, Caroline saw, was very still. "Had you," Caroline asked slowly, "formed an opinion as to what the tests would show?"

Gates leaned back, pulling herself more tightly together: it seemed clear to Caroline that what she was about to do violated her deepest professional beliefs. "My sessions with Mr. Arias," she said at length, "indicated intense self-absorption; a profound lack of empathy for others; a disrespect for social norms and accepted rules of behavior; a tendency to project his own faults on other people; a lack of interest in anyone else's feelings or beliefs; a high degree of dishonesty and manipulation in interpersonal dealings; a distrust of other people's motives; and, paradoxically, a tendency to see others strictly in terms of his own needs."

Gates paused, frowning, as if deciding whether to explain the man himself. "This kind of personality," she said at length, "*can* be very charming. Indeed, charm helps such a person get what he wants, and as long as people give it to him, he can be quite pleasant, even cheerful. *But* if someone opposes him, the result can be extreme anger and a series of actions—often outside accepted behavior—to strike back at the offending party. So it was with Mr. Arias."

Caroline gazed at her a moment. "That's an impressive cluster of symptoms, Dr. Gates. Does it happen to have a name?"

"Sociopath." Gates smiled with one corner of her mouth. "I could have told you *that* much without ever giving a test."

"And did you offer this analysis to Mr. Arias?"

Gates's smile vanished. "What I told him," she said softly, "is that psychological testing might damage his case."

Caroline raised an eyebrow. "And how did Mr. Arias react?"

"Predictably, on one level. He said that tests like that were bullshit, quote unquote, and became quite angry with me." Gates sounded somewhat chastened. "In truth, I *should* have predicted his more considered reaction. Instead of trying to compose his differences with Ms. Peralta, he redoubled his efforts to keep the evaluation from ever happening."

"How did he do that, if you know?"

Gates frowned. "By putting his charges about Elena in a legal pleading and filing it in court." She paused again. "At one of our sessions, he described at great length how he had served the papers on Ms. Peralta by waiting inside her apartment at night. He also thought the charges against Carlo Paget might drive her and Mr. Paget apart." She looked at Paget, finishing directly. "If Ms. Peralta was alone again, he seemed confident that he could break her down."

Caroline stopped for a moment, caught between fascination and the horrified realization that she had just helped Salinas develop Paget's motive for murder. "Did you respond to any of this?"

"Yes. I implored him not to do it, for Elena's sake, and to let the evaluation take its course." Gates shook her head. "He absolutely refused, of course; his rationale was that Ms. Peralta had given *him* no choice. Also predictable, I'm afraid."

"What about his concern for Elena?"

Gates gave the same ironic smile. "Mr. Arias could not seem to separate Elena's needs from whatever he wanted. It was somewhat akin to Mr. Arias's relationship with his own mother."

"Did he say what he would do *if* an evaluation actually occurred?"

"Yes. He didn't want one, he said. But he told me he'd been working overtime on Elena's teacher, trying to make the right impression, and thought he was looking pretty good." Her tone was dry. "As I said to Mr. Salinas, Mr. Arias tended to look ahead."

It was time, Caroline thought, to resurrect the idea of suicide. "Isn't it possible, Dr. Gates, that—faced with real scrutiny by a trained psychologist—Mr. Arias would contemplate suicide in order to avoid exposure?"

Gates's eyes narrowed in thought. "Possible? In some remote way, I suppose I can imagine it. But Mr. Arias wasn't anywhere near that point. Although Ms. Peralta's trip to Italy unsettled him, the last day I saw him he seemed quite hopeful that she and Mr. Paget might back down. In *fact*, he was intent on confirming his Monday appointment to discuss that further."

Caroline studied her. "Why," she finally asked, "did you keep on seeing this man?"

Gates frowned at her folded hands. "I asked *myself* that, continually. Fairly early on, I saw what his problems were. But I hoped that I could control his worst excesses, perhaps help him see things in a somewhat different light. That was why I gave him my opinion about what the test might show—to persuade him to stop using Elena as a pawn. At every step, there was *always* a reason for what I did." She paused, finishing quietly: "And, step by step, it seems to have yielded one bad result after another. To the end of Mr. Arias's life, and beyond."

It was a terrible concession, Caroline thought, simply stated. "I take it," she asked gently, "that you reached some conclusions about Mr. Arias's fitness to raise a child?"

Slowly, Gates looked up. "I don't know Ms. Peralta at all, Ms. Masters. I don't know much about Elena's circumstances, or Elena herself. But it is very difficult to imagine the circumstances in which I would give Ricardo Arias custody of a child."

Watching Caroline return to the table, Paget was buffeted by emotions in conflict. He felt a deep relief for Terri: however hard they had been for her to reach, her beliefs about Richie were right, and her decision to leave with Elena—and later to fight for her—had been vindicated. And closer to home, no one on the jury would convict Paget himself as an act of vengeance for a suffering father.

But Caroline had come no nearer to clearing Carlo. Furthermore, the Ricardo Arias who emerged from Gates's depiction—resourceful and pathologically vindictive—was a man worth killing. And the ultimate damage, which Victor Salinas was surely about to underscore, was that Gates seemed certain that Ricardo Arias had not decided to kill himself.

"There goes Richie," Paget whispered as Caroline sat next to him. But in her face he saw the same doubts he had.

Salinas was already on his feet. "As I understand it," he said, "you saw no sign that this psychological testing, whatever the result, had driven Mr. Arias to suicide?"

"None."

"Did you see any indication that it *ever* would?"

Gates contemplated him, looking suddenly weary. "Again, no. Mr. Arias was perfectly capable of weighing his self-interest and giving up if the price seemed too great. Including deciding to negotiate some new arrangement rather than face embarrassment." Gates paused for a moment and then quietly finished her answer. "The clear picture I had, from over thirty sessions with Mr. Arias, was of a man who'd harm another person before he'd *ever* harm himself."

Abruptly, Salinas sat down. Paget was still staring at the words of Richie's note when Judge Lerner's gavel banged, and then he realized that the first week of his murder trial was over.

SEVEN

PARKING IN FRONT of Rosa Peralta's, Christopher Paget got out, looking around him.

It was close to nine on Friday night; Paget had arranged to meet Terri at Rosa's so that she could put Elena to bed upstairs and, oddly, because Rosa had requested this. Paget wondered why Rosa wished to see him now; after all that had happened, this was the first time he would meet Terri's mother, or enter the home where Terri had been raised.

It was a modest two-story stucco, neatly maintained, with concrete steps climbing to a covered porch. Paget stopped on the sidewalk, gazing down the slope of Dolores Street. After the entombment of the trial, it felt as though he were reopening his senses. The night was dark, the wind chill on his face; the tall palm trees running down the median strip of grass swayed and rustled in the shadow of streetlights; the night had the fresh smell that came with a cold breeze. On the other side of the street were two dark figures beneath a palm—homeless men, Paget thought, or drug dealers. But in another part of Paget's mind, he saw Ramon Peralta walking his daughters to school at Mission Dolores while Terri's mother lay battered on the second floor.

Gazing up, Paget saw a soft glow from an upstairs window, which must be Elena's night-light in the bedroom where Terri had once slept. He could feel the muted tragedy that had run through from mother to daughter to Elena. Yet it was Ramon Peralta and Ricardo Arias who had died, and Paget who might spend his life in prison; at whatever cost, only the women seemed to endure.

What would Terri and he say tonight, or do? And whatever it was, would it be any more than the reflex of a man facing prison and the lover too loyal to desert him until the trial was over? He could already feel the difference between his desperation to escape, if only for one night, and the small moments, unconsidered and serene, that create the heedless rhythm of a couple's settled life.

Enough, Paget told himself. His task for the next few minutes was to meet his lover's mother, and to do it with grace. No matter what she thought of him, or he thought of himself, he was intently interested in Rosa Peralta.

He turned and climbed the front steps to the house.

But when the door opened, Paget was speechless.

Even in the dim light, the woman he saw startled him. She returned his gaze with silent dignity, as if the moment did not require words.

"I just found out," Paget said finally, "how Terri will look someday. In that, at least, she's lucky."

Rosa acknowledged the compliment. "Please come in," she said, and Paget stepped into the living room.

It was small and dimly lit, with a mantel above a fireplace framed in baked enamel. Paget felt the absence of the crucifix and the stiffly posed family pictures Terri had described; what had replaced them were more recent photos of Terri and her sisters and, Paget realized, a copy of the same school portrait of Elena that the police had found near Richie's note.

The other surprise was less jarring but was interesting for its own sake: an unframed oil painting, in the style of a Haitian primitive, of a native woman with a child in her arms, staring out to sea. Something in the woman's expression, cool and impassive, reminded Paget of Rosa Peralta.

They were alone. "Teresa is upstairs with Elena," Rosa explained, "and I wanted to see you. Please, sit down."

Paget took a chair across from the sofa. As Rosa sat, her face came more fully into the light. There were shadows beneath her eyes, as if to mark the passage of joy. But she had reached the equipoise between beauty and time which, for moments in the lives of certain women, gives a face an interest and refinement that can be neither hurried nor preserved. Perhaps only Paget would know to find the faint white line above her lip, the slight ridge in her nose, which was more crooked than the one she had once had and passed down to Terri. But then studying Rosa Peralta was important to him on several counts.

"You're different from your pictures," Rosa told him. "Golden, just as Teresa said."

Paget smiled a little; he did not know the rules for this conversation. "Less golden by the day."

Rosa nodded. "I'm sorry for what has happened to you. That is much of what I wished to say."

Rosa's English, while lightly accented, had the formality of someone who had learned to speak it carefully. It lent their conversation a certain air of diplomacy, two ambassadors from different worlds, searching each other out.

"It's been difficult," Paget said simply.

Rosa gave him a considered look. "You love my daughter very much, I know. For a time, I was not sure." She paused, arranging her skirt. "And she needed to be away from Ricardo, and to get *Elena* away. I understand that now."

Paget found that he did not feel like mere politeness. "Was that so hard to understand before?"

Rosa seemed to stiffen: there was something withheld about her, as if tempered by time and hardship, and Paget sensed that she did not care to be questioned. "I was afraid of what Ricardo would do. Getting away did not seem easy."

"It still isn't."

"Yes," Rosa answered in a level voice. "You are paying the price for us. I know that too."

Paget did not choose to argue. "What Terri did took courage," he said. "She broke away from Richie, against your advice and, whether or not you accept this, without my help. If nothing else, the trial has justified her."

Rosa raised her head. "Perhaps. But now she has you."

It was a probe, Paget sensed. "Perhaps," he answered. "Perhaps not."

Rosa appeared to study his face. "Do you think," she asked at length, "they will accept that Ricardo killed himself?"

The question surprised him; it could be understood on different levels. "No," he said finally. "In the end, they'll decide whether or not I killed him."

Rosa's lids lowered, half covering her eyes. "Why do you say that?"

"Because there is no one who believes that Richie committed suicide, and a medical examiner to say that the circumstances of his death add up to murder."

Rosa sat back, and then something in her face became remote and almost hard. "It shouldn't matter how Ricardo died," she said. "Only that he's dead."

There was in Rosa's voice the tone of absolute dismissal; the idea of Richie's death held no more awe or mystery for her than the swatting of a fly.

"I can never express to you," Paget said softly, "how much I wish he were still alive."

Across the room, Rosa Peralta regarded him impassively. "He *would* be," she answered, "if Teresa had not left him."

The words had an eerie conviction; Paget did not know whether they were offered in irony or consolation. Rosa Peralta, he had become quite certain, was not a simple woman.

Paget watched her. " 'Character is fate,' someone once said. I think that's true. For all of us."

Rosa was silent for a moment, appraising him. "Long ago," she told him in a quiet voice, "I stopped believing in God. But I still believe that, in some terrible way, there is a balance in life. I know Ricardo's death is part of that. Just as I know that, in the end, you will survive."

Perhaps it was her voice: for a superstitious moment, Paget felt as if a palmist had read good fortune in the lines of his hand. But when he gave a soft laugh, Rosa Peralta was not smiling.

"You will see," she said. "In the meanwhile, I will believe that for both of us. And for your son."

The mention of Carlo, accused of molesting this woman's granddaughter, startled him. And then he heard Terri's footsteps on the stairs.

Entering the living room, she looked from Rosa to Paget, as if surprised to find them together.

Paget tried to smile at her. "Relax," he said. "Your mother just told me I'll be acquitted."

Rosa shook her head. "No. I said you will be absolved. To me, it is not quite the same."

Terri gave Paget a veiled look, then turned to her mother. "We'd better go, Mom."

She bent over the sofa, kissing her mother; in profile, Paget could see how alike they were, yet how they might yet become different. At forty-nine, there might still be light in Terri's face.

"I'll be back in the morning," she told Rosa. "By seven at the latest, so Elena doesn't worry."

Rosa faced them in the pale light; Paget thought he saw regret and a trace of sadness on her face, though he was not sure for what. "You look well together," she said softly.

All at once, Paget felt this woman's love for Terri. "Thank you," he answered. There was nothing else to say.

Leaving with Terri, Paget was aware of Rosa Peralta watching until she gently shut the door behind them. It was a while before either of them spoke.

"What an interesting woman," Paget said.

Terri did not look at him. "Sometimes," she said at last, "my mother's like a mystic. Perhaps it's all the secrets she kept. Even from herself."

EIGHT

CHARLES MONK sat in the witness stand, wearing his trademark gold glasses, a crisp gray pinstripe that looked tailored for a football player, and a silk breast-pocket handkerchief Paget had never seen him wear before. He wondered if Monk, observing that Paget's own silk handkerchiefs had vanished for the trial, meant this as an ironic joke.

"How did it come about?" Salinas asked Monk, "that you first went to Ricardo Arias's apartment?"

Monk seemed to look about, as if orienting himself to another Monday morning. "I was contacted by a uniformed policeman on the scene," he told Salinas. "Mr. Arias's mother-in-law had called in: he hadn't been seen for a week or so, and she asked if we'd perform a well-being check. When no one answered, they broke in the door and found Mr. Arias."

"When you arrived, what did you observe?"

Monk gazed at the ceiling. "The body, of course. Near Mr. Arias's hand was a Smith and Wesson thirty-two safety revolver—the second model, manufactured between 1902 and 1909." Monk paused, regarding Salinas calmly. "The age of the gun was unusual. On inspection we found that one of the rounds had misfired and that the bullet which killed Mr. Arias was the second attempt at firing. Which meant that if Mr. Arias had killed himself, he was one determined man."

The sardonic twist caused Caroline to make a note. Sitting next to her, Paget saw Luisa Marin fold her hands and force herself to pay attention; it reminded Paget that Monk was perhaps the witness he most feared.

"Did you observe anything else?" Salinas asked.

"Yes. The dead man had been shot through the mouth, and there was a note on Mr. Arias's desk, next to a picture of a little girl who turned out to be his daughter." He looked briefly at Paget. "In addition, someone had turned off Mr. Arias's answering machine."

At the corner of his eye, Paget saw Joseph Duarte open his notebook, Marian Celler glancing over his shoulder. Paget decided to focus on Monk.

Salinas moved forward. "After you made these observations, what did you do?"

"Dr. Shelton and the crime lab people were doing *their* work— inspecting the body, lifting fingerprints. So we began to search the apartment."

"What did you find?"

"To start, there was no sign of forced entry. That could have meant suicide, but it could also mean that Mr. Arias had been killed by someone he let into the apartment, particularly because the building had an intercom for visitors. Then we started finding things that didn't add up." Monk paused, sipping casually from the glass of water in front of him. "Mr. Arias had a laundry ticket in his pocket, which turned out to be dated the last day anyone had seen him. It seemed kind of strange that a man who meant to kill himself wanted five clean shirts, with medium starch."

It was a blow, Paget knew at once. With an air of satisfaction, Salinas asked, "Did you find other anomalies?"

"Yes," Monk answered. "There was a full pot of coffee. Someone had set the automatic coffeemaker to brew some coffee that Mr. Arias never got to drink. When we got into his computer, we found a calendar showing appointments for after anyone had seen him *and*, we calculated from the pile of mail and newspapers, *after* he'd been shot." Monk ticked them off on his fingers. "There was a notation for eleven the next day: 'Coffee with Leslie.' Then there was an appointment with a Dr. Gates on Monday and, a hearing in the family court. If this man was winding up his life, he seemed to have left a few loose ends.

"Then there was nothing which tied Mr. Arias to the gun—no permit, no record of purchase, nothing. Not even any ammunition, or oil, or anything you'd need to maintain a gun." Monk peered at the jury. "Man wants a gun to kill himself, he's not going to make any secret about buying it. I mean, what's the point, especially when you mean to leave a note."

"Of course, it *could* have been a robbery. But the apartment wasn't torn up, and Mr. Arias still had his watch and his wallet, with cash and credit cards inside." Monk gazed down for a moment. "Also, in a gym bag in the bedroom closet, we found ten thousand dollars. Cash."

Caroline looked up from her notes. "Colt," Paget whispered. "They must have paid Richie off in cash."

Almost imperceptibly, Caroline nodded. "Watch Victor," she whispered back.

Salinas had paused. "So according to what you found, Mr. Arias *also* was not financially desperate."

Monk gave him an even stare; Paget sensed some private form of communication. "Sure didn't look like that," Monk said coolly. He stopped, as if interrupting himself, and then shrugged. "We also found a passbook showing another ten thousand or so. In an account at the B of A. So he had some money even without support from Ms. Peralta. However he got it."

"Brooks called Monk off," Paget murmured to Caroline. "Monk wanted to know where the money came from, and they made him stop when he couldn't trace it to Terri or me."

"Sounds right." Caroline made another note. "I wonder if Victor knows about that."

"And when," Salinas asked, "did you first speak to Mr. Paget?"

The prosecutor, Paget realized, had quickly changed the subject. "Victor knows *something*," he said under his breath.

"Three days later," Monk was answering. "At his home, after he and Teresa Peralta flew back from Italy. She was there too."

Paget leaned closer to Caroline. "I remember Monk asking if I still meant to run for the Senate. Maybe he was trying to tell me something."

"And what did Mr. Paget tell you?" Salinas asked Monk.

"Then? Only a few things." Monk glanced at Paget, then he faced Salinas. "I asked Mr. Paget whether he'd been home that Friday night, after the last time anyone claimed to have seen or spoken to Mr. Arias. I understood him to say yes. But when I went back to the office and replayed the tape of our interview, I realized he hadn't said a thing. Just nodded." Monk shook his head in wonder. "It was a stupid mistake. I don't know how many times I've told interview subjects to answer aloud. Including a couple of Mr. Paget's clients."

"What did you do about that?"

"Nothing, at first. Just started going over the papers we found in Mr. Arias's apartment." Monk adjusted his glasses. "I found a clipping from a tabloid, the *Inquisitor*, where Mr. Arias accused Mr. Paget of 'stealing' Teresa Peralta and breaking up his marriage. So I started in on the papers from Mr. Arias's divorce case."

Salinas stood straighter, folding his arms. "And what did you find there?"

"The last papers filed in the case were marked confidential, so the public couldn't read them." Monk touched his chin. "It was a motion by Mr. Arias to keep his daughter, Elena, from seeing Mr. Paget or his son. Mr. Arias's own affidavit repeated the accusations he'd made in the *Inquisitor*." Monk finished in a flat voice. "He also accused Carlo Paget of having sexually molested Elena Arias."

With every instinct of a father, Paget wanted to stand up to say that Ricardo Arias was a liar. But instead he fought to compose himself, aware of Marian Celler turning to watch him. Beneath the table, he felt Caroline lightly touching his arm. And then Salinas asked Monk, "Did you then go back to Mr. Paget?"

"Yes."

Slowly, Salinas walked back to the prosecution table and produced a black tape player, holding it aloft. "And did you record your second interview with Mr. Paget?"

"Yes."

Paget braced himself for the tape. But then, to his surprise, Salinas dropped the subject. "After you spoke to Mr. Paget," he asked, "what did you do next?"

Monk glanced at Paget again. "We interviewed a neighbor," he answered. "A woman named Georgina Keller, who lived next to Mr. Arias. She had gone on her own vacation the same day as Mr. Paget, to visit a daughter in Florida, and only returned ten days or so after we found Mr. Arias."

"And what did Mrs. Keller tell you?"

"What she *told* us," Monk responded, "was that she'd been taking out the trash to the garbage chute the night before she left. When she passed Mr. Arias's apartment, she thought she heard voices coming from his apartment. Two men, and then a thud. Like someone hitting the floor."

Caroline rose at once. "Your Honor, Inspector Monk is entitled to a certain leeway in describing the course of his inquiry. But we're in danger of getting a lot of undocumented information, a lot of it secondhand, and plainly hearsay. I move that the answer be stricken and that Inspector Monk be admonished to stick to matters about which he can claim personal knowledge."

"He *is*," Salinas retorted at once. "I am not asking him to testify for Mrs. Keller, who will be with us shortly, but to describe the evidence he gathered. Subject to proof, we are entitled to lay out his investigative processes." Here he turned to Caroline. "Particularly if, as we suspect, Ms. Masters intends to suggest that the police or prosecutor are somehow biased against Mr. Paget."

Salinas, Paget thought, was like a computer. There was no defense he did not anticipate, no testimony he was not armed to justify. "Motion denied," Lerner said promptly. "The prosecution may continue."

"Thank you, Your Honor." Quickly, Salinas turned to Monk. "What else did Mrs. Keller tell you?"

"That she went to her door and opened it a crack."

"What, if anything, did she report seeing?"

"A tall blond-haired man, in a light-gray suit leaving Mr. Arias's apartment. She saw his face, she said, because he stopped for a minute to look at his hand and then at something on the sleeve of his coat."

"Did she describe this man?"

"Yes." Monk folded his hands. "About six feet, six one, with blondish hair, a strong jaw, and a slight ridge on his nose."

Paget felt the jury turn to him, matching the description with his face. Joseph Duarte seemed to squint; next to him, Marian Celler put on her glasses.

"And did you then show her a photograph?"

"Yes." Monk paused a moment. "Of Mr. Paget."

"What, if anything, did Mrs. Keller say?"

"That this was the man she had seen in the hallway."

Paget found that he could not watch the jury.

"And what did you do next?" Salinas asked in a calm voice.

"Detective Lynch and I obtained a warrant to search Mr. Paget's house and impound his car."

"And what evidence did you find?"

Monk removed his glasses, wiping them on the silk handkerchief before he casually stuffed it back into the breast pocket of his suit. "Mr. Arias's landlord," he said matter-of-factly, "had installed new carpeting just before he moved in. All carpets leave fibers on the shoes of anyone who walks on them, and *new* carpeting leaves many more fibers." He put his glasses back on. "According to the crime lab, there were fibers from Mr. Arias's carpet on the Persian rug in Mr. Paget's entryway, the runner up his central stairs, and the Chinese carpet in his bedroom."

Salinas raised his eyebrows at this inventory of wealth. "What about in the carpet of Mr. Paget's Jaguar convertible?"

Monk peered through his glasses. "More fibers," he said evenly. "On the driver's side."

In the jury box, Duarte wrote this down, scowling at his notepad. Now Salinas looked almost eager. "Did you then take Mr. Paget's fingerprints?"

"Yes."

Paget could feel the stale air of the courtroom, hot and close. Salinas half turned to the jury. "And did you attempt to match the prints with prints found in Mr. Arias's apartment?"

"Yes." Once more, Monk faced Paget; this time, his eyes did not move. "Mr. Paget had left a full right-hand print, four fingers and a thumb, on Mr. Arias's answering machine. The one that someone had switched off."

There was utter silence. "Perhaps," Salinas said softly, "we should play the tape of your second interview with Mr. Paget."

For Paget, the next few minutes were a kind of death.

As if in slow motion, Monk identified the tape and began answering Salinas's staccato questions in a monotone. Paget had not before mentioned the charges against Carlo, Monk said, or even the *Inquisitor* article. Paget had said that he might still be running for the Senate. Paget had acknowledged, at last, his hatred for Ricardo Arias.

And then Monk switched on the tape.

Listening, Paget could remember his tautness as he answered Monk's questions. That he had never spoken to Ricardo Arias. That he had never even seen Ricardo Arias. That he had never been to Ricardo Arias's apartment. And that on the night before leaving for Italy, he had been at home alone.

His voice on the tape surprised him—cool, well-bred, a little bored. For Paget, and for the jury, it seemed to change everything.

The jury leaned forward, looking from the tape to Paget's face. Except perhaps on television, none had ever heard him speak: these words were to be the last they would ever hear from him. To Paget, his answers—terse and measured—sounded like lies.

"In short," Salinas finished crisply, "Mr. Paget had denied ever meeting with Mr. Arias, is that right? Let alone going to his apartment."

"That's right." Monk turned to Paget. "For a while after that, I even believed him. Until we did our job."

Cross-examination started after the lunch break. Caroline spent most of that time on the telephone; she did not say with whom.

Her opening question was quiet, almost muted. "You mentioned, Inspector Monk, that you'd tried to trace the Smith and Wesson revolver to Mr. Arias. Did you also try tracing it to Mr. Paget?"

Monk nodded. "We did."

"Could you describe for us *all* the steps you undertook to establish ownership of the revolver?"

"Sure." Monk sat back. "First, we checked the usual sources—gun dealers, records of sale, all the paperwork they've required for the last twenty years. There was nothing.

"So we worked backward. The Smith and Wesson factory in Connecticut had a record, by serial number, of every thirty-two-caliber Second Model they shipped. *This* one was shipped to Shreve's department store in San Francisco sometime in October 1906." Monk's voice took on an ironic undertone. "Department stores used to sell guns over the counter, just like perfume or slippers. But no one kept records then. Once Shreve's sold this gun to the first owner, it vanished for almost ninety years. Until we found it next to Mr. Arias's body."

"Did you take other specific steps to tie this gun to Mr. Paget?"

"Yes."

"Including question his housekeeper and his son?"

"Yes."

"And showing Mr. Paget's photograph to gun dealers in the city?"

"Yes."

"In fact, did you find a single piece of evidence connecting Mr. Paget with this or *any* gun?"

Monk folded his hands. "We found no evidence that Mr. Paget has ever owned a gun."

Caroline looked bemused. "Instead you simply assumed that—out of all the guns available as a murder weapon—Mr. Paget selected an eighty-six-year-old revolver, so unreliable that it misfired."

Monk shrugged. "Maybe he wanted to save money," he said dryly.

"Isn't there another problem, Inspector? The bullets?"

Monk's eyes narrowed. "That they're old, you mean."

"Specifically, that they're Winchester silver tips, which haven't been manufactured for a thirty-two-caliber weapon in roughly twenty years, true?"

"That's right."

"And, in fact, *these* bullets were rusty."

"Also correct."

"So Mr. Paget would have had to buy an antique revolver *and* rusty bullets. Does that seem likely to you?"

"Objection," Salinas put in. "Calls for speculation. How can Inspector Monk be expected to know the defendant's mental processes?"

Caroline turned on him. "We're talking about Inspector Monk's *investigative* processes, Victor, just as you predicted on direct. I'm just helping you flesh them out a little."

Judge Lerner looked from Caroline to Salinas. "Which cliché would you like, Victor? How about, "Sauce for the goose is sauce for the gander'?" He addressed Caroline. "You may continue, Ms. Masters."

She nodded to Monk. "I'm not able to tell you," he answered, "what kind of gun Mr. Paget might have considered an appropriate suicide weapon for Mr. Arias."

It was a shrewd rejoinder, Paget thought. But Caroline did not hesitate. "Or bullets? Isn't it true that the bullets showed signs of having been kept in a damp place for a long period of time?"

"Yes."

"Do you have any theory as to why Mr. Paget would buy wet ammunition?"

Monk shook his head slowly. "No, I don't."

Caroline paused. "Can you tell me what kind of noise this gun would make? When it fires, that is."

"Sort of a pop."

"Fairly loud?"

"Fairly. Yes."

Caroline raised her eyebrows. "By the way, Inspector, did you happen to check this venerable murder weapon for Mr. Paget's fingerprints?"

Monk's eyes widened in what might have been amusement. "Yes, Counselor. We didn't find Mr. Paget's prints. *Or* Mr. Arias's." He paused. "It's common not to find usable prints on relatively small metal surfaces. Like a gun."

Caroline smiled. "Just checking. In the course of your inquiry, Inspector, did you find *any* evidence of *any* kind that Mr. Paget had displayed *any* inclination toward violence?"

"No."

Caroline nodded briskly. "Then let's move on. When you searched Mr. Paget's home, you were looking for more than rug fibers, correct?"

Monk crossed his arms. "We were looking for evidence. Period."

"Isn't it true that you searched Mr. Paget's closet? For clothing with blood spatters or gunshot residue?"

"Among other things."

"Come up with anything?"

"No."

"Really?" Caroline paused. "How about rug fibers on Mr. Paget's shoes?"

Monk was quiet for a moment. "No."

Caroline put one finger to her lips, as if the truth were dawning. "So let's summarize your evidence against Mr. Paget. After all that effort, it comes down to rug fibers in his house and car, an eyewitness who saw a tall blond man, and prints on Mr. Arias's machine. Right?"

Monk gave her a pointed stare. "He *also* had a powerful motive."

One corner of Caroline's mouth flickered. "To *dislike* Mr. Arias, surely. But so did Ms. Peralta, correct?"

"I would say so."

"Did you consider Ms. Peralta as a potential suspect?"

"For a time, yes."

"And did you also search Ms. Peralta's home?"

"Yes."

Caroline took a step toward Monk. "And found rug fibers there? The same kind as you'd found at Mr. Paget's?"

"Yes."

"So you didn't pick Mr. Paget over Ms. Peralta because of rug fibers."

"No."

"And in fact, you *did* remove a suit from *Ms. Peralta's* closet, right? Because it had a stain on the front."

"Yes."

"And what did the stain turn out to be?"

"Ketchup." A small smile. "Seems like Ms. Peralta was guilty of eating at McDonald's."

"Oh, well." Caroline cocked her head. "So at *that* point, your case as to Mr. Paget was the same as against Ms. Peralta. Motive and fibers."

Watch it, Paget thought. Monk shook his head. "One big difference, Counselor. Ms. Peralta admitted that she was at Mr. Arias's apartment a lot. Mr. Paget denied being there."

Paget could feel the damage, even before he saw Joseph Duarte's silent nod. But Caroline looked quite calm. "And *that*," she said to Monk, "was why Mr. Paget's prints on the answering machine so troubled you?"

The question startled Paget; abruptly, Caroline had moved to the most damaging piece of evidence—Paget's fingerprints.

Monk regarded her with an air of interest. "Yes," he answered.

"Could you identify any *other* prints on that machine?"

Monk nodded. "Mr. Arias's and Ms. Peralta's."

"Why didn't *Ms. Peralta's* prints disturb you?"

Monk gave her a look of weary patience. "Because she had reason to visit the apartment a lot. And before that, she'd lived with Mr. Arias. You'd expect her prints to be on some of the things he took to his new apartment. Like drinking glasses."

Caroline smiled. "Or an answering machine?"

Why, Paget wondered, was Caroline pushing this? Even Monk looked curious. "Yes," he said.

"Do you happen to know the history of *this* answering machine? For example, if the machine had always belonged to Mr. Arias?"

Monk shrugged. "It was in his apartment."

"So it was. Did you happen to find Mr. Paget's prints anywhere else?"

"No."

"Did you find *other* prints besides Mr. Arias's and Ms. Peralta's?"

"Yes." Monk hesitated a moment. "We found several prints that we couldn't identify."

"Including on the answering machine?"

"Yes."

Paget tried to detach himself; beneath his apprehension, the professional in him admired the skill with which Caroline chipped away at the evidence.

"These unknown prints," she asked, "what did you do to identify them?"

"We ran them through the FBI print bank. And our own."

"Did that assure you that none of the unknown people who visited Mr. Arias's apartment had a criminal record?"

Monk touched his glasses. "All that this told us was that the prints didn't belong to anyone who'd been printed. At least by any agency we have access to."

"Didn't that trouble you?"

Monk considered her. "Mrs. Keller," he said, "identified Mr. Paget."

"Or so Mrs. Keller may think." Caroline's voice became very soft. "Tell me, Inspector Monk, when did you first discuss this case with the district attorney? Not Mr. Salinas, but the D.A. himself. McKinley Brooks."

Before Paget could even turn to him, Salinas was on his feet. "*Objection.* Law enforcement is the D.A.'s *job*. What Mr. Brooks *may* have discussed with Inspector Monk or *any* law enforcement officer is irrelevant to the evidence against Mr. Paget. Ms. Masters is simply trying to get a peep through the keyhole at our theory of this case."

"Hardly," Caroline said to Lerner. "We think that Mr. Brooks has everything to do with the case against Mr. Paget and, perhaps, with why there is a case at all. Justice will be blind, Your Honor, the day that district attorneys stop being politicians."

Salinas assumed an indignant look. "*That,*" he said, "is an unwarranted assault on the integrity of District Attorney Brooks."

Caroline smiled at him. "Think of how embarrassed I'll be, Victor, when Inspector Monk tells me that the D.A. fearlessly insisted that he follow the evidence, wherever it leads. Which, I'm sure, Inspector Monk would have known how to do on his own." Paget saw Monk arrange his face in a benign expression, and then Caroline turned to Lerner. "Just as Mr. Salinas's direct anticipated, the defense questions the objectivity of this entire inquiry. It's important to determine if, for whatever reason, the police or prosecution did not follow all the leads they should have."

Lerner wiped his forehead with a handkerchief, gazing at the courtroom clock. "I'll permit this," he told Caroline finally. "But if all you end up doing is making accusations in the form of questions, I'll cut it off."

Somehow, Paget sensed, that time would never come. When Caroline turned to Monk again, his face had become a blank. "When *was* the first time you spoke to McKinley Brooks?" she asked.

"Two days after we found Mr. Arias."

"And how did that conversation come about?"

Monk sat back, folding his hands again. "The D.A. called me."

"Please describe the substance of that discussion."

Monk gazed at the floor, choosing his words. "District Attorney Brooks wanted to let me know that the case should be handled carefully."

Caroline gave him a satiric look. "Isn't it your practice to handle your cases carefully? Or is the D.A. required to issue these periodic reminders?"

Monk's returning gaze was level. "The D.A. believed that this case had political implications."

"Which were?"

"That it involved Mr. Paget."

Caroline stared at him with an air of surprise. "How could Mr. Brooks know that?"

Monk appeared faintly puzzled. "Somehow, the D.A. was aware that Mr. Paget was involved with Mr. Arias's estranged wife."

"You hadn't let him know about Mr. Arias's death, had you?"

"No."

"So how did he know that Mr. Arias had died?"

Monk touched the bridge of his nose. "I don't know."

Caroline's expression became curious. "During Mr. Brooks's tenure in office, how many homicides have you investigated?"

"Around a hundred. Give or take a few."

"And on how many of these have you worked directly with District Attorney Brooks?"

After a moment's thought, Monk answered, "Two."

"*Which* two?"

"The high-rise massacre, a couple of years back, where a gunman killed six people." Monk paused. "The second was the Carelli case."

"That involved Mary Carelli, right? The TV journalist accused of murdering the novelist Mark Ransom."

Monk's eyes seemed to widen; the effect was of someone trying to maintain an absolute poker face. "That's the case."

"Would you say that was a high-profile case?"

"They're *all* important, and the victims are all dead. But the Carelli case got a lot of attention."

"And what was the result?"

Monk gave Caroline a droll look. "Mrs. Carelli got off."

"And who defended Ms. Carelli?"

Monk folded his arms. "Mr. Paget. And Ms. Peralta."

Caroline smiled. "And just for the sake of posterity, who was the judge in the case?"

"You were."

Caroline nodded. "In this initial conversation with the D.A., did Mr. Brooks mention the Carelli case?"

Monk nodded in turn. "He did."

In the jury box, Marian Celler gave Salinas a look of wariness and interest. "And what," Caroline asked Monk, "was the context?"

"That anything involving Mr. Paget was sensitive—that people might be watching us for bias."

"Did Mr. Brooks tell you that, as a result, he was keeping hands off?"

"No." Monk inhaled visibly. "What he told me, Counselor, was that he wanted me to report to him directly—on everything. Even though Mr. Salinas was being assigned to the case."

"Was this unusual?"

Monk seemed to consider the word. "It wasn't *usual*."

"Did Mr. Brooks give you any *other* reason that the case was sensitive?"

Monk took a sip of water. "What he mentioned was that Mr. Paget might be running for the United States Senate."

"Did he state a position on Mr. Paget's candidacy?"

Monk gave a half smile. "The D.A. and I don't have those kinds of conversations."

"Did he mention anyone *outside* the office who had a potential interest in the Arias murder?"

Monk considered her. "No one specific."

"In that first conversation, did you discuss the specifics of the *case?*"

"To some extent. I reviewed what we had found in Mr. Arias's apartment."

"Did Mr. Brooks comment?"

"Yes." Monk sat back, as if preparing for a long stay, and then said quietly, "He was interested in the ten thousand dollars in cash we found in Mr. Arias's closet."

Suddenly Paget saw where this was going; it was hard to suppress a smile. "What did you tell the D.A.?" Caroline asked.

"That I wanted to know where the money came from."

Caroline, Paget saw, had a faint smile of her own. "And how did Mr. Brooks respond?"

Monk webbed his fingers. "He told me to check Mr. Paget's and Ms. Peralta's bank records and then get back to him."

"And did you check?"

"Yes." Monk's voice was flat now. "We couldn't trace the cash to either one of them."

Joseph Duarte looked up from his notes. "Did you so inform District Attorney Brooks?" Caroline asked.

"Yes."

"And how did he respond?"

"That he didn't think the cash was relevant."

"Did he give you any specific instructions?"

Monk's eyes met Caroline's. "To drop trying to trace the money."

At the defense table, Paget turned to Salinas and slowly shook his head. Salinas spread his hands a fraction, as if to disclaim involvement, then turned away.

"Tell me," Caroline was asking, "did Mr. Brooks give you any instructions regarding your treatment of Mr. Paget?"

"Uh-huh." Monk folded his arms. "No favoritism."

"Was that a real risk?"

Monk gave her a long expressionless look. "What the D.A. said," he answered with a trace of irony, "was that it shouldn't seem like we were favoring Mr. Paget because of politics."

"No worry on that score, was there? Did you ever have a more specific conversation about what 'no favoritism' meant?"

"Yes." For the first time in a while, Monk looked at Paget. "After the eyewitness and the matching prints, the D.A. submitted the case to the grand jury, and an arrest warrant was issued. I asked him if we should contact you, as Mr. Paget's lawyer, and ask if he'd submit himself for arraignment voluntarily."

"Is that unusual?"

"No. Unless the defendant's a flight risk." Monk looked at Paget again. "Mr. Paget has a son. Didn't seem to be any point in putting the boy through all that."

"Indeed. And what was the D.A.'s response?"

"He repeated that he didn't want to be showing Mr. Paget any favoritism." Monk paused, then added with sardonic casualness, "You know, just because Mr. Paget was in politics."

A corner of Caroline's mouth twitched upward. "I see. Tell me, did you consider the ten thousand dollars you'd found in Mr. Arias's closet to be a suspicious circumstance?"

"Yes. I did."

Caroline donned an almost innocent expression. "In your experience, Inspector, are large amounts of money in actual cash often associated with criminal activities?"

"Objection." Salinas stood, angry now. "The question not only calls for speculation, but it's completely irrelevant to the question of whether Mr. Paget murdered Mr. Arias."

"But *not,*" Caroline shot back, "irrelevant to the question of whether *someone* murdered Mr. Arias."

The jury, Paget saw, seemed utterly enthralled.

"Ms. Masters' question," Lerner said to Salinas, "comports with *my* experience. And I'm anxious to hear Inspector Monk's answer."

In the witness chair, Monk folded his hands on his stomach, a distant, almost dreamy look spreading across his face. It was all Paget could do not to laugh: the money was surely Colt's; Salinas could say nothing; and Caroline was about to kill him with it. Salinas, Monk, Paget, and Caroline all knew that; only the jury was in the dark.

"Yes," Monk said solemnly to Caroline. "In my experience, large amounts of cash are often associated with activities that people don't want anyone else to discover."

"Is drug dealing among those activities?"

"Not always." Monk's expression remained deadpan. "But that's maybe the most common."

At the prosecution table, Salinas stared at the wall, as if willing himself to stay calm.

"And did you," Caroline asked, "happen to inquire into whether Mr. Arias was dealing drugs?"

It was, Paget thought, sublime.

"No," Monk said evenly.

"And in your experience," Caroline asked, "is drug dealing frequently associated with violence?"

"That can happen. There's a lot of distrust and double-crossing. And a lot of cash." With an almost professorial air, Monk adjusted his glasses. "Plus, you're not dealing here with the finest elements of society."

"Again, in your experience, are drug dealers inclined to carry weapons?"

"Sometimes."

"Do these weapons tend to be registered?"

"No. People who ignore drug laws don't make a habit of obeying the gun laws. It might start a bad precedent."

Caroline paused. "Did you consider the possibility that Mr. Arias was killed in a drug-related incident?"

Monk frowned now; Paget sensed Brooks's punishment was going too far for his liking. "I have to tell you, Counselor, that I had no reason to suspect that Arias was a drug dealer."

"Other than the cash?"

Monk shifted in the witness chair. "I couldn't explain it, that's all."

"Because Mr. Brooks stopped you."

Monk considered her; an experienced witness, he knew that she was trying to end her examination on a high note. In a level voice, he answered, "I don't know what would have happened. Maybe we'd have never traced that money."

For a long moment, Caroline looked back at him. "But it bothers you, doesn't it?"

Monk seemed to look amused, as if knowing that the truth was a gift. "Yes," he said finally. "It bothered me. But I don't believe it would have changed anything for Mr. Paget."

"Of course," Caroline put in smoothly, "Mr. Brooks didn't want to show Mr. Paget any favoritism. You didn't happen to show your eyewitness—Mrs. Keller—photos of any drug dealers, did you?"

"No."

"Did you show Mrs. Keller *any* pictures at all—other than Mr. Paget's?"

Monk fixed Caroline with a level gaze. "No."

"Is that your usual practice?"

"It is not."

"Then why, Inspector, this exception for Mr. Paget?"

Monk leaned back. "Mr. Brooks," he said, "wanted an ID immediately. To see if we could rule Mr. Paget in or out, he said." Another pause. "We also had a lineup, Counselor."

"Indeed you did. And where, Inspector Monk, did you find the *other* five members of Mr. Paget's lineup?"

"Mr. Paget found them."

"Where?"

"The county jail."

Caroline raised an eyebrow. "It is an unfortunate fact, is it not, that the great majority of the county jail prison population is nonwhite?"

"Yes."

"Besides Mr. Paget, how many members of the lineup were Caucasian?"

Monk scowled. "One."

Caroline put her hands on her hips. "And whose idea was it to have Mr. Paget choose among prisoners?"

Monk stared at her fixedly, a man who did not like giving excuses. "The district attorney," he said finally. "When I arrested Mr. Paget, the D.A. told me to line him up the quickest way I could. That was the quickest way."

Caroline's slow nod seemed a gesture of respect. She studied Monk in the silence. "Thank you, Inspector," she said at last. "I have no further questions. At least about *your* role."

She walked slowly back to the defense table.

The jury seemed to follow her to her chair. Sitting, Caroline looked quite calm, except that her eyes were unusually bright.

And then Salinas was up. In a quick series of questions, he established that Brooks had never told Monk to go after Paget and that the evidence against Paget was gathered by the police and the medical examiner without interference. But in the end, Paget thought, the jury would remember two conflicting strands: Paget's fingerprints on the answering machine, and the suspicion that, for reasons of politics and spite, McKinley Brooks had kept the inquiry focused on Paget.

After Salinas had finished, a weary Jared Lerner adjourned court for the day. With a final fathomless glance at Paget, Monk left the courtroom, a professional who had done his job.

When Paget turned to Caroline, he saw her beckon to Victor Salinas.

The courtroom was noisy and a little chaotic—reporters rushing to file stories, spectators talking, the jury filing out. Glancing over his shoulder, Salinas walked to the defense table.

"Cute," he told Caroline under his breath.

Caroline gave him a hard smile. "More than cute, Victor. I want McKinley's ass in court, as a witness." She stared up at him. "Tell Mac that, as a courtesy, I won't serve the subpoena on his wife and kids. We're not afraid of playing favorites."

NINE

"YOU REALLY ARE a miserable prick," Caroline said to McKinley Brooks.

They were alone in Brooks's office; the D.A. refused to have witnesses present. He stared back at her, as if waiting to choose his words with care. His voice was quite soft. "Sticks and stones, Caroline."

"Try 'obstruction of justice.' And 'cover-up' has a certain ring."

Brooks folded his hands. "You really don't care, do you?"

Caroline gave a humorless laugh. "This isn't about *me*. Once I put you on the stand, *you're* through in politics. Just when *did* Colt call you, Mac, to let you know that the stench from Richie's apartment might be more than just a stinking corpse? A day or so after they found his body?" She raised an eyebrow. "How do you know that *Colt* didn't have him killed?"

Brooks's face filled with anger. "That's bullshit."

"Just watch me." Her voice grew cold. "When you sold your soul to James Colt, you lost something dearer than your integrity. You lost control."

Brooks managed a thin smile. "You can't prove *any* of this."

"Because you'll *lie*?" Caroline gave him a look of mock amazement. "Oh, Mac, why didn't I consider that? Now let's see—you'll need *other* people to lie too, won't you? Such as a cop to say that *he*, not Colt, called you about Richie. Why do I keep remembering Richard Nixon?" She spoke quietly now. "You are *such* a fool. Drop the dime on Colt, and all you are is finished. Try to *lie* about it, and you'll do time." She smiled. "Our prisons really aren't all they could be. How do you fancy becoming the special friend of someone named Bubba, a lonely guy with a yen for law enforcement."

Brooks's eyes narrowed. "Paget will be right there with me. If you tie Richie to Colt, it's like writing 'motive' in neon lights. Our good friend Victor will get *your* client on the way to getting *my* job."

That might be right, Caroline guessed. But somewhere behind Brooks's opaque expression, a proposition was forming. "Assuming that the jury doesn't view Richie's demise as a public service," she retorted. "But *your* demise is a given."

Brooks sat back. "Spit it out, Caroline."

Caroline gave him a long, cool look. "I want this case dismissed."

Brooks's laugh was a curt bark. "Send me the subpoena. Like Victor, I prefer murder to suicide."

"Fine." Caroline stood to leave. "I wish I could say this was interesting. But it hasn't even been that."

Brooks shook his head in disbelief. "Quit the theatrics. You came here looking for a deal. Sit down and listen."

Caroline stared down at him. "Only out of respect for your office," she said, and sat again.

Brooks waited until she was settled. "One offer, my first and last. Are you listening closely?"

"Just speak slowly, Mac. So that I can keep up with you."

"You get your voluntary manslaughter. Sixteen years—in reality, Chris Paget will be out in eight." He paused. "I'll keep the offer open until the end of our case. Take a run at our eyewitness if you want. Then you can decide whether you want to take it or go for broke."

"And if we take it?"

"*You* drop the subpoena." Brooks paused for emphasis. "And you—*and* Chris—forget any thoughts you ever had about making my life hard."

Caroline pretended to think awhile. "Doesn't that leave me with an unexplained loose end? The money."

For the first time, Brooks looked genuinely amused. "The *drug* money, you mean? Make all the mischief you want with *that*, and I'll keep Victor out of your way. Which is what you've been planning on all along." Brooks leaned forward. "One stipulation. *If* we find new evidence against Chris Paget, our deal is off. I don't want to get hung out to dry."

That was reasonable, Caroline knew. "As long as you're not holding back some evidence yourself."

"We're not. If we were, and Lerner found us out, he'd dismiss the case."

After a moment, Caroline nodded. "I'll talk to Chris."

" 'If you could occupy any place in history,' " Carlo Paget read aloud, " 'at any time, what would it be?' " He put down the assignment sheet next to his computer, muted the Pink Floyd disc on his player, and turned back to his father. "Any ideas?"

Paget thought. "How about: 'I'd be President of the United States, with unlimited pardoning power.' "

Carlo gave him a pinched smile. "Not funny, Dad."

By Paget's estimate, Carlo would be on the stand in two more days. "No," Paget said. "I guess not. I gather that neither Marie Antoinette nor Ronald Reagan appeals to you much."

"Only as a couple."

Paget took a seat on the end of Carlo's bed. The scene felt familiar. Carlo's room, with its view of the bay at night; the plaques from his athletic teams; the framed picture of his mother, Mary Carelli. Carlo himself, baseball cap stuck backward on his curly black hair, scowling at the computer. And Paget, inveigled by his son to help with an assignment. But this time, Paget sensed that Carlo did not need his help; this was a safe way of killing time together.

It was fine with Paget. His alternative was thinking about Terri's testimony, beginning tomorrow morning. Or, more painful, Carlo's right after that. It was good to be with his son when the ostensible subject was not the trial.

Their dinner had been too quiet. Paget had refused to watch the news. But Carlo, he knew, had sneaked upstairs to watch in his bedroom. Paget was equally certain that the shaken boy at his dinner table had heard about the fingerprints on Richie's answering machine: when, once more, Carlo tried to open the forbidden subject of what his father would say as a witness, Paget sensed that he was hoping for an explanation of the prints. Calmly, Paget had repeated his reminder that Carlo was a witness, that his job was to state the facts, and that no conversation they had could be private. His son's worry and frustration was a necessary price to pay for sparing him the greater devastation of the truth.

"How about Ted Williams?" Paget said now.

Carlo turned from the computer. "For my essay?"

"*I'd* do it. Williams was not only the best hitter in baseball history; he was the only subject my dad and I could really talk about." Paget put his hands behind his head. "My father *loved* Ted Williams. The one special thing he did with me was to take me back to Fenway Park in Boston, when I was nine, to see Williams play in a four-game series with the Yankees." He smiled. "He did it for himself, really—I was just an excuse. But by the time those games were over, *I* loved Williams too. Because he was a truly great player and because my dad spent time with me."

Carlo gave him a look of interest; for years, Paget had told him more about Ted Williams than about his own father. "So *that's* how the Ted Williams thing got started." His brow knit. "Was that hard—not being close to your dad?"

Paget shrugged. "He wasn't really close to anyone. It's just that I was his son, so maybe it hurt a little more. But after twelve, I was in boarding school. You develop a kind of prep school toughness: I tried to view my parents as a pair of socialites in San Francisco, who didn't have much to do with me, until they became more of an absence than a presence."

Carlo studied him. "When they died in that car wreck, how did you feel?"

"Angry. It was such a joke of a death. Or would have been, had my mother not suffered for days before she died." Paget's tone mixed irony with regret. "My father was drunk as a lord. He'd found out my mother had taken a lover, and pulled her out of a party in some sort of rage. If he hadn't been so drunk so often, he would have noticed her lovers when I did—ten years before, when I was twelve or so and *asked* to go to boarding school. And if *she* hadn't been so drunk, she'd never have stayed with him. Or, for that matter, driven with him."

"How did you learn all that?"

"About the accident? My aunt told me. She wanted to make sure I didn't turn into another inebriate." Paget's voice turned cold. "And if *she* hadn't been such a malicious fool, she would have realized that drinking was the one way I would *never* be like them. Emotionally distant, self-protective, and afraid of intimacy—sure, I might become *all* of those. But a drunk? Never." Catching himself, Paget shrugged again. "Sorry. I generally don't think about them. But parent-child stuff dies hard, I guess."

Carlo looked into his face. "You've been a good dad, you know. The best."

Paget was touched. "That's because *you* were the best thing that ever happened to me. At the risk of being sentimental, I got a great kid to care about and to take me out of myself. You've paid me back a thousand times. . . . ."

Abruptly, Paget stopped; this was so true he could feel it in his throat. He had told Terri he wanted a family. But *Carlo* had been his family, a better one than most men had, and he was throwing it away.

All at once, Paget wanted to hug his son as tightly as he could.

"Are you okay, Dad?"

The telephone rang on Carlo's desk. Carlo still watched his father, concerned.

"I'm fine, Carlo. But maybe you could get that."

Reluctantly, Carlo answered the telephone. He listened briefly, then held it out to his father. "Your lawyer," he said in a flat voice.

Taking the telephone, Paget covered the mouthpiece. "Ted Williams," he told Carlo. "That's where all this started. If you don't want to impress your English teacher by being Louis Pasteur, try Ted Williams in 1941. He hit .406 that year."

His son tried smiling. "Four-oh-six," he repeated. "Adjusted for inflation, that's seven million a season."

Paget laughed, enjoying one last instant of this, a pantomime of their normal life. He took his hand off the mouthpiece. "Ted Williams," he said, "thought only of greatness." He held the phone to his face. "Isn't that right, Caroline?"

"My father," she said dryly, "lived and died with Williams. The Red Sox broke his heart."

Somehow this snippet of biography sounded right; it reminded Paget of how little he knew about Caroline Masters.

"What's up?" he asked.

"I talked with Brooks. He's made us an offer."

Casually, Paget strolled into the hall outside Carlo's room; the boy became too still, pretending not to listen. "What is it?" Paget murmured in the hall.

Quickly and clearly, Caroline explained the deal. "Choice one," she finished, "is to plead to manslaughter if Mrs. Keller stands up under cross-examination. Choice two is to turn down the deal and go for an acquittal. If we decide to do that, we also have to decide whether to savage Brooks, implicate Colt, and try to paint this as a political vendetta. At the risk of making Richie seem like your worst nightmare.

"Choice one caps your time in prison. As long as there's no new evidence, if you're convicted you'll still be out in eight." Her voice turned cool. "In other words, you don't die there. At least if you're careful."

"What new evidence," Paget asked quietly, "does Brooks have in mind?"

"I've no idea."

Paget thought for a moment. "This loophole about 'new evidence' bothers me. Do you think you can get Brooks to drop that? It's an excuse for him to gin something up and welsh."

There was a long silence; Paget could imagine Caroline in her office, wondering why he had asked the question. "If you're worried about new evidence," she said quietly, "you take the deal right now. Plead guilty, serve your eight years, and be done with it."

Paget gazed in at Carlo. In the light of his desk lamp, Carlo was poised at the computer, pretending to write about Ted Williams. Eight years, Paget thought. He would be fifty-four, and Carlo twenty-four. They would still have time.

"I'll take my chances," he said at last. "I figure Victor will be through in four more days. Let's see how we feel then."

Caroline swiveled her leather chair, staring out the office window at the skyline of the city at night—darkened towers, black glass, grids of light where someone worked late, high above the city. Only her desk lamp was on: at times like this she remembered growing up in New England—a girl who loved books and sailing and walks on the beach—and thought of how she had become who she was now, an ambitious yet prideful lawyer, the woman whom McKinley Brooks had called the cat who walks alone.

It might have been different, she knew. Less ambition, less solitude. But she had made her choice years ago: it was only at night, when the minutes slowed and a room grew quiet, that she wondered.

What untamed impulse, Caroline thought suddenly, had moved her to defend this case?

No good would come of what she had done, this treacherous game with Brooks, unless it was good for Chris Paget. Of course, that was what lawyers were *supposed* to do, protect their clients and not themselves. But how many really did that, let alone with the ruthlessness she had used on Brooks. Somewhere, James Colt had her name on a list; if Chris took Brooks's deal and Colt survived, she would have an important enemy for life.

Perhaps she had done all this, Caroline decided finally, simply because Chris Paget, who seemed so much like her, had let people into his life. With a fierceness she did not quite understand, Caroline did not wish for him to lose that.

It was not that she believed him innocent; Caroline had wavered on that question and did not choose to dwell on it. When her thoughts escaped her vigilance, she could not believe that Chris would be so stupid as to try to fake a suicide and yet leave fingerprints behind, or so blinded by hate that he could not find a better way to destroy Ricardo Arias than to kill him. Everything she knew about Chris bespoke a mind that moved coolly toward whatever it was that he wanted: the fact that what he most wanted was a life with his son, and with Teresa Peralta, made murdering Richie seem unthinkable. . . .

What new evidence? Paget had asked her.

Replaying his question, Caroline felt certain that there *was* something else out there and that Chris knew what it was. *That* would explain why Chris had insisted on rushing to trial in the face of conventional wisdom. Which could make him a killer with an unusually clear head.

But she would expect such a man to take his coolness all the way and testify. For although the law would not allow Salinas to say so, Chris's refusal to testify was the act of a guilty man, and a guilty man wishing to seem innocent would find a way to speak on his own behalf. And Christopher Paget knew this.

For a moment, Caroline wondered again if Terri had murdered her husband and that *this* was what Chris knew.

Those damned fingerprints.

There was a knock on Caroline's door. "Come in," she called. Teresa Peralta stood in the doorway.

Softly, Terri closed the door behind her. In the light-and-shadow of Caroline's office, she looked somehow remote. "Did you ask Monk those questions I gave you?" Terri asked.

Caroline nodded. "Yes."

"Good." Terri walked closer to the light. "Because I have an answer for you. The one Monk *didn't* have."

Caroline looked up at her. Quietly, she asked, "Is it the truth?"

TEN

WHEN TERRI TOOK the witness stand, she turned to Christopher Paget and smiled.

It was a good smile, hopeful and loving and filled with confidence in the man she gazed at. But the smile was for the jury: like Caroline and Paget himself, his lover had become an actress.

"They're looking at you," Caroline whispered.

Paget contrived a smile of his own. The jury could not know how it felt to remember Terri grinning across the table amid the gardens at the Splendido, just before the concierge appeared with Rosa's message. And then Terri turned, hands folded and shoulders squared, to await Salinas's questions.

She had taken care with her appearance. Gone was the crisp, almost severe look of the young professional woman; today Terri wore gold earrings, her makeup was applied with special care, and her black dress was simple but a little softer. The effect was to make her prettiness and youth more obvious, her poise a little less so. Paget was quite certain that she had discussed all this with Caroline; he was not sure what else they had discussed.

But only Paget, he was confident, knew that Terri's folded hands were a sign of nerves.

She turned to him once more: for a fleeting moment, she looked serious and sad. And then she smiled again for the jury, fingers tightening a little more, and Paget silently wished her luck.

Quickly, Salinas cut to the core. "How long, Ms. Peralta, did you know Ricardo Arias?"

Terri's voice was quiet but clear. "Nine years."

"How many years did you live together?"

"Over seven. And married for six."

"And your daughter is *how* old?"

Terri gave him a level look. "Six."

Salinas's voice rose slightly. "During all those years, did Mr. Arias ever discuss the possibility of suicide?"

"No."

"Did you ever suggest to *anyone*, in words or substance, that Mr. Arias might kill himself?"

Terri was still quiet. "No."

She was making a good witness, Paget thought; not sparring with Salinas, her dignity a contrast to the way he used his voice to underscore a point.

"Did you ever see or hear anything which, in your mind, raised the concern that Mr. Arias might take his own life?"

Terri seemed to consider this. "That's so hard to say, Mr. Salinas. I came to believe that my former husband was emotionally unstable. I'm not sure I wanted to think about everywhere that might lead." She paused. "Do you remember the poem they made us read in high school, 'Richard Cory'? It was about a wealthy man who seems to have everything and then shoots himself for reasons no one can explain. That poem came back to me when a law school classmate killed himself, and I realized that we can never really look into anyone else's heart. Even when we tell ourselves we know everything about them."

Paget could feel the simple beauty of the answer even before Luisa Marin leaned forward, turning her face to Terri. But Paget knew that Terri had rehearsed these words with Caroline; his only question was whether her last sentence was about Paget himself.

Salinas had stopped to look at her. "Did you speak to Ricardo Arias the night before you left for Italy?"

"Yes."

"For what reason?"

"To beg him to let me raise Elena—in person, if I could. I was scared for her, Mr. Salinas."

The answer, with its faint reproach, reminded the jury that Terri was a mother. Marian Celler gave her a look of sympathy: by exposing Richie's inner life, Paget realized, Caroline had earned Terri a measure of compassion.

Salinas looked unruffled. "And how did he respond?"

"That he had an 'appointment' that night and couldn't see me."

"Did he say with whom?"

Terri rearranged her hands. "No. But he made it sound like a date."

"Did he sound depressed or discouraged?"

"No." Terri raised her head, looking directly at Salinas. "But as I understand you've developed in this trial, Richie hid things. From his mother, his psychologist, Elena's teacher, from me—even, I think, from himself. As you've also developed, he was emotionally disturbed." She paused and then spread her hands in a gesture of helplessness. "Really, there's no fair answer to your question."

Paget saw Salinas consider moving to strike Terri's answer and then decide that she was still too sympathetic. "She's doing well," Paget whispered. But Caroline, eyes narrow with thought, did not respond.

"Did you believe," Salinas came back, "that Mr. Arias was emotionally disturbed at the time you lived with him?"

Terri regarded him calmly. "Only at the end," she said, "when I knew I should try to get Elena away from him."

It was another good answer, Paget thought, making the jury see Terri as a mother instead of Paget's lover, eager to desert her husband.

"In all of those years," Salinas asked crisply, "did you ever know him to write a letter in his own hand?"

Terri hesitated; Paget saw her deciding to concede the point. "No."

"Even a short note?"

"Not that I remember."

"You're familiar with the contents of the note found with the body, correct?"

"Yes, I am."

"Did you ever hear Richie describe himself as 'selfish and pathetic'?"

Terri shook her head. "No."

"And he certainly didn't on the night you last spoke to him, correct?"

Quite deliberately, it seemed to Paget, Terri unclasped her fingers. "That's correct."

Salinas had a rhythm now. "You also had plans to dine with Mr. Paget, true?"

"Yes."

"Which he canceled."

"Chris called me, to say that he was sick. He certainly *sounded* bad. So I decided not to make him feel guilty." Terri paused. "I'm sure I could have, Mr. Salinas. And then he would have taken me to dinner, and none of us would be here."

"Move to strike," Salinas promptly said to Lerner. "Unresponsive. I understand Ms. Peralta's sympathies, Your Honor. But I begin to see a pattern of tacking speeches onto whatever truthful answers don't help Mr. Paget."

"Not speeches," Caroline retorted. "Explanations. The sense of Ms. Peralta's answer is that *she* let Mr. Paget off the hook on dinner."

Lerner nodded. "I'm going to deny the motion." He turned to Terri. "But please confine your answer to a fair response to Mr. Salinas's question."

"Of course, Your Honor." Terri's expression was grave and puzzled; it suggested that it had never occurred to her to quarrel with Salinas. "Sometimes 'yes' or 'no' isn't really the right answer, that's all."

The remark was delivered with such innocence that Lerner, who knew better, smiled before saying to Salinas, "You may continue, Counselor."

"How did Mr. Paget seem the next morning?" Salinas asked promptly.

"Tired. But all right."

Salinas put his hands on his hips. "And between seeing him that morning and his phone call the night before, you don't really know where Mr. Paget was, do you?"

For the first time, Terri looked nettled. "I know what he told me."

"But you have no firsthand knowledge, do you?"

"No," Terri said softly. "But Chris is *not* a liar. Or a murderer. Which is what this is all about, isn't it?"

The simple statement of faith seemed to throw Salinas off. But before he could move to strike, Terri added with equal quiet, "I apologize, Mr. Salinas. I needed to say what I know in my heart."

Suddenly there was nothing that Salinas could do. For the first time today, Joseph Duarte had looked up from his notes.

"When you went to Italy," Salinas asked abruptly, "did you try to contact Richie?"

Terri folded her hands again. "Yes. No one answered."

"For how long?"

"Two or three days." Terri glanced at the jury. "I thought he was avoiding me. It was the kind of thing he *would* do."

"Did you call the school?"

"No. I called my mother and found out that Richie had never picked up Elena."

"Did you also tell your mother not to call the police?"

"Yes." Terri's voice was level. "Elena was happy with my mother, and Richie and I were in a custody fight. I didn't want to make him seem more responsible than he was."

For the first time, Salinas looked openly disbelieving. "Had Mr. Arias *ever* failed to pick up Elena?"

"No."

Joseph Duarte made a note. Salinas's tone sharpened. "This was *also* two weeks before the hearing on Mr. Arias's motion, correct?"

"That's true."

"To keep Elena from going near Mr. Paget and his son."

"Yes."

"Because he had accused Carlo Paget of molesting *your* daughter."

Salinas was firing his questions now. Paget saw Terri decide to slow him, taking her time to answer. "Yes," she said quietly. "Richie said that about Carlo."

"And with all of that, Ms. Peralta, did you have any concrete reason to believe that Ricardo Arias would start blowing off his custodial time?"

Terri's gaze was steady. "He hadn't in the past. Really, I didn't know what to think."

Salinas stared at her now. "Isn't what happened that Mr. Paget asked you *not* to find him?"

Yes, Paget answered silently. "I really don't remember that," Terri said. "It was *my* decision."

"Your decision," Salinas repeated softly. "Because you were afraid that your lover had murdered your husband."

Silence. "No," Terri said tightly. "I've never thought that."

She clasped her fingers again. "No?" Salinas asked. "Just how *did* Mr. Paget feel about Mr. Arias?"

"At first? I don't know. Later, Chris despised him. But not as much as I did."

Abruptly, Salinas changed subjects. "How long have you known Mr. Paget?"

For the first time in a while, Terri glanced at Paget; for Paget, the moment was shadowed with the untruths she had already told. "A year and a half," Terri said softly.

"And when did you become romantically involved with Mr. Paget?"

"A year ago, almost." Turning back to Salinas, Terri added pointedly, "After I left Richie."

Salinas gave her a skeptical smile. "How long 'after,' Ms. Peralta? 'A year ago' is cutting it pretty close."

Terri gave him a cool look. "Three weeks after, I would say. I can date it from the day I lost interim custody."

"So let's see. Within three weeks, you left your husband, lost custody of your daughter, and commenced an affair with your boss."

Terri stared at him. "You have a knack, Mr. Salinas, for making the most painful things in my life sound cheap. The only thing you've got right is the chronology."

"How did that happen, then—your involvement with Mr. Paget? Did you just happen to fall into bed one night?"

"No." Terri seemed to make herself be patient. "It wasn't like that."

"It also wasn't like he'd never touched you before."

"Do something," Paget whispered to Caroline.

"I can't." Caroline's voice was flinty. "I refuse to make this worse for you."

"No," Terri said quietly. "Chris had touched me."

"And kissed you."

"Yes."

"And when did *that* first happen?"

Terri sat back. "A few days after I left Richie."

"Getting closer, aren't we? Isn't it a fact that you were sleeping with Mr. Paget *before* you left Ricardo Arias?"

Paget could feel the jury watching Terri with newly withheld sympathy. "No," Terri answered firmly.

"Didn't Mr. Paget *ask* you to leave your husband?"

Terri sat straighter. "You really don't understand, Mr. Salinas. Chris never said or did anything. I thought the feeling I had for Chris was only *mine*, and I didn't even know *that* much until a few days after I left Richie." She glanced at Paget again, finishing softly: "Then I told Chris that I cared for him, and saw that it had happened to us both."

"Isn't it true that Mr. Arias accused you and Mr. Paget of having an affair?"

"Yes," Terri answered simply. "Just as he accused Carlo Paget of molesting our daughter."

Salinas stopped for a moment. Paget could see the jury consider anew that Ricardo Arias might be a liar; Marian Celler whispered something to Joseph Duarte, who nodded. And then Salinas was back again, holding a scrap of paper in the air. "In fact, Ms. Peralta, didn't Mr. Arias accuse you and Mr. Paget in the *Inquisitor?*"

"Yes." Terri's voice filled with disgust. "For ten thousand dollars. I guess that's the going rate for exploiting a child."

"How did that affect you and Mr. Paget?"

"We were both furious."

"And was that one of the reasons Mr. Paget changed his plans to run for senator?"

"No." Terri turned to Paget with a look of affection. "Chris was willing to give up politics, for me and for Elena. If you're trying to suggest that politics drove Chris to murder, you don't understand him at all."

Salinas looked annoyed. "But Mr. Arias also accused the defendant's son of molesting Elena. How did Mr. Paget receive *that?*"

"He was angry but calm. We both talked to Carlo. Not only did Carlo deny it, but he said that he'd face a trial before he'd let Richie use him to keep me from Elena." She turned to Paget again. "I think Chris was proud of that."

Salinas kept boring in. "What about the hearing on Richie's motion," he snapped. "He'd filed the papers under seal, had he not?"

"Yes."

"And, in them, charged Carlo Paget with molesting Elena."

"Yes."

"And *Christopher* Paget with taking you away."

"Yes."

"In fact, Mr. Arias told you that unless you gave up Elena, it was going to a hearing."

Terri's head bobbed. "Yes."

"And Mr. Paget knew all that, correct? Because you read these papers together."

Terri paused. "Yes. We did."

Once more, Paget felt himself ensnared by Richie's plans, now the motive for a charge of murder. "And wasn't that hearing scheduled," Salinas said, "four *days* after your return from Italy?"

"That's true."

"At which time all these charges would become public."

Terri folded her hands, looking steadily back at Salinas. "They would, yes."

"Mr. Paget knew that Carlo would have had to testify."

"Probably. Yes."

"And he knew that the charges about his *own* conduct with you would be open to the press."

"He understood that too."

"Did you discuss with Mr. Paget the possibility that his career in politics would end?"

Terri paused again. "Chris thought that it might. As I said, that wasn't as important to him as the people in his life."

"Speaking of the people in his life, Mr. Paget was also aware that the court might order you to keep Elena from Mr. Paget and his son. Because you discussed it with him."

"Again, the answer is yes." Terri was angry now. "We faced all of that."

"Did it damage your relationship?"

Terri started to say something and then stopped herself. "It was hard, Mr. Salinas."

"So hard that you talked about breaking up?"

Terri's shoulders drew in. "Yes," she finally answered quietly.

"Who initiated that discussion?"

"I did." She turned to look at Paget. "I love Chris. I didn't want him to go through all that because of me. And now he is."

* * *

Turning from Chris, Terri saw the faces of the jury, looking back at her with doubt and sympathy. She could see them all—the jury, the gallery of gawkers, the press corps, making their judgments day by day. How could she ever tell the jury how Chris had seemed to her then.

"It was Chris who changed my mind," she said to the jury, "in Italy. He told me that he loved me and that our future together was worth whatever he'd go through—"

"This was in Portofino," Salinas interrupted.

She turned to him; Salinas's face—the bright eyes, the mustache, the zealot's animation—filled the screen of her mind. Her palms, twisting together, felt damp.

"Yes."

"Eight days *after* you last spoke to Mr. Arias."

It was like being paralyzed, Terri thought; she could see where he was going but do nothing to stop him.

"Yes."

"Eight days *after*, according to the medical examiner, someone had murdered Ricardo Arias."

"You don't understand. Chris believed Richie was alive." Her voice rose. "All through Italy, we worried about staying together. Chris wasn't himself—"

"Just like a man who had killed someone?"

"*Objection.*" Caroline rose to her full height. "Even if that question weren't harassment, which it is, it can't be answered in any factual way. To paraphrase the court, it's an accusation in the form of a question."

"Sustained." Lerner's voice seemed to come from above Terri and from a distance. "Move on, Mr. Salinas."

Salinas came closer. "Wasn't the purpose of your trip to Italy to decide the fate of your relationship?"

"Possibly. Yes."

"And as of the night before you left, when you last spoke to Mr. Arias, you and Mr. Paget didn't know whether you would stay together?"

With piercing sadness, Terri remembered how that felt. "No. We didn't."

"And then, eight days later, Mr. Paget proposed that you get married."

"Yes."

Salinas smiled a little. "To your knowledge, had anything happened to make life better for you?"

"Yes. Chris and I had talked things through."

"But then, later that same day, you found that your husband had been dead for at least a week."

"Yes."

"And suddenly you had custody of Elena, *and* you were free of Richie, *and* Mr. Paget's career was still viable, *and* Carlo Paget was off the hook, *and* Richie's charges were sealed away. All true?"

"Yes. But not the way we wanted."

"No? Tell me, Ms. Peralta, how did Mr. Paget react to the news of your husband's death?"

Terri could feel Chris watching her. In a calm voice, she answered, "He was shocked and appalled. Chris is not the kind of man who would wish a death on anyone."

"Wouldn't you agree that Richie's death solved a lot of problems?"

It was time, Terri thought. She felt an almost unnatural calm come over her. "For one of us," she said to Salinas. "As terrible as it is, at least I got Elena back. Unlike Chris, whose son faces these charges *because* of Richie's death; whose political career *is* over now; who, if he loses this trial, will never live with me, or Carlo, or anyone. Who will never have the second child he wants." She turned to the jury, voice soft and clear. "If Richie wanted to hurt Chris deeply—and he did—the cruelest thing he could have done is to die the way he did. It's so senseless to think that Chris would bring all this on himself, on Carlo—"

"Move to strike," Salinas cut in crisply.

"You asked for this," Terri shot back, and then went on in a flat, calm voice. "*You*, and the district attorney. You *asked* me if Richie's death solved a lot of problems. However awful it was, it may have, but only for *me*. I have a far deeper motive than Chris ever did. But I don't fit the plan, do I? I mean, the district attorney doesn't care about *me* any more than he cares about Richie." Her voice grew hard. "This was always about Chris. You've always known it, I've always known it, and Inspector Monk always knew it. And that's why it ended the way it has."

Salinas turned from her. In a calm, cold voice, he repeated, "Move to strike, Your Honor."

When Caroline stood, Lerner held up a hand. "Ms. Peralta's answer was wholly responsive." He said to Salinas, "You *did* ask for it, until her final comments regarding the district attorney and his motives." Lerner turned to the jury, saying, "You will ignore Ms. Peralta's remarks about District Attorney Brooks," and then faced Terri. "And *you*, Ms. Peralta, will not repeat them."

"Yes, Your Honor," Terri said, and now Salinas came after her.

"Did *you* kill Ricardo Arias?" he snapped.

Terri did not answer for a long moment; Salinas looked disconcerted, as if expecting a quick and angry denial. "No," she said. "I did not."

"And yet you also tell us that you don't believe that Mr. Paget killed your husband."

"I *don't* believe that, Mr. Salinas."

Salinas smiled. "Has Mr. Paget discussed with you whether he went to Mr. Arias's apartment?"

He's setting up the fingerprints, Terri thought. "Yes."

"And what did he tell you?"

"That he had never been there."

"You intend to testify for the defense, do you not, that Mr. Paget is a truthful person?"

"Yes. I do."

Salinas looked almost pleased. "And if you were to learn that he *had* been to Richie's apartment, and lied to you, would that affect your belief as to Mr. Paget's honesty?"

How close would he come? Terri wondered. "That's hypothetical," she said. "Chris would never lie to me."

"But what if he *had*?"

Terri felt herself tense, and her voice seemed to come from a distance. "A lot of people lie, Mr. Salinas, for whatever reason. Far fewer people kill someone else. And Christopher Paget is far too gentle to kill."

Salinas's smile became cynical. "Of course. Just as he's far too honest to ever lie to you." He turned to Judge Lerner, saying in a dismissive voice, "No further questions."

Salinas, Terri thought, had gone for it. As she had thought he would.

Terri saw Caroline Masters smile as she rose, a slight narrowing of the eyes. Only Chris looked far away.

The first part, Terri knew, would be the simplest.

Caroline stood by Chris, as if to draw the jury's eyes to him. "You mentioned, Ms. Peralta, that Chris Paget would never do anything that would separate him from Carlo. I take it that you've had occasions to see Chris as a father."

Terri nodded. "Many times. It was one of the first things that drew me to him."

Salinas stood. "I'm going to object to this line of questioning. What kind of father Chris Paget may or may not be is irrelevant to whether he killed Ricardo Arias. And the time for character testimony is when the defense puts on its case."

"Why wait?" Caroline said to Lerner. "Ms. Peralta is here right now. As for relevance, the prosecution has suggested that Chris Paget was so inflamed by Mr. Arias's charges against Carlo that he murdered him. Our point is the precise opposite: that Chris's devotion to Carlo is a compelling motive *not* to murder anyone. And, equally important, that Ms. Peralta knows Mr. Paget as a gentle and loving person."

"Overruled," Lerner said promptly. "Motive works both ways, Mr. Salinas. As does character. And there's no point in bringing Ms. Peralta back later."

"Thank you," Caroline said, and turned to Terri. "What kind of father *is* Chris Paget?"

Turning to the jury, Terri smiled a little. "Chris is a great dad, patient and kind, and any woman who spends time with Chris has to accept that Carlo comes first. Carlo plays three sports, and Chris goes to all of his games. Except when Chris is in trial, they eat together every night. Chris reads his term papers, takes him on trips. They're both crazy about the Giants." She looked directly at Marian Celler, the mother of two successful children. "Chris told me once that as a father, he didn't have a moment to waste. Carlo is the center of Chris's life—the person who, in the end, Chris loves most in all the world."

Marian Celler gazed back at Terri; the small smile on her face, that of one parent for another, seemed tinged with reminiscence.

"And how," Caroline was asking, "did Chris react to Richie's charge against Carlo?"

"As I suggested, he was filled with contempt for Richie." Terri realized that she had folded her hands again; the subject of Elena was too personal and painful. "But Chris's ultimate feeling was that life is unfair and that a measure of Carlo's courage was how well he faced up to Richie." Her voice grew quiet. "What he said was that Carlo would be forced to learn character, because Richie had none."

Caroline nodded. "Did you have *any* sense that Richie's charges would drive Chris Paget to violence?"

"I can't imagine it. There's no way that Richie drove him to murder. He intended to use the legal process to vindicate his son." Terri turned to the jury again, giving the answer that she and Caroline had formulated. "That's why he came to public attention in the first place: by seeing the process through, even over the opposition of a President. Chris's entire life is a search for truth, through law and the courts, as an *alternative* to violence."

Caroline waited for a moment, letting Terri's words resonate with the jury. "What kind of friend is Chris?"

"The best friend I've ever had." Terri faced the jury again. "Before I knew how I felt about him, I knew what kind of man he was. Chris was great to work for—interested, encouraging, concerned. He asked about Elena a lot and seemed to worry that work might hurt my marriage to Richie." Speaking to Joseph Duarte, her voice grew firm. "Chris never, ever crossed the line with me. If he had, I would never have come to love him."

"When you became involved, whose initiative was it?"

"Mine, completely." Terri raised her head. "Chris wanted me to be sure about my marriage and be certain that I cared for him for the right reasons. I think he worried that I was too upset to know what I was doing, and that he was too old for me."

For the first time, Caroline moved forward. "Mr. Salinas," she said quietly, "seemed deeply concerned with determining when you and Chris Paget became lovers. How did that happen?"

In a trial, Terri thought, there is nothing private. "I came to *him*," she said simply, "the day after I lost custody of Elena. When Richie fooled the court into believing that I'd asked him to be the caretaking parent.

"I was devastated. But throughout it all, Chris had been the one good thing in my life. The next day, even with all the pain, I knew I wanted him. I waited for night, and I told him that. He was wonderful to me." However hard to say this aloud, Terri realized, it was good to remember. "Chris never tried to make me fall in love with him. He never tried to take me from Richie. He never offered me anything but kindness." Terri's voice grew quiet. "That was enough."

Caroline tilted her head. "And when you were in Italy, and worried about your future together, did Chris seem like a man who knew Ricardo Arias was dead?"

"No." Terri looked straight at Joseph Duarte. "I know Chris, and he's not that good an actor. For Chris, Richie was still alive."

"And during those eight days together in Italy, from the morning he picked you up until the afternoon you learned that Mr. Arias had died, did you observe *any* sign that Chris Paget had been in a struggle?"

Terri found it best to look at Caroline. "No," she said flatly.

"Did you ever know Chris Paget to own a gun?"

Terri shook her head. "Chris despised guns. That was a lot of why he ran for the Senate, to stop the flow of guns. He thought all the violence was so senseless."

Terri felt Joseph Duarte study her: but what about the fingerprints, she imagined him saying in the jury room, and then Caroline asked, "How do you feel about Chris Paget now?"

When Terri turned, there was a shadow on Chris's face. She looked directly at Caroline Masters. "I love him. But I'm testifying about the *reasons* that I love him, not testifying *because* I love him. There's a difference." She turned to Luisa Marin, finishing quietly: "Because I could never love a man whom I believed to be a murderer."

Luisa's gaze met hers. *Believe* me, Terri thought, please. "That's what I regret most," Terri added softly. "That by loving Chris, I brought these troubles to his door."

For a moment, somewhere in Marin's eyes, Terri thought she saw her answer. And then Caroline asked softly, "Including rug fibers?"

Terri turned to her. "Yes. Including rug fibers."

At the prosecution table, Victor Salinas had suddenly tensed. "Is it your belief," Caroline was asking, "that *you* tracked fibers from Richie's carpet into Chris's bedroom?"

"Yes. Because that was where we stayed together." Terri paused a moment. "Sometimes, after dropping Elena with Richie, I would go to Chris's. It was hard to be alone then."

Caroline moved still closer. "The police *also* found carpet fibers on the driver's side of Chris's car. Can you explain that?"

"Yes." Terri turned to Duarte again. "I'd never driven a Jaguar before. So Chris let me drive his car."

"Often?"

"Several times. Including after visiting Richie."

"And did Chris also visit your apartment?"

Salinas, Terri saw, was resting his chin on his hand, as if trying to divine where Caroline's questions were going. But unless he was much more prescient than most, he would still believe that this was all about rug fibers.

"We were a couple," Terri answered. "Chris came to my apartment quite a lot."

At the corner of her vision, Terri saw Chris's eyes narrow. Perhaps in doubt, perhaps in understanding. As if to bewilder Salinas, Caroline switched subjects abruptly.

"Did Mr. Arias have an answering machine?"

"Yes." Terri made herself sound very calm. "That was one of the frustrations of calling from Italy—he'd switched his machine off."

"To your knowledge, how long had Mr. Arias used this machine?"

Terri folded her hands. "This particular machine? About two months."

Salinas was very still now; Terri sensed that he knew that something was awry but was not quite sure what. "Do you happen to know," Caroline asked almost casually, "where Mr. Arias acquired this machine?"

Terri nodded. "From me."

"And where did you get it?"

Terri turned to Salinas now; she reminded herself of the police this man had sent to question Elena, and then, softly, she answered, "From my apartment. I gave it to Richie when I got a new one."

Salinas, Terri saw with satisfaction, looked as if he had been shot.

Caroline spoke in the same quiet voice. "And do you know, Ms. Peralta, how Mr. Paget's fingerprints came to be on that machine?"

"Yes." Terri now spoke to Salinas. "I'm quite sure that Chris touched the machine while it was still in my apartment. As I said, he was there all the time."

Was that even possible? Paget wondered.

It had stunned him. On the stand, Terri stared straight at Salinas as the prosecutor walked toward her.

One thing was certain, Paget knew. He had not been there "all the time" but, at most, a handful of times: he could never visit Terri while Elena was with her, and when the little girl was not, Paget as Carlo's parent would not leave his son alone for the night. The pattern of single-parent romance, dictated by children.

"You *knew*," Paget whispered to Caroline.

She gave him a sideways look. "Is anything wrong?"

When Paget did not answer, Caroline picked up her pen, ready to take notes.

"*Why,*" Salinas demanded of Terri, "have you never said this before? About the answering machine."

"No one asked me." Terri folded her hands. "And everything you have asked me, Mr. Salinas, has been twisted and distorted. You tore up my house, interrogated my six-year-old daughter, suppressed evidence about the money Richie had." Her voice rose. "I didn't come to you, Mr. Salinas, because you and your office don't care about the truth...."

"Didn't you want to clear Mr. Paget's name?" Salinas asked angrily. "Or were you waiting to give that little speech?"

Terri looked quite composed now. "I didn't know what your evidence was. *If* you had told me about Chris's prints on the machine, I *might* have told you how they got there. But you never asked."

Salinas looked rattled now. "Are you telling me, Ms. Peralta, that you never discussed these fingerprints with Mr. Paget?"

Terri smiled. "Let me rephrase that for you. Not only am I *telling* you that I never discussed the prints with Chris, but it's *true*. Which is all that Chris ever said to me about testifying—to tell the truth." Her smile faded. "You've made me a witness against the man I love and want to marry. We practice law together: any other case, and we'd be talking all the time. But Chris didn't want to do or say *anything* that looked like influencing my testimony. So for the last three months, while Chris went through this nightmare, we couldn't even talk about it. You can't imagine, Mr. Salinas, how hard that's been. But we've stuck to it." Her voice turned cold. "If you think Chris asked me to lie for him, you're mistaken. But it's not nearly as big a mistake as this whole miserable prosecution."

Eyes narrowing, Caroline Masters put down her pen. Softly, she murmured, "Victor's fucked."

ELEVEN

THE NEXT MORNING, Carlo Paget took the stand.

He wore a white shirt, a blue blazer, and one of his father's floral ties—he himself did not have much interest in ties, and his father's taste in clothes, he had once remarked, was much better than his taste in music. Taking the oath, he smiled uncomfortably at Paget and then stopped looking at anyone; in this formal setting, there were still traces of the awkward boy whose shirttail might come out. Circles were visible beneath his eyes; the night before, Paget had heard Carlo stirring in his room in the early-morning hours, unable to sleep. Helpless, Paget cursed himself for this moment, and then Salinas began.

After a few preliminaries, Salinas asked him abruptly, "Do you know Elena Arias?"

"She's Terri's daughter." Carlo paused, and then added, "She used to bring her to our house."

It had started. Salinas would try to legitimize Richie's "concerns," Paget knew, while making the possibility of molestation real enough to be Paget's motive. All that Paget could hope for was that Caroline had prepared Carlo well and that he would keep his poise.

"And did she sometimes *leave* Elena with you?" Salinas asked.

Carlo, Paget thought, looked paler. "Sometimes."

Speak up, Paget told him silently.

Salinas moved forward. "What did you do with her?"

Humor a child, Paget thought, while the adults gave them both a benign smile and turned their attention to each other.

"Mostly we played games," Carlo answered. "Whatever she wanted. Sometimes I took her out for ice cream, and once or twice to the park."

"Were you ever alone?"

"Hardly ever. My dad would be there, and Terri." His voice became stronger. "Sometimes my girlfriend too."

I'm not some pervert, Paget remembered him telling Terri—I have a girlfriend. Paget could not easily imagine the hardship for a sixteen-year-old boy, dealing with the deepening pulse of his own sexuality, accused of molesting a child. He could feel the weight of the courtroom on Carlo, the scrutiny of the jury.

"But you *were* alone with her," Salinas prodded.

Carlo squared his shoulders. "Only a few times. Maybe three or four."

"Did Elena ever kiss you?"

Carlo looked down. "Sure. Little kids do that stuff."

"Did you ever kiss *her*?"

Carlo seemed to wince, as if at the pounding of a headache. "Like you do to a *kid*, maybe. On the forehead."

Salinas, Paget noticed, was without theatrics today—his manner grave, his face and voice unchanging. Quietly, he asked, "Did you ever see Elena naked?"

Carlo's eyelids dropped, as if the moment he dreaded had arrived; to Paget, he looked like someone who had received a blow to the stomach. In the jury box, Joseph Duarte—the father of two girls—watched with taut vigilance. "Once," Carlo said. "She asked me to give her a bath."

"Was this the *only* time she asked?"

"Yes."

"And where was her mother?"

"With my dad. At a speech he was giving."

"So the *only* time Elena asked for a bath was one of the *only* times you were alone with her?"

Carlo folded his arms. "I guess so."

Salinas paused, as if disturbed by this coincidence. "Were *you* undressed?" he asked.

Carlo flushed. "No."

Paget turned to Caroline; she touched his arm, gaze fixed on Carlo. "Not *yet*," she whispered.

"Did you touch *her*?" he demanded.

Carlo had begun to look drawn. "Only with a washcloth," he said. "And maybe to help her into my dad's bathtub."

"Who undressed her?"

"*She* did."

"Did you watch?"

"*No.*" Carlo's voice was angry. "She was undressed before I even got there."

Salinas moved forward. Softly, he asked, "Did you touch her genitals, Carlo?"

Paget had to keep himself from standing. "*No,*" Carlo answered.

"Not even with a washcloth?"

"*No.*" Carlo's voice was strained. "You can ask me that a thousand times, and the answer will always be the same. I didn't touch that kid in any way that was bad."

"So that if Elena told her father you'd touched her genitals, she was *lying?*"

"*Objection.*" Caroline sprang out of her chair, turning on Salinas with a look of disgust. "There is no evidence, *anywhere*, that Elena ever said that. Not even *Mr. Arias* made such a claim. Frankly, Mr. Salinas, the biggest perversion I've heard so far is *your* effort to smear a teenage boy so that you can convict his dad of murder."

"That's offensive . . ."

"Really. Then *show* it to me, Victor. Show me where there's *any* basis for the question you just asked." Caroline stepped forward. "Want to take a break to look for it? Because we're all prepared to wait for you."

Lerner's gavel cracked. "That's enough." The judge turned to Salinas. "What's the basis for your question, Counselor?"

Salinas stepped forward. "It was another way of asking if the witness molested Elena Arias."

Lerner leaned over the bench. "Did you hear my question, Mr. Salinas? *What* is your basis?"

Salinas hesitated. Then said, calmly, "None, Your Honor. Other than I just explained."

Lerner stared down at him. Softly, Caroline said, "I'd like an apology, Victor."

He turned to her, angry. "For *what?*"

"Not to me. To Carlo Paget."

Watching, Paget felt his own outrage ease; Caroline was making Salinas pay. "I'll decide who I apologize to," Salinas told her, "and for what. It's certainly not clear *what* this witness did."

But Joseph Duarte, Paget saw, was frowning at Salinas. "Let's move on," Lerner snapped. "Objection sustained. And underlined."

Salinas turned to Carlo. "Did there come a time," he asked in an even voice, "that Mr. Arias filed papers charging you with molesting Elena?"

"Yes." Carlo seemed to have gained strength from Caroline. "He left a copy on my dad's doorstep. So we wouldn't miss it."

"Did you discuss this with your father?"

"Yes. Dad said we should stand up to him."

Salinas gave a first skeptical smile. "But how did *you* feel? You were the one who would have to go to court."

"How did *I* feel?" Carlo's eyes froze with remembered anger. "I thought Elena's father was a scumbag."

Salinas shook his head. "Did you want to go to court?" he prodded.

"No. I don't think *you'd* like being charged with molesting a six-year-old, either." Carlo turned to the jury, his expression wounded and urgent and sincere. "But I was ready to say then, just like I'm telling you right now, that Richie Arias was a liar. I didn't need anyone to say that for me, and I didn't need anyone to kill him, either. All I need is my father back."

"Move to strike as unresponsive," Salinas snapped.

Caroline did not even stand. In a weary voice, she said, "And I move to strike that motion as pathetic."

"Motion denied," Judge Lerner cut in. "Spare us the critiques, Ms. Masters. As for you, Mr. Salinas, perhaps you would have been better off apologizing."

With that, Paget thought, Salinas's punishment was complete. Expressionless again, the prosecutor asked Carlo, "These papers Mr. Arias filed, did you ever read them?"

"No." Carlo looked quite calm now. "My dad read them to me."

Salinas nodded. "When did he tell you that Mr. Arias had charged him with breaking up Ms. Peralta's marriage?"

Carlo darted another quick glance at Paget. "After he was arrested."

"So at the time you discussed with your dad Mr. Arias's charges against you, he didn't tell you that Mr. Arias had also made charges against *him?*"

Carlo seemed to consider this. "I guess my dad didn't want to upset me any more."

"In fact, if he hadn't been arrested, your father might *never* have told you."

"Objection," Caroline called out to Lerner. "Calls for speculation."

"Sustained."

But the point had been made, Paget knew: in ways small and large, Salinas had succeeded in suggesting that Paget was bent on concealment of whatever was inconvenient—from the police, from Terri, and even from his own son. And each question raised about Paget's character would make his failure to testify all the more damaging.

Abruptly, Salinas shifted subjects. "Let's discuss the night before your father went to Italy. You went out, right?"

"That's right."

"Around seven-thirty?"

"Yes."

"Did you tell your dad where you were going?"

Carlo nodded. "Out with friends."

"Does he make it a practice to tell you if *he's* going out?"

"Yes."

"Always?"

"Pretty much."

"And what did he say on *that* night?"

Monk, Paget remembered, had not asked Carlo that question. But Caroline appeared to have prepared him well; almost offhandedly, Carlo answered, "I think he was going out with Terri."

"Did he seem ill?"

Paget felt himself tense. "I really don't remember," Carlo said in a calm voice. "Dad's not much of a complainer."

Salinas seemed to give the boy a second look. "Did you tell your dad when you'd be home?"

Carlo nodded. "Twelve-thirty." His tone turned flat. "I have a curfew."

"When you spoke to your father," Salinas asked, "did you give him reason to *believe* that you'd be home any earlier?"

A moment's hesitation. "No."

Caroline, Paget noted, kept her eyes fixed on Carlo; she had not looked at Paget since the line of questioning began. "And did you return home at twelve-thirty?"

"Yes."

"And was your father home then?"

"Yes."

"How do you know?"

A first slight smile. "He waited up for me. He does that a lot."

"And did he seem sick?"

Another pause. "I couldn't tell. It was dark, and I couldn't see very well. The only light was in the library."

Salinas moved close to the witness stand. "Do you remember what he was wearing?"

"Jeans and a sweater, I think."

"Not a gray suit?"

Carlo hesitated. "No."

"What about when you *left*, at about seven-thirty. Was he wearing a suit then?"

Paget felt himself tense. "I *think* so," Carlo said.

"Do you remember what color?"

"No."

"After midnight, when you came home, did you notice any injuries to your father? Say to his right hand?"

Carlo's face went blank. Paget had known this expression since his son's childhood: Carlo used it when he wished to lie to him, or at least to conceal his thoughts or feelings. "No," Carlo answered tersely.

What, Paget wondered, did Carlo think he had seen? But Salinas could not know Carlo as Paget did. "Between seven-thirty and twelve-thirty," Salinas asked abruptly, "did you return home unexpectedly?"

The jury, Paget realized, had leaned forward with the question. But Carlo's voice was firm now. "Yes. I did."

"When?"

"About eight-thirty."

Salinas had become quiet again, surefooted. "And what were the circumstances?"

"A bunch of us were at a friend's house—Darnell Sheets. We decided to go to a movie, and I realized I'd left my wallet at home. I wanted to take my girlfriend out for a pizza later, so I decided to go home and get it."

Once more, Paget cursed his son's absentmindedness. "Did you see your father?" Salinas asked.

"Physically see him? No."

"Did that concern you?"

"I was in a hurry." Carlo hesitated, then shrugged. "I guess I thought he was out with Terri."

"Where did you find your wallet?" Salinas asked.

"In my bedroom."

Salinas, Paget thought, had his satisfied look. "To get to your room," he asked, "you walk up a central staircase, right?"

"That's right."

"And going to the staircase, you pass the living room and library."

"Yes."

"Was anyone there?"

Carlo folded his arms. "Not that I saw."

"Was it light enough to see someone?"

Another pause. "I think so."

"Your father's bedroom is next to yours, correct?"

"Yes."

"Did you hear anything in your dad's bedroom?"

"I don't think so. I was hurrying."

"Did anyone call out to you?"

"No."

"So at the point you climbed the stairs to your bedroom, you thought no one was home."

Caroline was watching Carlo with new intensity, Paget realized; like Paget himself, she had lost control. "I guess that's what I thought then," Carlo answered finally.

He was tense, Paget saw, hoping to give a helpful answer. "Salinas is going to sandbag him," he whispered.

Caroline's eyes narrowed. "He just has to stick to his statement. He knows that, Chris."

"In fact," Salinas said, "as far as *you* were concerned, no one was home."

"That's not true." Carlo's voice rose in anger. "I told the police I thought I heard a sound. And now that I know my dad was home, I'm sure the sound was him."

Salinas gave a too agreeable nod. "You told Inspector Monk that you thought perhaps you'd heard footsteps, right?"

"I'm sure I did."

"You're sure now?"

"Yes."

"Positive, in fact?"

"Yes."

"*No,*" Paget said under his breath.

Caroline had tensed. Salinas was leaning back a little, as if to look down at Carlo. "Tell me, Carlo, about how long after that night did you give your statement to the police?"

"I don't know. Maybe three weeks."

Salinas walked back to the prosecution table, picking up a piece of paper. "And at *that* time, according to the transcript of your interview with Inspector Monk, you said, *quote,* 'All that I remember is thinking maybe I heard footsteps in the attic, above my room,' *unquote.* Remember that, Carlo?"

Carlo shifted in his chair. "I guess so."

"And now it's about four *months* after that night, correct?"

Next to Paget, Caroline seemed to have stopped breathing. "I guess that's right," Carlo said, and then leaned forward, looking Salinas in the face. "That's a long time, Mr. Salinas, to think about you accusing my dad of murder. It makes remembering things more important. So I've replayed that night in my mind, over and over. I remember walking up the stairs, finding my wallet, and then hearing footsteps in the attic, where Dad and I keep our suitcases." He turned to the jury. "I've thought about it, and now I'm sure. I can hear the footsteps in my mind."

Listening, Paget felt almost sick. And then, as if he could not help himself, Carlo looked to his father for approval.

Paget tried to smile. But when their eyes met, Paget knew that Carlo saw there was something wrong.

"Did you ever tell that to the police?" Salinas asked.

Carlo's eyes flickered, and then he turned to Salinas. "No," he said. "The police never came back."

Salinas gave him a look of skeptical understanding. "Did you tell *anyone?*"

Carlo met Salinas's stare. Paget knew he would not look away now; it was the same trapped steadfast look Paget had first seen when Carlo was seven and he had caught him in a lie. "No," Carlo said.

"Not even your dad?"

Carlo shook his head. "He won't talk to me about the case. Because I'm a witness."

"Then how about his *lawyer*, Carlo?" Salinas pointed toward Caroline. "You know Ms. Masters, don't you?"

"Yes." Carlo hesitated. "We didn't talk about it, exactly. I knew I'd get a chance to say things here."

"In other words, you just decided to save it for the trial."

Carlo stared at him. "You asked me, and I just answered. It's the truth."

Paget felt cold inside. "Then you must have considered calling the police," Salinas said smoothly.

Carlo looked puzzled; it was the difference, Paget thought, between a normal person and a lawyer who could see the traps before they shut. "I don't understand," Carlo said.

"You thought your father was with Ms. Peralta, right?"

Carlo blinked. "That's what I *thought*."

"So weren't you concerned about a prowler?"

Carlo looked startled. "I don't remember what I thought, exactly. I was in a hurry."

"Did you happen to mention it to your dad," Salinas asked in a pleasant voice, "the next time you *did* see him?"

Carlo seemed confused now. "I don't think so."

"I don't think so, either, Carlo. Because you made it up, didn't you? To cover for your dad."

Joseph Duarte was giving Carlo a skeptical look. Carlo still met Salinas's gaze. "No," he said. "I'm *not* making it up."

"No? When you came home at twelve-thirty, did you happen to ask your dad how his night was?"

"I don't remember."

"Did he tell you he'd gotten sick and stayed home?"

"I don't remember."

Salinas shook his head. "Or did he simply tell you, Carlo, to come to court and lie for him?"

"No." Carlo's voice filled with anger now. "My dad would *never* ask me to lie."

Carlo, Paget felt, had just lost a piece of himself. A gift for his father.

Salinas shook his head in disbelief, looking from Carlo to Paget. "No further questions."

Beneath the table, Paget touched Caroline's knee. "Get him off of there. *Now.*"

Caroline did not move. "I can't do that to him," she said under her breath. "He'll know then. Do you want to destroy him?"

"Ms. Masters," Judge Lerner was asking.

Caroline turned to Paget with a look of urgency. "There was something that Carlo wants to say. For his sake, let him say it."

Paget looked past her, into the face of his son, looking to his father for cues on how to feel. Smiling at Carlo, Paget whispered to Caroline, "Then make it fast."

Quickly, Caroline was on her feet, moving toward Carlo with an air of confidence. "What kind of father *is* your dad?"

Carlo took a deep breath, as if to relax himself. "A great dad."

Salinas stood at once. "Your Honor, whether Mr. Paget is, or is not, a good father has nothing to do with the murder of Ricardo Arias."

"But it does." Calmly, Caroline addressed Judge Lerner. "In Mr. Salinas's words, it's perfectly all right to accuse Carlo Paget of child abuse without a shred of evidence and then to suggest that those charges drove his father to murder. The least the court can do is permit this boy a chance to say that his father is, in his considerable experience, a devoted father and is neither violent nor a liar. Under the rules both of evidence and of common decency."

Lerner nodded. "I quite agree. Proceed, Ms. Masters."

Caroline turned to Carlo. "Why has Chris been a good father, Carlo?"

"He's always been there." Carlo's voice grew husky and a little raw. "I always knew how important I was to him."

Caroline smiled. "By 'been there,' what do you mean?"

"For school, or my games, or to take me places or talk to." Carlo turned to Joseph Duarte. "It's more than that. He's my dad, that's all. He never loses his temper, and he's always straight with me. I don't know where I'd be without him."

"When did you start living with your dad?"

"When I was seven." Carlo's voice held a trace of wonder. "I was living with my grandparents—my mom's parents. One day Dad just came for me. Ever since, it's been the two of us."

Paget could remember that final day in Boston, scooping Carlo up in the darkened living room of his grandfather Carelli's wretched home, telling Carlo that he was his father, that everything would be all right. "What were things like for you before?" Caroline asked.

It was the wrong question, Paget thought, although only a parent could know that: children with neglectful parents tend to defend them, as a defense against the truth. But to Paget's surprise, Carlo said, "I was pretty young then. But I know it wasn't good."

"Why?"

Carlo looked at Paget. "Because any happy memory I have, my dad is part of."

Salinas was on his feet again. "I realize, Ms. Masters, that Carlo Paget loves his father. If nothing else, he's certainly proven *that*. But we're *very* far afield now."

Caroline turned to Lerner. "With your indulgence, Your Honor, I think I can show relevance."

Lerner nodded. "Go ahead."

Caroline waited for the jury's full attention and then looked at Carlo gravely. "You say that your dad has always been there for you, Carlo. Based on all you've been through together, can you imagine your dad doing *anything* to jeopardize that?"

Only a father, Paget was certain, could notice the look of wounded doubt that moved through Carlo's eyes. It was that which hurt Paget more than anything; he had last seen that look many years ago, on the face of an insecure boy.

Carlo stared straight at Caroline. "No," he said. "I can't imagine it."

TWELVE

WATCHING ELENA ARIAS play with the cloth doll that had supplanted the small plastic figure as "Teresa," Denise Harris sat a few feet away, pondering the black dog of Elena's nightmare.

Elena had never described her dream. But she had wakened screaming the night before, telling Terri for the first time of a black dog that always frightened her. It squared with Harris's best guess: that Elena's repeated nightmare, like Terri's own, was the key to some buried trauma. It was the first clear sense Elena had given that her thoughts were breaking closer to the surface.

Now Elena sat on the rug, playing in a patch of late afternoon sunlight filtering through Harris's window. Her mother sat outside in the waiting area, reading summaries of trial testimony; Harris had thought that Terri looked drained. But on the telephone this morning, Teresa Peralta had sounded intense and determined to get at the meaning of Elena's dream: if there was one thing Denise Harris believed about Terri, it was that she put Elena above everything else. There was nothing Terri would not do, Harris sensed, to give her daughter a normal life.

"Teresa's tired," Elena said of her doll. "She wants to lie down."

It was the kind of thing that a child, enacting normal domestic scenes, would say about a doll when assuming the role of parent. But Elena's voice sounded thin and a little apprehensive; it was as if the scene had shadows that Harris could not see. And after she laid the doll on its back, Elena seemed to think for a moment and then turned it over, face buried in the rug. Almost to herself, she said, "The robbers are outside."

Leaning closer, Harris said, "Maybe she'd like the alligator to sleep in her room."

Elena was silent; it had taken another session for her to accept the presence of the alligator, and the concept of a protective figure still frightened her. Quietly, Harris placed the alligator close to the doll. "Teresa will be safe now," she told Elena. "She can sleep as long as she wants."

Elena's brow furrowed. She reached for the doll; for an instant, Harris thought she felt threatened and would change the form of her play. But all that Elena did was to roll the doll on its back again and smooth its red cloth dress. Darting a glance at Harris, she said, "Teresa's sleeping."

By instinct and experience, Harris did not move. She felt the signs of tension in Elena—the tight voice, her surreptitious look—as the tingling of her own nerves. For what seemed long moments, Elena did nothing at all.

Harris sneaked a look at her wristwatch: in twenty minutes, she had another appointment. But all she could do was wait.

Elena gave her a sideways look, barely seeming to breathe. She was still for a moment and then leaned over the doll, fingers touching the hem of its skirt.

Slowly, Elena lifted the skirt up, above the doll's waist. Her face seemed intent and a little scared.

Silent, she stroked the doll's cloth stomach with two fingers of her hand.

Harris asked, softly, "What's happening?"

Elena seemed to swallow. In a small voice, she answered, "The robber is tickling Teresa's tummy."

Harris waited, watching. Elena's fingers moved imperceptibly downward.

"How does Teresa feel?" Harris asked.

"It feels good." Elena's voice became harder. "Sometimes she likes it. But sometimes she doesn't."

Harris said nothing. Deliberately and methodically, Elena's fingers moved across the stomach of the doll. Her hand did not go lower.

Through the window, Harris's senses registered the sounds of the world outside—cars in the street, a voice calling, the rattle of a gust of wind on glass. But Elena seemed removed from any place but the one she imagined, her eyes smaller, her expression focused. It was the dissociation Terri had described to her, when the Elena she had known since birth seemed almost to disappear.

Harris remained where she was. "When doesn't Teresa like it?"

Elena did not answer. Her fingers stopped moving, resting on the stomach of the doll.

"Is there something special the robber does that Teresa doesn't like?"

Elena stiffened. After a moment, she turned her head from Harris, and her fingers moved again.

With an awful fascination, Harris watched Elena slide one finger between the cloth legs of the doll.

Head averted, Elena stroked softly, rhythmically. "How does Teresa feel?" Harris asked quietly.

"She feels good," Elena said, and then her eyes filled with tears.

Elena's face squinted. Her finger seemed to move on its own.

Gently, Harris picked up the alligator and placed it beside the doll.

Elena's hand stopped moving. "It's all right," Harris said. "The alligator can help her. All Teresa has to do is call."

Elena shook her head. "She *can't*."

Her face was tensed; her eyes were shut. Down one side of her face, Harris saw the tears begin to run.

Harris knew better than to reach for her. She sat there, circumscribed by her profession, as she watched a little girl dissolve before her eyes. And then Elena Arias took the alligator and flung it across the room.

Harris moved next to her. Softly, she asked, "Did someone touch *you* like that, Elena?"

The little girl crossed her arms, turning her back to Harris. Helpless, the psychologist watched her shoulders tremble. It was the reaction Terri had described her having, Harris recalled, when Terri first asked Elena about Carlo.

"Was it Carlo?" Harris asked.

Elena flung herself on the rug, face pressed against it, and covered her ears.

"The California roll was good," Carlo said.

It was merely something to say, Paget knew; his son did not require an answer. They sat on the Persian rug in the library, with plates of sushi scattered across the marble coffee table. Returning from court, they had decided to order sushi in; somehow neither of them felt up to having other people watch them eat. Paget felt sadness take up residence inside him; the words of thanks he had given Carlo sounded hollow, even to him, and the half pitcher of martinis he had drained seemed like an act of cowardice.

There were times, he had learned, when it fell to a father to lie to his son, or for him. But he had never imagined the moment when Carlo would lie for *him*. Without meaning to, he had taught his son moral compromise; the lesson sat there, a silence between them, in a relationship that could never quite be the same. The mistake of a loving heart.

"I'm proud of you," Paget said.

That was not quite a lie, Paget knew, it was an evasion—worse than saying nothing, because it was becoming part of the fabric of their conversations, replacing truths that could not be spoken.

Quietly, Carlo asked, "Do you think they believed me?"

Perhaps about Elena, Paget thought. Not about me. "Yes," he lied again.

What else could he do, Paget thought bleakly: turn to his son and speak the truth? I know you lied, Carlo—it is for that reason, above all, that we can never talk about this trial. It is for that reason that I will never again be for you the person I seemed to be.

But there was, perhaps, something to be salvaged. "You faced up to this thing about Elena, Carlo. You said what happened and backed Salinas down. No one watching could possibly believe you'd hurt a little girl like that." Paget placed a hand on his son's shoulder. "Really, you were great."

Carlo's gaze, it seemed, had lit on his father's martini pitcher. "But what about you?" he finally asked. "How was I for *you?*"

You were terrible for me, Paget thought. And the worst was not that you looked like you were trying to save me. The worst is that I *know* you were. "You helped me, son. Piece by piece, Caroline is chipping away at this case."

Never mind that, next to Paget, Caroline was the most surprised person in the courtroom when Carlo, stubborn in his love for a father, had acted on his own. Frowning, Carlo still did not look at him. "I couldn't do that much for you," he said. "But once *you* testify, it'll be fine."

It was time, Paget knew; he had no stomach for more evasions. "*If*

I testify," he said casually. "It all depends on what Caroline and I decide. Once Salinas's case comes in."

Carlo's head snapped up; he looked his father in the face. "How can you not testify, Dad? How can you not *tell* them?"

Two sentences, Paget thought, with so many layers. *I* testified for you, Dad. I *lied* for you, and now I want us to stand together. I want to know you didn't do this. And even if you did, I want you to say you didn't. No matter what, I want you free. The look on his son's face, shocked and shaken, shriveled Paget's soul.

"It's strategy," he said calmly. "If the prosecution hasn't proven its case, you don't give the jury a chance to hate you, or the prosecution a shot at making you look bad. Which Salinas can do with the innocent as well as the guilty."

"You need to *tell* people, Dad. This isn't just about Salinas. It's about everyone."

Most of all, Paget heard Carlo saying, it's about *me*. Because I want to believe you. Watching Carlo's eyes, he saw the boy's sense of his father slipping away.

"You need to tell them," Carlo repeated angrily.

Slowly, Paget shook his head. "I have my own reasons," he answered. "I do things for you, or for me, or for Terri. Not because of what *other* people may think." He touched Carlo's shoulder again. "I didn't need you to testify to know you didn't molest Elena. I knew before you even looked me in the face and told me so. Because I knew *you*."

Carlo stared at him, and then he turned away. "Within this family," Paget said quietly, "there are certain things we know. We know you're not a child molester, and we know I'm not a murderer. And that's what counts."

Perhaps once, Paget thought. Perhaps even yesterday. But through Carlo, more surely than in the courtroom, justice had begun exacting its price. His own son would not look at him.

THIRTEEN

JACK SLOCUM, the political reporter, was a slight, sandy-haired man with sharp features, an assertive manner, and a voice that managed to be at once thin and scratchy. There was something unhealthy about him: his skin was pallid, his beard spotty, and his posture slumped; it was easy to imagine him in a bar or coffee shop, trading information and smoking a cigarette. The most lively thing about him was his eyes: he watched Victor Salinas—whose witness he was—with the wary calculation of a man gauging each question for hidden angles. To Paget, he looked untrusting and untrustworthy, a man in his thirties who had already earned his face. Paget loathed him on sight.

"What a little ferret," he murmured to Caroline.

She leaned closer. "This particular little ferret," she said, "is about to give you another motive for killing Richie. This time it's politics."

Slocum had not come willingly. Through the lawyer for his newspaper, he had claimed that his testimony was not relevant and would jeopardize his sources. But Salinas had asserted that Slocum was needed to show Paget's outrage at the damage Richie had done to him, political and personal. For reasons of her own, Caroline had not fought this, and Lerner had permitted the testimony within certain limits. In the end, Paget suspected that part of Slocum would enjoy doing harm to his defense.

"And after Mr. Paget began exploring a Senate race," Salinas asked him, "when did you first speak to him?"

"Late summer. I'd seen an article in the *Inquisitor*." Slocum darted a look at the jury. "Mr. Arias accused Mr. Paget of stealing his wife."

"Any why did this article interest you?"

"It raised certain questions about Mr. Paget's character, which I believed he should answer. What kind of people seek public office is an important issue, and private character can tell you a lot."

"And so you called Mr. Paget?"

"I did." Slocum shot Paget a resentful glance. "I told him about the article and gave him the opportunity to comment."

Salinas put his hands in his pockets. "And how did Mr. Paget respond?"

"He was very arrogant. As I recall, he told me that Mr. Arias had already found his natural audience, and he hoped that I wasn't part of it."

"Oh, Christopher," Caroline said under her breath. "*That* doesn't sound like you. No *wonder* he was so upset."

The remark made Paget smile. But it did little to dampen the disgust he felt: this man had tried to damage Carlo on the pretext that Paget's entry into politics had made his son fair game, and now, thwarted and officious, he had begun trying to send Paget himself to jail.

"Was he merely arrogant?" Salinas prodded.

"No. He was quite angry. He called the *Inquisitor* article libelous, and I would have to characterize his tone of voice as threatening."

"How did you respond?" Salinas asked.

In the jury box, Luisa Marin glanced quickly at Paget. Slocum folded his arms. "I told Mr. Paget I intended to report that the charges existed and that they could pose a problem for Mr. Paget's campaign."

"And did the item actually appear?"

"No." Slocum's voice became rougher. "The publisher of the newspaper, Mr. Devine, told my editor not to run the story. I had the impression that Mr. Paget may have threatened him with a libel suit."

"Move to strike," Caroline said promptly, rising to address Judge Lerner. "This is not only hearsay but double hearsay: Mr. Slocum was not party to his editor's conversation with Mr. Devine *or* to Mr. Devine's alleged conversation with Mr. Paget. And the likely reason this article didn't run is that no respectable newspaper wants its reporters feeding off the bottom of the journalistic food chain, let alone a garbage trough like the *Inquisitor*. Especially when *its* ultimate source is an estranged husband embroiled in a custody suit." Her voice turned astringent. "Let *alone* Ricardo Arias."

Lerner looked to Salinas. "She has you, Victor—at least on hearsay." He turned to the jury. "Mr. Slocum has no firsthand knowledge about what Mr. Paget may, or may not, have said to Mr. Devine. Beyond the fact that his editor directed him not to run the article on Mr. Paget, I instruct you to disregard his answer."

Salinas's frown, Paget knew, was for show: he had not expected the testimony to be admitted, but the jury would not forget the impression that Paget had gone to great lengths to kill an article that could damage him. "All right," he said to Slocum. "When was the *next* time that you spoke to Mr. Paget?"

"It was after Mr. Arias's death." Slocum seemed to choose his words with care. "I became aware that in Mr. Arias's custody suit against Ms. Peralta, some papers had been filed under seal, which apparently involved Mr. Paget and his son. So I called Mr. Paget—who was still a prospective candidate—and asked if he'd discuss the contents of the filings or, possibly, provide me with a copy."

"And what was Mr. Paget's response?"

"Again, he mentioned a possible libel suit." Slocum glanced at Paget. "He also said that the article would be damaging to him and expressed outrage that I would print anything about his son."

Salinas nodded. "The defense has characterized Mr. Paget in these proceedings as a very peaceable man. Was that your experience of this conversation?"

"Not at all. He has a way of talking that is very cold and very hostile. His tone of voice was extremely angry. All in all, this is a very threatening man."

"The little twerp," Paget said under his breath. "I didn't threaten him with anything. What does he expect—for people to fall all over him?"

Caroline kept watching the reporter. "That's the general idea."

"Did Mr. Paget's anger deter you?" Salinas asked.

"No. Like before, I intended to run an article regarding any filings relevant to Mr. Paget's fitness for office or to his viability as a candidate."

"And did you run *this* article?"

"No." For the first time, Slocum smiled. "Once more, Mr. Devine—my publisher—called and told us not to run the item. Because Mr. Paget was withdrawing from the race."

Glancing at the jury box, Paget saw Joseph Duarte make a note:

the jury would not like the notion of an influential man threatening the press, and the article in question was directly tied to Ricardo Arias.

"Did you agree with this?" Salinas asked.

"No." Slocum spread his hands. "I don't want to be vindictive, but this guy might want to run for office again. I thought people should know *why* he was getting out."

"Bully for you," Caroline murmured. But her eyes were narrow: as she had feared, Paget's efforts to protect Carlo were becoming evidence against him.

Pausing, Salinas had the alert posture and voice of a lawyer underlining his ultimate question. "In your opinion, Mr. Slocum, could Mr. Paget's candidacy have survived exposure of his alleged adultery *and* the claim that his son had sexually molested Ms. Peralta's daughter?"

Caroline was up quickly. "Objection," she said. "That calls for not only speculation but fortune-telling. There's no way that this witness can predict the reaction of several million voters over a year *after* he runs whatever swill he feels is fit to print."

Salinas shook his head. "Your Honor, that objection is ill taken *and* misinformed. As Mr. Slocum is prepared to testify, there are many factors which can end a candidacy well *before* an election— factors which Mr. Slocum, who has reported on politics in the state and city for over five years, is well equipped to address. As, I believe, the defendant acknowledged by telling Mr. Slocum that his article could damage him."

Lerner pondered this with an unhappy look. "Overruled," he said finally. "You may answer, Mr. Slocum."

Slocum nodded briskly, as if pleased at this acknowledgment of his expertise. "The short answer," he said, "was supplied by Mr. Paget himself. By getting out *before* my story could even appear.

"He was smart to do that." Pausing, Slocum tried to look sententious. But the pleasure in his own importance, Paget observed, showed in a certain brightness of the eyes. "Even a man as wealthy as Mr. Paget needs money to run a statewide campaign—money from unions, agricultural interests, wealthy individuals, and the like. No one as canny as these big contributors will give money to a wounded candidate. And once *we* report *that*, and elected officials and party activists *read* it, a candidate is dead. Period." He turned to

Paget. "This particular aspirant faced a charge of adultery, perhaps survivable in itself. But add that to raising a boy believed to have molested his new lover's five-year-old daughter, and I can guarantee you that he couldn't stick it out. Why humiliate yourself politically while dying a slow death? That's the reason Paget tried so hard to kill this story. Because, in the end, this story killed *him*."

Slocum's voice, casual and a little contemptuous, suggested that Paget was yesterday's news. The only thing about him still of interest was the murder of Ricardo Arias, and Jack Slocum had just provided the definitive explanation of Paget's motive.

"There are some days," Caroline murmured, "when I truly like my work."

Rising, Caroline looked at Slocum with faint distaste. The courtroom was very still.

"You're not exactly a supporter of Mr. Paget's, are you?"

Slocum sat back a little. "It's not the function of the press to support anyone, Ms. Masters. Our role is to inform the public on things they need to know."

"So you don't feel you treated Mr. Paget unfairly?"

"Not at all." He shot a look at Paget. "If anything, this man got off light."

Caroline raised an eyebrow. "Am I correct in understanding," she asked, "that if Mr. Paget had supplied you with a copy of the papers filed under seal, you would have published Mr. Arias's charges?"

Slocum nodded. "Yes."

"And how did you intend to verify whether the charges were true?"

Slocum hesitated. "Well, if Mr. Paget had been willing to talk to me, I'd have asked him. Or his son, for that matter."

Caroline looked puzzled. "If they had denied the charges, would you *still* have printed them?"

"Along with the denials, yes."

"In fact, you don't know whether it *is* true that Mr. Paget had an affair with Ms. Peralta, do you?"

Slocum folded his arms. "No."

"And you *also* don't know whether Carlo Paget, then aged fifteen, molested a little girl."

"I know that the charges were made."

"Yes or no," Caroline snapped.

Slocum's mouth became a stubborn line. "No."

"That's better. Is it fair to say, Mr. Slocum, that these charges are hurtful to Mr. Paget and his son?"

"I already said that."

"And that Mr. Arias—as the contestant in a custody suit—might wish to hurt them both?"

"I suppose so."

"Then why don't we also suppose, Mr. Slocum, that these charges are false? Do you think printing false and denigrating charges is fair to Mr. Paget *or* his son?"

"Objection," Salinas interjected. "Ms. Masters is badgering this witness to no purpose, about complex journalistic judgment calls which have no relevance to this case."

Caroline shook her head. "We believe they do, Your Honor. Just as we believe that this witness has been less than candid. With the court's permission, I believe that I can demonstrate both points. Both of which, I might add, suggest that Mr. Slocum is biased against Christopher Paget."

Lerner looked perturbed: Paget sensed that his natural solicitude for the press was at war with his concern for Paget's own rights. "You may continue," he said, "for the moment. But unless you show relevance in fairly short order, Ms. Masters, I'll cut you off without prompting by Mr. Salinas."

"Thank you," Caroline said, and turned back to Slocum. "*Do* you," she demanded, "think it's fair to print false charges?"

Slocum sat straighter. "There's the public interest to consider—in this case, the interest in the character of people running for office, including the desire to cover things up. The fact that charges are made is important for its own sake. Put simply, it's news."

"Would you also say that there is a public interest in the character of people who *report* the news?"

"Objection." Salinas stood. "This is not only irrelevant, it's harassment."

"Irrelevant?" Caroline asked. "Not to *this* witness."

"Sustained." Lerner leaned forward. "Please be warned, Ms. Masters—this is not a forum for your views regarding Mr. Slocum's reportage."

"I understand, Your Honor." She turned to Slocum. "Am I correct that one of your reasons for calling Mr. Paget was to get a copy of Mr. Arias's papers?"

A moment's pause. "Yes."

Caroline put her hands on her hips. "But didn't you already *have* a copy?"

Salinas, Paget saw, was poised to rise. On the stand, Slocum looked to the prosecutor, then to Lerner. Quietly, Caroline said, "Just answer the question, Mr. Slocum."

"Your Honor," Slocum said to Lerner, "I believe this may come within the California shield law. Entitling a reporter to protect his sources."

"When I want to ask Mr. Slocum for his sources," Caroline rejoined, "everyone here will know it, and Mr. Slocum will not have to use the shield law simply to shield *himself*."

Lerner smiled a little, turning to Slocum. "You may answer the question, Mr. Slocum."

"I'll be happy to repeat it," Caroline said. As she faced Slocum, her voice turned hard. "When you called Mr. Paget, asking for a copy of Mr. Arias's charges, you already *had* a copy, didn't you?"

Slocum shifted in the witness box. "Yes," he said finally.

"So when you suggested to Mr. Paget that you needed a copy, you weren't exactly candid, were you?"

"I didn't think I needed to tell him everything."

"Is that also true of Judge Lerner and the jury? When, not half an hour ago, you suggested that you had called Mr. Paget again at least partly to secure a copy."

"I never said I didn't have a copy." Slocum turned to Judge Lerner. "In both cases, I was trying to protect my source."

"No," Caroline snapped. "You were *lying*. But let's move on. I take it that the person who provided you with the papers was *not* Ricardo Arias. Or you would have called Mr. Paget about their contents long before you did."

Once more, Slocum looked to Lerner for assistance. "Your Honor, I really believe these questions impinge on my sources."

"At the time of your call," Caroline said in acid tones, "Ricardo Arias was *dead*. If *he* gave you the papers, it really *is* news."

Salinas, Paget thought, was curiously inactive; for whatever reason, he seemed content to let this pass without protest. "You may answer," Lerner told Slocum. "Did you receive these papers from Mr. Arias?"

Slocum shook his head. "No, Your Honor."

"That's a relief. Proceed, Ms. Masters."

Caroline moved closer. "How *did* you get them, Mr. Slocum?" She gave him a chilling smile. "No names, please. I wouldn't want to reveal your sources."

"A third party gave them to me."

"And did this nameless someone tell you where *he'd* gotten them? Seeing how they weren't publicly available."

"No."

"You didn't think your source got them from Mr. Paget, did you?"

"I guess not."

"And Ms. Peralta had also refused to give you a copy, correct?"

"Correct."

"That pretty much leaves Mr. Arias, doesn't it?" For a split second, Caroline paused. "Dead or alive."

"Objection." Salinas said reflexively. "Calls for speculation."

Caroline turned on him. "As to *what*, Victor? Whether Mr. Slocum's nameless source received the papers from Mr. Arias in a living state or *after* Mr. Arias was deceased? In which case I would think that the district attorney would be even more enthralled with talking to this person than I am."

It was lovely, Paget thought. In one deft response, Caroline had introduced the anonymous source as a party to shady dealings with Ricardo Arias and, at least possibly, to his murder. Even Salinas looked nonplussed: he was suddenly confronted with the prospect of protecting Slocum's source—certainly in the best interests of his boss, McKinley Brooks—while permitting Caroline to suggest that he was concealing a key witness. The alternative was to expose the source as an agent of James Colt and demonstrate that, however lethal the man's political designs might have been for Paget, literal murder was not among his assignments. Whatever Salinas's choice, Paget did not envy him.

"Let me suggest this compromise," Salinas said to Judge Lerner. "The district attorney will, of course, explore this matter with Mr.

Slocum in private. For present purposes, I suggest that he identify the source by occupation only, but testify fully and completely about the content of their conversations."

This was shrewd, Paget saw: it preserved Salinas's options until he spoke to Brooks, while permitting testimony that might make the unknown source seem a little less sinister. As for Caroline, she might move to dismiss the charges if the source was not revealed, arguing that a material witness was being withheld; on the other hand, revelation of the source—if this was her reward for cornering Brooks— might be far less useful than a shadowy figure. Watching from the stand, Slocum looked somewhat diminished and completely lost.

"Very well," Caroline told Lerner. "If that solution is agreeable to the court, why don't we at least try it. Until we've *all* had time to think."

Lerner steepled his hands. "For the moment, we'll proceed. But this has to be resolved, by agreement or otherwise, before this trial is over. I'd like to minimize the risk of reversible error."

As Caroline turned to the witness, Paget saw that the jury was on edge. "How," she said to Slocum, "did you come to know the source who gave you Mr. Arias's papers?"

Slocum considered his answer. "I knew him before. From previous campaigns."

"And what is this person's occupation?"

"Political consultant." Slocum paused, then added quickly, "Self-employed."

"And how did he get these papers into your hands?"

Slocum glanced at Salinas. "My source called and asked to meet me confidentially. At my home."

"When you met him, what did he tell you?"

Slocum cleared his throat. "That they were papers concerning Mr. Paget. And that I could judge for myself whether they were newsworthy."

"Yes," Caroline said dryly. "I'm sure that he didn't want to compromise your journalistic integrity. Did he happen to mention what *his* interest was in seeing that this material got published?"

"No. He wouldn't say."

"Did you at least form an impression?"

Slocum appeared torn between the desire not to answer and the fear of sounding disingenuous. "What I assumed," he said at length, "was that my source represented someone hostile to Mr. Paget's candidacy."

"Didn't it bother you, Mr. Slocum, that you were being used by a politician to help torpedo a candidate he disliked?"

Slocum tried to summon a superior smile. "In my business, like yours, you learn useful things from a lot of people whose motives may not be the best but whose *information* serves the public interest. *My* only interest was the quality of the information itself."

Caroline raised an eyebrow. "I thought you didn't care whether the information was true or not."

"Objection," Salinas said. "Badgering the witness, mischaracterizing prior testimony."

"Oh, never mind," Caroline said carelessly. "So to summarize your testimony, you received this information from a political consultant who refused to reveal his interest, after *you* agreed not to reveal his identity *or* his motives. Is that it?"

Slocum stared past her. "Essentially, yes."

"And after *that*, you decided to print the information this person fed you—which you concede would damage Mr. Paget—without knowing the credibility of that information?"

"Yes." Slocum's voice rose. "I decided the story had value as it was."

"So much for journalistic integrity. Now let me call on your expertise on another area—political disaster. Would you say that it would be damaging to whatever politician had your 'source' leak this information if the *politician*'s identity was known?"

Slocum hesitated. "Maybe."

"Potentially fatal, even."

Slocum's voice had become a monotone. "I can't really say."

"Oh, you really *can*, Mr. Slocum." Caroline's New England voice carried an undertone of contempt. "You were certainly less bashful when Mr. Salinas asked you if the information *itself* would ruin Mr. Paget's campaign. So why don't you give me your best assessment." She paused again. "In the public interest, of course."

Slocum still did not face her. "It might be damaging, I suppose."

Caroline paused for a moment. "Did *Mr. Arias* appreciate that fact?"

Slocum looked startled, and then his face closed. "He was *dead.* Just like you point out."

Caroline smiled. "He wasn't dead, was he, when you first talked to him?"

Slocum glanced toward Salinas. "Did you," Caroline snapped, "ever talk to Mr. Arias?"

Slowly, Slocum turned back to Caroline. "Yes."

"And when was that?"

"After I saw the article in the *Inquisitor*. When I was planning to write about it."

"So Mr. Arias didn't point out the article himself?"

Slocum's eyes flickered. "No."

"Who did?"

Another glance at Salinas. "My source."

Caroline nodded. "Your friend the 'consultant.' I rather thought so. And during this *first* conversation, what did your 'source' say?"

"Just sent me the article. To see if I was interested."

"And when you subsequently called Mr. Arias, he didn't happen to ask you for money, did he?"

"Not exactly." Slocum looked down. "He did ask if we paid for interviews."

"And what did you say?"

"That I didn't think I could."

"And how did Mr. Arias respond to that?"

Slocum paused. "He wanted to know who else might be interested and whether I'd talked to anyone like that."

Paget felt a surge of contempt; glancing at the jury box, he saw Joseph Duarte's mouth thin in distaste. "And what did you tell him?" Caroline said.

Slocum looked away. In an affectless tone, he said, "That I couldn't reveal my sources."

Caroline stared at him in silence. "But you *did* pass on Mr. Arias's interest to your 'source,' correct?"

A long pause. "Yes."

"Well," Caroline said with disdain, "then it looks like you helped set up a blind date, anyhow. And you've already agreed, I believe, that anyone who knew about your 'source' 's role—or the politician he worked for—might be in a position to damage that politician seriously, correct?"

"I suppose, yes."

Caroline waited a moment, then, quietly asked, "Including Mr. Arias? A man with a proven gift for extortion?"

"Objection," Salinas said. "The question calls for speculation."

"Sustained." Lerner turned to Caroline. "I think you've made your point, Counselor."

Smiling slightly, Caroline gave the judge a nod of respect. "I'll change subjects, Your Honor," she said, and turned to Slocum. "Beyond your appetite for such morsels as your 'source' provided, you decided to print them at the risk of your life, correct?"

Slocum faced her again. "I don't quite follow you."

"I mean, given how scary Mr. Paget can be on the telephone, weren't you concerned for your personal safety?"

Slocum folded his arms. "I didn't say that. I said he was angry."

"You didn't worry that Mr. Paget was going to do away with you?" Caroline said in tones of mock admiration. "Very brave, Mr. Slocum. Tell me, do you have any reason to believe Christopher Paget to be a violent man?"

"I don't know."

"Yes or no," Caroline snapped.

Slocum paused. "No. Not specifically."

"And do you happen to know Mr. Paget's position on violence in our society? Including gun control?"

Another pause. "Yes."

"Did you also happen to attend Mr. Paget's speech to the California Society of Newspaper Editors, given shortly after a deranged father with an assault rifle slaughtered seven children in a recreation center?"

"Yes."

Caroline turned to Judge Lerner. "Your Honor, I would like to show the witness a videotape of that speech—it's only about ten minutes—and then ask a few brief questions."

Salinas stood. "I object, Your Honor. This is a murder trial, not a political rally. And Mr. Paget's self-serving speech has no probative value for *either* purpose."

"Nonsense, Your Honor. The speech was given well before Mr. Arias's death. I believe that Mr. Paget's distaste for guns, *and* for violence, is more than a little relevant to whether he shot Mr. Arias with a handgun." She turned to Slocum. "As is whether this witness—who has been so willing to inflate his response to Mr. Paget's understandable indignation into an act of heroic journalism—knows of *anything* in Mr. Paget's life inconsistent with these stated beliefs."

Lerner touched one finger to his lips. "It's been an unusual day," he said with an air of bemusement. "Roll 'em, Ms. Masters."

Within moments, the courtroom was dark, and Caroline was sitting next to Paget, watching the introduction to his speech. In the darkness, the television screen flickered in black and white; the jury seemed as focused as patrons in a movie theater.

"Any thoughts so far?" Caroline whispered.

"A couple," Paget whispered back. "You've not only decimated this guy, but you turned his 'source' into a real problem for the prosecution. I can't believe Victor couldn't see it coming."

Caroline turned to him. "I think he *did*, Chris. There's a very deep game going on here. My guess is that Victor set McKinley up, for reasons which have nothing to do with you. *Or* this case."

Suddenly, to his surprise, Paget found himself fixated by his own image on the screen—a man in black and white, speaking with passion on a day when children had died.

"I don't own a gun," he heard himself say. "Outside the army, I've never fired one. Perhaps that makes it easier for me to notice that the chief use of handguns in America is domestic violence and robbing the corner store. . . ."

His voice had been soft with anger; Paget still remembered the feeling. But now, listening, he felt less angry than sad. Sad once more for the children who had died. Sad that he could no longer speak out. Sad that, now, the only use for these words was to defend him against a charge of murder.

Paget turned to look at the jury. In the half-light, they appeared as a silvery frieze: Marian Celler seemed to nod at the screen; Luisa Marin looked more accessible than ever before. Next to Paget, Caroline Masters still watched.

"In the end, you wouldn't have made a politician," she murmured. "But it really is too bad."

Suddenly Paget felt grateful to Caroline; she had found a way for the jury to hear from him other than as a voice on Charles Monk's tape. And he knew that, whatever else, this had become a bad day for the prosecution.

When the tape ended and the lights came on, Caroline Masters stood facing Slocum.

The jury seemed drawn to her stillness. "Well," she said to Slocum, "I'm sure we're all relieved to know how hard you worked to spare us Mr. Paget's candidacy. And now, if you will, a few more questions."

FOURTEEN

"WE'VE GOT TO TALK," Paget told Caroline.

"Concerning what?"

"About this eyewitness Victor's putting on tomorrow. And, beyond that, about what kind of case *we* put on."

They were in the elevator on the way to the underground garage, evading reporters by arrangement with Judge Lerner. Caroline leaned back against the wall, briefcase in hand, giving Paget a curious look. "About our case," she said, "there are all sorts of choices. Starting with whether you testify."

Paget found himself smiling; Caroline had a subtle mind, and he was confident that she had worked out their options to the last permutation. And that, depending on Salinas's final witness, she knew precisely where she wished to go. "I just want to keep you from getting confused," he said.

Caroline gave a sigh of mock relief. "Christopher," she answered, "I would just be lost without you."

Her voice, a parody of admiring femininity, made Paget laugh out loud. "If only Mr. Slocum could see you now," he said. "A vulnerable woman, tormented by the burdens of her job."

Caroline flashed a wicked grin. "I really didn't like him much."

"It showed," Paget answered, and then the door opened.

They walked to the car. "Okay," she said. "Where do we go?"

"I'd like to check out Carlo for an hour. He's not doing all that well." Paget got inside the car, adding as Caroline took the driver's seat, "I'd ask you over to dinner, but I don't want him to overhear our conversation. For several reasons."

Caroline nodded. "I'd like to shower, anyhow." She turned on the ignition. "Would you mind coming to my place? It would be a little easier, at least for me."

Paget turned to her, surprised; Caroline drew such a line between her professional and private lives that Paget had never imagined himself inside her home. "I don't mind at all," he said. "Tell me where to find you."

Where to find Caroline Masters turned out to be the penthouse of a four-story building near the top of Telegraph Hill. Wearing gray wool slacks and a black cashmere sweater, Caroline let him in with a faint aura of self-consciousness, and then Paget found himself gazing through floor-to-ceiling glass at the bright outline of the Bay Bridge and the high-rises of the financial district, where Paget and Caroline had their offices—the brightly lit Transamerica Pyramid, the four towers of the Embarcadero Center, moving in a row of staggered heights to the sudden inky darkness of the bay. It struck Paget that he had not seen much daylight lately.

"This is beautiful," he told her.

"Thank you. Care for a glass of wine?"

"If you have something open."

"A Montrachet. Do you mind?"

"Hardly." Paget smiled to himself: a fine French wine sounded right for Caroline, stubbornly eccentric, as if drinking California wine would be too easy. He followed her through the living room, noting their surroundings as he went. The decor was tasteful but not ostentatious: Caroline's furnishings combined the very modern with carefully placed antiques—a rocking chair, an oak rolltop desk— which Paget guessed were inherited rather than purchased. It reminded him that he knew nothing of Caroline's background, except that she was a New Englander. But from Caroline's flat he surmised that, like Paget himself, she must have family money: there was simply no way that she could have bought such a place based on twenty years as a public defender or a judge, or, for that matter, even on six months' income from Kenyon and Walker.

The kitchen was spacious and bright and neatly ordered, the cooking space of a single person who knew how she liked to keep things. Caroline passed him a glass of wine. "Thank you," he said.

She sipped her wine without answering, seemingly preoccupied. After a moment, she said, "Would you care to go up top? It's a pleasant night, and we've been stuck inside."

She did not wait for an answer. Following her, Paget saw that one corner of the living room featured a spiral wrought-iron staircase, which climbed through an opening in the ceiling. At the top, Paget discovered, was a small enclosure that opened to a roof garden, with shrubs in wooden containers and a table and four chairs. The garden was walled in by glass, to break the wind; from here, Caroline could see for miles in any direction. It was as if she had arranged the semblance of a perfect world, a kind of retreat. Without Carlo, Paget thought suddenly, he might have lived this way.

He walked to the edge of the garden. "Incredible," he said to Caroline.

"Do you like it?"

When he turned, she was standing on the patio, some distance away. "Very much," he said.

She walked back to the entrance, flicking on an outdoor light. The effect was to cast light and shadow on the trees and shrubs surrounding them.

As he sat across the table from Caroline, her face came into the light, aquiline and elegant and hard to read. "Could you tell me something?" he asked.

Caroline smiled. "It depends."

Paget leaned back on his chair. "Why in the world did you become a criminal lawyer?"

Caroline gave him a look of tolerant understanding, as though the question were expected but a little superficial. " 'What's a nice girl like me . . . ,' " she said dryly. "Perhaps I should have been a law professor, writing tomes on the antitrust laws. Or maybe a bond lawyer in a Wall Street firm. Like *you* should have been."

"Oh, *that's* different. With the conspicuous exception of Mary Carelli, I've generally defended the kind of people who don't use guns and have never met a street cop—investment bankers and the like. But for the better part of your career your clients were murderers, rapists, armed robbers, and car thieves."

Caroline sipped her wine. "There's no doubt that you represented a more polite class of criminal. Which is why defending *you* has been such a treat."

Paget laughed in surprise. "It's a pleasure to see you laugh," Caroline said. "Even if it's only at some irony of mine, instead of at the joy of living."

Paget gave a wry smile. "That's because, as you point out, you're having all the fun. Incidentally, you never answered my question."

"About criminal law?" Caroline turned from him, looking out at the night sky and the distant glow of lights from Marin. "There wasn't any plan, really. At some point in my twenties, I understood that what I was doing was redefining myself, choosing things that weren't predestined by who I was or the life I'd been given. So that, in the end, I'd have made my own way. Criminal defense seemed to fit that." Consciously, she seemed to pull back. "Anyhow, I'm pretty good at it."

The last dismissive phrase reminded Paget of what he had felt about Caroline at other times: the teasing sense that he was on the edge of it, but never would know her. And yet now this elusive woman held all his hopes—and Carlo's—in her hands.

"Not just 'pretty good,' " Paget said finally. "Among the best."

Caroline shrugged and smiled but did not argue with him. Between grown-ups, her silence suggested, there was no point in dissembling.

Paget sipped his wine, dry and flavorful, lingering on the tongue. "How's Teresa?" Caroline asked.

He studied his glass. "Do you mean how is *she*, or how are *things*?"

Caroline considered that. "Both, I suppose."

Paget told himself that he had no obligation to be candid, and then found that he wished to be. "For Terri, things are hard. Part of it is Elena. The other part is what makes it hard for *us*." He paused, facing Caroline directly. "In her heart, she's not sure I didn't do it."

Caroline gave him an ambiguous glance; Paget sensed her wishing not to look at him. "Ambivalence in *lawyers*," Paget told her quietly, "is the norm. It's not so good in lovers."

Caroline smiled with one corner of her mouth. "So I'm forgiven?"

"Always."

"And Terri?"

The question took Paget deep within himself. "I don't know," he heard himself murmur. "I really don't know."

Caroline studied him. "She did well for you in court. Remarkably well, if what you say is right."

In Caroline's voice was an unspoken question: had Terri lied for him? Now it was Paget who did not wish to look at Caroline.

"When the trial's over," he said at length, "perhaps this will all make sense to me. Perhaps my *life* will make sense. But it doesn't now."

Caroline waited for a moment. "There's a bit to do between here and there. You wanted to talk about it?"

Paget nodded. "I did," he said, and then realized—a glancing thought—that Caroline had once more avoided talking about herself.

"All right." Caroline finished her wine. "Tomorrow is Victor's last witness—the woman who claims to have seen you leaving Richie's apartment. As of now, where do you think we stand?"

Since leaving court, Paget realized, he had thought of little else. "You have to take this a piece at a time," he said. "And our *first* defense is that Richie killed himself.

"Salinas has done well there. Liz Shelton was strong on the medical evidence of murder, and no one Victor put on—whatever damage they did to Richie's posthumous reputation—believes that he was suicidal. Neither, in truth, do I." Paget paused. "We should still make use of suicide as a defense. But if you asked the jury what they believe, odds on they pick murder."

"I agree," Caroline said with dispassion. "Which would leave us with reasonable doubt."

Paget nodded. "That breaks down to several parts. The first is whether I had a motive. That's kind of a wash. On the one hand, *if* I were homicidal I certainly had reason enough to kill him. But so did Terri, she made clear—whether I wanted her to or not. And you've done a very good job of making the case that I would *never* kill this guy, if only because of Carlo."

Caroline considered this. "Also," she said then, "you've never owned a gun. Not unless your family passed it down—which would explain the age of the bullets and gun. But they've found no proof of that."

"True."

"So let's take the evidence they *do* have," Caroline went on. "They thought they might have you with fibers in the house, but Terri explained those. Ditto the fibers in the car." She looked at him intently. "And of course, there are the fingerprints on the answering machine, which Terri neutralized so neatly."

When Paget did not comment, Caroline continued as if she had not paused. "In terms of your whereabouts, you're weak on the night before you left for Italy. If anything, Carlo hurt you there— the fact that it looked like he was lying underscores the fact that no one can say you *were* home." She looked at him sharply. "Except, of course, you."

It was a probe, Paget knew. Again, he chose to ignore it. "On the other hand," he countered, "you've parlayed Richie's ten-thousand-dollar payoff from Colt into murderous drug dealers and homicidal politicians, who have gone undetected because of the meddling of a biased D.A. and a self-promoting reporter. Whose source, we both agree, is far more useful as a phantom suspect than as a witness." Paget sat back in his chair, stretching his legs in front of him. "If my whereabouts are a loose end, so are the implications of Richie's cash. As even Monk admitted.

"Finally, you've taken Richie from a struggling Hispanic underdog to the kind of slimy con man who sometimes lives a very short life." Suddenly restless, Paget stood. "I doubt that anyone on the jury is lusting to avenge him. And it may well have occurred to them that Richie is someone whom people routinely imagine murdering."

Caroline smiled a little. "Suppose," she said after a time, "the jury were to vote tomorrow."

Paget had an answer, although it made him apprehensive to speak it aloud. "I've been wrong before," he said finally. "But on *this* evidence, I think they acquit me. Lerner might even direct a verdict."

"Agreed." Caroline spoke more quietly now. "What if tomorrow's eyewitness swears beyond doubt that she saw you leave Richie's apartment. *And* I can't shake her?"

Paget began pacing. "Then everything changes."

"*Then,*" Caroline said behind him, "you have to think about testifying. Or whether you take Mac's deal and plead to voluntary manslaughter. Because you'll be in real trouble."

Paget felt the words in the pit of his stomach. He did not turn. "Suppose," he said finally, "that you *can* shake this lady. What kind of a defense do I put on *then?*"

"What do *you* think?"

He turned to her. "None. That's how you've been figuring it, all along."

Caroline raised an eyebrow. "Have I?"

Paget nodded. "The whole pattern of your cross-examination has been to put our case on through Victor's witnesses. Pretty much the way we'd do it if I choose not to testify.

"First, we'd consider calling a forensic expert to quarrel with Liz Shelton. But we can't find a good one who doesn't agree with her on the essentials, and you've already done the best you can on cross. For the jury, Shelton was a long time ago, and a bad expert of our own might only remind them of how persuasive she was. So in the end, we wouldn't call one.

"What we *would* do is try to damage Richie. Which, of course, you've already done."

Caroline, Paget saw, had begun smiling again. "Finally," he concluded, "we'd consider calling character witnesses to say that I'm a kind and gentle person, incapable of murder. But the two best witnesses for *that* are Terri and Carlo. You not only got them on during Victor's case, but you've even sneaked in that film today, my outburst about guns." Paget paused, adding quietly, "And calling more witnesses to say I'm wonderful would only serve to remind the jury that I'm not speaking for myself, wouldn't it?"

Still smiling faintly, Caroline poured herself a second glass of wine, lids lowered, carefully measuring the amount. "What about putting Mac on the stand?"

Now it was Paget's turn to smile. "You never intended to do that, Caroline. Not for a second."

"Why not?"

"Because Mac's more useful as a sinister puppeteer than as someone the jury can see—an amiable-looking politician fully capable of sounding righteous and aggrieved." His voice softened again. "You only threatened him to get a manslaughter deal. In case I needed it."

Caroline gave him a long, considering look. "So," she said at length, "if I can break this woman down tomorrow, we're agreed?"

"Of course," Paget said with a trace of irony. "You've already written your summation, haven't you? 'Ladies and gentlemen, Mr. Salinas has indeed made out a case—for Mr. Paget.' "

Caroline was not smiling now. "And if I *can't* break her?"

Paget was quiet for a moment. "But you will," he answered. "As I said, you're among the best."

* * *

Driving home, Paget knew that he would not sleep tonight. He hoped that Caroline could.

His house was dark and had a curious quiet. Usually, he could feel the presence of Carlo, imagine him studying or talking to a friend or watching sports highlights on ESPN. But tonight their home felt hermetic and airless, as if its life had crawled into a corner.

Paget climbed the stairs. Although it was only ten-thirty and Carlo was a night owl, no crack of light came from beneath his door.

Paget stopped in the hallway. Before he had left for Caroline's, Carlo had seemed withdrawn, uninterested in where his father was going, happy enough to see him leave. He had mentioned no plans to go out himself.

Paget knocked softly on his son's door.

There was no answer. Cautiously, as if expecting to find a body, Paget opened the door.

Carlo lay on his bed, in a T-shirt and jeans. His upward stare at Paget was both defensive and profoundly uncurious. It took only an instant for Paget to smell dope.

"Since when," he said to Carlo, "have you been smoking this stuff?"

"And you *didn't*?" Carlo sounded lucid enough, but his voice was slowed down, as if he were listening to its echo. "Or does it bug you that I'm doing it at home?"

It was like hearing the taped replay of the baby-boomer parent's nightmare argument, a son or daughter confronting a parent's hypocrisy: "Do you mind that I'm living with Johnny, Mom and Dad, or do you just want me to pretend not to fuck him while we're visiting?" All at once, Paget knew what was wrong.

It was plain enough. The relationship of a parent with a teenager is shot through with ambiguities and hypocrisies, large and small— the child's dependence and resentment, the parent's self-indulgences and prohibitions. But somewhere within this uneasy mix, in the best of families—his and Carlo's—both parent and child know which lines should not be crossed: the child's sense of privacy, the parent's sense of propriety. A delicate balance preserved until, as adults, both sides can either laugh about it or forget it.

Quite deliberately, Carlo had crossed the line.

"What the hell are you doing?" Paget asked.

Carlo shrugged lazily. "You've got martinis."

Carlo's eyes seemed fixed, his pupils a little wider. "That's pretty puerile," Paget answered. "But I'm not so sure you'd get that right now. This is about *you*, not me."

Carlo shrugged again. "This isn't hurting anything."

"It isn't helping, either. For example, what about the basketball team?"

Carlo's eyes widened, as if he had just been given a glimpse of the surreal, and then he began to laugh. "What about the *basketball team*," he echoed with amazed derision. "What about *your trial*, Dad?"

Paget sat on the edge of the bed. "Okay," he said at length. "That was truly dumb. What I should have said is that I love you and I want to know what's happening."

"What's happening?" Carlo's voice was still amazed but a little less hostile. "Give me a break, Dad. I'm getting used to things here as they're going to be. You know, when you're not around anymore."

Paget's nerves seemed to go dead. "I'll be around."

"Sure. And they weren't going to indict you. Then, when they did, you were going to take care of it all. And then I saw you can't." His son's voice rose. "What do you think I was trying to *do* the other day? You've been bullshitting me, Dad. Don't you think I *know* by now when you're feeding me a crock of shit? Do you think it's only *you* who sees things about *me*?"

The words jarred Paget; the time had passed when he could lull his son, and he had been too preoccupied to face that. "All right," he said at last. "I'm in trouble. But not because I killed Richie." He shook his head in despair. "God, Carlo, I don't want you to be any part of this."

"I *am* part of it." His son sat up on his elbows. "I'm tired of pretending for you. Just how much do you think I can take?"

"I don't know."

Carlo's voice hardened. "There are a lot of things you're not telling me."

Slowly, Paget nodded. "There are some things I'm not telling *anyone*, Carlo. Because I can't."

Carlo studied him. "Why not?"

"Because, in the end, they don't have to do with me. And because it would do me no good to say them." He paused. "You're the only person, son, to whom I've even said *this* much."

Carlo gave him a look of doubt. "Including Terri?"

In the tangle of events, Paget wondered, had Carlo come to believe Terri was more important to him? "Yes," he answered. "Including Terri."

Carlo was quiet. "You're going to break up, aren't you?"

"I don't know." Paget felt a wave of sadness. But even the future they could have had, he realized, was not as real as this boy in front of him. "Maybe whatever role we were supposed to play in each other's lives was also supposed to end. But you and I aren't supposed to end. Ever."

Carlo stared down at the bed. "It's like we've been so distant."

"I'm sorry. I did something careless and haven't known how to get out of it. If I could tell you about it, I would. But as I said, it's about someone else."

Carlo looked up at him. "Do you know who killed Richie?"

Paget watched his son's expression as Carlo hoped for an answer that would exculpate his father. "I'd only be guessing," he said finally. "I'm not even sure that Richie didn't kill *himself*." Pausing, Paget finished with emphasis. "But about this trial, I'm doing everything I can. If you believe nothing else, believe that I'm a smart lawyer and know what's best to do. I haven't lost that."

Carlo shook his head. "This is *hard*, Dad. I can't sleep anymore. I can't even talk to you."

"You *can*. About everything but this. And even about this, you've at least told me how things are." He clasped Carlo's shoulder. "In a week, maybe two, this really *will* be over. One way or the other."

Carlo simply watched him, taking this in. It was so strange, Paget thought, that this talk had begun with his son smoking marijuana. "About the dope," Paget said finally. "I smoked it for a while, and then I stopped. There wasn't that much point to it, and for the most part, it makes you slow and kind of dumb."

"There's a point," Carlo said flatly.

"Reality avoidance? That's just a problem."

Carlo rubbed his temples. "You're never going to testify, are you?"

"No. I'm not."

Carlo appeared to reflect for a time. And then he reached beneath his bed and pulled out a sandwich bag full of grass. He cupped it in his hand for an instant, then tossed it in his father's lap. "You can throw this out, Dad. It wasn't that good, anyhow."

FIFTEEN

TO PAGET, all the energies of the courtroom flowed toward Salinas's final witness: the jury, mute and attentive; Caroline Masters, watching with preternatural stillness; Salinas himself, asking his warm-up questions in a manner that seemed stiff and tense. Even Jared Lerner could not take his eyes off her.

Georgina Keller was an ordinary woman: a widow in her seventies, a rail-thin former teacher with her thinning hair dyed black, a mottled face, and the slightly agitated manner of a hypochondriac. But the burden of her importance here showed in her dazed look at the jammed courtroom, the way she kept blinking, as if dragged from a dark place into a room filled with klieg lights. Even her voice, low and raspy, filled Paget with remembered alarm: it was that of the woman, coming from the darkness of the police auditorium, who had picked him from the lineup. Next to her, on an easel, was a black-and-white photograph of Paget himself.

The questioning began in earnest. Caroline picked up a pen, poised it over her pad, still looking at Georgina Keller. In the jury box, Joseph Duarte did the same.

"And where *is* your apartment," Salinas asked, "relative to Mr. Arias's?"

Keller pursed her lips. "I'm at the end of the hall. Mr. Arias is, or *was*, the apartment next to me. On the left-hand side, if you're facing out."

"And how many feet, approximately, was Mr. Arias's door from yours?"

"Perhaps twelve feet. Fifteen at the most."

"And did there come a time, on the night before you left on your vacation, that you became concerned about Mr. Arias?"

"There did." Pausing, Keller gave a blink of nervousness, touching the bridge of her nose as if to push up glasses that were not there. "I heard a noise in Mr. Arias's apartment—the walls aren't very thick, and I could hear when he listened to music, or even sometimes when he talked to his little girl. But this time I heard voices and then a thud. Like something, or someone, hitting the floor."

"Did the noise worry you?"

"Yes." Keller looked vaguely at the jury. "Because of the voices, you see. It was two men speaking like they were angry. They were muffled, of course. But one of them sounded like Mr. Arias." Keller continued more quietly. "What disturbed me was what happened *after* I heard the thud. Suddenly I couldn't hear any voices at all. Just silence."

"And what did you do, if anything?"

Keller looked apprehensive, as if her memory of the moment was colored by Richie's death. "I went to the door," she said in a brittle tone, "and cracked it open. As far as the door chain would permit."

"And what did you see?"

In the jury box, Marian Celler leaned forward to hear Keller's answer. "Nothing, at first." Turning, Keller almost peered at Paget, and then her head snapped away. "A noise frightened me—a door opening in the hallway. I flinched so hard that the door chain rattled."

"And did you look out again?"

Keller glanced quickly at Salinas, as if in a nervous pantomime of the action she described; Paget suddenly imagined her, peeking fretfully through the crack of a door. "Yes," she said slowly. "I *did* look again."

The courtroom was still. With her quirky mannerisms, Paget realized, Keller was an oddly effective witness: she seemed less to describe the scene than to inhabit it. As if sensing this, Salinas had begun nodding his encouragement. Quite gently, he asked, "And what did you see *then?*"

"A man." Keller's voice went soft with dread. "Coming out of Mr. Arias's apartment."

"And could you describe this man?"

"Yes." There was a tremor in the words. "He was tall, in his mid to late thirties. He wore a gray suit, double-breasted, and his hair was kind of blond. Copper almost."

Keller held her head rigid now, as if straining to look not at

Paget but into her memory. Watching her, Caroline's face seemed quite calm; only her posture, rigid and unnatural, betrayed her tension.

"Did this man *do* anything?" Salinas asked.

"He stopped—for a moment. I thought he saw me. But he hadn't." Keller swallowed. "He was holding something, like a notebook or a journal. Then he put the journal in his left hand and began staring at his other hand. The next thing he did was odd."

Keller stopped abruptly.

"What was that?" Salinas prodded.

"He shook his hand, like it hurt. And then he touched the sleeve of his suit coat and turned it over." Keller stared at the floor. "As if he were looking for stains."

Caroline, Paget realized, intended to let all this go. With an air of solicitude, Salinas asked, "And during that time, Mrs. Keller, did you see the man's face?"

Keller stared straight ahead now, head cocked, as if peering through the crack again. "Yes."

"Can you describe him?"

A nod, and then a moment's silence. Paget felt the jury wait. "It was a *strong* face," Keller said. "With a ridged nose and a cleft in his chin."

As if by reflex, Luisa Marin turned to Paget. The other jurors followed; helpless, Paget could feel them studying the features Georgina Keller had described.

"Had you ever seen this man before, Mrs. Keller?"

"No. Never."

"After looking at his sleeve, what did the man do next?"

"He turned away." Keller's eyes closed briefly. "But I was afraid to shut the door, because he'd hear me. So I leaned against it, listening to his footsteps, until he disappeared."

Her voice had fallen. Quietly, Salinas asked, "Did you call the police?"

"No." Keller hung her head. "It was none of my business, I thought, and I was leaving the next morning. To visit my daughter in Florida. Until I returned, three weeks later, I didn't know that Mr. Arias was dead."

"And did there come a time, after you returned, when the police came to your apartment?"

"Inspector Monk did." Keller thought for a moment. "*And* his partner. Inspector Lynch. I was shocked, of course."

"And did you tell them about the man you saw?"

"Yes. They had me describe him, over and over."

"What happened next?"

"They showed me a picture. From a newspaper, I thought." Fretful, Keller passed a hand through her hair, still looking everywhere but at Paget. "Right away, Mr. Salinas, I knew I'd seen the face before."

Salinas walked to the easel with the photograph of Paget—a head shot, taken at the time of the Carelli trial. "And is *this* the photograph Inspector Monk showed you?"

"Yes." Keller gazed at the picture. "It was the man in the hallway."

"You're certain of that?"

A jerky nod, face averted from Paget. "Yes."

A grimness had begun settling over the courtroom. Paget had seen it before: a turning point, when a jury begins to accept a defendant's guilt. Since Keller began, Caroline had not even looked at him. She had made no notes at all.

"And did there come a time," Salinas asked, "when Inspector Monk took you to a lineup?"

"Yes."

"Could you describe what happened there?"

Keller sounded vaguely mystified, as if describing the arcane rites of an obscure South American tribe. "They took me into an auditorium, at the police station. It was almost like a play—the stage was lit, but all the seats were dark.

"There were six men on the stage, dressed in orange coveralls and holding numbers to their chests. Each of them stepped forward, turning to the left and the right, while Inspector Monk asked if I recognized any of them."

"And did you?"

"Yes." Keller spoke more firmly now; still she did not look at Paget. "I asked the man to step forward twice, just to make sure. But I knew him the moment I saw him."

Salinas stood straighter, jamming both hands in his pockets. "And do you *also* see that man in the courtroom, Mrs. Keller?"

For the first time, Georgina Keller turned to Paget. She paused for a moment, as if checking each feature, and then raised her arm to point. "Yes, I do. The defendant. Mr. Paget."

Beginning, Caroline seemed muted. "This crack in the door," she asked in a tone of pleasant inquiry. "About how wide was it?"

Frowning, Keller held her hands in front of her face, peering between them. "Like so."

"About two to three inches."

"I would say that. But the door opens on the right side, and Mr. Arias's apartment was to my left. So I was looking straight at his door."

It was a very good answer, Paget knew. Caroline seemed to search for another avenue. "About how long," she asked, "would you say that this man paused, looking at his hand and sleeve?"

"For a time." Keller reflected for a moment. "A good ten seconds."

"You were frightened, yes?"

"Yes."

"That can make time stand still, Mrs. Keller. In fairness, could it have been less than ten seconds?"

Silence, then a grudging nod. "I suppose it could have."

"Perhaps even five?"

Keller shook her head. "It couldn't have been that short a time. He looked at his hand *and* his sleeve."

Caroline tilted her head. "Did *you* look at his hand?"

"Yes."

"Could you see anything?"

"I thought maybe it was injured. As I said, the man shook it."

Caroline nodded. "And when the man looked at his *sleeve,* did *you* look at it too?"

"Yes.

"Could you see anything?"

Keller gave a nod of satisfaction. "He was right beneath the overhead light in the hallway. I thought I saw a stain—dark speckles on the sleeve."

Each answer, Paget knew, was that much worse; for the first time,

Caroline seemed to be floundering. "About how long, Mrs. Keller, did *you* look at this man's hand?"

Keller squinted. "A few seconds, at least."

Caroline nodded. "About how long did you look at his *sleeve* before noticing the stains?"

"Another few seconds."

"And during the time you were looking at his hand, and then his sleeve, you *weren't* looking at his face, correct?"

A slight pause. "I suppose not, no."

"So out of the ten seconds—or maybe less—that this man was in front of Mr. Arias's door, how long did you actually see his face?"

Narrow-eyed, Keller sucked in her cheeks; it gave her a hollow, gaunt look. "I can't say."

"Less than five seconds?"

"Maybe."

"Less than three?"

"I don't know." Keller's raspy voice rose slightly. "All I can tell you is that I saw his face, clearly."

"Clearly? It was in shadows, right?"

"What do you mean?"

"It would *have* to be, Mrs. Keller. If the light was right above his head."

Caroline had captured the jury's attention now. But it seemed more polite than vigilant; to the jury, Paget was certain, the photograph and lineup had damaged him, and the in-court identification had finished him off. In a recalcitrant tone, Keller said to Caroline, "I can't remember shadows. I saw him, that's all."

To Paget's surprise, Caroline nodded agreeably. "And you'd never seen him before, correct?"

"Correct," Keller affirmed.

Somewhere in the last two answers, Paget suddenly sensed, Caroline had set a trap. But he could not yet see where it was.

"And how much time passed," Caroline was asking, "until Inspector Monk dropped by with the picture you identified?"

"Perhaps three weeks."

"And how long after *that* did you identify Mr. Paget in a lineup?"

"Maybe another two weeks."

"In other words, at least five weeks or so from the time that you saw the man leaving Mr. Arias's apartment."

Keller touched her cheek. "I guess so. But I *knew* that I'd seen him before."

Caroline looked curious. "How do you know that you weren't identifying Mr. Paget in the *lineup* because you recognized Mr. Paget from his picture?"

Keller shook her head, impatient at Caroline's obtuseness. "Because I'd seen the man in the picture *before* that. Just as I told Inspector Monk."

For the first time, Caroline smiled. "Then perhaps you can humor me, Mrs. Keller, by looking at some other pictures."

In moments, with the aid of Lerner's courtroom deputy, Keller was gazing at a pasteboard with seven color pictures—Paget's conscripts from the county jail, wearing jumpsuits and holding numbers one through six, and a group photo of them all. Paget's great white hope, the Southern inmate named Ray, stood out from the pasteboard as suspect number three. But compared to Paget, his face was pale and weak.

"As Mr. Salinas has stipulated," Caroline told Keller, "these are police photographs of the men included in the lineup. Can you pick out Mr. Paget?"

"Yes." Keller pointed. "The second from the end."

"In fact, isn't it fair to say that—in terms of height, build, hair and skin color—Mr. Paget stood out from the others?"

Keller squinted at the board. "Except for the third man."

"And didn't you, in fact, also ask Inspector Monk to have *that* man step forward for a second time?"

Keller hesitated. "I believe I did."

"For what purpose?"

"Because at first glance, certain things about him generally resembled the man in the hallway."

"What things?"

"Well, this man's hair color was different—too reddish—and his face was softer than the man in the hallway. It was more that the height and build were the same."

Caroline, Paget saw, was being matter-of-fact and unthreatening, more an academic in search of clarity than a bristling cross-examiner. More and more, Paget guessed that Keller was already in trouble, although he still did not know how or why.

"And so," Caroline summarized, "the man you saw in the hallway was slender, about six feet tall, with hair on the blond side and fair skin. Correct?"

"Yes."

"*And* about thirty-five years old?" Caroline asked innocently.

"About that."

Caroline smiled. "As opposed to Mr. Paget's forty-six?"

Reluctantly, Keller gazed at Paget again. "He looks younger."

Caroline gave Paget a mock-critical once-over. "Not *ten* years younger, I would say. Although I'm sure that Mr. Paget appreciates your charity."

There was mild laughter; it seemed a small point, and even Salinas smiled briefly. Keller settled into the chair again.

"Are you," Caroline asked, "familiar with a case entitled *People versus Carelli?*"

A short nod. "That was Mr. Paget's case."

"And *mine,*" Caroline said dryly. "As you may recall, *I* was the judge."

"I know. I *thought* I recognized you."

"Really? How?"

Again, Keller looked at Caroline as if she were slightly dense. "From *television,*" she said impatiently. "You were *on* every day."

It was *he,* Paget suddenly realized, who had been dense. "So," Caroline said amiably, "if you were to put me in a lineup with five other women, do you think you'd still know I was the judge?"

Paget could not help turning to Salinas. The prosecutor was on his feet, a portrait of alarm. "Objection," he said. "Calls for speculation. And until Ms. Masters is charged with some crime, whether this witness remembers her isn't relevant to anything."

But Lerner's eyes were bright now, a trace of the smile he had to suppress. "Overruled. You may answer the question, Mrs. Keller."

"Maybe." Keller said to Caroline. "I recognized you *here.*"

"Because you'd seen me before. On television."

"Yes."

Caroline skipped a beat. "Just like Mr. Paget."

Keller looked around her, blinking again. "When I identified Mr. Paget I didn't realize it was him. Even at the lineup."

"But before the lineup you *had* seen Christopher Paget before, correct? On television."

A stiff nod. "Yes, I had."

Caroline looked curious. "Tell me, Mrs. Keller, do you think Mary Carelli did it? You know, murdered Mark Ransom?"

Keller shook her head. "I couldn't tell. I changed my mind from day to day."

Caroline raised an eyebrow. "You watched *every* day?"

"Almost."

"The Carelli trial was about two weeks long, right?"

"Objection," Salinas called out. "Irrelevant."

Lerner held up a hand. "Be serious, Mr. Salinas." Turning to Caroline, he added, "Please continue."

"Mrs. Keller?" Caroline asked.

"Two weeks long? About that."

"So before Inspector Monk showed you the picture, you *had* seen Mr. Paget before—every day, for two weeks. On television."

"That's true." Keller's voice turned stubborn. "But I'd never seen him in person."

"I quite agree," Caroline said dryly. "But at the time Inspector Monk showed you this picture, you *knew* you'd seen Mr. Paget's face before."

"That's right. I just didn't place him."

"And when they put on the lineup, you'd already seen Mr. Paget's *picture*. As well as seen him on television."

Keller had begun looking confused. "That's true."

"And once more, you *knew* that you'd seen him before."

"Yes."

Caroline's voice became very quiet. "But when you saw the man in the *hallway*, you didn't recognize him as anyone you'd seen before, did you?"

In the witness box, Keller seemed to go blank. Paget recognized it: the moment of helpless confusion when a witness begins to lose her will. Caroline moved forward. "Do you want the court reporter to read back your prior answer, Mrs. Keller? Where you told us that you'd never seen the man in the hallway?"

Absently, Keller twisted a lock of hair, then caught herself. "I *said* that, yes."

"So when you saw the man in the hallway," Caroline repeated, "you didn't recognize him as *anyone* you'd seen before."

Looking down, Keller shook her head. "No."

"Let alone Christopher Paget."

"No."

"And until you saw his *picture*, you didn't recognize *Christopher Paget* as anyone you'd seen before, either. True?"

"I guess not." Keller shook her head. "I'm confused now."

The jury, Paget saw, was transfixed; Joseph Duarte flipped his notebook back a page and drew a line through what he had written. But Caroline still had points to make.

"No," she said to Keller, "you're not confused *now*. Tell me, isn't it true that you recognized Mr. Paget's picture because you'd seen him during the Carelli hearing?"

Keller twisted her hair again. "That might be *one* reason."

"So isn't it also true that when you identified him at the lineup, you recognized Mr. Paget from his picture *and* from television?"

"Anything's possible, I guess." Keller's voice turned obstinate. "But I *still* think I recognize Mr. Paget from in the hallway."

Caroline stared at her and then plucked a plastic bottle from the pocket of her suit, holding it up for the jury to see. "Is *this* anything you recognize, Mrs. Keller?"

"I believe so." Keller glanced at Salinas. "It looks like the bottle for my sleeping pill prescription."

If he were not a lawyer, Paget thought, or on trial for murder, this might have been too terrible to watch. Caroline moved close to Keller. "In fact, it is. Just how long have you taken them?"

"Almost a year."

"Every night?"

"Yes."

"At about what time?"

"A half hour before I go to bed. Sometime between nine and ten."

"How do they affect you?"

Keller's voice turned flat. "They help me sleep."

"By making you drowsy?"

"They do that."

"And perhaps a little less observant?"

"Maybe. I've got no way of telling."

"Tell me this, then. The night you saw the man leaving Mr. Arias's apartment—for maybe five seconds, perhaps with his face in shadow—had you already *taken* your pill?"

Keller touched her forehead. She seemed to have drawn inward; she no longer looked out at the courtroom. "I don't remember."

"But it's possible? Please, this is important."

Keller furrowed her brow, as if trying to retrieve some image of that night. "I can't remember," she finally murmured, "one way or the other. So I'd have to say it's possible."

"So would I," Caroline said softly. "About how long after you saw this man did you fall asleep?"

"I don't know. I remember being tired. Maybe a half hour."

Caroline tilted her head. "You also wear glasses, do you not?"

"Yes. But only for reading. Not for any distance."

Caroline, Paget saw, was edging toward the easel. "Were you wearing them the night you saw this man?"

"No. As I said, I use them just for reading."

Caroline put her hand on her hip. "Do you think you could look at the lineup picture again and tell me Mr. Paget's number?"

Before Keller even turned, Paget knew that she would squint. For the long moment of Keller's silence, Paget could feel the jury watch her. "Five," she said finally.

"It is indeed." Caroline said dryly. "Let me return, for a moment, to your testimony that you heard voices and then a thud, like someone falling. How good is your hearing, Mrs. Keller?"

Keller sat straighter. "It's very good."

Caroline nodded. "And after this thud you heard, and before seeing the man in the hallway, did you hear anything else?"

Keller looked puzzled. "I don't believe so."

Caroline paused a moment. Quietly she asked, "Not even a gunshot?"

Duarte's head jerked up from his notes. There was a long silence as Keller considered the question. "No," she answered slowly. "I did not."

Caroline smiled briefly. "Thank you, Mrs. Keller. I have no further questions."

She turned, walking back toward Paget. Though her eyes were bright, she kept her face expressionless now; it would not do to look pleased.

As she sat, Paget whispered, "That was classic."

"A minor classic, at best." Watching Salinas rise, Caroline kept her voice low. "Once Keller's neighbor told Johnny Moore that all she could talk about for two weeks was the Carelli case, this poor lady was as dead as Humpty Dumpty. Not even Victor can put her together again." She turned to Paget. "No deal?"

"No deal." Paget paused a moment. "And no defense."

Redirect was over quickly, as Caroline knew it would be.

Salinas did his best. Yes, Keller affirmed, she believed the man in the hallway was Christopher Paget. At the time, she had not recognized the man in the picture *or* the lineup as Paget—to her, he was the man in the hallway. Wearing glasses to see would have done more harm than good, and she was too frightened to be drowsy. Listening, Caroline had no more idea who Keller had seen than did Keller herself; for all Caroline knew, it *was* Chris Paget. But that mattered as little as Victor's redirect; as the key prosecution witness, Georgina Keller was damaged goods.

When it was over, and the jury excused, Caroline asked Judge Lerner for a meeting in chambers.

Glum, Salinas seemed to know what was coming. They sat in front of Lerner's desk as the judge, leaning back in an overstuffed chair, comtemplated the prosecutor with a certain sympathy. Caroline had been in Victor's place; she knew too well what it meant.

"It's Friday afternoon," Lerner said pleasantly to Caroline. "You're not planning to make me work, are you?"

Caroline smiled. "Not until Monday morning, Your Honor. But I wanted to discuss our plans for the defense."

The judge nodded. "Go ahead."

"We have none." Glancing at Salinas, she saw that he was determinedly stoic. "Under the circumstances, we plan to present no witnesses. But before final argument, I *would* like to move to dismiss this case for lack of evidence."

The judge nodded again, as if he had expected this. "Eight o'clock Monday morning, then. But be prepared for final arguments." He looked at Salinas. "Anything else, Victor?"

Salinas shook his head. "Not at this time."

"Then there's one thing *I* want to raise—this matter of Mr. Slocum's source." Lerner turned to her. "Is any part of your motion that the prosecution—or this reporter—denied you a material witness? Whoever this 'source' is."

Caroline shook her head. "No, Your Honor. *If* there's final argument, we intend to make a point of the uncertainty this creates. But we've chosen to accept Mr. Salinas's compromise." She turned to Salinas, pinning him to the wall. "That is, if you *and* Mr. Brooks still stand by it."

Salinas looked like a man concealing some deep emotion: Caroline was certain that Brooks had ordered him not to let Slocum's source become a witness and to accept the problems this created. She could well imagine the fury of someone as competitive as Salinas. "The D.A.," he said finally, "has decided to let Mr. Slocum protect his source."

Lerner nodded his satisfaction. "That's it, then. See you Monday morning, for Ms. Masters' motion."

That was all. "For the record," she told Salinas on the way out, "we're not taking McKinley's deal. But you can tell him he's off the hook."

Salinas merely shrugged. His expression was unfathomable; perhaps Caroline only imagined his disappointment. They trailed out of chambers, Salinas quiet, Caroline quietly pleased.

Lerner was the right judge; her strong sense was that, come Monday, he would dismiss the case.

Christopher Paget was almost home.

SIXTEEN

PAGET SPENT the weekend quietly. Unlike Caroline, he seesawed back and forth, believing that Lerner would either throw out the case or let it go to a jury about which Paget still had grave doubts. The prospect of a quick exit—the case closed, the pursuit of new evidence cut off—both tantalized and tormented him. The hours passed too slowly.

It gave him time to think. But the summing up depressed him; that Carlo and Terri had lied for him was deeply painful in itself *and* because neither relationship could ever be the same. He cared much more about that than about the world at large, personified by the camera crews posted outside his door. But he had paid a price there too: even if he was acquitted Monday, the first thing people would think of when they met him was Ricardo Arias.

He saw Terri only once. There had been a call from Elena's therapist; Terri seemed quite troubled, although she would say little. But for the first time, Terri appeared to be uncomfortable in his home; encountering Carlo, she was distant and preoccupied. She received the news that Paget would not testify with dead calm, wishing him luck and asking no questions. She left shortly after.

Whether he won or lost, Paget knew, there would be a reckoning between them. There were wounds and doubts, perhaps for both of them, which had yet to be addressed: Paget sensed that what would preserve their relationship for a time was a conviction, because Terri would feel obliged not to desert him. But that would be, Paget intended to tell her, no consolation at all.

The one bright spot was Carlo. Paget saw Caroline's dismantling of Georgina Keller for what it was: the guile of a gifted lawyer who knew that eyewitness testimony, which seemed so damning to lay people, was often not hard to discredit. But Carlo chose to seize on it as vindication, as if to fill the vacuum created by his father's silence. The knowledge that Carlo's optimism was an act of will did not entirely dampen Paget's pleasure: with his future in the balance, any lightening of Carlo's mood afforded some relief.

He had been right to choose Caroline, Paget thought. Despite the restrictions he had placed on her, she had done an extraordinary job; Paget wondered if he himself could have done as well. There had been a real comfort in Caroline's presence; her coolness and self-confidence were much more bracing than constant solicitude or burning zeal. And he had come to like her. Sometimes Paget wished that he could tell her the truth.

But between them, perhaps the truth did not really matter. Caroline was a professional; he knew she would spend the weekend preparing and would make an excellent argument. By Monday morning, Paget had half convinced himself that, within hours, he would be free again.

The first sign that something was wrong was the look on Salinas's face.

They were in court, waiting for Judge Lerner. The jury was not present; reporters, notified by Lerner that Caroline's motion would be heard, already packed the courtroom. But Salinas did not appear edgy and combative, as Paget would have expected; he seemed almost detached, and there was something in his bland expression that suggested a half smile. He looked like the only person in the courtroom who knew what was happening.

Paget turned to Caroline. "What's with Victor—?"

"*All rise,*" Lerner's courtroom deputy called out. "The Superior Court of the City and County of San Francisco, Judge Jared M. Lerner, is now in session."

Lerner ascended the bench. "All right," he said crisply. "Our first business this morning is the defendant's motion to dismiss all charges. Ms. Masters?"

Salinas stood. "Pardon me, Your Honor. But within the last forty-eight hours there has been a development which renders this motion premature, at best. The people ask leave of court to reopen the prosecution case, to present another witness. After disclosure of the prospective new evidence to Ms. Masters, of course."

Paget was stunned: Salinas had underscored the words "new evidence," to tell him that the deal with Brooks could not be retrieved. "He's *sandbagged* us," Caroline murmured in a taut voice, and quickly stood. "Just how did you discover this witness, Mr. Salinas?"

"*She* discovered us." Salinas's voice had a shade of irony. "She recognized Mr. Paget from television. A news report of Friday's court proceedings."

All at once, Paget knew what had happened. But Caroline, of course, did not. "Who *is* this?" she asked Salinas. "Surely not another keyhole peeper."

Salinas shook his head. "This person met Mr. Paget in an entirely different context. A charitable donation, in fact."

Caroline turned to Lerner. "A moment, Your Honor, if you please." She sat, turning to Paget with a look of worry and annoyance. "Do you know what this 'new evidence' is?"

Paget felt sick. "Yes," he answered. "I do. And any chance for a deal with Brooks is gone."

Lerner gave Caroline the morning to prepare; the witness's testimony was simple and straightforward and would not take long. At two o'clock, Anna Velez took the stand.

Except for a black suit, she was as Paget remembered her—lovely brown eyes, gold earrings, and vivid makeup, pleasantly plump. He had been a fool to hope that she would not remember *him*.

Salinas still seemed calm, almost matter-of-fact. "And where do you work, Ms. Velez?"

"At the Goodwill outlet on Mission Street."

Paget's memory of that day, he found, had a dreamlike quality: shaken by Monk's questions, he had drifted through the next several hours, from one haphazard solution to another, settling on the most foolish. When, as fate would have it, he encountered Anna Velez. Of that, his memory was perfect.

As, it seemed, was hers. "And in November of last year," Salinas asked, "did you encounter the defendant, Christopher Paget?"

Velez had a face made for smiling, Paget recalled, but now it was somber. "I did," she said. "At the store."

The jury, Paget saw, was attentive but mystified: they understood only that this was important. Quietly, Salinas asked, "And why did you choose, at this late date, to bring this to our attention?"

Velez folded her hands. "I was watching television on Friday night—only because my sister turned it on. The newsman was talking about this case, and they showed a film of Mr. Paget.

" 'I know that man,' I said to my sister, and so I started paying attention." Furtively, she glanced at Paget. "It was about this lady who thought she saw another man leaving this dead man's apartment and that he wore a double-breasted gray suit with maybe something on the sleeve. And suddenly it all made sense."

Salinas seemed animated now. "*What* made sense?"

"The reason I knew Mr. Paget is that he came to my store with three suits and a new pair of shoes." Velez's voice conveyed a certain horror. "One of the suits was gray and had a stain on its right sleeve."

"*Jesus,*" someone murmured. In a few brief hours, Paget thought bleakly, he had gone from the verge of acquittal to facing a life in prison. The jury seemed startled, as if their sense of the case had just turned around.

"Was there a particular reason, Ms. Velez, that the defendant stuck in your mind?"

She nodded. "It was the whole thing—him *and* what he brought. At first, it was that he was good-looking and that the shoes and suits were so expensive but he didn't seem to care. Like he was rich. He didn't even want a receipt for taxes." She paused. "After we closed, I looked at the suits again. They had foreign labels—Italian, I think—and the wool was like I'd never felt before, light and very soft. It really amazed me that someone would just give away what seemed like a thousand-dollar suit. And then I saw the stain."

"Could you describe it?"

Velez nodded. "It was like spots. Or a spatter of something."

Everything she said, Paget thought, made things that much worse: even her ingenuous touches—his wealth and carelessness—would be deadly with the jury, and Caroline could do nothing.

Salinas paused for attention. "What, if anything, did you try to do about the stain?"

Velez spread her hands. "The suit was so nice, Mr. Salinas, that I decided to take it home and try to clean it."

"And did you?"

"I tried. I used soap, stain remover—everything, even cold water. It wouldn't come out." Her eyes narrowed. "It was like ink, I remember thinking. Or blood."

Caroline glanced up but otherwise did not react; to move to strike the answer would only drive it home.

"You also mentioned shoes," Salinas said. "Could you describe them?"

"Not as well as the suit. But they were black leather and soft to touch." Velez glanced at the jury. "What I really remember is that they were almost brand-new. Like even the heels were barely scuffed."

"At the time Mr. Paget gave you the shoes, did you ask him about this?"

"What he told me was they didn't fit right." Velez frowned, then shook her head. "I remember thinking *I'd* take them back to exchange."

Did you find fibers on any shoes? Caroline had asked Monk. Paget wondered if the jury was following this, and then he saw Joseph Duarte make a note.

"Do you know where the shoes are now?" Salinas asked.

Velez shrugged, shaking her head. "I couldn't find them at the store. So I guess we sold them or gave them away. From our records, you can't be sure."

Salinas paused again. "What about the suit?" he asked softly. "With the stains like ink. Or blood."

Paget felt himself tense. In the jury box, Marian Celler turned to Velez, awaiting her answer. "No," Velez said. "It's gone too. We don't know where it is."

For a moment, Paget closed his eyes.

"Did you have a receipt," Salinas asked, "from Mr. Paget's visit?"

"We have a copy."

Salinas held up a small square of paper. "Your Honor, by stipulation with the defense, I would like to introduce this as People's Exhibit 17 and ask the witness to identify it."

He passed the scrap to Velez. "Is this your handwriting?" he asked.

Velez held it gingerly. "It is. This is the receipt I gave to Mr. Paget."

"And could you tell us what it shows?"

Velez nodded. "It shows that on November 1, Mr. Paget gave us three suits and a pair of shoes. Just like I remember."

Salinas took the slip, proffering it to Caroline. "We've seen it," she said, and then Salinas walked to the jury box and handed it to Joseph Duarte. Duarte read the receipt, and then gave it to Marian Celler. Paget watched it begin passing from juror to juror—a piece of paper with lines for each item and the word "Padgett" scrawled at the top.

"No further questions," Salinas said.

Rising, Caroline looked puzzled, inclining her head toward the jury box. "I'd understood you to say that Mr. Paget didn't *want* a receipt."

"He said he didn't *need* one. But I told him he should have it."

"And what did *he* say?"

Velez looked at the ceiling. "I guess I don't remember," she said after a time. "But he must have taken it."

"How did you get Mr. Paget's name? To put at the top of the receipt."

"I asked him." Velez paused. "I remember wondering how to spell it but not wanting to ask."

"So he wasn't trying to hide who he was."

Velez thought about the question. "I don't know," she answered. "But he gave me his right name. I just didn't spell it right."

Caroline nodded. "When Mr. Paget was in the store, did you talk to him?"

"A little bit."

"How did he seem to you?"

"Nice." For the first time, Velez seemed to feel bad about what she had done. "He wasn't superchatty, but I thought he was real nice. I remember joking with him about something or other."

"Would you say he was friendly?"

"I'd say so, yes. He wasn't stuck-up or anything. Or really quiet."

It was all Caroline had, Paget thought: to make him seem an amiable man, running a routine errand. "Did he appear nervous?" Caroline asked.

"Nervous? No. I never thought that."

Caroline moved closer. "And so, at the time, the impression Mr. Paget left was that he was generous?"

The word seemed to puzzle Velez. "You mean, giving away new things?" She considered for a time. "Yes, I guess I thought that was generous. I mean, you don't usually get things that nice. Even the suit with the stain."

Caroline nodded. "About that stain—you have no idea *what* it was, correct?"

Velez hesitated. "That's right."

"On a gray suit, you couldn't even tell what *color* it was."

Velez shook her head. "Except that it was darker than the suit."

"So when you said the stain reminded you of ink or blood, it was because it wouldn't come out?"

"That's what made me think of it."

"And ink, or blood, were just *examples* of stains you think are hard to get out?"

"That's right."

"You don't claim to be an expert on bloodstains?"

"Oh, no."

"Or, for that matter, stain removal."

Velez grinned. "I guess I'm not. I couldn't get *this* one out."

For the first time, Caroline smiled. "So in summary, a pleasant man came to your store, turned in a pair of shoes and three suits, one of which had a stain you can't identify, joked with you a little, gave you his name when you asked, and let you fill out a receipt recording his visit. Is that right?"

Velez seemed to tick off the points in her mind. "That's right."

Caroline's smile faded. "When you found out, over the weekend, that the man you met had been charged with murder, were you surprised?"

Velez looked troubled. "Yes. I was."

"Because he seemed so nice."

"That's right."

"And because his behavior *didn't* seem suspicious."

Velez pondered that. "I thought he was *careless*, in a way. About his things. But he *was* nice."

Caroline smiled again. "Some millionaires are like that, I suppose—careless but nice. Anyhow, I guess he didn't seem like a homicidal maniac."

Salinas stood at once. "Objection. Lack of foundation, calls for speculation. Murderers come in all shapes and sizes, Your Honor. And guises."

"Sustained."

But Caroline had made her point. Casually turning back to the witness, she asked, "By the way, Ms. Velez, do you like red wine?"

For a moment, Velez looked bemused. "Sometimes," she said. "Especially Rioja. You know, from Spain."

"Ever spill any?"

Velez grimaced. "Yes. On a new cotton skirt."

Caroline smiled in sympathy. "How was it to get out?"

"I couldn't," Velez said, and then nodded. "Wine—that's hard to get out too."

"I've always thought so," Caroline told her. "Thank you, Ms. Velez."

"It was all I could do," Caroline said at last.

They were in Caroline's car, driving Paget home. She had not asked where he wished to go but simply started driving; the atmosphere in the car was close and tense, and Caroline's voice was flat with withheld anger.

"I know that," Paget answered.

Caroline stopped in front of the house. The only light came from streetlamps. But there was a yellow glow inside the house; Carlo was already home.

Caroline stared ahead. "I set Victor up," she said, "and then walked right into my own cross on Keller. All that stuff I did about the man leaving Richie's apartment and Keller looking at his sleeve instead of his face. Pure suicide."

"You didn't know."

Caroline shook her head. "I'm sorry, Chris. But you really fucked this up."

Her tone was factual but not unkind. Suddenly Caroline sounded tired. They were quiet for a while.

"This changes everything," she said.

"It can't."

She turned to him. "Spell it out for me, then."

His own voice was tight now. "I can't testify, Caroline. How much clearer do I have to be?"

She stared at him. "You don't," she said finally.

Paget felt a burst of anger. "If you think this has been easy for me, *you* try it. Compared to my role, *yours* is light work."

Caroline's eyes narrowed. "So you want me to stick to this—no defense. Even after today."

"Yes." Paget paused. "I have no choice."

Caroline turned away.

Perhaps, Paget thought, she had wanted him to be innocent. Perhaps she did not know with whom she was angry—Paget or herself. After a moment, she leaned back in the seat. "Then it's closing argument tomorrow."

"Yes."

"I suppose I'd better go, then."

Paget's own anger had died. He touched her shoulder, then opened the car door and got out. It was a while before Caroline pulled away from the curb.

Carlo was in the library.

The television was on, a film clip of Anna Velez leaving the courtroom. When Carlo turned, there were tears in his eyes. But what Paget saw was worse; for the first time, his son believed him a murderer.

Awkwardly, Paget hugged him; stiffly, Carlo returned it. There was nothing either could say.

SEVENTEEN

When Salinas rose to give his closing argument, Terri and Carlo were together in the courtroom.

The idea was Terri's. She had called the night before; Paget told her of Anna Velez and that he still would offer no witnesses of his own. Terri did not argue; days before, she had stopped asking questions. After a moment's silence, she said that it was important that the jury, before cloistering to reach a verdict, remember the people who loved Paget most; if the case was over, she added, there was nothing to keep her or Carlo from the courtroom. Terri had called Carlo herself; almost defiantly, Carlo had insisted to his father that he come. Now they sat behind his father, her lover, where the jury could see them.

The symbolism was effective: not only did these people need Paget in their lives, their presence said, but Terri did not believe Richie's charges against Carlo. Only Paget would realize how little they spoke to each other, compared to a half year ago, or how tired Carlo looked. As for Terri, she had waited until the jury filed in to lean forward and squeeze his hand; even when she smiled, a part of her seemed elsewhere.

"You'll be all right," she had whispered.

But he did not believe that, nor did Caroline seem to. This morning she was unusually quiet; the professional élan had been replaced by a certain inwardness. On the day before what perhaps would be her most important closing argument, she had been dealt a surprise that unsettled her equilibrium and made her task far more difficult. It left no time for chatter.

As for Paget, he felt alone. What made it worse was that this was no one's fault but his; from the first time Monk had come to his home, he had begun stumbling blindly down a path that now, abruptly, had closed behind him. He could not talk to anyone, no matter how deeply he wished to, and he did not know if he ever could. All that he had left was the jury.

They seemed more alert, perhaps a little surprised to be awaiting closing arguments instead of Paget's witnesses. It was a bad sign that so few looked in his direction; even Marian Celler, whom Caroline had wanted so much, kept her gaze straight ahead. Joseph Duarte was reviewing the notes that, Paget well knew, ended with the damage done by Anna Velez. Only Victor Salinas appeared at ease.

"Mr. Salinas," Jared Lerner said gravely, "you may begin."

Gazing at the jury, Salinas looked solemn and self-contained, a serious man doing a necessary job. There was no trace of showmanship.

"*This,*" he began, "was a murder. And from the moment that he killed Ricardo Arias to the final and devastating moments of this trial, Christopher Paget has been trying to get away with it."

He paused, letting that sink in. The jury watched with open faces, ready to believe him.

"The mantra Ms. Masters will repeat to you, I am sure, is that you *must* believe that we have proven Christopher Paget guilty of murder beyond a reasonable doubt, or you must find him innocent. So let us talk—right now—about what we're *not* required to show.

"We *don't* need a witness who saw Mr. Paget shoot Ricardo Arias. That hardly ever happens.

"Nor does *every* witness have to be sure about *every* scrap of testimony."

This was clever, Paget thought with apprehension: it would be Caroline's strategy to slice and dice the case into a thousand facts and then to cast doubt where she could. "No," Salinas continued, "our job here is to present sufficient proof, accumulated in the form of circumstantial evidence, to satisfy men and women of common sense—the *same* common sense that Ms. Masters asked you to bring to this courtroom—that Mr. Paget *is* guilty. *Guilty,*" Salinas repeated, "beyond a reasonable doubt.

"Is there a reasonable doubt that Ricardo Arias was murdered? There is not.

"The medical examiner spelled out for us the medical evidence."

Holding up his hand, Salinas ticked off his points one by one: "The absence of blood spatters on Mr. Arias's hands.

"The absence of gunpowder on his hands.

"The strange position of the body.

"The curious angle of the bullet.

"And all those things Mr. Arias plainly did *not* do to himself—the abrasion on his leg, the gash on his head, the bloody nose.

"Mr. Arias did *not* beat himself up." Pausing, Salinas gave a first grim smile. "Nor did he pirouette around the living room, taking pratfall after pratfall, and then shoot himself in the mouth from the most uncomfortable position he could imagine after wiping his nose to make himself presentable.

"He did *not* make a coffee date to tell Elena's teacher that he had decided not to kill himself.

"Or make an appointment with Dr. Gates just to keep his options open.

"Or take five shirts to the laundry to provide a choice of fresh clothes for the funeral."

Pausing, Salinas slowly shook his head. "No, ladies and gentlemen—*this* was a man who expected to live until the moment that he died, and no one who knows him believes otherwise.

"Not Elena's teacher.

"Not his own mother.

"Not the psychologist he saw perhaps *forty* times.

"Not even, it is obvious, his wife. Christopher Paget's lover."

Turning, Paget glanced at Terri. Her gaze at Salinas was a silent challenge. But the jury did not see her; they were wired to the prosecutor. Even Caroline seemed absorbed, her ultimate compliment.

"Which brings us," Salinas went on, "to the defendant. Christopher Paget.

"As Judge Lerner will instruct you, motive is not an element of the crime. But does anyone doubt that Mr. Paget had *several* motives? The only 'reasonable doubt' is which one was the strongest—political ruin, personal exposure, the loss of his relationship to his lover, or public knowledge that his son, Carlo, was charged with molesting Ms. Peralta's daughter."

Carlo Paget stared stonily at the prosecutor. But Terri appeared as if her thoughts were elsewhere. Neither Terri nor Carlo looked at each other.

Salinas spoke to Joseph Duarte now; like Caroline, Paget guessed, Salinas must be expecting Duarte to become the foreman. "Ms. Masters," he said, "tells us that Mr. Paget loved his son far too much to murder Mr. Arias.

"It is equally fair to ask whether he loves his son too much to see him publicly labeled as the molester of a five-year-old child.

"Ms. Masters tells us that Mr. Paget loves Ms. Peralta far too much to leave her.

"Perhaps, instead, he wanted her too much to *lose* her.

"And then there are those far less worthy motives—ambition and self-protection—which Mr. Paget had in such abundance. Just as surely," Salinas said with sudden harshness, "as he had abundant opportunity for murder.

"For, as became so abundantly clear to us all, here is a man who cannot account for several critical hours on the last night that *anyone* saw or heard from Ricardo Arias.

"Because, for those same hours, no one at all saw Christopher Paget. Not Ms. Peralta and *not* his son—however hard he tried to *hear* things.

"In truth, there was no one home for Carlo Paget to see *or* hear. Because someone else *did* see his father, leaving Ricardo Arias's apartment." Salinas turned abruptly to Caroline Masters with an air of challenge. "Georgina Keller, who described Mr. Paget perfectly—*before* she saw a single picture."

Salinas faced the jury again, speaking with quiet irony. "As one lawyer to another, I should pause here for a moment and pay tribute to the true sophistication that Caroline Masters has brought to Mr. Paget's defense. The way, for example, she suggested that Ms. Peralta—somewhat like Typhoid Mary—might have tracked fibers from Mr. Arias's rug into Mr. Paget's home, ground them into the driver's-side carpet of Mr. Paget's car, and, better yet, made Mr. Arias a gift of Mr. Paget's fingerprints.

"So that it was no surprise, at least to those of us who admire her, when Ms. Masters suggested that Mrs. Keller had summoned Mr. Paget from her television set."

From Caroline, Paget saw, there was a brief, thin smile, the tip-off to how unamused she was: adroitly, Salinas was trying to lead the jury to view her with skepticism.

"It's a touchy point for the defense," Salinas continued, "because if Mr. Paget was at Mr. Arias's apartment that night, he not only had every chance to kill Ricardo Arias but he lied to Inspector Monk about it—a telling admission of guilt. So it was doubly important that Ms. Masters discredit this critical eyewitness. And she tried *very* hard; suggesting not only that Mrs. Keller had confused a real man in a gray suit with an image on a screen but that Mrs. Keller had spent far too much time watching this man examine an injured hand, and a stained sleeve, to truly take note of his face.

"Here, I can only sympathize," Salinas said with the same irony. "For little did Ms. Masters know that her very best work, transmitted through television, would summon Anna Velez into our midst. The woman to whom, shortly after the police began their inquiry, Mr. Paget made a gift of a pair of shoes and a gray wool suit coat with a stained sleeve."

Salinas's voice turned hard. "With *that*, there is no doubt anymore that Georgina Keller saw exactly what she said she saw— *Christopher Paget* leaving Ricardo Arias's apartment, examining his injured hand *and* the stained sleeve of his gray suit coat."

Paget felt numb; in the eyes of the jurors, locked onto Salinas, he had a premonition of the verdict. Next to him, Caroline's face was blank.

"Like his lies to the police, ladies and gentlemen, this charitable 'gift' is an admission of guilt. Part of a cover-up which began with Mr. Paget's trip to Italy and culminated in his defense." Salinas paused for an instant. "Such as it has been."

It was the nearest that, without reprimand, Salinas could come to reminding the jury that Paget had not testified. "An admission of guilt," Salinas repeated, "by a guilty man.

"The man Ricardo Arias was waiting for, when he told Ms. Peralta he had an appointment.

"The man whose trip to Italy, like his trip to Goodwill, is the alibi available to a man who is as careless of money as he was careless of life."

Salinas spread his arms. "And yet after *all* this, ladies and gentlemen, Ms. Masters will ask you to look at what isn't there. She will ask you, for example, why we never tied Mr. Paget to the gun that killed Ricardo Arias." His voice grew quiet. "But all you need is common sense. And with *that*, you can ask Ms. Masters, 'Are you seriously suggesting that Mr. Paget would buy a revolver over the counter, register it in his name, then plant it with Mr. Arias's body as part of a fake suicide?' And then, armed with the same common sense she recommends to you, you will answer her, 'No. It is Ricardo Arias who, *if* he meant to kill himself, would not bother to conceal the purchase of a gun.'

"Common sense, ladies and gentlemen. It really is all you need to penetrate the smoke and mirrors which is Mr. Paget's defense. It is all you need to know that someone who lied to the police—let alone an experienced lawyer like Mr. Paget—did so for a reason."

Salinas's face and voice had become commanding now. "Mr. Paget's reason," he concluded, "is that he killed Ricardo Arias. There is *no* reasonable doubt about it. And, for that, Christopher Paget must pay the price.

"I implore you to return a verdict of guilty. Guilty of *murder*, in the first degree."

Finishing, Salinas gazed at Joseph Duarte. Instinctively, Paget turned to Terri and Carlo. Terri was still looking at Salinas. But Carlo saw his father; the way he tried to smile made Paget feel that much worse.

When Caroline rose, she walked to the jury box and stood silent, gazing from one juror to the next.

"Did you notice," she began, "how Mr. Arias disappeared from Mr. Salinas's closing argument? Yet when his case opened, Mr. Arias was the purehearted underdog, battling for the safety of his daughter against the rich and arrogant Chris Paget—wife stealer, protector of child molesters, and, of course, killer of the less fortunate."

Caroline paused, letting her startling first words make their own impression. "The banishment of Mr. Arias, members of the jury, is the key to this case. For the one thing that Mr. Salinas *has* proven beyond doubt—and these were *his* witnesses, remember—is that the one decent man in this case is the one he asks you to convict of murder."

She looked directly at Duarte now. "But let us consider *why* Mr. Salinas has banished Mr. Arias, and why that is so important to the decision you must make here."

rose suddenly. "But there were traces of blood and GSR on Mr. Arias's hands, if not enough to satisfy Dr. Shelton. And there are *also* smears that suggest he wiped his nose—which, if true, shatters the notion that someone knocked Mr. Arias to the ground, shoved a revolver in his mouth, and pulled the trigger.

"I don't know *how* Mr. Arias got the abrasion on his leg and the gash on his head." Caroline paused for emphasis. "And neither does the medical examiner.

"But I *do* know that the way she wrapped up the medical evidence, trying to explain everything, is just a little too neat. As neat," Caroline said with sudden quiet, "as believing that Ricardo Arias found someone sticking a gun in his mouth and decided to wipe his nose."

Caroline spun on Duarte again. "We don't even know *when* he died, do we? But Mr. Arias may well have died when Christopher Paget was on a plane to Italy. Think about *that* when you consider the prosecutor's plea to convict him of murder."

Duarte's face seemed attentive but skeptical; Paget implored Caroline to move on. "But let us assume for the moment," she continued, "as you *cannot* assume under the law, that someone murdered Ricardo Arias.

"If so, why Christopher Paget?

"The prosecution's case is founded on the notion that what Mr. Arias did was so ugly that Chris Paget abandoned the training of a lifetime and shot Ricardo Arias with an ancient gun and a rusty bullet.

"Why on earth should you believe this?

"The *two* people who know Chris Paget better than anyone—Teresa Peralta and Carlo Paget—say that he's not a killer.

"They know him to be a kind and decent man.

"And, in Carlo's case, he believes he heard his father at home that night." Pausing, Caroline continued in measured tones. "Mr. Salinas asks you to conclude that Carlo Paget, after thinking about what did not become the most important night in his life until weeks *after* the event, cannot be believed. But if Carlo Paget is right, and yet you believe him disqualified by the love of a son for a father, then you will become part of a double tragedy. The failure of a son to help his father with the *truth*, and the conviction of an innocent man."

Carlo raised his head to face the jury. But the jurors were drawn

It was a good opening, Paget thought; in less than a minute, Caroline had turned the tables on Salinas and reminded the jury of who Ricardo Arias really was. "The *real* Ricardo Arias," she went on. "A man who was twice accused of stealing.

"Who was fired from at least four jobs.

"Who exploited his own wife and cheated his own mother.

"Who used his six-year-old daughter to collect ten thousand dollars from a tabloid.

"Who, it is clear, engineered his custody fight as the paid hireling of Mr. Paget's political opponents to torpedo Chris's candidacy for the Senate.

"Who insisted on putting Elena through an unnecessary hearing, despite the fact that his *own* psychologist implored him not to do it." Duarte, Paget noticed, seemed to watch Caroline with interest. Her voice grew quiet. "A man who did that because the psychological evaluation—if Ms. Peralta continued to insist on it—would expose him as a compulsive liar, cheat, and worse.

"In sum, Ricardo Arias was a man who hid his motives *and* his fears from his mother, from his wife, and from everyone else he ever met."

Glancing at Terri, Paget sensed the pain beneath her unflinching gaze at Caroline. She had been married to Richie for six years, shared a child with him, and now he had been revealed as someone she had understood too little and too late.

"And Ricardo Arias," Caroline went on softly, "had so very much to fear. A life at the margins, unemployed and unemployable. A future of financial desperation. Exposure as a sociopath.

"And, almost certainly, the loss of his daughter—his *only* connection to the one person who could still take care of him and keep his life together. Teresa Peralta."

Caroline turned to Marian Celler now, tone passionate and imploring. "Why is it so important that we focus on the real Ricardo Arias? First, because Mr. *Salinas* is so certain that Ricardo Arias did not kill himself.

"*I* say, who can know? But when someone is as troubled as Ricardo Arias, I defy *anyone* to say anything else beyond a reasonable doubt.

"The medical examiner," Caroline went on, "cites the lack of blood spatter and gunshot residue on Mr. Arias's hands." Her voice to Caroline now, the eyes of some flecked with the first traces of doubt.

"Let us stop for a moment," she said softly, "and consider Carlo Paget. There is not a shred of evidence, anywhere, to suggest that Carlo Paget molested anyone. But that has never stopped Mr. Salinas from smearing this boy, in front of this jury and the national media, in order to convict his father. Because this is *not* a prosecution, ladies and gentlemen. It is a witch-hunt, and it is utterly without principle.

"*Why,*" she demanded suddenly, "is the testimony of Leslie Warner and Sonia Arias that Ricardo Arias would not kill himself so worthy, and the testimony of Carlo Paget and Teresa Peralta that Chris Paget is not a murderer so unworthy?

"I cannot tell you. Not when it is so obvious that the *real* difference is that Carlo and Terri truly know Chris Paget and that Ms. Warner and—sadly—Mr. Arias's own mother didn't know Ricardo Arias at all."

With a brilliant thrust, Paget realized, Caroline was back to suicide. But Paget could not look at Terri or Carlo; whatever Caroline said, he knew their own doubts too well.

"That's what sociopaths like Richie do," Caroline went on. "Fool people. But no one has disputed that Christopher Paget is a gentle *and* nonviolent man. And, for that matter, a skilled trial lawyer." Here, Caroline paused again. "A skilled trial lawyer, who knew what Ricardo Arias knew: that he wouldn't hold up under the cross-examination that Christopher Paget intended to inflict on him in the fight for custody of Elena. And then the supposed affair, and the alleged abuse, would turn back on Ricardo Arias—a pathological liar whose character was, at last, about to catch up with him.

"So when you look at motive, ladies and gentlemen, consider that Ricardo Arias had a better motive to kill himself than Chris Paget ever had to kill him." Abruptly, she turned to Duarte. "And then you must ask yourself this: has there ever been a more unlikely murderer than Christopher Paget? *And* this: if there was any evidence that Christopher Paget had ever committed a violent act, wouldn't Mr. Salinas have found time to mention it? But he has *nothing*.

"*That,*" she snapped, "leaves us with the 'evidence' on which the prosecution, which *itself* has ignored so much, asks *you* to ignore every doubt you should reasonably have and convict Chris Paget of murder."

Caroline's voice filled with scorn. "A fingerprint. But no one disputes that Chris Paget touched the answering machine while it was still in Terri's apartment.

"Carpet fibers. But no one disputes that Teresa Peralta left them in Mr. Paget's house and car, *just* as she did in her own."

Caroline focused on Duarte again. "An eyewitness," she said evenly, "who *heard* everything but a gunshot. In truth, we don't know if this unknown man leaving Ricardo Arias's apartment—whoever he was—had come with a gun. And the only time Mrs. Keller *failed* to recognize Chris Paget as a man she'd seen before—on television, as it happens—was when, according to Mr. Salinas, she saw this stranger leaving Mr. Arias's apartment carrying, she tells us, some sort of journal." She paused. "Without gloves, she *also* tells us. And yet, once we eliminate the answering machine, *without* leaving a single print that was Christopher Paget's. Nor, you will recall, did the police ever find a journal in Chris Paget's possession, or ever explain what it was or why he would even care to have it."

In all his notetaking, Duarte's surprised expression said, *these* were points he had not considered. Caroline's voice had become softer yet. "Most damning of all, Mr. Salinas suggests, is that Chris Paget gave some clothes to charity. And *then*, just to conceal his evil intentions, Chris *also* gave them his name, so they could record it." Her voice filled with irony. "Oh yes, and one of the suits had stains on it—a pretty good reason, if you're financially comfortable, to give a suit away.

"There are stains, ladies and gentlemen, and there are stains. After all, the high point of the police interest in *Ms. Peralta* was the day they found a suit in her closet with stains on it." Caroline paused for a moment. "Ketchup stains."

Careful, Paget told her—don't remind them that *I*, like Terri, could explain this by testifying. As if she had heard him, Caroline went on. "But while Mr. Salinas touts *all* of this evidence, there is *one* piece of evidence he treats like a dead mouse on the kitchen floor. And that's the ten thousand dollars in cash about which his superior, McKinley Brooks, has shown such a driving lack of curiosity."

Salinas stared straight ahead, Paget saw, as if he had been steeling himself for this.

"Ricardo Arias lived a funny life," Caroline told the jury. "How many of *you*, I wonder, keep ten thousand dollars in cash sitting around *your* house?" Her voice became rhythmic, compelling. "But drug dealers do, and people with secrets do. Perhaps drugs, or secrets, got Ricardo Arias killed. Perhaps he was killed for this mysterious journal. But who among us knows?" For the first time, she turned to Salinas. "Certainly not the prosecution."

Caroline was going for Brooks's throat now, Paget realized. "But the district attorney," she continued, "does know *some* things. He knows that Christopher Paget embarrassed him in the Carelli case. He no doubt knows, as his reporter friend Mr. Slocum knows, that other politicians did not want Chris Paget to be a senator and that Ricardo Arias wanted money from them. And he *certainly* knows that, win or lose, Christopher Paget was through in politics the day he was charged with murder. Just as he knows that the unknown politician he seems so determined to protect would have been through in politics if Ricardo Arias had ever turned him in." Her voice became dry again. "It surely sounds like motive to *me*. At least for ignoring *all* the things that the prosecution has chosen to ignore."

As Caroline turned to Luisa Marin, Paget saw why Caroline had wanted her. Could hear the young Hispanic woman quote her dead policeman father, disenchanted with his job: "They pass good laws, and then we enforce them against people we don't like."

"Inspector Monk," Caroline said quietly to Marin, "wanted to know where the cash came from. But McKinley Brooks called him off, so *you'll* never know.

"Mr. Slocum *knew* who gave him copies of Ricardo Arias's papers, weeks after Richie's death. But McKinley Brooks told Mr. Salinas not to ask who, so *you'll* never know.

"How and why did this man get those papers? *You'll* never know.

"*You'll* never know whether Mr. Arias was dealing in drugs, or politics, or both.

"*You'll* never know," Caroline said with sudden scorn, "because the D.A. didn't *want* you to know." Just as quickly, her voice softened. "And because of the district attorney, you will never know who pulled the trigger. Even if this was murder."

Luisa Marin regarded Caroline intently. "If the district attorney had done the job he should have done, with integrity and honor, perhaps Mr. Salinas could look you in the face and ask you to convict Chris Paget. Perhaps, at least, he could tell you that this is not a vendetta more insidious and dishonorable than any pursued by Ricardo Arias. But he cannot."

Caroline stood straight, gaze sweeping the jury. "From the beginning of this case, when McKinley Brooks reined in Inspector Monk, Christopher Paget has been his only target. Now *you*, each one of you, are Christopher Paget's only hope of justice. He is a good man, and a good father, and he means a great deal to Ms. Peralta and to his son. And when the district attorney cannot do right, it falls to you to protect the man he has so grievously wronged.

"*That* is your job now. The absence of doubt you need to convict Chris Paget of murder should be no less than the certainty you would need to take a life-support system from someone you love, knowing that he and those who care for him would suffer an irreparable loss. For a sentence of guilty will, for all practical purposes, remove Christopher Paget from the lives of those who love him."

Pausing, Caroline turned to Joseph Duarte. "This case," she finished softly, "is what the district attorney made it. If you cannot condemn Christopher Paget to a life in prison, confident that you are doing justice, then you must let him go free.

"Thank you."

EYES OF A CHILD

FEBRUARY 17–FEBRUARY 19

ONE

BY THE NEXT MORNING, the jury had begun its deliberations.

For Paget, the hours of waiting became a collage. Lerner had instructed the jury; they listened with sober concentration and then filed out in silence to elect a foreman. The courtroom seemed to decompress: it was like a slow leak of tension—spectators talking quietly, muted by uncertainty. The knowledge that what mattered now was out of his control, and would happen out of sight, hit Paget hard.

Trying to smile, he told Carlo and Terri he would see them later. They left together, not talking to the press or to each other; suddenly Paget and Caroline were two people with nowhere to go. When Paget suggested that he buy her lunch, she seemed almost grateful; whatever the strains between them, they were still bound to each other by the experience of the trial, and she did not seem ready to face the office.

Evading the press, they drove to Sam's, a venerable seafood institution, and got a booth with a curtain they could draw for privacy: Caroline phoned in their number to Lerner's courtroom deputy and then drew the curtain and sat, mustering the first semblance of a smile. "So that I can drink at noon," she said. When the waiter came, she ordered a double Scotch on the rocks.

Paget asked for a martini. They sat in the booth like a pair of conspirators, in need less of each other's company than of not being seen or questioned. Caroline looked tired.

Paget touched his glass to hers. "You were terrific," he told her. "This morning, and throughout."

Caroline took a large swallow of Scotch and then set it down, staring into the glass. "I think I lost Duarte," she said. "I just want to hang this one."

The kind of bald comment one lawyer makes to another, it was

Caroline's honest reaction to what had happened, and the fact that Paget was also her client did not stop her. This was, Paget knew, the residue of Anna Velez.

"You think I screwed you," he said.

She looked up from the glass. "I'm only your lawyer, Chris. This isn't about me." She shrugged. "Maybe there was nothing else you could do—I suppose I'll never know. It's just that we went awfully far down the road, with me trying to make them wonder if you were even there that night, for this Goodwill lady to pop us. But then that's why you wanted a speedy trial, I suppose. Hoping they wouldn't find her."

Paget did not answer. Caroline drained her Scotch and put it down emphatically. "I might as well have another one," she said. "They won't be in today, I don't think. Maybe, even, Duarte won't be the foreman."

Paget finished his martini; something in him wanted to reach out to her, explain himself. But another part held back. "If the jury hangs," he said at last, "Brooks will try me again."

Silent, Caroline pushed a button in the wall; the waiter came, a bespectacled veteran in a white jacket, and she ordered a second round of drinks. The waiter seemed to know better than to mention food. When he was gone, Caroline said to Paget, "Maybe not."

Paget smiled at this; in their fatigue and distraction, they had fallen into the pattern of old friends who can remain silent for minutes and then pick up the thread of an abandoned conversation as if it had never been broken off. But the subject itself depressed him. "Oh, they'll retry me," he answered. "Victor will go to school on his mistakes and figure he can win next time."

For a moment, Caroline toyed with the nondescript black watch she wore only for trials. "Mac's in trouble," she said after a time. "If we really go after him—put him on the stand next time—I can make him look like he's covering for someone. Even if that didn't scare him, and I think it does, *Colt* may call him off."

Paget considered that. "It's possible, I suppose. But the local media would be all over him."

Caroline smiled slightly. "Our friend Slocum has problems of his own. At least one part of the local media may be content to let Ricardo die."

She gave him a veiled look above the smile; for an instant, Paget saw her wonder if she was drinking with a murderer.

"Care to eat?" Paget asked.

By five o'clock, when they ceased deliberations for the day, the jury had not come in.

Paget picked Carlo up after basketball practice; as much as possible, he insisted that they follow a normal routine. But when they arrived home, there was a cluster of reporters and TV cameras on the sidewalk, looking for a quote.

"I hate them," Carlo said.

"You're not alone."

They parked in the garage and entered the back of the house without acknowledging the media. Two cameramen scurried up the driveway, to film them as they disappeared. The murderer, Paget thought bitterly, and the child molester.

Paget flicked on the kitchen light; it was dark outside, and the room seemed suddenly bright, reminiscent of the winter evenings when Paget would cook and Carlo would loiter at the kitchen counter, looking over his homework or, if it was done, eating potato chips and talking to his father or watching sports or news on the miniature television. The memory led Paget to the thought that by this time tomorrow, the verdict might be the lead story on the evening news. He felt a lump in his chest; this might be the last night that, however tentatively, he and Carlo could hope that their world would somehow return to normal. Only last night, Paget had bought Carlo more potato chips.

"Why don't I make chicken piccata," he said.

It was Carlo's favorite. Although the boy did not seem hungry, he answered, "Sure."

Paget fell into their ritual, thawing the chicken, scattering the capers and slicing the scallions. For once, he did not ask after Carlo's homework.

Carlo leaned on the counter. "So what do you think they'll do?" he asked after a time.

What should he tell him? Paget wondered. That he himself could not judge, or that his own lawyer thought that the best she could do was hang the jury? And then, looking into the face of his son, Paget knew what to say.

"I don't know," he answered. "I only know that you helped me."

Carlo's eyes flickered with hope. "Do you think so?"

Carlo was still so young, Paget realized; the cruelest thing he could do was refuse to accept the gift of his son's lie or to let Carlo wonder—perhaps starting tomorrow—if he had helped Victor Salinas convict him by not lying well enough. "Yes," Paget answered. "The way Caroline told the jury to believe you was one of the finest parts of her argument. That's what they'll remember."

Carlo gazed at the counter; somehow it reminded Paget of Caroline, staring into her drink for answers. "I haven't been sure," Carlo said at last.

"*I* am." It was all that Paget could give his son; there was no good way, after Velez, to tell Carlo that he had lied for an innocent man. "That, and coming with Terri today, were all you could have done for me."

Watching Carlo, Paget saw the boy remember his own discomfort with Terri, perhaps consider that she might be no more certain of Carlo's innocence than Carlo was of his father's. "Will she be here tonight?" Carlo asked.

"Later."

Carlo nodded but did not answer. Paget was somehow certain that Carlo would go to his room and remain there. And then Paget saw him turn away, gazing at the blank screen of the television.

Paget reached into a cabinet and pulled out the chips he had bought. "Here," he told Carlo. "Have some of these."

Never, when making love with Terri, had Paget wished to imagine that he was anywhere else. But now, as he entered her, he found himself amid a fantasy where Richie's death had never happened and where, as their two children slept in Paget's quiet house, Terri and he would create a child of their own.

For the few moments that he was able to believe this, the escape lent their lovemaking a certain sweetness: each movement in the dark seemed slower, each sensation of her closeness to him—her breasts against his chest, the smell and feel of her hair, her hips moving with his—was more intense. When he came inside her, some part of him imagined her smiling into the eyes of their child, and then she lay next to him, quiet and still, and Paget was in the present.

Gently, Paget kissed her.

She had come to him with a simple warmth that said without words that, at least for this night, she had resolved to put all else aside. But Paget knew that her warmth could no longer be instinctive and unthought of; it was an act of generosity and not of impulse. He could not say this: he could only accept what she could give him, as he had accepted her lies. There was no graceful way to thank her.

They lay silent in the dark. The moonlight came through his window; its frame was cracked open, the crisp winter air reminding Paget of college winters in New England, so that even the murmur of cars passing by, muted by distance, began to sound like wind or waves. When he touched her face, Terri seemed far away.

All at once, he had the desire to tell her what truths he could. "I wonder," he murmured, "if this is anything like the fear of dying."

Her eyes widened. "How do you mean?"

"To drift back and forth between wanting to take each moment and imprint it in your mind, so as not to lose it, and remembering what you once took for granted as precious."

She touched his hair. "Is that what you're doing, Chris?"

"That, and wishing for what I've never had." He kissed her forehead, adding in a tone of irony, "Perhaps if I *do* face something really profound—like truly dying—I'll manage to rise above self-pity."

Terri did not answer. After a time, she said, "Caroline was terrific, you know. Perhaps, someday, I'll learn to be that good."

Paget found that he wanted to know what Terri thought, at least to talk again as professionals if they could not go deeper. "How were final arguments?" he asked. "From your perspective, that is."

Terri seemed to search for words he might believe, yet that skirted what could not be said. "They both did what they had to do, I think. Salinas handled his evidence well." Terri paused; she did not need to tell Paget what she meant. "Caroline was far different, and more emotional than usual. Where she was strongest was making them distrust Brooks and despise Richie. It's easier for a jury to think about reasonable doubt if they hate the victim."

The last comment, flat and dispassionate, gave Paget a sudden frisson; they were lying in bed, talking about her dead husband, the man Paget was accused of murdering. Silent, he touched her skin.

Wind rattled the window. After a time, Terri said quietly, "If you want me to, I can stay."

Part of him, Paget realized, desperately wanted her close; part of him was suddenly haunted by her presence. "What about Elena?"

He felt Terri watching him in the dark, face on the pillow next to him. "My mother's with her. She said she'd stay the night."

"Then be with me. Please."

She moved closer to him; it seemed less spontaneous than hopeful, as if by doing this they could feel closer. But what Paget felt was all that had come between them.

"I haven't said this enough," he said quietly. "But I hate this for Elena."

It was strange, Paget thought; Terri felt more distant. It was not that her body had moved; it was just that she seemed very still now, within herself.

"I know you do," she said.

It was the last they spoke.

At some point, deep into the night, her quiet became sleep. Paget never slept. When he looked at the clock at last, hoping it was near dawn, the time was just past three.

In six more hours, the jury would begin again.

At ten-forty the next morning, Caroline called him at home.

"You'd better meet me down there," she said. "Lerner's deputy just called. The foreman sent Lerner a note—the jury wants to see him."

"They're hung," Paget said automatically. His nerve ends tingled.

"Maybe they just want more instruction," Caroline answered. "But hurry."

By the time he arrived, pushing through a crowd of reporters, the word had spread; the courtroom was filled with media people, and Salinas was there. Almost as soon as Paget arrived, the deputy led the jurors back to the box. The jurors looked strained and silent; Marian Celler and Joseph Duarte, who often chatted during breaks, did not look at each other. Luisa Marin, next to Celler, whispered something in her ear.

"All rise," the deputy intoned, and then Lerner took the bench.

He looked from Salinas to Caroline and then to the jury. "I have a note," he said, "indicating that you have been unable to reach a verdict." He found Joseph Duarte, asking, "Is that correct, Mr. Foreman?"

Duarte stood, gazing straight ahead. "Yes, Your Honor. We're evenly divided."

Paget tensed. "Good," he heard Caroline murmur.

Turning, Paget saw that Victor Salinas was openly disappointed. His own palms felt clammy.

"I'm going to ask you a series of questions," Lerner said to Duarte. "I want you to listen carefully and answer each question without explanation or elaboration. Is that clear?"

The careful admonition seemed to increase the tension. Duarte merely nodded, as if reluctant to make a sound; in twenty-four hours, his air of confidence had frayed.

"They're pissed at each other," Caroline whispered.

"Mr. Foreman," asked Lerner, "how many ballots have you taken?"

Duarte stood straighter. "Three."

"Without indicating whether the votes were 'guilty' or 'not guilty,' what was the division after the first ballot?"

Duarte paused a moment. "Seven to five, Your Honor."

"And when did you take your last ballot?"

"At about nine-thirty this morning."

Lerner frowned. "Is there anything the court can do, by providing a rereading of testimony or further instruction on the law, to assist your deliberations?"

Slowly, Duarte shook his head. "That's not the problem, Your Honor."

Lerner folded his hands. "Is it your impression, Mr. Foreman, that you cannot reach a verdict?"

"Say 'yes,' " Caroline whispered under her breath. "*Please.*"

"It is," Duarte answered.

Lerner looked from juror to juror, as if seeking confirmation. "I'm going to poll each of you," he said at last.

Slowly, one by one, Lerner asked the jurors whether they believed they were deadlocked. The first five answered yes; the sixth, Marian Celler, hesitated before agreeing.

Lerner faced Luisa Marin. "Do *you*," he asked, "believe that this jury cannot reach a verdict?"

Marin hesitated; watching, Paget was quite certain that she had never been the focus of this much attention, except perhaps in the hours after finding her policeman father dead. Through his anxiety, Paget felt for her.

"No," she said in a shaky voice. "It's only been two days. I think we should talk more."

Paget tensed; did this mean, he wondered, that she was preparing to change her vote? "Let them *go*," Caroline whispered at Lerner.

Lerner raised his eyebrows. "Do you believe," he said to Marin, "that there is a reasonable likelihood that further deliberation will lead to a verdict?"

Marin nodded with an air of stubbornness. "We need to talk," she repeated.

Duarte had turned, staring at Marin. Marian Celler frowned at him.

"Duarte's voting against us," Paget said under his breath.

"I think so too. But what about Marin?"

On the bench, Lerner folded his hands. "Members of the jury," he said. "This trial took two weeks. However difficult your discussions may have been, your deliberations have lasted less than two days. . . ."

"*No,*" Caroline whispered. At the prosecution table, Victor Salinas sat up, alert with hope. Lerner did not have to push them, Paget knew, but Luisa Marin had given him a reason.

"Under these circumstances," Lerner continued, "you may not have considered all of the evidence. I would like you to return to the jury room, deliberate with mutual courtesy and respect, and see whether you can reach a verdict."

Slowly, Duarte nodded. Marin folded her arms, looking at no one. Paget felt his eyes close.

By the end of the second day, the jury had not returned.

TWO

AT ELEVEN-FIFTEEN the following day, Caroline called Paget at his office.

"They're in," she said.

Paget felt his chest constrict. "I'll be right down."

Replacing the receiver, he looked around his office. Part of him, he suddenly knew, did not wish to leave; only as long as he stayed here was he allowed to hope. In a kind of stupor, he put on his coat, fumbling with the buttons.

At his insistence, Carlo was in school. Paget had promised to call the principal's office directly after the verdict, so that Carlo would not hear it from schoolmates or reporters before Paget picked him up. No matter what, he resolved, he would keep his promise.

He pushed open the door—it seemed like an act of will—and hurried to Terri's office.

It was empty.

Her secretary, May, sat outside, a pleasant Chinese woman with framed pictures of her children arranged across her desk. "I thought Terri was here," he said tersely.

May glanced at the calendar on her desk. "She will be, except for the next hour. She has a doctor's appointment."

Paget felt suddenly alone. "With Dr. Harris?"

May nodded. She started to say something and then gave him the oblique watchful look Paget had come to associate with his wait for the jury. In a tentative voice, May asked, "Shall I tell her to come find you?"

"No," Paget answered. "I won't be here."

* * *

When Terri entered Harris's office, the psychologist looked like someone who could no longer hide bad news.

"What is it?" Terri demanded. "You were so strange on the telephone."

"Sit down, Terri. Please."

It was only then that Terri realized she was standing. She took a chair across from Harris.

"I've been keeping this for over a week," Harris said without preface. "Because of Chris's trial. I'm sorry, but in good conscience I can't wait anymore."

Terri felt herself inhale. "All right."

Harris leaned forward "I now believe," the psychologist said slowly, "that Elena has been sexually molested. And that it may be at the heart of her problem."

Tears came to Terri's eyes, as if from a sudden sting. "How do you know?"

"Play therapy, in part. Do you know the motif of the abandoned girl? Last week, when I asked what the doll was afraid of, she pulled up its dress and began tickling the doll's stomach. And then Elena turned her face from me and stroked the doll between her legs." Harris paused for a moment. "The things she said about it, that it scared the doll and yet sometimes felt good, were very real. As if she knew exactly how that was."

Terri could not speak. All that she could see was Elena with her face turned to the wall, refusing to answer when Terri asked if Carlo had touched her. "Tickling," Harris went on, "can be a metaphor for molestation. And quite often, that's how it starts—the molester makes it like a game and then slowly crosses the line. Just as Elena did with the doll."

Terri found her voice again. "Are there other things?" she asked.

"Yes." Harris's own voice was firmer now, as if she was relieved to talk. "Her prior behavior—the withdrawal, the pseudomaturity, the disinterest in other children—is consistent with sexual abuse. So is the playground incident that her teacher reported to you and Richie." Harris folded her hands. "But what struck me, even before last week, is that Elena always portrays the doll as helpless and in danger—like some trust has been abused, Elena's sense of boundaries violated. Add to that my belief that she feels guilty because she was part of something wrong and yet remembers that, as terrified as she was, she *also* experienced some pleasure. Just as any child discovers when first touching herself."

Terri felt a faint nausea. "Has she told you how it happened?"

Harris shook her head. "Elena," she said finally, "has never *told* me anything. But I'm morally certain she's been abused. *And* that it's probably why she seemed to feel at fault for Richie's death: she thinks she's a bad person. Once children feel *that*, they make themselves responsible for every bad thing that happens."

In the eyes of a child, Terri remembered Chris saying, everything that happens is about herself. But it was no use remembering what a fool she herself had been. "How can I help her?" she asked.

"By being patient." Harris spoke more softly. "Whoever did this, I think, told Elena that awful things would happen if she ever told anyone. Secrecy, and shame, are terrible burdens for a child to carry. That may be the meaning of why the little girl is afraid to talk to the alligator."

"Will she *ever* talk to *you*? Or me? Or tell us who it was?"

"I don't know." Harris was still quiet. "After she touched the doll, I asked Elena if what happened to the little girl had ever happened to *her*. She turned away and wouldn't talk. Just as she did when you asked her whether Carlo had ever touched her."

Terri found that she felt both anger and despair. "She's my daughter, damn it. Isn't there *something* I can do?"

"Spend whatever time you can with her. The fact that she acted out her trauma through the doll is progress. Next week, or next year, she may talk to me *or* to you." Harris gave her a look of deep compassion. "I know that's all you've been doing lately—waiting. But it's all that I can tell you to do."

Terri stood without answering. For an instant, she flashed on Carlo, walking to the park with Elena. And then all she wanted was to see her daughter.

Murmuring something to Harris, she walked quickly from the room.

"All rise," the courtroom deputy called out, and for the last time, in *People v. Paget*, Jared Lerner ascended the bench.

His face was grim. He took in the scene before him—the reporters quiet and waiting, Victor Salinas standing with his hands in front of him, seeming to fidget without moving. Next to Paget, Caroline seemed to draw a breath and hold it. Paget's stomach felt hollow; the jury, silent and staring at the judge, would not look at him or at each other.

They've found me guilty, he thought.

Joseph Duarte stood stiffly, appearing pale and a little smaller than before. "I understand," Lerner said to him, "that you've reached a verdict."

"We have, Your Honor."

Lerner turned to his bailiff, a uniformed sheriff's deputy with a broad chest and a bushy mustache. "Mr. Bailiff, will you collect the forms of verdict."

Silent, Duarte handed the man four slips of paper: verdict forms, signed by the foreman, for each of the four counts against Paget—first- or second-degree murder, voluntary or involuntary manslaughter. The bailiff walked across the courtroom and handed them to Lerner. Except for his footsteps on the wooden floor, there was no sound.

One after another, Lerner read the four slips of paper. With the first slip, his eyebrows rose and stayed there. When he was finished reading, he handed the forms to the courtroom clerk, a round-faced Irishman to whom Paget had hardly given thought and who now held the jury's verdict in his hands.

Lerner faced them again. "Members of the jury," he said calmly, "my clerk will read each verdict aloud. Thereafter I will ask each one of you whether this is your true verdict."

Duarte nodded. Behind him, Paget saw Luisa Marin raise her head. Next to Marin, Marian Celler silently took her hand.

Paget turned from them. For an instant the faces of witnesses flashed before him—Terri and Carlo, Charles Monk and Jack Slocum, Elizabeth Shelton and Georgina Keller. Anna Velez.

The clerk began reading. "In the Superior Court for the City and County of San Francisco, Case Number 93-5701, *The People of California versus Christopher Kenyon Paget*, on the charge of murder in the first degree, we the jury find the defendant, Christopher Paget . . ."

In profile, Caroline shut her eyes. The deputy's pause seemed endless.

"... *not* guilty."

A stunned murmur. Numb, Paget braced himself for the second count. The clerk's voice seemed to come from far away.

"On the charge of murder in the second degree, we the jury find the defendant, Christopher Paget, *not* guilty."

Caroline threw her head back, a first smile on her lips.

"On the charge of manslaughter in the first degree ... *not* guilty.

"On the charge of manslaughter in the second degree ... *not* guilty."

The courtroom exploded in sound.

Caroline turned to Paget in triumph. Clasping her shoulders, he said in a shaky voice, "You're wonderful."

Caroline grinned as if she would never stop. "Yes. I am."

Lerner banged for silence. "Members of the jury," he intoned, "I will now poll you individually."

Silence fell.

The next few moments were only impressions: Duarte's phlegmatic "yes"; Celler's calm affirmation. It was only when Luisa Marin, smiling slightly, answered "yes" in a firm voice that Paget guessed what had happened.

"*She* turned Duarte," he murmured.

Caroline nodded. "I think so. Wonders really *do* never cease."

As the polling ended, Victor Salinas stared down at the floor. And then he squared his shoulders, facing Lerner again. Paget began imagining Carlo and Terri when he told them.

Lerner turned to his clerk again, saying, "The clerk will record the verdict."

The clerk took each form. He raised a metal stamp above the first form; the stamp descended with a thud. It fell three more times, resonating in the silent room, and the trial of Christopher Paget was over.

"The defendant is discharged," Lerner intoned. Facing Paget, he smiled slightly. "Mr. Paget, you are free to go."

For the final time, Lerner gazed out at the jury. "Ladies and gentlemen," he said, "I would like to express the court's thanks for your service in this difficult case." He stood, looking out at the courtroom for a moment, and then left the bench.

"Jesus," Paget murmured. "Jesus."

Beneath the table, Caroline touched his hand. "Steady, boy," she whispered. "You've got things to do. Like figure out what movie to see this weekend."

Turning to the jury, Paget saw four sheriff's deputies shepherding them out the door, to ward off reporters. Briefly, Joseph Duarte nodded to Caroline; Luisa Marin glanced at Paget and then turned, smiling, to Marian Celler.

Abruptly, they were gone.

In the noise of the gallery, Victor Salinas walked across the courtroom. "Congratulations," he said to Caroline, and held out his hand.

Silent, they shook hands. And then, to Paget's surprise, Salinas turned to him and extended his hand.

After a moment, Paget took it.

Salinas faced Caroline again. "You outlawyered me," he said. "I learn all the time."

Caroline shrugged. "Mac screwed you, Victor. No help for that."

Salinas smiled a little. "Not now, anyhow." He glanced over his shoulder at the watching reporters and went to face them, stoic.

What, Paget found himself wondering, had Salinas meant? But it hardly mattered now. He was rid of the specter that had haunted him since he first had lied to Charles Monk; thanks to Caroline Masters, and his own resolve, he had got away with it.

"Ready for the press?" Caroline asked him.

Paget was quiet. Another thought had struck him: no one would ever answer for the death of Ricardo Arias.

"First, I need to call Carlo," he said softly. "And Terri, of course."

Seeing her mother at the classroom door, Elena gave her a look that combined surprise, apprehension, and pleasure in such rapid sequence that Terri wanted to pick her up.

Instead she walked over to the teacher. "I'm sorry," she said pleasantly. "But Elena has a doctor's appointment. I forgot to call."

"Oh, of course." Turning, the young blond woman beckoned to Elena. The little girl took a few tentative steps from her desk, and then Terri smiled. "I'm here for you, sweetheart."

Elena looked at the teacher for permission. The woman nodded. "Your mother's taking you to the doctor, Elena."

The little girl turned to Terri again, obscurely worried. "Dr. Harris, Mommy?"

"No." Terri smiled. "Dr. Mom."

The teacher gave Terri a puzzled look. But Elena went to her mother, touching her skirt; something about this simple gesture filled Terri's heart with love and sadness. Terri took her hand, and they left.

Outside, Elena blinked at the sunlight. "Where are we going?" she asked.

"For ice cream. I was hungry."

Elena turned to her, delighted by the surprise, and then frowned at another thought. "You didn't tell the truth, Mommy."

"I guess that wasn't good, was it?" Terri smiled down at her daughter. "People don't always tell the truth, you know. But next time, I will. I'll just tell Mrs. Johnson that I missed you."

"Did you?"

"A lot." Terri opened the car door. "Moms are like that, you know. Much more than kids."

Elena paused by the door, turning to look up at her mother with Richie's black eyes. "*I* miss you." She paused, and then added, "I missed you when I was with Daddy."

Terri knelt by her daughter. "You don't need to miss me now, Elena. I'll be with you always and take care of you."

Elena's look mingled hope and fear. "You're not going to die? Everyone dies, Mommy."

Terri felt words stick in her throat, felt sadness for Elena, a sudden stab of worry about Chris's trial. But she managed another smile. "*I* won't for a long time, sweetheart. Not until *I'm* so old that *you'll* be a grandmother. Like Grandma Rosa, only older."

There was a troubled look in Elena's eyes. "Let's have ice cream," she said abruptly. "I want chocolate marble, like Daddy used to get me."

They went to Rory's on Fillmore Street, double-parked, and bought two cones. Then they drove away in companionable silence, each licking her ice cream, to Terri's apartment in Noe Valley. It was only there that Terri thought of Chris again.

Mercifully, there were no reporters waiting.

They climbed the stairs and entered Terri's apartment; for an unwelcome moment, Terri remembered the night she had returned to find Richie waiting inside, with the papers accusing Carlo. She turned to Elena. "We'd better wash our hands, Elena."

The little girl looked up at her. "How come you never call me Lainie? Like Daddy did."

What, Terri wondered, was *this* about? "Because Elena's a beautiful name, and I picked it myself. Elena Rosa, so you could have Grandma's name too."

Elena gave her a serious look. "Mommy," she asked in a quiet voice, "did you and Grandma hate Daddy?"

Terri hesitated and then shook her head. "No," she said. "I didn't love him anymore, and he didn't love me. But I never hated him." Saying this, Terri felt a stab of guilt; perhaps she had hated Ricardo Arias too much to listen to what he was saying. On impulse, she asked, "Would you like it if, sometimes, I called you Lainie?"

Elena looked down and then slowly shook her head. "No," she said quietly. "Only Daddy called me that." And then she looked at her sticky hands and went to the kitchen to wash them.

Terri followed her. They stood at the sink, washing together. "What do you want to do?" Elena asked.

"I don't know. What about you?"

"Play Candyland."

The board game from hell, Terri thought wryly. "Okay," she answered. "I think you're still the champion."

"I *am*."

Elena, Terri thought, seemed much more communicative; it was odd that, on this painful day, their interaction had the veneer of normality. "What else would you like to do?" Terri asked.

Elena looked up at her. "You're not going to leave me, are you, Mommy?"

The little girl's voice had suddenly filled with apprehension. "What do you mean, Elena?"

The child looked around. "You know," she said finally. "Leave me at Grandma's tonight."

Terri picked Elena up and hugged her. "Not if you don't want me to."

"I don't, Mommy. Please."

The kitchen telephone rang. Suddenly remembering Chris, Terri carried Elena across the kitchen and grabbed it.

"Terri," Chris said. "I've been looking for you."

He sounded strange. "Where are you?"

"In the car, with Carlo, playing hooky." His voice rose. "They *acquitted* me."

She felt herself trembling, with emotion and sheer relief. "Oh, Chris"—her voice was choked—"that's *so* great."

"What *is* it, Mommy?" Elena's eyes were serious and almost accusatory.

"It's wonderful," Chris was saying through the phone. "Listen, can you get a sitter for Elena tonight? Carlo and I want to take you out to dinner."

Terri felt suddenly numb. "Dinner with you and Carlo?" she repeated in a shaky voice, and then saw the look on Elena's face.

"Sure," Chris answered. "We'll go to Stars."

In the whipsaw of her emotions, Terri could not find words. "I can't," she temporized. "I just promised Elena." She tried again. "I hate to be elliptical, but it's been a difficult day. For both of us."

There was a long silence. More softly, Chris said, "Getting acquitted is once in a lifetime. I hope."

"I know." Terri felt her eyes cloud. "I'll buy you dinner tomorrow night. That way we can really talk."

"All right." In his disappointment, Chris's tone became neutral. "We've got all sorts of time, after all."

She heard the question in his voice. "I'm so happy, Chris." Listening to herself, Terri imagined her own voice as a tinny echo on Chris's car phone. "Please trust me when I say I should stay home."

"It's okay. Carlo and I will have boys' night out."

Terri felt Elena's gaze. "I wish I could tell you how I feel," she said to Chris.

"Then I'll call you tonight," Chris answered with attempted casualness, "and you can tell me then."

He sounded all right. But when he hung up, Terri realized that she had not told Christopher Paget that she loved him.

"What *is* it?" Elena asked.

Terri's eyes shut. "Nothing," she said softly. "Chris just wanted to talk."

Wriggling, Elena grasped a piece of her own hair. "It's not about Daddy, is it?"

Only in the sense, Terri thought, that Chris was just acquitted of his murder. All at once, she felt alone. "No, sweetheart. It wasn't about Daddy."

Elena stopped wriggling. Quietly, she asked, "Then was it about Carlo?"

Terri felt a wave of guilt and shame. She set Elena down, watching her daughter's worried face. No one, she silently promised Elena, will hurt you now. Ever again.

"I'm here with you," she told Elena. "And I'm *staying* with you." Terri tried to smile. "So let's play Candyland, all right?"

THREE

STARS was a sprawling bright-lit three-level restaurant with high ceilings and splashy Parisian posters on the walls. It was jammed with people from black tie to punk, who crowded the tables and lined the mirrored bar two deep, talking and listening to a pianist at a sleek black piano set amid the diners, their voices mingling with jazz notes in a festive cacophony. Paget had gone there frequently with Terri; the food was superb, the bar was a San Francisco street show, and they could come in after the ballet or opera and eat and drink until one. Paget's choice of Stars was both instinctive and deliberate: he wanted to go there, and if a lot of people noticed him, both they and he might as well get used to that. But one look at Carlo, and Paget realized that—for tonight—Stars was the wrong choice.

They were sitting along the wall at a table that let them talk alone. But Carlo seemed painfully aware whenever someone stared at him; he looked uncomfortable and a little pinched, as if the bright lights hurt his eyes. When a bleached blonde with her hair combed back like Annie Lennox pointed them out to someone else at the bar, Carlo murmured, "It's like we're zoo animals."

Paget sipped his second martini. "Forget them, if you can. Soon enough, they'll forget you."

Carlo gave him a look that was both steady and opaque. "How are you going to live with this?" he asked under his breath. "People still think you *killed* someone."

Paget knew where part of the question came from: an interviewer had caught up with Joseph Duarte in time for the evening news. "I didn't vote *for* Mr. Paget," Duarte had said with a frown of dissatisfaction. "In the end, other jurors persuaded me that the conduct of the D.A.'s office had itself created a reasonable doubt." But beneath this, Paget knew, were deeper doubts of Carlo's own.

"I'll be okay," Paget told him. "Caroline was right when she said I wouldn't make a politician: when it comes right down to it, there aren't many people whose opinion I much care about. Especially people who only know me through television. There's nothing I can do about them, except live my life."

Carlo shook his head. "I'm not like that," he said. "What people think bothers me a lot."

Paget looked into his son's face, too young to be stoic, and wondered what to say. "I never said it didn't bother me," he finally answered. "But I know what I did and didn't do, why I acted as I did, and who it is that I really *do* care about. Starting with you." He hesitated. "A long time ago, I learned the painful truth that you can't look for how you should feel about yourself in the faces of other people. You have to have your own standards, both for how you act and for whom, besides yourself, you should answer to."

Carlo looked at him impassively. "Are you ever going to answer to *me?*"

Paget felt his eyes narrow. "I already have, Carlo. I told you that I didn't kill Richie and that the things I *haven't* told you may involve someone else. If telling you everything I might know or guess would change this business with Elena, I'd do it in a heartbeat. But it won't, so you're just going to have to trust me."

Carlo did not look away. "This may be selfish, Dad, and I'm gladder you got acquitted than you'll ever know. But *you've* shut me out of knowing why this ever happened. And no one is ever going to find *me* innocent of pulling Elena's panties off and playing with her while you and Terri weren't looking." His voice rose slightly. "Admit it—not even *Terri* is sure I didn't do it."

Paget flinched inside. "Terri's been through a lot," he said softly. "She's still *going* through a lot, with both Elena and whatever this child psychologist is trying to accomplish. So give her time." He put his drink down. "*I* know you didn't do it, and so do all your friends."

A shadow crossed Carlo's face, the belief that Paget was living with *his* own doubts. "Maybe you can deal with it," he said. "But this thing with Terri is something *I* can't live with."

"I'm not asking you to."

"I *mean* it." Carlo's voice shook with sudden feeling. "I'm not going to be around someone every day who thinks I molested a six-year-old girl. Imagine dinner—all these silences. God knows what Elena may have said to her, for whatever screwed-up reason a kid says anything." His voice steadied. "What you and *I* don't talk about, I guess I'll have to live with—you're not giving me a choice. But I don't *have* to live with Terri, and I won't."

Paget breathed in audibly. " 'Happy acquittal, Dad. And have a nice day.' "

There were sudden tears in Carlo's eyes. "Do you *understand* me, Dad?"

For a moment, Paget felt his own pain. Then he reached across the table, touching his son's arm. "Yes, Carlo. I understand you."

Terri pulled the comforter beneath Elena's chin, placed the book they had read on the child's bedside table. Turning out the light, she kissed Elena's check. The little girl's skin felt soft, her hair and face smelled fresh and clean. At that moment, Terri could not imagine loving another person as much as this child, the vulnerable person Terri once had carried inside her.

On the table, the elephant night-light flickered, casting light and shadow across Elena's face. The light was dying, Terri realized; tomorrow she would replace it. "I love you, Elena."

"Can you stay with me, Mommy?" The little girl's arms reached out for her. "Just for a while, okay?"

Terri smiled at the child's bargaining. How many times, she wondered, had Elena said "just a minute" or "one more time"? And how often had Terri spent the time Elena needed?

"Okay," she said, and lay down on the comforter.

"Get inside the covers with me, Mommy. Please."

Terri slid beneath the covers and turned on her side. Automatically, Elena turned and curled her legs and back against her mother, waiting for Terri to put her arms around her. Terri felt an almost primal familiarity: she and Elena called this "making spoons," just as Rosa had, lying next to Terri when she had been so young that she now remembers little else. Lying beside Elena, Terri still half expected to hear her father's angry voice, feel the rage that had driven Rosa to Terri's bed, until she herself had not known who was giving or receiving comfort.

"I love you," Terri said again.

Elena burrowed closer. "I love you too, Mommy."

Gently, Terri stroked Elena's hair until the child's breathing became deep and even, the pulse of sleep.

She herself should not fall asleep, Terri realized. She might have the dream of Ramon Peralta and cry out in fear, making Elena's own nightmare that much more frightening to her. It is the adult's job to seem strong and competent, Terri told herself. At least until the child is old enough, and secure enough, to accept the doubts beneath.

Chris and Carlo were out tonight, celebrating the escape she had prayed for but felt much more deeply as relief than as elation. Silently holding her daughter, she thanked God that Chris was free.

Chris and Carlo. Thinking about them, she knew she would not sleep. For Elena, at least, that was good.

Next to her, she felt Elena stirring.

Elena Arias awoke in a pitch-black room.

She was alone. The night-light was gone; Elena sat up in bed, stiff and fearful, eyes adjusting to the light.

She was in her grandmother's house. Her mother was gone and could not help her.

There was banging on the door.

It was the black dog; Elena was certain of this, although she had never seen him. Her mouth was dry.

The dog had never come through the door. But tonight, Elena knew, he would.

The knocking grew louder.

Elena began to tremble. Tears ran down her face.

She already knew what the dog wanted from her.

Desperate, Elena turned to the window, looking for escape. But it was nailed shut; even in the dark, she remembered that Grandma Rosa feared the men in Dolores Park.

The door began to splinter.

Elena tried to scream. But the cry caught in her throat; suddenly she could not breathe.

He was coming.

The door burst open.

The pale light in the hallway was from candles. Shivering and silent, Elena could hear and feel the dog's breath. But still she could not see him.

Elena hugged herself, and then his shadow rose above the bed.

It was more human than dog. For an instant, Elena prayed that it was Grandma Rosa, and then his face came into the light.

Standing over the bed, Ricardo Arias smiled down at her.

Elena woke up screaming.

In the flicker of the night-light, Terri saw her daughter's eyes as black holes of terror.

"*Sweetheart,*" she cried out, and held Elena close.

The little girl's heart pounded against Terri's chest. "It's *okay,*" Terri urged. "I'm here."

She could feel her own heart race. Elena's trembling arms held Terri like a vise. "It was just a nightmare," Terri said in a soothing voice. "Only a nightmare."

Elena could not seem to speak. Softly, Terri stroked the little girl's hair again, and then Elena began to cry.

Terri kissed her face. "What was it, Elena?"

The little girl kept on crying, softly and raggedly, pausing to breathe. After a time, her keening became half spasm, half hiccup, the residue of fear.

All at once, Elena was still.

Gently, Terri pulled away a little, cupping one hand at the side of Elena's face. Fearful, the child looked back at her.

"Tell me what it was," Terri said softly, "and maybe you won't feel alone."

The little girl watched her face, afraid to look away. Her mouth opened once, closed, and then opened again.

"Yes, sweetheart?"

Swallowing, Elena said softly, "Daddy was here."

"In the dream?"

Elena nodded. "I saw him."

Terri wondered what to say. "It *was* a dream, Elena. Daddy's dead now. He died in an accident."

Slowly, Elena shook her head, and then tears began again, ragged and shuddering.

"What happened?" Terri asked.

Elena clutched her mother's nightdress with both hands, voice suddenly higher. "I was *scared*, Mommy."

"Why?"

Elena's lips trembled. Half choking, she whispered, "He was going to *hurt* the little girl."

Terri felt her skin go cold. In a calm voice, she asked, "How?"

Elena looked away. Her voice was small and shamed. "He was going to take her panties off."

Terri felt herself swallow. "What else was Daddy going to do?"

"Touch her." The little girl's face twisted. "It was just their secret."

Terri stared at her. "Why is it a secret?"

"Daddy feels lonely. Sometimes he needs a girl." Elena looked into her mother's face. "To put his peepee in her mouth and feel better. Because he's all alone now."

Terri's sudden rage was almost blinding. "Did he do anything else to you?"

"That's all, Mommy." Elena's eyes shut, as if at what she saw on her mother's face. "But he let me light the candles for him. To make it special."

Terri pulled her daughter close.

She did not know how long she held Elena. Terri asked her nothing more; through her grief and shock and impotent anger, Terri knew that she should not push her. It was some time before Terri realized that she, too, was crying—silently, so that Elena could not hear her.

Perhaps, the reasoning part of Terri felt with pitiless shame, she had always known this. Perhaps she had simply chosen not to believe it, with the same preconditioned numbness that had protected her since the first day that she discovered, as a child smaller than Elena, that to know Ramon Peralta was to know a fear she could not endure. So that she, Ramon's daughter, was able blindly to live with a man who could do this to her own daughter.

"Elena Rosa," Terri murmured at last. "How I wish you could have told me."

Elena seemed to shudder. In a thin voice, she said, "I did tell."

Through her grief, Terri looked at Elena in confusion. "Who? Dr. Harris?"

Elena shook her head. "No, Mommy." The child paused, as if afraid, and then whispered, "I told Grandma."

Terri felt the child's tremor as her own. It was a moment before she spoke again. "When, Elena?"

"A long time ago." Elena's voice grew firmer now. "Before Chris murdered Daddy."

Christopher Paget stared at the bedside clock.

The illuminated dial read 10:45. He could not sleep; relief warred with confusion, pain over Carlo with sadness about Terri, hope with a deeper sense of loss. Before the trial, he would have known whom to call.

Impulsively, Paget picked up the telephone and dialed.

He lay back on the bed, staring at the darkness above him, listening to the phone ring in Terri's small apartment.

"Hello?"

A woman's voice, but wrong. Paget considered hanging up. And then he asked, "Is this the Peralta residence?"

"It is. But this is Terri's neighbor Nancy. Terri's not in right now."

Paget hesitated, surprised. "This is Chris Paget," he said. "I was expecting to hear from her tonight."

A moment's silence. "I'm sorry," the woman said. "But Terri had some emergency. She was too distracted to say what. As soon as Elena was asleep, she rushed out the door. She didn't know when she'd be back."

Paget sat up. "Do you know where she went?"

Another pause, the sound of reluctance. "She's at her mother's," the woman said.

FOUR

TERRI BANGED on the door.

Her mother's porch was shadowed, and the house was dark. The only sounds were Terri's fist slamming the door, her arrhythmic breathing. The drive to Rosa's had seemed like the last moments of a drunken evening, fractured images in the subconscious. Her thoughts felt more dangerous than clear.

Light came from inside, the soft sudden glow of someone switching on a lamp. Terri's fist froze in the air. She imagined, but did not hear, her mother's footsteps.

In the window beside the door, someone drew aside a curtain, fingernails scraping glass. The curtain closed again, and then Terri heard the rattle of a latch and chain.

The door opened. "Teresa," her mother said softly.

In the doorway, Terri could not see Rosa's face. Slowly, her mother drew aside, stepping back into the house.

Terri entered. Like an automaton, she turned and locked the door behind her, facing Rosa. Neither spoke.

The room was dark. Only the stairway light was on. But Terri knew the house by touch. Without looking, she reached behind her and found the light switch beside the door.

Her mother was in a robe and nightgown, her hair down as Terri had not seen it for years. Without her makeup she looked older and harsher, her face that of an Aztec statue. Her deep black eyes seemed beyond surprise.

Rosa stared into her daughter's face. "Elena," she said simply.

Silent, Terri nodded.

"So you know." Rosa's voice was quiet and clear. "Did she tell you about the candlelight, Teresa? That's how she knew that Richie meant it to be a special night."

All at once, Terri felt a calm, cold clarity. "When did she tell you, Mom?"

The two women faced each other, a few feet apart. Still quiet, Rosa answered, "The night before you left for Italy."

Before Terri could find words, Rosa walked across the living room to an end table, opening a drawer. When she turned to face Terri, there was a small burlap bag cupped in her hand. Stiffly, she drew back her arm and tossed it underhand to Terri.

Terri reached out and caught it. The bag clicked in her hand like a bagful of marbles. But Terri knew better.

With trembling fingers, she loosened the drawstring and emptied the bag into the palm of her hand. One of the bullets fell to the wooden floor.

Terri stared at them. They were dull black, tinged with a coppery rust. Terri found that she could not look up.

"For years," Rosa told her, "I hid these in the basement, with the gun. So that if Ramon ever harmed you, or your sisters, I would have a way." Her voice grew softer yet. "Do you remember the night Ramon took me from behind and raised his hand to you?"

Terri looked up. With equal quiet, she answered, "Do you think I could forget?"

Pain crossed her mother's face. "I promised myself then that if Ramon ever touched you, I would shoot him." She paused, adding coolly, "With Ramon, it never came to that."

Deep within her, Terri felt a chill. She cupped the bullets in her hand. "Why did Elena tell *you*?"

"Elena asked why you were leaving her." Rosa's voice assumed a bitter calm. "And then she asked when her father was coming for her. When I told her Sunday, she started crying. It took perhaps an hour to find out why. Her father had said that if *she* told anyone, the courts would take her away from him, and he would go to jail. As if the courts would ever help her." Rosa's face hardened. "I gave Elena a sleeping pill and held her close. By the time she fell asleep, I knew that I would never let him come for her."

Terri felt herself wince. "You should have told *me*."

Rosa's eyes flashed. "So that you could go to *court*, Teresa? Just as you did before?" Her tone became steely. "It would have torn Elena apart. Her own father had made sure of that."

"*I* could have made him stop."

"Just as the police stopped Ramon?" Her mother stood straighter. "No, Teresa. *I* made him stop. Now Elena is safe from him and from the courts. As well as from her own shame."

Terri felt her fists clench. "It's not *her* shame. She needs to face the truth, not bury it."

Slowly, Rosa shook her head. "When my own husband beat me and abused me, do you think I felt no shame? My shame died only with Ramon. If then."

There was an eerie certainty to her mother's words, as if she had faced implacable truths that Terri could not know. It placed Rosa beyond argument, or even remorse. Softly, Terri asked, "How did you do it, Mom?"

" 'Do it.' " Rosa coldly smiled. "Kill Ricardo, you mean?"

"Yes."

The smile vanished. "Then sit with me, Teresa. Instead of staring at me like a stranger." Turning, she walked to the couch and sat in one corner, gesturing at the empty space. "*Sit* with me, Teresa. *I* am your mother, and *this* was our home."

Terri walked across the room and sat at the opposite corner of the couch. The moment carried echoes back to childhood: Rosa and Terri, sitting on this couch, reading stories or dealing with the trials at hand. "All right," Terri said in a cool voice. "I *am* your daughter. Just as Elena is *mine*, although you seem to have forgotten that. Or do you think I haven't been beaten enough to earn your respect?"

Rosa seemed to flinch. "You can be cruel, Teresa."

"I can never explain," Terri cut in, "the cruelty of what *you've* done—especially to Elena. Richie is the least of it. But let's start there."

A first hesitancy flickered in Rosa's eyes, reflecting Terri's power to hurt. She folded her hands. "What should I tell you, Teresa?"

"The truth about what happened that night."

Turning from Terri, Rosa gazed out at the dark living room. "It began simply enough. Watching Elena as she slept, I was afraid to leave her. And then I realized that because of the pill, she would sleep without waking. At least for a time." In profile, Rosa's eyes lowered. "When I went to the basement and took out the bullets and gun, it was as if *I* were sleeping.

"For fifteen years, I hadn't touched or even looked at them. I had trouble loading it—I kept dropping bullets on the cement. I remember crawling on my hands and knees, beneath a bare light bulb, trying to pick them up. I couldn't be sure the gun would even fire.

"When I went back to see Elena, I felt drugged. I would think of Ricardo, and then Ramon—I think it was holding the gun again." Rosa seemed to stare into her memory. "When I walked to your room—Elena's room, I mean—it was as if I expected to find you. Looking down at Elena, I saw the gun in my own hand.

"But she was asleep." Rosa's voice grew soft. "In her sleep, Teresa, she looked very much like you. To me, she always has." Rosa shut her eyes. "You were damaged in this house, Teresa. I've always known that. I could not let it reach Elena."

Oh, Mama, Terri wished to say, that was *my* job. But she did not let herself say anything.

Rosa's eyes opened. "I picked up the telephone," she went on, "and called Ricardo's number. When he answered, I knew he would be there.

"I hung up. And then I got my black raincoat, put the revolver in its pocket, and went to the car.

"Driving to Ricardo's, I wondered if he would still be home or might have company. It was only then that I realized that if I killed him and was caught, Elena would know why.

"What happened to *me* made little difference." Rosa turned to Terri, looking into her face again. "There were so many times, Teresa, when I might have killed *myself* except for you—more, even, than your sisters. Times when Ramon beat me and I lay there as he did it, wondering how it would be to simply put the gun to my head and leave him forever." Her eyes narrowed with remembered hate. "Driving to Ricardo's, I found myself wondering if *he* had done that to Elena—shamed her so much that she wished to die.

"And then I saw the poetry of it. Ricardo would remove himself from Elena's life, and she would feel no blame.

"A kind of peace came over me. When I parked the car in front and pushed the buzzer, I felt calm. The sound of his voice over the intercom made me want to smile. Because I suddenly knew that Elena would never, ever hear that voice again."

Terri looked into Rosa's eyes with dread and awe; Rosa's life *had* led her places where Terri would never go. "When Ricardo heard it was me," Rosa said with quiet irony, "he buzzed me in. After all, what harm could I be?"

Rosa paused; Terri was uncertain whether she wished to hear more. As if sensing this, Rosa turned from her, voice tired and drained of feeling. "I went to the door and knocked. When Ricardo peered through the door, face behind the door chain, his nose was bleeding.

" 'You're too late,' he told me.

"At first, I didn't know what he meant. And then I realized he must be talking about Elena." Rosa's face turned to stone. "He stared at me. For a moment, I didn't know what would happen. When he opened the door and let me in, it was like the beginning of a dream.

"I closed the door behind me," Rosa said quietly, "and took out the gun."

Simply and sparingly, Rosa described the next few minutes.

As Terri listened, her mother's voice became a monotone. As if in a silent movie, Terri matched words with images—Richie backing fearfully from his door to the desk, picking up a pen, putting it down. Saw her mother, with lethal irony, placing Elena's picture by his note. Compared her mother's story to the medical examiner's flawed imaginings: the nosebleed when Dr. Shelton believed Christopher Paget had struck Richie in the face; the bruise on the leg and gash on the head when Richie had fallen backward. Except that Richie had been running from the gun in Rosa's hand.

"While he lay there," Rosa said with terrible calm, "I put the revolver in his mouth. I wanted him to die knowing how Elena had felt.

"The last thing he said was, 'Please—' "

Terri could feel her own silence. Reaching for her daughter's hand, Rosa Peralta closed her eyes and pulled the trigger, in memory.

Richie's eyes froze in shock.

A fine red mist rose from his mouth. Only then did the muffled sound of the gunshot register in Rosa's brain.

As Richie's head popped backward, she began to gag.

A deep breath. The nausea stayed where it was.

Swallowing, Rosa stared down.

There were specks of blood and black powder on her wrists and hands. Sliding from Richie's mouth, the gun left a trail of powder on his lips. The bullet had done little more than end his life; it had not, Rosa guessed, gone through his head. He looked innocent, even frail, surprised that life had not been fair to him.

They stayed there, killer and victim, staring at each other.

The telephone rang.

Rosa started. The phone rang twice more and then stopped. Gazing at the dead man, Rosa heard his voice.

"Hi there. This is 769-8053. I'm not in at the moment, but I know I want to talk to you. So please leave a message, and I'll call back. . . ."

His eyes seemed black and shiny. For a moment, Rosa imagined they were wet with tears, and then she realized that the tears were not in his eyes, but in hers; wept not for him, but for Elena.

"Bye now," his voice finished.

Richie stared emptily. And then a second voice echoed in the dark. "Richie . . ."

Rosa jerked upright, turning toward the voice.

"It was *you*, Teresa. Begging him to see you that night."

Terri felt the words in the pit of her stomach. Her mother's hand tightened on hers.

"I listened to you plead for Elena, while I looked into Ricardo's face. And then I placed the gun in his hand, wiped my fingers on the raincoat, and went to the machine.

"When you finished the message, I turned off the machine and erased the tape." Rosa turned away. "I didn't want them thinking you might have come there, you see. They might have suspected you.

"It was the last clear thought I had. It took all my strength to walk to the car and drive home.

"I went to the basement and put my raincoat in a garbage bag. The garbage men were collecting the next day. By the time they found Ricardo, the raincoat would be gone.

"I climbed the stairs and went to Elena's room."

There were tears in Rosa's eyes. "She was having a nightmare," she finished simply. "And so I held her, as I once held you, until she fell asleep."

Terri stood staring out the window at Dolores Street. Behind her, Rosa sat on the couch, silent and still. It was deep night. Terri did not know how much time had passed.

"You let Chris go to trial. You let Carlo believe him a murderer." Her voice trembled with shame and anger. "You let *me* believe him a murderer."

"It seems you're always misjudging men, Teresa. First Ricardo, and now Chris." Rosa's voice was soft and sad. "Never did I suspect what would happen to Chris. Either that they would arrest him or that you would believe him guilty."

Terri turned from the window. "And when it happened?"

"I had Elena to think of." Rosa's tone grew firmer. "My silence was harsh, I know. But Christopher Paget is an unusually strong and resourceful man. Meeting him, I could feel that."

Terri walked toward her in silent fury. Standing over her mother, she asked, "And Carlo?"

Rosa stared up at her. "Carlo," she answered, "is not my grandchild."

Terri jerked her mother upright, grasping the front of her robe. "*Carlo,*" she spat out, "is not a child molester." She drew her mother's stiff face close to hers. "You could have sent Chris to prison."

Rosa did not struggle. "No," she answered with quiet dignity. "I would never have permitted that. But now he is acquitted, and Elena need never know."

"What about *me?*"

"I would have told you, Teresa. In time."

"But you didn't." Terri's voice grew soft again. "You did what you thought was right. And so can I."

Rosa gave her a weary look. "And will you tell the police, then? Send me to prison and traumatize Elena? For what—Ricardo Arias?"

Terri shook her head. "For Carlo, and especially for Chris. For the rest of his life, people will think him a murderer."

Rosa's face went from fatigue to fatalism. "Ask him, then. Let Christopher Paget do justice."

Slowly, Terri released her mother.

Gazing calmly into her face, Rosa said, "There's more, I think. You called Ricardo *twice*, didn't you? That's why *you* believed Chris guilty, and why you feel so guilty now."

Terri did not answer. Looking at her, Rosa nodded at what she saw. "At the trial, Teresa, you told them you had called Ricardo around eight-thirty, and that he told you he had an appointment. But you never told them you'd called a *second* time, much later, and that Ricardo hadn't answered.

"That was why, in Italy, you were so worried when you could not find Ricardo. It's why you concealed from the police that you'd called him again. Because you were certain that Ricardo had died between your first and second calls." Rosa paused. "You thought that *Chris* had erased your message. That was what you could never speak of. Especially to Chris."

FIVE

CHRIS ANSWERED the door in a white sweater and blue jeans. It was two o'clock.

"I have something to tell you," Terri said.

He looked into her face. "It's okay. I was waiting up for you."

They walked through the silent house to the library, the room where Chris came to think. It was dark; by the glow of a dying fire, Terri saw a snifter of cognac on the table.

He flicked on a small lamp and sat on the couch, looking up at her in the half-light with an expression of inquiry, intent but not unkind. "Cat got your tongue?" he said softly.

Terri did not sit. "You didn't kill Richie," she said.

There was the barest trace of humor in his eyes. "Yes. I know."

"Chris, it was my *mother*."

His expression changed but slightly, a narrowing of his eyes, and then he nodded.

She watched him take this in. "You *knew*."

"I suspected. *Knowing* is something very different." Chris seemed momentarily to withdraw deep within himself, and then he looked up. Something in her face kept him from going to her. Quietly, he asked, "Do you want to talk about Rosa?"

If he said or did anything more, Terri thought, she would lose control. "Yes, and no," she said at last.

The fire spat, embers dying. "Tell me how she did it, then," Chris said. "I already know the why."

It startled her. "You *knew* about Elena?"

His face changed, becoming watchful. "I know that Carlo didn't abuse her."

Terri felt shame overtake her. "No," she said softly. "*Richie* did."

"Richie?" For the first time, Chris looked surprised. "Your mother *knew* that?"

"Yes."

He stood abruptly, staring into Terri's face. "Then she let Carlo hang there."

Terri did not flinch. "She let *you* hang there."

"I'm not sixteen." Chris's voice was quieter yet; it was as if he felt too much for anger. "You'd better tell me everything."

The sense of his self-control, maintained at a cost, made the moment that much more terrible. Looking into his face, she told him all she knew, without emphasis or inflection. His expression never changed. His body was unnaturally still.

When she had finished, Terri felt exhausted.

Softly, Chris said, "Does your mother understand what she did?"

"No." Terri's voice fell. "I want you to clear yourself, Chris."

A first ironic smile. "I thought I had."

"You know better." Terri paused, and then made herself finish. "I was afraid that you'd killed him."

He looked into her face. "What about Carlo?"

"I wasn't sure." With so much lost, there was no sparing the truth. "That's why you should do it, Chris. At least you'll salvage Carlo."

"You're right. As far as *that* goes." He tilted his head. "But you're leaving out Elena."

Terri felt herself draw breath. "If my mother had told me about Richie, we could have confronted him. *I* would have gotten Elena, and Richie's charges against Carlo would have vanished."

"All true. It has a certain irony, if you enjoy the ancient Greeks." Paget paused, as if to check his anger, and then shrugged. "But your mother didn't do that. So here we all are."

Terri went to him, looking up into his face. "There's no 'we' anymore. It's time for you and Carlo to bail out and let me pick up the pieces of my family. As best I can."

Chris stared down at her. "One of the pieces is Elena. If it were up to you, this would never come out."

"No. But that's not the point."

"Isn't it? The only thing your mother got right is that this would devastate Elena. That's not a decision I'm prepared to make by myself." He paused, finishing quietly, "Nor, in the end, is it *my* decision. Or yours."

Terri stared at him. "You'd involve Carlo?"

"Yes."

Through her exhaustion, Terri felt a flash of anger. "You can't do that to him."

"Your fucking mother did it to them both." Chris stopped himself, and then said more calmly, "Carlo's sixteen, Terri. Elena's only six."

Terri shook her head. "I can't permit that. Even if there weren't also *you*."

He gave a short laugh. "Me? I deserve whatever I get. If only for my own stupidity."

Terri looked into his face. "For what? Loving me?"

"No," Paget answered softly. "For being at Richie's that night."

Ricardo Arias opened the door.

Paget looked at him—the hint of a smile, the thin, clever face, the bright eyes that seemed to Paget somehow feral, as if Richie saw without feeling. In the car, Paget had wondered how the reality of Richie would seem to him: this man had once lived with Terri; slandered Paget; used Carlo in a despicable way. But the first thing he felt was distaste and unease, as if he was entering the presence of someone too troubled, and too lacking in conscience, to be dismissed.

"Come on in." Richie's voice was oddly pleasant, that of a new neighbor or a helpful salesperson. "I've been looking forward to this."

Silent, Paget stepped into the living room. Though the apartment was new, Richie's things made it seedy—a worn desk; a lamp with its shade askew; a cheap coffee table; dated posters on the wall, faded with time. Pieces of the life that Terri once had shared with him.

Richie closed the door behind them.

Paget turned to face him. Paget had worn a suit: wearing jeans was how one called on a friend. This, at best, was business.

"You told me what you had," Paget said. "I want to see it."

There was a certain pleasure on Richie's face, as if Paget had confirmed the importance of the moment, and of Richie himself. "I have copies," Richie said. "So don't even *think* about doing anything crazy."

"Show it to me," Paget demanded.

Richie walked to the coffee table. On the table was a red-bound journal, its spine cracked with use. Richie picked it up and gave it to Paget. "Read the last entry. It's all you'll need to know."

The journal felt heavy in Paget's hand. When he opened to the first page, there was the faint smell of mildew.

The writing was feminine, careful and precise, recording the events in the order they occurred. That the language was flat, without emotion, made the entries worse.

Richie waited anxiously. "That's not the good stuff," he said.

In that moment, Paget wondered if it was possible to hate another man this much. He did not look up, kept reading at his own pace. Richie's silence was like a caught breath.

Paget reached the final entry. When he stopped abruptly, staring at the page, he could feel Richie's eyes.

Paget finished the entry and then read the words again, trying to distance himself from their impact.

"Well?" Richie said.

Slowly, Paget looked up at him. "How did you get this?"

"I copied a set of Terri's keys." Richie's voice held no apology. "So what do you think?"

"Of you?"

Richie's eyes glinted. "It's not too good for *her*, do you think? Makes you wonder what kind of mother she'd make." His smile held a certain pleasure. "If *I* were still sleeping with her, I'd sleep with one eye open. Although I *did* teach her how to give good head."

Paget placed the diary back in Richie's hand. Softly, he said, "She was fourteen."

Richie's smile faded. "A hundred thousand dollars," he said. "Cash."

Paget did not trust himself to speak.

Richie seemed to misread this. "If she's not worth it to you, maybe we can negotiate some sort of global arrangement. Covering all our outstanding issues."

Paget stopped to consider just how he would respond. Knees bracing, he felt himself relax.

"Your choice," Richie said. "Maybe we—"

With all the force he had, Paget swung.

His fist crashed into Richie's face.

The shock ran through Paget's arm. Richie clasped both hands to his face, moaning, and fell half-sitting on the rug.

Gazing down at him, Paget felt his right hand throbbing. Softly, he said, "Carlo."

Richie's hands still covered his face. Between his fingers, Paget saw a trickle of blood.

The diary lay at Paget's feet. He kicked it toward Richie. "Hand that up to me."

Slowly, Richie looked up. His nose was swollen and bloody. "Pick it up," Paget repeated.

Staring at Paget, Richie looked dazed and nauseated. He bent forward, crawling mutely to the diary, then he thrust it toward Paget.

As he took the diary, Paget sent the back of his hand cracking across Richie's face.

With a short cry, Richie fell sideways, one arm upraised to protect himself. Paget flinched at the pain in his hand. It felt tender, perhaps broken; blood from Richie's nose speckled the arm of his suit coat.

"I suppose I should stop," Paget said softly. "I'm getting you all over me."

Richie's eyes had begun to water. Only now, remembering, did Paget seem to recall turning from him and then, as he walked toward the door, facing Richie again, resting his damaged hand on the answering machine on top of Richie's desk.

There had been something more to say.

"If I let you do this," Paget told him, "you'd be in our lives forever. So you may wonder what I'll do to *you* if you ever try to use this diary, or to ruin my son's life, or Terri's. The truth is, I have no idea. Because, whatever it is, it will be something I've never considered doing to anyone."

Richie stared up at him, balanced on his hands and knees. Only his eyes moved.

"I'll let myself out," Paget said. "You just stay there. From all that I can gather, it really *is* your best position."

Turning, he opened the door and left.

Terri studied his face.

"Why were you there?" she finally asked.

He shrugged. "To talk to him, just as *you* wanted to. Perhaps to see whether we could make some end to this. It was foolish, of course."

Terri shook her head. "No more lies, Chris. This isn't the night for it."

Paget did not answer.

She clutched the front of his sweater; as she did, it struck her that she had done this to Rosa. "I just found out that my mother is a murderer and that my husband molested our daughter. So don't bullshit me about whatever *this* is." She stared into his face. "You thought you knew why she killed him. But you didn't know about Elena."

Chris's gaze was steady. But the look he gave her was one she had seen before, on the night she had lost Elena. More softly, she said, "I want to hear *everything*. Just like you did."

For a long time, Chris simply looked at her. When he spoke again, his voice was flat. "He tried to sell me information."

She nodded. "Some sort of journal—the one Georgina Keller saw."

"Yes."

"What did you do with it?"

For the first time, Chris turned from her. He stared into the fireplace, darkened now, and then walked to the mantel. "It's here."

"Where? The police turned the house inside out."

"Not quite." Chris knelt, pushing the brick backing of the fireplace; a line of bricks turned sideways, exposing a square compartment. "The man who built this place was paranoid," he said quietly. "And the cop who searched it very young. I managed to distract him."

Terri felt herself tense. "Why?"

Reaching into the square, Paget withdrew a journal. He stood holding it in both hands, as if still deciding what to do. And then, hesitantly, he gave the journal to Terri.

She walked to the sofa, sitting beneath the light. Chris stayed by the fire.

Terri opened the journal. The handwriting was her mother's. The first entry was dated shortly after Terri's birth.

"Last night," her mother had written, "Ramon beat me until my cries awakened Teresa.

"It seemed to stop him. When he let me go, I went to the bathroom to clean my face, and then tried to comfort Teresa. After a time, she stopped fussing.

"It was dark, and she is only an infant. She could not see me."

Tears stung Terri's eyes. Suddenly she wanted to reach across the years, to the woman Rosa had been. To the nineteen-year-old girl who had written this.

Terri turned the page, and then the next. She felt Chris only in his silence.

Day by day, for fourteen years, her mother recorded what Ramon Peralta had done to her.

The words were flat, emotionless. But it was only here, Terri realized, that Rosa could tell her story. There had been no one else to tell it to.

Some of the entries stirred Terri's memory. Most did not. Only rarely did her mother's words raise a sudden image, vivid as a welt. When Terri reached that night in the living room, Ramon beating her mother, she set the book aside.

How could she have lived? Terri wondered bleakly. But part of her knew the answer: She lived for *us*. She lived for *me*.

Chris came toward her. "*No,*" Terri said. "Let me finish."

He stayed there. She resumed reading the march of words, one after another, as relentless as Ramon Peralta's hands and fists.

Before she reached it, Terri knew the date of the final entry.

She felt a tremor running through her. She breathed in once, and then out again. But when she began reading, she heard her own soft cry.

"I cannot be certain," her mother had written, "that the shadow was Teresa. Or, if it was, what she chooses to remember."

There was someone in the house. Half asleep, Terri could hear this, a whisper in the silence. Just as she knew that the sound was not made by her sisters, too frightened of the dark and of her father.

Perhaps it was Ramon Peralta, returning filled with whiskey and the poison of his own rage. But Terri knew his sounds—the stumbling irregular footsteps, the shallow breathing as he climbed the stairs. *This* sound was like a parting of a curtain, the footsteps of a cat.

Perhaps it was a dream. But the crawl of fear across her skin drew her into the hallway, to seek her mother. Or, perhaps, to know that Rosa was safe.

Her parents' door was ajar. Her mother was not there.

Terri was frightened now. Part of her wished to believe this a dream, to return to her bed, where dreams belonged. It *felt* like a dream: an empty house, sounds she did not know. And then, again, the whisper.

She would not abandon her mother, Terri decided. Not after all that she had seen. She must know that Rosa was safe.

Slowly, feeling her way along the wall, Terri crept down the stairs. As if in a dream, her feet made no sound.

The living room was empty.

Terri stood there, listening. Felt, rather than heard, someone else.

A creak, somehow familiar.

It made Terri shiver, even before she could place it. And then, gazing into the dining room, she saw something. A difference in the quality of the darkness.

It was the back door to the kitchen. That would be the creak; the door opening, to admit light.

Terri stood there, afraid to move forward, yet fearing to return upstairs. And then, remembering Rosa, she crept through the dining room.

Her goal was merely to reach the alcove between the dining room and the kitchen. To peer around the corner, at her fears.

Softly, she skirted the dining table, so that she could not be seen. Then crept along the wall. Until, heart racing, she reached the alcove and gazed into the kitchen.

A crack of light. A shadow, standing in the doorway.

The shadow faced the porch. But Terri knew it, slim and still. And then her mother turned a fraction, and the porch light caught her face.

She was staring down, through the doorway. Terri followed her gaze.

Ramon Peralta stared up at her. There was a trickle of blood on his face; his eyes were stunned, beseeching, like an animal's. "Please," she saw him whisper. Less with his lips than his eyes.

Silent, Rosa gazed down at him. Terri saw the blood beneath his head now, black in the half-light.

Rosa seemed to consider him. Then she straightened, closing the screen door. A whisper.

The latch clicked shut. In the light, Terri saw her father's hand, clawing at the door. His nails scraped the screen.

The image froze there: her father's hand, her mother staring through the wire. And then, it seemed quite calmly, Rosa Peralta switched off the light.

Terri felt herself gasp.

The shadow spun, facing the darkness where Terri stood. It was less movement than sound; without light, Terri could hardly see.

With blackness between them, Terri and her mother faced each other. Terri could not be sure if Rosa saw her; without the light, her mother's shadow was a lingering image on the retina, vanishing quickly.

There had been something in her mother's hand.

Terri was still. *Go,* she imagined her mother saying. I'm giving you time now. Go back to your room, and dream.

It was a dream, Terri told herself. A dream.

She turned without speaking and tiptoed across the dining room. There was no sound behind her. And then, reaching the foot of the stairs, she heard the wooden door of the kitchen softly shut.

As if walking in her sleep, Terri climbed the stairs. A dream, she told herself. A dream, made vivid by her own desires, the ones she could not confess.

"I'm sorry," Chris murmured. "I'm so sorry."

As he reached for her, Terri crumpled.

She sobbed against him uncontrollably, her body shuddering. Cried as Christopher Paget held her—cried for Elena and for Rosa, for Carlo and Chris and all the things that had come between them. And for herself, the child Teresa.

"It's all right," Chris kept saying. "In time, everything will be better."

In her grief, she did not know how. But she clung to this, even as she wept for all that she had never forgotten, as fiercely as she had wished to forget, and paid for her wish in dreams.

Somewhere, in the minutes of the night, Terri found herself again.

At least she could look at Chris, and speak to him. Tomorrow she might start to face the rest.

"Why did you do all this?" she asked.

He smiled a little. "Because I'm foolish, as I said. But that's not for tonight."

Terri nodded; whatever it was, she did not believe she could comprehend it. She felt unspeakably tired.

In her lap, where it had fallen, was her mother's diary. "What shall *I* do with this?" she murmured.

Chris's eyes narrowed. "Take it to your mother," he said. "Tell her it's a gift from me."

There was a certain tone in his voice, the absence of mercy. And then Terri remembered Carlo.

"Carlo needs to know," she said. "About Richie, and about Elena."

Chris nodded. "I meant to tell him."

Terri sat straighter. "We both should." She paused, adding quietly, "If that's all right with you."

He did not answer. But when he climbed the stairs to Carlo's room, Terri was at his side.

THE FAMILY

APRIL, THE FOLLOWING YEAR

ONE

IT WAS OVER a year before Chris and Terri returned to Italy, and when they did, it was not to Venice but to the hill town of Montalcino.

Terri did not know why she was relieved that the church on the hillside was as before: little about Montalcino had changed in centuries. But that the church matched her memories pleased her deeply. So many of her memories, retrieved from the darkness of her childhood, had been difficult.

They took in the view together, quiet. The spring morning was fresh and still; the trees surrounding the white stone church were in the first vigor of renewal, and the valleys beyond were verdant, rising and falling in green undulations until, miles away, the last ridge met the sky.

Chris turned to her. "We've earned this, don't you think?"

Terri smiled. "If we *haven't*, I don't want to know."

This made him laugh. But so much did now: it was something else she was still learning about him. Terri fell quiet again, happy in their shared contentment, gazing at the church.

"It really is as I remembered it," she told him.

Chris smiled again. "From which life?"

"The twentieth-century version. You remember—the one I have with you." She turned to him. "You didn't go inside the last time, did you?"

"No. As Carlo would say, I generally don't do churches."

Smiling, she took his hand. "Come on, then. I'll show you. It'll be all right."

* * *

That night a year before, when they told Carlo all that had happened, Terri had thought that nothing could be all right.

Carlo sat up in his bed, back against the wall; Chris sat at the bottom of the bed with Terri. Carlo was silent for a long time, looking from one to the other with a mixture of astonishment and vulnerability and some other emotion, deeper and more obscure, which Terri could not quite read.

"I'm sorry," he said to his father. "But you should have told me."

Chris could have justified himself, or at least tried. But he seemed to know that he should not. "Will you forgive me," he asked mildly, "for not killing Richie?"

"Don't play games with me, Dad. You let me believe you were guilty. This wasn't just about you. Or Terri."

Terri felt overwhelmed. Part of her dealt by rote with whatever was in front of her; another part recoiled from the shock of what she had learned. "At least I know," she said to Carlo, "that you didn't hurt Elena."

"I *always* knew that," he snapped. "Do you expect me to be thrilled with you?" He turned to Chris. "*Or* you?"

"No," Chris answered coolly. "But I expect you to remember all that Terri's gone through and *will* go through. If you want to blame someone, make do with me. I've earned it."

Carlo folded his arms. "Do you know who *I* feel sorry for?" he finally said. "Elena. She'll be left holding the bag a long time after *I* get over it." Pausing, he looked at Paget. "What are *you* going to do about Terri's mother?"

"For myself? Nothing."

Carlo studied him. "So you two are hanging *me* with this. If I say we should let the truth out, *I'm* the one who's sent this kid's grandmother to prison, and made her feel responsible for everything."

Chris's eyes narrowed. "No," Terri interjected. "We're not putting this off on you. I won't let you, *or* Chris, pay the price for Richie and my mother."

Carlo regarded her intently. "Thanks anyhow," he said at last. "I'm screwed here, that's all, and I'll just have to deal with it." His voice grew hard. "Just don't expect me to pretend this didn't happen. *Either* of you."

* * *

It was five o'clock before Terri got home. Elena was asleep; Terri's neighbor Nancy slept on the couch.

Terri apologized to Nancy, showered in a kind of trance, and had a quiet breakfast with Elena. Mercifully, the child had slept; she did not even seem to know that Terri had been gone.

Softly, Terri asked, "Do you remember what we talked about last night? With your daddy?"

Elena nodded at her bowl of Happy Loops. She did not look at Terri.

Terri took her hand. "I'm so glad you told me, Elena. I know how hard it was."

Slowly, Elena looked up. "Was it wrong, Mommy?"

You know it was, Terri thought sadly. "Very wrong, of your daddy," she finally answered. "That's not how parents treat their children. You were just trying to be nice to him."

Elena looked down again. That morning, they said nothing more about it.

All that Terri could think to do was to treat this like a normal day; she was too drained to go on anything but instinct. And it was instinct that led her, after she dropped Elena at school, to return to her mother's. It was only on the way there that she remembered her mother's journal, secreted in the trunk of her car.

Rosa had not collected the morning paper. The headline PAGET ACQUITTED stared up at Terri from the doormat. When her mother answered the door, she was dressed with care, her makeup applied. Only the hollows like bruises beneath her eyes were left to mark what had happened. She saw the journal that Terri held, and then stared into her daughter's face.

"May I come in?" Terri asked.

Silent, Rosa opened the door. When Terri was inside, Rosa extended an arm toward the couch. The gesture was courteous and oddly formal.

They sat at opposite ends, as they had the night before. It was strange what daylight did, Terri thought wearily; it was possible to imagine that what happened in darkness was a dream, if the truth was terrible enough.

Without speaking, Terri handed the journal to Rosa.

Her mother seemed to flinch; the journal lay in her lap, untouched.

"You have read it," Rosa said.

"Yes." Terri's voice was soft. "Chris says that you should consider it a gift."

Rosa folded her hands: Terri could feel, more than see, the depth of her mother's humiliation. Rosa's voice was parched. "Then Ricardo had it."

"Yes. He duplicated my keys and, apparently, decided to prowl through your house—perhaps to see if I kept papers here. Instead he found *this*." Terri paused, finishing quietly. "I suppose he overlooked the gun."

Rosa gave a small shrug. "Perhaps he didn't think it was important."

The quiet remark, so lethal in its irony, left Terri silent again.

Rosa gazed at the journal. "I never knew that this was gone," she said, "until after that night. I thought that *you* had taken it but could not bring myself to ask."

All that silence, Terri thought. "Do you think I'd have said nothing?"

Slowly, Rosa looked into her face again. "What do you remember?"

"Everything." Terri watched her. "What were you holding, Mother?"

"A wrench." Rosa's voice was soft. "*His* wrench. To use if I needed it."

Terri felt a wave of sickness. "We *killed* him, Mama."

"*I* killed him, Teresa. You simply protected me, and then tried to protect yourself. As best a child could."

It was strange, Terri thought: about her own future, Rosa had asked nothing. "So you see," her mother finished, "Ricardo was not new to me. Long ago, I learned that I was capable of murder. Because when Ramon lay on the porch, reaching up to me from amid his own blood and vomit, I knew that he must die if we were ever to be free."

But they had never been free, Terri thought, and were not free now. In that moment, she felt the burden of her family's past, with full knowledge of what that meant, pass from Rosa to her. She squared her shoulders. "Chris will say nothing, Mama. Neither will Carlo."

Her mother stared at her, silent and still. "Does this mean," Rosa finally asked, "that you and Chris will be together?"

The surprising question brought Terri close to anger; only the look in Rosa's eyes, still hopeful for Terri's happiness, kept her under control. "Just the two of us and our secrets?" Terri asked with bitterness. "I can't imagine it. But if we were, I'm sure that Chris would never want to see you."

Rosa studied her. "The boy."

"Yes. Even if Chris could forgive you for himself."

Her mother turned away. "What about you, Teresa?"

Terri watched her mother's profile: how many times, she wondered, had she studied this face for clues as to how to feel, or to be. Softly, Terri answered, "You're my mother."

Her mother's eyes closed. "And Elena?"

"I'll bring her to see you. As much as is possible, we'll act as we did before. We've become quite good at that, over the years." Hearing herself, Terri finished evenly, "Elena's your granddaughter, and she loves you. I don't think she can take another loss."

There was nothing else to say; Terri found that she could not stay inside this house. Without waiting for Rosa's answer, she stood and walked out the door.

Denise Harris touched her eyes. "Incredible," she murmured.

Shaking her head quickly, as if to clear it, Harris stood, then walked to the window. It seemed minutes until she turned to Terri.

"Have you slept at all?" she asked.

"No."

Harris shook her head again. "You can't keep carrying the mail for everyone else," she said. "In certain ways, you're the strongest woman I know. You've taken care of your mother, Elena, Richie— even Chris, at times. But you're going to need help now. A lot of it."

"That's exactly what I don't want—help." Terri stood now. "*I'm* Elena's mother. I can't ask *her* to cut me slack, or Chris or Carlo to live with the mess I helped create."

Harris walked over to her; for the first time, the psychologist simply put her arms around Terri and held her. In her surprise, Terri found this warm and comforting; she had to fight to keep herself from crying. "Then I'll help you," Harris said softly. "We'll do this thing together. If it ever gets to be too much, call me. Day or night."

After a moment, Harris let her go.

Terri backed into a chair; sitting, she felt as if Harris had released her exhaustion. "I could go to sleep right here," she said tiredly. "But there's so much to think about. Elena . . ."

Slowly, Harris nodded. "Let's start with some simple things," she said. "Elena can't know—not now. And you're right: you shouldn't keep her from seeing Rosa. Not only would it damage Elena's sense of security, such as it is, but she'd understand intuitively what was wrong."

"Then what do I tell her about Richie's death?" Terri felt a wave of despair. "For all I know, she'll ask me about Richie on the way home from school."

"Two things. First, that Chris is innocent and that what he went through is unfair. Second, that Richie's death was an accident and no one's fault." Harris leaned forward. "On some level, Elena is relieved that Richie's dead. That's probably why she was so eager to blame Chris."

"And about what Richie did to her?"

"So far, you're doing fine. Just keep telling her, as you did this morning, that it was wrong. Instinctively, Elena knows that: her father did more than abuse her physically; he abused the trust between parent and child. And having her please *him* would make that all the more shocking." Harris paused for emphasis. "Beyond that, keep on reassuring her that she can talk to us about anything—*Elena* shouldn't have to keep *anyone's* secrets, as you did for Rosa and Elena did for Richie. Adults protect kids, not the other way around."

"And when Elena's grown? What do I tell her then?"

"That's light-years away. Our mission is to get her through the next few months. And you." Harris became openly pensive. "About when Elena's an adult, I really can't say. You'll have to trust your judgment. Maybe, by then, she'll have sensed something. Maybe not. And your mother may well live for another thirty years." Her voice grew quiet. "Sometimes the truth is hard at any age. As you're beginning to learn."

Terri shook her head. "How could Richie *do* it?" she asked. "Elena was his *daughter*."

Harris gave her a look of compassion. "The hard truth may be that Richie did it to get back at you. If Richie was a sociopath, as Dr. Gates suggests, then he would tend to view life as a ledger book: 'If you do something to offend me, I get to do something back.' " Frowning, Harris tried to make her tone sound clinical. "Perhaps, as you believe, Richie wasn't molested as a child. But the occasional pedophile whose sexual interest in a child may coincide with an interest in adults is trickier. Richie was slapped around by his father and made a love object by his mother, so neither of them respected the lines between parent and child. Between them they helped create someone who saw other people—including his *own* child—solely in terms of his own needs and desires." Harris paused, then finished quietly. "The fact that she was also *your* daughter may have made it that much more enticing."

Terri felt an impotent anger, at Ricardo Arias and at herself. "To accuse Carlo . . ."

"Oh, Richie was clever, in his way. After this Leslie Warner raised child abuse, he must have felt quite desperate about how to divert suspicion and avoid an evaluation of Elena that might very well expose him." Harris gave a small grimace. "When Elena said that Carlo had given her a bath, Richie probably saw a way to solve both problems—blame Carlo and then use that to bludgeon you into giving up. But you didn't."

For a moment, Terri was still and silent. "Would *you* have ever caught it?" she asked at last. "Dr. Gates didn't."

Harris shrugged. "She doesn't specialize in abuse cases. I do. That's why Alec Keene wanted me to do this." She paused a moment. "Alec is supposed to be neutral. But when he called me about Elena, he said that there was something wrong with Richie— like a very good actor trying to play a real person. 'Spooky,' Alec called him."

Terri felt ashamed. "I should have seen it."

"Terri, Alec Keene has a Ph.D., and he's seen just about everything. But to most people, let alone a twenty-year-old girl, a con artist like Richie could look okay for quite a while—"

"No," Terri interjected. "Part of me always knew better."

Harris folded her hands in front of her. "You're a perceptive woman, Terri. But your mother taught you to suppress the truths within your family, even to forget them. And Ramon Peralta was your first model of a man." Harris's voice became very soft. " 'The truth shall make you free,' they say. As terrible as the truth is, you're free now. You've broken the chain, for Elena and for yourself. All you have to do is make a life that really *is* your own."

One more person deserved to know the truth. A few days later, with Terri's consent, the telling fell to Paget.

Caroline leaned back in her chair. "*Rosa,*" she murmured. An astonishing range of expressions crossed her face—amazement, deep thought, and a profound seriousness that bespoke a sense of tragedy. And then, to her plain surprise, Caroline Masters began to laugh until her eyes danced.

"*Rosa,*" she repeated. "God, Chris, I just love assisting justice by accident. It expands my sense of the possible." She touched her forehead. "It isn't funny," she managed. "I don't know what's wrong with me. Really, I don't."

"Take your time, Caroline. I'm pretty well out of cosmic jokes. So you might as well enjoy *this* one."

Through her laughter, Caroline gave him a long look that, after a moment, turned wholly serious. "Will you please tell me," she said at last, "just what you thought *you* were doing?"

Paget shrugged. "Oddly enough, I thought I was protecting myself." He sat back, watching evening settle onto the city. "I'd already lied to Terri about being at Richie's; I wasn't prepared to confront her with what I'd learned about her father's death, at least until I thought about it. Then, suddenly, there was Monk questioning Terri. All at once, I sounded like a man who'd lied to her in order to build an alibi—"

"But *lying* to Monk . . ."

"Stupid, I know. But I didn't remember leaving prints and didn't know that Mrs. Keller had seen me. So I made the split-second calculation that Monk wouldn't have a case unless I told the truth." Paget's voice took on an ironic inflection. "The truth being that I'd been knocking around the blackmailer who'd smeared my son—on the very night someone killed him—but had taken care to leave him still alive.

"You can also see now why I wouldn't take the stand. I refused to lie to the jury—to say I wasn't there—and admitting that I *was* there would be to admit lying to Monk. Which, with Brooks and Colt after me and no other suspect except Terri, might well have been fatal."

Caroline considered him. "Not to mention that you would have had to tell the jury about Rosa—and Terri. So you decided to take the chance that your disgruntled but gifted lawyer could walk you on reasonable doubt."

"Just so." Paget gazed out the window. "But when the Goodwill lady *did* show up, I was stuck—your entire cross-examination had been based on suggesting that I wasn't there. If I'd taken the stand after *that* and said I *was* there, they'd have convicted me for sure."

"Probably." Caroline gave him a quizzical smile. "Is that why you kept the diary? Because you thought it was Rosa's motive?"

"One reason. Of course, I wasn't at all sure that Rosa had killed Richie. But if I'd been convicted, she and I were going to have a little chat." His eyes went cold. "Even then, I put myself ahead of her. Not to mention Carlo. I wasn't leaving him behind if I could help it."

"And Terri?" Caroline asked.

"Was, to me, an implausible murderer. But it had to be Rosa or Terri. Never for a minute did I believe that stuff you dreamed up about drug dealers and homicidal politicians, and I assume you didn't, either."

"Of course not," Caroline said. "To the extent *I* considered it, I thought it was either *you* or Terri. After Terri's testimony, I even considered a possible conspiracy. *Both* of you, with Terri providing extremely clever testimony you'd auditioned in advance."

Even now, the remark hit Paget hard. "Jesus," he said.

Caroline gave him a look of compassion. "So perhaps you can forgive Teresa for suspecting what *I* suspected rather frequently." Another brief smile. "That I was representing a murderer I liked rather more than I should."

Paget did not smile. "You're forgiven, Caroline. Terri I'm still working out."

Caroline tented her fingers, as if considering whether to speak. "Is there any hope for that?" she asked finally.

"Aside from the fact that Terri went for months believing that I was a killer? Consider Carlo, then, or Elena. We'd be asking *her* to live in a family with a stepbrother accused of molesting her, and a stepfather who some people will always believe killed her real father. How could we make a child do all that? Or, for that matter, Carlo."

Caroline considered him. "Because Terri's who you want?"

Paget was quiet for a time. "It would have to be right for our kids," he said. "And that's pretty hard to imagine."

For a moment Caroline looked reflective, almost sad. "There, regrettably, I'm out of my depth. Although I had a goldfish once."

Paget smiled. "Mine always died."

"Mine too." Caroline stood abruptly. "I hate to run, Chris, but I have a partners meeting—something about what we're paying all of us next fiscal year. Prudence suggests that I should show an interest."

"I imagine so." Standing, Paget thrust his hands in his pockets. "Somehow, I don't think I've quite managed to thank you. At least adequately."

"Oh, I should thank *you*." Caroline took him by the arm, steering him to the door. But when he turned to say goodbye, she slid her hand behind his neck and kissed him, slowly and sweetly, on the cheek. And then she leaned back, eyes bright again. *"That,"* she said, "was for being innocent. Now go and get some good out of it."

A few weeks later, when Terri found that she and Chris were still together, she asked Carlo to dinner.

They went for sushi in Chris's neighborhood; the restaurant was bright and quiet and had sushi that met Carlo's standards. Eating his way through the menu, Carlo was equable and somewhat distant, as he so often seemed with Chris these days. Terri had the sense of someone who had begun living his own life and keeping his own counsel, becoming more like his father than Chris had ever wanted for him. Next to Elena, the relationship between Chris and Carlo struck her as the biggest casualty of Richie's death.

"Somehow," Terri admitted finally, "I was hoping to help make things better between you and your dad, if not between you and me. Even *I* miss how things were."

Carlo gave her the same look she had seen from Chris: a disconcerting mixture of directness, detachment, and a certain lack of sentiment. But they're *not* the same, the look said, so wishing for that is pointless. Aloud, Carlo answered, "Things happen, that's all. For years, I depended on my dad. But you can't stay a kid forever."

Weaned affections, Chris once had said sardonically, referring to his feelings about his own parents. But Chris deserved better. "Do you think you'll stay this angry?" Terri asked.

Carlo shrugged. "Who said I'm angry?"

"No one. And Chris has never said he's angry at me. So I guess that he must not be."

Carlo raised his eyebrows. "Dad?" he said with irony. "He's too cool to be angry."

"Are you too cool?"

Carlo gave her a long look of scrutiny, as if deciding whether to be candid. "No," he said finally. "I'm not."

Please, Terri thought, talk to me as you did before your father and I became lovers. "Is it more Elena? Or what your dad chose not to tell you?"

Carlo contemplated a piece of California roll and then put it down. "Elena," he said finally, "I'm learning to live with. I've sort of figured out that if you show up somewhere and *you* know you're okay, people will accept that." He paused, and then shrugged. "Anyhow, Katie always knew I didn't do it."

The last remark, quiet but pointed, struck Terri on several levels: that Katie had believed in Carlo more than Terri had believed in Chris; that Terri had also wondered about Carlo; and that Carlo, at sixteen, had emotional connections to his peers as real and immediate as to his own parent. "Has it been hard," she asked, "not telling Katie what really happened?"

Carlo considered her. "I never felt like I needed to," he answered.

Terri watched him. "But your father *did* need to, didn't he. So when he felt he could, he told you everything."

Carlo's eyes hardened. "He left me out there for a long time."

Terri nodded. "I understand how you feel, Carlo—it was exactly what he did to me. But you were a *witness*. If Chris had told you the truth, you would have had to choose between lying about what you knew or possibly convicting him." Terri paused, adding quietly, "Besides, do you think he should have told you about *me*? Or do you tell *him* everything about Katie."

Carlo inspected her. "No. But this involved me."

"*And* me." Terri softened her voice. "I'm not saying your dad was right, and I know he put a lot on you. I also know that he feels like he did you, *and* his relationship to you, permanent harm. Which is the thing that means more to him than anything. Or anyone." She touched his arm. "You *do* know that, don't you?"

"Basically, yes."

"Basically? Chris adores you." Terri looked at him intently. "Part of growing up is being your own person. I think you're getting that much pretty well down. I'm not so sure about the other part."

Carlo gave her the remote gaze that, in Chris, Terri recognized as a kind of challenge. "Which is?"

"Accepting Chris as he is—a flawed person who loves you and who's done pretty well by you without a road map from his own parents, or help from a partner." She looked at him intently. "You were upset about nearly losing him, and I don't blame you. Instead you still *have* him. Does that make him less worth loving?"

Carlo reached for the California roll, chewing it with a narrow-eyed look and then washing it down with a sip of Terri's beer. "Nope," he finally said.

There was the first trace of a smile around Carlo's eyes. Emboldened, Terri added, "But try not to be *too* much like your dad, okay? Not everyone can pick up the signals."

To her surprise, Carlo grinned. "Mr. Warm and Fuzzy, you mean? Yeah, I wish he weren't so emotional all the time. It's embarrassing."

In her relief, Terri laughed aloud. "I know. Especially in front of company."

The moment reminded Terri of their first common bond—a gentle mockery of Chris, based on shared affection. But then Carlo asked, as he would not have a year before, "What about your mother?"

It startled Terri into quiet. "It's not the same," she finally said.

Carlo had stopped smiling. "You've got *that* right," he said coolly. "How are you dealing with it all?"

Terri shook her head. "Badly. I don't have nightmares anymore. Just flashbacks from my childhood, and terrible guilt." She looked into Carlo's face. "It isolates me, in a way. There's this horrible thing, the biggest thing in my life, and I can't talk about it to anyone but Chris. Who's the person everyone blamed for it. Including me."

Carlo considered her. "Yeah," he said. "About that, I know what you mean."

It was several months before Paget encountered Victor Salinas, and then Salinas came to his office unannounced.

"I didn't know if you'd see me," Salinas said without preface, "and I think we need to talk."

"Who did I murder now?"

Salinas gave him an edgy, delayed smile. "McKinley Brooks?"

Paget stared at him. "Sit down."

"Can we talk about this in confidence?"

"Yes."

Sitting, Salinas looked around for a moment, taking in Paget's paintings and the small sculpture on his desk. To Paget, he seemed more muted than in the bleak environs of the Hall of Justice, his home. "I'd like to run for district attorney," Salinas said.

Paget nodded. "Let me see if I follow you, Victor. After what Caroline did at my trial, McKinley's anonymous friend became too gun-shy to find Mac some higher office. On the other hand, Mac is insufficiently wounded not to run for D.A. again. Which leaves him in your way." Paget paused, and then his voice became dry. "You're not here to ask me for money," he went on, "because taking it would be so unseemly. So you're wondering whether I want to screw Mac so badly that I'd help you become D.A. in some *other* way—say, for example, by digging up more dirt on how Mac tampered with the Ricardo Arias inquiry. You can't use the cops to help you: you're not the D.A., and Charles Monk won't play ball with anyone. On the other hand, *I* could probably ask Johnny Moore to see what he could find—like the nameless 'source' who no doubt contacted McKinley Brooks *after* the cops found Richie dead." Paget leaned back, his expression one of polite inquiry. "Is that about it? Or is there some subtlety I've missed?"

Paget could not help but admire Salinas's calm; his surprise had shown only for a second. But then Salinas was, as Paget knew, a capable trial lawyer. "You're in the ballpark," he said.

"In the ballpark?" Paget gave him a deprecating smile. "That kind of information would ruin Mac politically. He might even get indicted. All you'd need is to feed the 'source' to the U.S. Attorney, and a grand jury would have a field day, to use another sports metaphor. As would you, the last honest man."

Salinas's eyes flashed at the hint of condescension; Paget had reminded him that he would not forget the trial, and that there was no point in coyness. "All right," Salinas said at length. "It's what I need. So will you help me?"

Slowly, Paget drew a manila file from a drawer and placed it on the desk between them. "It's all here, in Johnny's report to me. The 'source' who called Brooks is the same man who funneled the information to Jack Slocum and, no doubt, the ten thousand dollars to our late friend Ricardo. It's yours, if you want it. In the public interest, of course."

Salinas stared at the file. He began to reach for it, and then stopped, looking at Paget's face. "What do *you* want?" he asked.

"James Colt."

Salinas sat back, still watching Paget. "This 'source' has ties to Colt?"

"Yes. To a certainty, Colt is McKinley's secret friend. The one who tampered with your case."

Eyeing the file, Salinas did not move or speak. After a moment, Paget nodded. "Your caution does you credit, Victor. Because once you let this particular genie out of the bottle, you lose control. Even if it were possible, Johnny and I will never let the damage stop with Brooks. The larger question, which the U.S. Attorney will be quick to see, is what politician the go-between Slocum and Brooks protected was working for." Paget paused for emphasis. "Never once did Caroline Masters remind me that she was making a powerful enemy, who might well be able to deny her a federal judgeship. But that result is unacceptable to me. So if *you* accept this information, you're committing yourself to Colt's political demise. Which will make him *your* enemy as well." Paget's voice became flat. "You help get Colt, Victor, or he'll get you."

Salinas remained silent. But Paget could make out his emotions—fear, ambition, prudence, and the sudden knowledge that this, which he had seen as his chance, might instead be his ruin. And then he looked into Paget's face again.

Softly, Paget said, "Yes or no?"

Salinas's faint smile, mingling pride and calculation, lingered for a moment. And then he reached across Paget's desk, and took the file.

Paget lined up the cue ball, carefully aiming at the black ball numbered 8. With a smooth stroke of the cue, he propelled the cue ball; there was a soft crack, and the eight ball glided away at a right angle and fell into the corner pocket.

"There," Paget said with satisfaction.

Carlo stared at the spot where, a moment before, the last ball had resided. "Another game," he announced. It was not a request.

They racked up the balls again. In the last nine years, they had shot countless games of pool in Paget's basement; over time, Carlo had become Paget's competitor and then his equal. But Paget was reminded less of that than of the way he and Carlo, when Carlo was too young to talk much, had communicated by throwing a red rubber ball—and, more sadly, that in their recent silences, Paget thought of all the men who could not communicate with each other except through sports and games.

Paget put down his cue. "Look," he said abruptly, "I know I screwed things up."

Lining up the cue ball, Carlo did not look at him. His cue flashed; the white ball sped into the pack, sending them flying at all angles. Two balls at the corners disappeared into pockets.

Paget felt his son's rebuff. "Nice shot, Carlo."

His son scanned the table. "You didn't screw things up," he said. "You *screwed* up. There's a difference."

"Which is?"

Carlo lined up his next shot. "You screwed up the Richie deal, all right? What made it worse is that, since I was a kid, I expected you to be perfect. When you weren't, I was scared—and pissed." Carlo made the shot and glanced up from the table. "You're really lucky, Dad. Of all the people in the world, you're the one I have the hardest time being fair to. Because, for a long time, you were the only person I could expect much from. Just like I said at the trial."

Paget looked at him. He did not know what to say.

Turning, Carlo eyed another shot. "Guess being a parent's a shitty deal, huh?"

The ball disappeared. "Only sometimes," Paget said. "Other times, it's not so bad."

Carlo smiled, and made a bank shot. "I'm getting older, though. You can't make your whole life out of worrying about me. Or annoying me."

"I didn't plan to, actually."

A moment's silence. "So what's happening with you and Terri?" Carlo asked, and sank his fifth shot in a row.

Paget raised his eyebrows. "I didn't know you cared," he gibed, not joking.

"Terri and I had dinner again the other night. I've decided to declare amnesty." Carlo smiled again. "You know, before I push things so far you really get fed up with me."

Slowly, Paget shook his head. That Carlo had protected Elena made him sad and proud at once; from what Terri said, it might yet be the saving of her. "You'd get a lot of points for Elena," Paget said seriously. "Even if I didn't love you so much. You've shown more character than Terri, or I, had any right to ask."

Carlo shrugged and then made his sixth shot running. "Terri's a nice person," he said. "A lot better than her life."

Paget hesitated for a moment. "What made *that* occur to you?"

"I remembered why I used to like her," Carlo answered, gauging still another shot. As it slid toward the pocket, he murmured, "Seven," even before it fell.

"And why is that?" Paget asked.

"Two reasons." Carlo sank another ball and then smiled up at his father. "First, she can honestly talk about how she feels, sometimes in complete sentences. Second, she doesn't talk to me like a parent. But then she's closer to *my* age than yours." The grin widened. "That was eight, by the way. You lose."

"I want to go outside," Elena said.

It was a crisp fall day, nine months or so after Chris's acquittal. Leaning through the window, Elena stuck her face into the sun; in her interest in the world, more constant now, she was a shade closer to the extroverted child she once had been. When she mentioned her father, it was rarely about his abuse of her; for good or bad, Elena clung to memories of when they had all been together, a family, before Terri left him. In one way, Terri acknowledged grimly, Rosa's solution to Richie had been perfect: Elena did not have to deal with her father, feeling guilty and ambivalent, trapped within whatever supervised regime of visitation the family court would have parceled out to him. As for Terri, who struggled with enough, she would never have to look at Ricardo Arias again.

"Why don't we go to Golden Gate Park," Terri said.

"Okay." Turning from the street below, Elena seemed to hesitate. "Do you think Carlo could go?" she asked. "He never plays with me anymore."

As Terri looked at her more closely, Elena's eyes flickered. The question was disingenuous, Terri knew: in some way, Elena had pieced together the reason she did not see Carlo. "What if Carlo isn't home?" Terri asked. "Can Chris come?"

Elena looked at the ground. "All right." She seemed to know that Terri would not ask Carlo.

When Chris met them, in a large grassy field surrounded by oaks, he was holding a kite.

"Carlo always did this," he explained. "I thought Elena might like to try."

Elena looked dubious. "*I'd* like to try," Terri said. This was true; her memories of childhood did not include a kite, and Terri doubted she had ever flown one.

It turned out that she was a natural.

Within moments, she had the kite aloft. After a moment of self-indulgence, Terri turned it over to Elena and sat next to Chris. They watched from a blanket, drinking coffee, while Elena flew the kite, flicking its string from side to side in imagined feats of steering. Seeing this, Chris smiled.

"Did Carlo use to do that?" Terri asked.

"Uh-huh, and so did I. As a kid, kite flying was one of my major talents—it's something you can do alone, and San Francisco is great for wind." Chris smiled. "Of course, Carlo always wanted to do it all himself. Floating somewhere over China are several perfectly good kites which somehow escaped his grasp."

His tone was relaxed, matter-of-fact in his fondness for Carlo. But he did not look at her; Terri wondered if they would ever have a conversation about their children that was not shadowed by Richie's charges.

There was a sudden gust of wind; the kite slipped from Elena's hands, rattled upward, and became snagged in a nearby tree. She gazed upward, lips tremulous. When Chris and Terri got up to help, she considered them both, then turned to Chris, hesitant. "Can you please get my kite down?" she finally asked. "You're tall."

Chris nodded. "I can *try*."

Terri sat down, mildly amused; by the age of seven, she thought, girls learn that men are supposed to be good at things. And then, with sudden bitterness, she thought of Richie.

The kite was easy enough for Chris to reach, Terri saw; with a few twists, he could get it down. But after working the string loose from a couple of branches, Chris stared up at the tree, his hands on his hips.

"I need some help for the last part," he said. "If I hold you up, can you get it loose from that branch?"

It was just the opposite, Terri thought, of what Richie would have said. Elena stared up at the string, caught on a branch perhaps five feet over her head, as if it were at the top of a building.

"I won't let you fall," Chris told her.

Elena paused again. Then, turning to Chris but looking away, she held out her arms as she once had to Richie.

Chris held her aloft. Elena's head disappeared amid the leaves; Chris held the string in one hand, to prevent mischance. But when he lowered her, Terri saw Elena's delighted face, and then the kite.

Chris smiled. "Thanks," he said to her. "That would have been hard by myself."

Firmly gripping the kite string, Elena appraised him. "Do you know Susie Goldman?" she asked.

Chris tilted his head, as if trying to remember. "I don't think so," he said.

"She's in first grade with me." The little girl frowned. "Sometimes we're friends, and sometimes we fight."

It made Chris smile again. "Sometimes friends are like that." He knelt to wrap the string around her wrist. "You're a good kite flyer, Elena. At least as good as Carlo."

At the mention of Carlo, the little girl scurried off with the kite again.

Chris sat down again. "I thought you weren't any good with little kids," Terri said.

He picked up his coffee, took a sip. "I never said I was no good. I said I'd had no practice. Especially with girls."

Terri gave him an amused look. "You *are* good, though—letting her get the kite was a true lesson in self-esteem."

Chris smiled. "It's easier to resist impressing women," he said, "when they're in grade school."

Terri smiled back and then wondered for a fleeting moment if this was a sardonic allusion to Richie. She found herself staring at Chris.

He gazed out at Elena; somehow, Terri knew that he was conscious of her scrutiny. "I honestly think you still wonder," he said, "after what Carlo went through, how I truly feel about Elena."

It was disconcerting; Terri could not tell if, because she looked at him, Chris had guessed her thoughts. "I know you feel sorry for her," she said quietly. "But yes, I suppose I do."

He turned to her. "What happened to Elena was a tragedy," he said. "How can I possibly blame her for it? So don't make things any worse than they are, okay?"

Could you ever *love* her? Terri wanted to ask. But she was not sure that the question mattered.

Just before the November election, McKinley Brooks was indicted by a federal grand jury.

The formal counts included conspiring to violate the federal campaign laws, as well as Christopher Paget's civil rights. But the essence of the charge was that, at the apparent instigation of James Colt, Brooks had prevented the police from following leads in the murder of Ricardo Arias. The witnesses included Jack Slocum and a political consultant, George Norton: Norton had received immunity for describing his conversations with Brooks, Slocum, and an aide to James Colt.

On the day of the indictment, Paget met Johnny Moore downtown, to watch the evening news. The two friends sat at a mirrored bar beneath a television, Paget drinking a Tanqueray martini, Moore his usual mineral water. "Does drinking that stuff ever bother you?" Paget asked.

Moore smiled. "All the time. By ten o'clock, I'm not half the wit I used to be. Nor do I have those wonderful epiphanies, where I suddenly go for the political throat of whoever's sitting nearest me, in flights of scorn and eloquence. Worse yet, the surviving drunks bore me to tears."

"Maybe you should develop a new passion, Johnny. Like going to the gym."

Moore gave him a look of distaste. "And start lifting weights in front of mirrors? At least alcoholism can be shared with others. Besides, I can experience narcissism vicariously. Through you."

Paget smiled, and then the news came on.

The lead story was Brooks's indictment. The anchorwoman, a blonde who looked something like Marla Maples, spoke in a voice typically reserved for kidnappings and mass disasters. "San Francisco District Attorney McKinley Brooks was indicted today, on five counts alleging obstruction of the Senate race and subsequent murder trial of prominent San Francisco lawyer Christopher Paget. . . ."

The picture changed. A grim McKinley Brooks appeared hurrying from the federal building, flanked by his own lawyers. For once, Brooks did not speak to the press; over the film, the anchorwoman went on.

"The case against Brooks centers on the testimony of political operative George Norton, who allegedly spoke to Brooks on behalf of gubernatorial aspirant James Colt. According to sources close to the grand jury, Norton claims he funneled campaign moneys to Ricardo Arias, the estranged husband of one of Mr. Paget's associates, Teresa Peralta, to make sensational charges against Mr. Paget and his son in Arias's divorce case. After Arias's mysterious death by gunshot, Mr. Norton—supposedly at the instance of an aide to James Colt—again contacted District Attorney Brooks, to ensure that the police did not discover the ties between Ricardo Arias and the Colt campaign.

"At his home in Bel Air, James Colt denied all charges. . . ."

On the screen, Colt appeared, standing beneath a palm tree, tense but composed. He was surrounded by cameras.

"He looks a little peaked," Moore remarked. "Rather like an albino, in fact. It seems the attention doesn't agree with him."

Paget nodded. "I wondered where my entourage had gone. I've missed them."

Colt began speaking. "These charges," he said in tones of anger, "are the work of those who oppose my efforts to bring a better

quality of life to all Californians, rich or poor. We expect total vindication and are confident that it will come quite soon. . . ."

"Two to one Mac sells him out," Paget murmured.

"Two cases of Perrier water against a bottle of Tanqueray. Are you
serious?"

"Sure."

On the screen, Colt's lips were moving soundlessly. "However,"
the anchorwoman narrated, "there were reports this evening that
McKinley Brooks is negotiating for reduced charges, in exchange for
testimony regarding his conversations with James Colt. While the
outcome of these negotiations is uncertain, the damage to Colt's
candidacy may be immediate and severe."

"Colt is toast," Moore said. "Whether Mac deals him or not."

"What about the bet, Johnny? Any takers?"

"No, thanks. Winning something should be fun. And Mac *will*
deal him. It's just a matter of establishing the market rate."

The anchorwoman reappeared. "Today's indictment seemingly as-
sures the election of insurgent candidate Victor Salinas as district attorney. Asked for comment, Salinas said, quote, 'The Ricardo Arias
matter was a travesty. This indictment reaffirms the principle
that justice should not be sold, no matter how rich and powerful
the bidder.' "

Moore, Paget saw, was grinning at his mineral water.

"As for Mr. Paget, who has been silent throughout, his only comment was, quote, 'I'm sure they'll treat Mr. Colt more fairly than he
treated my teenage son. Of course, he'll need that.' "

Moore looked sharply over at Paget. "Nasty," he said, "to stick
Colt with Richie's dirt."

Paget shrugged. "It had a certain elegance, I thought." He raised
his glass. "In any event, we've made the world safe for Caroline."

Moore touched Paget's glass. "Very selfless of you, that. Although
I couldn't help but notice that you've also redeemed Carlo's reputation. And, to some extent, your own."

Paget smiled. "We do have to live here, after all. Terri too."

"True enough." Pausing, Moore gave him an appraising sideways
look. "*So,*" he said softly, "who *did* kill Ricardo Arias?"

Paget smiled again. "James Colt, of course. Didn't he do
everything?"

* * *

Teresa Peralta lay beside Chris in the quiet of his bedroom.

It was just past Christmas; Elena, happy with her toys, was spending the night with Rosa. Fourteen months after Richie's death, Elena showed no sign of knowing the truth; for Elena, the security of Rosa's love, and of her life with Terri, seemed more and more to define her world. Sensing this, Terri was content. The subject of Richie, so potentially explosive, might be dormant for a time: Terri felt Elena, with a child's instinct for self-protection, establishing the touchstones of her new life before she could face the past. For once, what the absence of a father meant was safety.

The last thought, as it always did, made Terri sad. She turned to Chris again.

He slept lightly, his face calm and dreamless. A while ago they had made love, sweetly and unhurriedly, until the moment Terri lost herself and then lay back on the pillow, grinning at Chris out of sheer surprise and pleasure at the way this always happened. Making love was so much better, Terri thought, when it was not just an escape but a destination. Except that, until some moments afterward, she had not been sure where they were going.

"Remember the first time we made love?" she had asked.

Chris had smiled. "Tonight, you mean? Of course."

"I meant *the* first time."

Slowly, he nodded. "You'd lost Elena. But tonight was about *us*. It's not the same."

She looked into his face, serious now. "But are *we* the same?"

He slid away from her, turning on his elbow to watch her. "We'll never be the *same*," he said. "We've been through too much."

The elliptical phrase made Terri as sad as the memory of sadness she read in his eyes. "Such as," she answered, "the fact that I thought you'd murdered Richie."

He regarded her without anger. "It's there. I guess it will always be there. However much I may have deserved it."

"You didn't deserve it, Chris." She shook her head. "What hurts is that I came out loving you that much more, and you came out loving me a little less."

"Is that what you think?"

"Yes." Terri's sudden tears surprised her. "Damn it, I love you so much it hurts. Ever since we found out what happened, you've been endlessly kind, all right? And it's helped me a lot. But every day, the better *I* get, the more I feel how much I may have lost. I've gotten rid of the nightmares, I'm coming to terms with my father—somehow I can even live with what my mother did, then and now, and how she came to it. I can *stand* all that. What I can't stand is the idea of losing you."

"You haven't lost me, Terri."

"I haven't *got* you, either." She felt her voice rise. "God, I didn't want our life to be about Richie. But it still *is*, isn't it? Because you'll never forget what happened."

"No, I won't." His expression was not unkind; Terri thought it was the gaze of a man too honest to lie without good reason. "So what do you want for us?"

You, Terri thought, the way you were before. She felt more vulnerable than she could remember ever feeling. Quietly, she said, "I want all the things you said *you* wanted in Portofino. I want our child, and for you to love me. And Elena. Just as I answered you then."

He studied her. "Do you think we can do that? Make a family?"

"*I* can. The question is whether *you* can. Or Carlo."

His eyes softened. "You've already won Carlo over," he answered. "Did you think I don't know who helped bring him back to *me* again? It's hard for me to ask things for myself, or even to arouse much sympathy. It's not the way people see me—even Carlo."

She touched his face. "*I* see you, Chris. Except for those four months, I always did."

"I know."

"Don't sound so accepting, okay? Do you think that's easy work?"

He smiled a little. "I just said it wasn't."

She shook her head again. "It's like there's part of you, now, that's out of reach. I can't quite seem to touch it."

"Then keep trying." His smile faded. "Because if you ever stopped, I don't think I could stand it."

Terri looked at him, confused. "There's been damage," he said softly. "And hurt. But we've come through things that few people ever face." He kissed her forehead. "I believe in you, Terri. I always have. If *you* believe that we still can make a family, then we can. Because I still love you far too much not to try."

There it was, Terri thought, after months of wondering. She could not understand the tears in her eyes.

Christopher Paget held her close. "So are you going to marry me?" he said. "Or do I have to ask you?"

Terri found that she was smiling against his shoulder: anyone who could feel all these things at once, she thought, must surely be crazy. "No," she managed, "I'll marry you. But what about Carlo?"

"Carlo? Oh, I did ask *him*, a few days ago." His voice softened. "It's okay by Carlo. But he said to tell you no baby-sitting."

Now, as Chris slept, Terri smiled at his face.

She would love him, she knew, more than he had ever been loved. And so, in time, would Elena. For whatever else life brought to her, Elena's image of a father would not, in the end, remain Ricardo Arias. For this, and for herself, Teresa Peralta felt deeply grateful.

For the first time, Paget entered the church in Montalcino.

Carlo and Elena stood at the altar. But an almost equal wonder was that Terri had persuaded a priest to marry her to Paget, the non-Catholic. He could only hope that it did not involve some terrible deceit.

As they approached the altar, he turned to Terri, whispering, "You didn't lie about me, did you?"

She smiled up at him. "Of course not," she said innocently. "Your fingerprints were on the rosary, weren't they?"

"God," he murmured. "I hope this is legal."

She gave him an ambiguous smile. "Believe me, so do I." And then they stood in front of the priest, a stocky man with a peasant's face and warm brown eyes, their children beside them.

The church, Paget acknowledged, was simple and lovely. Even if, as he deeply suspected, no one really lived here. And then he looked at Teresa Peralta, and the thought did not matter.

She gazed gravely at the altar, and at the priest, her face beautiful in the light and shadow. The mysteries of the human heart were deep, Paget thought; as much of her childhood as she cared to leave behind, this much was part of her. Paget was happy to share it.

The vows began.

The priest spoke in broken English, for Paget's sake; with her

Spanish, Terri could follow Italian well enough. But she wanted Paget to know, she had said that morning, the moment that they were married.

When the moment came, Paget smiled to himself, and felt the pressure of Terri's hand. He kissed her then: from the side, Elena Arias looked up at him solemnly, as if he were a new discovery.

Carlo was the second to kiss Terri. "Nice going," he told her. "You guys are even starting to look like a couple."

Terri smiled. "It's a miracle."

Beside them, Elena began tugging on Terri's yellow silk dress. "Can we go outside now?" she asked.

The priest smiled down at her. "Go ahead," he told Chris and Terri. "I'll give the papers to your son."

This was better, Paget thought. He nodded to Carlo; in his pocket, Carlo carried Paget's check for ten thousand dollars in lire, for the preservation of the church. Paget did not require thanks in person: in some sublime balance, it seemed right that Paget, the nonbeliever, should honor this place for opening itself to them. And so Paget and Terri thanked the priest and followed Elena into the sunlight.

Outside, on the bench where they had sat during their first visit, was a bottle of cold champagne and a dish of fresh strawberries. But before they could retrieve them, Elena asked, "Mommy, can we go get some ice cream? Yesterday I saw a place in the town."

Terri smiled. "Not now, Elena. We just got married, remember? We have toasts to drink."

Elena pondered that and then turned to Carlo as he emerged from the church. "Maybe *you* can take me, Carlo. You're my step-brother now."

Carlo gave her a droll look. "Does that mean I have to take you places, Munchkin?"

The old nickname made Elena's eyes crinkle. "Yes," she announced firmly. "You have to now."

"Oh, all right. But *after* I drink some champagne."

"Are you old enough?"

Carlo smiled at her. "For champagne? Sure, Munchkin. We're in Italy, remember?"

Quietly, Terri took Paget's hand and walked away a little, to the bench.

They sat there for a time, watching Elena reattach herself to Carlo; it was probably good, Paget thought wryly, that Carlo was traveling to Rome tomorrow, to meet his mother.

"Do you think," Terri asked, "that Carlo and Elena would mind if we drank one toast alone? Now that we're married, I have something to tell you."

As soon as he looked at her face, smiling yet watchful, he knew what it was: roughly two months before, when Terri and Elena had moved in, Terri had thrown out her diaphragm. Paget was forty-seven, after all, and there seemed no point in waiting.

"A baby?" he asked.

Saying it aloud seemed strange. Terri grinned at him. "Uh-huh. What do you think?"

Paget sat back, taking this in as he looked out at the lush green hills of Tuscany, then at his family. First at Carlo and Elena, still talking to each other. And then at his wife, Teresa Paget, the mother of the child who would become part of them all.

He *was* forty-seven, Paget reflected. He would never be a senator, or do all that he might have wished to do. But he would be this woman's partner, their time together still ahead, filled with joys and sorrows and surprises and, most of all, people whom he cared for, their lives interwoven with the fabric of his own.

Taking Terri's hand, he leaned back on the bench, feeling the sunlight on his face, at peace for perhaps the first time in his life.

"A baby," he said again. "Seems like enough."

only does she type the manuscript, but Alison—a particularly insightful reader—tells me what seems right or wrong. The next book is for her.

Finally, there are Fred Hill and Sonny Mehta. Fred has been my literary agent, and friend, for fifteen years. He is what writers, at their most idealistic, hope an agent will be—a discerning reader, a supportive friend, and a superlative mediator between writer and publisher. With every book, Fred has helped me make the best possible arrangement, including a meticulous concern with which publisher and editor would be right for me. My career would be far different without him.

When we learned that Sonny Mehta was interested in my last novel, *Degree of Guilt*, Fred advised me to go no farther. It was, perhaps, Fred's best single piece of advice. Sonny is a superb editor, a committed and creative publisher, and a brilliant promoter of emerging writers. Because Sonny and his gifted coworkers at Knopf worked hard to communicate their enthusiasm to booksellers and to the public, I have been able to reach the audience that any writer wants. And because my career has become intertwined with the talents of Fred Hill and Sonny Mehta, I am free to write the best that I can. I am deeply grateful to them both.

ACKNOWLEDGMENTS

Like Blanche DuBois, I often depend on the kindness of strangers—and friends.

Assistant District Attorney Bill Fazio and defense lawyers Hugh Levine, Jim Collins, and Jim Larson contributed numerous valuable suggestions about the trial of a complex criminal case. As before, County Medical Examiner Boyd Stevens and Homicide Inspector Napolean Hendrix lent me their expertise. Karen Jo Koonan, of the National Jury Project, helped explain the valuable services performed by jury consultants in assessing jury panels. And Assistant District Attorney Al Giannini not only gave great advice but reviewed the manuscript. They share the credit for authenticity; any errors, or simplifications for narrative purposes, are mine.

The child custody process is interesting and unique. Marjorie Kaplan and Brian Johnson were generous with their advice, and Dr. Erika Myers helped me understand the conduct of a family evaluation.

Spousal and child abuse are difficult subjects. Drs. Howard Gillis, Rodney Shapiro, and Teresa Schumann, and counselor Cecilia Moreno, were invaluable in helping me. While there is no single psychological profile for either victim or perpetrator, I hope I have treated these subjects fairly and informatively.

Others helped as well. Clint Reilly, political consultant; handwriting experts Pat Fisher and Howard Rile; gun expert Dennis Casey; and blood-typing experts Dr. Ben Grunbaum and District Attorney Rock Harmon, all shared their knowledge. And legendary private investigator Hal Lipset was generous in explaining how he would help defend the case I have presented here.

As usual, several perceptive friends read various portions of the manuscript. Without Philip Rotner, Lee Zell, and—particularly—my wife, Laurie, the task of writing this novel would have been far more solitary and difficult. And, throughout, I was buoyed by the support and confidence of my friends at Ballantine Books, Linda Grey and Clare Ferraro.

One of my great pleasures has been working with Alison Porter Thomas. Not